The
Golden
Honeycomb

Novels by Kamala Markandaya

Nectar in a Sieve
Some Inner Fury
A Silence of Desire
Possession
A Handful of Rice
The Coffer Dams
The Nowhere Man
Two Virgins
The Golden Honeycomb

The Golden Honeycomb

a novel by

Kamala Markandaya

Thomas Y. Crowell Company
Established 1834
New York

Manufactured in the United States of America

Library of Congress Cataloging in Publication Data

Markandaya, Kamala
  The golden honeycomb.

  I. Title.
PZ4.M3447Go3   [PR9499.M367]   823'.9'14   76-27642
ISBN 0-690-01208-X

1 2 3 4 5 6 7 8 9 10

For my daughter

Prologue

When Warren Hastings, Governor-General of India, was brought the news of the surrender of General Burgoyne at Saratoga in 1777 during the American War of Independence, he remarked:

> If it be really true that the British arms and influence have suffered so severe a check in the western world, it is the more incumbent upon those who are charged with the interest of Great Britain in the East to exert themselves for the retrieval of the national honour.

These exertions eventually resulted in the Queen of England being proclaimed Queen-Empress of India.

Both before and after this Proclamation the importance of India to Britain was acknowledged. Lord Randolph Churchill was one among many statesmen to do so. He appealed to Members of Parliament to

> ... watch with the most sedulous attention, to develop with the most anxious care, to guard with the most united and undying resolution, the land and the people of Hindustan, that most truly bright and precious gem in the crown of the Queen, the possession of which, more than that of all your Colonial dominions, has raised in power, in resource, in wealth and in authority this small island home of ours ... has placed it on an equality with, perhaps even in a position of superiority over, every other Empire either of ancient or of modern times.

To preserve this precious gem the British operated a system of subsidiary treaties and engagements between themselves and the ostensibly independent Princes of India. Under this system a British-controlled force was planted within the Princely States to safeguard them against attack, the Ruler of the State paying a subsidy for the upkeep of the garrison within his borders and usually in his capital.

In effect it was a Catch 22 arrangement. Refusal to pay the subsidy risked annexation of the Prince's dominions in lieu, while payment ensured the support of a force that virtually guaranteed his subjection. It also, of course, protected the Princes against popular uprisings, so that there was no great pressure on them to be sensitive to the wishes and welfare of the people they ruled. Despite the system, some States were models of administration and advanced beyond anything achieved in British India. Some were not.

As the Princely States covered roughly a third of the sub-continent, these levers of British control, the garrison forces, were scattered like strategic confetti across the face of India . . .

PART I.

Rajahs are kept to a certain extent in leading strings until they have proved their capacity for ruling.

Marchioness of Dufferin & Ava,
Vicereine of India

1

The British have chosen the Maharajah. In fact they have had two stabs at it, choosing a merchant first, a victualling *bania*. The man is worthy. He supplies the oxen that haul the gun-carriages of the British armies that have been scrapping lucratively from end to end of the sub-continent. The *bania* does more. He provides fodder for the beasts and grain for the men. He is quartermaster *par excellence*. In his trail entire villages are devastated as if by a visitation of locusts. The British cannot do without him.

The Political Agent has himself picked the man, on the recommendation of his advisers. He considers it an excellent choice. 'I am unworthy, Excellency,' the *bania* murmurs. Inwardly he contests the demeaning sentiment. His jowls, the roll of fat that flops over the brocade cummerbund that encircles his waist, are quivering in anticipation of confirmation of his worth.

The Brahmin Minister sidles forward. The verb is the Agent's. He does not like this lean Brahmin whom he suspects. He does not suspect him of crime or conspiracy, but of something far worse: he suspects his intellect, whose keenness he simultaneously suffers and utilises. The Brahmin's ubiquity is what has retained him in his position through the alarums and excursions of wars and the tepid endorsement of successive Agents. He sidles forward.

The *bania*'s ears are flapping. He is straining to hear; the urgency is such that his whole body cranes, moves him from the spot on the chessboard assigned to pawns like himself. The Political Agent waves him back. The man smells like one of his grain shops, which is not surprising, but the Agent's nostrils twitch. The *bania* retreats, back to the white square of the marble floor of the audience hall. He feels aggrieved. He suspects that his interests—his *bania*'s interests which are encompassed within and integral to his own entity—are at stake. His instincts are sound. The Brahmin Minister is in fact harping on the *bania* quality of the *bania*.

'A *bania*, Excellency,' he murmurs.

'What? What's that?' The Englishman is testy. He is accustomed to having his decisions dismantled by the stringy Minister but not in public audience. It is like sacrilege in church. He is a High Church man. His hand flutters to his nostrils, covers and hides his thin and, he suspects, plainly querulous lips. He is reluctant to give away a single trick to his annoying adversary. The Minister observes the gesture, interprets it with an ease born of familiarity, but he has a duty to do. He represses his bony shoulders, which are itching to rise to a shrug.

'Not of the ruling class, Excellency,' he murmurs. He selects the word *class* with care, meaning it to fall, with reverberations, within the vocabulary of the Agent. The Englishman understands. It has come to be like a duel between them, to which he is not averse. He believes he is never averse to playing a game when the odds are evenly balanced.

'I think, perhaps, Minister, you mean *caste*,' he says, allowing his hand to fall, to reveal the curl of a disdainful lip.

'As you wish, Excellency,' the Brahmin rejoins. His hands withdraw purely, into the wide fluted sleeves of the severe, milk-white muslin robe he affects as his uniform at Court.

The Agent wishes. He cannot conceive that the foul connotations of *caste* can possibly attach to *class*. He believes in the latter, though he will never be crass enough to say so; the importance of the former he only concedes because he does not want a revolution on his hands.

The *bania* whose *caste* or *class* is under discussion is sweating. He feels the drops rolling down his torso beneath the tight white silk maharajah coat he has blundered into wearing. The brocade cummerbund feels clammy, and he understands that mental sensations are poignantly commingled with the physical. Stubbornly, he resists. He is a stubborn man. Were he not, he would not be in the position he is in, that is to say within an ace of appointment as maharajah. He tells himself he will make as good a maharajah as the next man, which is probably true. Stupidly, he goes further: he tells himself there is no good reason why he should not be made the maharajah. This one sticks. Try as he will he cannot get it past the mighty word *caste* that has been uttered, which has been wafted to him across the distance he maintains, and is expected to maintain, from Political Agent and Minister. Rebelliously, he straightens his craven backbone; but already the treacherous vertebrae are caving in, one by one, under the crushing weight of centuries. He slumps. Indeed, he is not fit to be maharajah. It has been an aberration, brought on and abetted by the British, even to imagine so. He is what he is: a *bania* like his father before him, a merchant of the Vaisya caste. Rulers of kingdoms are born in the Kshatriya caste mould. Even the British cannot shatter the caste mould into which a man is born. In time they will underwrite the system to ratify and shore up their own imperial presence, although now, in this present instance, it baulks them.

The *bania* is concerned with the future. His entire being is engulfed in the bitterness of the present, which overflows, gives bile-coloured tinges to his brownish flesh. He has suffered the worst blow in his life, he considers, since entering this audience hall clad in the murderous coat on which the royal seal was to fall. Already, mentally, his podgy fingers are wrestling to liberate the thirty-five buttons from the thirty-five sickle loops which splice it together from collar to hem. The maharajah coat is done for. The *bania* knows—he plans it in the crescendo of dashed hopes that roars in his ears—he will be vindictive with this garment which has been torn from his shoulders.

The Minister eyes the minion. He considers him a British booby, yet he experiences a passing pity for the man. The Agent eyes him too. Someone, somewhere, he perceives, has blundered. Before his gaze the *bania* dwindles. The combination of heaven-sent solution to a succession problem and emblematic embodiment of services rendered and crowned with appropriate seals becomes what he is: a corn merchant. The Political Agent rises. His move has been anticipated by the Minister, who nods to the Court usher, who bangs on the floor, twice, with his silver-mounted ebony staff, preparatory to making the announcement.

The audience is at an end.

The Political Agent has immured himself in what he is pleased to call his den. The room is as large as a tennis court. The windows, which have gilded frames, overlook a verandah that is chockful of stone urns crammed with beautiful blooms. The Agent does not see them. He is an unhappy man, bereft, he feels, of counsellors. Yet ample provision has been made. Himself at apex, the Political Agent for Devapur State, he can call on the services of his Military Adviser—but the man has a general's rampant enthusiasms for quartermasters, which has already resulted in this near débâcle. There is the Naval aide—but the young man is a sea-dog, ill-attuned to the nuances of the country in which he is newly landed. There is his Private Secretary—but he, seconded from the Civil Administration, is expert at sitting on fences from which no one, in living memory, has succeeded in dislodging him. The Agent frowns. He feels digging in his flesh the thorn which is, in fact, the Governor-General. His Excellency has already twice requested to be informed of the name of the maharajah who is to take the place of the maharajah who has been deposed. A third missive has been despatched and lies like a bomb on the rosewood table. The Agent capitulates. He hits the bell at his elbow, which emits a single, peremptory *ping*.

The Minister (Native) has been summoned and enters. He has bathed and changed; it is his custom after the hurly-burly of audience to rid himself of the scent of natives and *feringhi** (but especially *feringhi*), which is apt to clot in his nostrils. He has put on a fresh, equally dazzling robe of Surah silk and smells clean. The Agent is made irritably aware of his jaded white duck, which he has not had time to discard.

'Minister,' he says.

'At your disposal, Excellency,' the Brahmin assures him. He is suave. The Political Agent is sour.

'No doubt, Minister, you have your own nominee,' he says, coming straight to the point.

Indeed the Minister has. It is his practice to keep vigilant tab on candidates. He understands his job as Minister is made infinitely easier and richer if the occupant of the *gaddi*** has cause to be beholden. His choice has fallen upon a young man, barely past boyhood, malleable, caste unimpeachable, who fits his bill, but he will not presume to name names until invited. He inclines his head to acknowledge the existence of the nominee.

'The matter is urgent.' The Agent, who is fast losing patience,

*European; overtones of the Hellenic 'barbarian' in later Indian usage.
**Throne.

snaps. 'I am sure you appreciate, Minister, the necessity to settle the question of succession without further delay. Whom may I ask,' he demands starkly, 'have you in mind?'

'There is one Bawajiraj, Excellency.' The Minister, bearded, steers himself away from his beloved obliquities. 'A young man . . . a scion of the Ruling House . . . a youth of irreproachable character.'

'Suitable?'

'Eminently.'

'Caste?'

'Princely.'

'Acceptable?'

'Entirely.'

'To the people at large?'

'I can assure your Excellency he will be completely acceptable to the people at large.'

'I shall have to take your word for it, Minister.' The Agent sighs. 'No doubt you know your own countrymen best.'

'I was born in this country, Excellency.'

The Minister is gentle. He thinks of the land out of whose dust he has been created, on which he is firmly planted. He is aware it steadies him, gives him an advantage over the Englishman whose caparison cannot disguise that the ground he stands on is alien, and apt to be shifty.

The Agent has taken the point. He rises, a trifle stiffly.

'Sometimes, Minister,' he says, 'I have it in mind almost to envy you.'

The Minister bows. He is a man not much given to bowing. He is a Brahmin, and even kings must bend to touch his feet.

* * *

Although he is invariably addressed by the Agent as Minister, the Brahmin is in fact the Chief Minister, or Dewan, of Devapur State.

It is also a quirk of Devapur State to employ the honorific 'Excellency' to address resident English presences. Excellency, Highness, Grace (for many exalted personages are State visitors) are equally regarded as permissible. The title of 'Honour,' however, is strictly barred.

This ban will in time, when it dawns, irk the Honourable the Resident.

On the other hand, the Dewan is not actively enthralled either

7

by the 'Minister' that remorselessly falls from the Agent's lips, although he is prepared to tolerate it from the Maharajah.

Both sides endure, not without grace. India is a capital country for instilling the virtue of endurance.

* * *

The three men with whose lives the British are juggling have never set eyes on each other. They are also widely dispersed. The smarting *bania* has taken himself off to the fount of his fortune. In this ancestral village at the northernmost point of the kingdom, whose fields he owns as far as eye can see, he hopes to heal the lacerations which have come close to breaking what he calls his spirit. In time he will succeed. Already, in the space of a few days, as he has shrewdly calculated might happen, a view of these golden expanses, which his industry has earned him, is spreading its balm on his soul.

The view from the window of the island fortress in which the British have lodged the ruler they have deposed is entirely different. It is a vista of cobbled courtyard, peopled by sentries whose Indian feet have been painfully crammed into boots which resound on the cobbles. It is a planned effect. The ruler, intemperately torn from his *gaddi*, is indifferent to it, as he is to the view, which, aesthetically speaking, is not worth a second look. Were it pleasing, however, it would still be incapable of impact on a mind which is exclusively occupied with schemes. These schemes revolve around one central desire: to re-ascend the throne of Devapur, which the martial valour of his forbears, in ancient times, has won for him, and, pre-requisite to this end, to be rid of the British presence which has tipped him off it.

It is this latter aspect that has alarmed the British. They are indifferent as to who occupies any native throne. Their protégés in course of time will include, among other indulgences, a sadist, a pervert, an infant or two, and a prince who to all intents and purposes is a brilliant amateur jockey. But they are concerned to ensure that the occupant does not raise levies to eject them from the kingdom as the incarcerated maharajah has devoted his considerable energies to doing.

Scheming is what the British are afraid of. Schemes are the stuff of dreams which nourish the restless man who paces his narrow cell, which is as well, as they are to sustain him until his death from old age, in this same cell, in this island fortress the British have constructed to safeguard their many interests, which are grouped, for convenience, under the general heading 'trade.'

The young man upon whom the Dewan's selective eye has fallen knows little of the cares that beset his relative, the relegated maharajah, and nothing at all of the trials the *bania* he has ousted has undergone. In distinct contrast to them he is a carefree youth, eighteen years old, newly married, with the exuberance that often accompanies the two conditions. He is named Bawajiraj, after the erstwhile ruler. Some notion of basking in the glory of their princely kinsman has inspired the parents in their choice of name, although the connection between the two Bawajirajs is so intricate that family charts have to be got out to trace the precise lineage. Though minimal in influencing his decision, the name has also struck the Dewan as felicitous. Streets, squares, parks, markets, called after the banished ruler, proliferate in Devapur State. He envisages some little saving of revenues if wholesale change is avoided.

On this day of momentous decision—which is fine and sunny, a gentle breeze rippling across the valley and into the modest ancestral home—the family gathers to consider the commandment, which out of courtesy has been couched in the form of a proposal. Parents and grandparents are there, hampered by the presence of the unworldly (in their view) young man and his wife, who in turn are inhibited by the presence of their elders, although sustained to some extent by each other. Covertly, jointly, they study the Envoy the Dewan has selected and the British have sent. He is an experienced man, of infinite patience. He sits cross-legged on the rosewood plank they have laid for him, supping the dish of crushed sweet almonds and cream they have set before him, which is excellent, and allows them to thresh it out.

'Me, a rajah?' the young Bawajiraj says. He exchanges glances with his wife, who is a fair, round-eyed thirteen-year-old. Husband and wife giggle.

'A great, a *maha* rajah?' he asks, to improve the risible situation. This time the pair are almost convulsed.

The elders are incensed. This unseemly levity is a strain, but the hint of refusal of the glittering prize is unpardonable.

'You are a Kshatriya,' the frosty father reminds his son. He means it is the caste from which kings are sprung.

9

'It is an honour,' he says.

It is clear he expects his son to spring into this honourable role, by which deed he will fulfil his destiny.

The son holds back. The argument is strong, but the instincts that rein him in are stronger. His instincts warn that nowhere in the kingdom will he find a place that assuages his spirit as does this delightful valley in which he has been born. He does not want to leave it. He does not want to leave the long-legged little colt he plans to school and train himself. He has an unfathomable sense that the company that embellishes the Court will not approach the companionship he now enjoys, youths of his age and sympathies with whom he swims and rides and pits himself against in tournaments.

The elders are thinking aloud.

'It is your duty,' the grandfather says.

'An opportunity. Think about it carefully,' the mother reinforces.

They have considered it with great care, these elders. They have concluded they want wealth. Thinking about it most carefully, they want to give away their dearest possession, the lack of material riches. Their combined desire presses against the young man like a wall; he is almost overborne. The Envoy, who resembles a barometer in his sensitivity to such pressures, judges it time to intervene. He finishes the dish of almonds first.

'You bear the star on your forehead,' he says, to clinch the matter. None care to work against destiny.

Bawajiraj goes to Court. He is installed on the *gaddi* as Bawajiraj II. Agent and Minister interpret the Roman numeral to the masses as a happy symbol of continuity. It is a sop with which they calm *vox populi*, which is stridently clamouring for Bawajiraj I.

Bawajiraj II is unaware, and Minister and Agent are there to protect his innocence. Innocently he takes pleasure in his new riches and privileges, in the manner of his elevation, which is arranged with pomp and circumstance. Few are better at this than the formidable combination behind the throne. Brahmin and Briton are equally skilled in ceremonial; and the British are past masters at puppetry.

Bawajiraj does not know this. Knowledge, in driblets, will be his before the day of his death, but in this present a great many things are hidden from him, including the fact that he is a puppet. He thinks of himself as the ruler: not, perhaps, a *great* ruler—the modesty that has made the title *maha* rajah laughable to his healthy mind does not altogether desert him—but an effective one. After a fashion, perhaps, he is. During his tenure no convulsions rend Devapur State, and some slight amelioration in the conditions of the peasantry are directly traceable to his efforts. The powers that control him concede the gratification of these whims and fancies. For them it fulfils at once three desirable objects: it keeps the young man happy; it preserves intact those straws which, broken, lead to revolutions; and it safeguards the coffers of the State from indiscriminate dissipation.

Bawajiraj is unaware. His life is full, except for one corner which to the end belongs to his birthplace. Sometimes there are jarring notes, longings which resolve themselves into creaks and aches, reveries in which he is pacing his little colt, which in actuality has had to be left behind with its dam. On the whole, though, he believes he is happy. He puts on his robes of state and presides at durbars. A hundred beggars are fed daily, by his decree, at the Palace gates. The stables hold a score of thoroughbreds and half-Arabs. Above all he has the fair Manjula, blossoming at his side.

Although there are beauties in plenty at the Palace, from whom, it has been intimated, he can take his pick, Bawajiraj has no eyes for anyone except his wife. She, fortunately, is equal in beauty to any at Court, and if her simplicity suffers before the sophistries of the great courtesans, she has one irreducible advantage over them. In her flesh, in the fragrance of her hair and the depths of her eyes and in the cadences of her speech and voice her husband discerns and worships the very essence of the valley left behind. She is sprung from it, as he is. Like him a corner of her being cleaves to it, and will do so to the end. They share their memories.

'Do you remember the taste of the water?'

They pick on this most innocuous thing most frequently; it is a material substance and as such has least power to pierce the spirit.

'Sweet.'

'Sweet as anything. I can taste it still.'

'It sparkled. The water here is flat, and hard.'

The hard, flat water is trained to pretty effect in the water-gardens around which they stroll. It issues, gurgling, from innumerable crystal spigots, spouts from the pitchers of statuary artistically grouped around the emerald pool. They remember only the water that comes up stone-cold and crystalline, in buckets, from the granite bore a hundred feet deep. In the ardour of the moment she slips her hand, under the eye of the Palace gardener, into his. He crushes the tender flesh, consumed by a consciousness of their common being into which he feels himself dissolving.

At night she lies beside him, in the four-poster bed of ornate mahogany, in a night-robe of finest mull. When he parts the mull, which is split downwards from the embroidered corsage, and places his hand between pubes and navel, he can feel the lunge and thrust of the child she is carrying. They engulf him in a medley of emotions: of love for his wife and the pulsing life he can feel, and awe for the dynasty which he believes between them they are creating, and lust that seizes his loins as his fingers encounter the springy pubic curls. It makes him ache; he longs for the consummation that is forbidden. Her body is sacrosanct; it has been so for one lunar month and will be until she is delivered and cleansed after birth. He will not breach the interdict. It is not only the life of the child which is at stake but, it has been impressed on him, the continuity of the royal line. The size of it overpowers, sharply exacts obedience. He groans and buries his face in her breasts, nuzzles the warm plump flesh. A thin colostrum issues, beads against his cheek. It seems to him like an anointing.

* * *

The child who will one day be Bawajiraj III is born. The year is 1870.

The infant is handed to his mother, who cradles him against her breast. An intense emotion suffuses her, of which the predominant part is a violent protectiveness towards the helpless scrap, which manifests the moment he is placed in her arms. Against her thick white opaque skin, which has the texture of camellias, the infant looks wrinkled and dark. His eyes, which are a dusky blue, are in fact his mother's; in a matter of weeks they will turn to amber, a rich hue which occurs pertinaciously in her line and is one ingredient of her extreme beauty. His genitals are perfect. The midwife has examined them with care and cannot fault the organs upon which a dynasty depends, which lie limp yet bulking disproportionately large and forceful against the tiny body.

The father is summoned and enters, walking as if eggshells are strewn in his path. The union is so fervent that midwife and attendants withdraw, leaving the trio to their bliss.

In an ante-room the Minister and the Agent wait. The Minister has no certain notion of why the Agent has sent for him. He has obeyed the summons, but he will not enter the birth chamber—if that is the Agent's intention—until after the purification. The Agent's intention is precisely this. He is a Victorian. Relying on memory and precedent, he believes that Ministers should be in at the birth, as at death. He is in morning dress for the occasion, which he envisages as a happy one with the barest political underpinning: a puppet may found a dynasty, but the dynasty has to be consecrated by the British presence before it can achieve its full potential. By presenting himself, he has hoped to fuse symbol and reality in one person. The presence of the native-born Minister is to sugar the foreign pill.

The Minister baulks him.

'It is a simple matter, Minister, of conveying our felicitations to their Highnesses in person,' he says coldly. 'I must say I really fail to understand your objections to so harmless—indeed pleasing—a course.'

'It is not done, Excellency,' the Minister answers.

He chooses his reply with his usual care, to ensure maximum impact on the Englishman who himself, he is aware, operates within a system of complex codes. In a sense he succeeds. Underneath his frosty exterior the Agent boils. He cannot allow to others what is appropriate, he considers, to himself. What is not done by them accordingly becomes a perversity to him.

The Minister is cool. His name is Narasimha Rao, his father's was Tirumal Rao. The two names pepper the pages of the kingdom's history, as none is more aware than he. They will continue to recur with the persistence of the Maharani's amber irises while Agents come and go and Princes rise and fall. The Minister's calm has solid foundations.

The Agent is nobody's fool. He will not batter himself to pieces against rock. He inclines his stiff body slightly and has himself ushered, alone, into the Maharani's chamber. Bowing to the suffused pair, he delivers his oration, which takes on a genuine warmth as he observes the happiness that irradiates the young couple. Briefly his heart flits back to England, his green and gentle birthplace, in which wife, children, an entire supporting

13

web of blood relations reside. In such moments not all the pomp and power of his Indian position—which for the rest of the time suffice—can compensate the angular Agent for the voids and losses of his life.

The Maharajkumar is a lively infant. His infancy is happy, passed between doting parents and wet-nurse, who treats the child as if he were flesh of her flesh. The installation of the wet-nurse in the Palace represents a defeat for the Maharani. She wishes to nurse her child; she considers the choice a mother's prerogative. To her surprise, she finds this elementary right belongs to the Palace. The Maharani is tearful. She appeals to her mother, who has trundled two days and nights by carriage to be with her daughter, but the good lady's certainties, about which she is vocal enough in her own home, are reduced in these lofty surroundings.

'Perhaps they know best,' she is driven to uttering, by which she means the ladies of the bed-chamber, who are aided and abetted by the medical contingent.

The Maharani weeps from frustration. She places rough hands upon her breasts and squeezes them brutally. The milk spurts out rich and abundant; the bed-clothes are drenched.

'The waste, the waste,' she cries furiously. 'You expect me to waste this precious fluid! *Vandals!*' She rips the lacy wraps with which the maidservants are endeavouring to cover her.

The Maharajah comes in on the disorderly scene. He has had to dislodge a score of supernumeraries before he can do so. He kneels by the bed.

'Perhaps they know best,' he soothes his dishevelled wife.

The words are identical to those his mother-in-law has chosen. The difference is that he speaks with conviction. The expressed wisdom of the advisers who surround him is so evident, their experience so encompassing, that he feels himself ill-equipped to oppose them. Between this feeling and fact, there is little distance; in no time at all he will traverse the small stretch that remains.

'For my sake,' the Maharajah begs his wife. The words are inspired; they drip like honey from his tongue.

The weary Maharani capitulates. The wet-nurse who has fled from the scene steals back. The infant sucks and thrives. The mother's milk is dammed and after some agony suppresses itself.

'It was for the best,' the parents assure each other.

14

Another fetter, which both notice, but do not correctly label, has been riveted onto their lives.

The label they select is sacrifice. They have been given to understand, and understand, that sacrifice is expected of them in the name of the Ruling House. Neither Maharajah, nor on the whole Maharani, proposes to sell short.

They continue happy. There is a great deal to keep them happy, indeed a great deal is done to keep them in this state. Nevertheless, certain truths begin to filter inward, lie accumulating in their bones. When the Agent, upon whom the climate is beginning to tell, is brusque, or the Minister, under the stress of encroaching years, resorts to plain speaking, the sediment stirs, assumes disturbing forms. In these brief moments they glimpse the pattern, the intricate marquetry of figure-heads the British have laid over the face of the sub-continent of which they, the royal pair, are one.

But this is in the future. Life revolves around the present.

The young Bawajiraj grows and flourishes. He is, in general consensus, the light of the Palace. He is a merry, lively child, whose amber eyes and sunny nature make up for his dark skin, which has been an initial disappointment.

At the age of two—a week has passed since his birthday, which is marked for him by the big bangs of the guns they have fired in his honour, which still reverberate in his eardrums—the wet-nurse is withdrawn. There is no further need for her. The child eats well; he ingests rice, wheat, *dhal*, mutton, fruit, vegetables, eggs, and wool off the nursery Khelims, all with equal ease. Breast-milk, at this age, is the preserve, for different reasons, of the children of princes and paupers. In Bawajiraj's case it is now a luxury. He has reached the age for it to be withdrawn.

The wet-nurse weeps. She is a poor relation, of unexceptionable caste if reduced fortune, and as much to the point, a fecund young woman of curving hips and heavy breasts that have given suck to a dozen infants. Of these a number have been her own, but she has loved them all equally and wept over each removal. For the last time she offers the Maharajkumar her breast, which he takes with his usual greed. Tears roll down her cheeks, plop down on the curly head. He does not notice or feel them. His eyes are closed, his sucking mouth has created a world of intense sensation in which he is the only, the supreme incumbent.

In the morning her absence is forcefully brought home to him. He finishes his plate of mashed banana and looks round for his human comforter. She is not there. In her place he is handed a dummy. He screams with rage. He rolls on the floor, drumming his heels. The women servants flock round him like doves, cooing and concerned. They promise him a thousand things which are in their gift: sweets, a picnic, a ride upon their backs, upon the resident Palace camel's. The one thing he wants is not within their authority to give.

Between pauper and prince there is a vast acreage: hundreds of thousands of children are indulged their whims and necessities by their middle strata parents. Bawajiraj—such is the star they have pronounced him to be born under—alternately endures strictures which fall upon only the children of the poor and luxuries which can only be lavished on the sons of princes.

At five, Bawajiraj is withdrawn from the inner apartments, where he has flourished in the company of women, and placed in the schoolroom, which is a male precinct. Between one dawn and the next he has lost his fluttering doves and acquired this thin, dry, learned Pandit who, at the insistence of his mother, is to teach him the rudiments of his Hindu inheritance. If the exchange is unpleasing (as it undoubtedly is) the child knows better than to succumb to frenzy. He sits at his desk, which the Palace carpenters have knocked up, sniffing the new wood smell, which is agreeable, and diverts himself by alternately listening to what the Pandit has to say and gazing up at the ceiling, which is painted and has cornices of an intricate palmette design which is wholly absorbing. In this way he imbibes a little geography, a little philosophy, a good deal of arithmetic (the Pandit's pet subject; he is a dazzling mathematician), and a fair amount of Sanskrit, the only discipline that has not first been vetted by the Agent, the language being, to his chagrin, entirely outside his scope.

Bawajiraj's eighth birthday—eight bangs this time, the dovecotes are emptied, flustered turtle-doves rise, circle the cupolas of their erstwhile quarters on distracted wings—dawns delightfully. There is a pony. The *syce* leads it in and stands it in the portico, which is ordinarily reserved for coach-and-four. It is a palomino filly, thirteen hands, a stunning creature of creamy velvet coat and pale-gold, streaming tail. Its lashes, two inches long, are fitting companion-pieces to a pair of the warmest, most melting eyes the boy has ever seen.

The Maharajkumar stands entranced. A stableful of horses

does not compensate, apparently, for not having one of your very own. A slow ecstasy wells up in his breast; he can hardly dare to believe this exquisite creation belongs to *him*, until the grinning *syce* steps forward and relinquishes the reins into his frozen hand.

The pill, which is reserved till later, takes the form of an English tutor. The education of a young Indian prince and future Maharajah is adjudged too important to be left any longer in the hands of an Indian, however learned. The information that the Pandit can impart is suspect—not from any intrinsic shortcomings which have been detected in the man, but because a particular representation of facts is required to produce those attitudes of esteem and admiration which in time will result in loyal and acquiescent Rulers.

Nor is the Englishman bent on misrepresentation. He simply imparts values and attitudes his own education has inculcated in him. He has a touching and unshakeable belief in the soundness and moral integrity of Empire and is convinced, in all sincerity, that India can do no better than to submit to the British presence. This view he is transparently eager to transmit to his pupil.

Mr. Barrington is a charming, dedicated young Englishman, carefully selected and specially imported from England under the aegis of the Political Agent to, in his own words, introduce the young prince to the mores and usages of a wider world.

In the opinion of the Maharani, the confines of the subcontinent of India constitute for the present a wide enough world. She fails to see why these boundaries should be advanced, when there is a good way to go before her son even touches the limits of his native land.

'Let him learn about his own country first!' she cries. The words, which she considers to be hers, in fact embody sentiments adrift in the atmosphere, which are sawing at the edge of the nation's consciousness.

In the Agent's opinion her attitude reinforces the view that Indian women are backward. He overrides the Maharani.

The boy who will one day be Bawajiraj III learns about England, its geography and history, its constitution, its manners, laws, and customs, and about its explorers, generals, and statesmen who, from the highest motives, have annexed a third of the world.

The chronicles of his own country are, inevitably, curtailed, beginning summarily with the European connection; and of his own ancestral history he is given the barest bones. The plight of his deposed kinsman, the manner of his deposition, are disposed of in a few sentences; but the story of the Great Queen, the human circumstance of her accession in girlhood and early bereavement are so vividly portrayed, the wisdom and benevolence of her rule and that of her Ministers so enthusiastically communicated, that it becomes a matter of pride to consider himself her subject.

The tutor is painstaking. Counting it an honour to have the malleable young prince in his care, he throws himself into the task with unsparing energy. In the mornings before breakfast, after a cup of tea, he accompanies his charge on the daily ride. There is little he can teach Bawajiraj about horsemanship—the boy has considerable inherited skills. He cannot, he finds, ride bareback and barefoot in rough country as prince and *syce* do with the utmost aplomb; but on their return, under a hot sun, he instructs Bawajiraj in the art of tent-pegging, at which he excels.

Afternoons are for sport. The tutor, who is far from acclimatised, and possibly is too blond ever to become so, sweats it out with grace. He coerces the *mali* into constructing a grass-court on which he and Bawajiraj play tennis. He forms a team and coaches him at cricket—not just how to win, but how to lose gracefully. This is excellent practice for the prince, who will have to give ground, later on, on a grand scale, but is not undertaken in this spirit. It is simply that the teacher instils in his pupil standards of conduct by which he himself abides.

This fresh and eager, devoted young Englishman is, in truth, a nice young man. The Maharani eyes him askance. She cannot say what is excessive, or lacking, in Mr. Barrington—there is nothing. She only feels that her son is being moved away from her, from her *self*—which encompasses her country and her people, which are also his country and his people—though she has no notion how. This nebulous commission she pins to the innocent tutor's door.

Mr. Barrington, however, is but the first step in the alienating process. He is followed by Chiefs' College, whose principal is an Englishman, while for the future there is the British-officered Military Academy.

Bawajiraj emerges from this process tall, handsome, dark, and charming. Fresh air, sport, and rugged living have improved his physique—he stands a good bit taller than his father and is broad in proportion—and accentuated his colour.

* * *

A touch of the tarbrush, memsahibs in the past have been known to say, murderous behind their fans. They mean, these English ladies who have caught a glimpse of the child, the low-caste girl with whom the prince's father, a kindly man, has been seen to associate. This is an outdoor servant, a fragile creature who sweeps the congeries of paths and drives around the Palace and one day collapses as the Maharajah is riding by. He dismounts and picks her up—his humanity is intact; it is after all not that long since he was one of the people himself—and places her in the care of his own physician.

When she is recovered he finds he has acquired a slave, a thin waif who, it touches him to see, trails after him whenever it is feasible (outdoors naturally; her calling does not permit her to enter Palace confines), undeterred by the threats of the Palace staff.

The Maharani has taken to joking about it.

'Your *inamorata*,' she ribs her husband. The word has been culled from the ladies, whose fans are no obstacle to Manjula's sharp faculties.

'Not at all,' the Maharajah disclaims. 'A human creature who, as it happened, fainted at my feet.'

'Overcome by the Maharajah's presence.'

'By the heat, and the rigorous nature of her toil.'

'At the very instant of your passing.'

'These things happen.'

'Very conveniently.'

'No one can control the timing of their fainting fits.'

'You believe that? You believe the girl?'

'Why shouldn't I?'

'She is very attractive.'

'The poor child is young enough to be my daughter.'

'Or your mistress, they say.'

'Tittle-tattle!' the Maharajah snaps. This moonstruck servant girl who shadows him is beginning to try his patience.

The Maharani sails away, pleased to have breached her husband's calm. They love each other steadily. The marriage has been cemented by their translation from the beloved valley, which makes them cling to each other; by their lively child; and by passing time, which underlines the fortunate circumstance of this arranged match. It confers the freedom for such sallies and tilts.

* * *

As the years go by Manjula, in the eyes of many and certainly in those of her husband, appears to grow in beauty. At thirty-three she is, perhaps, more beautiful than she was at thirteen. Possibly she reflects the serenities of her marriage. Possibly it has something to do with her eyes and the matchless quality of her fair and unflawed skin. The English ladies ponder: skin colour is their preoccupation. At assemblies and receptions, where she is available for inspection, they study her narrowly. The Maharani's camellia hues cannot be faulted, but the thick waxy quality of skin which rosy tints cannot permeate is picked on by these nodding English roses. A rose complexion, then, is deemed to be the pinnacle.

Into a country already obsessed by colour a new dimension has been added.

* * *

The Maharani, in due course, begins the search for a fair bride for her son. She sends her emissaries—her clan is an extended one—far and wide in search of a girl whose qualities she has precisely catalogued.

The Dewan, who has an interest, which he does not declare, has also despatched emissaries whose commissions are equally strict. His concern is to secure a union which will strengthen the realm, by which means he hopes to trim the sails of the British, whose power, he fears, has grown overweening. At the same time he has no wish to strengthen the realm to the point where he, the Dewan, is rendered a cipher. The balance to be struck is a delicate one, requiring some agility and considerable skill. Narasimha Rao does not doubt himself, but he is a preoccupied man.

The third power in this game is the British Agent, who feels, with some reason, that he has been dealt a poor hand. For he has no one to send forth. Overt British intervention in this purely Hindu transaction is unthinkable. He knows it will only earn him a reprimand in those aloof quarters which expect results without obtrusive meddling. Indeed, he has little liking for such interference. The extravaganza that is his opinion of Hindu marriage rites offends his penchant for orderly display. Nevertheless, he is committed. The Empire he represents cannot sanction or ratify a union whose combined strength could threaten the British presence in one of the most lucrative markets it has ever cornered. He has, of course, power of veto, but he is chary of wielding a weapon which is apt to turn in his hands into a blunderbuss. What is left to him, then, is to remain behind the scenes and exercise what influence he can.

He remains, carping at his Minister from the wings.

'Like an Eastern bazaar, this procession of damsels—if I may be permitted to say so, Minister,' he grumbles. 'Is there to be no end?'

'It is an Eastern bazaar,' the Brahmin replies. 'If I may venture, Excellency, Eastern flavours are to be found—are they not—in all marriage markets.'

The Agent frowns. He cannot bring himself to downright lying, yet he would dearly like to dispute the point. At such moments he actively dislikes this stringy man with whom he is fated to ride tandem. Abruptly he changes the subject.

'Of course you will be aware,' he declares bluntly, 'that alliances of this nature are affairs of State. I trust I may leave it to your good offices, Minister, to ensure an outcome to the negotiations in progress that does not run counter to the interests of the Crown.'

The Minister inclines, slightly. He makes no promises. He owes no duty to the Imperial Crown which Victoria wears. To him it is a costly bauble, improperly won and worn, for which there have been many contenders, including the British, who happen to be, for the moment, in possession. He leaves it to others to interpret as they will their duty towards this transient symbol.

* * *

A girl is found, eventually. She is a compromise solution and as such encounters a tepid approval on all sides.

Her father is the Rajah of a neighbouring State. Such power as he wields is his own and his Ministers'; there is no resident overseer in the shape of Agent or Resident. This pleases Narasimha Rao. His cousin is one of the Ministers.

The docility of the girl enchants the Agent. He feels, sourly, he would be doing his successor a disservice to bequeath to him a woman as contrary as Maharani Manjula. There is, of course, the girl's father, the Rajah, but the Agent believes the prince's tutelage is sufficient to neutralise any undesirable influences from that quarter.

Manjula is satisfied that her criteria have been met, more or less. Shanta Devi is pretty, and when she is unveiled in the inner

apartments the Maharani detects qualities of stability and fruit-
fulness in the future bride that she calculates will stand her son,
and his kingdom, in good stead. Spirit, perhaps, is lacking.
Manjula sighs, but rationalises: spirited responses are not conducive to happiness under the British Raj, and happiness is what
she must seek for her son.

At last the young man concerned is consulted. He echoes the
approval that he hears expressed on all sides. The girl is fair
enough, and he is a pliant young man.

The Maharajkumar's birthday falls on an auspicious day in
June. The Minister, with an eye on Treasury funds, has decided,
but frames it as a proposal, to combine birthday and nuptials in
one mammoth celebration.

'The hottest, most dreadful month!' The Agent is aghast. It is
his custom—it has become a rule in these, his later years—to take
to the hills in the hot weather. He trembles to think of the
ravages to his constitution if he is forced to endure the blistering
plains. This year his sights are on Simla: its iced air and scented
forests are in the nature of a vision whose allure soars the instant
it is menaced.

'Quite impossible. An impossible month,' he says firmly.

'It is the marriage month,' the Minister comes back smartly,
and recruits the Maharani to his side.

The Maharajkumar is betrothed at eighteen and wedded on
his nineteenth birthday.

The nuptial ceremonies are everything the Agent has feared
they would be and the couple's parents have desired. The festivities go on for a month. In that time there is hardly a corner
left which the sounds of revelry and rejoicing do not penetrate.
Time itself is upset, as firecrackers turn night into day with the
marked approval and connivance of the populace. It wearies the
Agent, whose constitution wilts before these scenes of unremitting enthusiasm. He retires to his den and despite the heat closes
the shutters.

As a matter of pride both States contribute to the celebrations,
although in lesser families the burden would be thankfully left to
the distaff side. The dowry the bride brings with her is handsome. There are forty chests of brocade and fine linen, a retinue
of two hundred servants in full equipage, jewellery valued at
several lakhs of rupees, and a casket of loose emeralds—unset,
but matching, each the size of a ram's eye—on which no jeweller
has cared to set a price. In turn she receives the Summer Palace,

which has been specially built for her and furnished down to the last golden goblet, a troop of horse, a park of a thousand acres stocked with peacock and gazelle, and a framed portrait of the Queen-Empress, which is the Agent's gift.

At the end of it all the Dewans of the two States compute costs. The ledgers are full. The industrious clerks at the Treasury have recorded in meticulous copperplate items of ordinary and extraordinary expenditure. The latter predominate. There are entries for the enormous *shamianas* that have been erected on the Palace grounds to take the overflow of guests; for tents for their attendants; for gold plate and silver *howdahs* and horse and elephant trappings; for triumphal arches and priests' emoluments and feeding of the poor.

Narasimha Rao casts a disparaging eye. A waste, he observes, drily. He is at that time of life when it is seemly for a man to withdraw his suckers from the earth he will soon be leaving. Only the uninitiate cling; it is not a dignified performance, nor one even remotely within the scope of himself, the twice-born Brahmin. His counterpart—another Rao—agrees, with one exception. The feeding of the poor, he says. He does not have to say much, meanings are readily taken in this company.

The poor themselves—the masses that storm the bastions of the Palace with simple joy—do not regard their ceremonial feeding as a safety valve that preserves this very Palace and the British who are its protectors. Possibly, at this stage, they would not rise as revolutionaries were they to be deprived of these feasts that fill their bellies at intervals. Nor do they know that the taxes of people less than one remove from themselves will pay for the right royal handouts—there has even been a distribution of one piece of new cloth for each destitute family—they are enjoying. They only savour the moment and call down blessings on the heads of those who have arranged this great *tamasha* for their benefit.

The Minister and the Agent, having, each in his own way, satisfactorily closed this chapter in the life of the heir to the kingdom, settle to a consideration of their own destiny.

There is a pearl that each man keeps in his mind, a grain which the passing years overlay with nacreous coats. Worn close, guarded well, the pearl gleams; it has acquired the very sheen of those ardent desires that animate each man.

The Agent has a vision. It is his pearl, which he brings out shyly to exhibit to the Indian.

'A place in the country. Really quite small, a few acres. Nothing to all this, of course.' He waves a hand that simultaneously takes in and repudiates the magnificence of Palace and Residency. 'There's a trout stream, well-stocked I'm told, and the shooting's excellent . . . I hope to . . .' he falls into a reverie, rouses from it only through a civil consideration for the other man. 'And you, my dear chap, what are your plans, you must have them?'

The Minister hesitates. His pearl is an *ashram*, built under a banyan tree, in an outpost of the province that has been the fount of generations of Narasimha Raos. It is a place of stony and monastic character, crumbling, roots and vines encroach and are splitting the stonework. It is also a place of silence and solitude in which he hopes to recoup his spiritual reserves for those further excursions of his soul, for which, as is proper, he is preparing himself. Indeed, the process is well advanced. His wife is at one remove from him, although he continues to treat her with courtesy. He is detached from his family, even the son who has been groomed to step into his shoes. Increasingly he surveys with a remote and wondering eye the vanities and luxuries of his present existence, which bear less and less relevance to his inner being.

The pearl is radiant, but his worldly eye is not wholly dimmed; it sees that a dilapidated *ashram* will convey, if anything, only a suspicion of declining faculties to the Englishman.

'I have one or two dreams, Excellency,' he says gently.

'Well, I wish you fulfilment of them, whatever they may be, Minister,' the Agent replies with a gentleness that equals.

The two men part. They are of the same calibre and, basically, informed by the same decencies. It is possible, even likely, that had they been permitted to meet as equals they would have been friends, but the dominant/subservient roles written into and essential for the survival of Empire, of which this kingdom is a part, preclude such meeting. In the circumstances, each man has done the best he can.

* * *

At twenty-one Bawajiraj III accedes, suddenly, to the throne.

Bawajiraj II is out riding. It is a balmy day, freshened by a shower of rain. The chestnut gelding ambles along, sniffing spring scents, its glossy coat rippling. Presently it is hankering to trot. Bawajiraj feels the stirring muscles, gives the horse its head. Man and beast are cantering; exhilarated by the sweet season they are galloping like the wind. The *syce*, taken unawares, rides some distance behind but equably; his master is an excellent horseman.

Disturbed by hooves a cobra emerges. The frightened creature extends its hood and hisses. Hostile and erect, serpent tongue flickering, it is a truly terrifying sight. The terrified gelding rears, gets the bit between its teeth, and bolts.

Bawajiraj is thrown. His back is broken, he lies where he has fallen. The cobra, which could have administered the coup de grâce, retracts its hood and glides away; it has no malice towards the peaceable. When the distracted *syce* rides up he can see no reason for the accident, and Bawajiraj, who has been rendered speechless, cannot enlighten the man.

A palanquin brings the Maharajah back to the Palace.

The Court physicians wait. They are like the cobra, in that it is within their power to administer the coup de grâce. They prefer not to exercise their power but prescribe this and that. Suffering, especially in royal circles, is a medical money-spinner, which they are not renowned for lightly casting away.

Manjula dismisses them. She gets rid of the supernumeraries. She is a strong woman, this Maharani; the doctors quail before her scorn. The servitors, who have no cause for guilt, disapprove the method but respect the woman in this queen of theirs, in whom, at last, they recognise flesh of their flesh.

When all are gone, and she has closed the door on the last one, Manjula kneels beside her husband. They are fortunate, or blessed, in that there is no need for words between them. In any case it is not possible, since the Maharajah's speech centre no longer functions. Wordlessly, then, she offers her husband the potion which has figured in the artless love-compact they have made, she at the age of thirteen and her husband five years her senior. Wordlessly she administers it. Then she covers his body with her own and waits until it is time, she judges—the soul almost fled, most tenuously attached to its habitation—for the priests to take over as enjoined upon her by the scriptures. She rises then, relinquishes to them her place beside her husband.

It is dusk—the last dregs of twilight are barely tinting the marble of the outer courtyard—when the Maharani emerges. The women waiting in the ante-chamber in silence have intended to break into weeping and wailing, but are quelled by her appearance. She is like wax, an unlit candle. No tears have coursed down or marred her countenance. She walks between the women—none dares aid her—and enters her sanctuary.

* * *

There is a routine that takes care of every aspect of a prince's death. Prayers are said. The Treasury is sealed. The Heir assumes the royal mantle and sword and is named and acknowledged by nobles and commoners. Commanders of troop and Heads of State are advised and alerted. The Palace flag is lowered to half-mast. A lone conch blows from the Palace Lodge.

In the royal bed-chamber the dead Maharajah has been prepared for his last journey. He lies like a common man, on a litter constructed of bamboo poles and palm fibre, which emphasises the universality of his experience. His eyes are closed—they have not re-opened since Manjula lowered the lids over his acceptance of her offering. The unbleached cloth in which he is covered finally extinguishes whatever finery his body is entitled to. It is of coarse linen, daubed with sandalwood paste and *kumkum*, and is drawn up to his chin. Above it his face, exposed, is unnaturally white and composed, yet it is not that much changed from the fresh visage of the young man who departed his valley to become a king. Manjula has looked upon, and acknowledged, the unaffected, unchanged nature of the Maharajah not only in the hour of his death but throughout the lifetime spent in his kingdom.

She prepares herself, this marble Maharani, who will not permit one single maidservant to invade her privacy, to match the state of her husband, insofar as she can. There are in fact guidelines laid down for the bereft, which she is not reluctant to grasp. Standing in front of the mirrors that adorn the room she removes her jewels, returns each to its velvet-lined casket. She will not wear them again; they are no longer hers—they have never been hers except on lease. Now they descend through the daughter she has never had to the granddaughters she hopes will be conceived in the future. Only the *thali*, the necklace with which she has been wedded, is left encircling her throat, and upon her wrists a few recalcitrant, coloured glass bangles. When the last casket is closed Manjula unpins her hair. The thick glossy tresses, which reach to her thighs, have been the delight of her husband and have figured in their love-play. With an impersonal hand, although the sacrifice has not been demanded of a queen, she takes up the scissors and shears off her locks. It is not done well. A coarse uneven stubble is left, which prickles against the ear-lobes and will, later, irritate the Maharani. At present she is unconscious, or careless. Uncaring, she lets fall her sari, steps over the heap of tumbled silk, over the shorn hair that litters the floor, and enters the bath-chamber where cauldrons of water are waiting.

The water she throws over herself is like ice. She does not notice. She dries herself patchily, with a transient pity for the assembly of parts in its comely frame which will never more delight another, drapes around it the coarse white sari which in its simplicity rivals the cerements that encase her husband. Barefoot and crop-headed, the sari clinging in parts to the imperfectly dried torso, the Maharani surveys herself. She continues to look, and what the widow sees now is not herself as she is but as she was, the thirteen-year-old bride.

The image fades; or, rather, past and present are telescoped to present the reality of time. The bride/widow rouses; there are other duties to perform, as the receding images remind her. She kneels, and bringing her wrists together pounds them on the stone floor. The fragile glass bangles are shattered, and fall. She raises her hands to her throat and tugs at the *thali*, which has not been removed since the day it was tied. It breaks. The broken cord is in her hands when the anaesthesia of shock suddenly lifts. Her anguish begins.

The women outside have heard and are paralysed by the terrible sounds. When the Maharani emerges they are scarcely able to tell husband from wife, so close is the similarity between these two dead, drained individuals. But while the Maharajah's blood has long congealed, the Maharani's wrists are seen to be bleeding. Only one in the assembled company dares to move, intending to staunch the wounds; but she, too, falls back when she sees how it is.

Towards evening the funeral cortège begins.

The Maharani keeps watch, from the crystal gallery below the dome of the Palace to which she has ascended, alone, for these last views.

The procession is a mile long and torch-lit. It is led by caparisoned beasts and followed by eminent men on foot. The Agent is there, in black; and the Dewan in his pure vestments. Between them walks the young Maharajah, her son, on his right hand the British Envoy, on his left the Indian Minister. Priests, princes, nobles, ministers, and military commanders follow the bier, which is borne on a gun-carriage, with an escort of cavalry, muffled drums beating. Before and behind are buglers, drummers, standard-bearers, and the mourning host of common people. The Maharajah has been a popular man. He has also been a man whom the panoply of State has invariably reduced to laughter, an emotion he has shared with his wife.

Laughter, then, at last brings the tears. Tears stream down the Maharani's face, and for all that she tries will not be stemmed. It is morning, a watery sun rising, the glow of the funeral pyre dying on the horizon, before she leaves her crystal tower.

2

The child who is the protagonist of this story or history was born in January 1895, the natural son of the Bawajiraj who acceded to the throne as the third of his line.

At this moment, a fine day in the spring of 1894, he has yet to be conceived. He lives, divided, between his future: between his mother and his father to whom the present is all-powerful. They lie, entwined, in the tall grass on the verge of woodlands that form part of the Palace estates. The woman is pale and lithe. Her shyness has gone with her virginity, which Bawajiraj has taken a full month since. It allows her to use her limbs in a manner which brings them both to the pitch of ecstasy. When she raises her legs and crosses them over his torso both are lost. Neither can control the dazzling issue of their climax, which in the prelude has actually been their intention.

Afterwards—a little afterwards—they lie quiescent in the grass, which their energies have tamped down into a bed. Bawajiraj, loving and langorous after consummation, strokes the fair body on which he has lain, his fingers are proprietorial when they encounter the dampness he has left, where they have come together.

The woman, being woman, is apprehensive. She takes the stroking hand and holds it still. Her eyes reflect the passing clouds.

'What if there is a child?'

'There won't be.'

'There may be.'

'Think of that when we come to it.'

'Think of it now.'

'Now! Now is for *us*!'

He rolls over onto her and bites her lip. She rouses and answers his vehemence. Quite soon a fresh orgasm is achieved.

Afterwards—long afterwards—they pinpoint this as the moment of conception of their child. The child does not know—except perhaps in that incandescent instant of fusion when his two halves are joined; but the triumphant, dolorous paean, if there is one, is buried and lost in the womb.

* * *

The womb, having received, embeds the child in its wall and closes its mouth. It is an organ of great purpose and tenacity. The plug with which it seals itself off will not budge until birth is imminent or the obdurate cells are forcibly raked out. There is no flow.

'Are you sure?'

'Naturally I am sure.'

'You may be mistaken. You're inexperienced in these matters.'

'The midwife is not.'

'It's too early to tell, surely.'

'It's three months.'

The Maharajah gloomily surveys the woman, whose name is Mohini. She shows nothing; there is little to see except when she is naked and draws his attention. There is a slight flaring of the nipples. The belly on which he has bounced—as flat as a board within his memory—is slightly rounded. It is difficult to believe these rudimentary signs can possibly indicate an infant. Mohini gives him a date, to ram it in.

'In less than six months' time,' she says.

The Maharajah becomes defensive.

'What will you do?' he asks, preparing to shift his responsibilities.

'You mean what will *we* do,' she corrects. Her mouth is resentful; she cannot for the life of her understand why, when the pleasure has been shared, the burden should be single and borne by her alone. To do him justice neither does Bawajiraj, once the proposition has been put to him. It is just the enormity of the joint burden that appals, makes him long for her to assume it in its entirety, which she will not do.

She is a spirited woman, this Mohini. She is ward to Manjula, the Dowager Maharani, and some of the older woman's fire

30

smoulders in her. There is, too, a blood-tie. She is a distant relation of Manjula's, sent as retainer and companion to the widowed Maharani. The bold airs of that remote valley play about the young woman's head. They will not be swamped by the rarefied, royal atmosphere.

In fact, there is little to be done, since neither will tamper with what they have set in motion, their awe in the face of creation is too strong. Indeed, as the months go by they are reconciled to sequels and consequences, each ceases to question what the other will do. It is even conceivable that in moments of ultimate freedom both savour a tentative delight in the forthcoming birth, which is a product of their love for each other.

Mohini's pregnancy is the result of a first affair. Bawajiraj, on the contrary, has used his privilege as a prince to the hilt and indulged in a string of liaisons. None of them has ended in a pregnancy. None of them, he tells himself, has been like this one. He has never loved his other women—he has certainly never loved his wife, the tepid Shanta Devi—as he loves Mohini. He sighs, kisses her beautiful hands, and bemoans his fate.

'If only I had known you before!'
'Before what?'
'Before my wife.'
'What would you have done?'
'Married you. Made you my queen.'
'And been happy ever after.'
'Yes. Why do you laugh at me?'
'Because it's a dream. No one can be happy forever.'
'I would have been, with you.'
'Until the next woman.'
'There wouldn't be another woman. I wouldn't look at another woman.'
'And I would end up like the rest. Sit in the women's apartments waiting for my husband to come to me.'
'No.'
'Like Shanta Devi.'
'I give her everything.'
'Except yourself.'
'How can I? I belong to you. Why do you torment me?'
'You are the tormentor. You torment women.'
'Why do you say such cruel things?'
'Because of my plight!'
Mohini raps her pregnancy and sheds a few tears not so much

for herself as for her sisters who, in her position, would certainly be in a cruel plight.

But Mohini is fortunate. Her circumstance is such as to make her pig in the middle. A poor, low-class girl who gets herself pregnant—so the phrase goes—can look forward to being set adrift on the general tide of humanity. A nobleman's daughter endures disgrace and humiliation, a marriage to the man who has dishonoured her, forced by an avenging father. Mohini sits in the middle. She is not a low-class girl. There is no powerful, avenging family. The formidable Dowager Maharani is her guardian, and the woman on whom the favour of a Maharajah has fallen need fear no reprisal. It is not lost upon this graceful, resourceful girl, who now prepares to parry her lover's further assaults.

'Ah, Mohini!' he sighs again. He has taken to pleading with her; it is becoming quite an exhausting business. 'I beg you, will you not marry me?'

'No.'

'It would make me the happiest man alive.'

'I can make you happy without that. I have no wish to be your official wife. I have no wish to be your second wife either.'

'Can you not think of the child?'

'I often think of the child. It is precisely because I think of the child.'

'I cannot understand your objection.'

'I've explained it to you.'

'I must say I find it difficult. Even princesses do not baulk at becoming Junior Maharanis.'

'I am not a princess.'

'You could be a *queen*.'

'I don't want to be your queen. I want to be free.'

'Am I not free?'

'Of course you're not free.'

'As far as I'm aware—'

'You're aware of nothing. The British have tied you up hand and foot and you don't even know it. Do you want me to be shackled like you? Do you want my child—'

'My child.'

'Our child. Do you want our child to become like you?'

Frankly, Bawajiraj sees no objection. He is not an immodest man, but he believes, certainly in all truth, that he has served an onerous apprenticeship to fulfil his role as ruler and can say in all humility that he has always done his best for the State and will conscientiously continue to do so.

32

This modest claim is also true of his father. The difference is that Bawajiraj II has felt the strings the British attach to their protected Maharajahs and has at least glimpsed the extent to which they have kept him from realising his full potential. For he, unlike his son, has come of age as a free man. His translation to the *gaddi*, following the unsuitability of their first candidate, which the British still hold against the luckless *bania*, has been at the age of eighteen, long after the basic pattern has set. Subsequent changes, therefore, are in the nature of fringe alterations to an edifice whose inner structure has remained untouched.

Bawajiraj II has died not wholly unaware that the British have appointed, and he has been little more than, a figurehead.

No such intimations reach, or trouble, Bawajiraj III.

He feels he is the ordained Ruler. The history of his father's translation has been skimped by his tutor and is now forgotten. There is a hymn to which the Englishman has been much addicted, which informs him that the rich man in his castle, the poor man at his gate, God made them, high or lowly, and ordered their estate, and so informing, reinforces his view of pre-destination. There is his upbringing. As heir to the throne he has gone, barely touching common soil, from the hands of his assiduous tutor to Chiefs' College, an exclusive establishment for the sons of princes and noblemen founded on British principles and initiative and intended to function as an Indian Eton. Thence the Indian Etonian has gone, on the advice of no less than the Viceroy, to the Military Academy, which is officered by Englishmen and from which he has graduated with distinction. His education has been rounded off by a training in Civil Administration, undertaken by Mr. Hammond, a distinguished member of the Indian Civil Service, a service in whose upper reaches not an Indian is to be found.

In this process he has become eminently fitted to fill his special role.

This is no accident. The British have early understood the importance of the Native Princes, the one class in the country bound to them by every tie of self-interest, in the Imperial scheme. They are concerned to devise buffers which will protect them against the wrath of the masses and to ensure the emergence of Maharajahs amenable to their purpose. The matter receives attention at the highest levels. Viceregal edicts are issued which set out criteria for the instruction and education of Rulers' sons. There is no person more powerful than the Viceroy, who is the Sovereign's Vicegerent.

These criteria are wholly admirable. They call for exemplary standards of conduct and duty to the people. The most able and devoted Englishmen are found to man the élite establishments that inculcate such virtues and foster such qualities. Bawajiraj himself has been polished and turned out by such a system. He is, with the important difference of the colour of his skin, a very passable imitation of a young English nobleman. The trouble is that he is the Indian Ruler of an Indian State.

At eighteen, at the end of the formidable course he has run, the doors which would have opened to the young English nobleman he so closely resembles are closed to Bawajiraj. The regulation of the State of which he has been proclaimed Head, that would have engaged and occupied his energetic ancestors, except in minor respects has never been available.

Many things have been hidden from Bawajiraj II, the father. The curse, or gift, in more acute and disastrous forms is handed down to the son, Bawajiraj III, who has no notion that the British have taken him from his birthright.

* * *

Mohini, her pregnancy seven months advanced, has begun to consider the future of her unborn child. It is possible she has heard, through the Dowager Maharani, who keeps her ear close to the ground—the British are convinced of an extensive zenana spy system—of certain intrigues. These revolve around denying the child official recognition until the union of the parents is regularised. There have also been some rumblings about the naming of the infant.

'What shall we call him?' Mohini leans, langorous, against her lover in a flowered muslin scented with patchouli, which stirs his senses but leaves her unmoved. Her sexual inclinations these days, he has noticed, are secondary and subservient to her maternal role.

'Must we think about it now?' He caresses her. He can think of no more agreeable pursuit than to spend a balmy afternoon dallying with this girl but is aware of a lack of empathy. The silken hammock in which they are idling tilts alarmingly as she sits up.

'Why not now?' She is abrupt.

'There are other things.'

'I don't want to talk about other things.'

'As you wish.'

'I want to talk about our baby.'

34

'All right.'

'What shall we call him?'

Distantly, Bawajiraj hears authoritative voices, clipped accents. These have advised that, in the event of a son, the chosen name must not reflect any connection, however tenuous, however remote, with dynasties that have ruled, or are ruling, Devapur State. They have impressed upon him the undesirability of extending this honour indiscriminately to illegitimate offspring, to offspring whom the mother persists in rendering illegitimate, to natural sons of unmarried mothers upon whom they fear, not without reason, they cannot exercise the desired degree of control.

'Of course Your Highness will understand . . .' they murmur, these worldly, steely men, to the Maharajah.

But even they do not care to tackle the wayward, headstrong concubine. They leave this task to the Ruler, who now sets about it cautiously.

'If it's a boy,' he begins. The opportunity to finish is snatched from him.

'If it's a daughter then I can fend for her myself, call her what I like, do with her as I please, she will be mine alone, is that what you're saying?'

'No, no.'

'A miraculous conception.'

'No, of course I'm not saying that.'

'Or if its imperfect—a cripple or a monster—then I'm the mother, but you're not the father.'

'No, *no.*'

'But if it's a fine handsome son, then naturally you are the father.'

'Why are you so hard on me?'

Bawajiraj III is pained. The very daring that has attracted him to this girl, among all the others at Court from whom he could have chosen, is becoming a trial. He wishes he had never seduced her, although the advent of a child (he already has three—all girls—by his wife) always fills him with the tenderest emotion.

'If it's a son we'll call him whatever you like,' he says placatingly, smothering distant voices.

'What about Bawajiraj?'

The Maharajah flinches—this is categorically opposed to advice—but recovers himself.

'If you like,' he concedes, nobly.

Now, however, Mohini turns contrary.

'No! Why should he bear the name of your line?'

35

'Why not?'

'Because you won't recognise him.'

'How can I, if you won't consent to marry me?'

'I shall never consent.'

'Then how——?'

'You're the Maharajah, aren't you? You tell me often enough you're free to do what you like.'

'So I am.'

'Then why can't you recognise the child?'

'I've told you why!'

'The truth is you're not master in your own house. You're only a *nam-ke-vaste** king.'

'How can you be so silly?' The Maharajah heaves deep sighs. 'You're a woman, women don't understand these things.'

'I do. I understand very well. I'm not like your other women.'

'If you did, you would understand that Maharajahs have standards to uphold,' says the annoyed but controlled Maharajah. 'I am sure you would be the last one to wish me to default.'

Bawajiraj continues controlled, even urbane. Views of himself, and his supremacy, are rooted opinions in his mind, although not necessarily fed in by himself. They have come from outside, from a plethora of sources, and have lodged from the lack of any determined uprooting even by the astringent Manjula, who sees, perhaps, but perceives little purpose in afflicting her only son.

The view to which Bawajiraj most often and fondly refers is an unsolicited testimonial (he has had it framed; it hangs in the Hall of Private Audience) from his English tutor, the dedicated Mr. Barrington with whom he is still glad and privileged to correspond.

> *I have seen His Highness grow* [the enthusiastic Mr. Barrington has written] *into a tall young man whose distinguished appearance can be said to match his inner quality. A fine horseman, an excellent shot, a first-class cricketer, and unrivalled at polo, His Highness is equally the most charming of hosts.*

The tutor is, certainly, the most discriminating of men. He has unerringly selected those pursuits in which the Maharajah

*In name only.

36

excels, at which he shines in the most accomplished company, and from which he derives the most transparent pleasure.

The ruling of Devapur State is another matter, for the areas in which the Ruler can shine are quite precisely delineated. Its sufficiencies, of which there are a few, certainly stem from the Maharajah; while its deficiencies, of which there are many, cannot in all conscience be laid entirely at his door.

The curious factor in all this is that whereas the British, who have devised the system, believe (as does Bawajiraj) that the Princes of India enjoy a great deal of latitude, in fact no move by them which infringes British interests (these are manifold and growing) is permitted.

The Resident keeps close watch to ensure that there is no breach. That is the reason for his appointment, and for his residence, in some style, in the Residency in Devapur City, the capital of the State. Also in the capital, but independent of the State, under a Commanding Officer virtually chosen by him and entirely at his disposal, is the Garrison Force, permanently stationed in the cantonment. This well-trained, highly disciplined, British-officered force can be called upon, if necessary, to enforce his decisions. That the Resident has not had cause to do so can be fairly equally divided between the very existence of this force and the carefully groomed and conformist Ruler of the State.

True, the Resident does not appoint the Chief Minister of the State. That is the prerogative of the Maharajah; but no Chief Minister has yet been appointed of whom the Resident disapproves.

The Dewan appoints his ministers; but he is a shrewd man (another Brahmin; the Brahmins have collared the best brains— they have proved it can be done by a system of sufficient ingenuity and singular dedication) who is very well aware of the presences in the cantonment and Residency; and he chooses his men accordingly.

Bawajiraj III cannot raise levies.

He is forbidden to make treaties.

The first priority upon State revenues is not the State, or even the Maharajah, but the upkeep and maintenance of the Garrison Force.

He cannot travel abroad without the Viceroy's tacit approval; for the Viceroy's plain view of the Princes, which is also withheld from him, is that they are a set of unruly and ignorant and rather undisciplined schoolboys, who cannot be let loose too frequently on the pleasure trail abroad.

On the other hand the citizens of the State are entirely at the mercy of the Maharajah, who is given a free hand to levy what taxes he pleases. The only restraint here is the Dewan, who is called upon to judge how much can be extracted from the people without actually precipitating a rebellion.

It is strange to note how, in all that pertains to this State, two conflicting, if not diametrically opposed, views are held and expressed. Thus Bawajiraj, who has the Palace, the Palace estates, the three Guest Houses, the Summer Palace, the Jewel Chamber, a score of hunting and shooting lodges, his cavalry, his elephants, and in time the fleet of Daimlers and Rolls-Royces, considers himself on the verge of beggary because the Dewan has advised against raising taxes above their present levels. The beggars, on the other hand, of whom there are more than a few in the kingdom, consider their Maharajah to be a man of untold riches. It is an opinion—not a subject for envy or action. Indeed, their conditioning is so extreme that they actively and enthusiastically support their Maharajah.

'The upkeep of it all!' Bawajiraj often groans. 'How little the people know what it all costs!'

The Dewan cocks a disparaging but not unfriendly eye. He considers the Maharajah a thick but entirely genuine young man.

'They do not all own palaces, Highness,' he observes in his dry voice. A second observation rises to his lips—that Bawajiraj himself has little notion of what it actually costs—but this one he smothers out of a mixture of prudence and courtesy.

* * *

Despite the considerable handicaps foisted onto his innocent and cheerful shoulders, Bawajiraj contrives to be a good ruler. He places himself unsparingly at the service of his people. After prayers each morning—at noon—during the innumerable festivals that crowd the calendar, he is available for *darshan*, allowing his people a sight of their Maharajah. Thrice each week he holds durbars in the great Durbar Hall where, sometimes seated on his throne in full panoply, sometimes with the utmost simplicity, he receives his subjects, who flock here with their petitions, or grievances, or gifts, and sometimes just for the fun of it.

Rain or shine, he shirks little. In the worst season he can be seen, coated with dust, or drenched by an early and unforecast monsoon flurry, on an elephant, under a silver umbrella, heading whatever procession, religious or festive, he is required to head. The function or occasion is rare on which he is expected to be present but fails to fulfil expectations. No one can fault the daunting score of dreary foundations notched by His Highness.

Nor does he avoid his less spectacular obligations. Punctiliously, if without enthusiasm, he attends to what he calls Affairs of State, as do his Ministers, who lay before him imposing documents drawn on parchment and bearing rich and interesting seals. Bawajiraj executes these instruments of administration dutifully and conscientiously. Often by the end of the day his hand is cramped; he has to remove the heavy rings, set with emeralds from the fabulous dowry his wife has brought him, to rub his tired, diligent fingers. Ministers—the redoubtable Dewan himself—have never had cause to complain.

As for the people of Devapur, they have little but praise for the Maharajah. His sunny, transparent nature, which his parents have early discerned with pleasure, equally captivates his subjects. He has several little pleasing ways, a kind word here, a joke there, a basket of tempting provisions for some ailing child he has noticed, help with the dowry of some otherwise unmarriageable girl that has come to his attention, all of which convince the Devapuris of their good fortune. There is no doubt but that they worship their Maharajah.

The Maharajah's supreme yet humble pleasure is to dwell on his people's devotion to him. Any possibility that what accrues to his personal quality, and to the quasi-mystical state conferred by royal birth, is not an immutable flow (does not occur). Nor does he pause to differentiate between matters of fundamental import to the State and activities that absorb his energies but are essentially trivia. His life is crammed with trivia. That he does not recognise it for what it is is in a way his salvation, for the hollow shells do not compose themselves into a mocking ruin around him, as they would in a man disastrously equipped to identify them with precision.

Bawajiraj III is a Ruler; but most of the ruling that matters has been taken from his hands. He contrives to fill the inevitable gaps—happily unconscious of contrivance—with hunting, cricket, polo, his horses, his motor-cars, his newest love, the delectable Mohini, his children, including the one he has recently fathered, and his innumerable duties. In this way he is certainly wholly admirable.

* * *

Mohini's son is born. He is a bonny infant, fair-skinned like his mother, amber-eyed like his father, those matchless irises that have come down from Manjula. The parents drool over him.

'Isn't he lovely?'

'Adorable.'

'Just like you. More like you every day.'

'No, like you. He's a boy, do you want him to look like a girl?'

'The last thing.'

'Well, then.'

'He's lovely! He's lovely!'

Bawajiraj crushes mother and child to his breast. He feels he is bursting with love for this limpid woman who has returned to his bed, for the son he has at last achieved, which he takes as a vindication of his masculinity.

'What shall we call him?'

Mohini returns to this unresolved subject. It is certainly time. The infant has been nameless for a scandalous number of days; he cannot subsist (it is claimed on his behalf) on pet names and other effusions of love forever. Priests, moreover, are murmuring.

'Call him whatever you like.'

Bawajiraj is reckless. It is impossible for him to be less within the warm embrace in which the three are basking, and which has quite dissolved the disapproval of the Establishment.

'We'll call him Bawajiraj after you.'

Mohini tests her lover, who by now is lost to all caution.

'Anything you say,' he declares fondly.

'Do you mean that?'

'Of course.'

'Really?'

'Don't I always mean what I say?'

'By no means.'

'I try. But sometimes considerations of State . . .' Bawajiraj is lugubrious. He is also a little pompous, a recurrent quality which exasperates Mohini.

'Do you mean what you've said just now?' She throws off his encircling arm.

'Every word.'

'I've changed my mind.'

'It's your privilege.'

Not for the first time Bawajiraj ponders his wisdom in picking this girl. No one in the entire State treats him as peremptorily. When he looks at her, however—she is lying on a bed whose sheets and coverlet are rose silk, her bare shoulders against them are the purest alabaster, her lustrous hair he compares to a mane of silk—he is utterly lost.

'Anything, anything!' he cries.

His desire to please is so evident that Mohini relents. She twists a finger in the curly mop that rests against her bosom.

'Perhaps some ordinary common name. If it'll make life easier for you,' she says, shrewdly.

'It would, yes.'

'Or perhaps not entirely ordinary.'

'All right.'

'We'll call him Rabindranath. Do you like that?'

'It's a fine name.'

'It's the name of a poet, who is also a great man. Her Highness suggested it.'

'Her Highness!'

It astounds Bawajiraj. The tepid Shanta Devi scarcely voices an opinion of her own; her husband privately doubts that she has any. Also between husband and wife a fiction has been manufactured and crystallised that Mohini as mistress does not exist, that her son has never been born. They do not talk about either, and since reality requires a shoring up at several levels to become a force, it is possible that Shanta Devi avoids the worst abrasions of truth.

'Her Highness the Dowager Maharani,' says Mohini. 'Her Highness has a great respect for this man.'

'Is he a prince?'

'He is a poet, which is greater than a prince.'

'I have never heard of him,' Bawajiraj confesses.

'But that is no reason,' says Mohini, and settles the matter.

After some initial uneasiness—there has always been some distance between the dissident Manjula and her conforming son—Bawajiraj accepts Mohini's choice, which has been made via his mother. 'Rabindranath' has a fine flourish to it, and if it is the name of a poet or whatever whom his mother admires, he is not greatly concerned. His imperative, at the moment, is peace with Mohini, which gives him access to her bed. To Bawajiraj III, moments, and momentary fulfilments, have always been imperative. Forced to conform on so many issues—indeed, a cooperative conformist—his discipline scarcely functions when rules are absent. Bawajiraj has a distinct tendency to burst out in matters in which he is allowed his head.

Bawajiraj's wife, the Maharani Shanta Devi, lives a life apart from her husband. It is also subservient, in that in almost every aspect of it it is indented and adapted to allow for his development. If in the process she is herself stunted or warped, partly she is unaware and partly she is reconciled. Indeed, she believes—it has been bred in her, and in her kind, immemorially—that a woman's supreme attribute lies in her ability to submit to men in general and to her husband in particular.

The distortions that have been worked in her to accommodate him are, by a bitter if inexorable twist, the very attributes that most irk Bawajiraj. He thinks of her, when he thinks of her at all, as tepid and timid. He expects no surprises—that vital commerce that might have revivified their relationship—either from her mind or from the body she dutifully unclothes and surrenders to him. For the fire he needs he flies to other women. She, for her part, feels his apathy even when he lies with her, which he does as a matter of routine and convenience, and is angered, a sullen anger that turns her leaden in every aspect of their intercourse. They resent each other.

Bawajiraj has a favour to ask of his wife.

He wishes his mistress to be lodged in the Summer Palace, which has been a wedding gift to Shanta Devi. So far Mohini has dwelt as his mother's ward in a wing of the Palace which the Dowager Maharani has occupied since her widowhood. Now there is the child. Bawajiraj's heart fills when he thinks of the boy; he wishes to honour the mother of his son; he can think of no better way of doing it than by providing a residence that matches her status. To do so, the facts of life have first to be admitted. The glassy fiction that husband and wife between them have crystallised is about to be fractured.

'The Summer Palace,' Bawajiraj begins. 'You hardly ever use it.'

'The Palace is adequate for my needs,' says Shanta Devi.

'It is a pity to leave it empty.'

'So many things are. Half the rooms in the Palace are empty.'

'The Summer Palace though . . . perhaps if I could— if you could—'

It strikes Bawajiraj as ridiculous that he should have to ask his wife's permission, yet somehow he cannot bring himself to instal Mohini without first asking. In these flounderings Shanta Devi gets wind of what he is after.

'Is it for your use?'

'Not strictly speaking—'

'For your paramour then. For you and her.'

Dull and leaden, the words are out. Shanta Devi lowers her eyes over the rage she feels that he should have brought upon her this dreadful hurt of acknowledgment, which she does not wish him to see. He does not; but there is the atmosphere that claws at him.

'For the child,' he offers her nervously.

'If you like.'

'It's true.'

'It's for her.' Shanta Devi raises her heavy eyelids to confront him. 'A love-nest for her and her son in which you will be welcome. That's what you want. That's what you're asking me for. Why do you ask? I don't want to know. Take what you want. You will anyway. You always do.'

Shanta Devi turns away. She tells herself that one of the perquisites of marriage for men is mistresses. She accepts the position. Her own background has early informed her that Maharajahs have more than one wife and sometimes more than one mistress. She remembers that even her mother-in-law, so rumour has it, despite her love marriage has not been exempt. The difference is that Manjula has been able, within the security conferred by her comparative freedom, to joke about, and often to overlook, her husband's affairs. For Shanta Devi there is only the bitterness of truth that is so brutally thrust upon her.

Bawajiraj creeps away. He has got what he sought. His triumph may be muted, but it is there. He sends for his comptroller to set in train a complete overhaul and refurbishing of the Summer Palace. Rabindranath, who is now three months old, will celebrate his first birthday before it is finished.

When it is done he tries to make a present of it.

There has been a picture in the schoolroom, hung there by Manjula, stubbornly kept there by her throughout his intensive English education, which shows Krishna as a child holding the world in his palm. Such acts are for Gods. Maharajahs, suitably scaled down, are in Bawajiraj's mind not dissimilar. He has a distinct sensation of the entire Summer Palace resting like a globe in the palm he extends to Mohini.

'I have a present for you.'

'Another one! You're always giving me presents.'

'Why shouldn't I give presents to the love of my life?'

'Am I?'

'Need you ask?'

'What is it?'

'Something befitting you.'

He kisses her hand. He offers his plan for her life as if it were a rare jewel. She thrusts it roughly away.

'That mausoleum! You want to maroon us in it? In the middle of nowhere?'

'It's not ten miles from the Palace!'

'It might as well be five hundred.'

'Less than an hour by runner.'

'Do you think I'm a runner? Do you think I'm going to come running to you?'

'No, I'll come to you. Haven't I always?'

'You come to me now. But when I'm shut up in your Summer Dungeon?'

'I'll come to you there too.'

'What's wrong with continuing as we are now?'

'I would like you to have an establishment of your own. Where you and the boy can live in style, on your own—'

'Why don't you wall us up then, like your ancestors did with their enemies, if you want to be done with us? If all you want is to be rid of us?'

'Rid of you! Never!'

'Yes, what else? Out of your sight and out of your mind!'

'You can visit the Palace whenever—'

'Yes. And when I do shall I be allowed to peep at you from behind the curtains when you sit on your *gaddi*? Or would that be counted too great a liberty?'

'You know it would not be like that.'

Bawajiraj is subdued. He has an inkling it will be something like that. Peepholes and curtains have certainly flitted through his mind. It is also humiliating, in that this girl who is the love of his life has grasped the substance of what has only been nebulous to him. He is as proud as ever of his son, the wish to honour the mother of his child is no whit abated, yet he understands, belatedly, what she has already perceived and is determined to resist: the process of phasing her tempestuous presence out of his orderly life which he has tried to set in motion. In the face of her vehemence Bawajiraj jettisons this embryonic plan.

Rabindranath continues to reside in the Palace with the two women who in combination have routed his father the Maharajah.

It is a happy life. He and his mother occupy the set of apartments in the East wing known as the Pearl Suite, partly from the pearls with which it is liberally decorated, partly from the delicate hues the structures assume at sunrise. This is the time the infant is most wide awake. He is lingering over the dregs of his first feed, but is known to discard even this primary pleasure to gaze at the sunlight which turns the red sandstone of the outer bastions to crimson, tints with a pearly rose the pierced marble screens of the inner apartments. The colours are so entrancing that the child stretches out his arms and crows with pleasure, his own face suffused with these tender and rosy lights.

The Palace is indeed a place of unfolding delight for child and grown-up alike. It is an ancient, weathered structure of considerable beauty, which gives an impression of having arisen from the very soil of Devapur. The impression is generally truthful. The granite blocks that compose the edifice have been hewn from Devapur quarries not a hundred miles from the capital. The marble that embellishes it comes from farther afield, but local craftsmen have fashioned it. Local craftsmen, whose descendants can still be found in Palace employ, are responsible for the finely carved brackets and columns, for exquisite marble traceries and the delicate gold-leaf gilding, although the hand of distant artists—Persian, Mughal, Venetian—can also be traced in elegant inlays and tilework and mosaic, and in the little garden pavilions set among brilliant lawns and pools.

Marble and stone combine to ravish the eye. The same quarries, the same stone, yield different textures from weathering, different colours from red-rose to garnet to gold, which are mirrored in artificial lakes which are a feature of this landscape.

The whole conception of the Palace, certainly, might have been devised to capture the imagination. Within vast encircling walls is a whole labyrinth of courtyards and passages, winding streets and arcades and dark underground granite-faced vaults, which offer endless scope for fascinated exploration. The Palace itself is full of secret chambers, panels, passages, which enrapture the growing Rabi.

Still more engrossing to the boy are the lofty barracks, which once housed the old Maharajah's troops, and even, he learns from his grandmother, war elephants. In this decaying structure he plays war games with his friends, swooping in and out of the echoing rooms and up and down the polished ramps that lead to the upper storey. Down them he slides, shouting—half in terror, they seem precipitous to his small body. He learns, also from his grandmother, that his ancestor is responsible for building these ramps, up which, one momentous, moonless night, the war elephants are ushered . . .

The child always hushes at this point in the narrative. The barrack floors, Manjula tells him, have been strengthened with girders and beams to take the weight of the beasts and keep them there until the British, with whom the Maharajah is at war, surround the Palace. It is their strategy to gain possession of the Palace, which houses the Treasury, and the zenana, which will yield a clutch of desirable hostages. When the order is given the huge beasts come out of hiding and thunder down on the foe. The British are routed, Manjula tells, but they learn from their defeat. When they fight again they bring up cannon, heavy 18-pounders right up to the walls, nothing can withstand the flying, terrible cannonballs.

'Not even elephants?' The boy can scarcely breathe.

'Not even armoured elephants.'

So the Dowager Maharani tells her grandson who is three years old, who is avid for tales, who will listen absorbed hour upon hour to anyone who has this kind of time to expend on him, so that his education is eclectic.

'And then?'

'They defeated your ancestors.'

'Because they were better warriors?'

At this point Manjula always has a struggle. The struggle is to admit those faults which have delivered up a sub-continent to the invaders.

'No,' she says at last, 'they were not better warriors, but their training and discipline were better. And we foolishly allowed them to divide us. If we had stood together they would never have conquered us, not with all the bribery and plotting at which they were experts.'

'And afterwards?'

The child gazes at her, rapt. It is both disturbing and calming for Manjula to look down into eyes that by some awesome chemistry are so exact a continuation of her own.

'Then they pulled down the ramps so that no more elephants could go up or charge down.'

'But my grandfather built them up again.'

'Yes. He instructed his Dewan.'

Manjula is briefly returned to her youth. Newly wed, newly installed, she and her husband are strolling in the ornamental garden under the orange trees beside the nenuphar pool. The water-lilies are in full flower, the trees are smothered in creamy blossom, it is a still and beautiful scene; yet, as they complete their round there comes into view—as they have known it will—the vast, neatly piled mountain of rubble which represents the destroyed ramps.

'That eyesore! Can't something be done? It jars one's aesthetic sense.'

'Yes, as soon as agreement is reached.'

'What about?'

'The construction, I believe.'

If Bawajiraj is unable to enlighten Manjula more fully it is because the key issue is deliberately fuzzed. Even the Minister and the Agent indulge in veils, although each knows what the other is about.

'Sandstone surfaces, Excellency, will preserve the harmony of the whole,' the Minister propounds, the formidable Dewan Narasimha Rao himself, who utilises every opportunity to shore up the power of this British-supervised State in an effort to curb the growing insolence of Empire.

'No question, Minister, no question of that at all,' the Agent replies. 'The only stipulation—I'm afraid I must insist upon it—is for a glazed surface.'

A slippery slope, no good to man or beast, is being conceded. The Minister eyes the Agent. The Agent returns the look coolly. He is the master now, and both Englishman and Indian are aware of the shift in power.

The ramps are surfaced with polished stone. For good measure grids are inserted at the base, whose rods once revolved in their sockets fit to deter any animal but now are immovably fixed by rust. If Narasimha Rao thinks about these deterrents at all, in his *ashram* detached from the world, it only confirms him in his conviction of the evanescence of mortal concerns. Time has rendered immaterial the blocked routes of elephants, as it has their armour, as it will the bastions of the Palace. Only the ill-will of man is so intense that it gives their ingenuity an implacable power. Nothing can withstand it except an internal strength which is so shy and elusive that only a few seek or foster its existence within themselves. Narasimha Rao concedes a flicker, a crinkling of skin over the cooling cup; but that, too, is transient.

'So then there were no more war elephants.'

'What? What did you say?'

Manjula is lost. The vivid lunge of her past has throttled the present. She gazes, hardly seeing, at the child who is tugging at her sari to attract her attention. The white cotton slips from her head, reveals the widow's crop. The stubble has streaks of grey, but the overall hue is still black. Manjula, past forty, looks like a boy. She pulls up the sari to cover her head and returns the grandmother to the waiting, wondering child.

'No more war elephants,' she confirms. 'But there were lots more battles . . .'

She takes the boy on her lap.

* * *

'Why do you tell him these stories?'

Bawajiraj is none too pleased with his mother, who he feels interferes with the proper education of his son. He is booted and spurred, on his way to a hunt. The boots, and the riding-crop with which he flicks at his calves, give him the confidence to tackle the Dowager.

'Why shouldn't I tell him these stories?'

'They're so half-baked! They're only legends!'

'Legends are the blood history of a country.'

'He'll learn history properly, when the time comes for it.'

'Your kind of history.'

'My kind of history! History is *facts*!'

'How can you be so naïve?'

'Me—naïve? It's you! You've believed every story your nurse-maid ever told you.'

'Nursemaids are as truthful as tutors.'

'Do you mean my tutors were liars?'

'They saw the truth differently.'

'Facts are *facts*.'

'They can be slanted.'

Bawajiraj strides away. His boots clop on the marble floor; he sounds like a centaur. He seethes as he strides. He feels that honourable men, like the tutor who has testified to his qualities, have been impugned. He would like to take his riding-crop to his mother, although in fact he has never taken his riding-crop to anything in his life. But he likes to imagine, and fully convinces himself, this is what he is itching to do—his obedient fingers have even come up with the appropriate sensations. Bawajiraj is certainly an appropriate man, totally devised to yield the proper responses that are a bulwark against the shattering effects of unpredictability.

48

The Resident, the present avatar of the old Political Agent, calls Bawajiraj III an admirable Ruler, and means it. The more thoughtful, or perhaps articulate, members of the populace, on the other hand, have been heard, here and there, to refer to their Ruler as an expensive cipher. Both are opinions. Both reflect the truth as it is seen by each party.

For a great deal has changed. The old Political Agent has long been gone to his shooting and fishing nirvana. His successor is a tall, thin man, with something of a stoop acquired from his courteous habit of inclining his body in converse with his shorter Indian colleagues. He is blue-eyed and fair-haired, with a clean line to his jaw and a high-bridged, acquiline nose. In profile, at certain angles, he bears a peculiar resemblance to the Minister, a circumstance that jolts each man when he fleetingly encounters the one an ivorine, the other a pink pastiche of himself. His name is Sir Arthur Copeland. His official designation is the Honourable the Resident, although like his predecessors he is commonly known, within the boundaries of the State, as Excellency, an honorific to which he is not entitled. He is invariably so addressed. Apart from his wife, and a few close friends, hardly anyone calls him by his first name. In his absence he is referred to, by his colleagues, who have picked up the Indian habit, as His Ex, or more simply H.E. Indians prefer not to abbreviate. They are not, in any case, encouraged to be on familiar terms with their masters.

The Hon'ble the Resident, for his part, scrupulously addresses the State Ministers as Minister, and Bawajiraj as Highness, or more often Maharajah Sahib, a practice from which he does not depart except in such intense, intimate moments as when, say, the two are out on a tiger shoot, lurching side by side in a howdah on an elephant, knees knocking against a gun-rack. Then the Resident is known to call the Maharajah Waji, a diminutive which Bawajiraj cherishes, believing it establishes a kinship with the English which it is his fond and mild ambition to achieve.

Bawajiraj's schooling has fitted him for friendship with the English. Indeed he is most ardently at home with them; he feels he is one of them. What he does not realise is the one-sided nature of the situation that has been created.

The Dewan is also new. He is Tirumal Rao, son of the Narasimha Rao who pampers his soul in retirement. He is a sharp, handsome man, with finely carved features, hands whose structure reveals the long and finical process that has bred these delicate, useless bones in which he takes an inordinate pride. He will, clearly, never make a soldier or a labourer; but the breeding that has shaped the bones has also fashioned his intellect. Tirumal Rao knows he could be—one of his forbears has been— a competent general; but he has no ambition in this direction and fully understands that within the Imperial scheme there is no scope.

Having been groomed for office virtually from infancy, Tirumal Rao slips smoothly into his father's shoes. Bawajiraj, whose prerogative it is, has nominated him. The Resident has confirmed the appointment. He has no reason not to. Tirumal Rao is a man of outstanding ability who has held virtually every portfolio in the realm. Nevertheless, he suffers bouts during which he questions the wisdom of his action. It is not that the man has failed in any way, on the contrary. What unsettles him is that which has also plagued his predecessor, a suspicion of his intellect.

Sir Arthur worries at it. He goes over, in his mind, the bland, ivory-tinted and textured, impassive countenance of the Brahmin, and finally believes he has it. It is the turncoat nature of the Minister that seeds his distrust. For what manner of man, he reasons, can serve the British, the Maharajah, and the people—as Tirumal Rao claims to do—and yet call his soul his own? The Resident purports to do something very similar, but he is also perfectly aware of the quite distinct demarcation between saying and doing. Whereas the Minister apparently believes what he proclaims. It calls up in Sir Arthur's mind abstruse reflections on God and Caesar, and of what should be rendered to each, and narrows his view of the Brahmin. By comparison, he feels, the amber-eyed Maharajah (Tirumal Rao has impenetrable black irises) is a stream of clear running water. For sheer relief he is known to turn to Bawajiraj, although for other purposes he has perforce to return to the Dewan.

Tirumal Rao takes in and absorbs the Resident's view of himself with the competence of one amoeba ingesting another. He or his forbears have served Afghan, Mughal, Persian, and British usurpers, as well as rightful Rajahs, as also the people, with a skill which no one has been able to assail. What matters and will continue to matter is the country itself: its stability and continuity are of far greater moment to him than the colours and banners of its temporary masters. It will endure, and he will serve it. This vision is pellucid in his mind. What he finds difficult to penetrate is the Resident's reasoning, which, while applauding the political neutrality of his own home administration, yet despises the versatility of a minister whose care is equally the continuity of service. Tirumal Rao boils it down, as others have done, and notes that different standards prevail for Englishman and Indian.

Face to face, in daily encounter, Resident and Dewan get on well. If their outlook is differently orientated, both have lively minds that are often in harmony. Each in his own way is fastidious to a rabid degree. The Brahmin goes to great lengths to keep a distance of six paces between his person and that of the Englishman, who enjoys the consumption of animal carcasses. The Englishman is given to resorting to a cigarette if his nostrils suffer so much as a whiff of curry.

Both, indeed, are fanatical about cleanliness, an obsession that drives the teeming population, given to tossing its filth around, into more seemly, hygienic ways. Men of iron, both conceal their metal beneath casual visages and modulated tones. The Chief Minister has a naturally soft voice, which ensures him silence in which to be heard. Even in debate the Resident has never been known to raise his low bass note. From the mellifluous exchange presently proceeding no stranger would guess that the two are now in collision.

The subject is Rabindranath. They are warring, not for possession of the little boy, but over the best means of emasculating his undeniable presence.

The Resident is in favour of the process that has turned out the admirable Bawajiraj—suitably scaled down for his natural son. This will, he feels, ensure in the boy an amenable cast, with the added bonus that he will not too readily identify with the people as disaffected sons of ruling houses are known to do. Sir Arthur shudders to think of it. His prayer is to preserve the status quo, to hand over to his successor in due course a State as loyal and peaceful as he has received it.

The Minister's objection to this course is that the Exchequer cannot support another like Bawajiraj—not even a scaled-down version. He wishes the child could be spirited away, back to the anonymity of the valley from which his mother and grand-parents have sprung. As this cannot be done—both parents have reacted like tigers when the theme has been broached—the Minister opts for an ordinary upbringing that will fit Rabindranath into ordinary, un-ambitious slots. He has in mind the Commissariat. He does not think a son of Bawajiraj can make the grade as a clerk.

The Resident breaks the silence into which discussion of the subject has plunged them.

'A tutor, in due course, Minister,' he proposes. 'It is, I think, the only solution . . . although, of course, I am always open to advice.'

'As you wish, Excellency,' the Minister replies. 'As you wish, although I understand the mother—' he makes a deprecating gesture with his delicate, birdbone hands.

'Well?'

'Favours a local Pandit. . . . I believe she has in mind the very man.'

'She can be dissuaded.' The Resident is abrupt.

'It is possible,' the Minister agrees politely. He does not think it possible, for the Resident has no levers of persuasion to apply to Mohini such as are available for bringing Bawajiraj into line. They eye each other, and exchange their thoughts in a transaction that leaves them outwardly impassive and inwardly querulous.

'If only, Minister, Her Highness were to be blessed . . .' the Resident murmurs, in a heartfelt way.

'If only, Excellency,' the Minister echoes without a single false note.

The two men, bent on a masculine pact, placate each other by making a common scapegoat of the Maharani.

If only she would produce a son these wearisome conflicts between them need never arise. Their irritability concentrates on Shanta Devi, while Bawajiraj, whose sperm sexes the child, is not even named. As Mohini alone is adjudged responsible for the birth of the embarrassing boy, so Shanta Devi alone carries the obloquy for failing to bear a son.

Neither man, in his calculations, takes into account the women in the boy's life who are poised to upset their design; nor do they, from a candid assessment of the Princes of India, which Briton and Brahmin share, consider overmuch the young prince himself.

* * *

The two women who are sculpting the boy's life are, predominantly, his mother and grandmother.

There is an unexpected third: the Maharani. Shanta Devi is basically too sweet-natured to work out on a child, as she is certainly in a position to do, the resentments she bears his father. Rabi is drawn into her family circle, and from a quite early age he understands she will be impartial arbiter in his squabbles with his half-sisters. Sometimes he thinks she is his mother. She often wishes that she was. Bawajiraj is pleased for his son, on whom he dotes. He is also greatly relieved. His life is too full, he feels, to be subjected to the strains of petty domestic disharmony. Yet the very qualities in Shanta Devi which have led to this happy outcome cause him to despise her further. He knows, and takes pride in it, that he would never accept a child of his wife's that he has not sired. That she accepts his he considers both natural and his due.

* * *

'How kind she is!'

Mohini is eating peaches on the terrace. Her sharp white teeth bite into the soft fruit, the juice trickles down her rounded chin. Bawajiraj watches her tenderly. It gives him pleasure to witness her pleasure. At the same time he is critical; he considers her earthy to consume with such avid enjoyment. He compares, unfavourably, her uncouth way with the fruit to his own. At this moment he is engaged in peeling a peach for himself.

'Whom do you mean?' he asks. He is *au fond* a kind man, who would wish to reward kindness in others, especially towards the mother of his son.

'Your wife, Shanta Devi,' says Mohini.

Bawajiraj's benevolence seeps away. His wife's kindness points up certain meannesses of his conduct towards her. He is a Maharajah, of course, covered by a certain licence. But still. Bawajiraj is not altogether happy. It is a conspiracy of women of which men are ever the victims, he convinces himself, and manages to wriggle his way out. A detritus of unease remains. He puts down the knife with which he has been slicing his peach—it has a silver blade, which does not discolour the flesh—and pushes away his plate.

'In what way, kind?' he asks.

'So sweet to Rabi,' says Mohini.

'It is a woman's instinct.'

'Isn't it also a man's?'

'Of course! Am I not kind to my child?'

'Would you be if you weren't his father?'

'But I am. Am I not?'

He seizes her roughly. Her flesh, which bruises easily, shows the impress of his fingers on her arm; the five deep imprints are already reddening. The pain gives Mohini an exquisite sense of her power. It lies with her to cause him the utmost misery, as it rests with him when he hovers on the brink of relegating his favourite. She elects not to use it, but plays her lover as she would a fish.

'Is it so important to you?'

'You know it is.'

'How important?'

'Need I say?'

'I like to hear.'

'As important as my life itself.'

Bawajiraj is prone to exaggeration. Nevertheless, Mohini understands his anguish is unfeigned.

'You are a ninny,' she laughs. 'You have only to look at the boy. Rabi, come and show your face to your father!'

The child, who has been playing on the frizzled lawn below the terrace, comes willingly enough. He is fond of his fond parents. His eyes light up when he sees the peaches, which he loves. He reaches for the peeled, uneaten slices on his father's plate.

'No, no, not that!' His mother guides his hand to the whole fruit. 'Eat it properly, not like your father—the skin and the bloom are the best.'

Rabi bites into the fruit. His lips are in delicious contact with the downy skin, while his teeth sink into the soft flesh. He agrees with his mother. He consumes a second peach in the same manner.

The basket of peaches has been picked in the hills to special order. The labourer who has picked them has to labour one month to earn as much as the fruit in the basket has cost. The labourer does not think to begrudge his Maharajah.

His son does. He is a child of nine who watches, the sharp saliva welling up in his mouth, from the lawn where Rabi has abandoned him, the three who sit on the terrace and devour peaches.

Rabi plays with Das, the child of the labourer. He plays with the Palace children, the nobles' children, and with the children of the servants of the Palace and its estates. His is a roving, adventurous spirit, which takes advantage of the confusions of elders and statesmen who are unable to decide on the bastard's niche.

Whether he benefits is an open question. At four he is too young to know.

He marches down the steps to the lawn. Beyond the lawns are the water-gardens and the nenuphar pool, whose stock of gold-fish is to be replenished. Das is to assist the *mali* in this operation and has promised to allow Rabi to assist him. There is, however, no sign of Das, who is forbidden, somewhat laxly, to walk on the lawn for his own amusement. Rabi wishes his friend would return. He pokes about in the flower beds to see if he is hiding and flushes out a peacock. The child, very willing to be diverted, gives chase. The bird, which is used to and loathes children, puts on a fine burst of speed. In its flight it drops a feather. Rabi stops and picks it up. He strokes the diadem eye, which is gold and velvety blue; it parts into fronds, comes together again at his touch. It is as fine a feather as any in the Peacock Fan, which is his father's fan. This fan has a special fan-bearer, and is used only for him, and only on special occasions. Rabi has seen it swishing slowly, like a palm tree, over his father's head. At these times his father ceases to be what he is. Rabi cannot think of him as his father or even as a human being. He looks up to him as the Maharajah.

With the feather in his hand he becomes curious to experience what it feels like. He waves it slowly over his head and pretends to be Maharajah, but there is a difficulty that he traces to the absence of a fan-bearer. Ignoring his parents, who desire his company and are calling him, he runs off to look for Das.

Bawajiraj watches from the terrace and frowns. He loves his son, but he would like the boy to obey him.

'It's time Rabi had a little discipline,' he says to the mother.

'Discipline? He's too young.'

'Not at all. It's never too young to start.'

Bawajiraj looks back on his own schooling and finds in it virtues which have not been apparent to him at the time.

'The boy's running wild,' he says. His opinions, like his speeches, are ominously reminiscent of the Resident's.

'Nonsense.'

'I've noticed it for some time.'

'How could you? He's hardly more than a baby *now*!'

'At his age I could read Sanskrit.'

'Recite it parrot-fashion you mean. It is still meaningless to you, you told me so yourself.'

'It's the discipline that counts.'

'Discipline! Are you trying to make him a sepoy or something?'

'I have the boy's best interests at heart.'

'So have I! I don't want him trussed up like you.'

'Am I trussed up?'

'Do you imagine you're free?'

'Of course I'm free,' says Bawajiraj wearily.

Mohini jingles the bangles on her wrist. She thinks him thick, but continues to love him.

'Those men have been getting at you,' she says shrewdly.

'What men?'

'You know.' She motions with her hands. Bawajiraj gets the picture of the tall stooping Englishman and the fine-boned formidable Brahmin. The fact of her knowledge unhinges him.

'How do you know?' he falls back weakly.

'I can guess. I can put two and two together.'

'Well, they have to think of the boy's future.'

'You mean they want you to.'

'It's the same thing.'

'Not at all. They want to catch him early. They want him to be their creature. *You* ought to want something better for your son.'

The very words 'your son' are evocative. Bawajiraj melts before the image. He forgets the merits of discipline and reflects instead on the evanescence of childhood. These reflections submerge the Sanskrit and re-float those palmette cornices that schoolroom fatigues have scored into his mind.

'I want the best for him. I want him to be happy, you know that,' he declares warmly.

'I have heard of an excellent local Pandit,' says Mohini. 'We can engage him nearer the time . . .'

* * *

Rabi's quest for Das is unsuccessful; it often is since Das has to work for his living. The failure does not throw him. His day is chockful of possibilities. At the same time it is long enough to accommodate his designs on it. He is pressed neither by a sense of the shortness of time, nor byhits *longueurs*. Each day is the present perfect, which he savours as it comes. Rabi crosses his arms upon his sturdy chest and ponders the agreeable alternatives.

Two gravelled drives, each a mile long, sweep past the nenuphar pool. They loop round the Palace and are bordered by shrubs and trees, which a contingent of thirty-six gardeners maintains. The paths that meander in artistic a-symmetry be-

tween periphery and centre are raked and swept by another of
Rabi's acquaintances, a girl called Janaki. She is a grandchild of
that same frail creature who fainted at the feet of Bawajiraj II or,
as some still persist, in the very arms of the Maharajah. She is
built like her grandmother, from whom she has inherited her
job as well as her physique. In a high wind, which pins her rags to
her matchwood figure, she has been seen to totter. When she
smiles, as she often does, being only nine years old, so closely
does her pared face follow the contours of the lurking skull that
she is quite hideous. This same quality in her grandmother has
haunted the youthful Maharajah, fresh from his valley: she is a
living demonstration of the self-perpetuating nature of their
deprivation.

Rabi pushes her around. It is a game they play, in which she is
expected to succumb to his might, but on occasions when the
desire to fall down deserts her she finds she cannot master the
four-year-old.

'You're so strong, Maharajkumar!'

She pants, lying on the gravel on which he has thrown her. She
often calls him Maharajkumar, which is the proper title for the
only son of a Maharajah. Rabi, however, has already been made
to understand that he may or may not become the future
Maharajah. He is not greatly concerned. As for the girl, she has
no doubts about the matter at all. Even in their play she reminds
herself now and again that the boy is the future Maharajah.

'I am, aren't I? I am a mighty warrior-king.'

Rabi is flushed with triumph. He looks so pretty that Janaki,
who is maternally inclined, feels she could scoop him up and eat
him.

'Get up and let me knock you down again,' he invites.

'No, Maharajkumar, no,' she pleads. The gravel is flinty and
digs into her back. 'Please let me get up.'

'What will you give me if I do?'

'What would you like? Would you like a flower?'

'You're not allowed to pick flowers.'

'Only one that's been blown down.'

She reaches for a blossom from the refuse she has raked up
and presents it to him. He is pleased to accept it. In turn, he
makes her a gift of his feather.

'Ah, Rabi, it's so pretty!' she sighs.

'It is the prettiest thing I have.'

'Then you must keep it.'

'No, I want you to have it.'

The two children look at each other, their eyes brimful of the emotion they feel. Rabi takes hold of her hand; he wishes to keep her by his side.

'Let's go and feed the doves,' he says.

'No,' says Janaki dolefully. 'I have to finish the paths first, or the head gardener will thrash me.'

'I'll clout him if he does.'

'You go on, Maharajkumar. I'll come later.'

Janaki sighs again. At nine realities press closer than they do at four.

Rabi takes her at her word and runs off without a backward glance. Janaki's amiability turns to resentment. She cannot bring herself to resent the child himself, but she blames his class for this easy abandonment.

'Go on, run! Run away like the whole sodding lot of you always do!' she shouts after him in her high, shrill, gutterbred voice. She sobs a little as she takes up her rake, but already her anger, which has more froth than substance, has begun to evaporate.

Rabi hears her cry. He cannot distinguish the words but he registers the note. He runs on. His mind is intent on the dove-cotes, which are close to the Palace gates.

Mohini is apt to declare that the world of reality begins outside the crested, gilded, guarded, ornamental gates of the Palace.

Rabi's world, on the contrary, is contained almost wholly within them.

The Palace and its environs are indeed an entire city. It is surrounded by an enormous fortified wall, built of bricks from local kilns whose fires, it is said, have not been allowed to die in the five centuries since they were kindled. This wall has been shot and shelled, battered down, patched up, re-built—the scars of these assaults and engagements can be traced in the weathered bastions, and often are for the boy's pleasure by his grandmother. The present state of the wall is forlorn. It has been breached at strategic intervals by the British; one of their afflictions, inherent in the situation, is never to be able to trust an ally; and the State is forbidden by treaty to make good the damage.

Within these battered boundaries reside close on a thousand inhabitants. Of these a hundred, perhaps, are personages. The remainder wait upon them. They are servitors and retainers of one kind or another and artists and craftsmen who are retained to support and embellish the Court. In the course of a walk Rabi can look in on not only the cobbler, carpenter, embroiderer, saddler, silversmith, potter and jeweller, but can also call in at the dairy, distillery, bakery, flour mill, or at the pastrycook's.

Rabi has a preference for the baker. He loves the smell of the bread, and he likes the baker who is a huge man with hairy arms and soft, floury hands. If, when the metal bread-trays emerge from the glowing ovens, Rabi can spot so much as a speck of charcoal on one of the loaves, the bread becomes his. He likes this to happen, and it does not occur to him to be surprised that it so invariably does.

'That one, that one!' he cries, and the baker dusts off the speck before placing the loaf in his triumphant hands. When he tears it open it steams; the smell is so delicious that sometimes he eats it on the spot. Sometimes, though, he takes it to share with Janaki, who he knows is always hungry. So are the pigeons. He saves his crusts for them, but Janaki, he has noticed, never leaves so much as a crumb for the birds.

* * *

Rabi in due course is six years old.

When his father the Maharajah has a birthday the guns are fired. Rabi can remember three such salutes and the havoc they have created in the dove-cotes. He does not expect such salutes for himself—he has been told not to—but when the Palace flag is lowered on his birthday he draws the wrong conclusion.

'Is it for me?'

It is a fine day. The sky is blue and the air sparkles. Rabi is on the terrace, having a lesson. His teacher is the Pandit Mohini has had her eye on. He is a young man, twenty-five years old, who comes from the world of reality that to Mohini begins outside the Palace gates. He often tells Rabi about this world, which the boy finds absorbing. He also has an excellent repertoire of stories, and, like his grandmother, can always find time to tell them. Rabi likes his teacher. He likes him enough not to ask for a holiday even on his birthday.

'Is it an honour for me, Panditji?' Rabi tugs at the loose sleeve of the coarse white shirt the young man is wearing.

'Is what an honour?'

'The flag.'

'No. Not an honour. Not at all. It is to mark the death of the Queen of England.'

'Queen Victoria?'

'Yes.'

'She's the Queen of India too.'

'No. Queen-Empress. She was the Queen-Empress.'

'Is that different?'

'Quite different. It means she became what she was through conquest, not by the will of the people.'

'What is the will of the people?'

'What they want. I'm afraid they never wanted her.'

The people have not wanted her to the extent that their more exuberant elements have set upon her statue and tarred it. In faraway England the Queen, being told, is said to be distressed. In India her loyal subjects are incensed. Her statue is, of course, as indifferent to these reactions as to the posse of Indian labourers who are scrubbing the tar off her person. (They work behind screens, and there is a European in charge to see that the coolies don't take liberties.)

This long-forgotten episode returns to the Pandit, who wonders whether to relate the story to his pupil; but the face that looks up at him is too young, he feels, too innocent to fathom in the dastardly act the desperation that has prompted it.

'Why didn't they want her?' Rabi has to twitch for attention again. He does not often have to, Panditji is usually attentive.

'Because she ruled as a conqueror. Conquered people don't like their conquerors.'

'My father likes—liked her. He has a signed portrait, he says it's the most precious thing he has.'

'Your father is not one of the people.'

'The people liked her too. The baker has a picture hung up in his shop next to my father's. The silversmith's got one too, he puts garlands round it.'

Panditji gives a little groan.

'Palace people! They don't think! But they are beginning to think. Yes, I can definitely say that even in our State they have begun to think for themselves.'

He has this way of considering, aloud, matters about which he is not entirely sure, which makes Rabi respect his opinions. He also has a way of standing things on their head in order, he explains, that they may be viewed from all angles. Sometimes, to this end, he tucks up his *dhoti* and stands on his head on the terrace and invites Rabi to do the same. It is not too easy for Rabi. When he manages it, the sky, the clouds, the trees, his own toes in the air above him are strangely altered, the world certainly wears a different aspect.

Rabi watches his parents. He rounds out what he hears by what he sees for himself—his living is a continuous process of rounding out and filling in.

He watches his mother and grandmother at prayer in the temple. They often go. There are a good many festivals. He puts his hand over his eyes and peeps at them through the slits between his fingers. They do not notice him; they are too absorbed in what they are doing. Sometimes he becomes absorbed too. When this happens he forgets about the peepholes he has made. He even forgets about himself, except for a feeling that he is floating away to some faraway, murmuring place. It is always a shock when he opens his eyes and finds he hasn't moved at all. Sometimes he has to grip his mother's hand tightly as they walk out into the sunlight. There is a murmuring here too, but it is louder, and shrill; it comes from beggars who are clustered outside the walls. They slap their stomachs and hold out tins and wooden bowls and when he puts a coin inside—he is always provided with a purseful of coins for the purpose—the shrill noise becomes melting and gritty, like sugar before it turns to syrup. He notices they have a strange, humble kind of look on their faces.

Rabi watches his father.

His Highness Sir Bawajiraj Bahadur the Third, G.C.S.I., G.C.I.E., is holding a durbar. He often holds durbars. Sometimes it is held in the Private Audience Hall, which is very rich and elegant, like the Maharajah himself. He sits on his throne, and his nobles and courtiers approach one by one, swords half drawn from their scabbards, and he touches the hilt and says a few words. Then they bow and retreat without turning their backs. The grandest noble, he has been told, is not allowed to turn his back upon his father.

Sometimes the durbar is for the people and is held in the Hall of Public Audience. This is a huge hall, and he can see it has to be, for a great many people come; they often overflow into the courtyards. The Maharajah dresses up for them just as much as he does for his nobles.

This morning he is wearing apricot silk, with a brocade coat that buttons right up to his throat. The coat looks gold, but when he moves an apricot colour breaks through the gold. His turban is apricot muslin with gold lace bands, and there is a spray of diamonds in the centre that trembles as the fan-bearer swishes his fan. At his side is a sword with a curved blade; it has a jewelled scabbard and hilt on which the Maharajah rests a hand as he waits for his subjects to come up.

They advance one by one, as the Court attendants call their name, to the foot of the glittering throne where his father sits. Some of them have scrolls of paper, from which they read. Some of them bring little squares of orange linen, with a coin in the middle, which they offer in cupped hands. The Maharajah touches the coin and returns it to the giver. He listens to what they say to him; he replies. Rabi cannot hear what anyone says; he is too far away, but he sees the expressions of gratitude, benign on his father's face, humble, like the look the beggars wear, on the people's. It is clear that the Maharajah, as well as the people, are glad and grateful for each other.

When each man is done he touches his breast and forehead and shuffles off backward from the Maharajah the whole length of the hall. Rabi admires them for doing this. He knows how difficult it is, having tried it himself. He supposes they must practise before coming, but even so there are those who stumble, and all have pinched and anxious faces. It quite wipes away the glad expressions they had before they began to retreat.

* * *

'Here, come and sit beside me.'

The Maharajah dismisses the Court and calls his son to him. He is relaxed, now that the durbar is over. He undoes the top buttons of the stiff coat and weaves his neck around to get it comfortable again. He feels the voluptuous exhaustion—he has been at the service of his people for close on three hours—of a man who has not skimped his duty. It induces in him a mood in which he would like to convey to his son the subtle, semi-mystical nature of the relationship between a Maharajah and his subjects. He pats the throne's purple cushioning in invitation—it is wide enough to accommodate a man and his heir.

'Here. Sit beside me.'

'Why?'

'Wouldn't you like to?'

'I would like to sit by myself.'

Bawajiraj sighs, but he has never ceased to be an indulgent father. He unbuckles his sword and lays it aside, which enables him to sit on the carpeted steps to the throne. Rabi ascends and takes his seat.

'There! How does it feel?'

'I don't know yet.'

'Pretend you're the Maharajah.'

'No.'

'Why not?'

'I'm not your heir. I can never be the Maharajah. The English won't allow it.'

'Ah, my son, my son! Why do you say these things? If I want you to be the Maharajah then one day you will be the Maharajah.'

Now it is said, Bawajiraj sincerely believes he has the power, provided Shanta Devi does not produce a legitimate heir. So far she has not.

'I don't want to be the Maharajah.'

'Just pretend!'

'No.'

'All right then. I'll be Maharajah and you be my people.'

'I don't want to be your people. Your people are always hungry.'

'Nonsense, nonsense!'

The Maharajah is bluff. There is no hunger—what can the child know about hunger? But there have been some mutterings in durbar. It is all so upsetting to Bawajiraj, who has still to get his message across.

Rabi can see his father is miffed. He offers the olive branch.

'I like your throne,' he says. He runs his hands over the arms, which end in a pair of carved, gilded, magnificent lions' heads.

'Do you?'

'Yes. It's not a real one, is it?'

'Of course it is! What do you mean?'

'It's only gilt.'

'It's gold.'

'It's gilt. The old one was gold. The British took it away, my grandmother says, from my ancestors, after they were defeated in battle.'

'That old story!'

'Isn't it true?'

Bawajiraj is flummoxed. Devapur State has not always been allied to the British. In unwise earlier centuries it has resisted them, and suffered in consequence. The throne is in fact a replica. The original, a massive and unwieldy construction of pure gold, has been broken up and distributed as war booty in reprisal for a raid by the first Bawajiraj, who has paid in other ways for his temerity. British soldiery have gouged out the precious gems that once sparkled in delicate inlays on these very walls. The Golconda Diamond, which has once blazed in this very room, now adorns the Imperial Crown. Marble by the ton (to the concern of a civilised Political Agent of the period) has been stripped from the Palace and auctioned under the orderly and vigilant eye of Prize Agents, who have also supervised the orderly distribution of Prize Money, seized from the Treasury, in strict order of rank from British general to British private.

The denuding of jewel and treasure is carried in the memory of Devapur State, which Bawajiraj cannot escape. He does not, however, care to think about it much. Indeed, he feels, with the Resident, that it is bad form to bring up these subjects at all.

'I suppose it's true in a manner of speaking,' he says, dismissively, to his small but trying questioner. 'But you must remember it all happened a long time ago when standards were quite different.'

It is by stout referral back to the standards and morals of the day that the conscientious young Englishman, the Maharajah's tutor in youth, has been able to justify to his pupil, and to his own affronted conscience, the grosser actions of the early empire builders. Bawajiraj accordingly believes that morality, far from being an absolute, is open to interpretation.

* * *

The British bestow on Bawajiraj honours, privileges, a status second to none but themselves. They protect him from unfriendly assaults, real and imaginary. Their military strength is prodigious; Bawajiraj is entirely dependent on it. His alternative is to go to the people, whose strength, being derived from the country itself, may well prove to be a good match. Bawajiraj shudders at the prospect. He is devoted to his people, not even the irreverent Mohini questions that; but the opportunity to test and develop a mutual confidence has been taken from him. Bawajiraj would not dream of entrusting his future to the unruly, affectionate crowds that besiege his carriage and the gates of his Palace and beg for a sight of their Maharajah. He sees his destiny as bound up with the British.

The British refer to the Maharajahs as partners in the solemn act of governing the country. In franker moments they see them as handy tools with which to subdue the nation. In some cases they have created these tools; in others they have picked up what has lain ready to hand and shaped and polished them. Their motive is to preserve themselves as an Imperial power.

To sustain the Imperial Presence in India certain standards are obligatory, which by their very nature are far removed from the people.

The Viceroy, symbol and embodiment of this Presence, sets these standards. His salary and expenses total several lakhs of rupees. Even these lakhs, however, cannot support an entourage of nine hundred, summer and winter capitals, State balls and dinners, levees attended by a thousand guests apiece, bodyguard, band, French chefs, hothouse flowers, and vintage wines. His Excellency, it is made known, has to dip into his private pocket.

Janaki, the servant girl, has no private pocket to dip into. Nor has she any status to speak of to maintain. Her main preoccupation is to sustain her present state, which, since it includes one fair meal a day and one new piece of cloth each year at Deepavali time, on the whole she regards as satisfactory. She is paid one rupee per week. The Paymaster's assistant drops the coin into her cupped palm and tells her—the man is a bit of a wag—not to spend it all at once.

The Hon'ble Sir Arthur Copeland, Kt., C.I.E., the Resident, First Class, cannot and does not aspire to the resplendent state maintained by his illustrious superior. His entourage numbers, perhaps, no more than a hundred persons, and his household expenses seldom exceed, even in years that support the Viceroy's Tour, those of the Maharajah. Nevertheless it is incumbent on him to maintain a certain style. Sir Arthur feels he owes no less to his office, and would indeed regard it as a breach of duty to skimp, in whatever circumstances, the traditional standards expected of the Resident. These standards are such that none who has observed them has been known to choose a lesser adjective than magnificent.

The Residency is magnificent. It stands in sixty acres of the choicest land available. The major slice of this lush acreage has been seized from the deposed Bawajiraj I. Of the remainder, part has been surrendered by the succeeding Maharajah in compliance with an Order-in-Council; and part, since it is now an era of peace and friendship, is a gift freely given by the overwhelmed Bawajiraj III in return for the Star bestowed on him in acknowledgment of his munificent contribution to certain causes close to the Resident's heart.

It is a vast edifice of colonnades and porches that outdoes, and has been designed to outdo, the Oriental splendours of the Palace. The Grand Portico (Corinthian) is fifty feet long and forty feet high. The Durbar Hall is the same size and is lined with Ionic columns. On the same noble scale are the reception rooms, the two drawing rooms, the twin galleries, the Ballroom, the Banqueting Hall, the guest suites, and the private apartments of Sir Arthur and Lady Copeland in the East wing.

These rooms are splendidly appointed. There are moulded friezes and doorcases, embellished ceilings, and carved and gilded cornices. The floors are paved with marble, which are polished daily, by ten crouching men, each wielding two coconut halves. The Ballroom glitters; it is lined with mirrors, and there are lustres and girandoles of which the centrepiece is the great Teardrop Chandelier whose crystalline rays are reputed to lure into matrimony the pair upon whom they fall. At Residency Balls, which are held once a fortnight during the season, there is much clustering of nubile young dancers under the Teardrop Chandelier. It has cost, including shipping, from Waterford, in Ireland, one thousand pounds.

The costs of the Residency have been and are borne by Devapur State. A system of high finance—such as would need a battery of revenue officials to unravel and explain—obscures the fact that the entire expenses of the Residency continue to be billed to the State Exchequer. It is past belief, but nevertheless a fact, that only once has the Ruler been known to cavil, on the ground that these recurring expenses have clipped his own life-style. But this has been an aberration of his youth: Bawajiraj III has long redeemed the single wild oat he has sown. When he recalls the occasion he is covered with confusion and an embarrassment that verges on guilt.

There are, equally, certain concrete embarrassments felt by the Resident. He does what he can in amelioration. There are all those field-pieces, mortar and cannon, captured in past skirmishes. Except for a quartet, drawn by Mongolian gunmetal dragons (fierce beasts for which Sir Arthur has a special affection), that flanks the magnificent flights of stairs that curve up to the portico, the rest are carefully concealed among the canna beds. There is his Treasury, housed in a miniature fort in the compound and guarded night and day by a detachment of his own troops. Sir Arthur has felt the jarring notes introduced by this structure and has suppressed them by banishing the whole outfit to the basement.

And there is the watch-tower.

It has been erected in the era of mutinies and campaigns, and offers not only a commanding view of the countryside but also of any incipient insurgency. Sir Arthur shudders when it catches his eye. The squat tower bulks against the skyline. It outrages the pure profile of his noble mansion and offends his aesthetic sense. Nor does it serve much purpose. The idea of insurgency in peaceful Devapur under Bawajiraj and himself is quite unthinkable. Nevertheless, he cannot bring himself to order its demolition. There are memories that his blood carries, that are reinforced by the haunted memories of his wife, and the presence of their infants. Few can resist such mighty forces.

Sir Arthur has a way, when the watch-tower offends, of directing his gaze to the splendid South front, the entrance to which is guarded by a pair of enormous arched gateways gilded and crowned with rampant stone lions. For these portals carry, enclosed within stonework and arches, rich and abundant memories. Through them upon taking up his appointment the Resident has processed, on an elephant, in a silver howdah fitted with crimson cushions, with a mounted escort clattering behind on the cobbles, preceded and followed by a splendid retinue, to present his letters of credence to the Maharajah. Under them, in a procession no less glittering (purple and gold, to the Envoy's silver and crimson), the Maharajah has passed to return the call.

The Resident remembers, as if it were yesterday, going forth to receive the young Ruler, and the favourable impression formed then that he has never had occasion to change. The memory is shared by Bawajiraj, who often recalls with fondness the unaffected manner in which Sir Arthur has advanced to meet him, leaving his attendants behind and walking down the entire, immense flight of stairs alone, with his hand outstretched in greeting.

Indeed Sir Arthur has no need for affectation—apart from what is thrust upon him by his imperial role. Unlike his predecessor, the Political Agent, whose shining goal has been his country seat, his trout stream, and his few acres, Sir Arthur is no stranger to the resplendent. His family interlocks with the aristocracy. Birth, and links with empire, have bequeathed him extensive estates in England and Scotland. His Indian connections, like his wife's, have sprung a general here, a proconsul there, and the magnificence of his Indian Residence may over-shadow, but does not eclipse, the modest splendours of the country mansion to which he will in good time retire.

Withal he is a man of simple tastes; not, perhaps, as simple as those of his predecessor, who has now been laid to rest in a modest plot in a country churchyard, but basically similarly inclined. Nothing gives him greater pleasure than to rise of a morning and saddle up, without benefit of *syce* or peon, and gallop off alone into the wooded estates that surround the Residency. It is a genuine irritation to him to have servants material-ise as they do, fore and aft, for the simplest exercise—the umbrella-carrying minion who dogs his shadow as he strolls in the garden, the *syce* who trots behind when he is out riding, the sentries who spring to attention at every door he enters, the attendants who accompany his carriage when he and his wife are taking the air in the evening.

Sir Arthur could easily dispense with these props to his pres-tige and self-esteem.

The difficulty is that he is locked into the conception of his own situation, which is to benefit the peoples of India by preserv-ing and perpetuating the British Presence. Such a policy requires a pomp and ceremony, the visible symbols of power, to overawe and dazzle the vassal States into an enthusiastic con-nivance in their own subjection. As Sir Arthur sees it, it is by its very nature a sacred trust. He can do no less than honour its terms down to the last item of deadly, if dazzling, tedium.

There are escapes however—occasional solitary excursions, interludes of peace usually at daybreak, sometimes late at night after the last dispatch has been signed and sealed, when he manages to elude his solicitous attendants, when the trappings of his high office fall from his shoulders and he is able, briefly, to savour the freedoms of the ordinary man.

He is out early one morning, enjoying the solitude, the warmth of the sun on his back, which is pleasurable at this hour before the brazen heat begins, when he perceives he is not alone. Sharing the woods with him is a boy on a pony, both so involved in their partnership that they do not immediately notice Sir Arthur.

The child is splendidly mounted and is executing a compli-cated manoeuvre, a contracting figure-of-eight that weaves about a bandana thrown on the scrub. Sir Arthur, no mean horseman himself, reins in to watch, noting with pleasure the skill with which the rider handles his mount and applauding when, low in the saddle, in a final turn, the boy retrieves the bright silk square. Admiration overcoming his earlier petulance—he does like having the woods to himself—he canters up to the pair.

The rider is Rabi. He knows it is the Resident—his father has often pointed him out, though usually from a distance. He has been told, not by his father but by Panditji, that this is the most powerful man in Devapur State, more powerful than the Maharajah. Rabi has not believed it at the time, although he respects Panditji's opinion, and he is even less able to do so now. The man is perfectly ordinary. He is wearing an open-necked shirt and faded jodhpurs, and he is bareheaded and windblown. There is no sign of gold braid or plumes, or even of sword, which everyone knows is the symbol of authority. There is not even a *syce* in attendance. The Maharajah would as soon think of riding out without a *syce* as he would of flying. It leads Rabi to the conviction that Panditji has definitely made a mistake. No man who looks like this can possibly be powerful. He is, however, polite. His father often urges on him the special duty of politeness towards inferiors.

'I like your horse,' he says politely.

'I like your pony,' the Resident returns.

He is not sure who the boy is. The face is familiar, but he cannot put a name to it—there are innumerable children about the Palace, all with unpronounceable names, with whom he has little contact; they are no more than merry faces seen from a distance. The child for whose possession he has fought Bawajiraj, and with an even nobler intrepidity the concubine Mohini, has never had a face. He is a symbol: the natural son of the Maharajah, with the potential for peace or upheaval in the State, and as such to be shielded from populist contact and carefully reared. The parents have seen fit to do otherwise; they have taken the boy's education and supervision—at least for the time being, for the Resident has by no means finally conceded this battle—out of British hands. The Resident, accordingly—his own two children being confined to the British enclave—has had little to do with and does not recognise Rabindranath.

The two are joined by horseflesh.

'Fine animal you've got there.'

'Yes, isn't he? I chose him myself.'

'That was nice.'

'Did you choose your horse yourself?'

'This one, yes.'

'Is he your favourite?'

'Yes, as a matter of fact.'

'Do you always ride him?'

'Not always.'

'Why not?'

'Well, there are the others.'

'How many?'

'Quite a few.'

'My father has quite a few too.'

'Really?'

'Yes. So many he can't count them.'

Sir Arthur thinks he spots the bravado of childhood. He steers the conversation away from quantity to quality.

'It's a fine beast, that pony of yours,' he says kindly. 'And I will say you certainly deserve to have him.'

Rabi glows.

'I got him for my birthday,' he confides.

'Did you? That must have been delightful.'

'My birthday's the day Victoria died.'

'Victoria?'

'The Queen of England.'

'Her Majesty the Queen, Empress of India,' the Resident says, and straightens himself in the saddle.

'Nobody wanted her to be,' Rabi assures him. 'She became Empress by conquest; the people never wanted her.'

The boy's solemn amber eyes meet the blue, somewhat frosty gaze of the Englishman. Sir Arthur, with a slight shock of recognition, suddenly places the striking coloration. This bold, sturdy youngster is the Maharajah's natural son. He wonders fleetingly how such a father could have produced such a son, but his more pressing concern is to discover the source of the quasi-seditious opinion he holds. Before he can do so Rabi wheels his pony round and with a brief farewell gallops off.

* * *

'Waji, that boy of yours.'

'Rabi?'

Bawajiraj is guarded, even in these mellow moments as they stroll off the polo grounds together—both have scored for the winning team and are headed for the pavilion where delicious, and merited, refreshments await. He is proud of his son, but the very qualities that win his admiration, the boy's independent spirit and argumentative turn of mind, are precisely those he finds most tiresome when personally in feud with them. His admiration functions, as it were, in a vacuum. He respects his son's virtues, so long as they are exercised in the proper place. The proper place is definitely not within the stern, limelit precincts that a Ruler inhabits.

'Rabi, yes. I ran into him the other day. Fine youngster.'

'He is, isn't he.'

'Running a bit wild, though, don't you think?'

'Running wild, precisely! Those were precisely my words to his mother!'

Bawajiraj is delighted by the concord of their thought. The doubts that Mohini has sown in his mind about what is best for his son dissolve entirely. He wonders what in the world has made him accede to her wishes—the narrow will of a woman, confined to women's quarters, bounded by a woman's narrow horizons! He wishes, fervently, that Shanta Devi could take the place of Mohini. Then, without question, the upbringing of the boy would exactly follow his own. Then, there would be no tiresome acrimony, no coldness between him and this admirable Englishman with whom he sees eye to eye. Then—and this is most important of all—the Viceroy will recognise his son as heir-apparent, which, on various grounds (he suspects the 'running wild' the Resident has cited), he has hitherto neglected to do.

'What would you advise?' he asks.

'You know my thoughts on the subject,' Sir Arthur says with a hint of reproach, subduing the asperity he feels.

'I know, I know,' says Bawajiraj. 'But Mohini, she's as stubborn as a, as a . . . she insists on this Pandit of hers.'

'A peculiar man.'

'I absolutely agree.'

'A man who holds the most subversive opinions, which he does not hesitate to communicate to the child.'

'I will speak to him.'

'Speak to your child's mother.'

'Her. Yes.'

'If she has Rabi's interests at heart—'

'She has, she has.'

'She might re-consider a boarding establishment. There are one or two excellent institutions.'

'No, we couldn't. No.'

Bawajiraj rallies his wilting forces. He cannot abide the thought of parting from his son, which alone gives him the strength.

'In any case he is much too young,' he says. 'The boy's not seven yet.'

Sir Arthur's heart sinks. The iced champagne in his glass has turned flat, insipid. He thinks, like a Jesuit, that the boy's thought-processes are already set firm, that he is quite lost. Nevertheless, he cannot give up; he endures the clamminess of his sweat-soaked shirt, which the humid air has clapped to his shoulder blades, to pursue his duty.

'My children are too young as yet,' he says. 'But when they reach the age of seven—perhaps earlier—we shall have no hesitation in sending them Home. As parents, my wife and I feel no sacrifice is too great for our children.'

Bawajiraj is flagging. Against Sir Arthur even bubbly, he feels, has no power. More than ever he sorely needs, he feels, his bath, his tired muscles are agitating for the attentions of Bhima, his excellent masseur. After bath and massage he has planned to review some Argentine ponies, which have just been imported. He has his eye on a thoroughbred, which he hopes to secure for 2,000 rupees. His last Argentinians have cost him 1,000 rupees apiece, but the price of good polo ponies is going up all the time. This one looks like a bargain. Bawajiraj's mind, whose bent is towards the blithe, flits away from the tedious Sir Arthur.

'Later, H.E., later,' he says testily. 'I promise you I'll deal with it later.'

Later his conscience reminds him. He accosts Mohini.

'Sir Arthur is concerned about Rabi. He thinks the boy's running wild,' he tells her.

'Who cares what Sir Arthur thinks about my son?' asks Mohini. She has a bowl of soapy water and is blowing bubbles with Rabi; both are in merry mood.

'Well, I do,' says Bawajiraj, shortly.

'I know. You have to. It's your cross, my treasure,' says Mohini. She blows another bubble, which taxes Bawajiraj's patience. He bursts the shimmering sphere with a testy finger.

'I wish you'd be serious.'

'Why?'

'Well.'

'All right. Rabi, sit down. Your father wants a serious talk.'

They lay aside their soapy clay pipes and plump themselves down on a pink silk bolster on which there is room only for mother and child. Bawajiraj is left standing. He feels a little ridiculous, towering over the pretty, innocent pair.

'The Resident feels, and I entirely agree, that Rabi should broaden his horizons,' he brings out.

'Broaden—? Of course he should. It's what I'm always saying. It's what Her Highness your mother has always said. I'll arrange it at once.'

'Arrange what?'

'A tour. For him to see the world. Panditji has travelled widely throughout the country; we can safely leave the arrangements to him.'

'You know I don't mean that.'

'What do you mean?'

'I mean his education. He ought to be under a proper tutor—'

'Panditji is a proper tutor.'

'—or go to a proper boarding establishment.'

'You mean send him away from us?'

'Not now. Later. When he's older. In a year or two.'

Bawajiraj backtracks. The idea is none too attractive to him either; he hopes only to offer these sops to the Resident in the name of trying. It's the trying, not succeeding, that's important (he hopes).

'Send him away! In a year or two! No! Never!'

Mohini locks vehement arms round her squirming child. 'I'll never send him away.'

'For his own good! Parents must sacrifice themselves for the good of their children.'

'You want to sacrifice him for *your* good.'

'No. I'm only thinking of him—'

'You're thinking of yourself. You don't care about Rabi.'

'I do.'

'If you did you wouldn't want to send him away—'

'I don't *want* to!'

'—to some dreadful place—'

'Handpicked. A select establishment.'

'He doesn't need a select establishment! He doesn't need to become select. Only Maharajahs are select.'

'Why can't you think of the boy?'

'Why can't you? Do you want to break his heart, parting him from his own flesh and blood?'

'You're so emotional.'

'Do you expect me to be calm?'

'How can we discuss anything—'

'There's nothing to discuss.'

'All *right*.'

'But since you've brought it up I tell you straight I'll *never* let him go! I'll go away myself and take him with me. We'll go to my great-aunt's, do you think we have no one to turn to? You may be the Maharajah but don't think we're dependent on you—don't think we're orphans! Just say the word and we'll go.'

Tears sparkle like diamonds on Mohini's long lashes. Her cheeks are flushed. She looks ravishing and knows it. Bawajiraj is utterly vanquished. He needs Mohini as greatly as ever. The need is reinforced by his wife's pregnancy; Shanta Devi is eight months gone and forbids him her bed.

'We won't ever talk about it again,' he says huskily. 'I don't want you to go away. I don't want Rabi to go away. In the whole world there's nothing more precious to me than you two.'

He gets down on his knees, cumbrously, and kisses her delicate toes, which peep from under the silk. It is the most abject act of surrender that he can think of, or that there is, short of kissing the dust. Even his subjects are not expected to do that. He offers the act in the guise of a love-gift and is relieved when she does not spurn it. Their relationship is such that they do not always come together as partners. Bawajiraj is used to being, and believes it is proper for him to be, the master in his amorous deals; it compensates him for his submission in other spheres. In crises, however, he is prepared to forgo his role and discovers, to his surprise, that the sacrifice rebounds in his favour and sweetens the bond between them.

Mohini has no tangible hold over him, neither marriage tie nor influential father, such as Shanta Devi can command; she has only her own, somewhat turbulent self. Yet despite the most extreme exasperation she frequently rouses in him, it is to her he returns time and again. Despite one or two side affairs, she has been his love for close on a decade, so much so that the Palace has dubbed her the constant concubine. It is not, however, the woman's constancy which has called forth their praise, but the astonishing constancy of that arch man, the Maharajah.

Rabi, who is used to skirmishes between his gay mother and his prim father, and similar resolutions of them, retrieves the clay pipes and hands one to his mother.

'I would like to travel,' he says.

'So you shall, my pet, so you shall!' cries Mohini, and stirs the soapy water vigorously.

'And so you shall.' Shrugging off the Resident, Bawajiraj places his regal seal upon their joint desire.

Iridescent bubbles the size of tennis balls stream from the open window of the Pearl Suite.

The Resident, out for a stroll before dinner with his Secretary, observes the pretty pageant and thinks benignly of young Rabi. He hopes he has secured the boy's future. He believes he has intervened in the nick of time to rescue him from the pernicious influences which are permeating the country, in which he sees the seeds of ruin for the child. He is glad that he has. Rabi has impressed him favourably. He would not be disappointed if his own infant son grew up like the sturdy Indian child. Sir Arthur grows a little wistful. When his son is Rabi's age he will be far away at school in England. He, the father, will be able neither to see nor influence him. It is another sacrifice that is demanded of him, and that he willingly makes, for India.

3

Mohini, brow furrowed, face flushed, is describing a somewhat idealised expedition.

'Everything. I want to show him everything—rivers, valleys, mountains, hamlets, all the grand cities and the little villages, and the people who live in these places. I want him to meet the people. What can he learn, cooped up in the Palace?' she declaims to the Dowager, who refrains from pointing out the size of the coop.

'And perhaps a pilgrimage to the shrine,' suggests the older woman.

'Of course,' says Mohini shrewdly. 'We'll start with the pilgrimage; it will give the Bania Sahib less excuse to meddle in our affairs.'

By 'Bania Sahib' she means the hapless Sir Arthur. It is what he is generally dubbed in the women's quarters. However, though he does not know it, the Resident does not suffer in isolation. The British Raj itself is widely and disparagingly referred to, in Indian circles, at moments of exasperation in particular, as the Bania Raj.*

Mohini is right. Sir Arthur, who has got to hear of their plans, can find no reason to scuttle the expedition, which comes under the heading of domestic affairs. He is not too happy about its composition—the rabid Pandit and the subversive Dowager are included—and he considers the boy would be better occupied in the schoolroom; but the religious sphere does not fall within his brief and he considers it unwise to include it now.

*trader or shopkeeper Government.

76

Bawajiraj is equally stumped. Search though he does, he can find no way to block the women's intentions. He has, besides, endorsed their wishes, never envisaging this speedy translation into action, which is in striking contrast to most Palace procedure.

'The place will be as empty as the tomb when you've gone,' he grumbles.

'Oh, nonsense!'

'It's not nonsense.'

'The place is swarming with people.'

'Do you expect me to make-do with these swarms?'

'Why don't you come with us then? Rabi would like that, wouldn't you, Rabi?'

'Oh yes! I would love father to come with us!'

Bawajiraj recoils. The family shrine is on top of a *ghat* which cannot be traversed by carriage. It will mean a long dusty ride, very probably on a mule, or being jolted up in a litter. At the end of this frightful journey is a small unimposing temple, tended by one priest, serving a few locals. Bawajiraj's filial ties are not so strong that he would wish to worship in such austerity, in a place hallowed only because some commoner ancestor—he is not sure who, the man goes back beyond the first Bawajiraj into virtually antiquity—has chosen to make it his springboard.

Firmly, but gracefully, pleading the call of a Maharajah's duty, he declines.

* * *

'Your grandfather, my husband, worshipped in this temple,' the Dowager Maharani tells her grandson. 'And before that his forbear, the first Bawajiraj—'

'Who died in the fortress-prison the British put him in?'

'The same. And before him his father, who was a gallant chieftain. He extended the dominions he had received from his father and handed them down to his children. . . . They put down stones to mark the boundaries, the boulders are still there, you can see them to this day. . . .'

The boy listens. He is drawn into and implicated in the spell of continuity his grandmother weaves. The past advances, reaches into his present. The present elongates into the future in a way he cannot quite envisage, but he sees as a whole the process he has been apt to chop into three.

They are riding in a carriage-and-four, he, his mother, his

77

grandmother. Bumping along behind them, in a conveyance outwardly similar but less well sprung, are Panditji and Parasuram the Brahmin cook-cum-guardian. The carriages are from his father's coach house, but the gilt and crests and other princely trappings have been scrapped. Even the plum plush has gone, which Rabi rather regrets; he loves the downy upholstery, which has distinct advantages over the stuffed horsehair, canvas-covered seats that have been substituted.

This is Mohini's doing. She has also dismissed outriders and postilions. She is not entitled to them in the first place—officially she does not exist—but the brimming emotions roused in Bawa-jiraj's breast by the impending departure of his loved ones have led him to command a cavalcade. It strikes Mohini as ridiculous. She is bent upon being a commoner. She has been brought up as one. The splendours of life with the Maharajah, received with rapture at early acquaintance, have in the years since eroded to the point where they positively chafe.

'All these flunkeys! What are we going to—a ball?'

'Only so that you can return safe and sound. You know I would never forgive myself if anything happened to you and the boy.'

'You know it's not that at all. They're only there for ornament.'

'Why shouldn't I provide ornaments for my beloved?'

'We don't need them.'

'For your safety then.'

'We're safer without. Ordinary people don't go for ordinary people—they only attack people like you!'

'I know my people. I can safely say my people respect and cherish their Maharajah,' says Bawajiraj stiffly.

The Dewan steps into the breach. He has more than a streak of admiration for the headstrong concubine, which makes him anxious for her safety. Commoner, Mohini might ardently wish to remain. The fact is that the gilding brushed off onto her by her princely association cannot be as arbitrarily expunged as the Maharajah's cipher. There is an insurgency abroad, the Dewan is well aware, that is beginning to question the expensive ap-purtenances of Princes no less than of the representatives of Emperors.

'My man, one Parasuram,' he proposes. 'He is a Brahmin, an excellent cook, apart from other desirable qualifications, who will be happy to accompany the party.'

Those concerned take his point, in different degree. The Brahmins have established a network, as invisible, as wide-spread, and as coolly powerful as anything the British have contrived, which secures immunity for those upon whom it falls. The British do it blandly. There is hardly a Governor, or Commissioner, or Resident, or Commanding Officer in the subcontinent with whom Sir Arthur, through school and club and country house association, is not acquainted. He refers to them, with total absence of affectation, as his neighbours, which, separated though they may be by a thousand miles, in spirit and essence they are. The Brahmin web is as fine-spun, of blood and marriage ties, of inter-connecting ministers and lawyers and teachers and priests, and the elaborate, authoritative codes of a subtle society. Those who shelter under either umbrella rarely feel the heat of the sun.

'An excellent idea. The standard of cooking outside the Palace kitchens is execrable,' says Bawajiraj.

'I can vouch for Parasuram's culinary excellence,' says the Dewan drily. His mind centres on guardian angels rather than cooks. He hopes the invoking of these invisible beings through his approved agency will ensure that Mohini and her party proceed in peace. He takes time off, however, as he often does, to wonder if Bawajiraj can be as dense as he appears. The podgy hands, the dark, sensuous face, all but convince the Brahmin, but the children he has fathered, the three charming girls and the little boy Rabi, qualify the estimate.

Tirumal Rao experiences a rare, acute pity for the Maharajah. The clay is right enough, he feels, but the alien potter has mangled the material.

* * *

Rabi has never travelled so far before. Contrary to the women's assumptions, the rigours of the journey hardly affect him. Unlike them, it is nothing for him to spend the whole day in the saddle. Like his father his life is split between the luxuries of the Palace and the extreme discomforts endured in hunting, stalking, and ceremonial elephant rides. Unlike them, he has not seen the countryside as it opens itself to him on the journey.

'What is that, Panditji?'

After the first halt Rabi has transferred himself to the lesser carriage, away from the dozing women.

'What is what?'

'That.' He points. It is an undulating field that seems to shiver with every passing breeze, even the draught of their carriage is enough to set off the quicksilver movement. He has seen these patches of emerald, from high and distant vantage points in the Palace, and once or twice in Devapur City, but never at such close quarters. They are not moving fast. His finger is still on the target when Panditji answers. This is not always so. Several items of incalculable interest have gone by, into oblivion, from a difficulty in pinpointing them to his tutor who, from familiarity with these vistas, cannot readily distinguish the extraordinary from the ordinary.

'That is a paddy-field,' says Panditji.

'It's so green.'

'Yes.'

'It's beautiful. I've never seen anything so beautiful before.'

The Pandit is moved. A sight so common as scarcely to merit a passing glance from an ordinary man has captivated this Palace child. At the same time he is severe. He does not approve of a cloistration that results in so poor a grasp of reality.

'It's not there for its beauty,' he says.

'What's it for?'

'For growing rice, of course.'

'Why of course?'

'What else should people grow but grain to feed themselves with?'

'My father grows flowers.'

'He's well-fed—he can afford to!'

'Aren't they?'

'Who?'

'The people who grow the rice.'

'No.'

'But if they grow it why can't they eat it?'

'They can't because they have to sell it, don't you see, they can't eat it!'

The Pandit is quite agitated. The blood rises to his narrow, sallow face, reddens and fills it out; it looks like a blotched peony. Rabi watches with absorption; he has not observed the phenomenon before. His day has been full of observation and interest.

'My father says everyone in his State is well-fed,' Rabi pursues the matter.

'He is entitled to his opinion.'

'Even if he's wrong?'

'Who is to tell him he's wrong?'

'I could.'

'Yes, you do that,' says Panditji. 'You do that.' He leans back in the carriage and closes his eyes. His face looks drained, the yellowish tinges have returned to his cheekbones. It is his normal look, which reassures Rabi. He has decided he does not really care for the peony phenomenon, for which he suspects he has been responsible. Nevertheless he cannot restrain himself forever.

'Look, Panditji, birds, hundreds of birds! On that island.'

The Pandit opens his eyes.

'It's a mangrove swamp,' he says wearily.

'A nesting-ground, Panditji! Look!'

The Pandit looks. The mangroves are clumped in the middle of a small artificial lake whose banks are fringed with reeds. There is a bund, constructed of rock and clay, against which the greenish water laps. The roots of the mangroves are below the waterline. Their branches are thickly interlaced, and nests by the hundred are cradled in the meshes. Birds are circling and wheeling overhead.

'Can't we stop, Panditji? *Can* we stop?' Rabi leans out of the carriage to shout at the coachman.

'Yes, why not?' says the Pandit. He sees it as an occasion to improve his charge's mind. He will, he resolves, suggest the superiority of bird-watching to bird slaughter, which is the Maharajah's extraordinary pleasure. He raps, authoritatively, with his malacca cane. The coachman trundles the stock of his whip against a wheel—rat-tat-tat-tat—as he reins in the horses. The carriages slow and stop.

But all is not as imagined. The birdcalls have altered, and are now strident and lamenting. Their flight has become frenetic.

'Wait,' says the Pandit, and restrains the boy.

'A jackal, after the eggs,' says the coachman.

'A jackal that swims, no doubt,' says the acid Pandit to the abashed servant.

The source of the disturbance reveals itself. Two men are concealed in the cover afforded by the reeds. They are Europeans, and they have guns which are cocked to fire. There is a loud report, then another and another. Bang-bang-bang. Birds, seeded with shot, are falling. There are small puffs of smoke in the air, drifts of feathers twirl down aimlessly.

At this point the deserted shores of the lake suddenly erupt. A swarm of villagers materialises and converges on the Europeans. The two men retreat onto the bund. One of them raises his gun, but his companion restrains him. They stand and wait. The villagers stream onto the bund in a thin line and surround the pair. They shout and shake their fists. The Europeans are shouting too. Confused sounds are carried across the water, but the words and meaning are lost. The anger, however, is palpable.

'Why are they angry, Panditji? It's a duck-shoot, they're only shooting ducks.'

There is a mysterious density to the scene that disturbs Rabi.

'A duck-shoot!' he wails. 'What is wrong, Panditji, what is wrong?'

'Drive on,' says the Pandit sharply.

'No, no!'

'Drive on.' The guardian, Parasuram, adds his authority to the Pandit's.

The coachman flicks his whip. The carriage lurches forward, picks up speed. Rabi kneels on his seat, presses his face to the oblong of mica that affords a view from the back of the cab. He is relieved to see that nothing has happened. He has expected—he doesn't know what—something, which has made his stomach churn. But the men are still as they were, villagers and intruders, clumped together. As he watches there is a renewed jostling, a glint of sun on metal. The two guns arc upward and fall. The water closes over them. Rabi wrenches his attention away from the widening ripples on the lake to the crowd. He is reluctant to do this—he does not know why—but he forces himself. He cannot see the Europeans except for their arms, which are raised. The four bare arms jut over the heads of the crowd. They are blue to the elbow with tattooed designs that run down from the wrist, and the fingers are spread-eagled. Now he wants to see more, an unfinished quality to the scene ravages his mind, but the coach is rounding a bend. Frantically he twists and cranes, but now a hill interposes between him and his quarry.

* * *

The carriages rumble on steadily, without incident. The sun climbs higher. The country through which they are travelling has begun to change. There are hills in the distance. One range of hills lies behind them; they are traversing a valley stippled with soft green shades. The air is crisp and revives the two dozing women.

'Ah, that smell! How delicious it is!' Mohini says and uncurls herself—that sinuous movement which is apt to overwhelm the Maharajah—from the cushions.

'It reminds me of our valley,' says Manjula, and lays her ringless, thinning hand on the rounded arm of the younger woman.

'You have never been back,' says Mohini. 'There are many in your home, madam, who would be happy—'

'My home,' says the Dowager gently, 'was my husband's kingdom . . . I have no other now. One learns to let go, or have one's fingers prised loose. Time, you know, is a ruthless master.'

She gazes at this ward of hers, who is still in her springtime, and numinous with it, and wonders if the words can carry any meaning at her age. Then she recalls what she has overlooked, the ripening nature of the fitful role as unlicensed consort to her son into which this girl has cast herself.

'And you, madam—?'

Mohini is gentle too. The years stretch lushly in front of her, but imagination and experience leaven the effect; she is not incapable of understanding.

The women are murmuring, sitting side by side, but even so it rouses the boy. Rabi, yielding at last, has left the Pandit's rattling conveyance (it carries cooking paraphernalia besides the cook) for the relative comfort of his mother's, and is asleep on the cushions she has arranged for him. He has slept for some hours, although it seems to him no more than a few minutes. He sits up, momentarily confused. His cheeks are flushed, and one of them bears the imprint of the canvas weave.

'Where are we?'

'In a coach, my lamb.'

'I've been asleep.'

'I know, you were tired.'

'I wish I hadn't gone to sleep. I didn't want to miss anything.'

'You haven't missed anything.'

'Are you sure?'

'I promise you.'

Rabi is mollified, rather than convinced. He is aware that he and his elders inhabit different countries, in which different standards of worth prevail; but as there is nothing to be done, he reconciles himself.

'I'm hungry,' he announces.

'Then we shall eat. At once.'

In the event they clatter on for another half hour while the coachman objects to one place and Manjula finds fault with another. Finally the ideal spot is found, a meadow beside a stream that manages to bubble with a modicum of water. The denuded stream creates something of an oasis in the wake of its meanderings. Elsewhere the land is parched.

Here the cramped travellers debouch from the mobile crates into which, in their minds, the carriages have been transformed.

They are hot and dusty; the arduous selection of a picnic site has made them cantankerous, but all are magically restored by their surroundings. These surroundings are merely as made, that is to say no man has had a hand in their design. Consequently there are treacherous bogs hidden in the meadow, and thorn bushes thrive amongst the shrubs. Nevertheless, the overall effect is of a total and pristine beauty that ravishes them all. There is not one who would not exchange the marshalled splendours of royal parks and gardens for the stray and limited loveliness they discover here.

Parasuram, in his lesser hat, is preparing a meal. He is a good cook but an unskilled fire-lighter. There is smoke, but no fire. He pokes about in the scrub for more suitable kindling but is thwarted by innumerable bogs and presently retires, prudently suppressing his loss.

'It's green wood! Can't you do any better?' He snaps at the coachman he has recruited as wood-gatherer, who has produced this useless bundle of firewood.

'I've done my best. Better than your worship if I may be so bold,' says the grinning servant, and holds aloft the waterlogged shoe that Parasuram has abandoned to the bog.

'Look at his shoe! Parasuram's shoe! It's horrible, it's dripping, yuk!'

Rabi is beside himself with pleasure. The ordered Palace permits few such happenings. Parasuram is not enamoured of the Palace, but its order begins to re-assert its appeal. He tucks his feet under him where they will not attract further attention and gets on with his preparations.

The Dowager and her ward are strolling in the meadow, hems raised above their bare feet, exposing their slender ankles. Both are rejecting with fervour—the one naturally, the other with deliberation—the constraints which fall upon them in the Palace to embrace these plebeian freedoms to which, as inveterate commoners, they believe they properly aspire: Mohini after close on a decade, which she considers a lifetime, Manjula after an actual lifetime of princely protocol. They have kicked off their sandals in affirmation, though the frail leather straps, which have laid paler crosses on their pale insteps, cannot be said ever to have constituted an infringement. It is a gesture nevertheless. It pleases them, this shedding of thongs, leads on to further, wilful flagrancies.

The Dowager has come upon a thicket of lantana. The shrubs are bright with flowers and clusters of glossy black berries, which she recognises from her youth. She is bent on sharing her tastes and pleasures.

'Rabi, see what I've got. Try some, they're delicious.' A handful of berries glitters in her palm.

'Highness!'

The wood-gathering coachman attempts to intervene. He is a man of the Dowager's age, to whom—despite her cropped head, her widow's weeds, even the advent of the present incumbent—she will always be the Maharani. He is a plainsman, suspicious of hill produce, especially of this wild, glittering nature.

'Highness, what if it's poisonous!'

'Poisonous, what nonsense! When I was a girl we used to eat basketfuls! Here, try some.'

The man blenches. The badge of his service urges him to accept, but he is not at all convinced. He is saved by the firewood, which occupies both arms.

'I will, presently, Highness,' he says, and retreats with his load.

Rabi eats the berries his grandmother offers him. They are not a novelty to him. He and Janaki have established a thriving commerce, whereby she brings him an apronful of berries gathered on hillsides that are barred to him, and receives in exchange plums and apricots despatched from Kulu orchards, which she covets. He is, consequently, more enraptured by his mother's discovery.

'Mimosa,' she says, of the feathery plant, half hidden in a thicket, which she has spotted. She touches a frond to show her son and the leaflets fold like a butterfly's wings.

'*Mimosa pudica*, the sensitive plant,' the Pandit finds it necessary to say. He is, after all, an educator; and he is a conscientious man. Rabi hardly hears—he is wholly absorbed by the mimosa. He touches, and waits patiently, and touches again. The tender, murderous leaves brush against his fingers; he has to hold his breath to feel the thistledown caress. When he tires of this game he invents another, touching rapidly to see if he can close up all the fronds at once, but the crotchety plant closes and opens stubbornly; he finds he cannot defeat it.

Parasuram, against all odds, has got on with the cooking. He calls to them that the meal is ready, and disposes himself to receive the plaudits he feels he deserves.

No one stirs.

He calls again—he is afraid the slightest delay will spell disaster for his dishes—and this time the metallic note that enters his voice puts an end to mimosa worship. The little plant is forgotten. The worshippers remember that they are, in a manner of speaking, starving.

'I could eat a horse!' declares Rabi.

'What a disgusting idea.' Mohini wrinkles a fastidious nose.

'I'm only saying! I don't really *mean* that.'

'I know, but it still disgusts me.'

'Father *often* says it, it's only what *he* says.'

'You don't have to copy everything he says.'

'Why not?'

'Why should you?'

Rabi swoops away. He does not wish to argue with his mother. If he loses the argument—it's on the cards that he will—it may spoil his day. His day has been near to perfection and will achieve that state, he is convinced, when his stomach stops pinching. He swoops back and perches attentively, his plate on his knees, while Parasuram serves him. There is rice, and a stew, and wheat-flour *chapathis*. The rice is golden, if somewhat smoked, the stew thinnish, like gruel, the *chapathis* wear charred frills about their rims. To Rabi it seems the finest meal he has ever eaten. He wishes he could eat more, as he is being pressed to do, but he has already had three helpings. Reluctantly he refuses a fourth. He has finished; they have all finished except the coachman who is just beginning his meal. It is his position in life to eat last and apart from his masters. He does not mind. Anything else, in fact, would acutely embarrass him. It would also embarrass the others, who can have but sparse correspondence, they believe, with a coachman. They are relieved—especially the Brahmin Parasuram—that Rabi, who is known to have an eclectic circle of friends, has not sought to draw the man into the general company. He and his companion, the driver of the lesser carriage, settle to their meal.

Rabi, as it happens, has been too occupied with the novelties and excitements that have crowded in on him to remember the coachmen. He lies in the sun, on his back in the grassy meadow, squinting up at the bright blue sky as he goes over each delight. Suddenly, then, it explodes in his brain: between emerald paddies and mimosa bursts the star, starfish hands on blue stalks that push into the bluish air above him and hang there, and will not be rubbed out. He lets out a cry.

'Rabi! What is it? What's the matter?'

'Star—starfish—'

'You're dreaming, my love. Wake up.'

'I'm awake.'

'There's nothing. Look.'

'There is—I saw.'

'A nightmare.'

'*No.*'

'Wake up, Rabi. Open your eyes.'

His eyes are open, and red from rubbing. He accepts the warm embrace of his mother's creamy, seductive arms, but will not offer up in exchange his own gritted will.

'What happened to those men?'

'What men?'

'On the bund. The English.'

'Nothing, nothing at all. Why do you ask?'

'I want to *know!*'

'You know,' says the Pandit, 'that nothing ever happens to the English.'

'It might.'

'How might it? They were armed, you saw the guns.'

'But the people—'

'People don't stand a chance against guns, you know that.'

'So many! There were so many people,' he wails. 'It's not *fair.*'

The Pandit's heart feels hollow. There is a curious inversion here that he traces back to the boy's father, to Bawajiraj's frequently evidenced, maladroit grasp of reality.

'It's not fair to turn guns on people either,' he says, coldly, to the frantic child.

Rabi perceives the justice of it, but he has seen the watery fate of the guns.

'They threw them away!' he cries. 'The English had nothing left.'

'If they had come with nothing, nothing would have happened,' says the grim Pandit.

It subdues Rabi. Try as he will he cannot sort out right from wrong. In this confusion he allows himself to be ushered into the carriage, the superior conveyance with the springs and cushions, which they plump up around him in the hope, or some such muddled notion, that they will ward off nightmare.

* * *

Bereft of his loved ones, Bawajiraj continues to conduct affairs of State. It makes him feel sacrificial. There is a distinct sensation that he alone is sticking to his post, while others indulge in frivolous pastimes. The rewards of such virtuous conduct are, however, elusive. He feels, not a sense of righteousness, but merely somewhat hard done by.

He keeps it, he believes, to himself. He believes it is incumbent on a Ruler to preserve an outward calm, whatever his inward turmoil; but the forlorn airs that invest the dutiful figure that pads about the Palace are apparent to all but himself.

The truth is he misses Mohini and Rabi as much as he has said he would. The extravagant protestations in which he has indulged have not, somewhat to his surprise, in fact been extravagant. The crammed and lavish Palace indeed feels as empty as the tomb. His wife turns to stone when he approaches. Shanta Devi hardens her heart against the man who has heaped so many humiliations upon her, not least the latest conception that lies low and heavy in her womb. She gathers her daughters around her and douses the pity his woebegone countenance kindles.

Bawajiraj drifts away. Except in sexual matters, which he considers his prerogative, he is not a man to impose himself. Sex is not what he seeks from his gravid wife—in any case it is forbidden—but company. He wanders into the Pearl Suite; but the fragrances and memories Mohini has left behind only heighten his sense of desolation. Nor is he helped by the women attendants, who turn their eloquent eyes on him, and sigh, and fluff up a bolster or two to emphasise the bitter-sweet quality of the deserted bower.

Bawajiraj goes away. He feels ill-used, more so than any mortal should be. Mohini has not even vouchsafed him a date for her return, to which he can look forward.

'How long will you be gone?'
It is not that he has not done his best to find out.
'I've no idea.'
'You must have.'
'I haven't.'
'A week? A month?'
'Longer.'
'How much longer?'
'As long as we feel like. Many, many moons.'
'Must you be poetic?'
'Can I help it if I'm a poet?'
'You're only a poet when you want to provoke me.'
'Not at all. I feel poetic. Journeys are poetic, have you no imagination?'

'Mohini, I demand to know—'

'You can make no demands of me.'

'I have a right to know.'

'You have no rights at all.'

'I have.'

'Compel me, then.'

He is angry. Ancestors have merely had to frown for heads to fall. Anger, however, dissolves in the sense of impending loss. Besides, there is always a fear she won't come back, and she has reminded him that he cannot compel her. The insecurity that has accrued to Shanta Devi in marriage, has, paradoxically, devolved on him through his lack of any legitimate hold over this girl. Bawajiraj casts a fervid eye on the marriage bond, while at the same time he understands it will destroy whatever tenuous security he now enjoys with his constant, delectable concubine.

'Mohini, please,' he says. 'Please listen. You know I have to make arrangements.'

'What arrangements?'

'For you and the boy.'

'Why? Is this some durbar we're going to?'

'Moneywise!'

It is enough to tax the patience of a Brahmin, which Bawajiraj is not. He is a Prince, and this commoner is needling him.

Mohini folds prim hands and rests them in her lap. She is a commoner, and common clay is not to be hustled by princes.

'It's a pilgrimage,' she announces. 'Pilgrims are simple people, they don't need your kind of palaver. Can't you understand?'

'My son—'

'Our son.'

'Rabi can never be a simple man.'

'He will.'

'He won't.'

'I'll make him.'

'You won't be able to. He's a Maharajah's son, even you can't alter that.'

'You'll see.'

'What will I see? Ah, Mohini, will you take my only son away from me?'

'How little you know me!' Mohini's eyes, which have been dangerous, are suddenly turned to velvet. 'Highness, your son is your son—do you think I would ever come between the two I love best?'

* * *

So they are gone; the two he loves most have taken themselves off and left him behind.

His Highness, at the end of his arduous day, feels not tired but deflated. Flat as a pancake, and a taste on his tongue as if he has been deprived of vitamins. Even cricket and polo, those unfailing restoratives, fail to help. He drifts around the place, convinced he is sickening for something, and certainly the symptoms of ennui are often distinctly alarming. Without Mohini, Bawajiraj is, and feels like, a ghost of himself.

The Resident notes the Ruler's dejection. Sir Arthur's private being, as distinct from his public persona, is sensitive to distress to a fine degree. It is made so, perhaps, by the very nature of his living, for he dwells in a most precious, most precariously wrought haven of domestic bliss. This dwelling, its paramount support, is his wife, Mary. They have constructed, these two, out of torrid and alien soil a home whose outward grace and inner harmonies soothe and sustain them both. It has nothing to do with the Residency, which is its external casing: not in form, least of all in spirit. It is a sanctuary within that magnificent edifice whose cadences in Sir Arthur's hearing are sweetened and magnified by the presence of his wife and the two infants, Esmond and Sophie.

When he is parted from these three, or any of them, Sir Arthur is, and knows himself to be, a shadow of himself.

The partings are annual. When the hot winds blow in from the desert, and the mercury climbs above the red line that sets a limit, at 90 degrees Fahrenheit, to the endurance of the European race, his wife departs for the cool, salubrious hills, taking the children with her. Sir Arthur remains at his post. There have been times when Residents have fled the entire summer, which stretches from May to September. Sir Arthur contents himself with two months' absence from the capital, which leaves an interminable span for him to get through, somehow, on his own.

There is the other parting, more formidable still, which looms on the horizon, when the children will be sent home for their education. Sir Arthur does not care to think about it too much. He will do it, that he knows. Sacrifice is part of his contract of service to India; it is a package deal on which he will not renege. It is only in weaker moments—at night, or when the heat is wearing him down—that he shivers and wonders how he will manage without them.

As, clearly, the Maharajah cannot. The man is dislocated. The dejected figure obtrudes on Sir Arthur's disciplined landscape and, after an initial exasperation, awakes in him a certain fellow feeling.

'I hope you are well, your Highness,' he says kindly, if formally. 'Of late you have looked a trifle—under the weather.'

'Well . . . as a matter of fact, H.E.,' the desperate Bawajiraj mumbles, 'I'm not too well . . . I have thought I must be going down with something.'

'Perhaps you should see your doctor.'

'That donkey! What does he know? Waits for you to tell him what's wrong, then wraps it up in long words to justify a two-figure bill!'

Sometimes Bawajiraj can be quite shrewd. Sir Arthur smiles. He says, with the utmost caution—the territory of emotion is a minefield to him—

'I expect, your Highness, you miss your—your son, and—and—'

There are many words for Mohini; none of them suit the occasion, or the woman herself. Sir Arthur ducks out of naming her. The Maharajah, who is palely aware, rescues his Adviser.

'I expect I do. Perhaps that's what's wrong with me, H.E. I miss them.'

Bawajiraj's podgy fingers with the rings and stubs of nails drum on the table. The forlorn little tattoo touches off humane impulses in Sir Arthur, who is, indeed, no stranger to them. His office is such, however, that he is often called upon to stifle his humanity. This time he succumbs. The misery that exudes from Bawajiraj is so close to his own experience—so near the bone—that he cannot resist. With the utmost sincerity he offers what is most precious to him.

'You must come and see us, Waji. The children—you haven't met them, have you?—are at the most delightful age. Perhaps you would care to join us for dinner one evening? My wife—' he coughs—this is an area of uncertainty—but recovers and carries on gallantly—'and I would be most happy.'

'I'd love to,' says Bawajiraj.

He speaks the simple truth. His ambition—secretly nursed, since he cannot admit qualifying clauses to the belief that he is one of them—has been to receive just such an invitation. Indeed all manner of energies in the country are acutely centred on the issuing and receipt of invitations, from Collector, Commissioner, Governor, upward to His Excellency the Viceroy himself, whose invitation is the most coveted in the absence of the Sovereign. These august personages are themselves plagued by considerations of whom to invite—the most unsuitable characters have been known to inscribe their names in the Visitors' Book. At every level it arouses the utmost anxiety and agitation.

Bawajiraj's concern is not with these public summonses, of which he is assured as Head of State. He aspires to enter the charmed circle of personal relationship beyond the public portals of the Residency to which the most junior European cadres have access but to which he has never been admitted.

It has, at times, troubled Sir Arthur. Waji is a decent old stick. He has never been tiresome, unlike some rulers. Native, of course, but you would hardly notice . . . and they are good friends, no doubt of that at all. The difficulty is—Sir Arthur sighs; he knows it does not apply in this case, but he cannot quarrel with the principle—that errant Maharajahs have to be hauled up and rebuked, which you cannot do, however gently, to an inner circle friend.

A distance has to be kept—that is the official line. Sir Arthur's grounding has been as thorough, in its way, as Bawajiraj's, so that he never wastes any energy pondering the source of the questionable whiffs it indubitably gives off from time to time.

* * *

First Sir Arthur, now Lady Copeland is troubled.

She sits on a rustic bench in a little pergola set on a grassy knoll in the English garden. The garden is her creation. It has been coaxed and plucked out of an unsuitable soil and takes the place of the cultivated wilderness she has inherited. Only the plaintive memories of the older gardeners, and a stump or two that serve as bird tables, contain and recall the bamboo and wild date thickets, the banyan and tamarind and wood-apple trees that have once flourished here. Lady Copeland's memories have felled them. She has hankered for a softer, ordered landscape in which such choking, exuberant growth has no place.

The trees have been chopped down, or survive, a few, in the middle distance. The noisome huts that cluttered the farther reaches of the garden estate have been razed and cleared. The vistas that flow from the little pergola now are guileless and entirely charming. There are arcades of climbing roses, shady walks bordered with lilac and laburnum, banks and beds of sweet-smelling balsam and lavender.

Memories can create as well as destroy. These verdant monuments have been raised to commemorate placid recollections. The very substance of Lady Copeland reposes in this delicate fabrication, so that when she ascends the little knoll, and surveys her artless kingdom, she leaves behind the encroachments and exaggerations of the clanging continent and steps into the cool, charming, scented gardens of a romantic girlhood.

Only sometimes it does not work.

Her soul will not be soothed. She can feel the fretful sawing that accompanies the impositions of her public life. Mary Copeland folds her hands and rests them in her lap to still the dreadful chafing. To try, though her face has begun to burn.

It is not—she teases out the strands of feeling—that she has anything against the Maharajah. She hasn't. She has often met him. There are innumerable State functions at which it is impossible not to meet. She has accepted his invitations to Palace banquets, to those impulsive but lavish parties that Bawajiraj, overcome by some success in the hunting field, is apt to throw. He has attended receptions at the Residency. On these occasions she has found the Maharajah irreproachable. His manners are impeccable. There is nothing on which she can lay a finger.

But then, fingers do not lay powerful ghosts. Lady Copeland's ghost is called not one of us. Her lips spell it out, there in her little pergola. Not one of us, never will be, since it is an affair of the soul to which she will never play traitor.

At the bottom of the knoll, which it is not permitted to ascend, the diminutive, submissive figure of the ayah waits.

Lady Copeland puts aside her cares and rises. It is time to dress for dinner.

Ayah assists the Lady Sahib out of her bath and hands her warmed, fluffy towels. She carefully disposes the peignoir of figured silk, in sweet-pea tints, about her shoulders before she begins to brush her hair. Her dense black hands wield the hairbrush expertly, the diamonds worked into the monogram on the back flash rhythmically, like fireflies. She is a trained woman. She has been trained in Lady Sahib's mother's household, serves her now as she has once served her mother, and has accompanied her upon marriage as part of her retinue.

Lady Copeland is lulled by the woman's care. Not unlike Sir

Arthur, she feels she can relax in hands trained and trusted by her mother's establishment. She has surrounded herself with the devotion of such servants, which suppresses discordant notes as effectively as interring cannon in the canna beds.

The *syce* who saddles the children's ponies has trained as a boy in the stables of the old Colonel, Lady Copeland's grandfather. The cook traces his line back to the same establishment. So does the grizzled ancient who heads the batch of twenty gardeners who tend the English garden.

For Lady Copeland's is an old India family. Four generations have served the country, have unquestioningly devoted to it the best years of their lives. Their bones—those who have died in their beds, as well as of those whom the country has suddenly turned on and savaged—the blood debt of their suzerainty, which all the British suspect they may ultimately be called upon to pay—lie buried in distant Indian plains, in graveyards as neat and regimented as the British themselves. Their spirit is entwined in her; it reaches out from the past and makes her what she is. She herself is unaware of internal ivy; but the externals of her connection she readily admits and openly cherishes.

The room in which she sits—the Blue Room in the North wing (the South wing overlooks the gaudy, Oriental Gateways, for which Lady Copeland has little taste)—proudly attests, amid the cornflower and cerulean hues that compose it, to the mettle of her connections and recollections. There are campaign ribbons and medals, miniatures of fierce and delicate ancestors, mementoes of picnics and battles, the rosettes of horsemanship and the trophies of sport—Lady Copeland can recount in affectionate detail the history of each single object. Disposed on Chippendale, among the Sèvres, in silver frames, are the family photographs: of her relations, and Sir Arthur's, of the Colonel, mounted, and his lady, in a wide shady hat; of ponies and dogs and children at gymkhanas and fêtes, of Esmond and Sophie, and Sir Arthur himself: Sir Arthur as a young Secretary, smiling, in the sunshine, on the lawn of another Residency, not dissimilar to the one she now inhabits. Lady Copeland's features soften as she dwells on this treasured portrait of her husband.

There is a lot between these two that does not have to be said. And yet.

In the looking-glass that has framed her mementoes Mary Copeland discerns her husband, in the flesh, his masculinity stressed by her frippery (a mere male, Sir Arthur is fond of saying) behind which he bulks. She smiles at him through pale blue net, which he parts to enter.

'That will do, Ayah.'

Lady Copeland has something to say. It cannot be said in front of the servants.

'Memsahib.'

The woman glides away. All the servants in the Residency exhibit, or have been schooled into, this quality of noiseless locomotion. It contrasts with the Palace's domestics, who tend to pad in their bare feet, or even—in the Dowager's suite—squeak on the marble tiles.

'Ready, my dear?'

'Almost. How do I look?'

'As beautiful as ever.'

Sir Arthur rests a hand on his wife's shoulder, which is bare, and bluish-white from the flares released from the blue boudoir. He would like her to incline her long swan's neck and brush her lips against his knuckles as she usually does. Instead he feels, and interprets, the faintest tremor under the collarbone on which his fingertips are hopefully roosting. Sir Arthur drops his hands and starts to navigate the room, which has begun to glare from a sudden glut of twilight.

'Arthur.'

'Yes, my dear.'

'It's not that I mind, but—'

'I know.'

'One has to—'

'Of course.'

Sir Arthur is still pacing in circles, around the room stuffed with objects that normally exude a soft reassurance, but now are emanating, or so it seems, though he is not given to imagining things, a baleful light. The silver, especially, is throwing off sparks.

'Waji isn't a bad old stick,' he brings out, fending off the forces that are palpably butting against him. 'He's been a—bit lost, since his—his—'

'Paramour?'

'Yes. Since she went away, on this pilgrimage or whatever, something very odd I must say.'

'She's an odd woman.'

'Unusual. Inspired the most unusual devotion in Waji.'

'Mmm.'

Mary Copeland has pins between her teeth; she is bent on an artless, but taxing, coiffure for the evening.

'He seems—utterly devastated without her.'

'Mmm.'

'The boy too. I can imagine,' Sir Arthur bursts out feelingly, if surprisingly, 'what he feels like. I thought . . . our two . . .'

Mary Copeland fixes the last lustrous, honey-coloured coil in place.

'Of course. This once . . . ?' she asks, or lays down.

'This once. No question.'

'Because—'

'I know.'

'We must—'

'Naturally.'

'Keep . . .'

Her voice trails away. She will not define. It is not in fact necessary, or possible. She has constructed in this room, this house, in the very bowels of steamy alien territory, a richly lined and insulated casket that nourishes their living. It is in effect a womb she offers, which sustains them and is sustained by them, which she suspects—it is laid down in her bones—will rupture if penetrated by foreign organisms.

Lady Copeland has sound reasons for resisting the intrusion of a foreign body.

So has Sir Arthur, who has been temporarily overcome by human, though princely, dolours, but is now re-admitted to the fold. His wife is holding out her hand to him. He advances and clasps it, turns it over and uncurling the fingers kisses the fragrant palm.

'Do me up, Arthur, will you?'

He obeys. His eyes melt into his wife's in the silvered glass, which also reflects the unity of all that is assembled and concentrated here. They are distilled products, these two, of what is and has gone before, a fact that gives them a perfect luminous understanding of each other.

* * *

Bawajiraj bustles happily into this world of half notes, semitones, and nuances. He is wearing white satin; he has been told that dress will be informal, and this is the least his wardrobe has yielded. His tight white trousers have pearly straps at the instep, which are decently hidden by his pumps. His rajah coat (not unlike the one the wretched *bania* has attempted to copy) is fastened with pearl studs that remind Lady Copeland of the pea-buttons on her shoes, which the ayah has to coax through leather loops with a hook. They are the bane of the ayah's, as of Bawajiraj's dresser's life, of which neither owner is aware, but if aware would be heedless. There are unsuspected areas of affiliation even between these two.

'Your Highness . . . so pleased . . .'

Lady Copeland, in delphinium chiffon, floats towards her guest, murmuring.

'Delighted, delighted!'

Bawajiraj's fervid, podgy paw closes around the pale digits she offers, bids fair to break the latent bones with the weight of his feeling. His pleasure is so patent that Sir Arthur experiences a twinge or two, which spur him to his guest's side.

'Only too pleased, you know that, Waji,' he says, and taking a shimmering arm propels the enthusiastic Maharajah into the drawing room.

The drawing room of the private suite of the Resident and his lady has been planned to pacify body and spirit—to anticipate and fulfil the wants of the human frame and the hankerings of the soul in exile. As such it does not awe; it is not meant to; there is no necessity to stun with imperial thunder those who penetrate these purlieus. Bawajiraj is consequently somewhat dismayed. He has a penchant for crimson and gold, for shimmer and dazzle, all of which are conspicuously absent. Instead there are sofas covered in chintz, cushions cosily opulent with goose-down, roomy chairs of a comfort that has to be experienced (Bawajiraj does, and is somewhat compensated for absences) to be believed. Mild, Anglo-Saxon airs prevail, aided by the calm spaces that the walls enclose, whose surfaces are clad in some kind of thick and silencing material, spaces clearly impermeable to tumult except by leave, in muted forms. The tone is plain—that of a bell whose lucid tongue is not heard outside these quarters.

These quarters are a place apart. They are set in the Residency, but cannot by any stretch of fancy be imagined a part of it. To those, purblind, to whom the division is blurred, or even invisible, there are the coils and trusses of double-twist to remind, presided over by a sentinel in the livery of the House, with the monogram of its Head worked in scarlet thread upon white drill, and a silver cockade in his turban. On his passage to and from official functions Bawajiraj often sees the loops of yellow silk rope that cordon off the Private Suite. They have assumed in his mind the properties of a hurdle, or even a vaulting-horse.

* * *

'Not everyone, you know, Minister.'

Bawajiraj has attempted to crow over his Dewan, who has never been honoured. Tirumal Rao, who is embedded as deeply in privacies as precious as any the Resident commands, cocks a sardonic eyebrow.

'Indeed an honour, your Highness. But,' he asks, this niggling eagle, 'is it advisable?'

'Advisable! What has advisable to do with friendship? It is a friendly gesture!'

'You might find it difficult after this, Highness, to refuse a favour,' implies the Minister.

Bawajiraj is disgusted with such vulgar cynicism. What, he wonders as he marches off, makes him keep such a common creature in his employ?

The Dewan aches with suppressed laughter, an effect the transparent Maharajah often induces in his servant. He could, but does not, and never will, enlighten his royal employer. Tirumal Rao is not a man given to over-loud comment on British chicanery. Those he has uttered have been intended, as it were, for light consumption, for if Bawajiraj has given away a trick, so has Sir Arthur. Discipline and drawing-rooms do not ride well together. The Dewan is aware, and vicariously pleased. He is, in his way, attached to the capricious Ruler.

* * *

'Don't know why we keep him on.'

Bawajiraj unbosoms himself from the depths of the sofa into which they have hospitably thrust him. 'The man's a jackass—he really believes the most unlikely things.'

Sir Arthur can cite a dozen compelling reasons, but does not care to, any more than has the Minister. He does not greatly care to talk shop either.

'People do, these days, I find, don't you?' he says. 'Another drink, Waji?'

'Can't say I'd mind.'

Bawajiraj holds up his silver goblet as if it were a shining chalice. His eyes are brimming. He is full of warmth, from the whisky, which he finds much to his liking (it has been despatched from a distillery in a Scottish glen), and this Englishman's castle, which he has been permitted to penetrate, and these people who are his friends.

'And this—' his charming hostess hands him a snapshot, '—won first prize at the Flower Show. The first time I believe we have ever beaten you, am I right, your Highness?'

'Waji. Please call me Waji,' begs Bawajiraj, gazing in rapture at the bulbous marrow that has, apparently, eclipsed the Palace's fortunes.

'If you like—Waji,' says Lady Copeland, and passes another faded print.

'The Poona point-to-point.' Sir Arthur cranes over her shoulder. 'That was a good year, 1897 . . . wasn't it, my dear?'

'And these are the children.'

At this point the children themselves manifest, backed by an ayah apiece. Esmond is crawling. The chubby baby has wriggled free of his ayah, much to the woman's chagrin, and is rapidly advancing on his mother.

'Esmond Baba!' The mortified ayah swoops, her spotless sari flying. Esmond accelerates, and evading capture by seconds, grabs hold of his mother's skirts.

'All right, Ayah.' Lady Copeland picks up the gurgling child and sets him on her lap. 'This is Esmond,' she says to Bawajiraj, and turns her son—her arm about him has assumed the most tender, cherishing curve—towards the stranger.

'And this is Sophie.' Sir Arthur presents his daughter. 'Say how do you do, Sophie.'

The little girl considers. She is fair like her father, with his clear blue eyes and flaxen hair that curls about her face. It is the purity of this face, the utter vulnerability of this delicate porcelain figurine so miraculously flesh of his flesh that pierces Sir Arthur when he looks at his child.

'Sophie,' he says, and coaxes her out from between his knees where she has insinuated herself. This time the child obeys.

'How do you do,' she says, and entrusts the dimpled calyx of her hand to Bawajiraj.

'How lovely they are! Such lovely children!'

The Maharajah is enchanted. His emotion wells up and overflows into the room. It is totally unfeigned. He is the archetypal family man; children to him are the blossoms of if not the reasons for existence; he adores every one of the many he has fathered. His feelings are such, the mixture is so rich and incandescent that it kindles a blaze in which the three disparate creators can be, and are, briefly conjoined.

It is put out by Lady Copeland, who is afraid, always afraid, of encroachments, and horizons that close in, and most of all of the vacancies of loss that she encounters in her husband's gaze when, as now, he is forgetful of its nakedness.

'They are rather fun,' she says, 'but, I assure you, quite a handful.'

And surrenders the infants into the hands of the hovering and angelic menials.

* * *

In the year 1857 the people rebelled against their British masters. The rising was martial. It was called the Mutiny. Later on it came to be called, by the people, the First War of Independence. They were independent by then and were free to say such things.

On a May night in that year Lady Copeland's grandfather the Colonel was stabbed as he lay in his bed by a sepoy from the regiment he commanded. The Colonel, who woke before he died, recognised the man and had time to be jolted. It was the last thing he had expected from any of his men, whom he believed to be devoted to a man to their commanding officer. So aghast was he that those who found him had a job getting the lids down over his eyeballs, which were stark.

The Colonel's lady was saved from multiple rape (she imagined: the sepoys were not enamoured of white women's flesh and no evidence was ever produced to support her belief) by the same scoundrelly band by her terrified servants, who were alerted by one Ram Singh, also a sepoy, who had been the Colonel's orderly. He was moved to his act by certain human aspects an officer inevitably reveals to his personal manservant.

The servants were called loyal in the British camp but were reviled by the rebel soldiery and, later on, by the populace. The loyal sepoy lay low, that is to say he went off to till his patch of land until the regiment was safe once more for people like himself.

The sepoy who had stabbed the Colonel was fired from a cannon, together with two of his comrades, selected at random by the new commanding officer for a similar destiny as cannon-balls. The Colonel's lady attended the ceremony, mounted sidesaddle on the Colonel's sable charger. It appeased her to see the fleshy morsels flying, but did not lead her to an understanding of the events that had overtaken herself and the Colonel. So haunting were the perplexities of that dreadful period that she did try, in later years, to pierce the motives of the natives for their dreadful deeds, though not her own, or those of her countrymen; but as she could not, she concluded that the answer was a savagery latent in the nation.

The question of understanding continued to nag, however, even after she had supplied the appropriate solution. This she handed down, the solution that is, while omitting the riddle: a strange random creature that sprang full grown, dispensing with genesis, from her wounded side.

'Treachery, dears. Simple, vile treachery.'

'Savages, that's all. All of them, every single one. Never trust one. Not one. Ever.'

'Barbarians. No other explanation.'

For the need to understand, trailing from Lucknow to Bath, continued to plague.

'Beyond understanding!' was torn from the lips of the poor baited creature before the old lady turned her face to the wall.

Those gathered in the chamber thought it was peace she was after; they could not in any case have resolved the dying woman's craving to crack the riddle.

* * *

In Lady Copeland even the will to understand is absent. The lessons learnt at grandmama's knee eat deep. She holds herself aloof. The charming hostess Bawajiraj has beheld and whom he has reluctantly bid good-night has been, effectively, a zombie.

In the privacy of their bedroom she returns to herself. The shell is peopled again, and lit from within. The warm processes of living, which she has carefully repressed, are resuming their function.

'Glad that's over.' She frees an arm from her nightgown—the lace furls back in a pretty exposure of shoulder and clavicle—and rests it on her husband's chest.

Sir Arthur allows it to lie. He will not endorse a comment which he considers excessive. Bawajiraj's frank and unfeigned warmth for his children has touched a chord in his breast. It has also pointed up the sham performance in which Sir Arthur now considers he has indulged himself (he excludes his wife from an innate chivalry) at the expense of a guest. He lowers his lids, on whose inner surface lingers the exquisite cameo of his daughter, the fragile flower of her hands enclosed in a clasp as tender and cherishing as any he himself can provide.

Moments like these, which afflict him usually at night, push Arthur Copeland into exaggeration.

They also propel him, protesting, into a search of his soul.

Presently he can feel the symptoms of the disease coming on. He would like to toss, but is pinned by the weight across his chest. So he conjures up Shropshire fields, and Shropshire sheep leap over stiles in contracting enclosures, while his jeering mind goes about its business, which is elsewhere. Presently the constitution can tolerate no more. Sir Arthur begins to pitch and turn until the twanging springs of the marital bed threaten to rouse his sleeping partner. Then at last he subsides, and allows the burdens of his split office to possess him.

* * *

The carriages bearing the commoners from the Palace continue to rumble through the countryside. The valleys are left behind. The land is so arid the wheels do not raise more than a meagre dust. There is scarcely a rivulet to refresh the landscape. For this year was one of the worst, if not the worst, for drought. It followed a succession of such years, and moved the British Indian Government to debate a remission of taxes from one half gross to one half net of the peasants' produce. People starved by the hundred thousand and died by the hundred thousand. The consequences were plain for all to see.

Parasuram and Panditji are feeling the heat. The two men prop their sagging spines against the crumpled canvas and discuss the weather. Rabi sits on the opposite seat in solitary state, as he has been invited to do, and listens, when it suits him, to the grown-ups' conversation.

'It's so hot.'

'Hot and dusty.'

'My throat feels like a lime kiln.'

'It's these plains. Always parched.'

'Could do with some rain.'

'Not a cloud in sight.'

'Monsoon's late again this year.'

'If it's ever coming.'

'Could be disastrous if it failed again.'

'*Could* be?'

'They stopped the fountains playing after the pool was cleaned,' Rabi contributes.

'Do you consider that disastrous?' Panditji wants to know.

Rabi deliberates. Bawajiraj has declared it a disaster, but the son is becoming cagey where his father is concerned. He does not answer, because he is being asked for a judgment, he suspects, before he is in possession of facts that are in reality beyond him. Although they exist, he is convinced, only there is this impediment. Exactly what, he does not know, but is driven to incriminate his own unfurled innocence. It is an uncomfortable position to be in.

'Do you?' He counter-attacks cunningly.

'One must bear in mind the *scale*,' says his educator primly, 'before one can calculate the magnitude of achievement, or disaster.'

Scales can oscillate wildly, Rabi knows. His situation is even more intolerable. He slides down in his seat until his kneecaps knock against the Pandit's. Each time the carriage lurches on the stony road there are these bony collisions.

'Rabi, please sit up.'

'I'm all right as I am.'

'You can't possibly be comfortable.'

'I'm quite comfortable, thank you.'

'You *can't* be.'

'I *am*.'

Parasuram steps into the perverse breach man and child have created. He is, actually, resuscitating a conversation that has been well-nigh shot to pieces, although the assassin naturally has no notion.

'I've never seen so many walking skeletons,' he announces.

It engages Rabi's attention. The only skeleton he has seen is a dusty arrangement of bones in a glass case in the schoolroom. He drags his heels across the floor—the gritty scraping sets the elders' teeth on edge—and sits bolt upright.

'Where?' he wants to know.

'*Everywhere.*'

'*I* can't see.'

'*Men,*' says the frayed Pandit. 'Men.'

Lessons are learnt not only at grandmama's knee. Rabi's vigilance is assured, at least for a span. When he looks around—it is made easier when the coach stops—he does indeed discover an abundance of ribs. They are even more marked, he notes, than those that Janaki reveals when he tears open her bodice. She is his single comparison, for in the palatial city he inhabits the servants are clothed and fed. Even the gardeners are issued shirts and loincloths, so that only the long thin shafts of their thigh bones are evident.

Whereas the nakedness exposed here is a revelation.

But other aspects of life are more bewitching.

For now they have arrived at the foot of the sacred mountain. *Dholies*, in which they will ascend to the summit, are waiting. Rabi, barking his pained tutor's shins in his hurry, is out of the carriage in a jiffy and into the rustic conveyance. The two men who are to tote these human burdens up the mountain, seeing the eager child, hoist to their shoulders the pole on which the *dholi* is slung and swing it to and fro to give him a foretaste. The wickerwork contraption creaks and sways and with it the delighted Rabi. He squats, knees up under his chin, on a palm-leaf mat, and imagines he is putting to sea. Now and then as he journeys the mariner notices the flash of shoulder blades, bony deltas that slither about and thrust up sharply under the sweaty skin. It does not add to, or mar, his enjoyment. He only wishes it could go on forever, this novel ride, and their travels, and the experiences that make him feel he is being expanded like the water-lilies in the emerald pool in springtime.

Whereas the Maharajah is already counting the days, and the hours, and finally the minutes for the journey to be over and his family to be returned to him. He has been dressed since dawn to receive them.

'I trust you have had a pleasant journey, my treasure,' he says radiantly, as the leading carriage draws to a halt. He is standing, the most luminous in a group of luminaries, which has gathered to welcome the return of his *maîtresse en titre*, not to mention the Dowager, under a construction of roses the major-domo has commanded.

'Hot, and dusty, but interesting.'

Mohini leaps lightly—a gazelle—from the carriage, her very step a rebuke to these courtly sobersides who will not stir an inch outside the capital.

'Hot! And dusty!' Bawajiraj is aghast; he would not have a hair of his beloved's head harmed; his tone implies that he would have assumed control of these unruly elements had he been but present. He looks for Parasuram, the Dewan's creature, to whom he intends to speak his mind.

'But *interesting*,' says Mohini, picking off shrivelled petals of roses which are floating onto her person off the papery triumphal arch. (The dry spell has been disastrous for roses, despite the convoys of water-carts, as the gardeners have told their superiors, but there are some who will not be told.)

'It was so *interesting*,' continues Mohini. 'That's what's important, isn't it?'

'If you say so.'

'It's not only what I say. Ask your son. He's had the time of his life.'

'My son!'

Rabi arrives on cue, in the second carriage. Barely has it clattered to a stop than he is out, running, a puff-ball of energy and emotion, towards reunion.

'It was lovely! We had a wonderful time! I'll tell you about it, shall I? But it's lovely to be back too. Lovely, lovely, lovely!'

There is something, some shimmering quality, about these three. In face of it the lustrous personages who have prepared speeches, and even mustered a garland or two between them, are happy to drop their schemes and fade out of the family circle.

'And the men carried us in *dholies* all the way to the top of the mountain.'

'*Dholies!*' Bawajiraj shudders. He has seen the things.

'Yes. They're fun to ride in. Grandmother says at one time you went everywhere in them.'

'She, not I. In her day.'

Bawajiraj winces at the thought. He is not as enamoured of gratuitous discomfort as are Mohini and, it would appear, her son.

'It's the only way to travel,' avers Rabi.

'Not at all. There are many ways less barbarous.'

'I mean up the sacred mountain.'

'I must say, if that's the case, I wouldn't trouble.'

'But you'd miss so much!'

'Would I?'

'Yes. You've already missed so much.'

'Have I?'

'Yes. You should have come with us. We saw—'

Rabi settles down to recital. First he sips the grape cordial the waiting-woman has brought, which he knows he will need. His throat is dry from dust and excitement, and there is so much to tell.

Bawajiraj listens, now and then. He is not much taken with tales of the arid outer reaches of the country. Mostly he watches his son, the curved, ruby lips that the cordial has stained, the strong bare legs with the plum bruises (Panditji has returned knock for knock), and is lost in wonder of the small, handsome male he has sired.

'And then we went to the Fort.'

'Which one?'

He puts the polite question, to show interest, which he does not feel. There are a good many such monuments to anxiety in the State. Each strategic military or merchant point has sprouted a fort or fortress; there is even a cross-roads where they have put up a pillbox.

'Where our ancestor was imprisoned.'

'What? What's that?'

'The first Bawajiraj, whom the British unjustly gaoled, because they were afraid of him.'

Bawajiraj does not greatly care to recall the failings, or the perfidy, of the British. To do so (the ferrety knowledge barely scratches a corner for itself in the hinterland of his consciousness) would be to chip away at convictions on which his life is based. For Bawajiraj is a British creation. He is too robust, or implicated, to assist in a process that some lingering shreds of instinct warn him would end in his dissolution.

'The fortunes of war,' he says dismissively, and avoids the boy's eyes, which will certainly recall the Dowager. 'What else?'

'The sacred eagles,' says Rabi, who needs little prompting. 'We saw them at the shrine on top of the *ghat*, a pair of white eagles—they only come once at sunset.'

'Really?'

'Yes, really. There's never more, or less, than two, and the priest feeds them, and they fly away and nobody knows where they come from or go to.'

'Really?'

'Yes. But they're only there to remind us of the conqueror—'

'Conqueror? What conqueror?'

'The British, of course. When they've gone, the birds, they say, will vanish forever.'

'Who says? Such stories! Who tells you these silly stories?'

'Highness, it is a common legend,' says Mohini, 'told him by Her Highness the Dowager.'

Bawajiraj breathes noisily. It seems there is to be no end to invocations of his mother, not to mention Mohini. The two women, he feels, are bent on aggravation. He also feels, since there are limits, he would like to put a stop to it. But the ominous word *Highness* has been uttered. Mohini is usually careless of his titles and pre-fixes; if she uses it now it signals she will not be available when he wants her. He wants her badly; but women, he ruminates moodily, bundle up sex with their soulful emotions; it is not simply a cheerful, physical activity as he believes it is for him. He is not interested in the arid experience a withdrawn Mohini can provide; his life with his wife is chockful of such encounters. What he thirsts for—he is as tight as a drum with longing; only his son and decorum prevent him from instantly laying Mohini—is the total, encompassing experience.

In the interests of which he restrains himself.

In their ordinary intercourse Bawajiraj and Mohini find comparisons of the displaced Shanta Devi odious. It is a convention of some delicacy, to which both scrupulously adhere except, occasionally, in bed.

The pair are in bed, lying voluptuously relaxed side by side on a favoured ottoman, which the servants have dubbed the nuptial sack.

'Is she as good as me?'

'No.'

'Am I better?'

'Infinitely.'

'Don't exaggerate.'

'I'm not. She doesn't fit at all.'

'Do I?'

'Like a glove.'

Bawajiraj sighs. It is no more than the truth. Shanta Devi is fat and soft, and given to lolling on cushions (a penchant fully indulged during her last pregnancy) and nibbling Turkish delight and Bombay *hulvas*. And she has grown slack, what with all those daughters, the fourth babe but recently delivered . . . whereas the graceful nymph whose flank rests against his— ah yes, the supple Mohini is everything a man could want.

'I did miss you,' he says warmly.

'I missed you too.'

'Not as much as I did.'

'More, I assure you.'

'If you had, you wouldn't have stayed away so long. If only you knew what I felt like!'

'I felt like that too. But there are more things in life than love.'

'Nothing, nothing in the whole universe!'

'Why are you so fond of exaggerating?'

'I'm not exaggerating.'

'You are.'

'Well, six months is a *very* long time, by *any* reckoning, for a—a—couple like us to be parted.'

'Couples like us have to put up with it. How could we have seen the country in a fortnight?'

'People do.'

'People like you.'

The dialogue is canting dangerously. Bawajiraj tries to right it.

'If you'd gone by train, I did suggest . . . Much quicker, and so much more comfortable. The royal train was refurbished and ready, you know it would have been my pleasure—'

'But not mine! What can you see from a train? Almost nothing that matters! Whereas we—ah, there was so much to see, you should have seen Rabi—poor child, cooped up in a palace all his life—he was absolutely enthralled . . .'

Her gaze is dreamy, full of veils and exclusions, it seems to Bawajiraj, who longs to have been part of the experience the two who mean most to him have apparently shared. Of which he has been deprived, he has convinced himself, by State obligations and his sense of duty, and is now to be denied even a tenuous, second-hand access. His chagrin is such he cannot resist reactivating the old argument. The grievance has, in any case, been festering for some while.

'And not a word,' he grumbles, 'in all that time, about when you were coming back.'

'I didn't know myself.'

'You must have had some idea.'

'If I had, why would I keep it from you?'

'Mohini, you know you like provoking me.'

A lapse from endearments and speech-arabesques to plain names can also act as a signal between them. Mohini accepts and responds sunnily to the wry tendrils of appeal he puts out.

'My dearest, if I'd known I promise you . . . but we planned from day to day . . . You know what your son and your mother are like . . .'

Bawajiraj is mollified, but indulges in a dying grouch.

'And you know how difficult it is for me—a man in my position . . . Sir Arthur has been at me, I can tell you.'

'What for?'

'Well, he has his difficulties too . . . A man in his position, he has to plan ahead—'

'Plan what?'

Mohini ruthlessly axes this exaltation of the Englishman, to which Bawajiraj is much given, especially since his admission to the Copeland citadel.

'The Durbar to be held in Delhi. In honour of the Coronation of His Majesty the King-Emperor. He has to request arrangements for those who will be attending. It is a *most* important affair.'

'Who will be attending?'

'Well, I shall, naturally. And Rabi, I hope.'

'And the Maharani.'

'Yes.'

'And I?'

'You too, I hope. Yes, certainly you too.'

Mohini is suspicious, of what she isn't sure yet. Led by purest instinct she hunches up her shoulders and conjures up the tall, slightly stooping figure of the Resident.

'Does the Bania Sahib know?'

'I wish you wouldn't call him that.'

'Why not? What does *he* call *me*?'

'Nothing.'

'Correct. I'm invisible as far as he's concerned. He can't even grant my existence.'

'It's not *like* that.'

'What is it like?'

'It's a matter of protocol. Sir Arthur—'

'I don't care about Sir Arthur!'

'—has to make suitable arrangements—'

'—to put me in my place, is that it? Some hole, for the kept woman?'

'Mohini, I assure you—'

'What can you assure me of?'

'If the arrangements were in my hands—'

'But they're not, are they?'

'How can they be? Hundreds of miles away? For a durbar in Delhi?'

Bawajiraj is riven for himself. He has planned—looked forward to—a night of voluptuous pleasure, and instead is reduced to fighting these rearguard actions. He throws up the sponge, but in a manner that will not ruin his designs upon this fierce woman who can also be—when the mood takes her and, it does occur to him, he does not mangle her human rights and frailties—the most pliant and felicitous partner.

'Please come,' he says simply. 'As my honoured guest. I promise you, no less. Come as anything you like, but please come.'

'I'm not sure I want to. These imperial orgies!'

'For my sake.'

'And the boy.'

'Of course the boy. In fact Sir Arthur suggested it.'

'I don't want him exposed to subversive influences. I don't believe in Emperor worship.'

'With his Pandit, then, if you must. To counteract whatever it is you fear.'

'In that case, very well.'

Bawajiraj is glad to feel the stony flank alongside his quicken into flesh. His own is plangent. It is, after all, a fleshly purpose, despite some soulful trimmings, that has brought them to lie on this ottoman. He opens his hand and runs a whetted palm along the silky curves that now, turning supplicant, encourage and advance the caresses with which he prepares them for coitus.

* * *

Such has been his passion, such is the langour that follows consummation, that Bawajiraj is barely aware that he has, in fact, conceded the intolerable. The Pandit falls under this head. Sir Arthur has made it plain. He has, indeed, himself suggested Rabi's attendance at the Durbar as an antidote to the indoctrination the boy has undoubtedly suffered on the extended pilgrimage or whatever at the hands of this Pandit. He has coupled the suggestion with a proviso that the Pandit be excluded. The man's presence at a function of this nature will have, the Resident indicates, a disastrous influence on Rabi. The boy's mind is plastic. It is highly desirable he should carry away from the Durbar impressions and interpretations of the most correct kind, whereas the tutor is known for the disloyal slant of thought, word, and deed.

Disloyal! The very word sounds a knell in the Maharajah's breast. Of all princely qualities he prides himself most on his loyalty, which has already earned him a Star. He entirely agrees with the Resident. He intends to stand by their agreement. Unfortunately, there are times when he ceases to be Sir Arthur's creature and becomes Mohini's.

Mohini is also Sir Arthur's cross. He has no control over the woman. A Junior Maharani would have fallen well within his competence. A concubine is well outside.

The tight net that restrains the regulars has these holes through which the irregulars slip. Mohini has given tart, vociferous, and repeated indications that she has no intention of regularising the position.

* * *

While his parents love, and fight, and come together and fly apart in the lively manner of their partnership, Rabi is engaged in a war of his own. He has at last captured Janaki. Both girl and boy are panting. It has been a hard chase, all along the gravel path to the dove-cotes and back to the shrubbery behind the stables.

'Rabi, please don't.'

'I want to.'

'You mustn't.'

'Why not? You used to let me.'

'That was months ago. I'm older now.'

'What difference does that make?'

'A lot of difference.'

'I only want to look at your ribs.'

She yields. Actually she has no alternative, for he has thrust her onto the ground and pins her there with a knee. He is so urgent that the buttons fly; it is a mercy that a girl's only bodice has not been ripped to pieces. Janaki squints up at Rabi and notes he is indeed doing only what he said he would. He is inspecting her rib-cage, which still heaves from her exertions, if not her emotions. The swell of her breasts, which has engaged her lately, seems to interest him not at all. She sits up abruptly.

'Seen all you want?'

Her fingers are furiously seeking the buttons that have shot from their moorings.

'Yes.'

'All that fuss, just for *that*!'

'I didn't fuss, *you* did.'

Rabi sits back on his heels. His indignation is tempered by the note of disgust she has sounded, that he divines he has provoked.

'Would you like to see mine?' He offers the *amende honorable* for whatever offence she indicts him, although it remains obscure.

'What for? Sprouted breasts or something?'

Fury renders her crude, grace leads her to regret it instantly.

'All right, Rabi. Show me your chest.'

'The ribs. Just look at the ribs,' says this bone-conscious boy.

'All right, I'm looking.'

'Can you see them plainly?'

'The fact is, Rabi, your ribs don't show up all that much.'

'I know. Exactly. That's what one should be aware of constantly.'

It is so novel that Janaki is moved from indulgence to curiosity. In her view such preoccupations do not belong in the realm of people like the Maharajkumar.

'Why?' she asks.

'Because it gives one a standard of comparison.'

'Really?'

'Really. Panditji pointed it out to me.'

'Well, you're doing all right then, aren't you.'

'But the people aren't. Hundreds of people. I saw them, they looked terrible.'

'I daresay.'

Janaki, indifferent, draws her flimsy bodice around her.

Rabi flings it apart again. The thin mull wings are now definitely wrecked.

'You aren't either, are you. *Are* you.'

This time his mental force is subduing her, its invisible thrust is as palpable as the compelling knuckle and knee with which he has floored her. But she resists. Some delicacy in this child off the scrap-heap of her destiny prevents her confessing to the milk-fed lamb the reality of her famished role that, in multiplicity, supports and is crucial to the society to which he belongs.

'I'm all right, Rabi. Really I am. Now don't you go worrying your head about it.'

And she draws his head onto her breast and plants generous kisses on it, for all the world as if they were equals, an illusion which the thick, sheltering shrubbery fosters and even, perhaps, turns into fact.

4

An act 'as traumatic to those it eventually embroiled as the slaughter of the Colonel as he lay in bed that dread night of the Mutiny in 1857 occurred on the 9th April 1902. It gained a place in the chronicles of the 9th Lancers, a brave and famous British regiment officered by the sons of dukes and gentlemen.

On the evening of that day Atu, a cook, was beaten outside the regimental barracks by—the man said—troopers of the 9th Lancers. The Commanding Officer was duly informed. He took no action.

Atu died from injuries received. He took a week to do it. The nun who nursed him marvelled at his constitution, although it was not this, but rather the man's will, which for seven whole days defied, in the powerful cause of those dependent on him, the massive outrages inflicted on his body.

A Court of Enquiry could not now be avoided. It declared itself unable to single out the culprits. The Court was composed entirely of officers of the regiment.

The Court had barely risen from its task when Bhola, a coolie, incurred the displeasure of a trooper of the 9th Lancers, who kicked him in the guts. The coolie died of a ruptured spleen.

* * *

The mainspring of the actions recorded lay not in any brutality peculiar to the 9th Lancers, but rather in the prevailing ethos of equality.

Equality, like morality, was widely considered in British circles to be not absolute, but relative. There were several bands, and most people knew to which they belonged, although it is true there was a certain squabbling and confusion in the middle reaches. There was no question, however, that the ruling class, the British, belonged to the top band and the labouring class, the coolies, to the bottom. The coolies themselves would have been the last to deny it. They claimed no privileges and were merely thankful to, as it were, continue to exist.

Only the threat to the continuity of his existence made Atu depose against his masters as he did.

In Brahmin households like the Minister's only a Brahmin could be a cook. He was entitled to (and exacted) the same honour as his employer.

No Brahmin would enter a regimental cookhouse. They pinched their nostrils as they went by in a pointed manner that officers and men alike found insupportable. There was nothing, however, to be done about this. The Brahmins were effectively protected by their own caste disdain. Officers and men, consequently, had to make-do with the lower orders. These lower orders had no caste, and few human rights, to safeguard them.

Atu was one of these. So was the coolie.

The men who assaulted the cook and the coolie did not consider them as human beings on any level that counted. Neither did their officers. It was this aspect that perturbed His Excellency the Viceroy when the matter came to his attention.

The Viceroys of India, of whom there were a succession, were human but also historical personages. There would be no place for history in folk chronicles, were not history, iron instruments, so vehemently insinuated into the lives of common folk.

At the time the events recounted took place the Viceroy of India was Lord Curzon. He was a man of brilliant intellect and high principle, qualities which no doubt earned him his label of most superior person. He was, and considered himself to be, as did others, a Christian gentleman. The difference between himself and others was that he was prepared to uphold, in speech and in action, those qualities which were inherent to the proposition, at least as it was understood within Christendom.

There were several discrepancies between the qualities attributed to Christians by those outside Christendom and those they assigned to themselves. Hindus, for instance, thought them not only unclean but ruthless, and not only ruthless but pious about it. As for the quality of their justice, in which they took immoderate pride, this, while arbiting impartially between Indian and Indian, became totally partisan when it came to holding the scales between Indian and European.

Lord Curzon, as a Christian (in his own austere view of the term), wished to put an end to acts of brutality perpetrated by British soldiery upon the natives of the country, which, he felt, were occurring with reprehensible frequency—the cook and the coolie representing but the tip of an iceberg. In other words he wanted those responsible for the murder of Atu the cook and Bhola the coolie to be punished.

The Viceroy was the most powerful man in all India. He got what he wanted. But it took a good deal of correspondence, persistence, and courage; and it earned him the implacable hostility of the Army in general, the 9th Lancers in particular, and a massive number of British civilians as well.

The punishment that provoked these reactions revolved around some curbing of leave and a reprimand of the regiment. A proposal that it be barred from the forthcoming Delhi Durbar parades was made, but defeated.

The reverberations set up by the death of the lowly pair involved not only the Viceroy and his Durbar but affected, in time, Rabindranath and his father, and the fortunes of their Ruling House, in a manner that none of those implicated could acknowledge until, much later, the air had cleared.

* * *

The Delhi Durbar, which has evoked the scorn of Mohini and reverence from Bawajiraj, is in fact a version, magnified beyond recognition, of Bawajiraj's own durbars. The tangled aims and emotions that pervade his State durbars also invest the Delhi Durbar, although understandably on an immensely grander scale. For India is the most precious jewel in the Imperial Crown, which has now passed from the Queen to her beloved son Edward. The splendour that attends his coronation in London may not be eclipsed by the sister ceremony in Delhi, but in the general view it must reflect the pomp and grandeur of the Imperial occasion.

The Dewan considers it a woolly and expensive enterprise.

'Mumbo-jumbo,' he declares, roundly, to his wife Vatsala, who being of his caste understands perfectly what is meant.

'The spin-off for the British can be valuable,' she says, thoughtfully, in her surprisingly up-to-date idiom. She is a woman of forward fashion, though not in Mohini's class. She will not, for instance, beguile her husband as the concubine is reputed to do, nor does she claim those freedoms that would establish her identity apart from him. But if she is content to live in the shadow of her husband, it is more form than substance that is conceded. The chemistry of breeding that results in cut-glass Tirumal Raos cannot in honesty (and shoddy has not been known to enter the high purpose of this purest of processes) by-pass the female line. This diamond mind perceives the realities of a loaded situation and persuades her to work from within her female role.

The shadow is in any case a substantial one. Tirumal Rao is the second most powerful man in Devapur State. Vatsala is entrenched in her position as his wife. She may not be titular head of the household, but over its management and control she retains a decisive grip. Nor, within the household, is the husband known to direct his wife. Tirumal Rao likes to believe that if the need arose . . . but it doesn't; between them the adroit pair ensure the occasion never arises. The Dewan preserves his belief, which bevels his masculine edges. The Dewan's wife is respected as the acme of Hindu womanhood without having actually to endure its rigours.

The two are engaged in the realities of the present situation. The conversation is pithy and frank and would surprise the Resident who is more usually treated to those tedious curlicues at which the Minister is adept.

'Shall I arrange for your attendance?'

'At this bun-fight?'

'Circus, you mean.'

'It would amuse the children, I suppose.'

'Undoubtedly. The British are unrivalled at pageantry.'

'At other things too. The children are at an age to be influenced.'

Vatsala's tones are thoughtful, subdued by the respect she feels for the adversary, the formidable British. The same goose-pimples overrun her as have erupted on Mohini's flesh. Bawajiraj is the object of their fright. All unknowing, and wearing the caul of his birth within which his very innocence assumes a fearful glitter, he is the spectre of British conditioning from which both women recoil.

'I don't think we need have any fear on that score.'

The Dewan dismisses the notion, as he has ground to do. Apart from what he, scholar and statesman as he is, takes time ungrudgingly to inculcate in his children, their education has been in the hands of a battery of pandits from the earliest age of comprehension, which is confidently ascribed to infancy. Whatever twists and turns polity may induce upon conduct, at least he is as certain as any man can be that his issue will never lack the clear vision he himself enjoys.

'In that case perhaps one ought to go. For the children's sake.'

'For the sake of the spectacle, which it will undoubtedly be.'

The Dewan is merry. His wife succumbs to his mood. They have developed between them a keen appreciation of the incongruities the British dominion so effortlessly provides. These shared humours refresh their alliance and add those touches of spice which, in Tirumal Rao's view, pep up a marriage.

He is especially content with the state of matrimony at times like these. His gaze is benign as he watches his wife's sleek head bent over her task, which is preparing his post-luncheon *pan*. He is sitting on a rosewood swing hung from silver chains, she on a rosewood plank with silver rosettes at each corner. This lower plane has nothing to do with her lesser rank: it is merely more convenient to deal with the *pan* paraphernalia from floor level.

'Here you are.'

She hands him the neat little parcel she has made of scented nut and leaf.

'Delicious, delicious.'

The Dewan throbs like a turtle-dove. He is particularly fond of this hour, with his lunch agreeably inside him, and the smell of freshly watered *khus-khus* screens wafting in through the windows, and the cat-nap in which he indulges casting a haze on his brow.

But there is something.

Through the haze he becomes conscious of something that has been insinuated. Something very like grit, or perhaps closer to the pea that a princess can feel under a plethora of mattresses. The Dewan is no princess, but he is an old married man. He tracks his unease to the angle at which Vatsala is holding her head, the electric speed with which her nimble fingers fly to stem and string the inoffensive vine leaves. It is normally—it has begun as—a tranquil operation.

The afternoon is not to be, after all, as expected.

'I suppose,' says Vatsala, and rips off a vein. 'I suppose *she's* going.'

It could have been Lady Copeland speaking.

The Dewan sits bolt upright. He has not often heard her ladyship speak except on polite, polished occasions. But there have been times, less fenced, more fraught . . . and a tone once heard, or especially overheard, is not forgotten. It is part of Tirumal Rao's office, as he sees it, and certainly an ingredient in his success, to record such nuances. The inflections of his wife's voice, the Dewan is aware, exactly match those of the English milady. It makes him weak. He has a sneaking admiration for the irregular Mohini.

'Do you mean—?' he asks.

'I do.'

His wife is so flat the Dewan retreats into Court purple.

'His Highness naturally desires the mother of his son—'

'You mean she's going.'

'Yes.'

'So am I. I have made up my mind.'

Vatsala rises in a swish of silk. As a Hindu matron she wears nine yards of the stuff, which is capital for displays.

The Dewan registers the flouncy effect, as also the hostility she induces from inanimate objects, the silver rings that she wears on her toes, as she clinks out of his presence.

Whereas he is reduced to shuffling. For no reason at all, since he has not, and cannot have, the least carnal design on his suzerain's mistress. It is her *mind* he admires. But reduced all the same, the crutch of an urbane conscience unaccountably behaving like matchwood.

'And the children?'

He shuffles after her, calling. He has to find out; there is a whole brood to accommodate in a manner befitting. The Resident's Private Secretary has already been at him, nagging, in clipped accents behind which loom the fearful machinery of imperial carnival that has to be set in motion.

'And the children,' she throws back at him over a retreating shoulder. 'All of them.'

She hopes to be tiresome. The inclusion of the two youngest will almost certainly guarantee success.

And yet Vatsala understands there is no lecherous involvement. Her quarrel is precisely with an attitude of mind: her husband's, which not only condones but admires the concubine's bold assumptions.

It is an emotion common to the matrons of Devapur. Euro-

118

pean and Indian, between whom desperate chasms elsewhere yawn, are mentally united by what they see as a threat to the sanctity of marriage. The flagrancy of it, to be precise. For all are aware of affairs on the side, the clandestine peccadilloes that it is men's nature to indulge in. What they cannot abide is the open intimacy that Bawajiraj and Mohini embody, which their recent reunion has so shamelessly highlighted. For there is this insolence of her sex that infuses the concubine and puts these quintessential matrons in a flurry when she is around.

It is lucky for the princely partners that they are above the common herd and are allowed, and claim, their sensual privileges.

It is also a consolation the ladies draw from their own position, which permits no such concessions. Their marriage lines are clearly defined and defended with zeal. Affairs in the hill stations, during the long hot summer months, between gay young subalterns and grass widows up for the hot weather with the children, may be the fashion; husbands may take their fling, within the Indian fold, with a girl of dubious class; but neither camp, whose obsession is with appearances, will regard these episodes, so long as they do not break surface, as a breach of the nuptial contract.

The letter of the law is paramount to the ladies.

In the same spirit, with less clarity, they hope that Rabi will be kept from his inheritance—as certainly the Resident is empowered to ensure—until his mother regularises her position. This Mohini will not do. She has rebuffed all efforts (Court and Residency in close alliance) to make her the Junior Maharani. The years have only shored up the shrewd, but also proud, decision.

* * *

The latter half of the year leading up to the Great Durbar held in Delhi in January 1903 declared itself for a variety of people in a variety of ways.

For the peasants, the majority of the people, it was a good season. The long drought ended, the rains fell, the paddies were lush, the grain swelled pleasingly, the granaries were full. There was a rumour that taxes might be reduced to compensate for the long years of drought and famine just concluded, but even if rumour proved unfounded they would eat well, which was an unusual and delightful prospect.

For Rabi the event itself was one of the peaks of his experience. The peak was by no means of even composition. It had sweet and bitter faces, and at least one was touched with terror.

But when he looks back upon his childhood the memory most fraught is the appalling tedium of preparation, which includes being fitted out in a manner befitting princes.

The current feeling is shared and expressed in a gale of sighs from boy and tailor.

'Stand *still*, Maharajkumar!'

'I *am* standing still!'

'How can I fit you properly if—'

'Don't scratch me then.'

'You don't want me to botch your suit, do you?'

'I don't care!'

'What would His Highness say if it made you look like a buffoon?'

'I shall look like a buffoon anyway.'

'What nonsense. The finest material—'

'A velvet jacket! And velvet breeches! Like a peacock. No, like a musk-rat.'

'Maharajkumar, how can you say such things! Do you know how much velvet costs?'

The tailor is quite upset. He knows what the rich stuff costs: it would keep him in style for a month; but this is not the thought that preoccupies his mind. He is concerned that the boy should appreciate the fine quality of the material which he, the Court, and the Maharajah himself have had a hand in selecting. He runs it through his hands with a lingering love that is totally devoid of envy.

He is a good tailor. Even memsahibs are known to summon him to attend them. He is a short, nearsighted, dark-brown man, who sits hunched—at such times as he is not attending the Presences—clad in a sober white *dhoti* and jacket over his clacking Singer, in his dingy, cluttered one-room of a workshop, and conjures up out of such unpromising surroundings outfits of utmost elegance at rock-bottom prices.

He lives, mainly, on appreciation.

This, the Maharajkumar, rebelliously contemplating his own fate, stubbornly denies him.

'I think it looks dreadful. So do I. I look like a clown. Janaki will die laughing just looking at me.'

'A common servant girl! Why should Rajkumar care?'

'Why shouldn't I? She's my best friend!'

'Maharajkumar, please keep still. Tell me, does it fit here?'

'No, it's tight!'

'Where, exactly?'

'Everywhere! I can't move at all.'

Here the superlative child actor produces some wooden movements that are indeed those of a pinioned puppet.

The tailor is patient, as he is expected to be, but there is some inward fraying. He takes out pins as if they were molars, returning the extractions to his lapels, which are already bristling with pinheads. His fingers click for the minion whose sole function is to carry the measuring tape.

'Come on, come on! Do you think Maharajkumar has got all day?'

This is exactly what is reducing Rabi to despair. The woods, the doves, his pony, all, all are calling, and the light is fading, and the son of a Maharajah cannot obey the summons precisely because he is what he is.

Then there is the hatter. Mubarak Ali is a Muslim, but a man of eclectic custom, with a range that runs from the little round skullcaps he turns out by the dozen for the Armenian merchants in the city to the cartwheel hats that please the European ladies.

The request for cartwheels, these last months, has been phenomenal. The hatter has waited on virtually every bungalow in the cantonment. Virtually every memsahib has been invited or is going anyway. He has been to the Palace, to measure Rabi for his hat. He has also been to the Residency and has been accorded a vision, and one or two sepia photographs, of what the Lady Sahib, his most hallowed customer, has in mind, which he has to realise in chiffon and straw. It is his first summons to the Residency. He owes this good fortune not, as he fondly believes, to word of his reputation reaching these august circles, but to the fact that a ship carrying a collection—an entire trousseau: hats, dresses, shoes, veils, and gloves—from Europe has been insufferably held up in the Canal. One of those damn' Gyppos' obstructions, which will take time and a couple of gunboats to sort out.

Mubarak Ali has reverently taken the Lady Sahib's order to the forefront of his cluttered shop (which is as dingy as the tailor's, in a parallel alley) where most light falls. Here a space has somehow been cleared and a white sheet spread on which repose the components of vision that has yet to take form. The detail of it is clear. The creation is to be out of straw, of the finest quality, with asters around the crown and a lining of pleated flower-print chiffon through which the Delhi sun will filter, it is hoped, the most becoming shades upon the wearer.

But there is the composition . . .

Mubarak Ali ardently needs the space and light of his hard-won oasis. For the hat, he can tell, is going to be difficult.

Rabi's hat, by comparison, is straightforward.

It is not so simple as to absolve him from bouts of standing still and being fitted, but at least these do not make so much inroad upon his precious hours.

The finished object is of velvet that matches the suit. It is stiffened with buckram and lined with silk and is embroidered and tasselled in gold.

Mubarak Ali is pleased with his effort. It has flowed with a natural vigour from his hands, which are bred to the shapes and contours of a landscape to which cartwheels only intermittently and uncertainly belong. Uncertainty bedevils Mubarak Ali when he wrestles with floppy brims. Gauze asters are a foreign dimension. His hands have adjusted and can cope—he is a craftsman of high order—but the inner eye is dodgy; it swivels evasively and will not settle in judgment. So that Mubarak Ali, having no convictions, is entirely at the mercy of the memsahibs, which saddens the craftsman in him that demands that he be his own master.

Whereas with the boy he can tell the moment it is done. He would not, even under duress, alter a line or stitch.

He places the hat upon Rabi's head as if it were a diadem and stands back, a leaning tower of admiration. For he can tell it is exactly right. The workmanship is excellent, the embroidery faultless. The hat, in fact, fits. And when he looks at the visage beneath, Mubarak Ali is suddenly afflicted with the sense of endurance. For the bones that lie composed under the skin are leopards of a native stock that melt into the scene, and have moulded the features and flesh of innumerable portraits that adorn the walls of the audience halls of the Palace. The elderly hatter is moved, he does not know why, to stoop and touch the child's feet before straightening up once more into the ordinary airs of existence.

'There you are, Maharajkumar. Is that not fine? A perfect fit.'

'Yes, it fits, it's very fine,' says the impatient boy, and rams the hat into the shivering cocoon of tissue and linen in which it has been borne hither. '*Now* can I go?'

The bustle that is generated in the State by the distant Durbar naturally involves the Ruler. A Maharajah cannot escape the fate of the common people. Bawajiraj sighs, though he has never been known to grumble at what his training assures him is part of his duty. He has to decide on a costume. A wardrobe to which entire chambers in the West wing are devoted still cannot be expected to yield an outfit to match the glittering occasion. It has to be new and splendid. There is no difficulty here, the privy purse is ample. The trouble lies in the delicate balance of splendour, for it will not do to eclipse a senior Maharajah. To be eclipsed by a lesser is unthinkable.

'I suppose everyone will be going?' He consults Sir Arthur.

'The whole mob, my dear chap,' says Sir Arthur amiably. 'Why?'

'Oh, nothing. I just wondered,' says Bawajiraj. His entire face is hollow with effort. The mob referred to parades through his mind. The Heads of State, Bobbili, Cooch-Behar, Indore, Jaipur, Kolhapur, Mysore, are made to pass in alphabetical order. But what will they be *wearing*? He supposes he could ask them—several in the stately procession are personal cronies—but he suspects they will not tell him.

'It's a question, Resident Sahib,' he blurts out, 'of what to *wear*.'

'Wear? I wouldn't have thought, Waji,' Sir Arthur rejoins in a dry way, 'you had much of a problem in *that* field.'

Bawajiraj absolves the Englishman. There may equally well be, he allows, one or two matters of English protocol to which he, though one of them, is not privy. He really cannot expect Sir Arthur. So he turns the conversation to channels where both flow together on the tide of a mutual and innocent emotion. These have come to be the children, above all Sophie and Rabi, the deep love of whom each man recognises in the other with a leap, elsewhere hobbled, of simple fellow feeling.

Bawajiraj feels he can open his heart about Rabi and Sir Arthur will not only listen but understand. Sir Arthur returns the compliment. He has, indeed, once or twice broached the subject of his small charmer to Waji in the certainty of a devout hearing. In the present situation the little girl naturally enters the Maharajah's thoughts. He has it in mind to offer a token of the tender emotions she arouses, which have been brought to the fore by the impending journey he envisions with his son by his side.

'The State choo-choo,' he announces, surprisingly, 'is available, H.E., if you want it. Just say the word. You know,' he says from the pool of their common feeling, 'what children are, they love the things. . . . I'm sure Sophie will enjoy the ride to Delhi in the Special train.'

'That's civil of you, Waji.'

The Resident is moved by the noble but worried countenance that lightens and shines in the transparent pleasure of imminent giving. He would like to receive the gift less on behalf of the child than for the sake of the man, but his wife has tied his hands.

'But Sophie, I'm afraid, will not be going,' he says.

'Not going! *Everyone* is going.'

'Her mother does not think the climate of Delhi will be congenial to her health,' says Sir Arthur in one brave rush, and puts a distance between himself and the brimming Bawajiraj, which the invocation of his wife, even in her tender madonna role, can instantly manufacture. But it is not only the woman that creates but her accomplice the Colonel, his boots reversed in the stirrups of his sable charger, which a loyal *sowar* leads. There is even a sepia still, to remind, but not to be exhibited to maharajahs within or without the citadel.

Bawajiraj is aware of Lady Copeland's grandfather the Colonel (snapped in the act of pinning an outsize rosette to a winning pony's young rider) and (at the hands of his tutor, Mr. Barrington) of that shameful interlude in the history of the country, the Mutiny: but the effluvium that can coat patriot and traitor and even holders of the Star like himself is too outrageous to credit. Bawajiraj will not indulge outrages, and lacking indulgence he cannot unlock the mystery of sudden distances. The draught he feels—indeed he does, the bulge of his neck is cringing—creeping along those dreadful sunken corridors, he misinterprets. Such misinterpretations come readily to men of his education.

He has made, he feels, some gaffe. The question is, what? He gropes, and is not alone. Sir Arthur is also groping his way back from a distance which an innate sense of justice refuses to sustain. It is really going too far. Poor old Waji, he wouldn't harm a fly, it's not his fault he is what he is. And the soul of generosity. Sir Arthur cites the train, and is moved to think of the truly sumptuous rolling stock offered to beguile his small daughter.

'Sophie's a bit young,' he says kindly, 'but I'm sure your son will benefit from the trip. He's a most lively and entertaining youngster.'

All Bawajiraj's misgivings and anxieties dissolve. His face, his being, are radiant.

'You should see him,' he says, shyly, to the tender and acquiescent Englishman. 'You should see him when he's dressed up, in his Prince's costume.'

And claps his hands—the sounds cannon off the lustres disposed in niches around the room—to summon a flunkey.

Velvet, silk, gold, craftsmen and their art, have no power to dazzle a man to whom all these are, if not daily fare, commodities to be easily commanded. What captures the Maharajah is a vision of the son who will come after him, in sapphire, wearing the sword and mantle of his father—an irresistible image hung with the flowers of immortality that ravishes the royal parent. Under this pure and even loving animus the Ruler is impelled to exhibit the blue velvet suit to the Resident.

'Rather fine, H.E., don't you think?' he says, offhand, in tones belied by the reverent care with which he lifts it from its caparisoned box and holds it up complete with its interleaved tissue. The glowing miniature hangs, and is subtly incorporated into the rich interior from which it springs, which is its rightful concomitant.

The Englishman cannot but be affected. He is no stranger to emotions aroused by the continuity of line. He is in peril, then, of conceding what is most ardently sought: the seal of approval on the succession, which requires no more than a nod from him.

He stifles the human impulse. Princely participation in the British scheme is too important to be the subject of parley while in the grip of wayward emotion. The boy must prove himself worthy of ascending his father's throne before he can be recognised as the heir-apparent. Furthermore, the Resident has not given up hoping for a legitimate heir, with the admirably passive Maharani as mother, instead of the concubine who unfailingly tries his patience. Such an outcome will avoid all these awkward and disagreeable encounters with the Maharajah.

Meanwhile he copes with the present.

'Extremely so, Waji. Very fine indeed,' says Sir Arthur, with the utmost sincerity, and a genuine regret that he can go no further.

* * *

'That boy,' Sir Arthur remarks to Major Ponsonby, the Garrison C.O., at dinner. 'Uncanny, the resemblance. Living image, judging from portraits, of—um—the old Maharajah. The one we removed. Yes. I was quite struck. When he's dressed up—Maharajah Sahib showed me the costume today—it'll be a case of, well, a phoenix, really.'

'Peacocks, wouldn't you say?' says the bluff Major. 'To me they all look uncommonly like peacocks in their finery. I sometimes think they must frequent the nearest theatrical costumier.'

He comes close to appalling Sir Arthur, who has noticed that the Durbar dress of the Maharajah's son copies a pattern that goes back some centuries. The precise intricacy of embroidery can be followed in Court portraits to which the Major, no less than Sir Arthur, indeed has access, but little enthusiasm to pursue in ruined keeps the minutiae of dim and distant Indian Courts.

It is also possible that he does not wish to accord full measure of credulity to the orderly existence of such Courts. India, for him, flying in the face of historical fact, which he undeniably possesses, has a distinct tendency to begin, like justice, or order, with the messianic, if also somewhat operatic, entry of the Anglo-Saxons.

Confronted by such crusty assumptions in the otherwise astute Major, the Resident changes the conversation.

What with hat, and suit, and lessons, and rehearsals that Rabi learns are an ingredient of all durbars, there is little time left to him for his own pursuits. Complaining, he is given to understand—his father the Maharajah makes it plain—he must expect encroachments as he grows older especially if. If what? If a father's hopes for his only son are endorsed by God and the King-Emperor. What hopes? Little boys should not ask such questions.

Rabi is not interested enough, and anyway is too pushed to dredge. The time he has for himself has a quirky way of racing, whereas the tedium of durbar stretches dreadfully. Sometimes, with doves' wings fanning his face, or out in the woods with his pony when time flies fastest, he suspects *they* have the key, his elders who have their methods of tinkering with time.

So he hurries—at last, at twilight, he is free—to the shrubbery behind the stables where Janaki has promised to meet him. It is a spot chosen by joint acclamation because here, unobserved, they are left alone. Otherwise tasks are found for Janaki, who is not paid for leaning on her broom. Or Rabi is taken by the hand and led away to pursuits more fitting than gossip with an outdoor servant girl.

Rabi does not lightly submit, but he has found that Janaki has this supine way of fading from the scene when he is locked in combat, often at the crucial moment. For, as she has explained, she has her position to consider. Rabi considers her plaintive bleat unworthy, to him it is the principle that matters, a philosophy which his tutor and the unlikely Bawajiraj both preach. He fails to convince Janaki; he imagines it is because he cannot pin her down. Physically he can throw her, but she has this agility—he can seldom wring from her a plain statement so that he can hardly ever taunt her for reneging.

Circumstances have taught Janaki to sidle.

It exasperates Rabi, who can afford, and basks in, the forth-right postures that are a gift of his birth.

'It's all right for *you*, Rabi!'

Sometimes a cry is torn from her and it breaks open a window through which he can peer. But the aperture is small, it lets in—at his age—barely a glimmer. The main part is puzzlement.

But Rabi likes his friend. She is a rapt audience. He cannot hope to impress Palace sprigs, or the blasé Brahmin scions of the Dewan, or his own older siblings, whereas Janaki laps up whatever he has to tell. The way she listens strokes the masculine bud within him. He is too young to savour, as does his father, the pleasures that lie beyond domination. He enjoys his dominion over Janaki. It gives him pleasure to impress her.

'We shall be travelling a thousand miles!' he tells her impressively.

'A thousand! Are you sure?'

'Well, hundreds anyway. We shall be on the train all night.'

'Fancy that! Won't you be tired, sitting up all night?'

'We shan't. We shall lie down.'

'On the floor, Maharajkumar?!'

'On the floor!' he scoffs at her. 'On beds, of course.'

'Beds? In a *train*?'

'It's a special train. It's the Devapur State Special. It was specially made for my father.'

'That explains it then.'

'Yes. He designed it himself. He chose everything he wanted, except the paint.'

'What paint?'

'On the outside. He couldn't have the colour he wanted.'

'His Highness can have anything he wants!'

'He can, usually. But he couldn't, this time. He had to stick to purple.'

'Purple's a nice colour.'

127

'He wanted white. He couldn't have it because the Viceroy Sahib—' he rolls the words 'Viceroy Sahib' on his tongue: there is a mystery, as yet unresolved, that invests this figure who, he has been told, but does not for a moment believe, is greater than the Maharajah and the Resident put together— 'because the Viceroy Sahib has it for *his* train.'

'Ah well. White's an everyday colour. All us servants wear white.'

She looks down at her garments, which have certainly been white once, but cannot be called so now by the most well-meaning observer. Come Deepavali there will be new ones, she hopes, white naturally, but perhaps with a purple border. She quite fancies a white sari with a purple border.

'Do you think they'd give me purple next year if I asked, Rabi? A purple-border sari?'

'Yes, why not?'

'Would they let me have purple?'

'Of course, silly. People can choose what colour they want.'

'But your father the Maharajah—'

'That's different! That's a whole train!'

Janaki cannot visualise a whole purple train, or even a white one, come to that. And now Rabi is describing indescribable tents.

'On the great plains of Delhi, amid the crumbling tombs of vanished conquerors,' he declaims, after his tutor the Pandit, 'they are putting up tents for all the Maharajahs who will be attending the Durbar.'

'*Tents*, Maharajkumar? For Maharajahs?'

She gasps. She has lived in a tent once. In the year of storms in which her mud hovel among others has dissolved into soup, the Dewan has ordered tents, canvas, servants' camping category. She has crawled in, and been thankful for shelter, but it is definitely not for the likes of Personages.

Rabi remembers too. He has entered her tent, to investigate the exciting novelty. It has been exciting, but when the novelty has palled there has only been a damp and fearful discomfort. It is a depressing memory.

'Not like those servants' tents, you don't imagine?' he scoffs at her.

'I couldn't help wondering, Maharajkumar.'

'Quite, quite different,' he says dreamily, and since he is drawing from his imagination with a dash of the state his father keeps to complement it, he can go on forever. 'Of silk and gold, and priceless carpets from Isfahan, and bearskin rugs because the nights in Delhi are cold, even the Mughal Emperors found them cold, and my father the Maharajah will look like an Emperor, in brocade from top to toe, and at his collar the Paragon Diamond which is the finest—what is it?'

For the girl is quivering like a leaf. They are sitting side by side, sharing a stone slab, and her tremors are unsettling him.

He is not afraid. His childhood has been sunny. Dread is not, except for the one glancing blow he has been dealt, a part of his inheritance as it is Janaki's; but he cannot avoid the aspen experience she transmits—they are too close, flesh is touching—to him.

'What is it?' he asks, his voice is shrill.

'Nothing, Maharajkumar.'

She shakes herself, and argues she is imagining things. But the shrubbery, whose glossy thicknesses have nourished life-enhancing fantasies, has definitely thinned and begun to yield the precious assurances it previously offered.

And Rabi is dried up. The closeness that lubricates inter-course, even this touching between children, is gone.

'I'll tell you all about it when I come back, shall I?'

'Yes, Rabi,' she sighs. 'That will be lovely. Tell me everything when you come back. You will come back, won't you?'

'Of course.'

'Here.' She unknots the grubby tail of her sari where the precious globe resides and hands it to him. 'Keep it with you, Maharajkumar.'

'What is it?'

'Something to remember me by.'

The boy holds her gift in his palm. The solid glass marble has coloured stripes, like the score or more he already owns. He slides it carefully into his pocket.

'I'd remember you anyway, but it's a lovely present,' he says generously. 'I'll bring you back a present too, shall I?'

'A present? For me? What sort, Rabi?'

'You say.'

'I don't know. I've never had a present.'

'A sari,' says Rabi, inspired, 'with a purple border.'

'A purple—! Ah, Rajkumar, how kind you are!'

She raises the dark flower of her face to his. He is standing. She is at his feet. Defying her destiny, she locks her hands, lovingly, about his ankles.

5

The Delhi Durbar, to which Rabi is journeying in high excitement, this December of 1902, was part of the socio-political life of the British Raj.

The social life of the British in India, for which the standard was set by the Viceroys and Governors of India and their ladies, was a long saga of dinners, banquets, receptions, garden parties, picnics, pleasure trips, fancy dress balls, hunting and shooting expeditions, and polo and cricket matches. These activities countered the misery of exile (suffered at all levels from the most junior aide to the Viceroy himself) and the appalling *longueurs* of life in an inclement and uncongenial environment. They also served other, more important, purposes.

A proportion of these frolics and entertainments were official functions. They maintained, and testified to, the power and status of the Western potentates, as was the intention. At the Lord Sahib level they outshone anything the Maharajahs could do. As they had done with these Native Rulers, the newcomers took what they found and turned it to their own use. Oriental splendour was lifted out of the exclusive realm of Nawabs and Maharajahs and made an attribute of the British rulers.

The socio-political history of the British in India was similarly studded with Durbars, Jubilees, Proclamations, Depositions, Accessions, Investitures, King-Emperor's and Queen-Empress's Birthday Celebrations, and State Arrivals and Departures.

At these events it was a neck-and-neck contest as to who would mount the better spectacle. Sometimes the Native Rulers won; mostly the British did. They had a flair for pageantry, a taste for order excelled only by their Mughal predecessors, and an infinite capacity for taking pains which out-classed the baroque effects achieved by their exuberant Eastern rivals.

The constant losers were the people. They paid.

At the Durbar of 1903 the entire and immense costs of this lavish affair, as well as the hardly less extravagant expenditure of the Duke and Duchess of Connaught and their Suite, were borne by the country.

During this Durbar the Viceroy had wished to proclaim, in view of the successive famines of previous years, and the numerous wars and campaigns to which the country had contributed men and resources, a token remission of taxes. He was overruled from London. Taxes, including the hated Salt Tax, continued to be levied at old rates. The people of India continued to pay them. It was taxation without representation, although this cry was not clearly heard until later.

In the year in question, 1903, it was no more than a whisper, to which hardly anyone paid attention. The Delhi Durbar accordingly was not marred on this score. The mark it made on the Viceroy, and far, far down the scale on the Maharajah's son, arose from other matters.

When the wretched *bania*, whom even the magic wand of the British could not turn from sow's ear into silk purse, had amassed his corn and grain fortune, he built himself a palace. It was this elegant pile that gave rise to the dream. He dreamed he could be anything. The heady vapours that emanate from palaces persuaded him to answer the unreal summons, which he had half instigated and half been expecting, since the British were always ready, though sometimes ill-advised, to meet the aspirations of their supporting cast.

The *bania*, a mortified and by now an ageing man, has by retreat to the modest homestead of his beginnings, which overlooks the cornfield fount, regained a modicum of peace.

In similar vein Sir Arthur does pause to wonder, amid the expensive turmoil of the Durbar, which is steamy with intentions, some of them conflicting, the purpose of it all. He feels, but quickly stifles the emotion, that there are other pursuits, more engaging, less fraught, than this portentous undertaking in an eastern land.

These reflections are, possibly, shared by the Viceroy, whose brainchild the Durbar is. There is, however, one preoccupation, or awareness, or burden, that Lord Curzon carries alone: the knowledge that whatever public protestations of duty and loyalty to him the Durbar may call forth, he has earned himself the implacable hostility of his own countrymen. He has let the side down. He has called for, insisted upon, and obtained, the punishment of Englishmen responsible for the deaths of Atu the cook and the lowly Indian coolie. He will not revoke any part of his actions. He suffers no regrets. To uphold his princples this icy Englishman is prepared to pay the price. But it is a lonely man that travels in state in the dazzling, white-and-gold Viceregal Special.

* * *

So they journey, in their carriages and trains, lords and ladies with their entourages, Maharajahs and Maharanis with their retinues, sahibs and memsahibs with their retainers, the common people supporting each other and arriving, as usual, on foot.

The Dewan is, as ever, exquisitely aware that none of the ornamental bolsters mandatory for Resident and Maharajah are vital to him. He can go, if he wishes, as a grandee. His private coffers are full, the plush-lined caskets in his steel safe in the cellar of his residence contain a fine collection of priceless gems, his income (salary plus a percentage of State revenues) is such that neither he nor his descendants to the fourth generation need fear penury. He chooses to play the simple man, in the assurance that whatever his choice of outer rig he will continue to command respect. For Tirumal Rao is pretty solidly based on himself and his intellect, and knows it, and shows it, sometimes in a manner calculated to offend.

He has chosen, for Durbar wear, the simplest white: white muslin, white *surah*, the finest off-white Kashmir, and four dozen changes of each to meet the finical imperatives of his fastidious caste, which so exasperate the British.

One private secretary, one peon, one woman servant to look after the younger children, is the sum of his attendance.

The extent to which he pares himself down is acutely annoying to Sir Arthur. The process reveals an intellectual arrogance to the man that the Resident finds insufferable. He suspects the Minister of rubbing it in.

'No need, Minister, to journey like a fakir,' he says frostily, suppressing the bloody Benedictine that rises to Anglican lips. 'You're going to a celebration, not a funeral.'

'No need. A personal preference, Excellency,' says the Minister in his silky way—even his jowls are suave—and whips his wife and family smartly into the ordinary first-class coaches of the ordinary magenta mail train.

And shoves off, punctually (the Station Master, in a lather, personally ensures that the train leaves on the stroke), to Delhi.

The Maharajah follows cumbrously in purple, with his wife the Maharani, the Maharani's daughters, Mohini, Rabi, the Pandit, his Private Secretary, his private Physician, his personal Bodyguard, his fan-bearer, his guards, *syce*, peons, macebearers, cooks, the Band, which is to parade in the Review of the Ruling Chiefs' Retainers, ayahs, waiting women, and minions too numerous to mention who bundle themselves up and lie like logs in the corridors of the Special.

There are sufficient coaches not only to accommodate all these persons but to ensure a seemly division, where necessary, between the various parties.

The Hon'ble the Resident has his own efficient express. Unlike the Maharajah's, it is strictly functional. It boasts, for instance, none of those ingenious devices (a perfume fountain, a miniature goods train that trundles condiments around the dinner table, beds that tilt and rock at the touch of a button) that captivate children. The Resident's Special is designed to take, in severe compartments, in strictly graded degrees of seniority and comfort, his travelling suite.

This suite comprises his Personal Assistant, his Military Secretary, his Chaplain, the two aides, one Surgeon, several clerks, butler, chef, valet, steward, sentries, *syces*, printers and a press (for the issue of *ad hoc* Notices) Lady Copeland's ayahs (four under-, one upper), her dresser, and the dog-handler for the two little Pekingese who are travelling in a basket.

The horses travel in horse-boxes. Tantivvy, the Maharajah's favoured charger, and Caesar, the Resident's, have each a carriage for self and *syce*.

Both trains are so long, consequently, that each, the Maharajah's Special and the Resident's, is hauled by two locomotives, utterly reliable engines manufactured and shipped with admirable foresight from Birmingham.

With similar foresight the elephants have been despatched on foot, with their *mahouts*, and weighed down with their own durbar regalia, several weeks prior to the main exodus. They are fed and watered (peppercorn rates) at villages en route, by villagers resigned—it has gone on for centuries—to the passage of armies and rulers as they are to the visitations of locusts. In much the same spirit they cope with both.

All these disparate elements are to rendezvous on the Delhi plain, in a camp twenty-four miles in circumference, for festivities scheduled to last a fortnight, on a scale of free-spending lavishness intended to be unsurpassed, and succeeding.

In Delhi it is a field day for children and artisans. It has, in fact, been thus for several months, ever since the intention of Durbar has been declared.

The city has been cleaned, shined, polished, and forced into bloom. Flowers, at the command of an army of gardeners, blaze in banks and beds, in urns and baskets. Under the enamelled dome of sky, in this Indian winter, it is like a hothouse. It quite drains Lady Copeland, who is driven to wonder if her constitution . . . though, of course, when called on, it will stand up to anything, even this extraordinary flamboyance. So she settles her veil and lays the cool lilac tips of her gloves on an arm that hands her into the waiting landau, and drives from terminus to camp through teeming streets which are dressed overall.

Scarlet, blue, and white are the chosen colours. They are impressed into garlands, banners, and bunting, which labourers by the thousand have draped over balconies, bandstands, and innumerable triumphal arches. They are towering, these arches: elephants must pass. Squads on ladders have dressed these arches and lamp-posts and flag-poles. There has been a great deal of swarming and shinning up and down, and the heights have blossomed with garlands and wreaths, and imperial crowns in bronze and gilt, and banners conveying strange, but correct (relays of secretaries have checked the *munshis'* uncertain Latin) and honourable sentiments. There are a great many flags too. Each schoolchild has been handed one Union Jack. In mission schools the lucky youngsters have received two per head.

At lower levels a regiment of coolies has been recruited to tear down eyesores along the Processional route, which runs, circuitously, from Queen's Road to Viceroy's Camp. All hovels within sight of Durbar participants have been torn down and the bemused inhabitants hustled off into the hinterland. A few stout citizens who have resisted have been rewarded with a coat of fresh paint (free) for their offending shanties. In the Hospital, which lies on the Processional route, a complete ward has been cleared of its mouldering inmates. A detachment of healthy volunteers waits, ready to slip between spotless sheets at word of inspection. The order has come from the Medical Director himself, who wishes to spare the Distinguished Visitors.

The order of the day, indeed, is for the unwholesome to be banished and for gaiety to prevail. Such is the mood of the people, or perhaps such are the innate needs of their nature, that the object is realised. The very air is festive. Even the disinherited turn out, in their best tatters, to add their notes of ragged colour to the general jubilation. Even the most uncouth critics hold their tongues.

* * *

The Minister's derisive eye takes in the scene with an unusual tolerance. He is a relaxed man. It is not his show, apart from some fringe contributions by the impetuous Maharajah (the Band, a contingent of Devapur Lancers, two dozen elephants). Its mainspring and motivation are clear to him—he has himself sanctioned similar extravaganzas—but the wary balancing between the need for circuses and what the exchequer will stand (normally his lot) rests on other shoulders. Tirumal Rao is a free man, and as such permits himself to enjoy the proceedings.

He travels, lightly, with his wife and family in the somewhat sober victoria the Durbar Committee has sent to meet Prime Minister and Party at the Terminus. The day is a-sparkle, it puts him in high good humour. That gaudy exuberance from which Lady Copeland shrinks appeals to the Oriental streak in his austere Brahmin soul. The innocent raptures of his children, though they will undoubtedly eventually pall, are infectious. The glacial age, into which discussion of the concubine has plunged them, is over. He and his charming Vatsala have resumed the normal symphony (as rewarding as the muted duet between Sir Arthur and his wife) of their intercourse, which allows for a mutually agreeable exchange of views on all aspects of the occasion.

'Fireworks and Illuminations Night is, is it not,' says Vatsala, bobbing sedately beside her husband, 'on Friday?'

She has in mind what she will wear for the occasion: the sari of emerald-green Benares tissue and matching emerald necklace that the Dewan has had delivered to her following their little tiff. She has accepted his token of propitiation. Her sign to him is the circlet of dewy tuberoses (his favourite fragrance) that she has wound round her glossy chignon. It is not precisely a love-exchange; but it is certainly the working language of their harmonious union.

'Fireworks on Friday.' The Dewan consults the Programme of Events the Committee has provided him with. 'Elephant Procession on Monday, Polo Tournament on Tuesday, Assault-at-Arms on Wednesday, which brings us to Thursday the Great Day.'

'One can say, something for everyone.'

'One can. Impeccable organisation. You have,' says the Dewan (the impeccable detail has captivated his meticulous nature), 'to hand it to them.'

'Indeed, they are past masters.'

'Great showmen.'

'Unparalleled.'

For it is a quirk of the country for rulers and ruled to pay each other these compliments.

'I hear,' says Vatsala, tiring of the game, 'that Maharajahs' younger sons are to take part in some British ritual?'

'Are implicated,' confirms her husband, 'in carrying the ladies' trains, or some such nonsense. Although I cannot believe Advisers will not find some way to circumvent the folly.'

'Such weird garments.' Vatsala arranges sari pleats, which brush her toes, with a special grace. 'And gloves as well.'

'To spare them the touch of the hoi polloi.'

'If the hoi polloi get within touching distance.'

'Within touching—!' The Dewan is consumed. 'You couldn't touch them for a pie, they're worse than *banias*.'

'*Bania* lords and ladies.'

For the Brahmin couple this is really funny. The Dewan wipes his eyes.

'I remember my father telling me,' he says reminiscently, 'that poor *bania* they put up, his coat was killing him. . . .'

Vatsala listens amiably. It is an amusing anecdote, though she has heard it before. The Dewan recounts it with his customary skill, bringing it to a risible close as their carriage enters the straight for the run past the Flagstaff Tower to their Camp.

The illustrious Representatives of what is reliably reported to be one-fifth of the human race are accommodated in Camps within the grand Encampment that has bloomed on the great Delhi plain.

There are a great many Camps. They range, like pearls, in graduated splendour from the Viceroy's Camp (the apogee:

gulabar tents a hundred yards square, scarlet tent-flaps, and golden guy ropes) to Visitors' Camp No. 30 (P.W.D. issue tents, inmates of the category of State Engineers). Somewhere between are Native Camps for the Native Chiefs and Chieftains. A good many of these Chiefs and Chieftains are in fact Maharajahs and Nawabs, rulers of princely states and sizeable dominions. Titles, however, are a commodity controlled by the British, who for the occasion have corralled them all under the heading of Ruling Chiefs (Native).

The Chief's Camp to which they have assigned the Maharajah flawlessly fulfils his expectations. Its admirable trappings—his keen eye tells him they are entirely in keeping—stills certain tremors that have afflicted His Highness since leaving his Special. His rank and position, which are judged by such outward attributes, are very nearly as dear to him as his soul. It would never do, Bawajiraj feels, for that upstart in Ranjipur to be rated higher, or that rascally Mir, forever pushing his claims. He has made earnest representations on these lines through Sir Arthur, and it is not that he has no confidence. He has. He knows the British, their word is their bond. It is his peers he mistrusts, the bombastic nonsense they pour into British ears, which are not, with all due respect, attuned to Indian scales. Bawajiraj can imagine the dreadful consequences. He does. With a bulging eye, bolt upright on the shiny leather seat, he scans his rivals' camps as he is borne past in his carriage.

All, however, is well. The Durbar Committee, locked in conference over many a month, has produced this scrupulous gem that Bawajiraj cannot fault.

It rounds him out. He feels he is back on form. The flow is so strong he recovers a sense of his clothes fitting him, converting the apparel of some scarecrow into what, after all, it is: the robes assumed by a Ruler.

'Well, Rabi, what do you think?'

From under the sumptuous canvas, urbane in this rightful, urbane setting, he benignly surveys his son.

'I think it's lovely.'

'What you expected?'

'Better. Much better.'

Light in peony tints streams from silk linings upon the small boy. He looks up at the canopy and it is like the trumpet of an immense hibiscus. When he moves, the silver buckles on his pumps give off ruby glints. There are rubies studded in the golden branches of the candelabra that gilded cherubs bear, a pair each side of the tent flaps.

'I think it's the loveliest tent I've ever seen,' he says. 'Is it yours?'

'My dear boy, of course not.'

'Why not?'

'Well, it's not my durbar, is it?'

'Is this yours?'

'What?'

'This.'

Rabi traces, with a toe, the Persian beast on the Tabriz upon which they are standing. It is a beautiful creature. He thinks it is a doe.

'I couldn't say.'

'It's yours if you paid for it.'

'I really couldn't say what I pay for and what I don't. You'll have to ask the Dewan.'

That vulgar man is sure to know. He has a *bania*'s nose for such detail. The contempt he feels for these trader's traits, a disdain he knows he shares with the British, warms Bawajiraj. He says, genially, out of this happy cloud:

'What shall we do? What would you like to do now?' Spreading the treasure of infinite possibility before his son.

'What can we do?'

The child's acceptance teeters on his wary acquaintance with the concomitants of such largesse.

'Anything you like.'

'Can we do anything we like?'

'What a question! Of course we can.'

'I'd like to see the horses.'

Entourage begins murmuring.

'What horses?'

'All the horses. There must be hundreds, mustn't there?'

Murmurs are rising.

'Well, I'll have to see.'

'And the camels and elephants.'

The murmurs have become a prohibitive, well-bred lowing.

'It's a question of time, Rabi.'

'You *said* we could.'

'I know, but you know I have my duties.'

'You said anything.'

'You know duty is paramount.'

'You *said*.'

Rabi's desperate heels dig into the priceless Tabriz. There are outraged notes in his voice. Some young Taurus, Bawajiraj feels, that he seems to have sired. He would like to yield to the boy—it would be easier—but duty prevents him. At ten o'clock sharp he has to join the State Procession. It is eight o'clock now, which doesn't leave time for hundreds of horse. In any case he needs a clear hour to change. This is an Imperial occasion, not some minor junketing at home. It calls for immaculate standards. Already his mind is on the maroon outfit he is to wear and the cinnamon outfit chosen with some care for Rabi to complement his father's ensemble.

Ah yes, Rabi.

'I expect we can manage something, can't we?' he says brightly, to the entourage, avoiding the young bull's glare.

'No difficulty, Highness.'

A dozen skilled arrangers are at hand. The boy eyes them as if they were vipers. He wants his father, whose feel for horses equals his own, to share his delights with. No one, not even the *syce*, can take the place of his superlative, horsey parent.

'I don't want to just go! I want to go with you!'

Bawajiraj sighs. The boy does take after his mother.

'We'll get your Pandit to take you,' he offers, sacrificially.

That dreadful bounder, in his mildewed black buttoned up to his bilious throat, on whom his son seems to dote, for some unfathomable reason.

'Panditji doesn't understand *anything* about horses!' wails Rabi.

But here Bawajiraj is fully in command. He raises a finger and a smart young cavalry officer (an honorary ADC) detaches from the entourage to attend the Maharajkumar.

'We take up positions at ten o'clock sharp,' he says to the gilded sprig.

'Highness.'

The officer salutes. He has been seconded to the suite by Sir Arthur, and can be—Bawajiraj gratefully acknowledges yet another debt—relied on absolutely. With a surge of relief he hands the boy over.

And at ten o'clock sharp there they all are.

Standing in his shiny cinnamon outfit and patent pumps beside the ADC in the West Porch, which is the assembly point for the State Procession, Rabi wishes—in a sort of way, because of course she would never be allowed—that Janaki were here. She would love the Band, and the bright decorations, and all the grand people in their grand costumes. She often tells him she is a one for *tamashas*.

Whereas he is infinitely bored. The fearful tedium that has preceded the Durbar is as nothing to what he now endures. Rooted to the spot they have chalked for his feet. Standing attentive from ten o'clock sharp and it is now eleven-fifteen. In brand-new shoes that pinch. Waiting for people when it is more usual for people to wait for him. Circumstances that are enough to make his father's expressed rapture smack of perfidy.

Although his father does seem to be enjoying himself. He is standing a little way away, in a clump of dignitaries and fellow Maharajahs, and is smiling and cheerful. Rabi wonders how his father manages so well; his clothes are even more stiff and scratchy, but he is beaming happily and bowing to his Maharajah friends. Perhaps it is because he is a Maharajah. Perhaps it is the umbrella, which an aide has unfurled and is holding above him. It is a huge umbrella, lined in orange silk, and it throws a rather hot and fiery shade, but it is better than no shade at all. Rabi ardently wishes to be where his father is, but he cannot move from the special mark they have made for his feet. Besides he is surrounded by a flotilla of attendants who keep him in his place. He occupies himself by counting the pearls with which each spoke of the orange umbrella ends. He becomes so absorbed he almost doesn't hear his father.

'Rabi! Come here, my boy!'

Rabi obeys with alacrity. When he moves the flotilla moves with him, which slows him up, but at last he arrives. His father puts an arm about him and draws him into the peppery shade.

'Enjoying yourself?' he enquires kindly.

'Yes, thank you.'

'Great occasion.'

'Yes, it's lovely.'

Rabi doesn't think it's lovely, it's much too glary and hot, but he makes an effort for his father's sake. He doesn't want to disappoint his father, who he knows wants him to enjoy himself. He tries, standing as patiently as he can, and watches the herd of dressed-up elephants that *mahouts* are coaxing into line. Among them is Lakshmi, the elephant he usually rides at home in State processions. She is wearing a chain-mail coat made of little silvery discs and there are large patterns painted on her face. When she looks at him, rolling her little piggy eyes as she passes, a shiver of fellow feeling runs through him. He knows exactly how she feels. Foolish. In her coat that chinks and chanks as she moves, and those huge painted red and yellow circles round her eyes. He determines he will make it up to her when she stops for him, and is feeling in his pockets for sugar-lumps left over from feeding the horses when, incredibly, she clumps past him. He follows her with astounded eyes and sees her settling down on her rump opposite a yellow umbrella under which the Resident is nestled. Another beast lumbers up behind her and sinks down in front of the orange umbrella.

'Here is your elephant, Maharajkumar,' says the ADC.

'That's not my elephant. My elephant's Lakshmi. I always ride her.'

'No, no, Maharajkumar.'

'Why can't I have Lakshmi?'

'You have another elephant.'

'I don't want another elephant. I'd like my own elephant.'

Rabi turns to his father for support, but the Maharajah, his face grave, is engaged in other matters.

'This *splendid* elephant for you, Maharajkumar,' coaxes the ADC.

Lakshmi is just as splendid; in fact she is shimmering; but in her howdah perch the Resident and his Party. And there is this other howdah, on the back of some unknown beast, into which he is being bundled by a dozen courteous hands.

As they amble off to take their place in the procession his father waves to him gaily. He has ceased to be grave, Rabi notices, and is once more beaming and radiant.

Bawajiraj is radiant because he is enjoying himself. He loves durbars. They bring out, he feels, the best in him. He is at his best, his most responsive, when he feels the waves of adoration flowing to him from his people. He also feels he has the authority and skill to embody these emotions in his person and to transmit them, compressed into an ingot of shining loyalty, on behalf of all his people to the Viceroy and through him to the King-Emperor. The process, he feels, has this day been exquisitely consummated.

The day has not been without its satisfactions on lesser, if more human, levels. Rabi's behaviour has been exemplary. Despite some worry (the freewheeling way Mohini insists on bringing him up, which accounts for that slight contretemps about elephants), he has conducted himself like a Maharajah's son. Not a hint of impatience. Standing rigidly, like an officer on parade, though he is still quite a small boy. Even that dash of hauteur— he has observed the clash with the ADC—that is proper to his station. He gazes at Rabi, shimmering in the distance, and is quite overcome.

'My son, you know,' he says, casually, to his neighbour the
Rajah of Krishnapur.

'The lad over there?'

'The one in cinnamon. On the second elephant.'

'Handsome youngster.' The Rajah is quite impressed. 'Got
him down for the Corps?'

It makes Bawajiraj wistful. He has flirted, somewhat furtively,
knowing Mohini, with the thought. It grows on him, now that it is
put into words. Such a fine body, the Imperial Cadet Corps,
instituted by His Excellency the Viceroy himself, open only to
the sons of Maharajahs and Noblemen. He can easily imagine
Rabi. Before his ardent desire the durbar cinnamon gives way to
the splendid cobalt of the Corps. What a fine Cadet the boy
would make! In blue with gold lace, and the splendid turban,
and swan-neck spurs, mounted on a jet-black charger, like the
squadron that has just clattered past to take up escort duty.

'That is my hope,' he confesses.

* * *

'If you want to know, it was the idea of His Highness the Rajah
of Krishnapur himself,' Bawajiraj tells Mohini.

He and she quarrel afterwards in their tent. The subject, as
ever, is Rabi. It is a constant feature of their relationship that the
child over whom they jointly rhapsodise also sows the most
fervent dissension between them.

Emotion, and the carmine tent, have added the prettiest
touches to Mohini's enchanting magnolia. She looks delightful.
It calls forth only a sour response from Bawajiraj, who marvels
that anyone who looks so charming can bicker so outrageously.
This wonderment has been with him since his first assignation,
in the rose gardens of the Summer Pavilion, with his true love. It
has shown little sign of abating in the years since.

'If it was his idea then all I can say,' says Mohini, 'is that I don't
think much of him.'

'He is a Ruler of distinction and, if I may say so,' says Bawajiraj, 'an old and valued friend.'

'If he is, he did you a disservice.'

'In what way?'

'Suggesting Rabi should become a Cadet!'

'He didn't.'

'You *told* me he did.'

'He only *asked*! If Rabi was down for the Corps.'

'Putting such ideas in your head!'

'He didn't. I've always hoped. It's an admirable idea.'

'It's a frightful idea.'

'The Corps is meant for—'

'Lackeys!'

'—the sons of Princes.'

'I won't allow my son.'

'He's my son too.'

'Only half. Do you think you were entirely responsible for his creation?'

Bawajiraj often plumes himself in this belief. It is not physically true of course, but it is the spirit of the thing that one goes for.

'Mohini, you must allow me to decide—'

'Why should you? Why can't I?'

'I will not put up—'

'Neither will I.'

'I have stood quite enough.'

'So have I. So have I! Do you know what I have to put up with?'

Mohini is thumping the couch. The stretchers beneath, the very foundations of the *gulabar* below the Persian pile are beginning to groan. Bawajiraj is quite alarmed. There are a dozen Ruling Chiefs within stone's throw, ears pricked—he knows this crowd—for gossip.

'What?' he asks. Anything to placate.

'*Purdah,*' she answers.

'What do you mean?'

'You know very well what I mean.'

'If I did would I ask?'

'Screens!' she cries. 'They have arranged screens, we have to peep from behind them, like slaves in a harem!'

'It is customary for royal ladies—'

'I am not a royal lady.'

'I am not responsible for durbar arrangements,' says the weary Bawajiraj, and closes his eyes, and thinks of the days ahead, which are crowded with appointments, for all of which he has to be at the very top of his form. Women, he feels, have simply no conception.

Shanta Devi, in the next tent, with her sleeping daughters, listens to the impassioned exchange, which reaches her as a formless murmur, and wonders, with a curiosity bordering on jealousy, what any couple can find to talk about, to this extent, after so many years of living together. Her own communication with her husband has dwindled to monosyllables and silences. It lifts, when the children are present, to a pretence of animation. When they copulate it sinks, on his part, to moans and grunts. For her part she has long given up those cries of ecstasy feigned for his pleasure during early married days. Now she merely surrenders herself without ceremony and dissociates her mind, a technique she has perfected to meet the situation.

Tentage for the Maharajah and his women has likewise been planned to meet a situation. The Committee, diplomats to a man, have made the necessary arrangements for wife and paramour while clinging, fingerhold on precipice, to their ignorance of irregularity. There has been, in effect, a good deal of right hand not knowing what the left is up to, a skill which receives the silent plaudits of all concerned.

Rabi's tent is also contrived with some skill to take cognisance of his irregular status without undue emphasis. A standard flies, but the device is decorative and without significance. The furnishings are rich, but devoid of ciphers and symbols. Sentries are present, and spring to attention, but do not present arms.

If Rabi is entranced by his quarters it is less to do with them than the manner in which they match his pure imaginings. The magnificent carpets (not Isfahan but Kirman), the animal skins, the rich canvas, all are there much as he has described them to Janaki. It awes him to think he has conjured them up, mainly to impress her, and they have taken shape. It is, he feels, as if a wish had come true. How nice it would be, he continues dreamily, if all one's wishes came true!

Lying on his couch, the sumptuous fur stroking his chin, he wishes she were here, sitting on the carpet at his feet, exclaiming over the fur, the tent, the couch—she is much given to exclamation. But then, of course, she is quite easily impressed. Even that ordinary marble she has given him is special to her—he can tell from the way she has handled it and the special way she has presented it to him. With some difficulty—he is half asleep—he picks it out from the collection of indispensable objects he has assembled next to his couch. He knows it is pretty, but it is too dark to see. If it were made of brilliants instead of glass it would shine, you could see it even in the dark. He is disappointed that he can't. Tomorrow, though, will be filled with brilliants . . . brilliance . . . a brilliant day. . . . He falls asleep with the cold glass sphere already warm in his fist.

Under coarse patched canvas, in a truckle cot, in the sprawling encampment, the Pandit finally manages to fall asleep. Uneasiness invades even his slumbers, so that he pitches and tosses, a frail craft launched on waters inimical to its structure. Tomorrow he participates in the Durbar, a proceeding that in his view reduces every citizen who is implicated in its glittering coils. As he is. His very presence is an endorsement of a regime he is pledged to terminate. He, an educator of the young, is leading the way down such dubious avenues. The image of himself that springs to mind is even more disagreeable than the mildewed apparition Bawajiraj has brooded over. The Pandit groans, and pulls the pillow over his suffering head, and resolves to be as dissociate from proceedings as it is possible for a man to be, given his corporal presence.

While the humans achieve an indifferent sleep, jackals slink through the lines of the encampment, their flattened shapes merging into shadow before the advance of the watchmen's lanterns. The watchmen are afraid of these scavenging packs. It is the hereditary fear of their hereditary calling. They call to each other for comfort, hollow sounds that jar on tympana unaccustomed to these night airs. The jackals' calling is hereditary too. They are scavengers. On these very fields they have feasted off the flesh of warriors and beasts slain in battle. Human morsels are more difficult to come by, under Pax Britannica, but there are scraps that the cooks toss out for which, after dark, they scour the camp.

But the watchmen are not to be convinced, or outwitted. They perceive ancestral memories in these tricksters' eyes that glow, reddish, out of the darkness. The shrill, vulpine yelps confirm their perception of a lurid past. Shuddering they draw their shawls closer about their bones, and menace the flesh-eaters with their swinging lanterns.

* * *

The great day, Durbar Day, dawns in a welter of blue and gold, a sky of piercing blue, the sun like a gong, brazen. Lady

Copeland lies, eyes closed, in the pastel flounces of bed and nightgown, and shrinks from the light that penetrates the canvas linings (citron: an immoderate colour) and settles on her lids like dying yellow moths. She can hardly lift her eyes, though she will have to, soon. Her husband is already astir.

'Arthur.'

'Yes, m'dear?'

'Don't bang about, will you, there's a dear?'

Sir Arthur puts down the bolster with which he has been about to swat the anopheles that has somehow entered and is pinging around the mosquito net.

'Slept well, my dear?' he enquires, solicitously. Arthur Copeland is always solicitous for his wife. Though he knows better, her milky-blue hues seem unfitted to withstand the rigours of these torrid zones.

'Thank you. Yes.'

'Lovely day, from the look of it.'

Mary Copeland makes no response. She has hoped for mists, something to soften the stridencies of the long Indian day that lies ahead, but she can feel—her sinuses are already parched, the delicate hollows will soon begin to grate and ache—it is not to be. Not that it will affect her bearing or composure. Her slender frame, she has more than an inkling, is strung exceedingly fine, but with a great tensile strength that will carry her through anything. But just for a few minutes she lies, supine, until it is time, and her servant comes in with pads soaked in lavender water.

* * *

In the peony tent Mohini's warm, soft arms encircle and awaken Bawajiraj just as, he feels, he has at last succeeded in falling asleep.

'What is it?' he mumbles, peevishly.

'It's me.'

'Not time already, is it?'

'No.'

'Then what is it? You know I need my sleep.'

'You've slept beautifully.'

'Hardly a wink. All that yelping, all night long.'

'Oh, nonsense. I didn't hear a thing.'

'Mohini, you know you're not as sensitive as I am.'

He closes his suffering eyes—such an onerous day ahead—but

feels her breath. She is leaning over him, unfastening the froggings of his sleeping shirt one by one from collar to hem. At each
release she kisses the new exposure of flesh. Flaying him, he
feels, shuddering; and stops her there.

'Not now, Mohini.'

'Why not now?'

He cannot actually say, except that he feels there is a time and
place, and it is not here, in the very shadow of Imperial scarlet, in
the very dawn of Durbar. It would be, he feels devoutly, wrong.

'I don't feel it's the proper thing,' he says, primly.

'It is.'

'No.'

'Yes.'

'Is this a proper time?'

'Certainly.'

She kisses him again, her lips touch the fork of his body.

'I don't feel like it,' he cries weakly, against all the evidence.

'You do. My love, you do.'

She straddles him. Her voice is husky and triumphant, and
banishes tents and illustrious shadows. But all the time, in the
very vortex of his love-making, Bawajiraj is afflicted with a sense
of the sacrilegious.

The pyjamaed Rabi, shedding flunkeys on all sides, leaps over
guy ropes and past the guard—the startled sentry barely manages to spring to attention—and bursts into the carmine bower
of his parents' tent. Luckily they are through.

'Wake up, wake up,' he cries, gathering up armfuls of se-
quinned crimson netting that drapes the couch against the ravages of anopheles.

'We are awake.' Bawajiraj is dignified, though naked.

'Do you know what day it is?'

'Of course.'

'It's Durbar Day.'

He tells them anyway, he hasn't all that much confidence in
grown-ups' utterances, especially in the early morning, and
especially when they look as his parents do. A fuzzy look, he has
noticed in passing, that often comes over them, as if they are
inside cocoons they have spun round themselves. Like silk-
worms. There are silk-worms in cocoons on the mulberry trees at
home. When the cocoons are fat enough they are picked off and
thrown in boiling water and the worm is boiled to death but the
cocoons are left and silk threads are wound off them onto

147

bobbins. His parents, he fancies, could be worms in silk, although they are, of course, alive. Their eyes are open.

'Time to get up,' he cries, and leaps on the bed, aiming to wriggle his way into the cosy hollow between them. His father stops him.

'Stay where you are, Rabi.'

'Why?'

'It's time to get up, as you said.'

'I only meant it will be soon.'

'It's time now. Run along, Rabi. Never do to be late today, you know.'

'I know. I shan't be late.'

'You will if you don't hurry.'

'I won't. I shall be ready long before you. It takes you *hours*.'

'Nonsense. I can be ready in a jiffy except for special occasions.'

'Like this one?'

'Like this one. It's my duty to be properly dressed.'

'You mean you have to be.'

'I owe it to the people. It is a Maharajah's duty not to disappoint the people.'

'Panditji says clothes don't matter.'

'Well, the clothes he wears, of course it doesn't.' Bawajiraj snickers, though he is not altogether happy at this turn to the conversation.

'Panditji's right. Clothes don't matter. It's what I love about your father,' says Mohini briskly, and jiggles the boy off the bed with her foot.

Rabi runs off. He believes he understands what she means. He has deduced from their outlines under the sheet that his parents have not a stitch on, but, clearly, they love each other best as they are. It is easy enough to stretch the theory to the people. Although he does not make a conscious follow-up, this is the substance of the reassurance he feels. It is not the Maharajah's clothes that the people worship, they worship the Maharajah for himself. This assurance produces a warm, bright glow within his breast.

His new understanding of duty gives Rabi a better grace with which to endure the loathed blue outfit. He dons it with a modicum of fuss. He allows the flunkey to place the detested hat on his head, stifling his inclination to jam it on any old way.

And now here he is, in his regalia, on this brilliant morning, riding with his father in the gilded carriage that is taking them to the Durbar.

His father sits on the right. He sits very straight, his hand resting on the hilt of his sword, which is gold encrusted with diamonds, except when he raises it to wave to people. He waves quite often, and now and then he gives a little bow, and he hardly stops smiling at all. It is a very bright sunny smile, and his eyes are shining, and the rings on his fingers gleam when he raises his hand; he has a sort of total golden look, like a nugget.

Rabi likes this look. So do the people, he judges, from the way they whistle and cheer, and shout *'Maharajah ki jai!'* as their carriage rolls past. He resolves to copy his father—he feels he owes it to all these people who have gathered to watch them. He smiles and waves and people smile back and some of them shout *'Maharajkumar ki jai!'* Rabi enjoys this. He is sure the people are enjoying themselves too, from their jolly faces and air of festivity; in fact, he has heard grown-ups say pageants are held to keep the people happy. He can see he and his father, and of course all the other splendid Maharajahs too, are making them happy, dressed up in velvet and silk and cloth-of-gold, and their fine horses in jingling harness. He beams at the friendly spectators. They beam back, and the children wave their flags. There are hundreds of children. They all have flags.

'I wish I had a flag,' says Rabi enviously.

'No, no. Too vulgar.'

Bawajiraj murmurs, behind a jewelled hand. He does not want the postilion to overhear.

'Why is it vulgar? Those children all have flags.'

'Those children are not Maharajahs' children!'

'Are you sure I am?'

'Of course I'm sure!' The Maharajah almost snaps. Really, the boy has his mother's knack. The moment could hardly be less appropriate. He does not, however, permit his annoyance to mar his urbane performance. He, his form and lineaments, the sumptuous costume he is wearing, all are sublimated and dedicated to the service of the people, although these people strictly speaking are not his subjects. The Maharajah continues to smile and bow, although it is none too easy from the sitting position, and to raise his hand unstintingly, on this long ride, in a gesture that falls between a benediction and a salute.

Rabi is acutely aware of his father. Only now it is not his father at all but a shining warrior-king wrapped in a shining mantle beside whom he happens to be sitting. So he ferries himself outside to take a better look. It is not too difficult to do. Quite soon he is jammed in with the crowd, in the front rank of children; he even imagines he has a flag in his hand. The Maharajah is plainly visible. His turban is loaded with jewels. His jewels flash in the sunlight, throwing off fiery colours. His sword glitters in its golden scabbard. Rabi is quite carried away by the radiance of this warrior-king.

'Maharajah ki jai!' he shouts.

'What is the matter with you, Rabi?' The Maharajah asks, out of the side of his mouth.

But even this does not shake Rabi's devotion. He is devoted to the Maharajah. There is no one mightier than he, and by the greatest piece of good fortune he is the mighty Maharajah's son. A brilliant pool of feeling seeps up and warms Rabi. He is glad the people can see him sitting beside this golden, puissant figure. He wishes the whole world could see.

* * *

'Panditji, did you see us?'

In submission to Mohini's edict the Pandit has taken charge of the boy. The Maharajah has hoped that the nature of the occasion, and the august presences that grace it, would deter: but no, there is this mountebank, planted next to (admittedly on the periphery) the cluster of dignitaries waiting to receive him. Standing there, the Maharajah notes (despite his preoccupation with the implacable sword that is hampering all efforts at a dignified descent), with that insufferable brahminical nose-in-air attitude as if he is superior to all that is going on.

'None of your democratic nonsense,' he barks, above the polite paeans of welcome the courtiers are making, and hands the boy over to the tutor.

In fact the Pandit has had to muster every ounce of his cowed spirits to keep up appearances. His knees are knocking, although luckily the folds of his *dhoti* conceal the base movement. His lips feel tacky.

'Come on, Rabi,' he manages to say more or less normally, and follows the caparisoned cavalry officer who has been detailed to conduct the Maharajkumar and this *munshi* or whatever to their places.

Rabi keeps close to his tutor. He has been told not to take his hand and he dreads getting lost in this huge amphitheatre that reminds him of a circus. It is horse-shoe shaped, he observes, and painted blue and white, and has innumerable arcades and galleries and gilded cupolas that gleam in the sunshine. There are thousands of people milling about, though in a polite way, looking for their seats. There are thousands of seats too, but they can't just sit anywhere, each one has his special seat, with his own number on it. Rabi's seat is 200K. The number is printed in red on the ticket the ADC is holding. He is just wondering how in the world they will find it when there they are: Tier K, Seat No. 200.

'Maharajkumar Sahib.'

The aide-de-camp clicks his heels and bows, a bow that cuts out the *munshi*, attached though he is to the Maharajkumar. It is a tricky manoeuvre; it pleases the exquisite young officer who has just brought it off, and makes him reflect on the advantages of his excellent training.

Rabi inclines his head, slightly, stiffly. He too has an armoury of proper ripostes to every contingency, advantages that glance off onto him from his Palace upbringing, of which he is unconscious. He sinks into plush and looks round eagerly at the gay scene. Far, far down the tiered circles he spots his father. He is sitting in the front row of Maharajahs, conversing with his neighbours. The neighbours are very grand. They are wearing their best jewellery, diamond collars and necklaces and armlets, ropes of pearls, ribands encrusted with stars and suns, and sashes smothered with precious gems—the rainbow glints travel all the way up to Tier K; but none, Rabi is glad to observe, is grander than his father the Maharajah.

'Panditji, did you see us?' he asks again.

'See what, Rabi?' The Pandit, rid of the military popinjay, has just succeeded in settling himself, his haunches spurning the touch of plush, his hands resting severely on his abject knees, which have, he considers, let him down.

'Us, riding in State. The Maharajah and I.'

'You and your father. Yes, I did catch a glimpse.'

'It was splendid, wasn't it?'

'A very fine sight.'

'Why didn't you like it, Panditji?'

'I did like it.'

'No, you didn't. I can tell from your voice.'

'Well, I—'

The tutor, in his cheap black coat and bazaar sandals, in this sparkling assembly, any member of which can buy him out many times over, becomes conscious yet again, contemptibly, of the weight of opinion that is pulping his marrow. The pressure is such that he is, almost, tempted to throw overboard his most precious convictions. The very honesty of the child—those pristine, trusting surfaces: he feels that an amber lamp has been turned on his soul—saves him from these shameful excesses.

'I couldn't help wondering if it wasn't a waste of money,' he says. 'Yes, that's it. I was wondering whether it couldn't be put to better purpose.'

'Do you think it could?'

'What do you think?'

'My father has pots of money.'

'I know.'

'He thinks you think too much about his money.'

'*His* money,' says the annoyed tutor, and would like to launch into an exposé of the sources of the princely income but the occasion does not lend itself. It is altogether too brassy, he feels, too noisy and distracting for such expositions. Bands are playing. Guns are sounding. A salvo is fired from the ramparts of the Red Fort each time a Maharajah's carriage is sighted; another from the battery stationed in the park each time a Maharajah alights. There are some five hundred Maharajahs; at least there are five hundred States, give or take a few, and the Pandit cannot see many of their Heads resisting a Durbar. He curls a lip (he is almost restored to himself now) and raises a bony finger to his oppressed temples when the artillery grows too thunderous.

Rabi, on the other hand, has martial leanings. He loves cannon. He is something of an expert on gun salutes. He knows— Bawajiraj has gone into the matter thoroughly for his benefit— that the gun salute fixes the Maharajah's rank and position. His father has twenty-one guns, which makes him a great Maharajah. Rabi diverts himself by placing the other Maharajahs, as they arrive, in their order of rank.

* * *

As the last salvo dies the Band starts up a spirited march.

This is the moment—singled out like a hallowed flame on an altar—for which Lady Copeland has been waiting. She leans forward in her seat, in the noble tiers of the English, under the *quelques fleurs* shade of her straw, and fixes her burning gaze on the thin line of nondescript warriors that is filing in to the rousing strains of 'See the Conquering Hero Comes.'

Tottering, the Dewan describes it to himself. Ensconced in his distinguished box, cool in his extravagantly simple cotton ensemble, he feels he has never clapped eyes on such a rickety collection of aged gentlemen as are now attempting the long march to their reservation in the arena. Some are dressed in weather-beaten khaki tunics. Others are in rusty frock-coats, whose cut and style indicate to the Dewan the handed-down gifts of departed Sahibs. None can be under seventy, which is not surprising as all of them date from the Mutiny. Not one but has a chestful of medals and ribbons awarded by the British, which again is not surprising since these venerable men are relics of regiments that have stood by them during that dreadful uprising. They are present at the Durbar as a mark of honour for their service to the Queen.

Arms crossed on his unadorned, immaculate breast, eyes hooded against the glare, the Dewan ponders the suitability, in this country, of the chosen tune, and still more the wisdom of this triumphal parade of veterans whose services might be seen by the populace at large as, at best—he selects the word with care—dubious. The populace, however, for the most part barred as it is from the glittering enclave, has no means of voicing an opinion.

Whereas the assembly is vociferous. It cheers and claps, and baritones from the English enclosure call for three cheers for the loyal old sweats. The call is generously answered. The British lead, and the Maharajahs fall in. The arena rings to cordial hosannas for those whose support has enabled the chosen to continue to fulfil their destiny in the Indian sub-continent.

Limping (he has a rheumatic hip) but keeping up with his comrades is Ram Singh, the loyal sepoy who rescued Lady Copeland's grandmother from the fate (or even worse) that befell her husband the Colonel on that May night in 1857. He is a confused old man, who does not know what he did right, what he did wrong. The sahibs have commended him, given him all these medals, but his own folk have taken to acting sour; they don't want to hear his tales, or look at his decorations any more. Save it, old man, they say. Sometimes they even call him a traitor for what he did. What did he do? He isn't too sure, certainly not what they say. He could never be a traitor, no. Anyway, it is all hazed over, whatever he did, except for the woman. A white woman, with wild eyes, cowering in a charcoal *godown*: unbelievably the Lady Sahib herself, he perceives, under the fright and grime. He remembers her pale arms, warding him off, then, because he has no evil design, clutching him like a drowning woman. Succouring a woman in distress, surely a man can be proud of that? But the neighbours . . . you can never fathom what they mean. With the sahibs, though, how different it is! Just listen to them cheering! And always ready with a kind word, and once a month, regular as a soldier's pay, the runner comes with the pension money . . . yes, with the sahibs you never need to doubt yourself.

The old man raises his rheumy eyes, watery from the sun—he fervently hopes the drops won't slop over—and searches the rows of English for the face that, above all others, resuscitates him. For, in the manner of these things, the Resident's wife is a replica of her grandmother, the Colonel's lady. In Ram Singh's mind the two have been fused into one.

The impulses that move the old soldier also, in other forms, throb in Lady Copeland. She does not acknowledge them. She has no doubts at all of her role, her presence, her past, the part her forbears have played in wars, in conquests, in the Mutiny, in the sub-continent itself. But the profound mistrust that is a portion of her heritage, a lifelong hairshirt next to her skin, lifts briefly and mercifully when she looks down at the devoted soldier. Mirrored in the old man's swimming eyes Lady Copeland sees the battalions of the faithful. Her own are ardent: blue flames that warm and nourish Ram Singh's uncertain bones.

Salt of the earth, is Sir Arthur's verdict on the veterans. He doesn't share his wife's passion: he is a Gurkha man himself—tough little fighters, not a thought in their heads except absolute obedience to their commanding officers—but the Indians are a doughty lot too, no doubt of that. One has only to look at these old campaigners—can't be one under seventy, and most of them stiff as old pokers, but all of them marching doggedly, and even keeping up with the Band, like the fine old troupers they are. His genuine admiration moves Sir Arthur to raise a warm, spirited Hooray!

Bawajiraj is also cheering. He has been among the first to answer the call. 'Hurrah!' he cries, 'Hurrah! Hurrah!' not tearing out his lungs of course, but heartily, as he has been coached in youth. Though he does wonder about his turban. From boyhood on the question has plagued his mind and never been finally resolved. A quick look round, however, is reassuring; only one *pagri* raised (Pudur's: the man's a bit of a cad, with a pocket-handkerchief State). It is quite a relief to leave his in place. The last thing anyone wants is some contretemps with one's fiddly Durbar turban.

Rabi is quite prepared, and would like, to wave his cap in honour of the gallant old soldiers. Denied a flag, caught up in the death and glory mood that moves the audience, the pestilential thing has come into its own. He feels like sweeping it off his head—his hand has already grasped it—and flourishing it like a banner. His tutor stops him.

'No, *no*, Rabi.'

'Why not?'

'*Think* what you're doing.'

'I'm cheering the Mutiny veterans.'

'What *for*? You must stop and think.'

'For their loyalty of course. They're loyal old sweats.'

'They're traitors.' (Voice drops shamefully, has he no control?)

'What?'

'Traitors!' The Pandit almost bellows. (In this company. But there are things one has to do. The effort turns him grey.)

'What did they do?'

'They—' He trembles. He has been warned against democratic nonsense, and here he is embarked on treason. 'They acted against the country,' he manages.

'In what way?'

'They put down an uprising of the people.'

'Was the Mutiny an uprising of the people?'

'It would have been. But they stopped it.'

'Why?'

'I suppose they didn't think.'

'Why not?'

'Soldiers are trained not to think.'

'My father's a soldier. He's Commander-in-Chief of Devapur State Forces.'

'Hush, Rabi.'

The Pandit throttles the reply that vaults to his lips. His brief is for straightforward history: the Indian view, as Mohini describes it. Unless intolerably goaded he does not care to extend it to denigrations of the boy's father. He concentrates instead on the Programme, which is going like clockwork, on which the next event scheduled is the arrival of the Duke and Duchess.

Precisely at eleven the carriage carrying Their Royal Highnesses the Duke and Duchess of Connaught to the Durbar leaves the Viceroy's Camp. It is escorted by one squadron of British and one squadron of Native Cavalry. The cavalcade travels along Prince's Road and Review Road, whose entire length is lined by mounted men who hold back the enthusiastic spectators. As it turns into the arena the Bandmaster raises his baton for the National Anthem. The cymbals are still clashing as the carriage pulls up at the Central Dais.

At eleven-thirty on the stroke (the half hour allows for the watering of the dusty route of the cavalcade; it is also an interval of studied significance) the carriage conveying Their Excellencies the Viceroy and Vicereine leaves for the Durbar. It is escorted by a British Cavalry Regiment, a Regiment of Native Cavalry, the Imperial Cadet Corps in blue and gold, and His Excellency's Body Guard in scarlet and gold. As the gilded coach enters the straight for the run to the Central Dais the Band breaks into the National Anthem again, and the cannon bombardment begins.

Or so it sounds to the Pandit, who cannot tell one outburst from another; whereas to Rabi's practised ear the individual bangs and their messages are perfectly clear.

'Thirty-one guns! A Royal Salute!' he cries with rapture, his voice melting into the tumult of welcome that the distant gold and scarlet have already sparked.

Then they are standing. The entire congregation, as versed as Rabi in these matters, has risen to the guns as one man. The act is assisted by drums, which are rolling once more into the Anthem. It is also mandatory, laid down with simple clarity in the *Durbar Directory*, copies of which have been widely distributed. It is, nevertheless, seminally and essentially a tribute to an Emperor wrung from the lustrous assembly, a fact which does not escape the interested Dewan nor, to some extent, his humbler facsimile the Pandit.

ALL STAND is the firm injunction.

In a glare of jewels and a flow of silk and a hush of reverence the entire assembly obeys. It stands, and remains standing, while the Viceroy, preceded, or surrounded, or accompanied by the Vicereine and his Staff—such is the dazzle few can tell in what order—proceeds to his Throne. To many minds the procession resembles the serene progress of a sun, accompanied by satellites, the nimbus of each merging into a common and blinding radiance that blurs the minute distances that are meticulously maintained between these moving bodies. No regiment could have done better. Equally, none has been better drilled or put through its paces than this concourse of glittering elegance.

The Dewan retains his normal sight but once again suffers, and admits to, the pangs of a distilled envy. He is not to be distracted by suns. Rays can be traced to brass and steel, to brasso, blanco, spit and polish, plumes, pennants, swords, and medals. These are the merest garnishes. The true source of the miraculous performance he is witnessing, he acknowledges, indeed partakes of the miraculous. It is the spirit that feeds the absolute conviction that Providence has created the Empire for its own ends, and appointed a British Trustee. The Dewan wonders if, and can hardly believe in, any force that can be pitted against such consecrated armour.

* * *

The views of the Durbar by those who attended it—as subsequently recorded, and even at the time—showed a refreshing diversity.

The British view, which they saw no reason to change, was that it achieved its declared purpose. This purpose being manifold, the issue singled out for pride of place was the demonstration of unity: the drawing together of the disparate elements in the country under one flag, and the public acknowledgment by the Ruling Chiefs of their allegiance to the King-Emperor.

The various strands were spliced together by a symbolic device: the reading of the Proclamation announcing the coronation of the King, Emperor of India. Actually, the coronation had already taken place, in London, in the August preceding. No such considerations were allowed to modify the Durbar. In any case August, in Delhi, then as now, would have been an impossible month.

The Indian view was necessarily divided between the élite and the proletariat. Spokesmen for the proletariat were, later on, apt to call it a vulgar extravaganza that affronted the impoverished nation. The proletariat, however, at least that portion of it perched on the earth mound outside the amphitheatre thrown up especially for them—these lucky citizens from their grandstand view found it a thoroughly enjoyable spectacle. The élite, but for one or two carping dissenters, pronounced it an outstanding success.

Mohini's view was jaundiced. Bile sprang, not only from inner convictions that resisted imperious enactments, but also from certain constraints that she discerned in her position: specifically, physical restrictions, since her view of proceedings was through the latticed framework of the enclosed Gallery for Native Ladies. The nature of her seating—peephole, and humiliating, in her opinion—confirmed suspicions she had harboured and roused in her a fury that she was only prevented from venting by the distance that separated the Gallery from the front row where Bawajiraj basked.

But Rabi saw clearly, from his seat in Tier K. He saw very clearly indeed what went on.

* * *

But now they are standing, while their Excellencies advance, or rather are borne in state, in the living palanquin of their attendant suites, to the central dais surmounted by the resplendent domed pavilion. Slowly and with infinite precision the glittering procession progresses, along the immaculate aisle, up the crimson-carpeted steps to where, on a gold-embossed carpet, under hangings of a Roman splendour, the silver Thrones await.

There seems little to choose between these chairs of State, though the Dewan's eye does perceive minute distances that suggest the order of precedence. It is not, however, easily interpreted outside Court circles. The English avatar of Saxe-Coburg-Gotha travels poorly to Anglo-India, and even less well to India. Masters though they are in the art, even this élitist Indian audience cannot wholly unravel the punctilio of ceremonial that is observed. It accounts for a certain confusion as the Durbar proceeds.

No such confusions beset Bawajiraj. He has his upbringing to thank. He thinks affectionately of his English tutors, for whose elucidation of so many English manners and customs he cannot be sufficiently grateful. And of course Sir Arthur. The man's been an absolute brick. He has spent simply hours of his valuable time briefing him. But for that—Bawajiraj quivers: it's unlikely, but not impossible—he could easily blunder, like that oaf, Nawanagar, at the Investiture, who has behaved, really, as if it were a country durbar! The Maharajah adjusts his aigrette and dwells, not without some masochistic transfer of roles, on the blunders of his peers while he waits for his moment to come.

Rabi also waits, now and then stifling a yawn. A great deal happens of course, but there is a lot of time when nothing happens at all, when they are simply waiting for something to happen. At these times it can be boring. And hot. The cupolas are a glary white; it hurts to look straight at them. The air is wavery, which shows how hot it is. It is always hottest at noon. At home, at noon, it is coming up for siesta time, and the *malis* are watering the *khus-khus* blinds to keep the bedrooms cool. Then they go away to their *godowns*, to sleep. Janaki hasn't got a *godown* (she is hoping to get one next year: the head gardener has said he will see what he can do), but she curls up under the lime tree behind the stables and pulls her sari over her face like a veil and sleeps.

Rabi wishes he had a veil. He feels quite sleepy. If he had a veil he could have a little nap; it wouldn't be a disgrace as no one could see what he was up to behind the veil. He wonders how the soldiers manage to stay awake, standing out there in the open. He feels quite sorry for them, especially the soldiers drawn up in front of the Dais. They are the Guard of Honour. They are dressed in kilts, and their knees are bare, and the sun falls right on their faces. Their faces are red and blotchy, except for the ones who are going to faint, who turn a buttermilk colour. One or two have toppled already. They lie on the ground and you can see the backs of their thighs. A third man has closed his eyes and is swaying a little. When his shoulder touches his companions' they give him a tiny nudge, you can hardly see it, though of course you can guess they are trying to help, but there's not much they can do because the Herald is in the middle of an important announcement and they are standing to attention.

At last the Herald finishes. There is a silence. It wakes everyone up. The soldier stops swaying and opens his eyes, and his colour floods back to his face and turns it geranium red. Then suddenly a lot begins to happen. There is a fanfare from the trumpeters. The Guard of Honour presents arms. The Royal Standard is hoisted and flutters at the top of the flagstaff high above the arena. The Band plays "God Save the King" and the Salute is fired. It's an Imperial Salute: 101 guns. Rabi has never heard it fired before; it is quite awesome. He wishes he could tell Panditji, but it is too noisy. Then they are all standing, and sitting down, and clapping, and at last the moment comes which his father has told him to watch for, when all the Maharajahs will be honoured by presentation to the Viceroy.

Rabi looks forward to this. He sits on the edge of his seat in excitement, and he can see the Maharajahs are excited too. They are smiling and clapping and their jewels are flashing, and when the Viceroy stands up to receive them and places one foot on the little silver footstool near his chair, and waits to receive them, all of them burst into loud cheers. Rabi is carried away by the sound. He joins in, cheering as loudly as he can in spite of Panditji, who seems to be leering (his mouth is askew, which shows he disapproves) and who, in his dull black coat with mouldy tinges, is, Rabi cannot help thinking, a bit of a wet lettuce in this bright and jolly company.

Bawajiraj, awaiting his moment, is relaxed and happy. He will, he feels, be up to it. At least he has done all in his power. Unlike that booby—can it be Sonapur? it's unbelievable—who has just fallen up the steps. Clearly he has not bothered trying on his mantle, let alone walking up stairs in it.

'Tricky things, mantles,' he murmurs to his neighbour the Maharajah of Gurpur.

'Devilish.' The Maharajah concurs wholeheartedly. 'Won't have anything to do with the damn things myself.'

'They add a little something, you have to admit.'

'True. But tricky. Dashed tricky.'

'It's the yardage. Got to watch it, otherwise it's a disaster. Poor old Sonapur.'

'Sonapur? No, no, not Sonapur, not in a thousand years.'

'Precisely what I said to myself. Let's see now . . . ah yes, I see, it's—' he hardly breathes the parvenu's name '—Pudur.'

'One might have known.'

'Indeed.'

The two Ruling Chiefs are gently convulsed. And now there is more entertainment as Bukhor starts up a speech and has to be led away in mid-sentence by an ADC. And now someone—quite a few of these gaucheries actually—has seized the Duke's hand, completely ignoring the Viceroy! And still more entertainment as a Chief in bright green fan-pleated skirts presents himself, pleats swinging to reveal his dusky ankles as he marches up the aisle. Some hill kingdom, up north, Bawajiraj fancies, and joins in the titter that rises from the British circle. Then he puts levity aside. His moment is near. He hopes Rabi is watching. He swivels round to make sure and observes that the boy is attentive, his eyes are glued. It gratifies a man, a son like that. Bawajiraj waves reassuringly but gaily to Rabi—rainbow lights stream from his brocaded arm—as he rises and heads for the Dais.

His performance is flawless. When he goes over it, afterwards, he cannot really fault himself. He walks with a firm easy tread along the aisle, ascends the steps without a hitch, and advances to within six paces of the Throne before which His Excellency is standing. Here, holding himself with dignity, he pays homage to the King-Emperor's Representative, and, in a few well-chosen words, asks for his felicitations to be conveyed to His Majesty on the occasion of his Coronation. Then he bows deeply, three low bows, and retires in good order.

Well versed in the intricate ceremonial of his own Court, not to mention the Resident's, it has been a relatively simple exercise for him. A fair amount of timing and practice, of course, but that is part of his job, to which he has directed himself with his usual assiduity. Accordingly, his performance offers him a certain

satisfaction, rather than pride, and he brushes aside with a
genuine humility his peers' congratulations. Smiling and relaxed, pausing only to acknowledge Rabi, he resumes his seat,
preparing to enjoy the remainder of the Durbar as, he feels, he is
justly entitled to do.

For Bawajiraj his duty, for the time being, is ended.

For Rabi the rub of reality is beginning.

Leaning forward, gripping his seat with excitement, Rabi
watches his father. Sees him pause and speak and bow, three low
bows. Watches him retire. Sees the shining warrior-king retreat,
walking backwards. Backing away like a lackey, like one of his
own subjects at one of his own durbars.

The Maharajah is mighty no longer. He is a subject. The
sovereign is this man on the Dais called the Viceroy. He is like a
sun, dazzling, and the whole of this Durbar, all of it to the last
gold cupola, is there to do him honour. And his father in the face
of this sun has been frizzled up into nothing. A vassal, that is the
reality of it, who has to bow and scrape and back away from the
Presence. The vassal that his mother and grandmother have
proclaimed, and he has never believed, the Maharajah to be.

Rabi sits frozen in his seat. His face feels stiff. With stony eyes
he sees they have combined, although it is not clear to him how:
the gold cupolas, the silver throne with golden crowns, the
Guard of Honour, the glittering lances of the Body Guard, the
silver and crimson stool upon which the Viceroy's foot is
planted—all these have combined to reduce his father, who has
just, at this very moment, turned round to smile at him.

Rabi blinks back the tears that are threatening. Forcing the
parchment of his face he smiles and waves, and then he closes his
eyes, tightly, like the soldier. He can imagine his face turning the
colour of buttermilk, and even pictures himself pitching forward, onto the spiky epaulettes of the man in front, but he knows
in reality he won't because Panditji has noticed, and put his arm
around his shoulders and is holding him up.

* * *

'Rabi, are you sure you don't want to go?'
'Quite sure.'
'The finest polo teams in the country!'
'I know.'
'And you still—?'
'I don't want to go.'
Rabi dangles a listless foot over the side of the bed in a way that

161

baffles Bawajiraj. For here is a spread that any boy would jump at. As he would have done at Rabi's age, because, after all, durbars like this don't come round every day. But all Rabi seems to want to do is to mooch around in his tent. He simply can't make out what's come over the boy. He's already missed the cricket match, and the assault-at-arms, and now it looks as if the Polo Tournament. Bawajiraj has quite looked forward to watching the Polo Tournament with his son.

'Don't you feel too well?' he asks, kindly but cautiously. He is a healthy man himself—all that open air and good clean sport—and he dreads illness in another, especially Rabi, a fine sturdy youngster who takes after him. Though now he definitely looks peaky . . . perhaps a touch of the sun? Sun doesn't affect Bawajiraj—his skin is quite dark, but afflictions do have their saving side, as he likes to point out—but the boy has his mother's fairness, not to mention her intransigence.

'Are you ill?' he asks, less kindly.

'I'm all right.'

Rabi burrows deeper into fur. He wishes his father would go away. Then he would get up and go—on his own, he feels he would like to be on his own, as he often is at home—to where the animals are stabled; he likes being with them—it's as good as being on one's own. But his father is dug in. On the couch, frowning, the rings on his fingers gleaming in furry depths. So that Rabi is trapped, under the coverlet, which is beginning to stifle him, while his father has one more go.

'What is the matter with you, Rabi?'

'Nothing.'

'There must be.'

'I don't want to, that's all.'

'Why not?'

Rabi comes perilously close. He wants to shout at his father who pretends to be what he isn't, but grace, and gratitude, imprison him.

'Just don't,' he mumbles.

'You know I only want you to enjoy yourself, Rabi.'

'I know.'

Rabi gets it out, somehow. His throat is hurting horribly. He hates his father, but he loves him too, more than anyone in the world except his mother and grandmother and perhaps Janaki. He clutches her marble in his hand. It is hard and solid, and almost as comforting as if she were here with her steadfast cry of *Maharajkumar!*

Bawajiraj goes away. Outside he encounters the Pandit, whom

Mohini has despatched, and who is drooping uneasily at the entrance in the presence of the bristling sentry who has neither forbidden him ingress nor permitted him to pass.

'I suppose it's your doing,' he barks at the embattled man.

The Pandit has never been treated to other than canine notes from the Maharajah, and has long discounted as flattery rumours of a milder repertoire. Nevertheless, the assault is so unwarranted it provokes him to reply.

'Sir, I have done nothing!' he dares.

'Except ruin the poor boy's enjoyment!' snaps the Maharajah, and strides away, his riding crop whingeing and slashing the air as he goes towards polo.

The Pandit enters the tent. He is trembling a little. The encounter has upset him—not only the Maharajah but the guard. The man, taking his cue from His Highness, jaw out-thrust and bayonet clattering, has all but defied him to proceed. Only devotion of a high order to Mohini, his paymaster, and to his calling, enables the tutor to stick to his duty.

But when he enters, and sees the child's forlorn countenance, his sense of martyrdom is instantly quelled. Even the Maharajah is suppressed. The need to separate child from father, which is often pressing, is totally absent. The child alone fills his consciousness. He draws up a stool and sits beside the boy at his level.

'Well, Rabi, what shall we do today?'

'I don't know.'

'There's quite a choice.'

'I don't want to do anything.'

'Lots of lovely things.'

'I don't think anything's lovely in rotten Delhi.'

'You mustn't say things like that, Rabi.'

'Why not? Why can't I say what I think?'

'Because it isn't true, is it?'

'It is. I hate everything.'

The Pandit feels queasy. The Maharajah's accusation revives and begins to niggle. Is he indeed responsible for utterly wrecking the boy's capacity?

'That isn't true, is it?' he asks, anxiously.

'It is.'

'But you liked the illuminations, didn't you?'

'Yes.'

'And the elephant procession?'

'Yes. Some of it.'

'And riding in the carriage with your father to the—'

'No.'

'I thought—you said—'

'I didn't! I didn't!'

The boy's vehemence throws the Pandit. He has to trace back, and then he remembers that sudden pallor, on Durbar Day, which he has put down to the sun, which has clearly not been to blame. But he still cannot determine the cause, and Rabi, his mouth like a trap, he can see is going to reveal nothing. Unable to cure, he resolves to palliate, if possible.

'Let's do whatever you'd like to do,' he says as enticingly as he can.

'*Anything?*' Grown-ups' treachery—the weal is still livid—enjoins precautions.

'Anything.'

'Promise?'

'I promise.'

'I'd like to go to the Champ de Mars.'

'All right.'

The Pandit hasn't the foggiest, but he is game. Anything to prise the boy out of his misery. Even this warlike place, whatever it is, so long as it banishes these shadows.

'It's where the menagerie is,' Rabi enlightens him.

'I shall enjoy that.'

'Are you sure?'

'Of course I'm sure. I enjoy looking at animals.'

'And afterwards?'

'You say.'

'No, you. It's your turn.'

The Pandit considers. There is a Review scheduled for this afternoon. A parade of power, the Dewan has called it, such as to ravish peasants and children, and keep nawabs and rajahs in line. He has gone into considerable detail. Tirumal Rao takes a keen interest in military matters, in the manner of his ancestor the General, of whom he is inordinately proud. This General is the Dewan's secret weapon, which he often hurls at the unsuspecting Maharajah when Bawajiraj, in his paladin moods, snipes at his brahminical milksop of a Minister.

The martial detail, though lovingly conveyed, has been largely lost on the Pandit, who has a pure scholarly ancestry; but cavalry and cannon have lodged. Rabi, he knows, and regrets it, is an aficionado of both.

'We could attend the Review,' says the Pandit, marching against the grain.

'I don't want to.'

'Lots of cavalry.'

'State cavalry?'

'All sorts.'

'How do you know?'

'The Dewan told me.'

'And artillery?'

'I believe so.'

Rabi slides off the couch. Gun-carriages rumble through his mind, drawn by teams of bays.

'With you?' he asks, warily.

'If you like.'

'I don't want to go with my father.'

'Rabi, if your father wishes—'

'I won't, that's all.'

The Pandit says no more. The treaty is too delicate, he feels, to be subjected to any stresses. He has a fair notion that the Maharajah (the tutor gives the devil his due) will readily acquiesce in whatever serves the interests of the boy.

* * *

The Review of Troops which took place on the 8th January was, and was intended to be, a high spot in the Durbar of 1903.

It was an event of rich and splendid proportions, a gallant military show that so impressed many who were present that their memories still yielded up titbits fifty years later.

It was also a display of might, a message clearly received by many, although, so superb was the spectacle, a good few entirely missed the iron hand. Among the latter was Bawajiraj, who was enraptured by what he saw, and on his return attempted to match squadron for squadron, and manoeuvre for manoeuvre, in a way that drove his commanders to distraction, and dreadfully alarmed Sir Arthur, who needed all his diplomacy to curb the Maharajah's guileless ardour and retain the Devapur Forces at their ornamental level.

In the Durbar Review thirty-five battalions of infantry and sixty-seven squadrons of cavalry took part. It included the 9th Lancers, the regiment which had been disciplined for the deaths of the cook and the coolie at the insistence of the Viceroy, and to the fury of the European community.

It received from the Europeans, civil and military, as it approached the saluting base where the Viceroy waited, the greatest acclamation of all.

Lord Curzon was aware that the wild cheering that rose from

his countrymen at this point was one in the eye for him as much as it was an expression of admiration for a fine regiment. He was also aware, and recorded his awareness, that in that long line of men rode two murderers. As he had not flinched from his duty before, so now he allowed nothing to disturb his composure. Stiff and unmoved he sat his horse, in the loneliness of his eminent position, upheld by his moral convictions, and heard the verdict of his compatriots.

Rabi, like the Viceroy, was sharply aware of animus. Normally sensitive, the Durbar had left him in a state of abnormal and quivering sensitivity. He heard the cheering, but registered the baying notes, which had also been the prelude to those starfish hands that still invaded his dreams. He did not know the cause, any more than he had before, because he was too young, and the history books had yet to reveal, but he knew that a man was being hounded. It was then that he looked, full face and closely from his privileged seat, at the representative of the King-Emperor, and beheld an ordinary mortal.

It was in effect a confounding of intention, at least as far as Rabi was concerned. The reverent growth the Resident had hoped the Durbar might nurture was largely stultified, and the earthy aspirations of the Dowager and Mohini were at least partly realised. Not only was the Maharajah divested, but the sun-king before whom he had dwindled was himself reduced to common proportions. For Rabi, the divine ascendancy of the British, which had transfixed his élite elders, ceased to be tenable, and the process zigzagging wildly and indiscriminately made him equally aware of the human skeleton, rattling away stubbornly underneath the most abject rags and tatters. Gods and men, in a way, resumed their proper stature. It was a child's-eye view, of course, but the eye remained singularly suspicious, permanently on guard against illusions and sophistries.

PART II.

Love makes one ashamed of disgrace, and hungry for what is glorious; without which neither a people nor a man can do anything great or fine.

Plato

6

The Dowager wakes at dawn. Light filters in through the filigree marble of the chamber and rests on her eyes in rosy wafers. She will not dispel them yet. She lies, motionless, in her narrow bedstead, and allows her happiness to lap at her. She cannot trace it, momentarily. She does not try, it is enough to feel. At the summit of feeling it comes in a rush. Rabi and Mohini are coming home today.

Ah yes, Rabi. She has missed the boy. The one, to her, who carries the torch. Not her son, the lustrous satellite. Not her grand-daughters, four obedient little wax dolls, like their mother, the sallow and suspicious Shanta Devi, unlit from within. Retarded, the Dowager considers her daughter-in-law, a woman caught between the impositions of her marriage and the strictures of the Court and crushed into ceding her own development. Not, Manjula allows, that she has made a bad job of it. No one can fault Shanta Devi for not carrying out her duties. Dutiful woman has even bred four dutiful daughters who stand, round-eyed, and whisper—the Dowager has caught them at it—about the deranged views of their grandmother, or listen, politely and insipidly, to her stirring tales until suddenly she stops. Cannot go on. Cuts off in the very middle of narrative and sends them away, back to their polite, insipid mother who gathers her brood about her and whispers in her turn, presenting, to those solid but receptive skulls, for her own self-respect, the stunted and humiliating role that is hers as the ideal of womanhood.

They have departed for the Durbar, these budding little women, and the Dowager has barely noticed. But Rabi's absence she has felt as if part of herself were missing. As he is. He, not his father, is her true heir.

Heir to what though: the Pearl Suite, the Palace, the State, thraldom to the invisible Presence they, bag and baggage, have scrambled off to honour? Heir to identity by grace and favour?

Suddenly and urgently, then, she wants the boy beside her: to see what they have done to him, to question him and wrest from him answers, to gaze down into that topaz look he presents when she involves him in the past or the future: both, at his age, a foreign domain that the grave child surrenders to her to interpret. As she can. As she will. Her breast heaves with high purpose.

'Highness.'

A low, ruinous knock. Rubble, where king and castle were rising. If she lies doggo will the knocker go away, leave her to pick up the pieces before the shine dulls on those radiant surfaces? She will not.

'Highness, your water.'

The door opens. The Dowager relapses, defeated. In company with Sir Arthur she feels that Palace life is one long round. She watches the intruder, who is, in fact, her maidservant, padding around, setting out the paraphernalia of the morning's ablutions. Making, she observes, a meal of it. The woman's hands are sedulous as a priest's about the silver basin with its pierced cover through which can be glimpsed, floating on water, the crimson petals of roses. A beaten silver ewer, from whose lip curl wisps of steam, beside its companion-piece. Sandalwood soap in a silver lotus-shape dish. Pink, fluffy turkish towels, draped like a boa over the gnarled bark of the patient human tree.

When the Dowager's vitality soars she will not suffer these trappings. The whole outfit is dismissed. Enamel is substituted for silver, or even, if her mood is imperative and the Palace can rise to it, tinplate. Display is offensive to her not only because of her widowhood, which is in any case a permanent and accustomed state, or a hankering for simplicity that maturity accentuates, but due also to the zephyr that arising from the distant Durbar ripples across the country and is felt, in some quarters, as a distinct draught.

Manjula wriggles her bare shoulder-blades, which have begun to crawl with irritation. This morning, however, her roving reflections have blunted her energies. She says, wearily but irritably,

'How many times have I told you?'

'Told what, Highness?'

'You know what. That I am done with silver.'

'Silver is proper for a Maharani. She is never done with it.'

The woman is old, and stubborn. She has fought many battles with her mistress, lost a good few, but never conceded the ancient war. It is, in fact, necessary for her to continue the campaign that confirms her own deprivations, since her notch in the hierarchy of service depends upon the quality of the artifacts of daily living that surround her lady. Mud pots are for her ilk. Gold plate for His Highness and those exalted beings like him, the Lord Sahibs. Silver for the widowed Maharani. With stubby, mulish fingers, intent on preserving the immutable pattern, she lifts the precious cover from the petalled, and scented, but ordinary fluid, and proffers the gleaming utensil.

The very mode of presentation is compelling. There are times when Manjula understands and even forgives her son. To refuse seems not an exercise in decency, but the perversion of a barbarian on his bad day. The British are masters of inversion, and have innumerable apprentices, among whom, at different levels of skill, she counts her son and her maidservant. Bawajiraj is dreadfully afraid of appearing uncivilised in British eyes. The maid, on her mistress's behalf, has equally severe anxieties. The Dowager trounces them both, soundly if silently, and herself as well when she capitulates to these civilised buffoons. As she does. Too often, she considers, as she soaps herself under the woman's approving gaze.

After prayers she breakfasts on the verandah. It is a simple meal, served by a Brahmin who endorses, though he cannot ordain, these ascetic frugalities for the royal widow. There is a cupful of milk, a small pot of honey, a platter of fruit, peeled and sliced, under a starched napkin.

Sometimes Mohini, flushed from early rising, to which she is not devoted, but persuaded of its virtue, joins her for the meal, which at once discards its mundane aspects. For the young woman's exuberance transfigures the scene: the dawn is flawless, the air like wine, the grass viridian, the apples are golden, milk is ambrosial and honey turns to nectar.

The dry Dowager, not unused to the charms of daybreak, indulges, she believes, her ward; but her murmurs of consonance take on a depth and gilding that cannot owe all to indulgence. On occasion she acknowledges it: admits to vernal fields and florescent dawns, a new-mint landscape revealed to a fresh pair of eyes that is Mohini's boon to her.

Sometimes it is Rabi, on his favourite, a gleaming Arabian

beauty, who invades her solitude. Boy and pony, to all intents and purposes one, charge the flower-beds bordering the verandah. Pull up within inches and ascend the stairs, rider urging his mount—though the pretty creature hardly needs encouraging, its little polished hooves tittup purposefully across the ridiculous terrain until he reins in, executes a caracole, and salutes her from the saddle.

There is an object, aside from love, that prompts these graceful attentions. He flies, and she perceives, the delicate kite of desire: he asking, she fulfilling. It gives her a quite extraordinary pleasure to see the seraph's greedy, exquisitely chaste lips close over the diced flesh she offers him: ripe flesh of peach and mango, papaya and melon and apricot, according to season. The pony competes, scarcely handicapped in the charm stakes. Its soulful eye having pierced the napkin, it woos her; turns, well-bred, from nuzzling for apple under the damask to win her by grace, abandoning the peerless india rubber of its muzzle to her palm, snuffling softly of elysium glimpsed and—they share the knowledge between them—to be shortly attained.

Yes, Rabi. Life has seemed flat without the boy and his mother. Fizz absent, in the absence of the lively pair. The tick of clocks heard. The Palace denuded. This vast city, against all fact, has actually seemed empty.

In truth it is, of course, both amply populated and throbbing with purpose, as she can see from her elevated position on the verandah above the banked cannas and crotons. On the parade ground, by the West tower, a squad of stiff little marionettes goes through its daily paces. A string of ponies, led by *syces*, clops out to exercise. The *dhobi* troops past, through the tradesmen's exit, under the graceful scalloped arch, driving a quartet of donkeys hung about with bundles of washing. Gardeners are watering the shrubs and lawns. Peacocks fly, dislodged by the silvery floods, protesting raucously—pampered stupid beauties, surprised by their daily fate. Indoors a platoon, on its heels, half-coconuts cupped in palms, has begun on the marble. Soon the renewed surfaces will squeak and gleam and offer themselves to officious feet that bustle about the business of the Court.

The Court is always bustling. So, keeping its distance from its gypsy neighbour, gathering its staid skirts about itself, is the Court of the Hon'ble the Resident. Both establishments, bustling, have nevertheless evinced in these last months a certain infirmity of purpose. A distinct wobble, the Dowager sees it, as of a man on a bicycle who clearly remembers oiling his machine but has disastrously forgotten where he is going. Which no doubt the return of Sir Arthur will remedy. The Resident, the British pivot around which so much revolves. Already his standard has been raised. At least they are practising. Sir Arthur is known to be displeased if the flag sticks, as it has a tendency to do, halfway up the mast.

Presently the Dowager bestirs herself. Birds will be flocking, bright with assumptions, coral claws bickering for toe-hold on the crested perch, the finials of the ornamental gates. Rabi's doves, to which she has a duty, and no less to the boy, whom she has solemnly promised. Calling for the basket of bread and seed she rises, *paschmina* over her shoulders, bounty slung from her arm, and makes her way to the dove-cotes.

* * *

Lady Copeland's mornings have been not unlike the Dowager's. She is a grass widow, and she misses her husband. Duty has detained Sir Arthur. He is in Delhi overseeing Bawajiraj. Never know what peccadilloes . . . he murmurs to his wife, who agrees that these are best nipped in the bud.

Actually he cannot bring himself to believe in them. On the other hand Princes are known to get up to all kinds of pranks. There has been, for instance, that political incident (put years on the Resident concerned, poor fellow) when a Ruling Chief, following some trifling dispute about taxes, has trussed up a pair of the Viceroy's secretaries and presented the brace to His Excellency. Not that Waji. Not in a thousand years. But still. One can't be too careful. In a welter of trust, and suspicion, and disclaimer, and obsession, that springs so liberally from their close association, Sir Arthur remains behind.

Peccadilloes have hardly entered the blameless Bawajiraj's mind. His decision to extend his visit is perfectly innocent. He would like to look round Delhi. Durbar commitments have so far prevented him. He also wishes to show his womenfolk the sights. Mohini in particular. He is—he puts it frankly to himself—tired of listening to her pilgrim's tales. Marvels abound in elegant cities, he wishes to demonstrate to her; there is no need to sweat it out in savage outposts. Bawajiraj quite looks forward to capping some of her stories. He dispatches his efficient Dewan to cope with the State—he freely admits the man has a way of getting things done—and settles with his entourage to planning the sightseeing round.

Sir Arthur remains, now and then joining up with the

Maharajah. His wife returns. Delhi has drained her. Its haughty memorials, its domes and tombs and insolent citadels, even the exquisite water-gardens that homesick Timurids, yearning for Kabul and Samarkand in the heat of Hindustan (until Hindustan itself, subtle captive, became the object of passion), have constructed and left behind to mark their presence—all, the tender and the audacious, are reminders. Of what she doesn't want to know, but feels them brush against her soul, frail bird of truth, which cowers in its cage. Why, she does not care to find out. Never do to ask, in this wily continent. That way lies ruin, scattered with the rubble of monuments picked over by jackals and vultures. Lady Copeland shivers. She puts it down to the climate. She needs, she feels, her garden, her dogs, the children, the accustomed airs of the Residency. She needs, indeed, to retreat to what she has contrived: castle and keep, within a bowery framework, that offers those cool certainties and assurances that calm her fluttering spirit.

'Goodbye, Arthur.' She lifts the spotted net.

'Look after yourself, m'dear.' Sir Arthur kisses the cheek she offers, noticing the tints that India lays. Absinthe for the ladies, liverish tinges on a man. But the children—ah yes, the children. Angels not Angles, floats up in Sir Arthur's mind, a phrase from some child's book which strikes him as utterly apt. Fair and lovely, untouched by the climate, ushered away before a finger can be laid, they are the quintessence . . . The very bloom—Sir Arthur dares the lapidary—of faraway islands, in spring, on a clear day, can be glimpsed in their delicate countenances. Like his own dimpled exquisite Sophie, with her porcelain perfection, the cornflower eyes with which she bewitches him.

'Give my love to the children.'

Sir Arthur steps forward, the black umbrella, held by a brown man, moving with him, to call.

'I will.'

His wife blows him a kiss and lowers her cobweb visor to protect her eyes, which are very bright, and pricking a little, as they always do at such moments.

But she is glad, sipping her bed-tea, contemplating her day, to be back. Soon she will rise, and bath, and step into her morning gown—Ayah has laid out the daffodil lawn, perhaps not appropriate now the monsoon has started, but her favourite—and wait to receive the children. Then breakfast in the morning room—too wet for the terrace, much as she would prefer it—and afterwards the chef will come in to confer about luncheon. Something light, she resolves, none of those orgies to which the man inclines, no doubt from his early training at the Oriental Club.

This orderly pattern—it has reached the compromise stage: they have agreed on lamb chops, a fruit compote, and perhaps rice pudding for the children?—is hideously ruptured by Janaki.

Sobbing and gulping, her wet soles slithering on the marble, which is forbidden to the likes of her, but driven by the doom they have pronounced this very day, the desperate girl scoots into the morning room, a shade ahead of her pursuers, and falls at the Lady Sahib's feet. She is shivering and snorting, and a thin malodorous steam rises from her rags, which are soaked through and beginning to disintegrate indecently in places, but none of these things is apparent to her. She is only overridingly conscious that she has attained, is in, the presence of the power that alone can avert her fate. Suffused in sunflower hues, forehead on marble but greatly daring, she gropes blindly, in acres of lawn, for something to which she can cling and comes upon silken ankles. Blissfully she fastens a clammy grip around them and lifts her face. Hope overflows from eyes and her glistening shoe-black lips.

'Memsahib!' she utters.

Lady Copeland, bemused, looks down from palmy heights. An assortment of rags, it seems to her, blown in by the monsoon wind. But no. The sodden bundle is human. It is a girl, wild-eyed, wild fingers clutching her gown, there are sooty smudges all along the hem. With worse to come. Petrified though she is Lady Copeland can feel. She feels the hideous tentacle that this frightening creature has wrapped about her ankles. Dripping. Gibbering.

There are no words with which, possibly, the two might have disengaged humanely from each other. Not a word, in Lady Copeland's vocabulary, except imperatives to deal with Indian exigencies.

'Chup raho! Jao! Jaldi jao!' She screams, giving little kicks to free herself, her bones, the ruined flounces.

And Janaki, for her part, has only the language, also specially minted to meet her situation, of begging and blandishment.

'Memsahib! Burra Memsahib! Devi!'

The two are pulled apart, though not physically, by the entry of stalwarts. Peons, gardeners, grooms, and ayahs converge in strength, followed, though not closely, by the sentry whose boots have been killing him all day and who feels this last caper has definitely finished him. They crowd round the two women, expressing views in voices that induce in both, sisters under the skin as they are, though both would repudiate the charge, the symptoms of incipient migraine.

'Bad girl, memsahib!'

'No respect, these days!'

'Don't know their place!'

'Cheeky slut!'

They wave the big stick, figuratively speaking, over the transgressor, all except for the head gardener. This man feels he has a lien, in view of his responsibility—he has duly presented his report of scandalous goings-on in shrubberies. Stooping he delivers, one, two, each side of the head where he hopes it will do the most good.

So Janaki finds out what happens next—she has been wondering. Someone is boxing her ears, ear-boxes are singing. She opens her eyes—like Lady Copeland she has closed them against the frightful fracas—and sees it is that bane, that poison toad the head gardener, as one might have guessed. More to the point, she can see that the Lady Sahib has no intention. Her eyes, if not closed, are lying low under bluish lids, which Janaki admits she must have been mad to think. As if they could lift for her! She, the Lady Sahib, herself a cheap, garden-path sweeper. All at once details she has overlooked begin to pepper her hide like grapeshot. Her hair! Her clothes! The puddles they have left on the floor! And her flesh, peeping out in all the most outrageous places! As for that noise she is making, she can hear, plainly, what *it* sounds like. Suppressing herself as best she can—her snuffles, her shameful anatomy, the watery tatters—the naiad rises up, as they are roundly bidding her to do, off of the devastated floor and trails away to her ordained sphere.

While Lady Copeland, her gown in disarray, the morning awry, the floor about her feet disagreeably awash, returns to the menu. She doesn't feel like it. She feels like swooning. She is certain she can sense in the extraordinary manifestation, gibberish though it has sounded, definite if ineffable threats. But she carries on, as one must. Grandmama hovers, stiff as a ramrod in her bombazine (but that was after she was widowed). And there are others. Generations peek over her shoulder. One owes it to them. Forefinger to temple—the incipient throb is flexing itself—Lady Copeland finishes the session before she takes to her bed.

In the darkened room, between cool sheets, cologne-soaked pads on her brow—by now she has a raging headache—she accepts with gratitude the ministrations of angelic Ayah, who is armed with a fan, and a bottle of sal volatile, and lulling syllables, her minstrel's lay crowned by the placid swish of plumes, involuntary contribution of some tart bird.

'What was it all about?' Sleepily, jolting the tranced minstrel, she thinks to enquire.

'No you worry yourself, memsahib. Outdoors girl, doing bad things.'

Ayah, embroidering madly, does her duty. In any case she hasn't a good word, not for that pagan cow. She is a devout Catholic herself.

* * *

Janaki makes for the shrubbery when the deluge is temporarily halted. She is looking for a suitable stick. She is unlikely to find one in shrubberies, whose purpose is poles apart, but she pokes about all the same, among the fleshy leaves of dense bushes that have been, until he went blithely away to the Durbar, their refuge. Still obstinately claims to be, displaying thick glossy textures, bolts of deep green, like a flash salesman.

Indignantly Janaki aims a kick or two. Hasn't she always suspected the foliage? And is requited by a shower, chill from standing in leafcups, drops as bright as diamonds, that drenches the hemline she has just wrung out. Talk of shaking the pagoda tree! Janaki glares, as blistering as she can, but she knows when she is beaten. Squatting on the sodden ground, eyes taking on the glaze that has defeated all grades up to the head gardener, she dreams. For she has a vision, a pearl sedulously moulded around the merest grain. Like Lady Copeland, her inadmissible soul-sister, she too has a legendary grandmama. In this vision grandmama, who for the purposes of enchantment is a beautiful girl, falls in a swoon just as the Maharajah is riding by. Before she can hit the ground the handsome Maharajah scoops her up, on to his milk-white charger, and they gallop off into the sunset.

'Hey, you! Not gone yet?' The poison toad, where a Maharajah should be.

'I'm on my way.'

'Taking your time, aren't you?'

'My time, isn't it? Do what I like with my time.'

'You watch it, my girl. None of your lip.'

'You don't go shooting your mouth either!'

The shout rises shrill and extraordinarily powerful from the crimped shallows of her pigeon-breast. It is surprising what effects belligerence, or perhaps visions, can have. It surprises the gardener into silence, of which the brazen lass takes full advantage.

'Or I'll get the Maharajah to have you sacked!' she throws in his face as bold as brass and stalks away, riding high, borne up in fact by grandmama, to the bamboo thicket by the *hatikhana** which, she admits, is more likely to yield what she seeks than shrubberies, however enchanted.

Quite soon she finds the very thing, a bamboo cane that some lordly elephant has uprooted and stripped and discarded. She tests for suitability, balancing it on her shoulder, and is satisfied. The bamboo is supple, but not so lithe as to spring out of its bony groove. That can be deadly, she can well imagine, walking along with the cursed pole slipping every few paces, not to mention what depends on it, the very nucleus of her future life. Squatting down she slits and whittles away at the cane until it looks and feels right, and tests again. Once more, gingerly, this time with her bundle of clothes suspended from one end, her cooking pot and *lota* clanking at the other. All is well. The bamboo behaves. She looks round to see what else. There is nothing. She moves on, still somehow encased within her magical landscape or at least the few ramshackle frames that remain, so that she is quite prepared for the Maharajah (for the purposes of her vision he is the image of the Maharajkumar, only older) to materialise, and is willing to be wooed by him—but not, she resolves, too easily—into turning back. Although as she passes the shrubbery she does wonder who will listen to the boy, to whom he will pour out his wonderful tales of the great city he is visiting.

It is at this point that her breathing begins to stick and jerk.

* * *

In Delhi Rabi was shown a great deal that was wonderful. He also saw a good deal for himself. He saw mosques and palaces, and sensed in memorials and monuments that transience which had so affrighted Lady Copeland.

Emerging (quite soon) from the gloom into which Lord Curzon and the Maharajah between them had unwittingly plunged him, he went joyously with his vivid and intoxicating mother to bazaars and temples and boisterous street festivals, accompanied

*Elephant stables.

distantly by his father, and even more distantly by the Palace entourage. His tutor invited him to ponder on monuments raised to valour, giving a version of battles and sieges that did not tally with Sir Arthur's, so that Sir Arthur felt constrained to take the Maharajah aside. The Maharajah, accordingly, more than made amends, with the aid of the Military Secretary, by means of extended visits to the Military Academy, the Staff College, the Ridge, the Shot Tower, the Flagstaff Tower, the Headquarters of the Corps, and the Cricket Pavilion, over all of which the Union Jack flapped, and which, whether or not they were salutary, or intimidating, or provided antidotes, or whatever the inscrutable intention was, appealed immensely to Rabi's warlord streak, natural or inherited. His mother now distant, the non-violent Pandit positively out of sight, Rabi had a thoroughly good time, storing away the high spots for re-telling.

But apart from these exercises civil and military there were simple, aimless pleasures: picnics, and outings on lakes, and an apocalyptic first sight of the Taj Mahal, and the choosing of gifts for each other and those left behind.

These pleasures were exquisitely enhanced by the quality of their relationship. Bearing no valid seals, no social contract signed, status fluid and at the mercy of innumerable considerations of Empire and State, in the face of centrifugal forces of immense power, the Maharajah, his beloved, and their unlawful offspring nevertheless preserved themselves as a placid and innocent triad. Boiled down to man, woman, and child, they clung, bonded together by the voluntary nature of their interdependence, a compulsive glue whose irreducible element was, in effect, their love.

* * *

'I don't know when I've enjoyed myself more!'

Bawajiraj skipping, who would believe it, can't believe it himself but there it is. Small hand in large one masterminding the rhythm father and son are tripping it hip-hippety-hop lazily over the turf to the edge of some lake where Mohini sits. Eating, what else: what *better*, the sunny young woman is musing, feeding the ravenous maw that the crisp air has opened up, shovelling in the little green edible parcels as fast as she can go, elbow going like a piston, vine-leaf and spice smells fuelling her labours.

'Here, save some for us, will you?' The two wanderers *racing*, hippety nonsense ditched, eye beaded on the buttery mountain that is rapidly dwindling, homing in at speed.

'If you're quick.'

Between pearly molars, grinding away like mills.

'We're *here*.'

Groaning, attempting to slow down the rapt demolition, immobilised by muck, mucky fingers forbidden to touch food, meat-balls vanishing at a spanking rate.

'Here you are.'

At last, attention. Fingers hovering, washed, ready, greedy, glistening with juices, pouncing and popping. 'One for you, one for you, one for me.'

'You've *had* your share!'

'You should have come sooner.'

'We *ran!*'

'You should have run faster.'

Unrepentant queen, licking her tawny fingers over a platter picked clean as a bone. Her two outsmarted subjects toying with thoughts of revenge, but none too nimble actually, too many meat-balls downed, the shortfall has been wildly exaggerated. Somewhat bloated, the creative edges dulled, a saffron haze impeding, Bawajiraj is nevertheless driven to express himself.

'I don't know when I've enjoyed myself more!'

'So you said.'

'Did I?'

'A moment ago.'

'Well, I still feel the same.'

'So do I. It's perfect.'

'I wish it could go on forever.'

'Mmm.'

Reclining, sun in eyes, eyes closing, murmuring, the merest hold on consciousness, letting go luxuriously . . .

This idyll is broken by the most appalling sound. Yip-yip-yippe, it goes, yip-yip-yippe, ripping across the water.

Bawajiraj jack-knifes up from his tiffin torpor, bleary eyes sort out the source. A fisherman, choosing to announce some piscal triumph, is blowing—a Durbar trumpet is what it sounds like—but no, it's a conch, a huge bulbous thing from which lips to vent he is extracting these terrible blasts. Pleased with himself the virtuoso stands, clad in a cod-piece, black as pitch, balanced on the poop of his rickety cockleshell and smashing the peace to smithereens.

Bawajiraj, regressing, has thoughts of imprisonment without trial; but, more lucidly, it is not his State, or even his lake, off which the man can be ordered. So, quivering (those opening honks have really pierced him), he is compelled to endure this creature who reminds him, now he thinks of it, of one of those demon effigies that, quite rightly, the village children put on their bonfires at Dassara time.

To Rabi the scene, tilting differently, is utterly magical. He sees a splendid barge, riding stately across the lake, sails ballooning in a gentle breeze and a conch-blowing God in the stern. A God of flickering bronze, he could be, ablaze in the westering sun. Billowing canvas by sunset takes on the nature of revelation.

'That's it!' says Rabi on a note of deep conviction.

'What's what, Rabi?'

'What I want, exactly.'

'That *boat*?' Dotted lines running to the mangy object.

'The colour.'

'What colour?'

'The sails.'

That dingy calico? There is the silence, apart from the conch, of parents repressing themselves, manhandling the blame for the failure in communication from the boy to those atrocious sounds, from sounds to their perpetrator. Bawajiraj peevishly wonders if a word to Sir Arthur. Mohini, gathering up picnic detritus, wonders why it has to be her every time; should she suggest to His Highness to lend a hand with the empties? Rabi alone, or possibly the fisherman as well, insulated, these two natural beings by a selfish and glorious self-sufficiency continue rooted in their blissful occupation.

Carrying the colour in his mind, a dynamo of purpose, Rabi ransacks entire bazaars. Nothing will do but an exact match to the random purple a quirk of twilight has laid on a sail. It vexes Bawajiraj. None of the servants wears pure purple, only white, with touches. He regards it as his personal colour, in the same way that the British have nabbed scarlet for their own purposes. Besides, if his son is going to cart home presents for this unknown servant, is he to dig into his pocket for the remaining pack? It is worrying. In the name of equity alone he feels he ought to forbid Rabi, but the thought is repugnant. Bawajiraj is not a man to deliberately crush another's pleasure.

So Rabi continues his quest. Shopkeepers, too pleased, smiles gleaming, hair smarmed, oblige, sending a hundred choice lengths slithering across polished counters. Another hundred yards, or more, swirl and settle like fritillaries on the mountain growing from the starched linen floor. At last a match is made. Rabi selects, or at least he is sold, a sheer beauty of alabaster and purple such as no servant would dare, and which, assuming she wears it, will do nothing for Janaki's complexion.

The salesman bears it away, privately frayed, still gleaming gamely, nothing is too much trouble . . . In the poky back room he folds gossamer into tissue, into egg-white crêpe, into a cardboard casket with a lotus on the lid, finishes off with a twist of tinsel, delivers this creation to the impatient customer.

Rabi, the box in his hands, is transported. He pictures the presentation to Janaki. He can imagine her gasping, *Maharaj-kumar, you remembered!*—falling perhaps at his feet.

The boy's pleasure is so patent that Bawajiraj forgets his vexation.

'Got what you wanted, Rabi?'

'Yes! Oh yes, thank you!'

Touch of fervency there the Maharajah doesn't quite like.

'I trust your Highness is entirely satisfied!' Traces of anguish in the hollow proprietor.

On the very threshold the anguish gets through to Bawajiraj. Neither he, nor members of his household for that matter, ever handles the stuff, but if his purse-bearer can be found. . . . The proprietor finds him. Bawajiraj instructs the man. But really, he feels, as the shekels are counted out, people—his son, the shop-keeper who is old enough to know better—are much too passionate about small things . . .

* * *

So they returned, the Maharajah and his party, the Resident and his, the Palace and the Residency slowly filling, reflating, buzzing with a rediscovered sense of purpose, windows thrown open, mango-leaf garlands over doorways, dust-sheets folded away, beeswax and turpentine smells, the floral tints of fresh-cut offerings in crystal, weather-vanes veering smoothly in freshly oiled sockets, the two flags flying serenely to announce re-occupation.

'I suppose,' says Sir Arthur calmly, as his flagstaff hoves into view, 'I suppose when I'm laid out they'll have it flying from the top-mast.'

It's these little things, he feels. Here one is, the whole disorderly country tidily united—God knows with what effort—under one flag, to all intents and purposes, and one admirable Government: the finest Civil Service, the most disciplined Army, a system of justice acknowledged far and wide to be second to none—yet Indians do have this knack of upsetting the applecart. They will insist on botching the detail. It's a national failing. One does not, of course, allow these trifles to defeat one. In India if one did one would soon be raving. But—Sir Arthur runs a finger round his collar—there's no gainsaying their monumental capacity to irk.

When, however, he sees his Sophie, siren and seraph combined, waiting for him, dimpled arms ready, at the top of the curved flight, all the trials that the country so liberally trundles out are forgotten. Barely touching the step let down for him, leaving the old guard standing, he is up the stairs at a nifty pace to meet the small figure that flies, blue ribbons streaming, down the marble. They come together halfway. He scoops her up, delicious little-girl fragrances wafted to him, soft how-could-you-leave-me limbs clinging and hugging, petal face pressed against his. Behind them, beaming, Ayah: her water-melon smile, all her teeth showing, stretching from lobe to lobe.

'Sophie Missie missing Sahib,' she sibilates without a slip, this tongue-twist expert.

'Sahib missing Sophie Missie,' says idiotic, light-headed Sir Arthur.

* * *

Rabi's homecoming was, to start with, similarly ecstatic. He had his beloved grandmother, his doves, his pony, the adored Arabian Tara, she of the soulful looks, his favoured Lakshmi back from her Delhi trip, all of them eager to welcome him. But the blaze they kindled was doused, if not altogether extinguished, when he found out, or rather could not uncover, what had happened to Janaki.

The worst part, he discovered, was not knowing. No one knew.

He suspected no one would tell him.

He confronted the head gardener. But the man, primed, had his statement ready.

'Just went away, Maharajkumar.'

Bedding out the plants, he had his hands full, this time of year, such a busy season, why should Maharajkumar imagine? And back to flower-beds, marigold and tiger-lily, training the bougainvillaea and the under-gardeners, his deft hands with the warts on the backs, even His Highness would not dare to sack skilled poison toad (for he had heard what she called him) whatever an uppity sweeper-girl might think.

So Rabi re-traced, back to the stables, back to the shrubbery where her aura was strong. It gave him clues.

None of them was material. He could not have told what led him, but there he was in the strange, soft landscape of the Residency gardens, waiting. While Lady Copeland strolled between the scented borders, in flowing foulard, a parasol casting its shade, lacy patterns on her cool forehead and a pair of spaniels, unperturbed by smell of boy-next-door, frisking at her feet. They gave him away, a friendly swoop on the laburnum behind which he stood, so still she might have passed him by, in a dream of opening the coffer to which she held the key.

Lady Copeland was not alarmed, though her heart thudded at this unusual invasion. She knew the boy, if only slightly. The child was not much older than her own. She continued to advance.

Neither was Rabi alarmed, although he was well aware this precinct to which the trail had led was out of bounds. He stood his ground.

Of the two, perhaps he was more in command. Lady Copeland had her ingrown malady to contend with: she could not get behind any pigment other than her own. It had so warped her that when she tried, as she did sometimes, what took shape was distorted in proportion, and only presented gargoyles and ghosts, or at any rate figments that bore only the most tenuous resemblance to reality.

Whereas Rabi saw the ruling class, to which this woman belonged, not merely in the light of his wayward education, but with the extraordinary illumination that the Durbar had vouchsafed. Clay obstinately refusing to transform its qualities remained clay, including what was incorporate in Mary Copeland.

He continued to watch her, although there was little to see; the fluorescence flowed internally until as she drew closer it was so palpable he had no need to ask. He knew she knew: but from some block in her the knowledge she bore could not be tapped, it could not be poured into language. Though he tried.

'Janaki, did she tell you . . . anything? When you saw her? Before she went away?'

And she too tried, touched, even at her distance, by the great distress emanating from the child.

'Janaki? A friend of yours? No, she said nothing to me because, you see, I don't think I ever met her, not to my knowledge.'

And certainly this was true, for the soggy bundle in the morning room had never presented to Lady Copeland a human, admissible face. It had merely taken its place in a long line of confusing and upsetting episodes.

Rabi went away. It was like a death. He had never experienced a death, but he had never been taught to suck either. It simply came to him that this was what it would be like. Because it was so awful he tried to remember what *they* did, from their encompassing experience, to get over it. He threw the marble in the lily-pond. He shoved the pointless purple, complete with lotus box, away out of sight in a disused woodshed. Copying *them* he made a straw doll, wrapped it in a white rag, and reduced the crude parcel to ashes.

Nothing worked. It continued awful. He didn't tell anyone, not even his tutor. They noticed he was growing up, and sometimes they commented on it. And Rabi got on, as he had to, with the business of living.

* * *

So, of course, did other people. Bawajiraj was engrossed in planning an addition to the Palace, complete with all modern conveniences like electric fans and water-closets, such as had piqued his interest in Delhi, in which he visualised possibilities. It would enable him, for instance, to invite, without misgivings such as might otherwise plague, a Governor or two, or possibly even the Viceroy . . . No such visit was impending. On the other hand palaces, or even a new wing to them, cannot be built in a day. The Maharajah believed in forward planning. He was also a man of erupting enthusiasms, and this one was backed by Sir Arthur.

Originally Bawajiraj's enthusiasm had run towards raising a company or two, or perhaps a battalion or two, or possibly even a regiment, to be drilled and trained to the peaks of excellence he had so admired at the Durbar. A State Force, in fact, to challenge (metaphorically speaking!) the British Indian Army. The very thought was exhilarating. In military matters, however, he was bound by treaty to seek the permission of the Resident. Sir Arthur, delighted at the prospect though he expressed himself to be, dwelt, a shade reproachfully, on his absolute confidence in the State Forces as presently constituted, under their Commander-in-Chief. Perhaps, if his Highness so desired, he would have a British sergeant-major drafted in to neaten up the edges, he had noticed a ragged end or two on the parade ground. But as for—no, he really felt it might well upset the morale of the fine existing corps.

Initially disappointed, Bawajiraj soon accepted the point of Sir Arthur's argument. But his roused vitality would not subside. He carried, after all, the blood of energetic ancestors. He felt, as he put it, bubbly. It got so out of hand there were times he could not sleep for bubbles. Worse, he developed a restless leg, an extraordinary and elusive sensation that got him up and made him pace, often at the most inconvenient moments. He connected these miseries with sex. Shanta Devi was not available— some handy woman's disorder. And Mohini—if he could spill over into her whenever he wanted, he thought wistfully, all would be well. But there were difficulties. Sometimes her appetite was insatiable, even downright embarrassing (that morning in Delhi, in their tent, in the very heart of the Durbar Camp!) but sometimes she simply would not allow him, in her thoroughly selfish fashion, unless she wanted it too. Even more annoying she attempted to shift the blame.

'It's nothing to do with sex. You get plenty of greens,' baldly states this coarse woman. 'It's your *mind* that needs something to do with itself.'

He did not give it a second thought. He, with the whole of Devapur on his shoulders? But by then, battalions having been slaughtered, the new additions to the Palace were jostling to the fore. Bubbles continued to course as he pored over plans and catalogues of plumbers' fittings, but in a curious way they were invigorating now, and even his restless leg subsided.

Leaving the Maharajah to his frivolities, Tirumal Rao pursued his own interests. He was a poet and scholar of some distinction (and broadminded with it: Persian as well as Sanskrit), who could hold his own, and enjoyed so doing, with those carefully groomed and cultivated brahminical minds that administered a good many Indian States. His home, pleasingly set in a sufficiency of acres, and aptly named Dilkusha, was in its way as much an enclave as the Residency. Here, within the hospitable walls of his Heart's Delight, it was the Dewan's pleasure to welcome visiting pandits, gurus, poets, and ministers, with whom exchanges of some wit, some erudition, and much mutual understanding were possible.

Whereas in Devapur he had to contend with ignorance and illiteracy of truly stunning proportions: citizens who had to be reminded of their civic duties by means of town crier, peasants who could not read so much as a tax demand. It was, need one say, a frightful administrative inconvenience; but over and above that it offended a root-belief in him that equated the discipline of education with the dignity of a people. Quite frankly, as the Dewan often told his wife, he thought the illiterate masses a disgrace to themselves.

His revolutionary proposal was compulsory mass education up to the age of ten.

In actuality it was a handed-down plan. The old Dewan, Narasimha Rao, in the early days, long before he shoved off for his *ashram*, had inherited the dream of an educated proletariat. Not the kind the British had their sights on, by means of which clerks and petty officials would emerge by the thousand to man their administration. He dreamed, rather, of a sound, rounded discipline, rooted in the country to start with, its history, geography, geology, poetry, religion and mythology, which would burgeon to take in the rest of the world. But the time was not ripe. No one was ready for it, least of all the people; and his own kind, who would after all have to be the educators, were also dreadful hoarders, chary of disseminating their treasure too widely. And, of course, there was no money . . .

The old Dewan did not fret. If not in his time, there was his son, and after him, *his* son . . . the generations stretched serenely into the future, a long line beaded with Narasimha Raos under a variety of names. He took care, however, to burnish his plan and pass it on, together with his blessing and hopes.

Tirumal Rao, of course, had to make-do with what was in hand. The old Dewan's expansive notions, he accepted from the start, would have to be severely trimmed: mythology and geology would certainly have to be jettisoned; but what remained did at least ensure reading, writing, and arithmetic.

Even so the Dewan was ahead of his times, which thought it entirely proper that the lower orders should not open a book. It did not deflect him from his efforts. He had an instinct, a feeling of softness at the centre which convinced him that given a fair battering the walls would be down. It was the kind of battle which Tirumal Rao both enjoyed and excelled at, a creative exercise from which he derived the most prized, the most satisfactory essences of his office.

At home his life, if not heady, was harmonious. After some alarms his wife had been safely delivered of a child, their sixth, a little girl with inky eyes and wrinkled red skin that both parents devoutly hoped would fade to their own cherished ivory. As it did, long before the naming ceremony, while an initial trepidation, based on their last experience, was stilled by considerable evidence of a sunny disposition in this latest addition to the family.

They called her Usha: a pretty babe, much in demand for holding, a sweet-tempered child who endured with grace being passed from hand to hand. Children who had flocked to fuss over the last baby (Shanta Devi's) in the sprawling Palace now converged on Vatsala with their entreaties, usually not in vain. For by now she was a relaxed woman, who did not imagine the baby would fall to pieces. Indeed, in the midst of her busy life she was conscious of tranquillity seeping in, oases of stillness when she placed the infant in the arms of an older child, and saw tenderness transforming already tender features. Especially Rabi, she noticed. His forlorn air, whatever had pinched his face and made him walk like a ghost (she had never been able to discover what) lifted like a grey and obscuring curtain when he held her infant.

'Like babies, Rabi?'

'Yes.'

Rocking the warm bundle, arms full, inexpressibly moved by half-moon fringes resting on small, rounded, defenceless cheeks, the resolve to leave home in quest of his missing partner slowly began to falter. Though where the resolution actually fell down was that he did not know how to implement it. The seamy acres beyond the Palace estates, into which Janaki had boldly plunged, were as dense to him, as barely negotiable, as they were to the Maharajah.

The Resident came to call, in a wary way, when the baby was a month old. The invitation to do so had been as warily given by the mellowing Minister, and flew in the face of Vatsala's determination not to allow the impure one to cross her threshold. Perhaps he felt it. Treading as gingerly as if he were a trainee fire-walker, Sir Arthur, in his stockinged feet, entered the Tirumal Rao portals. He inspected the infant. He was not very good on scraps of humanity—his own two had had to wait six months apiece for recognition—but he courteously declared, and even perceived, the little girl to be charming. He had brought with him, selected by himself, a yellow teddy bear, which he carefully placed in the swing-cot beside one curled fist.

His goodwill was so transparent that Vatsala was surprised into almost welcoming his presence—at least a little warmth crept into the correct manner in which she was performing her duties as hostess.

It did not prevent her, later, from sending the silver cup, from which Sir Arthur had imbibed some revolting cordial (his lips touching the rim, Vatsala shuddered to see), to the silversmith's for melting down—a purification by fire that her husband thought extreme, particularly when the silversmith's bill for re-casting into another silver goblet arrived on his desk.

Sir Arthur was also surprised. His impression of the Minister's wife, formed during brushes at formal functions, abetted by some muffled instincts, was of a dour woman impervious to European overtures even at the shallowest, most innocuous social level. Whereas within the confines of her own home she turned out to be hospitable and even—yes, there had been distinct flashes—friendly. Walking away from the house— without a beat of drum, only one peon in attendance to stress the informality of the visit—Sir Arthur flirted, rather wistfully, with the notion of asking them back. But—the scent of the tuberoses that Vatsala affected strong in his nostrils, the rose-water with which the children had pelted him still freckling his jacket—he conceded his wife would never countenance such a move. A passing whim on his part which, perhaps rightly, she would not dream of indulging.

Nor did the Dewan think he would repeat the experiment, which had been somewhat fraught for him—a disagreeable and unusual experience for the assured Tirumal Rao. True, Vatsala had behaved impeccably, but equally easily she could have turned sour. It was much too volatile a situation for comfort.

The Minister and the Resident shared this in common: they suspected that but for the women they might have been friends, or at any rate reached the foothills, even if the peaks of friendship could not be attained within the imperial situation. But they did not go into it; did not reflect that none but men of gifts would have reached their present eminence: that, given their power, their highly developed diplomatic skills, it was not beyond their wit to devise and insist upon a less arid *modus vivendi*. It was simply that each found it easier, at best, to spare himself the battle and, at worst, to shuffle off the blame. They blamed the women.

* * *

Excitement in the Brahmin camp was followed by ferment in the British quarter. It was of an agreeable nature. Sophie was four. There was to be a birthday party at the Residency. Twenty-five children were invited, a total of well over fifty persons, including nannies, ayahs, and a *syce* or two for those who proposed to arrive on their ponies. The kitchens, never letting an opportunity slip, assembled a cake that would have been extravagant for a hundred people. The band (the Maharajah's Own, by courtesy of His Highness) practised nursery rhymes for musical chairs. And Sophie tried on, and looked adorable in, her frilled white organdie frock, with her new shoes of white glaće kid, and a blue sash in the approximate region of her waist.

The twenty-five invitees to her birthday party included, for the first time, two children from the Palace: Rabi and Bharathi, one of his half-sisters nearest in age to Sophie.

The origin of these invitations went back to the Durbar where views had been floated, no more. No directive, no statement of intent or policy; merely these balloons enquiring whether in a changing climate it might not be thought desirable to forge closer links . . . ? Not that anything was wrong with the climate referred to. It was said to be altering, that was all.

Sir Arthur needed no enlightening dirigibles. He was coming round to it himself. The distance between them being what it was he could not hear what the populace said; but he certainly invariably listened to the intelligence his scouts brought him, which had included a report of the disappointment of the people that the Viceroy had not announced, in his Durbar speech, a cut in their taxes. Of course this was in distant Delhi. There were certain differences between the subjects of the King-Emperor and the subjects of a Native Ruler; but disaffection did have an unhappy way of spreading, with or without just cause, from British India to the Native States. Sir Arthur wanted none of that. He hoped to avert it by closer ties with the Ruler, for he imagined that Bawajiraj, the subject of a forced weaning, through some racial affinity continued to enjoy the close confidence of his people.

Sir Arthur saw the party as a start in the desired direction. He hoped it would go better than the last effort he had made, which Bawajiraj had so enjoyed, which still made him, Arthur Copeland, wince. He also felt, obscurely, that it would be easier for his wife to begin with children, and two princelings at that . . . he had in any case quite a liking for Waji's sturdy son.

Lady Copeland, compelled in a manner of speaking, complied. She did it without pleasure, but also without rancour, dutifully stifling the sibylline voices that screeched within her so dreadfully at moments like these. There was, besides, the boy: the disturbing image of a stricken human at close quarters that, standing quite firm, he had compelled her to face. There were times when Lady Copeland distinctly felt herself molested, although it could also have been those apparitions from the past that took a beating.

Rabi declined the invitation. He did not give any reason. There was no need to anyway. There were two lines in bold print on the return portion of the card. One read: *I shall be delighted to come to your party*; the other: *I am sorry I cannot come to your party*. He crossed out the first line neatly and sent it back by the same *chaprassi* who had brought it without thinking about it twice. It was the unvarnished truth. There could be no delight for him where Lady Copeland was. It wasn't that he found her hateful, or unpleasant, or even remote. It was her presence, the thought of it, that made him feel he was suffocating, as if residues of terror and fright and helplessness had created a plangent field about her that he could sense: although of course it was not his experience but another's, and even of this he had no material evidence.

He was not sorry when it was done. Though he did admire the invitation card, which had a delightful design of kittens on the front, and a tiny gold pencil with a flossy tassel dangling on a pink silk cord from the spine.

Bawajiraj was devastated, doubly so as Bharathi flatly refused to go without her brother. He felt as stricken as if the summons had come to him and he had declined. He could not believe it of his only son, although past episodes were pressing belief on him. And when he tackled the boy Rabi simply took refuge in illness which, possibly, his psyche had been incubating since the shocks administered in Delhi.

Though the form it took was robust enough. What was diagnosed as influenza turned incontrovertibly into chicken pox.

He was covered in vesicles, body and face right up to the eyebrows. They put cotton mittens on his hands to stop him scratching and scarring himself for life. The storey above the Pearl Suite was cleared of the faded accumulation of Bawajiraj's and his tutor's fancies and manias: a vaulting horse, a rusty suit of armour, an unwieldy throne with a cobra canopy, a grand piano, a chintz-covered suite imported from Maple's, several javelins, several dumb-bells, an enormous carved wooden elephant whose stomach flapped open to reveal an outsize and markedly martial chess-set, and an assortment of wardrobes, trunks, camp stools, shooting-sticks, and military chests.

Here Rabi lay, hating the scrubbed emptiness that smelt of Lysol and carbolic, attacking with gauze clubs the blisters that swelled and filled and were at their most maddening as they dried out under scabs.

Mohini, anxious and tender, sat with him, indulging his cravings with foods that the doctor forbade like rose-petal hulva and breadfruit fries, quarrelling with Bawajiraj who was something of a stickler.

'Why shouldn't I give him what he likes to eat?'

'You know what the doctor said.'

'Dr. Hakim-quack said *congee* and whey. Would you like to live on *congee* and whey?'

'I'm not ill, am I?'

'That's just it! You can't imagine what it's like to be ill. Imagination's never been your strong suit.'

'I can imagine. I've *had* chicken pox.'

'Then you've forgotten what it's like. Nobody remembers horrible things unless they're silly, do they? Besides you know what doctors are.'

'What are they?' Bawajiraj, glutton for punishment, rises to it.

'They're sharks.'

'Not at all. Men of compassion.'

'You must be *addled*. Have you looked at the gutters lately? People lying and *dying* in them—'

'Is it my job to look at gutters?'

'—and *you* could lie and die and not *one* man of compassion, only you have these lashings to pay fat bills!'

'Mohini, you must not—'

'Why not? They're almost as rapacious as the British and that's saying something.'

'You really must not make these absurd statements.'

'And if you want to know, it *is* your job to look in gutters.'

'On my tours of duty—'

'You see nothing!'

'I'm not blind!'

'There's nothing to see, it's a complete whitewash.'

'I'm not that easily hoodwinked, you know.'

'You are! You're a complete ninny.'

No, no one in the kingdom. Bawajiraj fuming but restrained. Great restraint there, product of discipline and training. No point, however, in arguing with an overwrought woman.

He was, besides, a busy father. Three of his daughters had contracted chicken pox, and he had to spread his free time among them. Whereas Mohini had only one child to contend with, giving her the freedom to engage in this kind of acrimony. He actually thought of saying this, but by now he was out of the sickroom.

Marching along stark carbolic corridors Bawajiraj had the obscure sensation that he was strung between two poles, a position which made him helpless. He considered it bad form to engage in fishwife tactics, a debating art in which those near and dear to him were accomplished, while at the same time he had never quite mastered the dry subtleties of his English friends. Marching along aggrieved, his mood was not improved by encountering his mother, trailing down the corridor in her widow's weeds, carrying a suspicious basket. He could not actually tear off the lid, but he did ask pointedly. She answered equably.

'Something for Rabi to chew on.'

'Nothing unsuitable I *hope*.'

'Not at all. Sugarcane. He loves it.'

'But is it *good* for him?'

'My dear boy, of course it is. Sugarcane is *excellent* for chicken pox.'

Sweeping past, leaving him standing, suspecting and distrusting these folk remedies, which his subjects were resorting to on all sides.

For the chicken pox had spread. Half the children around were smitten—flushed spotty victims in the Tirumal Rao mansion, in the cantonment bungalows, in the servants' quarters, in the settlements around the Palace, in the carpenter's, the farrier's, the coppersmith's, the bakery—an unnatural silence fell as if someone had succeeded in decimating the crow population.

The Residency pair escaped. Lady Copeland saw it as providential that the Maharajah's two hadn't come to the party. Sir Arthur wouldn't go so far, but he admitted it had been a narrow shave. The thought of scars on young Sophie, even those of chicken pox, made him sick to the pit of his stomach. When it was smallpox—flaring in the bazaar districts, distant but never distant enough from the Residency—it was a waking nightmare, one of many one endured out here. At times like these he longed for his children to be safely at home in England, but this thought was equally nightmarish. During these periods of stress Sir Arthur felt most acutely the burden he bore, dwelt on the sacrifices he made, and speculated querulously whether the country was even aware, let alone grateful. He was not, however, by nature a querulous or even an introspective man, and for most of the time scarcely gave these matters a second thought.

Presently it was over. Rabi emerged, pallid and strained but largely unscarred, a pock or two under one eyebrow, a cluster about one shoulder—nothing to speak of. Unlike some of the children, in particular Das the labourer's son, whose entire face was pitted. Das said he did not mind. He was cleaning out the lily-pond prior to re-stocking and he sat back on his heels and looking up at Rabi who was watching told him labourers' sons' faces were of no account. His eyes were level as he spoke, but Rabi had a wretched feeling, a tang of aloes in his dried-up mouth. He wanted to ask why they hadn't wrapped his itching fingers in gauze, which he had been told prevented scarring, but he did not. He found there were a good many questions one could not ask; he saw it as a side-effect of growing up.

Growing up. What did it mean? What was the essence of this phrase so often on the lips of grown-ups? What did it hold within itself for him—me—I—Rabindranath—Rabi, the nouns and pronouns that slid into each other so mysteriously, and if he kept on long enough left him suspended, a particle of blue air, a part of the bright blue expanse of sky itself? Lying on his back in the coarse grass, filtering the sun through the livid membranes between his outspread fingers, Rabi journeyed back and forth in time and space, times and places remembered, times and places of the future shaping beyond the horizon but already sending out light, a distant glimmer that reached him, brought him trembling to the very brink of recognition.

'What will I be when I grow up, Panditji?'

The Pandit looking up, perceiving umber shades, himself a preoccupied man but hauling out to answer the appeal that was plainly unconnected with kingdoms and thrones.

'You will be yourself, I hope, Rabi.'

'I don't know what I am. What myself is.'

'Don't worry at it, Rabi. It'll come to you, as much as it ever comes. Things have a way of working themselves out, you know.'

'Always?'

'Eventually, yes.'

'That could take a long time.'

'It could take a short time just as easily.'

Turning it over in his mind Rabi found this basically acceptable. And from it rose a shoot, which perhaps had been his furtive object: a wry tendril of hope that it could apply to other matters, that what seemed endless could well have an end in sight.

* * *

Spring went by. The grass began to frizzle. The peacocks grew jaded, stumped around trailing their finery and allowed themselves to be captured by children rather than run for it. No silvery floods, either, to send them flying. Water was too precious to drench the canna beds. It came up in water-carts, in convoy, and was dribbled in soberly, from a kerosene tin, over three fingers of the gardeners' hands.

Copiously watered, lavish with the precious fluid that would sell by the glass to the populace before the season was done, the Residency lawns stayed green the longest. The limpid green vistas that here flowed incomparably were, possibly, no less vital to the inhabitants: a spiritual essential for souls in exile from their rightful vales, who in less blessed havens quailed before advancing deserts. Even so the sun won. Or perhaps it was the wind, passed before an open furnace, that browned the tips of those delicate blades for all that the bulbs were embedded in moist and enriched loam.

Lady Copeland was in retreat long before these first assaults upon the system. The Simla trunks were brought down and opened, her tweeds and cashmeres aired, the children measured for warm clothes, the gardeners issued with instructions to carry on during her absence, and the dog-keepers made to recite their duties towards the older dogs who would not be travelling.

When the smells of lavender and camphor and Keatings powder (fleas in the Simla blankets: no one knew how they survived from season to season, the lethal dusting that was their lot at each beginning and end), when this particular melange drifted up to him, Sir Arthur knew it was time to raise bulwarks. Which he did. Immersed in his darkened den, sending the peon to shout at the *punkah-wallah*, who was supposed to keep the infernal air circulating (those ridiculous petticoats strung from the ceiling worse than useless unless the sloth in a turban, whose sole job it was, pulled the ropes that swished them), he did his best to forget the annual exodus. And when it was over he began briskly counting the days to his own departure, now and then giving himself up to dreams, delightful intaglios in which he was riding down a mountain path to their summer abode, nestling between pines, log fires blazing behind gleaming fenders, where Mary and Sophie and Esmond would be awaiting him for tea.

These glowing enamels that his imagination, not really his strong point, somehow fired for him sustained Sir Arthur through the annual separations. Without giving it a great deal of thought—he did not believe in introspection, loathed the ruminant look, like one of his sacred cows, it gave rise to in the otherwise sensible Minister—he nevertheless suspected that, were he to be deprived of them, his life would verge on the insupportable.

No such sustenance was available for Rabi. Janaki had been sent away for good, that much he knew. He accepted that at his age he could not overcome the powerful grown-up fiat. No pleasing intaglios for him, though he did put up some defences. Avoiding the shrubbery he went directly to the stables, allowing the soft snuffling of horses to absorb other sounds, dodging the glossy looks of leaves, which were, in fact, meagre and dusty, left to survive, as they would, on niggardly dollops of water. He thought he was being crafty, but when the hot winds blew they scattered the mango blossom, starry scented flowers under his feet along the paths he trod.

'It's the worst time of year, Maharajkumar! You can't sweep them up off the gravel, you have to pick them up one by one, it takes all day I can tell you.'

Her voice as clear as if she were there in front of him, U-shape human picking up errant blossom, face tilted up at an acute angle to address him from somewhere around earth level, strands of mud-coloured hair streaming back to touch ground. Then he knew he was beaten. Crouching down he buried his face in his hands and wept, the tears washing over the sharp cameo that had been so swiftly and brutally engraved and thrust at him to keep.

7

But in time there was a reversal. The cutting edge of Rabi's cameo was trimmed, grew as smooth and buffed as a pebble so that in due course he wore it without injury, while the enamels on which Sir Arthur relied yielding up their assuaging powers became positively malign. Sometimes the flares that shot from these glowing surfaces all but excoriated him. Because he could not bear to look, he did not, not often. But with or without his complicity time raced, contracted, began to run out. It was forced in on him that days in the hills were coming to an end. That is to say with Sophie, who was growing up and would be going home.

His dimpled infant, not quite seven, leaving him?

The note of incredulous anguish echoed in Lady Copeland, but independently. They could not afford to chime together, these two, for fear of producing in unison some freakish, mighty orchestration of sound that would fell them both.

They talked about ponies instead.

'Shall Esmond have Star?'

'Bit young, don't you think?'

'I do. But who—?'

'H. H., perhaps.'

Mary Copeland dubious, looking for a Good Home, a European home by definition excellent, an Indian home definitely suspect, but what category a Prince's stables?

Into this area of uncertainty burst the effusive Bawajiraj, brimful of friendly offers.

'Are you sure, Waji? You're not just doing it for my sake?'

Sir Arthur uncomfortable, a phrase beloved of the Minister at his most sardonic whipping through his mind: *Your wish, Excellency, is my command.*

'Absolutely sure, my dear H.E. Just perfect for Bharathi.'

'For whom?'

'My third girl. Same age as your Sophie. Positively built for her.'

'Too kind, your Highness.' Lady Copeland murmuring, wondering about this Bharathi, would she mangle gentle Star's mouth?

And Bawajiraj, whose horses were as dear to him, almost, as his children, understanding fully and complimenting her ladyship on her natural anxiety, assuring her, plump hand on earnest heart, that Star would be one of the family.

So Star's future was settled, in good time, much as Sophie's had been, although her future had been charted, with the merest genuflections to the zodiac, long before her birth. Then it was only a question of waiting.

Waiting and watching. The menials noticed that of late Sahib could hardly take his eyes off his daughter. Only natural, they said, clucking sympathetically in the servants' *godowns.* It was the other impending act that struck chill, although about this they were less vocal. Sahibs had their ways, and who were they to criticise even if it seemed unnatural to them? But this they would say: Sophie Missie's mournful Ayah, plug of *bhang* lodged in one cheek, slow juices trickling to temper the misery of impending deprivation, possibly the loss of job, certainly relegation below Esmond Baba's Ayah, said it for them:

'Not if I were starving! No, even then I would cleave to my flesh!'

And closed her lips, a thin black line, over tombstone teeth, over the rank criticism that had been uttered, the first she had permitted herself in a lifetime of service.

Unlocking them, however, now and again, to pick at the mystery.

'What *for?* Don't they have everything, here in this very place, that heart can desire? But always they are sent away, always.'

Sir Arthur could have told her, despite some flames that licked at its validity, the plain reason, which was to do with the superiority of Sophie's race, jumbled up in his mind with the inferior quality of Indian schools. But he was a preoccupied man, moving through a landscape which had detached itself from him, or from which he had excommunicated himself. At least there were few connections he could detect.

Mooning in the garden one morning instead of attending to dispatches, especially the one the Minister had lobbed at him thick with proposals for educating other people's children, Sir Arthur discovered that Sophie and Rabi were acquainted. More than acquainted, to judge from the manner in which they were conducting some joint enterprise: the two heads touching, cosy breathless murmurs of shared experience rising above the clump of something or other—Sir Arthur left the botanical detail to his wife—in which the rest of them was buried. A similar cosy murmur, a maternal sound between a throb and a twitter, rose from the tangle of greenery. And a third, so frail he could not hear it if he breathed. Sir Arthur gave up breathing, such was the example of the children, to listen to it: a tap, and a scratching, and the great panting stillness of some weak creature working itself up to deliver the next assault.

An egg, Sir Arthur divined, about to hatch. One of a clutch, perilously cupped in a straggling nest cobbled together by some inept apprentice. The mother-bird, smug in a jumble of fluff and severed stalks, throbbing, cooing to the muffled captive within the chalky oval. The two children transfixed, caught in the framework of a common event. Or so Sir Arthur believed until, surprisingly, he found himself in the same state, hooked on to that charmed lattice as firmly as they, and waiting for life to crack its shell.

Chip-chik. Chip-chik. Miniscule pick at work, egg tooth chipping at white cliff.

'*Chir . . . ee . . . eep!*' Encouragement for the chipper.

'Mm . . . mmm!' From the captivated children as a network of cracks spreads over the chalk surface.

'Ah . . . h . . . h!' Sir Arthur unable to resist an accolade as inmate emerges, soft down plastered, muzzy eye blinking at first overwhelming glimpse of the world.

It could have been a communion that joined the four of them, sanctified by the sudden, shrill, jubilant *Che . . . eep!* of the fledgling.

'It's *lovely.*' Sophie's hushed treble.

'Mmm.'

'Shall I touch?'

'Better not.'

'I wish I could.'

'So do I. We'll come tomorrow.'

The children wriggled out of their hide. Still whispering, still linked by what they had seen, but out in the open. At this point Sir Arthur should have stepped out of cover. He meant to, certainly, but was arrested by what he saw, an illuminated picture of boy and girl. Both of them burning candles under tender skins. Glowing. Sir Arthur had a confused impression of beholding a shining whole, of which each part split could have been perfect, but in sum ascended to a wild excess: alabaster warmed and pointed up by gold, gold smouldering before those pure milky tones. A photographic image, positive to negative, it occurred to him, or a contiguity of two hemispheres. It was so unbearable, or so shattering, that this time he did come out from behind the climbing roses.

Although, in fact, they were merely holding hands, and continued this link.

'Bird-watching, were you?' Sir Arthur, dousing a flame or two, enquired mildly, although something had begun clacking inside him, the severe lips of some old gossip busily working.

'We saw it born. The baby bird. Oh Papa, you should have *seen . . .*'

His grave, translucent child, raving, clinging to this dizzy companion, bright shreds of a shared wonder thrown over the pair like a caul. Sir Arthur could have raged, had he been a lesser man. Instead he enquired:

'First time you've seen an egg hatch, Sophie?' (Having to ask! Perhaps he didn't spend enough time with his children?)

'Oh no, Papa. Twice here, and twice in Rabi's garden.'

'Really?'

Where had he been these years, not to know? About such things, about the commerce between gardens? Lulled, could it be, by the acreage between two enclaves? Though forest fires, contemptuous of man-made firebreaks, are known to leap impossible distances.

'And Rabi's found another nest.' Wide-eyed, informative Sophie. 'He's good at finding them, much better than me.'

'Ah, Rabi.' Turning to the boy, resolved to be affable, succeeding without difficulty. 'One of your hobbies?'

'Yes, sir. I like bird-watching.'

'So did I, at your age.' Continuing genial, no effort at all, now. 'Seem to remember I had a collection of birds' eggs. Before I had any sense, you know.'

He even twinkled at the boy, though he seemed to be, it did appear to him, retreating. As indeed Rabi was: in retreat less from the man than from the inflictions of the situation. Something was chafing: perhaps the invisible ropes of enclave, rubbing up disagreeably against sensitive skin. So he dropped

Sophie's hand and stood, awkwardly waiting for the getaway route to be indicated, as grown-ups knew how.

Certainly Sir Arthur knew; he dealt with innumerable such situations daily. But he could not bring himself. What he wanted to do, instead, darted uncontrollably into a picture in which he was gummed in the middle, grinning idiotically into the middle distance, with a smiling child on either hand.

A pure and innocent and totally unreal collage, he admitted, made out of shells and everlasting flowers, without a departure, or a parting, or a farewell, the whole dreadful packet, in fact, that lay in wait for him.

Though it was, when it came, really quite simple.

They drove to the station in a landau with Sophie between them and Star trotting behind, too loved to be left out of the finale. Sir Arthur returned alone, except for Star, who had behaved impeccably, a curtsey as the train steamed out, fine head dipped, a foreleg in graceful retreat, as Sophie herself had taught him. Sophie gone home to her Shropshire aunt. Star to become one of the Maharajah's family. It was as satisfactory as could be contrived in the circumstances.

* * *

Birds-nesting grew dull after that. You found it needed two, really, to kindle up. You missed sharing. You missed the adoration.

'Look what I've found, Sophie. Up here.'

'Oh Rabi, you are clever spotting that one!'

From being someone whom he would see, any moment now, skipping down the path towards him, she became with increasing acceptance a relic of the past. Receding daily, while the foreshore sprouted, grew dense with present preoccupations. When he looked back it was with a sense of perspective. He could see himself, a good head taller, humouring a small girl who had chosen to look up to him. As, it came to him, Janaki had done, submitting to him, older girl humouring the little boy that he had been.

Sophie's outline fuzzed, while Janaki's retained the utmost clarity. He had not the slightest difficulty recalling the exact shade of her skin, the angle of her tilted head, the bony deltas revealed to him. But then she went back as far as he could remember, broom-stick girl woven in and out of his doings—outdoors, that is, she had been an outdoors servant. Whereas Sophie—fuzzy golden Sophie—was a matter of months, fitful butterfly from an enchanted garden, centrepiece of birthday parties he had never attended (in fact he had only been asked that once), which stuck in his mind only because of the cascade of balloons released annually from the Residency terraces.

Both, vanished, had nevertheless left behind buoys, he discovered, to which he was anchored however far he ranged: those bright cascades that bobbed up in his mind, followed by the first frail spattering of early mango blossom.

But the flowers were palpable.

It was a visible fall, which could dry him up even now, he knew, if he allowed it to. He would not. Only sometimes when the fierce winds blew bringing down those heavy creamy drifts it was too strong for him.

Despite the foreshore. In spite of the years.

He stood there buffeted, the sharp grains of driven sand stinging his exposed skin, and became aware of another creature, as desiccated as himself, rattling in the wind beside him. A husk of a man, so dry it could have been a skeleton, except that it was on its feet.

'Ah Rabi,' the skeleton said, resolving itself into Sir Arthur. So pared away, though, it seemed a wonder the man could cast a shadow, as he undoubtedly did, an elongated shade lay half on the gravel, half across the back of the beast on whose saddle his freckled hand rested.

One of a pair, this Mongolian beast, planted one each side of the marble flight down which flew Sophie, blue ribbons streaming. Beast much favoured by Beauty, on its back in a jiffy, rising to a trot, working up to a gallop on gunmetal. Extraordinary. Only a child would punish with such verve its own tender bottom. Or was it insensitive? He would have liked to ask, but the rider had vanished, leaving him, and the beasts, to inherit the arid landscape. And one other, formed out of the same desert, so close to what he was that he felt he was talking to his split self.

'Sophie, you know . . .' He croaked, his throat parched by the terrible westerly.

'I know,' the dusty figure answered.

Then they simply stood, lashed by the gritty blasts, these two shattered human beings. Until Sir Arthur felt some urge to continue.

'It's Sophie, you know,' he said simply. 'I quite miss her. Sometimes I miss her quite extraordinarily.'

'I know.'

'Even now. Extraordinary isn't it? Sometimes I wonder if one ever gets over it . . . what do you think?'

'I don't know. I don't think so.'

'No. Neither do I. But then, you see, she was always with me. From quite a tiny baby, you know. It makes a difference, don't you think?'

'I can imagine.'

'Can you. I wonder. Though I daresay,' he acknowledged, though he would not ask, 'you have had your losses, whatever those may be.'

And peered to see, through those damnable flurries, while it slowly dawned that the distressed human he had assumed to be and addressed as a man was a child of eleven or twelve. So that he pulled himself together, rounding out into the shapes and syllables proper to a man of his station.

'I am afraid, my dear boy, you must think—' he began.

But Rabi was gone. He, too, was afraid, in a manner that went beyond idiom; some instinct warning, even at his age, against thoughts and revelations both would come to regret.

* * *

That was a bad year. Gusty winds swept the countryside, picking up heat and sand from the deserts they crossed, slapping it in the faces of the affronted citizenry who peered with reddened eyes, sandy eyelashed, at their puny crops, ready as ever to give up the ghost. When the winds died the sun glared down unchecked, out of a cloudless sky, so that a man could barely shoulder his hoe. Staggered off nonetheless, down to the fields to deal with the weeds, wild oats that, need one say, sprouted regardless. Especially the couch-grass, as sprightly as if watered daily by sprinklers such as could be seen, by those few privileged, or owning inordinately tall houses, working overtime in the Residency grounds. Water was the thing. The pensive Dewan, at his palatial desk (crafted and enthusiastically embellished by the Palace master carver), felt by no means for the first time that he would gladly have traded the Permanent Garrison for just one sound, well-built dam. Though he could see they were a fine body of men. As he did, gloomily, through the open window: sweaty stalwarts strutting in the heat like turkeycocks, their boots striking sparks off the cobbles of the distant quadrangle.

But efficient, he had to admit. Drilling in the sun long after the State Forces had legged it to the barracks. Of course the C.O. and Resident ensured they kept at it, in case of marauders. An elusive species, in the Dewan's view. Not once, in his tenure of office, had one such shown up. But undoubtedly the British believed in their existence. Or at least, since marauders were conspicuously absent, they had cast the people in this sinister role. A paranoid suspicion of the people. The Dewan did not object to paranoia. He did rather begrudge the hefty annual sums it cost the State. He also considered it extreme to pick on the people (the *people*, for God's sake) of whom a feeble procession, citizens and peasantry, trooped through his jeering mind.

'Scorcher, eh Minister?'

'Terrible, Highness. And little to mitigate the effects.'

The dry Minister eyeing the perspiring Maharajah. Maharajah eyeing back, daring him to go on. The Minister not without daring, but reluctant to bark his knuckles without some slim hope of a win. Echoes of an old encounter stinging both pairs of ears.

'Highness, if I might venture to suggest a cut in the British subsidiary forces—'

'Renege on my treaty obligations? Is that what you're suggesting? I would rather cut off my right hand!'

Would too, the Minister imagined: every bit as stupid. So should he present the reverse picture, enquire of the Maharajah would the British hack off their limbs rather than tear up a piece of paper?

He framed it differently.

'Ancient treaties, your Highness, are not treated as immutable in modern times by either party.'

'Ancient! Modern! What has that to do with it? It's my *izzat**
that's at stake! My *izzat*, Minister!'

The Maharajah's *izzat* intact while the country, depressed, slid into drought.

The town crier was despatched (the Dewan's education policy had yet to bear fruit) to proclaim it. He stood in the main square, named after the Maharajah, and beat his drum to summon the

*Honour, dignity.

204

citizens. They came—one never knew, it could be important. He told them, brave man, not to waste water. His listeners could have lynched him, only they lacked the energy. The country had worn them out.

Heat, drought, flies, taxes—they entertained each other with this recital.

The Maharajah shared their trials. He sighed, and told how sunshine and rain fell on rich man and poor alike. Mohini, detecting, she assumed, some biblical strains here, and tracking them easily, besought him to be less fatuous.

'No need to copy that silly tutor they say you had.'

'Who says?'

'Your mother. Lots of people.'

'Not silly. Most carefully selected. I revere his memory.'

But he did change tack, or at least the wording. He told all who would listen—many had to—that a Maharajah could not escape what Nature inflicted on his subjects.

He believed it was true.

Perhaps it was, to some extent. The penetrating quality of the dust was an imposition as much on the Palace as on humbler homesteads. It got into everything—food, hair, the waistbands of trousers. Bawajiraj's bare toes curled when, after a cold tub, he thrust his refreshed feet into the gritty depths of his slippers. He longed to flee, but where? He had no summer abode, only the Summer Palace. It would not do, not being elevated at all, only a miserable few hundred feet above sea level.

However, for some time now he had toyed with thoughts of Simla. Quite a few of his Maharajah friends—he had stayed with a couple—maintained establishments in this queen of hill stations. Pine-scented peaks. Air like iced sherbet. Slippers with slithery soles. A cosy little palace tucked away in the middle of all these delights, to which he could retreat as Sir Arthur did. Yet Sir Arthur himself, appealed to for advice, had murmured about cost. One agreed absolutely of course. One scaled things down a bit and, sure enough, Sir Arthur had written this summer from Simla, promising to keep an eye open. It encouraged Bawajiraj to go ahead—an Englishman's hint as good as anyone else's accomplished deed—with the outlines. Sketches of his requirements—drawn surreptitiously by himself; he didn't want the parsimonious Brahmin getting wind of what he was after—were already in Sir Arthur's hands. By next season, at the latest, he could see himself ensconced. Log fires. A spot of hunting. A drink at the Club as Sir Arthur's guest. It was the very stuff of dreams.

Meanwhile there was the season to be endured. Bawajiraj endured it, noticeably gritting his teeth in the darkened Palace. All day long the blinds were down, the heavy *khus-khus* grass screens watered by relays of Palace servants.

Soon after dawn the ice arrived, huge blocks hacked from the mountain buried in the underground ice-house, hosed down first to clear their sawdust coating. Coolies carried them in, floated the glittering slabs in the porphyry basin of the fountains that still played in the inner courtyard, overlooked both by the Pearl Suite and the West wing that accommodated the Maharajah. The icebergs smouldered, sending up life-saving airs that enticed the embattled Bawajiraj onto the overhanging balconies where, leaning on the delicate traceries, he could feel himself briefly revived. But icebergs could not win over the season. By midday they were spent, miserable slivers that tumbled about under the spray. At that clanging hour no one could endure another onslaught of coolies, threshing around in these inner precincts, the dreary sing-song they considered indispensable to hauling ice.

At night strong men carried the beds out onto the wide verandahs, or even into the gardens, mosquito poles teetering under a festoon of nets. Like a fleet of sailing ships, it seemed to Rabi, launched in the darkness and bearing them all away to unknown destinations: himself, his parents, his sisters, the auxiliary flotilla of sleeping servants.

Then they were gone, the girls and their mother to the Summer Palace. Bawajiraj followed. It was always a matter of delicacy, his going. Shanta Devi never invited his company, never forgot his arbitrary attempt to instal his mistress in her wedding pavilion, always remembered the humiliation with a muted fury. If he went, as he did, unable to suffer the sweltering capital any longer, it was with the dismal certainty of the uninvited that neither warmth nor welcome awaited him, apart from some slight offerings from his cautious daughters.

Mohini shared the evil memory, from her angle. Nothing would induce her to set foot in the place, even in the Maharani's absence, in which her exalted lover had hoped to immure his kept woman. *Kept woman, kept woman!* she screamed at him during their worst rows, though it had to be really fierce before she descended to that level. It was so unreasonable that the Maharajah often marched away, furious but baffled, for he had never ceased to offer to make her his Maharani.

Between the two women Bawajiraj often felt, righteously, that he might as well be rid of the thing. Sell it to Tirumal Rao perhaps. He was a man of property, owned half a dozen houses, he and his family, and had no doubt salted away a substantial acreage of land as well. He would jump at the chance, Bawajiraj imagined. Such salubrious sites were not often available except to Rulers. In fact, far from jumping, the Dewan shied away from this white elephant. Touching and idyllic in conception, it had all the qualities of a Maharajah's choice: uncomfortable, inaccessible, requiring a Maharajah's resources to run, and probably ruinous sums to demolish. Privately he called it the Summer Folly.

But actually Bawajiraj could not quite bring himself. Shanta Devi had received the Summer Palace as a bride, he could not strip her of the symbols however hollow the reality of the marriage. It irked though. The enormous place, which no one used except for a few months in the hot weather, eating up money for which he could find innumerable uses. . . . It was, however, better than his capital. After the usual upheaval, Maharajah and party proceeded.

* * *

When he was gone Rabi thought about his father. It was best done in his absence. When he was present there was an atmosphere: heightened, and even touched up, the colours and flavours were heady. Something always going on, or the delirium of preparation and anticipation. Not that he didn't enjoy it, he did. In fact, what he most liked to do, after lessons, and when he was done with the battery of tutors (Panditji much augmented these days), and none of those gamesmen who cluttered up his leisure (tennis coach, fencing master, wrestling instructor) were lying in wait, was to search out his father.

The Durbar Hall was a good place. Bawajiraj often made his way there, to rehearse the many speeches it was his destiny to make. He liked to mount his throne and declaim from this elevation, throwing his voice until it had shivered the drops of the farthest chandelier where his humblest subjects usually stood. That achieved he could concentrate on gestures, trying out what went best, most gracefully, with the speech, watching himself in the gilt mirrors and correcting errors as he went along.

Nothing worth doing, unless done well, was his motto. He

hated people who mumbled. And others of like ilk. Like Wikram Raja, so free with his arms, no wonder they called him Windmill Wikram!

Always prepared, though, to break off for Rabi.

'What ho, m'boy!' Booming robustly, in the vast reflecting chamber, over the heads of secretaries and aides, in a way that thawed those sharp crystals that were forming in Rabi.

'Done with the *munshis*, have you?'

'For today, yes.'

'Good, good. Worthy lot, m'boy, but all work and no play—you know what I mean.'

Winking, involving him in this delicious conspiracy, coming down from the regal dais to his level. Their heads close together, like plotters, plotting the next hour, the next day, days running together to make up their lives, those piercingly sweet moments when they acknowledged their kinship in a flow of sudden, warm currents.

One would never want to be cut off from that.

Only, one suspected nothing could be sorted out while it lasted. *It*? The fray, was the word that flew straight into his mind, and lodged.

Intervals were needed, and silences which existed outside the fray.

It took time.

Not clock time, that was the least. The requirement was for some unnameable dimension that began to form when the fluctuations ceased. One's self poised, neither coming nor going nor sounding nor silent, but still. Ready to receive. An aeolian instrument waiting for unseen currents to convert into statements. Letting in truths—if only the shapes, the names could come later—that were otherwise inaccessible: the fragments one scrabbled after, that were necessary to answer riddles.

From Who am I? he alternated, at times sick to the pit of his stomach, to Who is *he*? The two were connected, he knew, but the chains were kinked; he could not straighten them out. For the moment. Though in the end he would, the links would appear plainly: between himself and his father, the State, the Raj, and the spirit, or at least that nebulous flow for which he could think of no other name.

Or so he assumed.

Laboriously, and with the twinges a traitor might feel, he began fitting together some kind of jigsaw, at times supplying the pieces from within himself, sometimes supplied, unwittingly, by people outside.

'We sold out, you know. In all the confusion. All of us did. The whole continent.'

'Some of us weren't even *born* when it was done.'

'But we benefited from the transaction. You, I, Bawaji. He smothers even the conception.'

'What did we sell, Mataji?'

'Ah, Rabi. I didn't hear you come in. What a quiet boy you are becoming!'

'You move like a *thief*! Not a sound. Though the place is as still as the grave.'

The two women, fanning. Scrape of palmyra, tendrils of chestnut hair on his mother's pale forehead. His grandmother's a stubble, nothing would move that stubborn crop. Himself standing, awkwardly planted, something that wouldn't go away. So tall, in his grandmother's eyes (though at her age one shrank a little). His bones jutting. What she saw he could feel happening, his elbows and cheekbones felt raw, protruding so close to the surface.

'What did we sell?'

'Sometimes, Rabi, you can be as tedious as your father.'

'What did we sell?'

'Our *souls*, if you must know. Yes, our souls. Or our birthright, if you prefer. They're not unconnected, you know.'

Like a gong in his ears. Were they shouting, or was it the stillness? How still it was! The gusting winds had blown themselves out, not a leaf stirred. He could feel the heat banging against him, in between the rasps of air wafted to him by his mother's fan. Outside it would be hotter still, but he went all the same, heedless of voices predicting sunstroke, rejecting offers of topis from concerned servants.

He detested topis. His father had a stack, hung on a hatstand with antlers for pegs. They were white or khaki, with a knob on top and a brown leather chin-strap that could be raised to the brim when not required.

So had Sophie, he recalled.

Why did she swim into his mind now? Perhaps it was the strength of feeling they had shared, the common loathing of topis. She had never worn one; went bareheaded, or sometimes endured a white cotton sun-bonnet for Ayah's sake. Sometimes not even for Ayah. She tore it from her head and tossed it on the ground and ground it into the dust with a sandalled heel, while Ayah moaned, and then she ran like the wind, her hair streaming behind her. Her hair in the sun was golden. A good deal of her had been extinguished in his mind, but those golden flares remained.He remembered that, and the way she had revelled in the heat, at least its beginnings, before they whisked her off to the hills. He didn't revel exactly, the heat could be terrible, but there was something about high summer. A biting clarity. Views not available at other seasons, as if one were looking through to the bone.

It mesmerised him, what heat could do, the skeletal structures that the sun released. Trees splitting open, their bark ruptured to show sticky inner wands. The exposed stone-beds of streams. The veined filigree of dead leaves. Cracks in the earth, yellow down the shafts, ochre dust under the nails when your hand came up. Even bones crumbling away, falling apart in the fierce heat and ants scurrying in and out of the lacunae that had once sustained mouse or lizard, carrying away granules of dessicated marrow. The whole landscape as far as eye could see sucked up and dried out, reduced to its core.

* * *

In bad years the wells on the Palace estates ran dry. So did the springs that nourished the distant lake. One of them fed the nenuphar pool and that year when it failed they did not pipe in supplies as they had done before. Not politic at a time of drought, he heard them saying in the corridors of the Palace. The tenants were grumbling. Their wives had to march to the river for water for their cooking pots. It had to be a severe drought before they complained. However much they complained, it was new for them to be listened to, a new thing, in Devapur annals. The pool was left.

Rabi watched the waters subside. He trailed round to the pool each day and lay on the bank and peered down at the marker moored alongside. Two notches, three on a fierce day, could show up on the pole between one sighting and the next, between sunrise and sunset. By midsummer the bed of the pool was visible, wavery under barely a foot of soupy water.

The lilies survived, floated their thick fleshy pads on the dregs and sent their roots writhing for sustenance in the murky shallows. The fish had gone. Das came with a home-made trawl and took them away to an indoor pool as instructed. Whenever stragglers were spotted they sent for him again and he padded up silently, lowered himself into the slimy pool and walked up and down with his nets, in and out among the tangled lilies, driving the fish before him. Only a few minnows now, the carp were gone; but they were the most difficult to catch, these gasping panicky fish that preferred the certainty of their slime to the unknown beyond the nets, that raced desperately, choking and dulled in the bilious gloom, as if a shark, or more probably a memory of snapping carp, were after them.

Rabi would have asked, or offered, to assist, once. Once when exchanges had been light and easy, before they grew out of it. As one did, not at the same time, but of the two parties to a transaction, one defecting, withering the other without warning in the very act of advance. He was not inclined to put out a feeler now, risk having it nipped. Could not, in fact, bogged down as he was in some kind of tacky mess that they seemed to have manufactured jointly. He could not tell how. He knew only that something was set and solidified between them, which had yet to be resolved.

Das, once, would have invited Rabi. He often had in the past, grasped the small boy firmly by the shoulder and waded perilously, linked to his ardent but unskilled partner, among the slippery roots. Not any more. He did not feel disposed. So he went about his business, vengefully pursuing the fleeing fish and ignoring the figure sprawled beside the pool. Acutely aware of it, though. A fine, lithe figure, casually displayed in a cod-piece, sleek from prime food and rich sauces, such as he would have liked to command. Crammed, head to toe, with assumptions that one should loll about, another should labour. Not accountable for it, of course, any more than he, Das, was responsible for his lot, or his ridiculous stick-insect figure. But representative: the pair of them representatives, totems of their tribe.

Culpable, withal. Nevertheless and notwithstanding culpable! he hurled at the unwitting criminal on the bank.

Though it crimped him up inside to do it. He could feel his stomach knotting, and his rancour rose against the oblivious Rabi who had not, for very good reasons, heard the silent invective slung at his head.

Although, not being thick, he did feel bullets passing. He often did, as a matter of fact, when Das was around, so that mostly he kept out of range. Only now he did not feel like moving. It was pleasant beside the pool, the shady embankment if not the shrinking nenuphar, and the warmth had made him drowsy.

Torpid, Das fumed as he squelched up and down after a last but agile minnow. He would have bludgeoned it, had it been easier. His intentions transmitted to the fish. Something was up, it felt, swam for its life, like a maniac, demented loops and dives.

Das followed, blood up, but gingerly. There were things in that pool. Shards, and bits of clay gods that the retainers flung in at festival time. Palm wine and religion gone to their giddy heads, unable to tell Palace pool from tank in the town, unable to steer that far. O-oof! What could that be? A round hard object in the ball of his foot, violence done to a tender spot, shock zigzagging up his spine. Das fished out the object and laid aside his nets. He was through with trawling. He heaved up out of the lily bog and began to clean up the grimy thing that had scuppered him.

Scratchy sounds, in place of the lullaby of squelches, woke the slumbering Rabi. Das, scraping away industriously with his nails, abetted by a sliver of rusty razor blade. It looked interesting. Rabi levered up on an elbow.

'Found something?'

'Yes.'

'What is it?'

'Treasure.'

'I only asked.'

'I'm telling you.'

'Can I look?'

'Is that an order?'

'Please can I look.'

'If you must.'

Rabi did not bother. He dangled a toe in the water, where the tremulous minnow swam. It looked lost, a whole pool to itself. Its fellows were huddled together, a sullen crew in a pail, hating the clean water, longing to go back to soup. The feebler inmates were blanched and wheezing, preparing to give up the ghost. He didn't want them to expire; they had done nothing to deserve this fate.

'I think they'll die, if you don't transfer them soon.'

'Too bad.'

Concerned, however. The head gardener would have a word to say. The poison toad. Das suspended scraping and picked up the pail, slopping it as he went.

Rabi slid along to see what Das had found. It was only a marble. Rather grubby and faded. He dipped it in the pool and wiped off the last accretions and the colours came up a little. He knew what he was holding then. It made him feel dizzy, looking down at the small glass globe and seeing it expand before his eyes into a world that he and Janaki had once inhabited.

'What have you done with it?'

'Here it is.'

'It's mine.'

'No.'

'I found it. Finders keepers.'

'It's mine. Really.'

'You don't own everything you know. Not every single fucking thing you set eyes on.'

'I know, I never said—it's just that Janaki. She gave it to me, years ago—'

'Then you should have looked after it, shouldn't you. Your property, you know about looking after property. Not like human beings, is it, to be tipped out with the garbage.'

'I didn't, I didn't!'

'You threw it away.'

'Only because she—after she—she went away.'

Shuddering fit to dislocate his neck. His adversary aware, gripping the clattering vertebra, ready to snap the bony column.

'She was sent away because of you.'

His head was swimming. He fought to save himself.

'You've no right to say that.'

'I'll say it again. Because of you.'

Grinning, or something. His purplish lips barely contained his teeth. His cod-piece bulged, straining against the G-string. Such a huge thing, for his size. He was quite small really, small and ugly, one couldn't thump him as his fists were itching to do. So Rabi sat miserably, until it came to him, a slow welling, rather than a boiling up. Because of course he had known for a long time, since the day Das had refused to play with him. Abruptly, as if there had been a dawning, a mental opening up that went with his physical development. The youthful Das, then, from that day on averted, presenting a pock-marked profile sullen and curdled with resentment. You would have known from the mouth alone. He kept forgetting though. Kept on trying. Running eagerly to summon Das and coming up smack. He had been a small boy then, looking up to Das. Das was almost a man now. And he was no longer a child. Both of them were ripe for settlement, whatever it was.

'Why do you hate me?' he asked, so low, his voice like a husk.

'I hate you for what you are, Maharajkumar.'

It was so awful to have it confirmed that he was finished. He couldn't even disengage, so that it was Das who strode away from the scene.

Not every single fucking thing you know!

He had never claimed to. It came without claiming. He owned, or one day would own, a good deal of what eye could see. The eye saw a good deal, and the roll call of possession went far beyond what it saw to the far-off boundaries of Devapur State, all 20,000 square miles of it.

'All yours, my boy, one day.'

'All?'

'Of course. Provided the Viceroy, naturally. Except your mother's jewels, they descend in the female line. Some Hindu law, I believe.'

'Stridhanna.'

'What?'

'The law of women's inheritance.'

'I daresay you're right. Though what women want to inherit for I can't think.'

'I suppose for the same reason as men.'

'Ah Rabi, I can see your mother has been at you. But it's not necessary, my boy. Every single thing that heart could desire, we provide. Look at your mother now, is there anything she wants I would not lay at her feet?'

'You're rich.'

'I suppose you could say I'm well off.'

Bawajiraj detested bragging. He greatly preferred the British way: verbal understatement paired to the reality, both perceived and invisible, of a quite stunning order of magnificence. No need for a sun to proclaim it shines, was his private belief, though wild horses would not have dragged this dreadful piece of boasting into the open. Even in his mind it was largely unvoiced.

Actually he did not know. Even the Minister, to whom the most fearful complications of the princely revenues were plain (he had that squalid cast of mind), who had the Treasury at his fingertips, could not entirely have enlightened the Maharajah. There was so much that could not be valued. Those carpets, for instance. Up to the rafters, in the carpet room. Herat, Hamadan, Meshed, Qum. Two hundred knots to the square inch, and some large enough to cover the Durbar Hall. Whole life-spans of weavers between the fringes, scarcely computable in money terms. And the jewels. His Blue Diamond breastplate, for example. Not a stone much under fifty carats. He wore it, over a waistcoat of white buckskin, once a year at Dassara, otherwise he might easily have forgotten it. And the Moonlight Cummerbund: three thousand pearls, each as large as a marble, shimmering milk and moonshine. And the Gold Canopy, a canvas of gold mesh studded with rubies, sapphires, and diamonds. Successive jewellers had retired, unable to place a value. The Jewel Chamber was full of items before which dazed jewellers had retreated, whose value consequently remained conjectural.

Once Rabi, in the cavilling mood for which his female line was noted, less English than his father, had rebelled. Years ago, he must have been ten or eleven.

'You're not well off. You're rolling in the stuff.'

So vulgar. The very accents of Mohini, but then his blood was half hers. Difficult to eradicate, these blood faults.

'Not rolling, Rabi, Only hogs roll. Let's just say I have a sufficiency of the world's goods. Enough to see me out, shall we say.'

It would see him, Rabi, out too, if he lived to be a hundred, ethos and times permitting. The land alone, those endless acres that rolled away into the distance. He found it difficult to envisage, although the legend helped.

As far as your horse can ride, to you and your heirs, the divinity had promised. But it was no mere horse his ancestor rode but a steed with winged hooves. . . .

'Not one of your pocket-handkerchief States, you know.'

The Maharajah, basking in rare moments of pardonable pride.

Tirumal Rao, for once, was in harmony with the Maharajah. He saw it as his duty, or even a sacred trust, to preserve it as it was. As had his father. And grandfather. His friends— Brahmins of eminence throughout India—were similarly preoccupied. They presided like eagles—or intransigent goats, according to point of view—over the Councils of States they served, clinging to land rights, grimly resisting charters, deals, grants, exchanges, gifts, the innumerable masquerades and strategies of land acquisition, including straightforward annexation, at which the British—traders under the purple—were adept.

Not one of them would have bartered a bead. They listened to the roll call of land-grab and were chilled to the marrow. Shudders ran when the familiar names of seized provinces—Sind, Satara, Nagpur, Oudh, Jhansi, Jaitpur, or Sambalpur—were mentioned. As they frequently were, in these conclaves to which no European was allowed access. Tirumal Rao, like Narasimha Rao and Narayan Rao before him, was a graduate of this school.

Land-grab, it is true, had been in abeyance for some time. Nevertheless the Dewan, in common with his colleagues, would have considered it remiss to relax his vigilance by one jot. It was a subject to which they returned, and not without passion even in these rarefied circles, when they called on each other. At these purposeful, if congenial, meetings, they agreed that above all it would be fatal to underestimate the adversary, or to dismiss the co-existence of a bluff exterior and classical tenets with the enterprise and sharp practice of the marketplace. The history of their country provided evidence of the consequences of such crass errors. However credulous the British might be about themselves, the whimsical notion that the Empire had been acquired in a fit of absentmindedness—an idea to which Sir Arthur was devoted—raised the thinnest of smiles in these circles.

The tragedy, as these august men also agreed, was that wisdom had dawned so late. Late in the day as it was, however, they remained on guard against further encroachments.

The position was not without problems, in that Maharajahs were known to be carried away. Tracts of fertile land, in exchange for some Order or other. Caskets of precious gems in return for a signed portrait. Pledges of fully equipped armies, in return for some trifling courtesy in London. And wasn't there the rajah who had shipped an entire ebony throne to England as a present for the Queen?

Dwelling on these lunacies Tirumal Rao often felt he was one of the blessed. No alarming acts had been perpetrated during his rule. Though the Star, of course. Bawajiraj had raided the Jewel Chamber in gratitude; he had never confided in his Minister what he had abstracted. But that was his privilege, his private treasure. Land was another matter, precious above rubies and diamonds, altogether different. In Tirumal Rao's mind it assumed mystical qualities not inappropriate to winged hooves. It was soil from which he was formed, the very stuff of creation. He would not willingly have allowed a single sod to pass into alien hands. The most doleful emotions consumed him when he dwelt on his country's past.

In the Resident's opinion the Minister went altogether too far. For years he had coveted a certain plot, which he longed to call his own. A glen, he liked to call it, from certain Celtic echoes, full of streams and woods and wild rich views, on the northern edge of the kingdom. The Minister thwarted not Sir Arthur, but the spectre of the European settler implicit in him. It came to the same thing. The most Sir Arthur had been able to wring from him was a lease, the rights reverting to Devapur State after each lustrum. Bawajiraj, flushed and unhappy, backed his Minister. Some vestigial, ancestral instinct came to his aid, perched on his shoulder, the stern gaunt raven, and gave him the strength.

Sir Arthur could have prevailed; there were many ways, even if the days of naked pressure were passing. He preferred to bide his time—not vindictively, with nemesis in his sights, since spite was totally foreign to his nature, but simply waiting for Waji to see sense, perhaps after savouring, in Simla, similar pleasures of acquisition. . . .

For Sir Arthur profoundly believed that no country could be run on thumbscrew and rack. That kind of motion would have been altogether too jarring for his English sensibility. One didn't want, he often told himself, to shout at anyone, oneself. He even detested the atmosphere that, despite one's best efforts, sometimes grew up: a sense of carrot and stick, of penalties and rewards being handed out by a particularly harassed parent to a wilfully perverse child. But it didn't last. He saw to that. He was trained to see to it. Soon the old easy atmosphere was restored, not, he flattered himself, without some skill.

It was precisely skills like these that the Dewan and his colleagues recognised, and respected, and shuddered at.

* * *

The following summer was worse. The hot weather prolonged itself in the plains, while in Simla the frosts came early. Sir Arthur and Lady Copeland, and Master Esmond, by now a small energetic boy, returned to a scorched land.

Lady Copeland knew what to expect from the moment she caught sight, by mischance, of the first dead cow. Flies. Vultures. Beggars clustered round the walls of the Residency compound, banging away at their tin begging-bowls. It was forbidden, of course, and the peons leaped out from time to time and drove them away, but they always came back. She suspected the servants. Surreptitiously handing out alms, from some wretched superstition of gaining merit in heaven. It only encouraged these hordes. At times she felt she hated them, for the impotent misery they roused in her. Especially the children. Not accusing, that would have been a mite more bearable, but simply suffering. Those huge moist spaniel eyes. She had to hold her own child close to stave it off, locking her arms tightly about his chubby body as if to make up to him all that these others had been deprived of. One child, at least, safe. The converse of a solitary crucifixion offered up for the salvation of the whole of mankind.

It was, indeed, a nailed Christ that swam into her view at these confused and terrible moments. Mary Copeland, while averting her eyes, would have given anything to have these unhappy people well-nourished and healthy. As she could not—those seething masses defeated one's best intentions—she did the next best thing, dispensing tea and rice, sometimes in person, assisted by brave ladies from the cantonment, to orderly queues of starving.

Bawajiraj reacted differently, but tenderly. The holiday he had permitted himself was over. The image of the family man, he was returning from the Summer Palace with his wife and daughters conspicuously bouncing beside him in his open carriage. All the way from the outskirts of the city to the gates of the Palace he flung out generous handfuls of coins, right, left, right, left, shovelling them up from the gold-mesh sack that chinked and bumped at his feet. Now and then the girls got in the way and received a silvery shower, but it only added to the fun. The children who lined the route, irrepressibly merry, the thinnest of them, also found it fun. There was a great deal of scrabbling and competition for the coins that rolled in the dust, the only sour note being provided by the older people who got bowled over in the scrum.

While the detached Dewan, like Lady Copeland, also made-do with second-best: palliative measures, since the budget would not stretch to a cure. He reopened the grain distribution centres, closed since the last emergency, in the hinterland where distress was most acute. This done, he turned his mind to tentage for the inevitable floods. He knew his country. Equally he was familiar with, and would have raged except that the scriptures abjured passion, the ethic that allowed free play to acts of god, and the ethic that accepted it: government and people locked in this shabby compact, though it was abysmally clear to him, even in his swept and garnished premises, who got the better of the deal.

Once Bawajiraj, who vacillated between amazement at, and intense curiosity in, the workings of his Dewan's mind, had bluntly asked him what he dreamed about, since he simply could not think. He told his own first: the lustrous moment when he would present his son to the people at his coming of age, and hear them hail him as heir to the kingdom.

Maharajkumar ki jai!

He could hear them shouting it, thrice, as was the custom. His devoted subjects, acclaiming his beloved son. The scene was so powerful that his own lips moved, three barely muted *jais* that surprised the Minister.

'And your dream, Dewan Sahib?'

It was so abrupt that Tirumal Rao, somewhat off balance, answered with bald truth.

'I dream of controlling the seasons, Highness. In so far as it can be by mortals.'

The Maharajah thought it very high and mighty not to say expensive, though when it came to the fine detail he changed his mind, finding dams, canals, well-digging, and the other paraphernalia of the Minister's dream ineffably earthy, boring stuff.

More to the point, it was prohibitively expensive. The coffers had been recently raided for a good many purposes, including the marriage and dowries of two daughters, and if they had to run to the Minister's schemes, the remaining girls might, the lugubrious Maharajah felt, fare no better than beggar-maids.

* * *

'We do seem fated, don't we.'

Rabi plumped himself down on the cushion that bore his name: *Rabindranath*, worked in gold thread on jade satin by Vimala, the Dewan's second daughter. It was a long name, and it had taken her a long time, and she was definitely huffed when it was lifted all plump and warm from her loving hands and placed, not in the children's quarters, which was in bounds to her, but on the long low divan in the central room where the older members of the family congregated.

For Rabi had been promoted. From being a wistful boy whom the women mothered, he was more often to be seen by the Dewan's side. It had begun as a formal arrangement, with the object of acquainting him with the workings of Devapur State, which its Chief Minister could be allowed to know something about. But the formality eased, the arrangement expanded, spilled over beyond office hours and the confines of ministerial suites into the family home. For Rabi took to the Dewan—old sobersides, as his father had taken to calling him—finding the dry, ironic notes he injected an acceptable change from the coloratura maintained by the Palace. More important, the Dewan took to Rabi, who had hitherto merely occupied a niche in his domestic background, playmate to the children and the one most tolerant of the lively Usha.

A sprig of the Maharajah, for whom one entertained the most basic expectations. An inconvenient infant, if one went farther back, whom he, the Dewan, had recommended for speedy translation together with his mother to the remote point of origin. But metamorphosis imminent, not merely into heir-apparent (waiting only the final nod, so the word went, from the Resident), but into a youth not without possibilities. The Dewan's gaze—compared to agate by many upon whom it fell—turned to some lesser quartz when it rested on Rabi, sitting gloomy and cross-legged on his daughter's handiwork like a depressed tailor.

'Fated. In what way, exactly, Rabi?'

'Oh well. Drought. Famine. Floods.'

'Ah yes, those. But fate can be mitigated. As we are endeavouring to do. The tenders are in.'

'For tents?'

'For tents. Twenty thousand tents, which are sufficient for our low-lying areas.'

'I should think they're horrible to live in.'

'I daresay. Though—it is possible—they are better than nothing.'

Those carved nostrils flaring. Contempt for him? For the simple arithmetic that produced nothing?

Nothing.

That was the sum of Janaki's possessions. It enabled her to take off when told to with the freedom of a bird. It enabled the mud to ooze up between her bare toes. She wore a silver ring on the second toe. It had been taken off the corpse of her grandmother the moment she died, before she could stiffen, she told him. There had been a pair, but one was pawned for good. The other lay in the boggy mess of the low-lying areas where her sort lived. She squelched around in the slush, feeling with her feet, rather hopelessly. He had on thigh boots and he churned about with her until she asked him to desist, she was getting trodden on quite painfully. Then they went away, leaving the toe ring, to high ground where tents were sprouting.

'There was a girl.'

He couldn't resist. It was like a sore tooth, tongue forever ferreting to see if it could really be as bad as that.

'One of the servants, long ago, you wouldn't remember her. She—she took me into the tent they had given her. I asked her to. It was awful. So clammy. And the canvas smelt, frightful whiffs as it flapped up and down. I was enchanted.'

'Odd creatures, children. Find their raptures in odd things.'

'She wasn't in raptures. I can see that quite clearly now.'

'But sheltered, and, no doubt, grateful.'

So dry, you could have taken him at his word, swallowing the niggling particles as imaginary. Though you got to know, those very deserts were testing zones, you learnt to approach with caution, question in your turn to establish what kind of territory.

'Grateful, why should she have been grateful? I wouldn't have been, in her place. Would you?'

'What would you have done, in her place?'

'I would have complained, I suppose. Not that it would have done much good.'

'On the contrary. The State takes cognizance of all complaints. She would have been issued with a better tent, Class IV quality.'

The Dewan could have been smiling. Anything, really. Straight-lipped, his pointed hands folded in his snowy lap, no inflections to guide you. Briefly Rabi was joined with his father, who gave his opinion that old sobersides would excel at poker.

Since he was not to be helped he drove straight on.

'I think the State should cure the disease, not tinker about with the symptoms.'

The State is you. The unruly cry reached the Dewan's lips. He clipped it back. It was not time yet. He was not sufficiently convinced, yet, of the credentials of this wan and troubled convert to lay bare the conspiracy. It involved that arch-conspirator, the innocent Maharajah. Rabi was as fond of his father the Maharajah as his sons, the Dewan hoped, were of him.

It cost him something, though, to refrain from leaping in immediately to recruit from within the opposition itself support for his own cherished plans.

Rabi, staring at a portrait of a ministerial ancestor hung on the opposite wall (a Bishandas, in a rosewood frame), in lieu of any reaction from the Minister himself began to sense that something had shifted. Or someone. One of the pair of them had moved, or had been ferried over to the other side, so that now they were both on the same shore, or at any rate in the same boat. Although, of course, they continued to sit where they were, the Dewan on his couch with silk bolsters upholding him firmly in the lotus position, Rabi on the cushion whose scratchy letters were embossing themselves on his shin.

When they were rescued from themselves, and each other, by the entrance of Usha.

Something of an exasperating entrance, since Usha, a dressing-up enthusiast, had donned, and was entering these hallowed quarters in, a pair of her father's shoes, which that inept man had negligently discarded on some accessible verandah.

As Vatsala could see from the cell, monastic, but peppered with spy-holes, in which she had immured herself, being in the middle of her monthly. Hampered, as well, in that wife could not utter her husband's name.

'O-ho! O-ho!'

It was less than robust, considering what she felt like.

'My love?'

The Dewan, fluting; his voice inclining to trills when he conversed with his wife, in this mood.

'Usha! Look what she's up to!'

'Where?'

Flustered, and descending to futility; while his fastidious person shrank. Young children could be appallingly grubby with the greatest of ease.

'By the window. Right next to you!'

'So she is.'

A giggling but perfectly clean and wholesome Usha, he perceived with gratitude.

'She's wearing your shoes!'

'My shoes?'

'Take them away at once!'

The Dewan had relinquished the lotus position, but he could not stoop that far. Not to pick up a pair of shoes that had walked on heaven knew what filth. Made of cowhide, he had a nasty suspicion. The most he could manage was to slide his feet into them and wait for a peon to do up the buckles. Where were all the servants, come to that? Fifty of them on his personal payroll, but not one in sight in this emergency. The Dewan disdained to shout. He felt, like Sir Arthur, that one wouldn't wish to shout for anyone, oneself. He peered distastefully at the uncouth soles that had invaded his private hearth, although he was very fond of his latest daughter, while he waited for help to arrive.

'Shall I take them away from her, Father?'

Vimala offered her services, sacrificially, from the doorway where she was dutifully halted. She longed to enter these privileged premises, but parcelled up her desires so that they would not be thwarted as grown-ups were tempted to do, if they knew, if one were foolish enough to reveal to them.

'Yes. Please do. At once.'

The Dewan got in a shade ahead of his wife, who had been about to veto the proposal. Vatsala did not care for her daughters, at their age, to hobnob. Not Usha, she was only a little girl, nor even Vijaya, who was safely betrothed. But Vimala. The centre of some exceedingly delicate negotiations just barely beginning. The girl herself on the very brink, if she knew anything, all her boyish angles softening. While Rabi, with the looks, she had to admit, that a Brahmin could rightfully admire, and the physique of his kingly caste. For she had seen him sprawled by the pool. Springy curls escaping on all fronts from the skimpy cod-piece. His indolent organ in its chaste sheath lying soberly along one thigh. But liable to wild and instant conversions, orchid snout grouting for hymen like swine after truffles. The vulgarity shocked her, but try as she would the image refused to disperse. It was lodged in truth, as she saw it, set in the reality of what happened between men and women.

Vatsala shuddered again. She could imagine those fervid glances that youths and maids exchanged which started the whole explosive process, which she, if present, would intercept and extinguish. As one could not trust a man to do. As she could not do herself, having to keep apart. Vatsala groaned, and would have railed against her lot except that it made her shudder even more to think of mixing, as boorish lesser castes might do, while in her unclean condition.

So the Dewan was left, presiding benignly over the apartment which seemed to have burgeoned. That was his distinct impression as he surveyed the bright faces of the children who had infiltrated in Vimala's wake and distributed themselves blissfully on rugs and the plethora of low couches. A handsome lot, he thought—the atmosphere seeded such thoughts—gilded by the circumstance of birth, and further buffed by certain hues the room kindled. A room that roused Sir Arthur's ire, on the rare occasion when he penetrated, such were the exquisite lengths to which artistry was carried, reflecting in his view its finical begetter. But it perfectly fitted the Dewan, who delighted in the play of the finest fires, lights that streamed from pale inlays and the smouldering crimson Saryk hangings, from the glowing Herats he favoured, and his cherished collection of illuminated miniatures.

Relaxed in this setting, he listened contentedly to the silvery notes of the *veena*, which his daughter Vijaya was playing. The prim and occasionally flat notes pinged in from the music room on the first floor, now and then shivering the crystal curtain of bugle beads that hung by the door, which she had spent two summers stringing. A persevering girl, his eldest. Nothing would keep her from her daily practice, no amount of temptation. Whereas Vimala, who coruscated, in music as in other fields, could not be trusted to keep at anything unless madam herself selected the task.

Madam, in fact, was swaggering over the cushion to which she had apparently devoted her best years.

'It took me right through the holidays, you know Rabi.'

'I'm not surprised. It's beautifully embroidered.'

'If you can move your legs just a little, to the right.'

'There.'

'A bit more.'

'I'll get off, shall I?'

'No, no, you stay where you are. I just want to show you the feather-stitching, here, on the corner. Rather nice, don't you think?'

'Very nice.'

'Honestly?'

'Honestly. They remind me of those little tracks that quail leave. You know, when they're quite small, just beginning to run.'

'Me too. I never noticed that before.'

The Dewan listened tenderly. Invasion or no, he liked his children about him, it gave the place an air. He could scarcely contemplate without horror what it must be like in that enormous barn where the English resided. Of all the aberrations of which they were capable, this seemed to him the most wilfully perverse, depriving themselves of the pleasure of children. Sophie gone, Esmond destined, not long now. Simply because the schools were not good enough. Or the company inferior. Or the country inimical to health. Though his own brood thrived, on a diet of roots and nuts (he was acquainted with the British view) and could even be said to be a credit. As was Rabi, he liked the look of the boy. Hardly a boy any more, though.

At this point Tirumal Rao began to feel his wife was at his elbow; at any rate her astral presence was jogging him, he could distinctly feel some pressure. So he looked round to make sure, but the vulnerable Vimala was quite safely engaged in a game of patchesi with her brothers, and the suspect Rabi was innocently occupied with Usha, bouncing the little girl up and down on his knee. Dismissing astral injunctions the Dewan relaxed, reclining against roly-poly silk while he waited for *tiffin* to arrive, tasty morsels disposed on glossy leaf-beds, some sweet, some savoury. . . .

Chin on chest, Vatsala could see. After all he had said. How some Brahmins might rejoice to give their daughters in marriage to rajahs, but not he. How they must in their own interests steer clear of complications. Nodding, while complications were no doubt breeding under his very nose. So she clapped, rather louder than was necessary, and tinkled a hand-bell for good measure, to summon up *tiffin*.

8

My Dear and Beloved Son,

wrote Bawajiraj from Simla, capitals and flourishes, repressed in speech in the interests of understatement, thrusting up in his writing like delirious weeds.

You will I am sure be as Overjoyed as I am to hear that Magnolia Lodge is at long last near to completion. It is elevated Two Hundred Feet above Fairlawn which Pooky has purchased, and on the same level, but distant One Mile, from Glen View which Sir Arthur has made his Headquarters for the Season.

I am on Site every morning before the Races for discussion with Contractors and Decorators, and I am happy to tell you that our Dear Friend and Mentor gives me his invaluable Advice and Guidance on these occasions. I need not say that without his Help I could not have come so close to Heart's Desire.

I pray you will give your father the Pleasure of your Company very soon, as soon as the Building is done. *The Hunting is out of this World.*

Your Ever Affectionate
Bawajiraj III.

. . . an Avenue of Magnolias, [He wrote by the same post to Mohini.] . . . the Trees have arrived, they are each five feet tall, and their roots are balled in Earth and Straw to Preserve

them until the Holes are dug. Her Ladyship is Most Kindly
supervising the Depth and the Manuring, which are Essential
for growth. Some of the trees bear Blooms that remind me of
you, my Dearest Love, but you are Fairer by far . . .

Exaggerating as usual, Mohini told herself, but she tucked the
letter in her bodice next to the skin. Under the magnolia she
could feel her blood beginning to race.

As if in answer, or invitation, the telegram came the next day.

MAGNOLIAS PLANTED STOP   PLEASE COME IMMEDIATELY TO
VIEW.

'As if I could.'
Twisting the rope of pearls, pearls and slender neck knotted
up in the problem.
'Why can't you?'
'Well, Rabi. It's not easy, is it? For a woman? A hundred
things.'
'What things?'
Not a thing, actually, that a woman could lay her finger on.
Not, anyway, a woman like her, not with cartloads of servants.
But there must be things, she felt sure. She groped after them
while her mind, vile hedonist, had already danced away and was
busy loading the trunks.

Then it was Rabi's turn. Magnolia Lodge was ready. The
Contractors and Builders, propelled out of their customary
lethargy—no one had warned them of the abundant energies of
a Maharajah in pursuit of Heart's Desire—had completed their
task. Not by due date, that was unthinkable, but six months
thereafter, which was as well as the bulk of the furniture was
aboard a wandering freighter holed up somewhere in—a tart
Bawajiraj noted the opposite quality—the Bitter Lakes.
Spot of hunting, Bawajiraj began to feel, turning his attention
from building and planting. Do the boy good to get away from
tutors. Stuffy lot. He had not appointed and did not approve of a
single one of them. How much better if he and his Adviser had
been allowed their way! Chiefs' College, the Military Academy,
the Corps, one could depend on them to set a young man up. All,
all alas in the past, the future perfect wrenched from him and

this wobbly present substituted by his mother in league with Mohini, not to mention their crackpot Pandit. His surrender over that pallid creature had been, he could see, the fatal first step. . . . Bawajiraj skimmed over this part of history, which depressed him, and turned for a lightening of mood to pig-sticking, which he invested in the most engaging terms he could think of to lure Rabi away. Carried away himself, the phrases rolled from his pen.

> Excellent country, [he wrote] the Most Perfect you can imagine for our Sport, lies to hand in the valleys. I do believe there is no finer in the Whole of India, nor even in our Kingdom, an Opinion which I am gratified to say is shared by Their Excellencies . . . The Spears are now to hand, fifty of the finest weapons Heart could desire . . . the Blades have a broader channel as specially designed by me, so we shall soon see who gets First Spear, eh my boy? Now for the Horses—

The letter flowed easily to four pages. At the end he paused, then added a tailpiece that would, he felt, be irresistible. He had meant to keep it a surprise, but the mood he was in admitted no delay. He took up his pen again.

> From Magnolia Lodge I shall proceed to Bombay to super-vise the Disembarkation of the Rolls-Royce motor-cars which have arrived from England. We could, if you wish . . .

He grew radiant, thinking of possibilities. So much to show the boy. So much they could do together.

There were times when Bawajiraj craved the actual, physical presence of his son as acutely as Rabi required, at times, the physical and spiritual absence of his father.

This, however, was not one of them. Bawajiraj had been away for months, fussing over the Lodge—long enough for Rabi to advance along the circle he trod from not-wanting to wanting, from the desperate wish to be rid of that distracting conundrum, his luminous father, so that he could reach the periphery of an understanding of himself, to a frantic desire for that genial luminary to lift him out of his unquiet self.

Unquiet and obtrusive. Bilked increasingly of repose it howled disconcertingly, the dismal spirit, beset by questions sprung from within the pigeon-breast of a servant girl and the ramshackle rib-cage of sweaty coolies and explicitly in the surly invective of a labourer's son. A graduate of Chiefs' College, or the Imperial Corps, could have supplied answers that restored a rich, creamy, imperturbable peace. Rabi had only his tutors, models of rectitude no doubt, but also severely tried men whose lips let fall, from time to time, what the country was asking, more and more insistently, and with even a degree of insolence, so that even more questions bubbled up.

* * *

Problems, the courtiers said (and even the servants, who should have known better), that one grew out of. Bound to have them, at his age: we did. Putting it all down to flesh, and one or two giving their opinion that there was no need, quite a few girls around who would have been honoured. Dancing-girls, and the daughters of aging courtesans, and such-like.

B Class girls, Lady Copeland—she had a definitive vocabulary—would have called them, the cheap beauties who solaced the dregs left behind when the best people were in summer abodes in hill stations. But the comforters she had in mind (no-caste, low-caste riff-raff in the eyes of disdainful courtiers) were for Europeans, they did not encompass those shy, delightful gazelles, groomed exclusively for the nobles of Courts.

But Rabi did not want a girl.

He noted the mutations and manifestations of his threshing body, by day, by night, in dreams, the fierce heats and pearly effusions, but could not work them into wanting, or taking, a woman.

The thought left him cold.

He often thought his trouble was that he didn't know what he wanted. Preferred to be blithe about it however, who wouldn't? So he seized his chance, crackled the brimming missive from his father that nestled in his breast pocket and thought about Magnolia Lodge.

For Simla called. Like a siren, after years of lyrical evocation and imagined felicities. Air like wine. Divine country. Sport fit for a king.

Though he had more sense than to cite bloodsports in seeking his tutors' permission to depart.

* * *

'Pig-sticking?'

The Pandit, long ago, when they were new to each other. Unable to believe his ears, or this earnest child.

'You mean actually sticking the spear in the pig?' Gingerly, it seemed such a gratuitously vicious act.

'Yes. Here, in the shoulder, it's the best place.' Showing the ignoramus, who turned pallid with understanding.

'What for, Rabi?'

'Oh, well.'

Shrugging. It was something you either knew or you didn't, you couldn't explain it. Proceeding to easier matters.

'The object, well, it's to get first spear . . . you can prove you did because the blood channels, you see, they're full of blood and fat, that's what they're there for, in the blade, so you have the evidence . . .'

The squeamish Pandit, his flesh holed by spears with blood channels, reduced to a quivering silence.

It passed into the realm of what they did not discuss.

* * *

So Rabi omitted it from his plea, merely quoting suitable extracts from the letter.

'To help settle in. There's a lot to be done at the Lodge. And of course in Bombay.'

'Of course, if your father commands.'

The Pandit, stiff where the Maharajah was concerned, but correct.

'Of course I wouldn't dream . . . I mean if you didn't want me to, if you thought my work . . . I'd rather not go if you thought that.'

Feeling a prig, and wrung at the sacrifice offered up, but actually managing to mean what he said from being surrounded. A ring of astute educators whose attitudes one could not help absorbing, the suspicion lurking in potholes of the mind one plumbed from time to time that these attitudes were aligned to reality, more so than the attitudes struck at the Palace, or floated in like iridescent bubbles from Simla.

Then, after the Pandit, there was the Dewan to tackle.

First thing in the morning, Rabi resolved, when both of them were fresh, the Dewan like cut crystal from early rising and an icy bath which left him, in distinct contrast to his fellow men, in the ripe and mellow mood for permits and concessions.

Tirumal Rao was indeed favourably disposed. Simla he passed without a quibble, despite some private reservations. At Bombay, however, he stuck, surveying the supplicant with some incredulity.

'Bombay? At this time? Are you sure?' (Could even the Maharajah be capable?)

'Why not at this time?'

'Why rush to meet a hurricane?'

'Is there one?'

'If there isn't there's going to be.'

'Political, I suppose.'

'My dear boy, of course. All these upheavals are political.'

'In which case it would hardly affect us, would it?'

It was a matter over which the Dewan had pondered lately, and come to certain conclusions. Revolutions do not spare princes or show respect for frontiers, he thought of passing on, but it seemed so ponderous, so akin to pronouncements at Councils of State, that he could not bring himself to burden this transparently eager youth, on this pellucid morning that seemed specially minted for blithe doings.

'There is unrest. Keep out of troubled areas and I expect you'll be all right,' he said, lightening it, in his view, to soufflé proportions.

Bright as the morning Rabi walked away across the lawns to tell his mother. Dew lay thick on the grass, sparkling green turf in place of the droopy grey whiskers of high summer. Peacocks keened, displaying their fans—it was their favourite season too. Nearby a pair of cheetahs, eye on the birds, peacocks a favourite fowl, but chained, long chains that they knew would bring them up short of the quarry. Quarry knew too, strutted disdainfully, never pausing to think: What if a link should break? The hunters flattened to grass, only half pretending, in the peak of condition, muscles limbering up under svelte coats. In this season they hunted, were slipped from their chains to streak after black buck, the jungle was full of black buck, but nothing to say no peacocks.

Sometimes all that was left was the finery.

Rabi paused on his way, ravished onlooker: a combat of the jungle, enacted on lawns. Aware of scrutiny the cheetahs abandoned their role and sauntered up to greet him, rubbing up against him like cats, eyes gone to velvet, begging him to play: Look, no claws! So, gulled, he stopped for a game; they were only half-grown, creatures of so rare and extreme a beauty as might captivate, he felt, even their prey. Though the cuffs he received, even in play, and given with grace, felt distinctly like blows.

'Rabi, your arms! What have you been doing?'
'Those cubs. They don't know their own strength.'
Rabi rolled his sleeves down over reddening patches (no blood though; the animals had observed their pact) and sat down beside his mother, who was busy. One of those hundred things she hadn't been able to think of at the time, that crowd a woman's life . . .
She was making—it was the season sublime—rose attar. Or rather the roses were. They lay in trays of sweet oil and gave up their essences. By the thousand. Brimming baskets gathered that very dawn in the rose-fields of the Palace estates and brought in riding, queen of flowers, on women's crowns, dew still jewelling the damask. Women, another class, neither pickers nor bearers but handmaidens to the art, clustered around, bemused by ooze turning to attar.
Attar of roses was Shanta Devi's preserve except when she was away (as she was; she and her daughters were attending a wedding), when it devolved on Mohini; a capitulation to circumstance, an implicit *modus vivendi* that Maharani and concubine had contrived between them, even if nothing could close the gap, not after all these years of supersession.
'What a heavenly smell!'
'Yes, isn't it?'
Mohini poked about with a greenish wand, a peeled and sticky neem twig that she declared essential, releasing sweet heavy odours from the rose-jam.
'I simply had to, before going away . . . the roses will all be blown by the time we come back . . . I couldn't bear it if . . . Ah-h, the smell! I think it's the finest on earth, don't you, Rabi?'
'M-mm!'
M-mm! A-ah! Inhaling the incense together, like acolytes, at this time of year.
Always, at this time of year, those fragrances, suspended like crimson veils in which one or the other of them, his mother or the Maharani, was rosily embroiled.
'Though your father—I hate to say this Rabi, but he does strike peculiar at times—your father prefers pines!'
'Well, that's a-uh, nice smell too.'

'So *green*! It's a Simla smell. That's why he loves it. He's in love with Simla.'

'It sounds a lovely place.'

'That's why I'm going. One reason why.'

Under the skin, hue and cry beginning. Arum too thick for vivid show, but tinges evident, she knew, to the watching eye. So sharp, of late, that eye. So she drew her sari over the lower half of her face like a yashmak and met his gaze boldly over the edge of the voile, to out-stare her son, though what happened was that they exchanged their knowledge.

Round-eyed, peering starkly over the stretched cloth, she disconcerted him too. Wild ludicrous images shot off some spinning loom that they shared and rendered him speechless, apart from that electrifying exchange. Until between them, not without effort, they managed to hoist back on to ordinary lines.

'What about you, Rabi?'

'I'm going too. I've just seen the Dewan.'

'Soon?'

'Tomorrow.'

'So am I. Isn't that lovely? We can share the same train.'

'The Special?'

'I'm afraid so. Your father's wish. Since it gives him pleasure.'

But the Special, which had been shunted onto the reserved siding in readiness to convey them in state, had to be shuttled back to the workshops for repair, every pane of glass smashed overnight by a rabble of malcontents.

Mohini and Rabi left by the evening Express.

By an easier, lesser, slower train, cunningly chosen to emphasise the casual nature of his mission, went the Court jeweller. He had executed an order from His Highness for a pair of the finest diamond cuff-links. Rather well, he felt, opening (in his mind's eye) the little satin-lined box with his name, Kewalram, in gold on the red morocco, and the four huge square diamonds blazing inside, which reposed in the fob of his waistcoat. He also felt, somewhat patronisingly, that none of the respectable gentlemen who shared his carriage could possibly guess what their sober companion was worth. It gave him a certain mild pleasure as he was jolted along, box next to breast, Kashmir shawl at the ready to fend off the first nip of mountain air, to which he was unaccustomed.

'My dear Waji, what for! It isn't my birthday or anything, my dear fellow!'

'Oh, just, H.E. A token, let us say. Never have managed Magnolia Lodge on my own, not in a thousand years. Most— er—most.'

Bawajiraj, squirming. Avoid gratitude like the plague. Appreciation, possibly, *le mot juste?*

'A token of my appreciation, my dear Sir Arthur.'

'That's very handsome of you, Waji. Most handsome.'

Sir Arthur was quite overcome, not by the gift, which he did not care for and would not have chosen for himself, but by the kindness that prompted it. He could not bring himself to refuse, as was his usual practice. Dear old Waji, he said to himself; and shot his cuffs, inversely so to speak, hoping no English eye would fall on the somewhat flashy ornament.

The first eye that fell was Lady Copeland's, who wanted no part. But the blue fire drew her. It was too fine a gem to be condemned to those outré frames. Perhaps one day, she determined, she could have it re-set for Sophie . . .

The family was due the next day—the second lot, the son and, er, his mother, his Personal Assistant, after cautious enquiries, had informed the Resident.

Bawajiraj bustled about his preparations, bemoaning at intervals certain deficiencies in Magnolia Lodge which were due to circumstances beyond his control. Some Hun or other—tribal niceties escaped him—making trouble. Kaiser Bill, the Maharajah would say, if pressed, with distaste, in the manner of Sir Arthur. Kaiser Bill was preparing for war and what had gone like clockwork before was beginning to stick. Shipping lanes clogged. Consignments held up. China ordered from Harrods had still to arrive. Mappin's cutlery was in the same boat. A whole shipment of wine had gone astray; they were down to a couple of cases in the cellar. Worse to relate, Purdey's had courteously declined to give a date for the delivery of the 12-bore shotguns.

Rabi sympathised with his father, but bore these misfortunes with a certain stoicism. His eye, invited to dwell on disasters and deprivations, remained cool, and his voice, while doing its best, took on unintended ministerial inflections.

Mohini had remarked on the honing that was going on. So did Bawajiraj, but he dismissed it as a regrettable but passing phase, which he was prepared to overlook, and indeed found easy to do, such were the felicities of his nature; so that it was Rabi who felt raw, like some kind of assassin manhandling a child.

* * *

He was up by five the next day. The meet was at six. Showered and dressed he stepped out onto the balcony, which overlooked rolled lawns, the Magnolia Walk, massed rhododendrons, and a forest of pines in the distance. It was a brilliant, frosty morning, grass crystallised, spears glittering. At home it would be dew, more soft, as ravishing. How many shapes water could assume! Astonishing incarnations before which one would reel but for familiarity, most precious of all in its pure state. Those fish, gasping. Women walking five miles a day, sometimes, for a potful. Not a drop slopped, he had noticed, though when the drought ended they left trails of wet asterisks . . .

'Lovely morning, Rabi!' Maharajah, on Tantivvy, calling.

'Glorious!'

'Come on down.'

'I'm on my way.'

Off the balcony in a flash, racing down the stairs, boots clattering, new wool barathea going *wurf-wurf!* against brisk thighs.

Hunt assembling: riders, *syces*, horses: chestnuts and bays, a piebald, a roan, coats burnished, horse-breath like white smoke in blue air, leather squeaking, foot in laced basket of *syce*-fingers, up, mounted, feel like a king riding down to the valley.

'Should be a good day.'

'A field day.'

'Beaters out early.'

Beaters beating beasts out of their lairs. Sort of wickerbats, plus drums, gongs, clappers, din like kingdom come. Indignant beasts scrambling out—what is going on? Soon to find out.

It's a battue, sort of. Goes like this: five heats, four a side, should be five but it's the end of the season. Too bad for the young boar that's just been threshed out, piggy eyes rolling, curly tail perky: some kind of game, isn't it? No it isn't, not exactly.

'Come on, Rabi!'

The first heat's away, after pig, who has bolted. Rabi brings his horse round and pounds after him, heels encouraging speed, spear at the ready. He's in the lead, almost on pig. Pig stops dead, thundering hooves too close for comfort, and shows his tusks.

Horse stops too, not liking what it sees. Rider digs his heels in and urges it on. Straight towards Tusker.

Such a brave horseman!

The Maharajah's dark warm features are congested with blood, and marvelling.

It is not the horseman, actually, but the horse that is brave. Not even that, but those jabs in its sides. It thinks about its belly, which is at stake; gut to gullet it is naked. The horseman risks a leg, which is encased in a boot. Jabs come harder. Rolling its eyes like china balls the horse obeys, goes at pig who is charging.

Horseman, poised valiantly, veritable St. George, aims for the shoulder. But pig is not waiting. It swivels smartly. The blade enters an eye, withdraws with sludge in the blood channel. Proof of first spear, all right, but in the wrong place. Ghastly!

Pig runs on, it is running for its life, it has gathered. Pursuer pursues, spear gone wild, anything to finish. Anything not to, beast belts on. Liver, spleen, bladder, all are ruptured, all kinds of mysterious fluids are spurting. Bit of a shambles, actually. But on, trotters going like pistons, it must be possessed. One more thrust, *surely*. Yes. Pig falls. Please, please die. Anything to oblige, kind sir. One thing though, just one thing.

Before it gives up its piggy ghost it turns one furious eye upon the hunter while the second revolves with it, a blind, but glaring, red-jelly of an eye.

* * *

'What *for*, Rabi?'

'Oh well.'

This time the hunter is queasy; obstinate shoulders will not rise to a shrug.

* * *

Five before lunch. Not bad, eh? Two after.

They rode back, glowing from mountain air and their exertions. The beaters trudged back on foot. The pigs were carried, trotters strung to poles on bearers' shoulders, heads lolling from the springy bamboo. No one wanted them, really. Unlike tiger or leopard, pigskin lacked éclat. You couldn't drape it over couches, say, or hang it on walls. Not much good for anything

235

except wallets, which one did not carry, or possibly, the Maharajah supposed, for shoes.

So the pigs went to the underlings. The carcases were flayed and an outcaste cobbler sidled in, past the guard at the Lodge gates, whom he had first to bribe, to take away the skins. The flesh hung around, pink and somewhat gouged, neither Hindus nor Muslims would touch it; until with the help of a no-caste cook (he was a good Baptist actually) it ended up as rather high pork at less finicky tables. The remains went to the laughing hyenas, who nosed around at night, cackling, going haw-haw-heeaugh! shriller and higher as pork smells sharpened their appetites.

The hooves were acquired by the Lodge. Clean and polished, crevices neatly cleared out by hoof-picks, weighted with lead and mounted in silver, they were distributed in due course around the gunroom to add tone and patina which, the Maharajah could feel, this newish place lacked.

Long before this dispersal, though, they assembled on the verandah for the photographs. Pigs in the front row, snouts over the side to forestall puddles on the tiles, the more loathsome wounds tidied up for the camera (morticians *par excellence*, these hunt servants). Principals centred in the second row: the Resident, the Maharajah, the Maharajah's princely friends, the Military Secretary, one Governor, two ADCs, and the Heir-Apparent. Yes, the Heir-Apparent: the Hon'ble the Resident having that very day conveyed the glad tidings of His Excellency's recognition of the Maharajah's successor. In the third row, in this most punctilious hierarchy of the hunt, the senior *shikari*. Last of all the four-anna rabble, a grinning semi-circle of beaters and such, destined to be lost in a photographic haze. But the Principals stood out clearly in the photograph, which became the most hallowed in the Maharajah's possession.

He had a premonition even at the time, for when the prints were delivered he handled them with reverence, debating lengthily with himself before he took up his pen and wrote under them, in his best flowing copperplate,

Simla: An Unforgettable Day
With the Heir-Apparent
and Others.

* * *

Rabi received the accolade of viceregal recognition equably. The prize had been dangled too long—from the beginning of his uterine life—to make a shattering impact now. Whatever Sir Arthur might think, and it was clear Sir Arthur did think: an air of mellow bounty clung to him, coupled with sonorous rhythms when he raised a weighty glass to the Maharajkumar. Whatever, indeed, the Maharajah might feel, and it was plain what he felt: a pride that wreathed his brow in visible laurels, joined to the nuzzling gratitude that even a thoroughbred descends to as sugar-lumps melt on its tongue.

Thus impact was tempered, and Rabi's undeniable pleasure included vicarious elements in that he was pleased for the sake of his father, that somewhat portly figure that bustled about, endlessly entertaining, a kindly bumblebee.

And for himself? He experimented cautiously, to see. Heir-Apparent. Heir to the Throne of Devapur. The reverberations came all right, but oddly muffled by what had been amassed by secret unremitting processes at conscious and unconscious levels: those doubts, inflections, obliquities, what speech expressed and slurred over, the dry notes that entered the voices of Dowager and Dewan, his own observations of the bizarre, recorded mechanically and teased out later in the stillnesses of the mind: an accumulated charge that riddled the whole concept, making it a fragile golden honeycomb.

* * *

But if the accolade fell muted the days were charmed, living up fully to anything imagined during that period of deprivation before Magnolia Lodge blossomed in Simla. The Maharajah, superlatively skilled at coaxing pleasures out of the most unpromising situations—he even managed to enjoy the more arid durbars and garden-parties that stupefied a full three-quarters of the attendance—was in his element in this sparkling eden created for and consecrated to enjoyment.

An organising genius, Court and cantonment were wont to say, with a genuine admiration that sprang straight from first-hand involvement, of its Head. Privately Bawajiraj was inclined to agree. Faced with difficulties—delays, shortages, the rash of problems inevitable to a newish establishment—that would have felled a lesser man, the buoyant Maharajah emerged with colours flying. Entertainments, superbly planned and executed, fully up to doings in the State Capital, rolled smoothly off his drawing-board. Luncheons, dinners, picnics, battues, a moonlight Mystery Excursion—there seemed no limit to ingenuity. The Maharajah's guests—a wide circle, a good many of the Ruling Houses ran Simla establishments and came up for the season—said as much, often to his face, generosity a feature. At such times Bawajiraj could feel his ears positively burning. At times Rabi did indeed notice a dull red suffusing his father's earflaps, a turbulent area that could not be disciplined to the offhand hues the Maharajah would have chosen.

'Have to hand it to your old man, Rabi.'

The bristling warrior-Head of Sikh Dominions, a dab hand at frolicking himself, often seen in an amethyst turban charging at the head of his team, rapping out these handsome compliments. Pleasing, decidedly, but embarrassing. Deflect it slightly, only decent thing to do.

'Not quite doddering yet, you know, Pooky.'

'Come, come Waji. None of us gets any younger. Can't even pretend, not with these strapping youngsters around, eh Rabi?'

'No, Highness. Though I would agree with my father.'

'You would, would you?'

'Yes, sir.'

'Good for you, my boy. You stick up for the older generation, we could all do with a bit of support.'

'Pooky, you don't mean—? Ranjit isn't—?'

'No, no, no. Ranjit's a fine boy. Backs me to the hilt. But the younger generation, some of 'em, they're a bit, don't you know.'

'What?'

'A bit restless. No. Why should I mince my words? Disloyal.'

'Disloyal!'

'To the Flag! Impertinent cubs!'

Two flags, in fact; the Union Jack and the Standard of the State, though their fortunes were so intertwined they appeared as one. They gazed reverently at this entity, the two crumpled Chiefs, the mulled wine cooling in chilled hands, until the warrior moved to retrieve the situation.

'Ah well, not our problem, Waji, thank God.'

'You're absolutely right.'

'To Rabi.'

'To Ranjit.'

'Your very good health, Highness.'

'Ah, thank you, my dear boy. We rely on you youngsters, you

know. To carry the torch. When we have gone to join our
ancestors, your father and I, and the conches are lamenting
. . . then you must take up the baton.'

'Yes, sir.'

'In the relay of life, and bear it honourably. Promise.'

'Do my best, sir.'

'To our sons.'

'To the future.'

'I'll drink to that as well. Our sons and the future. Waji?'

'Mm?'

'Cup's empty, old boy.'

'Bearer-r-r!'

'Huzoor.'

More toasts, the golden wine flowing, chilled hands thawing,
chilled minds warmed, linings grateful for spicy oblations, a
richness of grapes and ginger colliding congenially with wood-
smoke. While the servant waited, a kind of glaze come over him
but somehow still on his feet, somehow still clutching the flagon,
the crest of his starched *pagri* cocky while the rest of him sagged,
under the drill, held up by belt and badges, man and outfit ready
to drop but gritting it out in the fervour of retaining this plum
job secured over the head of fifty contestants.

'Must go, Waji.'

'No, no. Night's young.'

'Night's over. Deuced enjoyable and all that, but over.'

'If you insist.'

'I do. Dawn is breaking.'

'Nonsense.'

'There, in the East.'

'As black as pitch.'

'No soul, Waji, that's your trouble. Rabi, heave me up, there's a
good lad.'

'Bearer!'

'Huzoor.'

'No, *no*. Not wine. His Highness's carriage, send for it, will
you?'

Bawajiraj resigned, some kind of hill-billy, where did the
comptroller recruit such specimens? No point in snapping
though, the man was doing his best.

So was Pooky, only his knees kept buckling. They had to hold
him up, Bawajiraj on one side, Rabi on the other, while they
waited for the carriage. Between them they bundled him in,
stood watching while it lurched away down the hill, its riding
lights glittering in the frosty air, Pooky's grateful face hanging

out of the window like a moon until it vanished abruptly round a bend.

They went in together, lingering a while by the dying fire, the Maharajah lambent. All in all a good evening.

'Enjoyed yourself, Rabi?'

'It was perfect.'

'Better next year, my boy. Have the flaws ironed out by then.'

'Weren't any, far as I'm concerned.'

'Truthfully?'

'Truthfully.'

'Ah well, you're a kind boy, Rabi. But even Pooky noticed—bound to, man's a perfectionist—only he was too much of a gentleman to say.'

'Too tipsy.'

'Well, maybe. Poor old Pooky! He only drinks up here, you know, with friends, he daren't tipple in his own State . . . that's why he goes over the edge. A sound man, though, my boy. As sound as they come. And he's perfectly right, you know, *in vino veritas* and all that—'

Bawajiraj clapped an affectionate arm about his son's shoulders, his voice gone shy, jibbing at these displays but helped along by the hour, and firelight and wine, and what this handsome scion had kindled.

'You are our torch-bearers, Rabi. Our inheritors. To you, my boy.'

Raising a last glass to his heir, who was suddenly seized, incapable of even the simple gesture required to respond to an inheritance. So stiff he could not, or could not bring himself to, because it seemed to him as if the muted years had suddenly begun to bell and toll in his ears. So he crouched, deafened, in the flickering light, with heavy-lidded eyes and shoulders that felt and rejected the weight of what was being bequeathed.

Though in the end he did manage to sip, and even to raise his leaden eyes to the glad Maharajah to whose blood he was tied, an element not easily disowned.

240

9

The next day they left for Bombay.

No *bandobust*, a private visit, a small private party, the Maharajah decreed; and after a pitched battle they whittled it down, not counting ancillaries like bearers and *chaprassis*, to fourteen. When the tiny company was assembled Bawajiraj did wonder, casting a doubtful eye, how he was going to manage, but cheered himself up with the thought that he was not, after all, casting off into some uncivilised hinterland such as Mohini might recommend, and such as was a feature of his State, but journeying smoothly to what was, he believed, the finest hotel in Bombay. Unbeatable service. Magnificence without vulgarity. None of that tinselly glitter bounders went for. A glow, rather. A certain *je ne sais quoi*. In short the sort of place one stayed at, the Imperial. He and his friends invariably did when, for whatever reason, an invitation from His Excellency (a summons to the Guest Suite at Government House *was* rather special) was not forthcoming.

Restored by the thought of the resources on which he could fall back, if necessary, the Maharajah settled himself into the pearly sueded interior of the limousine—nice change, automobiles, after trundling up and down hills in carriages (motorcars by decree, and quite rightly, only for Viceroy and C-in-C in Simla)—that had come to meet his train.

Three motor-cars, judiciously chosen for size without ostentation, conveyed the party from station to hotel. Not a cavalcade, of course, but still quite a procession, three sleek limousines, one with pennant flying, all with chauffeurs in white uniforms and peaked caps, purring along the streets of Bombay.

The odd thing was how few came out to look.

It struck Bawajiraj. He had taken up his usual position, on the right, with the hood down, so that he could wave back—he had never begrudged the people. But it struck him he need not have bothered. The number of people around was negligible, and of these the merest handful paused, and the cheers they raised were desultory, as if their hearts were not in it. Of course, he reminded himself, this was not a Durbar Drive. It was a private visit, no occasion for acclamation, one did not expect . . .

But as muted streets and mum citizens went by he did confess to a twinge or two. It was a little, well, disappointing, to be allowed to pass like any ordinary man.

The hotel, however, made amends. A full fifty yards of approach was lined with its staff, all beaming, and salaaming, and wearing his favour (knotted ribbons in the Devapur colours) pinned to their breasts, above the brass badges. Giggling children, posted at intervals, cried Welcome, welcome! in shrill uninhibited voices, pelting the motor-cars with assorted petals. Under the grand portico senior members of the staff were assembled, rather in the style of a guard of honour except that all of them were smiling, radiating a cordiality that warmed the cockles, nothing remotely stiff about *this* company. It melted Bawajiraj. Craning eagerly, but unobtrusively, over the crush hood, he sought, and detected, the cherubic features of the Head Chef, in the second row, under a tall hat. And some way behind him could that be—yes it was! his own table waiter, the same Madrassi rascal who had served him the year before. And there in the centre, bright as a ju-jube, was the Manager, his old friend Manekji, hair gleaming and teeth polished, shiny face splitting with pleasure, garlands as thick as ropes (out-of-season roses and lilies, netted in a criss-cross of silver) draped over a dapper sharkskin arm.

Glowing and golden, honey routing the disagreeable vinegar drip, Bawajiraj alighted. He felt he was himself again. He felt, almost, as if he had come home. Home from home, Pooky often said of the Imperial. One had to absolutely agree.

Surrounded, supported, feted, garlanded, somewhat in the manner of a Japanese flower-pellet placed in a tumblerful of water, the Maharajah expanded and bloomed.

In the morning there was, from the Maharajah to Mohini, a single flawless pink magnolia. It came up with the *chota hazri*, nestled in moss, among the early morning cups of delicate Spode, waiting to ravish the two silken humps that would—the servant, concerned that the tea should be piping, was rapping tenderly on a china rim with a golden spoon—shortly sit up and declare themselves to be human.

At breakfast there was, for Mohini, with the Manager's compliments, in a setting of emerald fern, a discreet bouquet of finest blooms picked from the hotel's Italian Garden.

For the Maharajkumar the management ordered and sent up a vast basket of fruit.

It was the first thing he saw when he woke, this multicoloured cornucopia, spilling out melons and pineapples and guavas with the abundance of earth itself, it seemed in those first few dazzled seconds. It was the arrangement less than the fruit, to which he was not unaccustomed: the artistic hand that had piled this horn of plenty. He was tempted, although by no means hungry, and was rolling over to reach for a guava when for no reason at all, none that he could discover, he was arrested. Arm at half stretch, roll half completed, open hand seized as if in the act of gluttony.

It happened to children. Or, rather, they did it to children, the small children of princes being taught princes' manners by the servants of princes. Used a tone, or tapped a chubby wrist intent on obeying primitive imperatives, or desperately removed a plate to stern and inaccessible heights.

'After Rajkumari, Rabi.'

'Not yet, Miss Sophie.'

His skin crawled, the parallel came so close. Yet he was not a greedy child, and the manservant had neither spoken nor moved, if anything he too seemed pinned in arrested time and motion.

The moment passed. It might never have been. Rabi resumed his roll and his fingers closed over the fruit. The stiff figure beside the bed unlocked its joints and began to function, on ball-bearings. Bed-table, fruit dish, fruit knife, finger-bowl, a napkin tucked under the Maharajkumar's chin over the braid froggings, back-rest behind the Maharajkumar's pillows.

'That's fine, thank you.'

'*Huzoor.*'

Rejecting the knife, Rabi bit into the guava, the scented flesh sweet to his tongue, but as he ate sweeter exchanges swam up. Saying to Janaki, *Here, just come in from Kulu*. Sliding the polished apples into her lap and receiving from her an apronful of tart berries that made his teeth squeak. *I picked them this morning, Rabi, I took only the ripe ones, I hope they're all right.* Assuring her that they were, loving this commerce while acid roughed up the incomparable inner glaze of palate and lips.

Such commerce was open to him now, he imagined. But when he tried his tongue grew obstinate, swelled and clove to the roof of his mouth, baulking at words as if they were poisons. So he continued to eat, jacked up against the back-rest, and it became obvious that something was over, or had shifted, as implacably as the lurch that had tipped him into the same boat as the surprised Tirumal Rao. Time in fact had run out, it came to him, for such exchanges. He was no longer a child, nor free to say, simply, Take, I would like you to share, as a child was free to say. He did not dare to.

It was the servant who dared. He dared to covet the fruits of the earth. He dared to assert the legitimacy of his desire. Unafraid he passed on the assertion, in those split seconds of standstill filched from another plane, since it had been no ordinary communication. All the while he knew his place, and kept it. He smiled and glided and served, he was a servant, trained by the Imperial, the ladies sighed over the matchless servants the Imperial trained; but under the starched white tunic he had unbound himself.

As Das had done, it came to Rabi now. The pock-marked, negligible youth in his tattered loincloth and this splendid man in his long white coat with an S-buckled belt and the fan-pleat in his turban, these two disparate people were, in fact, kin. They had shared the same emotions, felt the same bonds, and were now asserting, coolly, wordlessly, continuing to play out their allotted roles, their human rights. Prepared to weave round it though, a tacky web that rebuffed encounter while behind it the barricades were strengthened.

Nevertheless Rabi strove, from an impulse of friendliness that had never been rejected, with the one burning exception, within the boundaries of his State.

'What is your name?'

Making pale overtures, in the name of human contact, but drawing no response.

'Of no consequence, *huzoor*. You have only to press the bell. I will come, or someone will come. Day or night, we are at your service.'

'I wish to—'

It rose automatically, he had to pounce to re-frame the command.

'I would like to know,' he said, almost humbly, helplessly watching the simple rills of relationships he had known—with Das, and Janaki, and Sophie, in the congeries of the Palace that was a city—running away out of his reach to merge in desolate and vaguely hostile seas.

'It's a very common name, *huzoor*. Kapur. There are a hundred like us.'

Salaaming, withdrawing, yielding only that one small crumb of himself and even that in response to the—yes, he had to admit it—the exercise in humility that had been forced upon him.

And were there hundreds like him? A hundred Kapurs in these territories where his father's writ did not run, and even more disquietingly where it did, each with these hard knotted desires thudding against his rib-cage? He wondered, pacing, in his ruffled pyjamas, up and down the elegant room. Until it began to grate upon him, the gilding, the pearly floors, these bland shining surfaces that would never reflect, he felt, the cruder compositions of substance, the bowels, bones, and grimaces stitched up inside a reality that he knew existed. Only he did not know where he could go to find out, or how, or from whom.

* * *

The jeweller Kewalram was also a preoccupied man as he journeyed to meet the Maharajah. He was travelling, prudently, in a second-class compartment, where he attracted less attention than he would have done in the first-class compartment to which his ticket entitled him. Travelling first class made him conspicuous to his own countrymen, who went third, or at most second. It was also hazardous, since any European who came by and wanted the compartment to himself would have him thrown out, His Highness's courier though he was. Worse still, one's compatriots, these days, waxed belligerent on one's behalf, however much one wished they wouldn't. They would mill round indignantly, voicing their opinion of Europeans, and making a fearful commotion—especially if there was a Bengali around, Bengalis rejoiced in creating commotion. It ensured maximum exposure. Kewalram shuddered. He wished passionately to pass invisibly, or as near invisibly as his substantial proportions and—he secretly prided himself—presence would allow. For he had, disposed about his person in canvas pouches, under the baggy, deliberately plain high-buttoned coat, several thousand rupees' worth of black pearls and 18-carat gold fashioned into three small leopards as commissioned by His Highness, and commanded to be delivered in person at Bombay.

As Court jeweller Kewalram was not unused. He carried several thousands of rupees, even several lakhs, compressed into flawless stones, around with him in the course of business in Devapur State. But in Bombay? At a time like this? He had heard from his cousin that trouble was brewing in the city. Hot-heads. *Goondas*. Engaged in *hartals* and such, upheavals aimed at others that would, unfairly but inevitably he felt, embroil sober citizens like himself who asked only for peace. Feet neatly together, arms folded upon his severe bosom, the metal beasts surprisingly hard on the flesh of their creator, Kewalram peered nervously through the wire grille he had carefully lowered over the glass window at the delightful country through which they were passing, whose charm was entirely hidden from him.

Bawajiraj had given a good deal of thought to the design of these beasts, intended to adorn the three Silver Ghosts that had finally arrived, aboard the *Orient Queen*, and were awaiting collection at Bombay docks. He had pondered long and earnestly, consulting with his goldsmiths and jewellers, and engaging in lengthy correspondence with the Managing Director in Derby. Something of a purist, this man, Bawajiraj felt, carping passionately about what should or should not be mounted on the bonnets of his motor-cars. Naturally one applauded purity—were not Rolls-Royces the most coveted motor-cars in the world? But could not he, Bawajiraj, also be allowed to possess a modicum of taste?

Finally they arrived at a compromise. The gold leopards would share the place of honour with the Rolls-Royce mascot, in a bracket to be specially fitted next to it. Bawajiraj liked to think of it as an amicable arrangement, though sometimes he did wonder if it had not been won by attrition . . . but on the whole he could not really believe that the passionate Managing Director had been worn down merely by the flow of letters. Not at all. Possibly his enthusiasm was not total, but he had been persuaded by the essential fitness of the tableau presented to him, a tableau of twin emblems, Spirit of Ecstasy next to the leopards, sleekly disposed above the Greek temple with the State pennant fluttering between them.

Absorbed in these matters Bawajiraj hardly noticed the passing of time until luncheon was announced. Then he realised that Kewalram, essential cog in his plan, was missing, together with the leopards. These animals were vital. Bawajiraj wished to judge for himself their effect on the brand-new Silver Ghosts the moment they came ashore. He wanted the picture overall in his mind, without delay, at once. First impressions were so important. Indeed, he had resolved not to look at his motor-cars until the leopards were in place.

Somewhat chagrined, Bawajiraj sat down to his delayed lunch. He finished his coffee. His eyelids droopy (siesta hour), he went out onto the verandah and leaning on the whitewashed parapet scanned the terrain. Not a sign of Kewalram, who had been due at 10 a.m. sharp.

Frowning, a scowl marring his ordinarily cheerful features, the Maharajah rang for his Private Secretary.

The Private Secretary, Tawker, had just been informed of the fate that had overtaken the train in which Kewalram was travelling. It had been de-railed, some distance from Bombay. Agitators had removed a fish-plate. Of Kewalram himself, that purposely inconspicuous figure, there was no word. He had simply, thought the sour Tawker, vanished into thin air, leaving him the unpleasant task of conveying this and other items of bad news to His Highness. The Private Secretary had to brace himself before answering the summons.

About this time Kewalram was standing, dazed and trembling, beside the shattered sleepers and torn-up tracks. His coat buttoned up tightly about him he kept himself to himself, insofar as he could, hemmed in as he was by the crowd of fellow passengers who had tumbled out of the coaches as soon as the train had juddered to a halt. From all the confusion and hoarse shouting one thing penetrated. The accident was deliberate. Agitators (Kewalram translated it as *goondas*) were responsible.

Goondas, swarming down these rugged hills like Pindharis*— the apt comparison sprang instantly to the haggard jeweller's mind—to perpetrate these unsocial acts.

Even worse to contemplate than these ruffians was the Maharajah Sahib. His Highness would be waiting—how long

*Freebooters, Mahratta auxiliaries.

already? He, Kewalram, would go down in history as the man who had kept a Maharajah waiting. Kewalram longed to consult his timepiece, but this invaluable object reposed in an inner pocket and he dared not open his coat. Two hours, he surmised; and if he was any judge it would be another twenty before anything was done to get him out of this grim spot in which they were stranded. Appalled, quivering from considerations of the Maharajah, not to mention Pindharis, Kewalram began edging out of the crowd and towards a cart track a short distance away down which, at snail's pace, he observed a solitary bullock-cart approaching.

Striking a hasty bargain with the gaping owner, Kewalram clambered aboard this creaky vehicle, squeezing his prosperous frame in among the thousand mud-pots, or so it seemed to his quailing eye, that were on their way to some *shandy*. Alternately clutching his coat and the sides of the dusty cart—it was the first time in his life he had ridden in such a contraption—the shaken jeweller actually managed, as he was jolted along, to forget the Maharajah's plight.

'My dear Tawker, the man cannot simply have vanished off the face of the earth.'

'Highness, it is difficult to ascertain precisely—the situation is very confused.'

'I'm not *asking* about the situation.'

'Sir, I have endeavoured my best. The Chief Traffic Manager himself—'

The Private Secretary had a whole host of luminaries to cite, but the Maharajah cut him short.

'What you mean is, there is no trace of the man.'

'No trace, sir.'

'In which case one must proceed without him, that is all.'

'Proceed, Highness?'

The Private Secretary was wracked again. He had actually imagined he was to be let off lightly. His voice trembled.

'Proceed where?' He managed it, rather starkly.

'To the docks, naturally. What is the matter with you, Tawker?'

'Highness, it is not advisable.'

'Not advisable! Why not?'

'Sir, the workers are on strike. The cotton mills have closed. We have just received word.'

'My dear fellow, am I proposing to visit a cotton mill?'

'Sir, the trouble may spread. To the dock. The dockers—'

Gabbling, thought the vexed Bawajiraj. What trouble? He had seen none. Service at the Imperial was what it always was, and as for hooligans, they did have a passion for de-railing trains; it meant nothing. But some prudent streak asserted itself.

'Very well. I'll think it over,' he said, dismissing the perspiring Tawker.

* * *

'As if I haven't waited long enough! A whole *year*!'

Sunk in an armchair, in which in happier circumstances he would have indulged in an overdue siesta, Bawajiraj complained bitterly to Mohini. For by now prudence had given way to an itch, not unlike restless leg, that often overtook him when thwarted in the act of taking possession of whatever it was.

'A whole year!' He twanged, a disjointed instrument. 'I cannot, I shall not wait any longer.'

'If you've waited that long a few more days won't make any difference.'

Mohini, composed on a creamy sofa, her feet tucked under her, was cracking and consuming melon-seeds, a favoured pastime, which Bawajiraj privately considered fit only for parrots. It irritated him to see her sitting there, cool and collected under the long-stemmed fans—the same fans that did nothing for his fever—careless of what it meant to him.

'You don't understand, Mohini. I must say, you don't.'

'I do.'

She paused to anchor a tendril, loosened by the controlled gusts. 'The question is, do you?'

'What do you mean?'

'Is it sensible to rush out in all this disturbance?'

'A few hooligans! Do you think I'm afraid?'

'Mill workers are not hooligans.'

'In that case where is the question of trouble?' He was almost triumphant, but for one or two uncertain particles.

'You would provoke it.'

'Poppycock.'

'Like a sitting duck, in that finery you seem wedded to.'

'Utter poppycock.'

'If you insist on being silly at least take Rabi.'

In his curiosity, he passed over the insult.

'What for?'

'They won't stone him. You might escape too.'

'Because his mother is a commoner?' He attempted to jeer, but somehow the note fell out flat.

'He is.'

'He's the heir-apparent.'

'Soul. I'm talking about soul.'

'My dear girl, d'you think those ruffians—'

'Mill workers.'

'—are conscious of soul?'

'Would it surprise you if I said yes?'

Bawajiraj gave up. He had no more to say to his trying consort. All he could say was that he was not going to be intimidated by a gang of ruffians. Determination hardened on the instant, on the words. He did, however, take care to don the most sober outfit his wardrobe contained before setting off with Rabi to claim his little fleet. Mohini had all kinds of plebeian contacts (he had noticed odd comings and goings) and much as one longed to one could not dismiss everything she said.

* * *

The strike which began with the mill workers could have developed into a national strike. Its leaders intended that it should, acknowledging that otherwise their cause was lost. They did not understand that they could not succeed until they had come of age. Until that time they could not sustain what they had begun because they were not convinced of their own strength. Continual deprivation and humiliation had chipped away this elemental but vital faith in themselves. Mohini, having vision, was not wrong in her distant view. Equally Bawajiraj, though batting in the dark, was not wrong either in believing them to be unconscious of soul. Or, if they were not, they were unaware of the force that could be released from within it. They were not alone in this. The most powerful nations of the world fell into this pit. They misjudged the strength of the human spirit.

The mill workers who, among other things, disrupted the Maharajah's programme by striking did so because they were driven. What drove them was desperation, although sinister labels were found for this driving force. Nothing short of desperation, at this stage in their history, would have stirred them to challenge the established order.

This order, though world-wide, was at its worst, or at its organised peak of perfection, according to viewpoint, in those

250

countries that had fallen under the rule of foreign governments. It seeded an already pitiless system with even more dire elements. Because the newcomers were never absorbed but preserved themselves as an absolute élite, power was divorced from responsibility. Responsibility went first and overwhelmingly to the people of the home country. It ensured that those who laboured and created were underpaid and overworked to the greater glory of those who masterminded their efforts.

Mansions arose, palaces and guildhalls and custom houses sprang up like crops of mushrooms or poppies in Liverpool and London, in Calcutta and Bombay, in Cape Town and Durban and Lisbon and Atlanta and Amsterdam, on the fertile bonemeal provided by humble labourers.

Labour was cheap.

It was cheap because scores of thousands of people had been disinherited, some of them of their land, most of them of their spirit. They neglected to claim, or reclaim, a share in the equity that was their birthright. The rates these people were paid were determined by the free play of market forces. Few, even among those who had most cause to question them, understood the nature of this determined hoax.

* * *

The mill workers of Bombay—though it would have been no consolation to them had they known—were part of this larger pattern; that is to say they were the victims of market forces. No one set out deliberately to wreck their lives.

Some mangling was nevertheless unavoidable. It was only when even this mangled state was threatened that they jibbed. The threat came about because the price of cotton had dropped. It went on dropping until it was, at three annas per pound, grazing rock-bottom. To maintain profits, wages would have to follow suit, as far as the mill owners, and indeed the mill workers, could see. But as even the present levels barely kept body and soul together, the primitive urge to survive leapt into being. It was this that drove the mill workers to their desperate act.

The chosen hour was noon. At that hour the clacking of machinery ceased. The silence stupefied owners and managements. It was not that the strike had come without warning, or that the hour was in any way extraordinary—after all, there is some point at which any given action, even the most miraculous, must begin. What startled was a density to the atmosphere: some property, hitherto unknown, that had entered and altered its composition. If one moved, it would be uneasily, in this new element. Until, of course, one grew accustomed to it.

Unaccustomed, and possibly unwilling, the authorities nevertheless acknowledged in this distortion of the usual a strength, a meshing of wills that could suspend the flow of activities hitherto assumed to be as immutable as the course of the planets.

Castles, like kings, depend upon such immutability.

Some such revelation revitalised the workers who had streamed through the gates in the grey morning. The strength that such a crowd disseminates retracts when it is reduced to its component parts. The workers, reduced, each from within his cell contemplated singly and tremulously the act that was required of him. Until the distortion wrought by a collective purpose, which had already overwhelmed the authorities, began to breed explosive and unfamiliar energies, so that when the moment came each man discovered within himself the disciplines that were needed to straighten a back, control a jibbing muscle, throw a final lever, compel a wavery finger to still the clacking shuttle.

The discovery dazzled. Upheld by this new bright element compounded out of their own human and soulful crystals—indeed, the more imaginative felt themselves borne upon palanquins—the mill workers began to flow out, in shining good humour, chaffing a bemused guard or two who still pointlessly manned the grilles of open gates, linking arms here and there, and absorbing similar outflows and subsidiaries as they streamed along the streets to the rendezvous not so much selected as inevitable.

The dockers, who came out next, needed a little longer to stoke up. Their open situation, sea and sky, tended to diffuse their energies. They missed the noon apocalypse. But when at one o'clock sharp, in response to the wire trip from the Observatory the time-ball dropped from the Fort Clocktower, they too were approaching the same state of incandescent discovery as illuminated their comrades in the cotton mill district.

The faraway globe, visible for miles, twisting its innocent purpose in a manner that would, had he known, have prostrated the respectable and law-abiding Master Horologist, worked like a signal, or even a sign from heaven, upon the scattered men. Intentions, diluted by sea and space and queasy reflections, came together crisply in a single pure beam of purpose. Dockers and lightermen, stevedores, crane drivers, longshoremen, the

252

least spindly stripling who humped a sack, ceased to labour on the instant, arresting his act in mid-air or mid-execution as necessary.

Sounds worked themselves out. The last grain slithered down chutes and lay in heaps, soundless except for the rustle of chaff, rising and subsiding at the whim of passing breezes. Hawsers dangled over holds, idly, and grew still. Lighters, oars shipped, drifted. A last sack, dumped, burst noisily, spattering jangly metal canisters. Still, technically, aboard the *Orient Queen*, destined to be the first of the fleet, the Maharajah's Silver Ghost swung, in mid-air, suspended from a hook at the end of a jib of an abandoned derrick, rotating majestically in its coir snood, its urbane surfaces blazing where they caught the afternoon sun.

The man responsible, connoisseur that he was, numerous motor-cars having passed through his hands, could not escape a pang. Clambering down from his perch he had to pause, and heave a sigh for the elegant object his action had stranded, before running on, his thin calves flashing, to catch up with his fellows.

Chaupati Beach is uniquely the people's. As far back as anyone remembers this is the place to which they have come in their thousands to picnic, to pray, to fill their lungs with sea air and to raise their voices against laws, taxes, drought, money-lenders, the government, or whatever new burden it has been intimated they must shoulder. It is at once playground and sounding-off arena, and as such it is naturally selected as the rallying point for the strikers. The selection is less deliberate than by a process of osmosis. Without explicit guidance the entire insurgent force is irresistibly bound for Chaupati Beach.

First, though, a brief divergence is staged by the mill hands. One of their number proposes that they call at the temple to sanctify the enterprise. The proposal is carried—women out-number the men. *Mumbai-ah! Mumbai-ah!* they chant, these girls and women, a cry that is variously interpreted as an invocation of the temple goddess, or of the spirit of Bombay itself—both of which are in any case intertwined. From here, spiritually refreshed, jasmine and marigold adding brave touches, the fervid contingent wheels towards the Harbour to join, as pre-arranged, the work force pouring out of Alexandra, Victoria and Prince's Docks.

This was the phalanx that met the Maharajah and his party who were proceeding on their quest for the Silver Ghosts, and who had not long since left the precincts, or even sanctuary, some are beginning to feel, of the Imperial.

The Private Secretary, primarily. He knows he is not, but will be held to be, responsible for the Maharajah's escapade. For permitting same. Or not preventing. Already he can hear the steely Dewan.

'Surely, Secretary Sahib . . .'

Thin notes that slice through him like a knife through butter. Himself bleating.

'Dewan Sahib, I am doing my best.'

'Am I denying it? But sometimes your best, Secretary Sahib, falls a bit short, shall we say, of one's reasonable expectations.'

The Private Secretary can feel his scalp prickling. He settles his round black cap more firmly on his head and grips his umbrella for strength.

'Tawker.'

'Sir?'

'What is that?'

'Sir, it is a mob. A crowd of rowdies,' cries the embattled Tawker. 'Highness, please sit back!'

'Nonsense!' snaps the Maharajah, and grasps the strap to pull himself forward to the edge of his seat.

The crowd is boisterous rather than rowdy, though its mood is both liquid and changeable. A heady impression persists that it holds its future in its hands. There is a family atmosphere: a family on an outing. Men, women, and children—yes, children, some in the party are scandalised to notice—are to be seen in its ranks. It is also orderly, partly because the disciplines of rebellion still function, partly because of the presence of police who have just arrived, owing to some muddle at headquarters, in one smallish and inadequate truck.

The glum chauffeur decelerates and brakes with a resigned *troick*! He is a married man, disinclined for heroics; and in any case there is no room for manoeuvre, certain ebullient sections of the crowd have broken off from the main body and encircled the motor-car. In his driving mirror he can see, besides the popping features of the Private Secretary, a forest of admiring hands intent, for some reason, on touching the car, whose body he has spent half the morning polishing. He hopes those grimy paws, which have already defaced the sheen, will not ruin the paintwork as well. He also wonders that the police don't stop them. A wistful picture forms in his mind of a ruler rapping smartly on impertinent knuckles, as has been done to his schoolboy son and vividly described by the victim.

The police, from a better assessment of the situation, do not share the chauffeur's wonderment. They are, due to this official hitch, vastly outnumbered, and have no wish to provoke their own decimation. They stand, these guardians of the law, in blustering khaki and blunt heavy boots, and sincerely hope they will not be called upon to attempt the impossible. This knowledge of what is possible and what is impossible passes covertly, a neat if charged exchange between rebels and guardians.

The Maharajah is not alarmed. He is not unaccustomed to crowds. He is accomplished at handling them. As far back as he can remember, even as a little boy of three, people have thronged round him, and he has never once grudged to place himself at their disposal. Now, however, is simply not convenient. He is on his way, after delays of a trying order. Even so he does not entirely forget his duty, for all that these Bombayites are not strictly speaking his people. Banishing the frown that the day's cumulative vexations have etched on his normally sunny brow, Bawajiraj smiles and waves, confident that the crowd will give way, allowing him and his party to proceed peacefully.

But this turnout, being different, does not respond. Its good cheer, its family notes, are not far removed from those that are evidenced at State durbars; its proportions are certainly those of similar occasions; and certainly too the ingredients of entertainment are present; but within the familiar and genial framework, attitudes and assumptions are radically altered.

This crowd is bold. It has indulged in some scraping of scales and sees, not the Presence before whom it must bow and make way, but a portly gentleman and his son and one or two frightened flunkeys trapped in an enamelled cage. All of this it considers fair game, and it fully intends to extract from what heaven has dropped in its lap the last ounce of profit and entertainment. Bawajiraj does not know it, but he is bearing the brunt for the cumulative extravagances of uncaring, or irresponsible, proconsuls.

The more dedicated concentrate on delivering their message. They shout, and wave their placards, on which JUSTICE FOR WORKERS is written, furiously under the noses of their captive audience; now and then the poles descend, clump! on the sunroof which, mercifully, holds. Some, inquisitive, have got their faces up against the glass and are goggling, brazen as anything, at the occupants. The younger women, dissolving their personalities into the group, have overcome their personal modesty and are ogling the fair youth. One merry girl, bolder than the rest, is actually propositioning the young man.

'Ai, you,' she calls. 'Ai, Prince Charming, where have you been all my life?'

Her eyes are sparkling. She lifts up her thin arms and clicking her fingers like castanets, glass bangles clashing, executes a spirited little dance which she sprinkles with laughing invitations for him to get out and join her.

Rabi, ears burning, watches the fizzing, spindly little creature. He could, he feels, almost be tempted. His pleasure is so apparent that it touches the twirling dancer, who leaves off her pert manner and returns his smile, lips curved sweetly, a transparent human exchange that touches him in turn. It seems to him then that this turbulent assemblage in which she is implicated, extraordinary as it is, is nearer to normal, and possesses more natural contours, than the plush, but stuffy, cocoon in which they have become isolated.

The air is certainly stale. Secretary, chauffeur, and private detective have convulsively combined to dissuade His Highness from winding down a window.

Cooped up, Bawajiraj feels, by people unamenable to reason. His sunny opinion of them begins to fade. No respect for anything, flickers through his mind (a phrase but lately on the Copelands' lips)—he can hear them chaffing the Maharajkumar as if he were one of their number. And now they have begun rocking the motor-car, he fancies he hears the springs pinging. Someone else is thumping the mudguards, and, yes, a headlamp is done for.

It is going too far. He will not put up with it. Taking firm hold of the door handle, which the unhappy Tawker is attempting to wrest from him, he opens the door and steps out onto the running board as a preliminary to descending.

In no time at all a dozen hands have assisted him to the ground.

Bawajiraj adjusts his turban. His view is confirmed. A gang of hooligans, he sees, but he is unafraid of hooligans. He intends to advise them, if they have a grievance, the proper channels to make it known.

The crowd's view continues unaltered, but its mood begins to change. This tubby merchant, portly from good food and rich sauces, is attempting to restore *his* brand of order, an order which they have come together to destroy, an order that has come close to destroying them.

As Bawajiraj raises a hand for silence the first stones fly. First blood is drawn, and trickles down a gashed temple past the corner of an astonished eye.

It is a trigger, until one becomes hardened, to witness this wanton scarlet spillage. The colour alone shocks. Messages come wrapped in warning colours.

Rabi tumbles out after his father. *Hurtles*. A projectile, fuelled by explosive, if human, impulses. This man whom they have bloodied and whatever he or they may think of him, is his father. If they lay *one* finger on him. Just *try*. Thugs! Scavengers! Sons of bitches! He is swearing at them in the accents of Janaki and Das, in the coarse and strident language that belongs to, and is bred by, the harsh world in which livings are scraped.

To which this creamy youth, this milk-fed lamb, belongs?

'Never.'

'Not in the realm of—'

'When pigs have wings, that's when—'

'One heard, though.'

'Ears can deceive.'

'One's own ears?'

These incredulous stutters are smoothly joined by the pert little dancer.

'Well, who would have thought? Eh love? Who would have thought!'

She chucks him lightly under the chin, as she might a bold and admired younger brother, and whirling, fingers like castanets, the small pied piper in her faded motley leads off down the road. Which leads, after all, to their destination. Very soon they have all departed, a marching, singing company.

The motor-car stands, a meaningless diversion, like an abandoned toy.

* * *

The day, which has revealed abnormal glints, continues to slide into the extraordinary.

The Imperial, which believes itself to be under siege—a reaction which people on the move en masse invariably evokes—has trebled its guards. The ornamental, sadly, has given way to Gurkhas. Not because ornamental cannot be trusted to guard, but because it cannot be trusted. Who knows what kind of heart beats under a Bombay visage? The management is taking no chances. Fan-pleats are withdrawn, and in their place—the D.S.P. notes with approval as he tours the area—are these tough little mercenaries in Boy Scout hats.

In the hotel there is an air of suppressed reality. Reality, it is true, has always been suppressed to vanishing point: that is the purpose of service on castors, people who glide, palm court orchestras, Italian gardens, and the indispensable vigilante who flicks away beggars like flies off the plazas and porticoes of the Imperial. But now there is a grisly suspicion of deliberate muffling. The guests stroll about, and admire the flower arrangements that grace the cold table, and hope that pink gins will tide them over, and avoid each other's owlish eyes, which confirm they are linked in a conspiracy to deny what is ballooning outside the charmed palladium.

Which is nevertheless dragged in, in the shape of the Maharajah's motor-car, which anyone can see has taken a beating. They go into it over tea.

Tea is served in the Arcadian Room.

Darjeeling, China, Russian. Cucumber sandwiches and walnut cake from Davis's. The guests are disinclined, except for tea. It could be the heat; it is a hot afternoon. Or that dented hulk, which one cannot avoid, parked where it is, or even if it weren't one has heard. Some, more highly strung, are driven to barrack the guilty party.

'A bit indiscreet, don't you think?'

'Ill-advised.'

'Unfortunate.'

'Someone should have warned him, poor old chap.'

'I believe they did. But they're so *spoilt*. Like children, some of 'em.'

'Do you think it'll amount to anything?'

'What?'

'Well, er—you know.'

'Impossible to tell. Been here most of my life but blest if I know where the next eruption's coming.'

Absently fingering lemon butterflies, contrived by the servants in the teeth of crisis, that perch on the rims of tall iced glasses.

Training tells. Nothing like discipline to stave off the heeby-jeebies.

And here is bright ju-jube, the manager, in person.

He has restored his flesh, which a chance mirror has revealed to be flagging, to its suave proportions; and has achieved the effect of a face-lift. Crow's feet of strain (four best bearers vanished) show at the edges, but in front he blooms. There is a white carnation in his lapel. His small plump hands wash themselves in the pure air.

'Ladies . . . gentlemen . . . everything I trust is—ah—to your satisfaction?'

'Thank you, yes . . . yes, indeed.'

Gratitude wafts up. Dear Manekji, one can trust him, one feels one can leave everything safely. But, alas, cads get into the best places these days. Like this pair. Buttonholing the poor man. Booming, almost, in, need one say, the accents of planters.

'Look here, Manekji, what's going on?'

'It's disgraceful. That motor-car I mean. In full view. Can't you—'

'A little local trouble, sir. It will be attended to, madam. The matter is in hand, I assure you.'

The manager escapes, still gliding. But despite himself his hands have gone from washing to wringing, for it seems to him from what little he has been able to glean that the situation is sliding beyond redemption.

* * *

The electricity workers are threatening.

There is no hard news, but that is the rumour.

The bearers bring candles, in case. The holders are fine crystal, and are normally used in the Silver Falls Ballroom for candlelit suppers. No one comments. To do so would be to concede that the abnormal is rapidly overhauling what passes for normal. A resolute outfacing of what is happening is the true and tested remedy for all unsavoury situations. It prevents them developing.

Soon the bearers troop in again. Someone has remembered the emergency generator and sent them to collect up the candles, which will not be needed after all. The guests resolutely refuse to panic. They carry on in the role they have chosen, which is firmly spliced to what is passing.

But the clash of glass against salvers jars. It suggests chaos below stairs, at the very least. Some (those planters undoubtedly) even feel it reeks of the meaningless. The inward chafing is only marginally relieved by the thought that soon it will not be too early for a drink before dinner, although dinner unfortunately is still a long way off.

In the Maharajah's suite there is a chinking of ice-cubes.

The hotel physician has prescribed an ice compress and absolute rest for his Maharajah patient. To ensure that his orders are absolutely met the management has sent in a bath filled with ice, in case the refrigerators fail. The ice comes from Wenham Lake, Massachusetts, and has had a shorter, but more perilous, run in sawdust and tin-lined chests from the ice-house in Apollo Street where it is stored to order of the Imperial.

The blinds are down, but the sun is still powerful. It throws a smouldering light, which flares up here and there where it strikes brass or the silvered blades of the whirling fans. There is a hint of nimbus at the edges of the deep-blue blinds, which turns the bobble fringe into tiny golden balls.

Bawajiraj is sitting up in bed. An eye is puffy below the bandages, and the radiant outbursts make him wince, but he is more or less himself, a state of affairs accelerated by a return to an ambience that makes eminent sense to him.

Mohini sits beside him, in the space he has cleared for her on the four-poster. Her features are pinched from an appreciation of how close it has been, which he refuses to accept. Cannot, or will not: the question poses itself and hollows her out. Mohini has an overpowering desire simply to lay her head beside his, and weep, and wash away in these floods all that is threatening so that he may never be asked to yield what supports him. But as neither tears nor love will accomplish it she turns to physical matters.

'How are you feeling?'

'I'm all right.'

'A nasty gash, the doctor said.'

'It's nothing really. Just a scratch.'

'It's all my fault.'

'Nonsense.'

'I knew this would happen. I should have stopped you.'

'How could you have stopped me?'

'I could have tried.'

'You did.'

'Not hard enough. You might have been *killed*.'

'Oh, *nonsense*.'

'It's *not*. I *told* you not to go.'

'You just said you didn't really try.'

'Only because I know how pig-headed you are.'

'In fact you said I'd be all right if I took Rabi with me.'

'I thought you would! I was wrong. Is that my fault?'

'I'm not blaming you.'

'I blame myself.'

'Mohini, please be sensible,' the Maharajah says stiffly. The truth is, his head is beginning to spin.

'Highness, you might have been *killed*.'

She is swamped by misery and fright. Tears pour down her cheeks. She cannot, in fact, envisage life without her beloved duffer.

Bawajiraj is wrung by the sight of the weeping woman. Despite their long and enchanted union it continues to surprise and delight that he should be the object of her fierce love. These unassuming qualities are one of the richer aspects of his nature, and at least part of his hold over her.

'Please don't cry,' he says tenderly. 'I'm all right, really I am, and next time I'll listen to you, I'll be very careful.'

'Promise.'

'I promise. I won't take any more risks. And you were quite right.'

'About what?'

'About Rabi. He did stop those ruffians. In a way he— Rabi, come here a moment will you?'

'Coming.'

'Saved the whole situation, eh Rabi? Tell your mother.'

'There's nothing to tell.'

'On the contrary.'

Bawajiraj's pride in this son of his surges up. He reaches out a hand to the slender youth who stands beside the bed.

'It was magnificent,' he says. 'You showed 'em, eh my boy? Just got out and stood there and showed them who was master.'

His dark face is alight. Rabi has to look away before he can speak.

'No,' he says dully. 'I didn't show them I was master. I didn't show them anything. I spoke to them in their language, that's all.'

He disengages, quite gently, from his father's clasp and returns to his room.

This room is glary, by contrast. The sun streams in unchecked by blinds and buffs up pearly surfaces. The ceiling would dazzle; there are crushed sea-shells in the *chunam* wash; but the dazzle is broken by mouldings of fruit and foliage. Grapes far up in the cornices. If you were old you would have to squint to see the vine, if not the clusters. Such heights are planned: they encourage air currents. Like thought, in churches.

Thoughts can soar under such ceilings.

Rabi's heights are pinned to the street.

The quarry he has been circling since childhood—or has it been stalking him?—is out in the open. It is waiting to espouse him, out there in the alleyways, in the reality of dust, and abandoned looms and spindles, and the snapping fingers of a ragged dancer. He has only to take a step. One foot in front of another, like this. Years ago he had guided Usha, when she was done with crawling and intended to walk: those small imperious outstretched arms, forever demanding, mother and siblings sighing, no one could match that single-minded energy. But in a desert one has time. He came out of the stretch he was doing to respond: held her in front of him, a thumb gripped tight in each hand—how tight a baby's grasp can be! And they walked together, he steadying, she staggering on her short fat do-or-die bandy legs.

One step is all he has to take. The easiest thing in the world can also be the hardest.

Rabi leans against the window embrasure. The management has warned guests not to present themselves as targets. As if to justify their caution, there is a spattering of gravel against the pane. It is sparse and quite ineffectual, but it has taken audacity to puncture the hotel's defences. He peers out and spots the reckless culprit, a boy of ten or twelve, nimbly dodging between the topiary. When he nears the gate he puts on a spurt, his bare heels flicking up dust as he sprints past the surprised guards. It makes Rabi laugh to see. He sees in the cocky heels of the youthful offender the challenge of all his kind.

'Hi, there! You up there in the arbour! It's like this, come on down and allow me to show you what it's *really* like!'

'I'm on my way. I can't wait to find out.' (Or some such frothy and nonsensical exchange that his magically lightened spirit invents.)

Still smiling, and without fuss, the Maharajkumar lets himself out of the vinous chamber.

* * *

Fan-pleats would have recognised and parleyed. Boy Scouts cannot tell a Rajkumar from a rascal. The dejected figure drooping by the roadside (it is Kewalram the Court jeweller, who has made it to the gates) can, and does. His efforts are interpreted as a cunning plot between two unscrupulous rogues, one presentable, the other this tattered merchant from whom flows a stream of outlandish syllables. Kewalram is defeated. What language, he wonders, do these uncouth gorillas speak, in which a civilised jeweller can be expected to communicate? He sinks back on to the boulder from which he has lately and hopefully arisen, and puts up his umbrella for shade in the long hours of waiting that lie ahead, some of which he will use to dwell on the enigma of the Ruler's son, who for inscrutable reasons has elected to treat him as a total stranger.

Rabi slips away. He, too, is beset by enigmas that are rooted deeper and have festered longer than the one that engages the jeweller. He does suffer a pang, though. Poor old Kewalram, all he asked for was a flicker of recognition, even if in the circumstances this was the last thing . . . but he does not allow regret to detain him. In no time at all he is shot of the bewildered retainer.

10

In the streets there is an air.

It has been variously described as brewing, or simmering, or ballooning, or even pregnant, according to the various interpretations of events that have gripped the city.

There are even those who prefer to invoke the weather. It is stuffy, they say, and point to the thunderclouds that are rolling in over the Bay, and lay a finger to throbbing temples that tell them a headache is coming on.

To Rabi it is an air of expectation. This is not merely his opinion, but what he garners from the concentrate of emotion exuded by his co-citizens. They expect, these people: they dare to believe that by the end of this chapter they will have wrung, through their own exertions, an admission of the justice of their cause. Any other ending seems inconceivable, tantamount to an overturning of natural law. Their error, which will confound them yet, lies in confusing natural justice with what passes for it in learned, if malformed, institutions.

But as the future is hidden, they proceed jauntily, riding high on mineral hopes, like gold prospectors. Some even exhibit strange glints, a tinny light on ardent cheeks, though such glimmers can also be discerned in skin that is stretched too taut over bones.

Rabi goes with them, toes pointing the same way, feet marching in the same direction.

At first, true, he cannot find the crowd. The scene has recovered the remote tranquillity that has earlier lulled the Maharajah, and is indeed the view expensively procured for the hotel's guests. But when he moves away from this quilted region, and enters areas where livings are unlined, whatever iron has crimped the atmosphere sharply reasserts itself. This zone is electric. It draws the people into knots and clusters. People speak plain, and the sparks that fly from these blunt instruments get them moving. Clusters coalesce. A kind of sea begins to flow.

Flowing with it the whys and hows that have pushed up so liberally of late cease to harass Rabi. They are naturally sprung, he begins to suspect, from the incoherent element in which he lives, whereas the movement that now involves him has both coherence and purpose. He is at once with this tide. He trusts its intention. The crowd is bound for Chaupati Beach. So is Rabi, although he has never heard of it, and indeed has been steered away from this insalubrious and plebeian meeting-place. His only surprise—the merest trace, and soon despatched—is the speed and ease of his assimilation.

* * *

And now who should come to him but his grandmother. She is not marching beside him, but still, it is a quality she has made her own. She has opened her palm and is coddling his pony (his beloved and lustrous-eyed Tara) with quartered fruit while she converses with him, those quiet syllables that last and last, although a jingle of harness can muffle them.

'You see, Rabi, I didn't grow up in a Palace. And only barely in the State . . . a little valley on the borders, it was too far away to count. All we ever saw was the tax collector; he came after the harvests, to make sure of his tithe—he didn't trust the *ryots*, you see. So I had no idea, neither had your grandfather, what it would be like. We used to laugh about it. And when we got there it was so dazzling, all that panoply, far beyond anything we had imagined. But we weren't taken in, I don't think . . . we did understand about ordinary people, we *were* ordinary people, a few rungs up, perhaps a great many rungs up . . . but it didn't stop us seeing people.'

'I can see people.'

'Of course. You don't wear blinkers, no one has to.'

'Horses do.'

'Horses are forced to. Human beings . . . ah well, perhaps they are forced too, in a way. But not you, Rabi, never let anyone force you.'

The process, though, is insidious. How does one measure in oneself so stealthy a takeover? There will have to be some contortions, Rabi suspects, before he can judge with clarity.

* * *

All around him there are people. It is like a durbar crowd, except that in a durbar crowd he would not be packed in among them. He has, in the boundless curiosity of childhood, essayed to look in from without, to step out from the moving carriage into the cheering throngs, and because it is an age when imagination is powerful, has often succeeded. It intrigues him now to discover that the reality of that experience approaches what is fed into him from the actual stimuli of feet, shoulders, breath and massed and moving bodies.

He has marched like this before. It is the purpose behind the movement that is different. A durbar exalts and sustains the status quo. This multitude is on the move to declare that that state is no longer viable. The difference is as disturbing as a first emission, the inkling it brings, engulfing and incredible, of the staggering potential of which it is the herald.

When the hand touches him he jumps. It belongs to a short dark man with sharp eyes and a hook nose that gives him the look of a vulture.

'Ai, you. What are you doing here?'

'Same as you.'

'You're not one of us.'

'Didn't say I was.'

'You shouldn't be here then.'

'There's no law.'

'A spy. You're a spy.'

He can only mean *agent provocateur*. There is nothing to spy on here, it is all out in the open. Rabi shrugs and moves up the column but is not so easily rid of the vulture who moves up with him. He has a poor physique and has to struggle to keep up, which increases his spite. One hand, like a claw, grips Rabi's sleeve.

'Ai, you!'

'Leave me alone, will you?'

'Banchot!'

The lewd imprecation draws a frown from the woman walking

alongside, a mill hand in her middle years, her sari respectably swathed about her head and person.

'Keep it clean, will you? There're some of us as aren't used to your filth, can't you see? Nor care for it either.'

Her matronly gaze impartially includes all right-minded marchers, but especially herself, the young girls in the contingent, and the youth with the rarefied features (about the age of her own eldest son, she reckons) whom anyone can see doesn't belong here, but that's no reason to bawl him out or anyone else for that matter. Her reasonable sentiments are taken up and applauded here and there. Vulture, who has clearly earned some reputation as a bully, falls back rebuffed and unlamented. One man, to Rabi's surprise, is even moved to clap him on the shoulder.

'*Shabash, shabash!*' he cries, and another endorses him:

'He has a good heart to join us.'

'On our side, that's what matters. Good luck to him!'

There is a palpable re-statement of frontiers here that Rabi grasps, and it shakes him oddly. It seems to him that wholly without credentials he has been edging towards humanity, and now humanity is drawing him in without even asking to see his pass.

Rhythm reaches up from those marching feet, one pair of which belongs to him, to encapsulate the psyche.

Someone has come up with a drum. The trim *rum-pa-ti-tum* gingers up the joints. Feet tripping light fantastic (hot and flinty streets and pavements, actually, and only a few have sandals strapped to their soles) the miles fall away . In no time at all they are at Chaupati Beach.

Fifty thousand of them. Contingents have come from the mills, the factories, the docks, the railway workshops, the grain depots. The men are in white shirts and *dhotis*; the flimsy mull swirls up in the wind that blows in from the sea and suggests billowing canvas: a squadron of yachts inexplicably berthed on the sand. The women go for colours (once vivid, now faded from washing and wearing): orange, pink, indigo, saffron, and spotted cotton. This year dotted red-on-violet is very popular, especially among the girls.

Hemming in these colours of the country is the whipcord of khaki. Khaki is the smack of authority. It is worn by the army, the police, the belted *chaprassis* who man the courts and marshal, or cow, the citizenry into reverent and orderly files.

Khaki is thick on the ground here. The authorities are not to be caught napping twice. The military is in reserve. Police are deployed by the hundred: booted, spurred (a score of mounted police: man and horse an unbeatable combination for dispersing mobs), armed with steel-tipped *lathis*.

The two factions, neatly divided by hue and purpose, the one to impose its will, the other to thwart it, size each other up.

For the crowd it is a jubilee spree with numbers—50,000, at least. The noughts bowl one over; some men are even seen to embrace. The sheer weight of these ciphers has closed the mills, dislocated the railways, forced shops to shut, brought traffic and trade to a standstill. They feel entitled to ask what power can impede such a force and gleefully answer themselves that none can.

Khaki knows better. There is a whole science devoted to dismantling such blocks, driving in wedges to split the mass and systematically scattering the isolated fragments.

An officer rides by and considers that all is under control. He proceeds on his way, outriders clearing a passage, along Marine Drive, past the beach where this extraordinary meeting is taking place, and up the road to Government House at Malabar Point where he intends to deliver the sitrep in person.

* * *

Malabar Point is, by any calculation, the pinnacle of Malabar Hill, which is already ornamented with the immodest dwellings of the rich and powerful. Government House is imposing. It dominates, as it is meant to. Consequently there is little need for the incumbent to assert himself, and there is a marked lack of enthusiasm for what is privately referred to as throwing one's weight about.

The grounds follow a pattern that is similarly without vehemence. They are extensive and luxurious without being *nouveau*, like the textile millionaires' estates on the West side, and command some of the more pleasing views over the Bay and the city. The gardens are a delight. Successive Governors' Ladies have taken it upon themselves to create special effects, here a Walk, there a View, the overall achievement is enchanting. Maharajahs, among others, are known to covet an invitation to the Governor's Residence—though it can mean being quartered in the detached sleeping-bungalow in the compound—and suffer the most exquisite emotions when cordially commanded . . .

Such environs discourage fluster.

The Government indeed is playing it cool. The spot report is received by an ADC who undertakes to convey it to the Governor at a suitable opportunity.

His Excellency has guests. An opportune moment does not present itself until after tea, when the Governor appropriates a half hour to himself for a brisk constitutional.

'Everything under control, did you say?'

'I understand so, sir, yes.'

The ADC lopes after his Lordship. He is a fit young man, keen and ready for anything.

'Armitage, was it?'

'Yes, sir. And Major Holland's i/c the reserve.'

'Good.'

His Excellency pauses, as is his custom, at the spot where, on the spur of the hill, in a gap between the heliotrope, a magnificent vista opens.

'Fine view, Simon, don't you think?'

Simon, invited, peers between the foliage. Far, far below lazes the Arabian Sea, fringed by a line of creamy surf. Beyond is the wide curved beach, which at the moment is swarming with ant-like creatures who appear to be in a state of flux. He inclines his golden head.

'Indeed, sir. Quite beautiful,' he agrees enthusiastically.

The Governor casts an approving glance at the handsome young man (son of an old comrade-in-arms). Simon, he feels, should go far.

* * *

The agitation observed by the ADC was due to the police moving in to break up the crowd. They did so because their officers judged that the speeches had become dangerously inflammatory and were inciting the populace to acts prejudicial to law and order. Stones, it is true, had been thrown, and panes of glass, and other property, had suffered.

First, punctiliously, they invited the leaders to desist of their own accord from speech-making, and to disperse their followers in an orderly manner. The speech-makers were dumbfounded. The whole purpose of mustering was to speak out against what they considered the intolerable conditions imposed upon them. Silence for this host was the last thing. Look! they want to shout at the top of their lungs. Look at these miserable shoulders, these collapsed bellies, this faded rag that has to be washed and worn on the body because there is no other, although we are the ones who daily manufacture a thousand. Look at us! Our flesh and our children's flesh melt on the bone to provide you with trifles, look at us if you dare!

They were in the middle of this, and working up well, when the loudhailers called on them to desist and disperse peacefully to their homes. It enraged both leaders and followers and drove them to accusations, denunciations, and challenges of an extreme nature.

This was when the police moved in, employing their break-up tactics to scatter the meeting.

If this kind of action was new to the crowd, most of whom spent their days humped over looms and levers rather than tangling with the *sircar*, for Rabi it was a revelation to observe the limbs of government so deployed.

He has never seen policemen like this before. There is no connection between the benign and courteous paladins of his experience and this punitive horde pouring onto the beach. These men are *mad*, they are *rampaging*. They have unstrapped their *lathis* and are using these berserk clubs to strike down unarmed people. Flailing at them. The scene has manic overtones.

Police fell too, it has to be recorded. But Rabi's eye registered only what happened to those among whom, for the present, he had cast his lot.

He watches, dazed. Near him a man is hit. He has swaddled his head in a shawl but the *lathi* gets through to the skull, there is a *crump!* as the bone is shattered. The man screams and falls; his fingers, splayed on the littered sand, are ground into it by a boot, a second mangles it further. It is outrageous to see, even in the middle of outrage. It lifts Rabi out of his daze, but when he tries to help the intention is scuppered by the tidal flood of frightened people that intervenes. The human wave that sweeps him away rolls back from the edge of the sea where the makeshift podium stands, which a posse of police is demolishing. Men topple, or are thrown, from the flimsy structure. There is the sound of matchwood splintering. People are screaming. Some of the cries are high and shrill, the voices of women. Is hers among them, he wonders dully, the girl with the clashing bangles?

There is broken glass on the sand, blood, bits of rag, jagged stones, driftwood, ripped-off sandals. People race over this sharp detritus, sobbing and gasping. This crowd has lost its cohesion, all sense of purpose, all sense. A woman trips and falls. The herd, unseeing, or unable to control its impetus, keeps coming. Its members fall one by one, like spillikins, on top of the woman, who is buried in moments under a pile of bodies. The enormity of it does generate a flicker of lucidity. One or two stop, and begin heaving at the fallen, but now there is further trauma as a mounted column begins to work inwards.

Rabi cannot see the cause, but he feels the new and heightened panic that has been injected into the crowd. It turns his legs to water, implanting him in the path of whatever is coming.

'Run!' he hears a hoarse voice shouting. The man clutches his arm and drags him away from the human pyramid. His mouth is gobbling. It belongs, he notes with a faint surprise, to the vulture.

'Run, you fool, run!' he screams, and gives him a violent shove, knee in the small of his back, that sends him flying. Recovering his balance Rabi begins to run.

Where?

Anywhere to get away from Chaupati onto any road that leads to sanity.

The road that skirts the beach is lined with mounted men. Like a *chevaux de frise*, it does occur to Rabi, but the decorative element is totally missing in this relic of martial manoeuvring that has reverted to its original purpose. He can feel a thick suffocating fear that rises in him and binds him to the fleeing barefoot echelon of which he is a part.

This bristling line means business. It means to compel disintegration, and to do so by intimidation, and it achieves its aim perfectly. The echelon wavers and slows. It has only one object left: to gain the safety of alleyways that lie beyond the cordon of khaki. Since it cannot do so in its present form it simply falls apart, breaking up into ragged units whose single desire is to dodge between that taut combination of man and beast that is drawn up, reined in, and waiting.

Even more basically it is whittled down to a case of each man for himself.

For Rabi there has never before been a horse that he has feared, or needed to fear. But then he has never before approached a horse in such circumstances.

In circumstances like these it is monumentally different.

This animal is trained. It has been bred and schooled and trained to interpret its master's will, and suppressing its own nature it will do so with its entire and fearsome capacity whatever the consequences to its puny opponent. Its power is nakedly evident looked at like this, from the ground where one stands, looking up at this manifestation of strength. That immense girth. Those pounding hooves that can reduce human flesh to pulp. The correct stance for a man in this position is to grovel, to roll in the dust and beg for mercy. But then man has his spirit to contend with.

The rider notes the ember of rebellion in the feeble creature before him and signals his mount. The order is transmitted so secretly that Rabi would not be aware except that he, too, has given such commands. He sees what is intended: the pesade, a movement that is calculated to terrify the infantry. As the horse begins to rear he darts forward and seizing the bridle reverses the motion. The frightened gelding obeys. Its nostrils flare, it is showing the whites of its eyes, but the apparatus of fear, slashing forelegs and metal-shod hooves, is safely grounded.

Rabi releases his hold and slips past the animal. As he does so the rider twists round in the saddle and lunges at him. The blow opens his scalp.

Rabi keeps going, blunders on through the obscuring scarlet mist. How long he can keep on, though, is problematical, because the blood is flowing freely and he can't really see where he is going. Quite soon he will have to stop and staunch it, he realises dimly, but the thought is far from clear, the red veils keep falling and there is a feel of expanding cotton-wool in his head.

'Here, hold up. Put your arm round me.'

The voice of the girl, or woman, is urgent and, yes, anxious; the note of concern comes through the noise and confusion. She takes his hand and draws his arm about her shoulders. It is surprising what relief even this slight support affords him in his present perilous state. Wiping the blood from his eyes he looks at this rickety saviour whose bones he can feel jutting immoderately under his hand, and is convinced he sees, beyond all belief, the pinched and somewhat sharp features of Janaki. At this point he shouts her name, or imagines he does; the syllables are clanging like bells, his head is emptied of cotton-wool and becomes a resounding belfry. The clamour is so powerful that he slumps, or at any rate relinquishes himself wholly to her offices. The girl does not falter. She is, as it happens, used to assuming burdens. She half drags, half carries him along, this lame duck whom some stray impulse of pity has lumbered her with, her primary aim being to get them both off the violent, erupting streets.

* * *

'I'm not Janaki. Why do you call me that?'

'Because you are. Though you've changed.'

'No. Really I'm not.'

'You are. Why did you run away? I looked for you everywhere.'

'My name's Jaya. I don't know what you're talking about.'

'Why are you lying?'

'I'm not. Is it likely someone like you would know a mill lass like me?'

'I did. Before you became a mill lass.'

'It's what I've been since ever so long. From so high.'

'Please don't lie to me.'

'Why should I?'

'Please.'

'All right then. I'm your Janaki,' she says, and eases the mumbling figure back on to the mat.

When he wakes again it is dark. He can see a round piece of sky and it is inky blue. For some reason it doesn't surprise him to be able to see the sky through the ceiling, perhaps because it is in line with the fact that he is lying on the ground. It is vastly uncomfortable and there is no ameliorating it, he discovers; any position he assumes feels equally barbarous. His fractious movements bring the girl to his side, or perhaps she has been there all along, melted into the gloom in her dark sari. She has lighted a small lantern, keeping the wick low, the merest blue flame licks up from the metal cleft.

'How do you feel?'

'I have felt better.'

'That man! A real vicious swine.'

'You saw what happened?'

'I had my eye on you. Off and on.'

'Why?'

'Can't really say. Just noticed you, that's all. Want anything?'

'I'm thirsty.'

'I'll get you some water.'

She is gone for a while. When she returns she hesitates, holding the *lota* uncertainly.

'Will you take from me?'

'Of course. Don't be so silly!' he snaps.

'A young gentleman like you, you should know better than to say that,' she says reprovingly, but she does overcome their caste injunctions to pour him some water.

'Here you are.'

She supports him while he drinks; the water has the faint earthen taste of the mudpot in which it has been stored. Where his head rests, through the cloth she has wound round the injury, he can feel the fleshy mound of her breast and is seized with the desire to open her bodice and nuzzle down on her bosom. She lowers him onto a dried biscuit of a pillow.

'There. How do you feel now?'

'Dried out, like a kiln.'

'It's the fever, and losing all that blood. Hold still and I'll sponge you, there's a little water left. There . . . try and sleep now, you'll feel better in the morning.'

'How long have I been here?'

'Since I brought you in.'

'When was that?'

'Late evening.'

'What time is it now?'

She shrugs. She hasn't a watch, fancy thinking the likes of her, he seems to be raving slightly.

'It's night time,' she says. Surely that ought to be enough for any living creature? But she can see he is not satisfied.

He is not. He looks again at his watch, which has stopped. Night stretches, it can be anything. The girl seems part of the same fluid confusion in which nothing can be pinned down, but at least he can try. He gropes for her night-coloured sari and fastens on to it.

'Will you be here in the morning?'

'What do you think, I'm going to vanish like your Janaki?'

'Who told you about her?'

'You did. You told me about this sweetheart of yours a hundred times!' she cries.

Her face is looming over his. If she bent any closer, just a very little, the points of her breasts would brush the brown roundels of his nipples, which are sponged and clean and as concupiscent as the rest of his body.

She does bend, having seen; puts her mouth on his and moves his lips apart with hers, just a little, just enough for those match-less inner surfaces to touch; and withdraws abruptly.

'Ah, *bachcha!* Go to sleep now,' she says roughly, and extinguishes the lantern.

When he wakes it is well into day and the circle of sky is a
brilliant blue. The hut, or whatever this ramshackle structure is
called, is bleary with smoke, only some of which escapes from the
hole in the thatch. The girl is cooking, or at least she is watching
the pot. The thin sharp profile she presents reminds him again
of Janaki but confusion is absent, only the old tenderness floods
back and invests this avatar of a playmate. An old tenderness, but
laced. Man and child connect, but the man is structured to crave
and support the dizzy potential only sketched in the immature
apparatus of childhood.

Half rising up he calls, lucidly:

'Janaki?'

'My name's—'

'I know. It's Jaya. You told me.'

'Then why—'

'I'm only teasing.'

'You shouldn't.'

'Didn't you?'

'I never did. I—'

'Last night.'

'Nights are different.'

'Why?'

'Just are. Ask any woman.'

'None of them answer.'

'You're a bold one, *bachcha*.'

She laughs, abandons the cooking pot and squats by his side.
She has white even teeth and deep-set black eyes in a pointed
face. Her hair is scraped back into a careless and untidy bun.

'You haven't told me your name, *bachcha*.'

'You haven't asked.'

'Would you, if I did?'

'Of course. Why not?'

'Go on, then.'

'My name's Rabindranath.'

'That's a grand name.'

'I'm a grand person.'

'You don't have to tell me that, *bachcha*. I've a pair of eyes in my
head.'

'What can you see?'

He challenges her. There is a turmoil to being grand that
levity cannot exorcise. Like comparisons that stick in the gullet.

His, not hers. Holed thatch in place of grapes that are moulded into ceilings. Rough walls instead of lustres and glazes of whose perfection it is impossible for her to have any conception. She has, he imagines, no base for comparisons that seize one by the throat.

'What can you see?' He repeats, with an edge.

'Only that you're not one of us. That's plain enough, isn't it?'

Her eyes are very cool. She has taken away his clothes and washed them; he can see them blowing on the line outside, but there is his frame, under the thin sheet she has thrown over it, from which comparisons spring of which both are vividly aware. Her deficient construction, elbows and kneecaps like clubheads under the threadbare cloth. His own statuary sculpted regardless of cost, royal tools have chiselled and buffed this firm svelte form which one possesses, unclothes, displays, and uses with pride. Except sometimes. Exceptions breed, after childhood. Where have they fled, the easy acceptances that oiled his transactions with Janaki? Ball-joints grate painfully in their sockets. She has to help him to sit up.

'*Bachcha?*'

'Uh?'

'Don't think I hold it against you. Not anything.'

'You ought to.'

'I couldn't. Not personally. Not after I saw you right in the middle of that business. Question is, why?'

'I wanted to see.'

'See what?'

'What's going on. It's one's duty,' he says primly, a fatuous phrase, in his view, that suddenly twists, an astonishing magnet that acquires filings of dignity.

'You didn't see much, time they'd finished with you.'

'There'll be other times.'

'*Bachcha*, listen.'

'I'm listening.'

'Go back, love. To your own side. This side you'll only get hurt and why should you? It's not your fight.'

'It's mine if I choose.'

'It can never be that. We're fighting for our livelihood.'

'People's livelihood is our responsibility.' (Funny how clichés beloved of his father acquire standing and sense in these precincts.)

'Why? Do you belong to the empty-belly race?'

'If I like to belong—'

276

'But you don't.'

'It's up to me. It's been that way since I was born—they've never known where to fit me in.'

'You must be raving.'

'I'm absolutely clear-headed.'

'People are born. Do you think I could hoist up to your level simply by wanting?'

'I don't know what *you* can do. I only know what I can.'

'You mean well, *bachcha*. Have it your own way, love.'

She returns to her pot, whose rounded bottom is blackened with smoke; smoke swirls up and makes her cough as she fans the fire.

'It's nearly done. Are you hungry?'

'Starving.'

'Will rice do?'

'Do lovely.'

'Actually there's a bit of vegetable as well.'

'I could tell you were a rich woman in disguise.'

'And I knew at once you were a pauper in borrowed finery.'

She giggles as she serves him. When she smiles her sharp face loses its shrewish look and takes on a hint of muffled beauty. He feels he could love her the way she looks now. He eats slowly, rice and lady's finger, forgetting that he loathes this particular vegetable. She watches him eat, fetches in water for him to wash. When he is done she scoops his clothes off the line and brings them in over her arm, light and fleecy from airing. Kneeling she makes a present of it.

'For Rabindranath Sahib. Please to accept my gift.'

'Call me Rabi and I might.'

'Rabi, *bachcha*. Here you are, all nice and clean and fit for a young gentlemen. Please accept.'

'Do you mean you want me to leave?'

'Your family will be anxious.'

'I know about that. I'm asking about you.'

'I don't *want* you to go. But you must.'

'I'll come back then. Shall I?'

'You won't want to.'

'If I do. Will you let me?'

She doesn't answer. She picks up his shirt and eases it gently over the bandages.

* * *

The doctor who unwinds them is appalled by the quality, *vis-à-vis* the obvious rank of his authoritative, and indeed peremptory, patient who has rapped him for so much as enquiring his name.

'My dear sir, am I not entitled—'

'You're not. This is my body and it needs attention and it is your duty.'

It comes naturally to the son of a prince; there is no denying there are advantages, however much one regrets one's up-bringing.

The doctor purses his lips. He is unused. Usually he is a little tin god surrounded by worshipful acolytes, but the acolytes are strike-bound and who knows but that in these unusual times this noble youth won't resort to common violence? He removes the squalid cloth. The wound is clean and healing. No doubt the young man owes it to his own bursting health and not to the germ-laden bandages. Homily in mind, the doctor applies a fresh dressing.

'If I were you—' he begins.

'You're not, are you?' the patient slings at him, bunging rupee notes at the offended medical man who prefers discreet cheques, and who has just composed a judicious little cameo advising rest and better company.

* * *

Judicious conduct is very much on the mind of the Hon'ble the Resident.

It is not judicious for a Maharajah to offer himself as a target. It is outrageous of him to mislay a son, especially a son who has recently been recognised at the highest levels as heir-apparent to a sizeable State. Sir Arthur fumes inwardly, while not allowing so much as a wisp of steam to appear, all the way down from Malabar Point where he has been staying with the Governor—a stay already marred by the extraordinary events of this extraordinary week. Even the uplifting views have been meagre consolation, for it seems to him that the very basis of his appointment as Adviser—his judgment of character—is open to question.

'But surely, Maharajah Sahib, he cannot have vanished into thin air?' He enquires, thinly. His eyebrows are not so much questioning as accusing.

Maharajah Sahib! Bawajiraj is aghast. He is *Waji* to Sir Arthur, what can his friend mean? It is very upsetting.

'But that, Resident Sahib, is precisely what appears to have happened!'

Sir Arthur eyes the hollow culprit. Certain asperities spring to mind and are tempting, but the man is, after all, His Highness, and, it does occur to him, a distressed and anxious parent.

'Where do you think he's gone?'

He unbends a little, even removing the pith helmet under which he has found it necessary to conduct the alfresco interview.

'My dear Sir Arthur, if I only knew! But you know what young men are!'

Sir Arthur, happily, does not. His own boy is safe in the hands of an admirable housemaster. Esmond, besides, is that much younger, and has never given any cause (unlike wilful, exquisite Sophie) for anxiety.

'I shouldn't worry, Waji. I'm sure there's no need—he's always struck me as being perfectly capable of looking after himself. But he's not just anyone—is he?—to come and go as he pleases. Remind him, will you?'

Sir Arthur dons his helmet (this time for a different purpose, to ward off stony missiles that are, it is reliably reported, still flying) and returns thankfully to the haven of Government House.

* * *

The water-front is dark when Rabi makes his way back to what is also some kind of haven. The sea is inky under an overcast sky, the streets like pitch away from the glimmer of oil lamps lit by the indigent, the superior localities have been blacked out altogether by the action of the power workers. Only the hotel glares, fitfully, illumined by bursts of surging current from the erratic generator.

The guests are already complaining of eye-strain from these eccentric explosions. It becomes necessary for the Manager himself to soothe the distressed ladies.

Rabi has to pick his way. It is an unfamiliar city and the streets are littered with the debris of events. In due course the Municipality will send round carts (some days yet: the Municipality and Millowners Association is still reeling, its individual members have not got beyond declaring that they have never known anything like this to happen) but in the meanwhile there is assorted street wrack, tins, bottles, bricks, smashed bollards, broken staves, and shattered umbrellas to impede progress. Darkness hinders. He has a torch, and a good sense of direction, but the abnormal has taken over to an extent where it has altered even the physical fabric. Roads behave like heraldic serpents and swallow their own tails. Crescents become circles, dead-ends proliferate. He enters an alley—he has marched along it, knows it has an exit—and finds it blocked by a wall. He retreats, and makes for a main thoroughfare, which he imagines will be simpler to negotiate, but is thrown by a barricade, several feet tall, its jagged contours like menacing fingers against the skyline, that has sprung up impassably across the entire width of the roadway.

Soon he is floundering. There are only shadows to ask, which peel away rapidly when he approaches. Presently, exasperated, he pins one down firmly, a nervous shade against a convenient wall, that gibbers at first but is restored to intelligibility by reasonable accents.

'Where do you wish to go?'

'The mill district.'

'Where did you say?'

'Parel. The Weavers' Lines.'

'Ah, the mill area, where all the trouble started. Why—?'

'My business.'

'Of course, of course. You know what I thought at first? I thought you must be a *goonda*, can you imagine that? I—'

Garrulous from relief, the words flow. Rabi dams it brusquely.

'A *goonda* is no worse than a looter.'

'Sir, are you suggesting—?'

'I am. You are. I'm waiting for your answer. And if you direct me wrong I'll come back and get you, don't imagine for one moment that I won't.'

He takes the frightened man by the collar and shakes him till he rattles. It is not an act of normality for him. Still less so is the absence of any concern for his action, or for the terrified rabbit, bulging with loot, that he has trapped. The jamming of critical faculties might jar, in other circumstances. As it is he merely notes that whatever has garbled the physical landscape has worked on him too. The events of the night have moved, and are moving, to rearrange the internal stresses and strains of which he is composed.

He hears the muttered imprecation (rabbit has residues of spirit) and smiles as he turns away in the darkness. He has got what he wanted. A furlong up, turn left, turn right, and there it is, he has been directed to the mill workers' colony with great precision.

Still, there is quite a cluster of huts. It would be difficult to find, but a beacon is lit. There is a glimmer behind the thatch, and the plaited-straw door is held partially open by a raffia thong. The girl has, after all, believed in his return. He can see her in the pale light, sitting on her haunches with her back against the wall. Heels together, knees apart; the cloth across her legs is slack, it is the loose and abandoned attitude of a woman who believes herself alone. Straddling the doorway he calls her, somehow softly, though his heart is thudding.

'Jaya?'

'Is it you, Rabi?'

At once she covers herself, but not swiftly enough. He has glimpsed her thighs, those tender folds she has unwittingly exposed, and closed, but will unfold to his desires, he determines. He steps inside and fastens the door behind him. Forestalling escape he pushes her back against the wall and rips away the flimsy cloth she has pulled up over herself. Hands on her thighs, he forces himself between and enters.

His uppermost thought on completion, before he falls asleep, is that bodies are beautifully carpentered for their purpose. The thought falls neatly between relief and triumph, and blights the bud of a notion that there can be more to this natural act than inspired anatomy.

When he wakes Jaya is lying, awake, beside him. Their bodies touch at points: shoulders, hips, hers bronze, his creamy, the delicate sleeping triangle, the colour of pitch, that he has compelled to meet his ardour. Leaning up on an elbow he hovers over her, proprietorially.

'Was it good for you?'

'Very good. Rabi, *bachcha* . . .'

'Mm?'

'Was it the first time for you?'

'Do you mean with a woman?'

'Have there been boys?'

'No. There are other ways.'

'I mean with a woman . . . was it the first time?'

'Can't you tell?'

'Not always. Some men never learn. Some men are always bunglers.'

'I've never taken a woman before.'

'You weren't disappointed?'
'It was better than anything.'
'Rabi?'
'Uh?'
'Will you believe me?'
'Anything you say.'
'It can be better. Much better. Like this. Will you let me?'
Her face is close to his. Her eyes are brilliant, bearing down on him.

Like this. Erectile frills in the wake of her lips and stroking fingers. Like this. Moving in tender circles, apex like plush pushing up against him, her flesh like silk, like drawing slippery silk over polished cones. He is beginning to judder, but she holds and brings him into her rhythm. Coordinating superbly, they climax together.

* * *

'It was as you said it would be.'
'What did I say?'
She is up and dressed but oddly shy, turning her face away when she speaks to him. He finds it strangely touching, a delicacy by day that rounds out the experienced boldness of the night.
'That it would be much better.'
'Was it? Are you?'
She brings him a glass of tea, retreats, and sits at a little distance.
'It was. And I am. Come here and I'll tell you properly.'
'No.'
'I won't touch you, I promise.'
'Solemnly?'
'Solemnly. What're you afraid of?'
'You ripped my sari, you know. I don't want it ruined completely.'
'Nonsense. You were quite naked.'
'Before that. The first time. Look at that tear.'
'I'll buy you another.'
'So impatient, spoiling good clothes.'
'I wouldn't call it good. It was already in tatters.'
'Only because I tore off a piece for your bandage, if you must know.'
'You *didn't*.'

'I did. What do you think, this is some kind of palace?'

'Oh, *God*!'

'And I'm some kind of Rani, with chests full of clothes?'

'If I had my way—'

'I know, *bachcha*, love. Never mind, we'll pretend, shall we?'

'What?'

'Let's pretend the strike's over.'

'Is that all?'

'It's plenty. No work, no pay, that's awful. But when it's over, ah yes, then!'

'What then?'

'Wages, *bachcha*. Money. Money's what I think about most. Especially since my husband went.'

Rabi sits up. He sips his tea and considers her: this woman he has explored carnally and imagined he knows, who is drifting away, it is borne in on him, to totally unknown realms. The web of her living, her secrets, what she has withheld from him, become even more intolerable than his clusters of grapes.

'You didn't tell me you had a husband.'

'You didn't bother to ask.'

'You should have told me.'

'Why?'

Challenged, he can't quite say. Something to do with another man's property. Said baldly it grates: people cannot be equated with property. From down the years, overheard in childhood (children don't understand: but jug-handle ears are flapping, meanings arrive later), comes his mother's furious cry: *You don't own me, you know. NOBODY owns me!* Though—he has to smile at the memory—nobody could be more evidently her own proprietor than she.

'No reason. I would have liked to know, that's all,' he says.

'I'll tell you.' She moves up companionably. 'He's an agitator, *bachcha*. Or was. Like some of us, only he got caught, they put him away for five years, imagine that, just for giving out a few leaflets . . . that's his mat you're lying on but don't let it worry you.'

'I'm not worried. But what about you?'

'What about me?'

He doesn't know what to reply. The mores of her world are presently, or even forever, beyond him. She supplies the answer.

'You don't have to worry about that either,' she says roughly. 'I'm not a nun. No one expects me to live like one either, not around here. I fend for myself. I have to. Do you understand?'

'Do you mean you're for sale?'

'Put it that way if you like. But not all the time.'

'When?'

'When I'm short. Then.'

'Often?'

'Of course, *bachcha*. Of course often. What d'you think took all of us out to the beach, a *picnic*?'

She stands up and tightens the knot of her sari. It is the sum of her preparations for going out, he notes fleetingly, whereas his father—. But he doesn't wish to think about that; it is an intrusive thought and there are others more pressing.

'Where are you going?'

'Somewhere special.' She stands in the doorway, hands on hips, laughing.

'Don't look like that Rabi, *bachcha*. I'm only going for some food. We must eat, mustn't we?'

* * *

Some such thought occupies Bawajiraj as he applies himself to breakfast.

He owes it to others to keep his strength up. He cannot throw up the sponge, as another man might, merely because he feels like it. As he does feel. The trials of a parent, not to mention the acutely enhanced tribulations of a Maharajah parent. He sits, as impeccably garnished as ever (not a hair out of place despite everything—he can almost hear the respectful whispers of observers) and gazes lugubriously at his mistress across the laden table.

The Imperial has risen to the occasion. It has its pride, and is not to be cowed by the vulgar uproar outside. It has called on its reserves, which are of army proportions, and similarly organised. If anything, the spread this morning is even more lavish than in times of peace.

Bawajiraj nibbles a little toast Melba between courses. Mohini can hear the low moans he gives as he scrunches and is moved to pity.

'I'm sure he's safe and sound. He says he is.'

'Safe! What does he mean?'

'Naturally he means what he says.'

'He says don't worry!'

Bawajiraj smacks the disreputable chit his heir has scribbled and sent.

'Is it possible for a father, considering everything?'

'My love, there's no need to be upset. Rabi's not a child any more. Why can't you trust him to look after himself?'

'Leaving the hotel—running off as if he were a ricksha-wallah—does that inspire trust?'

'Young men have to find things out for themselves.'

'Does he have to behave like a ricksha-wallah to find out whatever it is? If only he'd been brought up properly—'

'As he has been.'

'One would have more confidence. As it is it's—it's—'

'What?'

'Too awful to think what he's up to.'

'What do you think he's up to?'

'Not what *I* think, it's what Sir Arthur—'

'Bania Sahib! I might have guessed. Is it important what he thinks?'

'Of course it is. Apart from his natural concern the whole question of suitability—'

'I don't care a fig.'

Sprigged voile billowing, Mohini rises from the table.

'I have every confidence in our son and his upbringing and if you had as much backbone as a jellyfish you would have told Sir Arthur so,' she says, and floats frostily off the terrace.

* * *

The shops were closed for the whole of that shattering period. The shopkeepers brought down the shutters sharp and kept watch from their poky upstairs apartments. Those who could left the city altogether, padlocked the premises and left furtively by night for the hinterland, taking with them as much stock as they could load onto creaky bullock-carts.

Rabi had to hunt hard for what he wanted. This side of him was perfectionist: his gifts had to match what his imagination pictured as fitting for the loved recipient. He could not, times being what they were, command acres of cloth to be slithered across counters for his consideration, but he did, after unsparing effort, track down what he wanted: a combination of popular taste, grafted on to the finest, richest silk that the most particular of his female relations would not have cavilled at.

* * *

On his knees he offers her the sari of red-spotted violet silk with the wide gold border.

'For Jaya Rani. A tribute from her humble servant.'

'For *me*?'

'Do you like it?'

'*Like* it!'

She whirls and settles, vernal honeybee sampling blossom, buzzing with amazement at first sip, can nectar actually taste like this? Why didn't anyone tell me?

'Rabi, it's lovely! It's not for me, is it? It can't be. Are you sure? Have you paid for it? How could anyone *afford* to! Ah Rabi, *bachcha*, you must be at least a Rajah.'

For her, a pleasure that dissolves even her radical scruples.

For him, confusion. It makes his head swim. For this has happened before. Himself, the gift, the girl. All, on some other planet, have been through these motions.

But no. Jaya's gift is quite plain; the shopkeeper has only been able to raise two frayed white tapes for embellishing, even the bows are perfunctory. Whereas Janaki's sari was done up in tissue and tinsel, with a lotus on the lid. But that of course was never presented, or unwrapped, or received swooning, except in his imagination. It languishes still, unless mice have been at it, in one of the Palace outhouses.

Slowly his head clears.

'Oh yes,' he says gently. 'It's yours. I bought it for you. I'm only glad that this time I—I—'

'Rabi, love, what's the matter?'

'I'm just glad that I'm able to give it to you.'

'I'll treasure it, Rabi. But I—'

'Yes?'

His heart is hammering. He wants to lunge forward, cram what she is about to utter back into her mouth, but some things are not possible.

'I didn't expect you to, you know Rabi. I didn't ask to be paid for what I did,' she says.

'I know. It wasn't in payment,' he says, gently enough, while what has been beautiful slowly begins to wither.

He traces back, afterwards, to this. This was the point at which he began to notice things about her. Things that could not come to light, he admitted with painful honesty, until the fusion of physical passion and intellectual ardour burned less brightly.

Things that were missing. Those fragrances, floral and clean, that clung to women like his mother.

Things that had always been there, and passed over. Quadrants of black lying under her ragged finger-nails, and grey-black backs to her heels. A smell of dust, and ochre streaks in the locks of hair forever truant from her untidy bun. Her way of squinting into a broken mirror, and indifferently accepting whatever was reflected, from rats' tails to smudges of charcoal and sweat.

He looked away. To make up for looking he went on the prowl in the nervous, shuttered city. Searching. Sometimes inwardly: huge areas of his psyche in disarray and calling for scrutiny, though his body thrived and bloomed. Sometimes savagely, ransacking the markets for atoning offerings, commanding traders to open up and deal on his terms, to his urgency, with the ruthless arrogance so effortlessly and even sweetly practised by Bawajiraj III. Lessons learnt at father's knee, when one was scarcely higher.

Daily he comes laden with the guilty cornucopia. Fruit out of season. Plump fish fresh from the paralysed harbour, where fishermen are having a bumper season. A sack of grain, hauled on a hand-cart by an urchin who normally trails after memsahibs out shopping. A lacy string of half-open jasmine buds. Salt, that taxed and expensive and coveted commodity.

'Rabi, how lovely! All this for me? You are sweet.'

Clasping her hands, her face rapturous.

'Rabi! I'll get diarrhoea if I eat all these things.'

'Why should you? You're not a sickly old woman.'

'Unused, *bachcha*. Use your head. Unaccustomed to rich food.'

'What it must cost! Where does it come from, all that money?'

Resentment rumbling, subterranean, an earthquake there, sending out these advance, detectable tremors.

And at last, sullenly,

'What will I do, *bachcha*, when you've gone? And I have to go back to the plain stuff? Have you thought about it?'

'Yes.'

'Do you care, that's the point.'

'Yes, I do care.'

'Ah well, maybe you do. Maybe you will remember—they do say one never forgets one's first.'

Lying on the mat, yawning, slack, naked arms up and crossed behind her head on the dingy pillow. The hair in her armpits is matted. It gives off an odour of day-old sweat that mingles disagreeably with the scent of the jasmine that reposes beside her. When she turns to him he shrinks; it is more mental than physical but nevertheless she divines it. The bond is still close.

'What's the matter, Rabi? Don't you want?'

'Don't feel like it.'

'I'll make you, *bachcha*.'

'No.'

'What's wrong, love? What have I done?'

'Nothing.'

'Then what—'

Her bewilderment goads him. He rounds on her and it comes out sharply.

'I wish you'd wash, that's all.'

'I do wash.'

'Not enough.'

'I do my best. Do you know how far I have to walk for water? How long I have to stand and wait for my turn?'

'I know, I know! I'm sorry, I didn't mean what I said!'

He embraces her fiercely, and indeed it is eclipsed by passion. But afterwards, there is an afterwards, he is conscious that they are working themselves out of each other. Running out of road, or steam, or simply unable to sustain what had come into being partly, if not purely, through external events.

She made it easy for him to leave. They made it as easy as possible for each other, because, basically, there was no quarrel. By then the strike had ended. It lasted the best part of three weeks. The worst part was going back. It was simpler for heads of families, who could cite their responsibilities, and offload guilt on to the innocent shoulders of wives and children. It was dreadful for those with none, who could only imagine it was their own lack of fibre, although, later, it did become pointless to hold out when the mass of the workers were returning.

Both wings tasted the bitterness of defeat. Both determined, never again. Never, until hopes could be raised on a more solid plinth than justice. Justice, people could see, was for gentlemen and judges. It counted for very small change indeed when it came to securing their rights. What they could not see clearly, at that stage, was what they could do about it, and what was needed to weld their strong but wayward emotions into a single and irresistible instrument of compulsion.

They suspected, though. The best of them—select members of the herd, alertness their keynote and function—were already scanning the horizon, and looking askance at the Government under whose aegis they had been broken.

When the trickle back to the mills and factories had become a flood, she announced her decision. He protested, pallidly, no heart in it since he could not see, any more than she, anything but vanishing options.

'I have to go back, Rabindranath Sahib. What else is there to do?'

'Sahib' edging back, no longer in play but in earnest, as the distance between them widened.

'On their terms?'

'Naturally on their terms. Winner's terms. It's quite usual for the empty-belly race.'

'Perhaps they'll be better than you think.'

'No Sahib, no sign of that. Signs are we'll be paid for the time we've been off and they'll put that in a frame. Picture of generosity. Ah well.'

She stands up in grey early-morning light and winds the skimpy remnant of sari about her. None of his horns of plenty has yielded anything as essential as a cloth to put on one's body. So like a rich man—not that she has known any rich men before, but anyone knows they're all alike—to overlook one's glaring needs. But perhaps she can sell this violet confection that a woman like her will never have occasion to wear. Though it comes hard. It is a very beautiful thing, and there will be times, she is certain, she will need it to prove to herself that her *bachcha* was not simply a dream.

'Well, Rabi, love. Look after yourself.'

'It's you.'

'I'll be all right, don't you worry . . . I ought to get going, never do to be late.'

'Is it far?'

'Some way.'

'I wish I were going with you.'

'No. You stay where you are. Rabi?'

'Yes?'

'It was good, eh *bachcha*? Between us?'

'Very good.'

'That's all that matters then.'

She smiles and walks away. Doesn't look back—a wave over the shoulder. Why should she? When she came back he would be gone. She knew. He knew.

He rebelled. He wanted to rush after her, pick up her courageous exploited body, cover her pointed face with kisses. Instead he sat, dislocated, with the flimsy door swinging on its thong. Because it was over. It had been over that day he came back from the Delhi Durbar and discovered she had gone. Janaki, his love, was gone. The finality he found unacceptable. Rebelled, then too. Searched from that day on, never consciously, always hankering vaguely for the piece that was missing; and pounced, imagining some other could be slotted into her space, although he could no longer offer the generous acceptances of childhood that had graced the early encounter.

Foolish endeavour. Fated. Belatedly, now, he closed the chapter that he should never have attempted to re-open.

It had started to rain. Rain slanted in through the hole in the thatch and hissed on the embers where she had brewed tea. It reminded him. He would see the Dewan about certain glaring holes in his own State. He was, after all, the heir. He had forgotten, it sat so negligibly on his shoulders. Meanwhile one did what one could. Always. Unless one wanted to be saddled with regret as well, as if the pack wasn't a deadweight already.

He assembled her possessions in the farthest corner and covered the lot with an empty sack. The rickety door had flapped itself off its fastening and was ushering in damp gusts. He hoisted it back into place, let himself out, and tied the thong securely. Anyone could get in, but there was little to tempt. The salt and grain were buried, and the beloved violet object was en route to the mill, firmly glued to its vigilant owner.

* * *

Fan-pleats were back, smiling, salaaming, too discreet, too Imperial-disciplined to raise so much as one hair of an eyebrow, though the Maharajkumar's absence had been noted.

His father said, after a tussle in which parental emotions extinguished Sir Arthur,

'I can't tell you how glad. Your mother and I—'

'I told you not to worry.'

'My dear boy, the worst thing for a parent is to be told not to worry.'

His mother said nothing. She gazed at him, full face, and he felt the slight collision of eyeballs. It transported him to the eve of Simla. Knew with precision how she had felt then, her urgent desire to conceal what she was giving away in a welter of rose-jam and traitorous pink splotches. Covering her face, vainly. Round eyes over modest sari, defying him to imagine the corybantic frenzy. He daring, the two of them exchanging images of the most vivid and explicit kind.

Both, now, party to the delirious secret.

She told her partner, who was not insensitive but absorbed in other aspects of his son.

'He's been with a woman.'

'Did he say so?'

'There was no need.'

'Well, that's a relief I *must* say. I was dreadfully afraid he had got himself mixed up with those frightful anarchists—'

'Millworkers.'

'Millworkers,' agrees the resigned Bawajiraj. 'But, you know, so *inexplicable*, when you think about it . . . I mean so many beauties he can choose from, my Court is simply awash . . . but no, he has to be peculiar. . . .'

* * *

So they were restored, more or less to their old selves, and—give or take a little—to their old places.

Of the Maharajah's embattled cluster perhaps the Rolls-Royce came off best. Left dangling for three weeks it survived in style, shrugged off wind and rain and the odd knock from a disgruntled docker with the aplomb of its breed and twelve coats of paint and emerged unruffled and gleaming at first flick of chamois. No one, afterwards, neither loving chauffeur nor besotted owner, could spot any difference between the one that had been so subjected and the remainder of the fleet.

Humans, though, devoid of twelve coats, did afterwards perceive nicks, putting it down to imagination, or even to what all of them, willy-nilly, had been through.

II

Seeing his princely employer more or less safely away, the Dewan had gone off to his ancestral village. He needed to be in the State Capital rather more urgently, he accepted, when Bawajiraj was around than when he was absent. In his absence the machinery of government could be trusted to function smoothly, considerable dynastic energies had gone towards this end, even the British in the heady throes of kingmaking and unmaking were not so rash as to dismantle the masterly scaffolding on which the State was hung.

But when the Maharajah was present one had to be on guard. An inventive and enthusiastic man, there were always schemes up his sleeve, some strange, some costly, some of extreme and imprudent benevolence, that could throw whole departments out of gear and induce trained clerks to hand in their notice in droves. All these disastrous proposals had to be tactfully shelved, or at least controlled, in the interests of the State. The Dewan liked to be around to do it. He was skilled and trained for the purpose, and Devapur State continued to be the object—these days Sir Arthur had an inkling, though he still found it a job conceding such emotions to the iron Minister—of his consuming if austere love.

With the Maharajah safely in the clutches, or embrace, of scented Simla and scintillating Bombay, Tirumal Rao could relax. He did not have to ruminate on whatever next, with which, a little too frequently for his liking, he began his working day. There was even time for his own concerns, principally—

Vatsala had brought it to his attention—the future of his beloved second daughter.

With a short valediction to his eldest boy, the youth who would one day (but not for a long time yet, one naturally hoped) take over the reins from him, and who was being left behind to accumulate experience, the Dewan and his family set off, at an auspicious hour selected by the *purohit*, in the modest but commodious family saloon for a periodic visit to what Sir Arthur called the Minister's country retreat.

Country it was; retreat hardly; for the rambling and unassuming house on the outskirts of the village was the hub of innumerable transactions of a personal nature. Even more important, it was the base for journeys the Dewan zealously undertook: those tours of inspection of his extensive landed estates that added substantial revenues to his already substantial income and, to some degree, contributed to the equanimity with which he supported his august employer's furious hints of relegation. Though infrequently, of late. Bawajiraj was mellowing: a different creature from the wilful young man who had balefully and openly wondered why one continued to employ such an egregious servant.

However. One liked to keep an eye, however secure one's position, on one's support system. In this the Dewan was aided by the erratic nature of his visits, synchronised as they were to the Maharajah's absences. No bad thing, he often reflected. It kept his lieutenants on their toes, and ensured a lively management of his spreading acres.

Estates, this time, had been ousted by Vimala. She took pride of place, being of an age for betrothal, the negotiations nicely timed for completion preceding the nuptials of her elder sister. It was his wife's plan, which the Dewan fell in with. She also took charge of the proceedings, although he was, so to speak, the titular chief, to whom one or two of the numerous intermediaries who came and went did, out of courtesy, defer.

Tirumal Rao did not really object. Brahmin women having, he conceded a little sadly, Brahmin minds, must be assumed to be eminently capable. Especially Vatsala. She had the whole affair well in hand, although for reasons not instantly pellucid to him she preferred to parley in their village rather than in the Capital. So that, her wishes being made known, emissaries came in flushed coveys with their photos and legends—not to glowing

Dilkusha, with its Herats and miniatures and ruby cordials in silver Kashmir goblets, but trailing down to the village, and having to be directed by yokels on the last lap to the rustic abode.

What for, the Dewan did wonder. Was not the ministerial establishment in the State Capital the fitter setting for negotiating an alliance for his fair and accomplished daughter? He fingered his chin, and felt his mind going soft, the brilliant cutting edge turned soggy as it strove to dissect the working processes of women's minds. Until his wife took pity, although it found expression in a somewhat flinty manner.

'Parents owe it to their children. To keep their wits about them.'

'I endeavour to—'

'Then surely you've seen.'

'I must confess—'

'Plain as—plain as anything to me.'

'What?'

'Vimala. She won't think of another suitor while he's there.'

'Who?'

'Rabi.'

'*Rabi*! D'you mean he's after her?'

'No. But madam is after him.'

'Aren't you imagining things?'

'Am I? Have you seen her drooling over that cushion with "Rabindranath" on it in gold letters? which she embroidered with her own hands?'

It threw the Dewan into a lather. Come to think of it, he had observed. But indulgently. Thinking what a fine couple—no, no, not couple, two single people who were, individually, pleasing specimens of their sex. The last thing was any connection to a Maharajah. Vandalism, in his view, to water the Brahmin intellect by union with a Kshatriya.

Some Brahmins might be flattered (Tirumal Rao fell back on old convictions, which time had if anything ratified) into yielding their daughters to such marriages, but not he. Not his daughter. Never. For her the son of a Dewan like himself, or respected lawyer, or scholar, but never the son of a Maharajah. Figureheads. Pinheads. Not that one was being personal. Rabi (here he mentally flourished the letter he had received that morning) was showing signs. But his blood. And what water could do, dripping, the most fantastic distortions gouged even in granite. Not to mention the British, superlative potters even by Brahmin criterion, who could shape and manipulate the most recalcitrant clay to their requirements.

Between blood and water and what the British could do the Dewan felt quite faint. He said, weakly,

'But Rabi isn't there to—to exert any influence over her.'

'His aura.'

'And when he comes back, what then. . . .'

Vatsala jiggled her *thali*, and sighed a little.

'By then, provided I have some co-operation, Vimala will be betrothed and being well brought up—an honourable girl—will not look at another man.'

So the Dewan did his best. Smothering deep and poignant feelings for his lands he forewent all the tours of inspection he had promised himself and, instead, made himself available to relays of envoys. Listening to eulogy—chopping the rhetoric in half to reach true conclusions—dwelling on horoscopes—his Sanskrit in fine fettle, although his familiarity with the heavens was limited, or rusty (some time since he'd gone into this sort of thing for Vijaya, his eldest)—he drew upon immense reserves of patience that his calling had developed to sustain his equilibrium. At his wife's request he opened portfolios and gazed upon solemn posed faces that looked to him as alike as a row of beans.

Raw ones at that, nothing to choose between.

But when presently, after a preliminary winnowing, he met the survivors in the flesh—young throbbing males, one of whom he was expected to nominate to penetrate and impregnate his child—surges of jealous and powerful feeling emanated, convincing him that not one was worthy of his young and charming daughter. Tactful, though. The fathers all men of standing, as otherwise none of the sons would have made it beyond the outermost portals.

At which point the search acquired a new tempo and momentum, to Vatsala's secret rejoicing. Confident she was of her own capability, but, no doubt about it, a man did provide incisive and desirable backing for one's efforts. Buckram behind the portrait. Tucking fresh-picked jasmine in her shining hair, bosom high and rounded out with her matronly purpose, she marched about the place in the reinforced assurances of her role, toe-rings going like small and silvery but masterful gongs.

When at last it was done, the Dewan, shedding those crisp energies that refreshed his wife, permitted himself to relax. He listened to birdsong. He collected his children about him and recited to them long passages out of the sacred texts—learnt in childhood by rote and impatiently, returning now to delight the singer if not the audience. In the cool of morning he sat on his string cot, set up on the edge of the wide shady verandah, and watched the squirrels feast off guavas from the trees that flourished in the artless garden.

A rich man's garden, even in its rustic simplicity, as anyone could tell. The freedoms of the rich, none of those stringy contraptions, worried cat's cradles of netting and twine that even a man like the Secretary Sahib, who was not poor, though not in one's class, flung over his peas and pomegranates. Hideous. One of life's joys was to be prodigal. Careless of depredations, as he could afford to be. Was. Squirrels came to dine. Birds. A dozen different delicate varieties, yellow-beaked, red-capped beauties among their perky little nondescript sparrow relatives.

Sir Arthur was a rich man, but he shot them. Gave orders, or did it himself. Spared the birds, pot shots at the squirrels.

Vermin.

Gone in a trice from trapeze artist to negligible cadaver carted away by the *mali* on a shovel. Smooth black ripple abruptly ended in the starry explosion, convulsed claw stiffly closed around the filched object. Blithe acrobat, no one ever told him singing for his supper wasn't enough. No one ever said the fruits of the earth were not his for the taking.

But learnt the lesson. Entire earth a monopoly. Claim staked by the most rapacious species ever to walk the surface.

Died, learning it. Not even vouchsafed a glimpse of nemesis round the corner awaiting one's teacher.

Destroyed, as heedlessly as one tossed pebbles in a pond. (Careful even there, and in due course taught one's children to be careful; and in time the thankless frogs grown bloated and throaty plopped up onto the bank and made the nights untenable with their quarking.)

Chasms yawned between him and Sir Arthur. Dialogues, unspoken, but no need to suppose meanings not taken.

'Assassin.'

'Bloody Hindu hypocrite.'

'Kill, as soon as look.'

'Wouldn't put a decent end to anything, every damn objection to a clean bullet.'

'Christian arrogance.'

'Sentimental nonsense. Impractical sentimentalist.'

The two men, products of not dissimilar processes, eye to eye on so many issues, as near to glaring as polish permitted. Abyss there, all right. Fundamental distance.

As with Rabi. Comparable distance, different abyss. Perhaps not abyss, settle for some lesser trench. Squinting along the same sights, sensors reading differently, view suddenly occluded.

Warrior ancestry. (True, one carried a General in one's knap-
sack, but that was a singular, brilliant deflection.) Brawn, and a
touching belief in the battering ram. Scant faith in the intellect,
and no referral whatever to perspectives, historical or impending.

'I'd just go ahead, Dewan Sahib. No other way to get things
done.'

'My dear boy, you must consider the difficulties and the consequences.'

'What for? Cross bridges when I come to them.'

'My dear Rabi, I beseech you, I insist, you must think in the
round.'

'Life's too short, Dewan Sahib. I can't think in abstractions. I
have to deal with what I see needs dealing with, straightaway. I
want things to happen while I'm still around to see them happening.'

Straight as an arrow. Bull's eye. Thwack!

Blunt. No subtleties *there* to ravish the mind. Wouldn't do at all
for one's daughter. And imagine (the Dewan's mind gave a mad
lurch) coming home to her unclean, ears and tails dangling,
hacked from some beast (one had not seen, and had no wish to
see, but one could imagine). The Dewan shuddered. No, never
do at all for one's decently reared daughter.

One day, one such contemplative morning, she came and sat
by him—he cross-legged on the string cot, she decoratively composed, fluid disposal of limbs and raiment on a pattern of tiles—
and asked after Rabi.

'Yes, I had a letter. He's well, he says.'

'Does he ask about me?'

'In general, yes. He hopes we are all well.'

'Is that all?'

'By no means. He's full of plans.'

'For what?'

'For the State.'

'What kind of plans?'

'To remedy holes, he says, in the fabric.'

'Which, in particular?'

'My dear child, who knows? So many need patching up, if not
remedy.'

'Will he be able?'

'We can try.'

'You and he?'

'He and I. Yes. I look forward to it.'

'Father, can you and he—work together? Properly?'

'Attempt to, shall we say. Though there are of course—bound to be—divisions.'

'Why?'

'You tell me.'

'You're more experienced.'

'Yes. I think one can say that without fear of contradiction.'

'Different ways of thinking.'

'Yes.'

'Rabi and I, you know, often think alike on things.'

'What things?'

'Any number.'

A frisson streaking through the Dewan, not unlike the one that had shot through Sir Arthur. How, in supervised enclosures, did all these numberless extraordinary girl and boy exchanges take place? Pass over it in silence: parental omniscience too useful to dent.

'My dear child, I'm well aware you do. Broadly similar. Naturally, at your age. But fundamentally—'

'Do you mean caste?'

'Let us say allied. Fundamentally there are divisions. At deeper levels. So deep our minds would have to be re-cast to—to find the richness and harmony that, say, your mother and I enjoy.'

'Rabi and I often enjoy harmony.'

It really alarmed the Dewan. He toyed with the thought of passing on what he had heard, which would cure her instantly. Tidings that had travelled here, as to Sir Arthur's eyrie, of Rabi's aberration. Some unwashed bazaar girl. Just to illustrate divergence of thought-processes, because no member of his clan—. However roused. Not an unwashed girl. Really, though, it was a mother's job, but Vimala's mother was not privy; he had considered it demeaning to repeat the distasteful gossip. So he mused, eyes hooded, hands hidden away in his wide cool muslin sleeves, and finally rooted up a platitude out of his own past.

'Believe me, your parents know best. The harmonies you speak of are as nothing to the concord you will one day enjoy with the partner we have chosen for you, your mother and I.'

Vimala pondered. In particular on her father. Known him all her life, but a certain quality. Pursue it long enough, come up against a stranger. Hands in retreat: lean almond shapes of which he was so proud, lurking, or reposing, under the flow of muslin. Cloudy. One could not imagine them cupping, say, the breasts of one's mother. Jawline strict, but the bones turned mild for her. Smooth as ivory, with touches of celadon. The way he wanted it. He got his servant to shave him close, docked the man's wages if stubble pricked up before evening. One heard complaints from both sides, one shrill, one low, both heartfelt. He hated the fall from standards, as irksome to him as some physical loss.

Her father, seated. On trestle and string. From where she was she could see the gentle dip of lattice-work. The merest curtsey of string between uprights to take his weight, the cord barely stretched, hemp in its twist, and the Dewan's own craftsmen. Strength in those frames. One knew, or guessed. Even the swaggering English, like the bandmaster, like the men who drilled the Garrison troops. Even the frosty English, incapable of swagger, disdainful ladies and lordships.

Their eyes grew guarded when they approached her father.

So Vimala surrendered. Or rather accepted her future. Questioning—as her sister had not thought to question—but stilled. Her parents patently loved their children. They never lied, basically. The promise of accord rang true. So she put aside play-acting (she had cast herself in the role of princess, she admitted with ruthless honesty), threw away the cushion, mentally speaking, and as an aid to pure thought set up the portrait of the chosen on her windowsill, flinging, when she remembered, the dull thing a glance or two of utter indifference.

When she had gone the Dewan continued to sit. Alone. Afflicted. Periodically it hit the three statesmen: the Resident, the Minister, and the Maharajah. These melancholy jabs, in a kingdom the size they administered, had a variety of causes: but the single unfailing common source was the disruptive influence of the irregular in their midst, not so much saboteur (though symptoms were developing) as catalyst.

As such the rules of battle fluctuated in a most upsetting manner. Anything but clear and dependable, containment in one quarter only inviting, it seemed, uprising in some totally different centre. Faith in their ability was not abated, but it did seem to the triumvirate, singly and collectively, that they could do better if the ground shifted less. The future, in fact, was flickering. Advantage, possibly, not always in their court. One had to be on one's toes.

Involuntarily the Minister's foot began to tap, a rhythmic waggle that was known to distract Sir Arthur. It also jarred the squirrels, boot-button eyes were popping. The Minister desisted to watch them. What pretty, nervous creatures they were! By no means all, however. One intrepid diner had settled on the verandah, impelled to bravery by succulent booty. Settling to guzzle, teeth into juicy pink guava, shivering with ecstasy, but interrupted. Pounced on, in mid meal, by his mate. No one else, surely, so brazen. The two creatures fizzing, disputing, balled, rolling, head over feathery tail until they tumbled, still madly entangled, over the edge of the verandah.

Squashed guava on the tiles. Quantities, luckily, still left to loot.

As he rose from his cramped figure-of-eight the Dewan made a mental note to instruct his manager. It was time for saplings to be ordered in to supplant, in due course, the mature trees. The man was an excellent manager, but the injunction on him to suffer plundering fowl and fauna in his fair garden he regarded as one of the more reprehensible quixotries. It made him too disheartened to keep it properly stocked. Sometimes he confessed it, to his master's face, only to be met with his employer's peculiar and perplexing silent, though evident, laughter.

It quite doubled up the Dewan at times.

* * *

Holidays over, principals returning, the usual afflatus of their varied establishments. A gilding of the Palace, gold-leaf on the cupolas, the Throne Room a-glitter for durbars in the offing, elephants dragged out of mud-baths and scrubbed clean, spanking new quarters for Tara and Tantivvy, *syces* standing by for a rub-down after the trials of horse boxes from Bombay—the Maharajah known to be most attentive to his animals' needs—and a sprinkling with rose-water of apartments and terraces.

At the Residency the customary combination: sparkling crystal, bowlfuls of flowers, dogs hysterical with welcome; and in the quadrangle the Garrison troops drilling with redoubled fervour, boots ringing on the cobblestones. Sir Arthur disapproved of slackness at any season; his wishes were known and complied with. As for Lady Copeland, it was widely believed that she would notice the demise of a single shrub in her spreading domain; relays of anxious gardeners had coaxed back to life the droopiest of plants.

The Minister's residence, unusually, had also entered the lists. This discreet mansion, which normally disdained such flourishes, from top to bottom had been painted a conspicuous buttermilk. The compound railings were lacquered black, the finials picked out in gold. The Minister's armorial device (privately the Resident doubted his entitlement, but actually it went back some centuries to the General), burnished and enamelled, blazed upon the gates, in addition to the same motif soberly carved in stone over the gatehouse.

Sir Arthur gasped as he swept past in his Daimler. The colour hinted at frivolities that he could not easily reconcile with the Minister. It reminded his wife of ice-cream. She compared it, with a touch of amusement, to a bombe, such as was a tour de force of the wizard at Malabar Point. Sir Arthur thought it apt. But when the motor-car drew up in the portico of the Residency, and the glaring pillars, as always after absence, and especially after refurbishing, made him blink a little, he began to wonder if the chosen colour was not a little kinder on the eye. Although of course the purpose of the Residency, being different, did call for drama. At any rate equivalent structures had never commanded less than floods of white, heights attuned to the soaring scale of trumpets, façades and surfaces of a stunning brilliance. Lady Copeland certainly found it a perfect foil, as much for the mantles and ribands she and her husband were obliged to assume from time to time, as for the cineraria and the tubs of red geranium.

All to do, the Dewan's effort, that is to say, with the forthcoming marriage celebrations of the daughter of the house. Sir Arthur learnt from local gossip, not directly since he had no such access, but relayed by his barber (client lathered up and compelled to listen), and presently confirmed by a clerk. It quite moved him, to think of the tiny infant, in whose cot—only the other day, it seemed—he had placed a teddy bear, grown to marriage size. Yielding to the amiable impulse he seized an opportunity to accost the Minister.

'I'm told, Dewan Sahib,' he said genially, and not without some traces of archness, 'that we are soon to hear the peal of wedding bells.'

The Minister simpered. Sir Arthur was loth to believe it, but there it was. Squirming a little, and distinctly coy sounds.

'Quite true, Excellency. Our eldest is to be given in marriage.'

And, distinctly, shimmied. Sir Arthur averted his eyes from the disconcerting phenomenon and moved on to facts.

'Is it to be soon?'

'By the end of the year. The date has yet to be fixed.'

'In that case, Minister, I trust you will convey to the young couple, in due course, my felicitations.'

Because in due course, before the end of the year, one would have gone. Departed from these shores in answer to the call from one's country.

Though, really, this was one's country too, bone of one's bone, not to mention certain incursions of the spirit. Somehow it entered. Grain by grain, and before you knew where you were a part of you was Indian. Not literally, of course. There was the gap, and, yes, fences. One put them up, it was essential to maintain a separate and distinct identity, not to say poise; the Indians themselves were the first to despise those unbalanced Europeans who aped them. Sound instinct, that; though a little give on their side did nothing but good, one didn't relish battling through out-and-out Indian thickets. But, no question about it, a portion did belong. When one had gone one would miss this land to which one had devoted oneself, given half a lifetime of dedicated service and—why deny it—come to love.

Tremors, like those that had shaken the Minister, shot through Sir Arthur, though fortunately contained by cladding in duck, which did not expose these quivers one's embarrassing emotions transmitted. It made him linger, however, in a manner that was unlike him and—the Dewan did notice—there was a misty quality to the gaze he bent upon his tandem-partner.

'Well, Dewan Sahib, all good things, as they say.'

'Indeed, Excellency.'

'How time flies. . . . Such a charming little infant—I can remember it as if it were yesterday—lying in her cot. . . . It scarcely seems possible she is now to be wedded.'

The Minister remembered too. It had been, he thought with shame, the only time they had asked the Englishman. He corrected Sir Arthur gently.

'That infant is still a small girl, Excellency. Too young to be given in marriage. The one now involved is our eldest.'

But Sir Arthur had no wish to delve into the Minister's marriage customs and arrangements, nor, really, could one keep track of the man's numerous brood. Mists, the Minister observed, were rapidly thickening to fog.

In no time at all, then, the two men were back on the rails. There were numerous matters, some of delicacy, to discuss: all the business of State, held up by various absences and accentuated by the Resident's impending departure.

* * *

There was one duty. Sir Arthur saw it as imperative, no less than what he owed to his successor, and beyond his successor what was owed to the Empire he represented.

In between social engagements that jostled one another so agreeably at Government House in Bombay, Sir Arthur had sallied out from Malabar Point to the spur on the hill where, from the gap between the heliotrope bushes, he had looked down at Chaupati Beach, which at the time had been crawling.

Like spying on ants.

But ants have qualities. They swarm, they sting, they prevail in a way not short of unthinkable. Sir Arthur had seen. A grown stag slowed by shotgun, but brought down, eventually, by these tiny creatures. It had been, and was, an ugly sight, which normally he kept shoved well down where he did not have to look. But that day, wedged between rampant heliotrope, it sprang into his mind, and stayed. He had to make binding promises before it would retreat and give him back a measure of peace.

Within weeks of his return these pledges were redeemed. The squat watch-tower that guarded the Residency, by now in some desuetude, was restored to its former vigilance and efficiency. Searchlights were wired in. Grim structures were built, efficient and deadly (embrasures in the brickwork), and fortified by two 15-pounders with an all-round traverse that the gunnery officer, a squad of sepoys, and an army of perspiring coolies finally hauled into place.

Sir Arthur did suffer twinges while they were at it. The panorama from this point—he ascended the tower to look— offered nothing but reassurance, the vistas that unrolled before him were utterly placid. No State could be more loyal.

But was the State the people? The niggly question—no bigger than a worm, admittedly—resurrected at Malabar Point, though hatched elsewhere and in another century, justified the precautions.

Meanwhile that other cloud no bigger than a man's hand had darkened entire skies. To this distant happening watch-tower and fortifications were linked, as a means of avoiding hurt to anyone's feeling.

The Great War had begun.

'One can't, Waji—don't you agree—be too careful.'

The Minister looked on, his sardonic talents barely leashed. It seemed a waste, whistling up sledgehammers to crack nuts. Peasantry did not require such thunder. On the other hand, if it was spirit one was after, no amount of ironmongery could squash so nimble and elusive an adversary. All that would happen, he feared, was the messy annihilation of a hamlet or two, triggered by a walk-out in some hapless cottage industry. Bill for damages, needless to say, to the Devapur exchequer. For there was this, and he freely allowed it to the British. No matter who incurred the expense, and whatever was the purpose of it, from Durbar to punitive expedition the country always paid. Sometimes the Minister, no mean hand himself at financial wizardry, had to stand back in admiration of his masters.

But apart from commentary the Dewan had no power. The Residency was British, and untouchable, soil. Additions and alterations, accordingly, were severely outside the jurisdiction of the Maharajah and his Ministers. It was only the Resident's unfailing courtesy, and a feeling for old Waji, that had led Sir Arthur to obtain his Highness's permission at all.

* * *

By no means only the Resident. The mill strike, throwing a wide lariat, also roped in the Maharajah and the Maharajkumar.

Bawajiraj bore visible scars. Pausing to adjust his turban, on his way to one or other official function, he often noticed the livid furrow that the jagged stone had left, just below the hairline. Then, glaring, the pride of his ancestry pricked, his eyes would darken, the clear resin, in which so much that was charming was harmlessly captured, would turn to coal, the glittering seamy surfaces reflecting a predatory and calculating stranger.

There were times when Bawajiraj could not recognise what he saw. He refused to countenance the signs. So did Mohini. When she lay beside him, her naked love, and, remembering, put up her hand to stroke his temples, the tips of her fingers encountered, under the thick springy hair, a hardness that could not be assigned only to scars.

Her pellucid beloved, developing these callouses.

Extraordinary that such sensitivity should lurk at the tips of members. Imagination purely.

But at night she moaned, her hands fought, sought to preserve what was precious. Not infrequently she snatched him from his own, disturbed, slumbers.

'What is it, Mohini? Wake up.'

Shaking her gently, gentle even in this wild awakening. Concerned.

'I'm all right. An unpleasant dream.'

Dragged into consciousness. Lying stark on the ottoman, perspiration beading her forehead, the flank that rested against his turned clammy. Flinging aside the silk then, entwining him with limbs and a sudden vehemence.

'Promise me you won't change! Promise!'

'Am I likely to? After half a lifetime?'

Sighing.

Pulling up the covers and, finally, subsiding under them, although both knew this was not what had been in question.

Feelings were roused on mornings after. Straightening the ruffled stripes, and thumping up the mangled bolsters, the eyes of the maidservants grew reflective and wary.

Soon afterwards the Maharajah instructed the Minister to outlaw strikes. Forbid them—issue a proclamation—whatever one did, but the gist of it was he would tolerate no more nonsense. Actually there was none. A clumsy stoppage or two, imitating happenings in the rest of the country, for better pay. A few walkouts, for similar motives, settled with a minimum of fuss and expense.

But official sanctions?

The Minister sucked in his cheeks and considered. As well command the people, he felt, to stop wanting. It did not lie in human nature, especially the kind of humans to whom the edict would apply. Humans whom Rulers, not to mention the Suzerain Power, had fleeced disgracefully despite the resistance of their local leaders and some faint bleating of their own. Bones picked clean—well, not quite, one must not exaggerate. But teetering, on the edge of pits into which, having once fallen, they would never emerge within their lifetime.

Endangered now, more than ever. Britain at war and therefore, willy-nilly, the Empire. The State (the Dewan pictured it as a still juicy orange) would be squeezed, if it did not embark on its own self-denying ordinances. Loyal notes were already being struck in the Palace.

And prices were rising. The Dewan had a list, compiled by his officers, that ran to two pages.

One could not at such a time snatch from a man the prospect of better days, a better wage on which he could string a few hopes. Unless one desired explosion. A melodrama, such as had already been acted out in the mills, wrung from desperation and occasioning insufferable inconvenience, according to all accounts, but serving little purpose.

Except as a beacon. Warning lights that people put out before they are goaded into wholesale and national rebellion.

Such were the unimpeachable sources the Dewan traced for disenchantment with his employer's wishes. But there were elements, which being of an emotional order he would not recognise, still less permit to sway his political judgment.

Beneath granite surfaces and the seals of high office the Dewan retained a sense of common affiliation: the properties of a common composition, which in Bawajiraj had been suppressed, that were, as often, at work.

He side-tracked, in his customary manner, the issue. This zigzag pattern, he had found, frequently proved the most conducive for his purpose. He proposed to summon the Council when, in due course, the Working Committee had reported on the Maharajah's proposal. The Committee had yet to be appointed. Its terms of reference would have to be debated. The drafting of appropriate clauses could be relied on to consume time. All this would while away the months, whittle down, hopefully, the Ruler's determination.

But Bawajiraj was not to be easily deflected.

One could tell, the way he crunched the gravel. Slashing with his sword-stick, though not a weed in sight. Boots like the sergeant-major's, and a note to match what hurtled across the quadrangle on broiling afternoons.

'None of your shilly-shallying, Minister.'

'I would not dream, your Highness.'

The Minister marched in step, a shade or two behind as required by the rules, without undue sound as he was wearing rope sandals which thwacked placidly at his soles. He continued:

'Although I would be failing in my duty if I did not inform your Highness the action you call for is inadvisable.'

'When I *need* your advice, Minister, I'll *ask* for it.'

'Nevertheless, Highness, even unasked I must tender it, as I am paid to do.'

'So long as you remember nobody is indispensable, Minister.'

'Naturally, Highness. That is always perfectly understood.'

An old exchange, all right, which he had supposed time had buried. Only, the tone was different. Both of them were aware of it, conscious of entering harsh new territory through which paths had still to be hacked. The Maharajah flushed, forbidding encroachments, the locked gaze of ancestral hauteur. Or incipient mania, the Minister felt, considering the circumstances, and the era that was catching up, after a sluggish start. He pondered, under his own glaze, glimpsing in the fleshy congested face that challenged him intimations of the kind that oppressed Mohini in her sleep.

It surprised him, truth to tell. Even accepting that men were complex. The spiteful streaks that had surfaced seemed so alien that they came close to confounding him. His heart felt crimped, for all his outward composure. Not daunted, exactly. He had strengths; but these strengths were what they were precisely because of bracing and underpinning, not to mention alliances, undertaken in good time.

There was, as it happened, the heir to the State.

Devapur State. The Minister's vision, enlarging, stretched to the farthest outpost of territories that his line had administered, and come to regard as its own. Carefully though: in the nature of a leasehold, title deeds held by another; and even that given up gracefully, in time. But this State, that had been nursed and cherished: that was as ably administered as could be managed and by common consent the least ramshackle of the Five Hundred: that was after all the only monument to men whose ashes would not rest under marble tombs nor in vainglorious abbeys but would journey on rivers to oceans: this kingdom could not easily be yielded to destructive whimsies. Then he concluded that Devapur must come first. Not above soul, certainly, but second to none else.

The Minister's pride, in its way, was as fierce as any.

Without fuss or show his determination grew that he and his officers would continue to defy infringement upon, or injury to, this entity.

Time, then, to usher the son, scion of this Ruler with the disturbing chameleon flashes, boldly into his camp.

Though he was of independent cast.

Prospect of intricate moves, a challenge not without appeal. Intrigue, strictly limited by the blunt British now that it had served their purpose, sparked the bleak Minister, drove strange hues to his cheek that compelled the Maharajah's attention.

Psychic exchange between the pair was minimal, but Bawajiraj could not help noticing, uneasily, peculiar inimical lights that seemed to stream from his Dewan.

Into this taut scene, unaware of struggle since both participants were civilised men, stepped the lighthearted Resident. Airy, having that morning seen duty done, and carrying a posy that some small smiling waif had pressed upon him on his way hither.

'Ah, Maharajah Sahib! Dewan Sahib! The very people. Mission, if I may say so, successfully accomplished.'

And waved the posy to where, in the distance, above the Residency, the tower bulked.

'Sleep more easily in our different couches, what? That is to say in our different continents.'

At which point, with customary faultless timing, there were inaugural bangs, accompanied by harmless puffs and recoiling muzzles; and scattered applause. In this disarming fracas the conflict between Maharajah and Minister, which had threatened to come to a head, dived sharply underground.

* * *

Soon after the farewells began.

The Hon'ble the Resident was a popular man. Not one from bottom rung to top that didn't have a good word, pleasant memories to enlarge on, a clap on the shoulder—so to speak: one didn't maul the Resident—for one of the very best.

Lady Copeland—well, the ladies in the cantonment were not too certain about her. They decided it must be her air. Not airs, mind you, though she would have been fully entitled, but something there. An invisible diadem, or core of ice, that made you remember distances, and keep them. None of the ladies could imagine tangling in a familiar way with the tall woman who glimmered palely, a bluish polar light, at their apex; or dream of exchanging with her at cosy get-togethers the warm, spicy gossip that enlivened Anglo-India.

But in the effusion of departure all was forgotten, or forgiven. They vied with one another. Parties, from all quarters and at all levels, were thrown at the Homeward-bound pair. It took the Resident's private secretary all his time, and tact, to sift through the invitations and arrange a manageable schedule.

'Hard to believe one is so popular.'

Sir Arthur was quite overwhelmed: a man of unquenchable modesties of spirit that he somehow spliced, credibly, to his high office.

'One isn't. You are,' said his wife, dry, but gentle, the gentleness that was habitual between them. Her faded cornflower hues were turning, lately, coming up a blazing blue. She could not wait to get out of this haunted continent.

There were numerous splendid and sentimental functions.

A party at the Palace, guest list a thousand, at which the Maharajah was seen, but forgiven, to throw an arm about the Resident. A second at the Residency, to which were invited Maharajah and Minister and their wives (both women, for different reasons, declined). Yet another at the Club, to which neither the Minister nor the Maharajah, to Sir Arthur's regret, could be asked, since no Indian, not even a guest—not even puissant Sir Arthur's—was allowed on the premises.

Social dealing in Anglo-India was known to turn strong men grey at the gills.

Finally it came to actual departure.

They lined up in strict order. Head of State, the Maharani, the Heir-Apparent, the Dewan, the Resident's personal staff, and the servants, indoor and outdoor, of the household. All but the sweepers, a noisome crew who had, unprompted, taken up positions in the open, downwind; and the chauffeur, in peaked cap and leggings, who stood smartly, ready to whip open, beside the shining Daimler.

All of them sad to see the Lord Sahib go. A good man, they said, who kept an eye, and saw that they were granted pensions —sizeable sums, not the kind of pittance Indian Sahibs dished out. Among them the old ayah. Bold black woman, breaking ranks to thrust herself forward for the master's attention. Hissing, her buck teeth truly beyond bearing.

'Sahib! Salaam to Missie Sophie, Sahib!'

'My dear, er, ayah, certainly. Certainly I'll convey to her . . .'

Sir Arthur rather vague—so many persons: who was this toothy woman?—but fastening on to her patent goodwill. Though it was all a bit much. In this heat. One would be glad to get it over.

Now down to principals. Some easy—straightforward handshakes. Some tricky—perhaps a slight bow for the Maharani? Sir Arthur moved smoothly, thoughts well hidden, in dove-grey, his silky topper artfully balanced in the crook of an elbow.

'Goodbye, your Highness.' (This stiff, unknown Maharani.) 'It has been a pleasure.'

'Goodbye, Sir Arthur.'

'Well, Rabi. Goodbye, my dear boy.' (Credit to his father; well, perhaps not. Not a boy either.)

'Goodbye, sir. Good luck.'

'Dewan Sahib.'

'Excellency. Goodbye, and godspeed.'

But Bawajiraj, who would not be denied, detached himself.

They walked together down the immense curved flight, down which Sir Arthur, alone, long ago, had come to meet the unknown Prince. The memory stirred both men. It dissolved flesh, and certain hardenings and accretions of which neither was wholly convinced despite what his looking-glass told him. The Resident saw himself—tall, tanned, upright, and confident—sword at his side, clattering lightly down these very stairs to take up burdens as he had been charged to do. The Maharajah stepped out fined and thinned. Slim handsome Prince, amber eyes clear and glowing, ascending to meet his destiny.

He had to come out with it.

'Been a long time, H.E.'

'Most happy. Some of the happiest, Waji, I don't mind confessing.'

'You must come back. When the war's over, H.E. I'll make the necessary—um—representations.'

'You mustn't flatter me, my dear chap. . . . But when the war's over, who knows? Maybe . . .'

'If you can—'

'I will. Goodbye, Waji. Look after it (Sir Arthur waved, a wide sweep that described the whole State) won't you, while I'm away, there's a good chap.'

'Goodbye, H.E. Do my best, you know that.'

The two men clasping hands, Sir Arthur's clasp as fervent as Waji's but detaching rather quickly, handing in his wife, bundling in smartly oneself in case (Waji's eyes suspiciously bright) anything boiled over.

Paths swept, gravel rolled, springs peerless. A last memory of those who had gathered was of Sir Arthur's top hat and the net balloon which enclosed Lady Copeland gliding serenely, hood thrown back, under the arched gateways from which the splendid pair of gilded stone lions looked down.

Sir Arthur had to turn as they passed. He had always had a fondness for the South front.

12

The outbreak of the Great War revived in the Maharajah, as if it were yesterday, certain sentiments of Lord Curzon at the Great Durbar of 1903.

'Is it nothing,' His Excellency had enquired, 'that the Sovereign at his Coronation should exchange pledges with his assembled lieges of protection and respect on the one side, of spontaneous allegiance on the other?'

Recollections of this noble compact roused in Bawajiraj emotions of intense loyalty to the Crown, and spurred him to place his person and the resources of his State at the disposal of the Paramount Power.

In short, an Expeditionary Force, drawn from the State Forces, augmented by recruiting drives, with himself as Commander-in-Chief. And as second-in-command—he was furtive about this—his son Rabindranath.

Bawajiraj was not alone. His fellow Maharajahs vied with each other, jammed the telegraph lines with their expressions of loyalty to His Majesty the King-Emperor and, perhaps more to the point, in their offers of services to the Crown in its hour of need.

For a time so did the entire country. It responded enthusiastically, at least in the early stages, to the call for aid. In return the people expected to be granted the right to rule themselves. Britain conceded the principle but, it became clear, had little intention of translating words into deeds. India, consequently, grew increasingly restive.

Devapur State was of course outside—separate and solemn treaty obligations—all this kind of pother, though some did wonder what manner of fence could prevent unruly thoughts, or even elements, from straying in over the border. Accordingly the Ruler felt no brake on his desire to place in the field a force—nothing less than a division, as he envisaged it—that would acquit itself worthily and bring honour and glory to Devapur.

As it could not do in its present condition, besides being woefully under strength. Inspecting his troops it became dismally apparent to Bawajiraj. He stalked about, sun and rain, topi jammed on his head, curtly dismissing the umbrella man, wincing at what he saw. Magnificent men; and accoutrements to match, he acknowledged, sniffing; but discipline and equipment of a kind that offended the eye of, after all, a one-time graduate of Military Academy.

What, he wondered, twirling his crop, the knob dull as a bullet in his palm, had ever made him suppose that such a collection? Where was the shining army he had imagined freely presenting to the Paramount Power? A bit straggly, Sir Arthur had agreed, that time after the Durbar when he, Bawajiraj, had observed shortcomings and requested permission, as he was bound to do by treaty. Permission had not been refused, as far as he could remember, but somehow nothing had come of it.

Then embers began to burn in the Maharajah's breast, flaring up here and there for all that he loyally tried to stamp them out, that it was perhaps to do with Sir Arthur. Magnificent fighting men, allowed the tinny equipment of toy soldiers. The State Force, which in its day had conquered redoubtable armies (Bawajiraj had to disinter and dust off numerous ancestors at this point), good for nothing so much as pageantry. But surely Sir Arthur? He couldn't possibly have suspected his friend Waji? It was too dreadful to contemplate. And why had he, the Chief, been blind? Confusing carnival with an efficient fighting body?

When the flares had been put out, and the misery subsided, it left more than anything a vast disarray. So poor a thing, the Maharajah felt, with which to come to the aid of His Gracious Majesty. And he curled his lip—somewhat unjustly, given to exaggeration as Mohini continued to accuse him—at the forces of which he was Head, and set about with his customary energy—and a host of recruiting officers, arms contractors, weapons instructors, and drill sergeants culled from a variety of sources—to overcome the years of neglect.

The war kept all of them busy.

In Bawajiraj's case zeal mounted not only because of His Majesty, but because the Maharajah wished to present the incoming Resident with a *fait accompli*. Whatever Sir Arthur's reason had been for keeping down the Devapur forces—cost, he had finally convinced himself; no other explanation was bearable—his successor should not have the opportunity.

Time was on his side. Some hitch or other—the war provided plenty—had held up the arrival of the new man. Six months of independence at least, Bawajiraj hoped for, with a glee that called up closely an unfettering of limbs. This disturbed him. He had never been fettered to his knowledge; and he did not like to think of himself as degenerating into a man given to imagining things.

Bawajiraj's cup would have run over, as the Expeditionary Force firmed and trimmed under his overall command, if he could have lured his son.

His only son. But this product of his loins, of whom he was justly so proud—requests for his services as ADC from Jaipur, Bikaner, the Governor, plus virtually a command from old Pooky—whom he could just see as his own smart deputy— cheerfully declined all invitations.

'Don't think I'm cut out for it somehow.'

'You are Rabi, believe me. Allow me to be the judge. Image of a soldier.'

'Image maybe. Pretty hollow though.'

'Don't you *want* to?'

'No, to be quite honest.'

It quite stung, inciting Bawajiraj to meaner thrusts.

'Your caste, Rabi. Warrior and all that. In the blood you know, you can't escape what runs in the blood.'

'I'll give it a try. Run like the wind, I'm good at running.'

Unseemly levity that made Bawajiraj quake. On one occasion white feathers actually fluttered. He had heard. Word of this tribal exercise had arrived. He knew it would not be long before it was emulated on these shores. Was it one feather the ladies presented? Final disgrace, whatever the number.

It spurred him to try harder, while his son retreated.

'What d'you say, Rabi?'

'Not the right man, Highness.'

So formal. As if they weren't father and son. As if they were in Court, on view in public, and it was necessary to make this formal avowal.

While wholly unnecessary reinforcements were brought up.

To be fair, came up, since Rabi, he granted, would never ask for them, that independent streak that was giving so much trouble.

Rabi's mother.

Rabi's grandmother.

The Dowager, so thin and bent these days you would hardly have thought her capable, but there she was, the Palace not big enough, really, to contain the two of them. Cruising round, *paschmina* trailing, cornering him in corridors.

'Rabi's almost of age, you know.'

'I know. I can count.'

Hardly brilliant, or even polite, but really his mother far from fading—widow and all that—was putting herself forward and making a monumental nuisance of herself. Humped in the corridor. Not actually blocking his passage—there was ample room to pass—but choking the free flow of his thoughts, his beliefs, his passions. Rebutting with her presence, it seemed to him, all that he was and all that he stood for, those very articles of faith he would wish to pass on. Himself flattened against the wall while her silences surged over him, wave after wave. He had a feeling of coming up for air each time it broke over his head. Though he was of course standing quite still, while his mind bobbed about in the wash as frantic as a cork.

When she moved he jumped. It galvanised a fly that had settled on his petrified sleeve. Dull thing, diaphanous wing gone to khaki on the cloth, but as it soared away the colourless light broke on those gauzy deltas into a kaleidoscope of whirling colour. Odd how seldom one noticed. No time perhaps, so many things on one's mind. Or perhaps it was the revealing quality of the light in corridors. Hard and white, its own colours stitched up securely inside until broken on a prism, while it searched out corners.

Laid one open, he felt. On the slab of her scrutiny. Though nothing there to shame a man.

But he continued oppressed, for all the assurances.

So was the Dowager, though the pressures were different. Sometimes she had to struggle for breath in the atmosphere he imported, for long of alien composition, but now tipping over into a totally inimical medium. Or perhaps she was older; time not what it had been, yards of the lovely shining stuff on endless spools, but limited. It made one long for magical solutions: swift conversion into an element where fair exchange was possible, meanings easily given and taken, instead of this suffocating miasma.

She might have let it go, but for certain considerations, not all to do with Rabi though rooted there. As it was she said, quite low, wrenching it out of herself:

'Haven't we given enough?'

'What do you mean?'

He was frightened. Perspiring. Sometimes his mother scared him to death.

'Are we to offer up our sons as well?'

That blinding stare of hers, it could unnerve a man. He had to make a supreme effort to come back.

'If you mean Rabi—'

'I mean all . . . all our sons. Dismembering them, body, mind, soul. . . . For what? You tell me. For what?'

She must be talking to herself, he decided. If not raving, as usual. But he could not make it stick, the gaze she turned on him was anguished but composed. Quite insupportable as well. Fending her off, figuratively speaking, he blundered past, his footsteps seeming to richochet from wall to wall as he strode along the labrynthine passages.

And Mohini said, cruelly, aiming to get under his skin:

'Why should he? He's Indian, isn't he? Not some kind of brown Englishman? Why should he get mixed up in their battles? For liberty? Hogwash. They're not even going to talk about our liberty. D'you think they're going to give up the most profitable thing they've got? They're not addled, you know!'

And again, of late they could hardly keep off the subject.

'What d'you think? Of course he doesn't want to become cannon fodder. He's got his head screwed on properly, no thanks to you.'

Cannon fodder. Was that all she could see? He almost pitied her, sitting there blinkered beside the orange trees feeding the goldfish, treating honour and glory in these brutish terms. Reducing the shining package to lumps of meat. Certainly it was an aspect of war, war was a serious game; but weren't there other aspects to contemplate, so rich, so redemptive that the most ordinary flesh could be seen to glow, brushed with a divine splendour . . . Thinking about it his heart began to trip and his eyes grew soft and lustrous and looked on carnage—even carnage that bloodied him—without flinching.

He was a brave man, effortlessly brave.

* * *

315

It was not, however, the thought of becoming cannon fodder that deterred Rabi. It could not, since he did not at any time even remotely consider becoming part of the Expeditionary Force, an outfit assembled by that remote man, the Maharajah. It was something to watch, not something to involve oneself in; got up in a cause earnestly proclaimed by this parent of his, which seemed, not unusually, of distant and exaggerated application. Somewhere, far away—the light came even now—sparkled the Sovereign's Representative; but its sources had been traced and could not awe; and there was little to delight, the connection grey and suspect set against the holed and pathetic fabric that was gradually revealing itself.

Even more simply he felt there was more to do at home. Immense problems that the Dewan sketched, the two of them hunched over the carved ministerial table while a common love flowered under electric light that sharpened as the evening wore on. A love for the land that both had inherited, though only one bore a legal claim. Problems that presented intractably, or even escaped the astute Dewan who could not accommodate unwashed girls except, perhaps, as part of his faceless flock; although, prodded, he now did so. Vast unexplored acreage: those immense tracts that opened beyond the ornamental gates at which, Mohini had maintained all her life, reality became suspended.

The Dewan went for brain. It was for him crown and meridian and fount, the source from which, given preparation and training, all things would flow. He had already secured, bludgeoning Maharajah on the one hand, populace on the other, compulsory literacy to the age of ten. Now with the first stage completed, and the ruler preoccupied, and the ruler's heir backing his efforts, he embarked on that programme of systematic expansion whereby the net was extended to embrace twelve-year-olds. The scheme had always been close to his heart.

Rabi was for water: an ubiquitous, everyday fluid that had been forcibly brought to his attention.

The life-giving aspects it assumed for others possessed him, even to the exclusion of those charming guises this ordinary flow could take on, or the beguiling effects achieved with it by the Palace.

'A half hour, for a thimbleful of drinking water.'

He told the Dewan, wondering if he knew, not about the girl, that was secondary, but about the circumstances of her living.

'She had to walk,' he rubbed it in. 'A quarter of a mile. It's too

316

much, no human should . . . a quarter of a mile for water so that she could wash.'

The Dewan blenched. He knew quite enough, one did not want all the squalid detail. Besides, this Bombay girl and her deplorable condition belonged to British India. Although it was only slightly better in Devapur State. Plenty of *izzat* here, and a lamentable shortage of piping.

'A dam,' he said firmly, and even poetically. 'To harness in times of plenty, and release when the heavens are unkind.'

'Floods, if not drought,' said Rabi. 'Poor girl'—these days he could bring himself to talk about her—'she used to be flooded out regularly.'

Yet another girl. The Dewan racked his memory, which finally yielded up the sweeper. A childhood crony, he remembered, dismissed for presuming. Still lingering, he saw. An enduring scar. But anything was grist to his mill. Opportunity here, he felt, to push ahead with schemes with or without the Maharajah's blessing in company with Rabi and these obscure females. Without further ado he recruited them to his side.

'Poor girl, quite reprehensible,' he said briskly. 'Now if one were to establish a measure of control . . . here, I'm told, would be ideal, where the river narrows . . .'

And he whipped out his maps.

Outside the Dewan's office the *chaprassi* stationed at the door eased himself off his high stool and crept round to the verandah from where he could take a peek. Both occupants, he saw, as surmised were engrossed in whatever it was. Heads bent over the table, that heavy drone like dizzy bees fussing around a honeycomb—he could tell it would be hours yet. Having satisfied himself he stole back, displaced the stool and settled himself in this space in a comfortable squatting position, rump just clear of the floor to aid circulation and, if obliged, a springy return to the stool. Then he took off his turban and fumbling in the dark folds (jade green actually, the Dewan's livery, drained to this shade by night, a time at which a servant ought rightfully to be in bed) located and extracted a wad of *bhang* which he expertly palmed. A routine look round, unnecessary at this godforsaken hour, but he believed in good habits, followed by a quick transfer to his cheek.

Chewing peacefully, the sappy juices trickling like a soothing potion, he fell into a light trance that would, he knew from experience, see him through the hours of waiting without ever toppling into the stupor that could cost a man his job.

317

* * *

They went on extended tours. Rabi mostly, being eager to see for himself, and accompanied by a battery of experts. The Dewan had his hand-picked officers, and believed in the art of delegation.

Rabi travelled by car, on horseback, on foot, and by elephant.

To outlandish places, the Maharajah concluded, and lost even vestigial interest.

To one spot in particular, deep in the jungle, where the dam was planned. Mounted on Parvati since Lakshmi—incomparable in processions, not batting an eyelash at the most frenetic of kettledrums, honoured, once at Durbar, with Resident and party by virtue of these very qualities—this splendid beast turned up her nose at jungle work.

Whereas Parvati was trained. She was a working elephant, and insofar as one could tell of an animal subdued or conned into irrelevant labour she revelled in her work. A grey lumbering beast, in these barbered precincts beside the Palace lawns. Some kind of a mountain you couldn't have missed in miles. But in her own environment the mountain became part of the landscape. They glided, it seemed to him; ponderous feet, huge scalloped toe-nails that featured so prominently on umbrella-stands, landing and behaving like butterflies. He had to strain to hear the crushed twig underfoot, though the scrub was thick. Overhang that might have swept him off his perch he saw only after it had been deflected by the solicitous, extraordinary trunk.

Detaching himself, as he had always been able, he could see them plainly: man and beast advancing in grey shade and stippled light in which the beast, and presently the man, were dissolved. Incorporated by soft and pearly processes into peaceful savannahs that one often suspected existed.

The querulous "I" stilled.

Questions yielding their shriller capacities, those frightful hooks fading.

One could absorb, in the encapsulated stillness. What could not be taught, nor learned, until one's rusty receptors were working. So he could feel himself alter, as he journeyed through the known and unknown landscape to which he had given himself, fitting into their subtler shapes instead of barging against them, that fretful banging and clanging that usually went on.

Then he began to feel he was close, or if not close, within range of taking up his heritage: those elucidations accessible to all, though his birth had precluded an easy or simple assumption.

318

* * *

No desire, observed the Court. Or little to speak of. Their gaze grew shifty, travelling downwards but obliquely, wishing to dwell upon the young man's equipment without revealing the slant of their thought. The older courtiers narrowed their eyes and compared son to father, who had tumbled girls like ninepins—a glutton for dalliance—until he fell captive to the constant concubine with fire in her belly. Or between her legs, they said slyly, enough to keep a man on the boil, although even so he was known to make forays. Naturally. Whereas this one. Not innocent, either. Bursting, they could tell (man to man they exchanged bawdy stories), but leisurely about it. Finical. Picking, as a prince had every right and entitlement, but at a rate that could only be described as odd.

And girls who had willingly—so they persuaded themselves—given up their rights and entitlements waited in satin apartments for noble and princely favours. Beauties who stroked their silky thighs, and wondered what tedious new position, and were consumed with boredom in bed and out of it.

But the new ones were tender, blushing under tuition.

Like pomegranates opening, the older courtesans, past it themselves, advised these charges, upon whose bodies a man might practise to bring himself to the peaks of skill and satisfaction. A language of sex that drew derisive hoots from the older girls; a language devised for virginal ears that reality, it was assumed, might stun.

* * *

What different tongues they spoke!

There were times when Rabi felt driven, biting his lip to stop himself from sharply silencing the inane, lascivious babbling.

But this one was tender. Coached, clearly, but had run dry. Licking her lips even to give her name.

'Leila.'

'Leila. You're not afraid, are you?'

'No.'

Lying huskily, a gallant liar, but trembling. In those ridiculous harem trousers considered a fitting garb, mock-chaste, infernally difficult fastenings about the ankles. A doll to dress and undress. But human. Begging for gentleness. Answer it. He said:

'I won't hurt you. Let yourself go.'

'I know. I'll try.'

He tried too.

But the small tight bud of a body resisted him. So dry, not a drop to be coaxed. Too green, he felt, or frightened out of its purpose, and would have gone away but she clung, this doll of a woman, out of pride, or the prompting of duty. Then he tried again, with a salve, salving the submissive shrinking female flesh, somehow still gentle although by now he was on fire. While she lay like a peony, suffering whatever he did and, he could see, dying of shame.

He should have given up then, he knew; but he was too far gone.

Ashamed, though, later. Nothing in it for her, not even the mechanical release that compensated him, edged though it was by a sour emptiness even at climax.

He grew circumspect after that. Saw to it that they were older. Seasoned dancing-girls, expert at more than their art. Pouting prettily to please a man—endlessly available, endlessly accommodating—where was their pride? It encouraged that abstinence that exercised the courtiers.

He had, he felt, finer models.

And eyed his mother.

Mohini, conscious of searchlights, was piqued rather than troubled. She felt she would like to take his head between her hands and crack it open, just a little, to look at what went on. But of course it was impossible and, besides, she had every faith in her son.

It grew with the years, while confidence in his father dwindled.

* * *

These physical pleasures, however, Rabi placed as the frills. Fulfilment lay elsewhere, outside the scope of barren encounters, and was to do with the passion he was beginning to feel for what was building in the jungle. A taste of honey, he put it to himself, in words that the Dewan's *chaprassi* would readily have endorsed: a sweet sense of creating that crowned each day's end.

* * *

The Dewan came to see for himself when the project was entering its second stage—art of delegation notwithstanding. To keep an eye, he convinced himself, since what was building was making healthy, if carefully scrutinised, inroads into the Exchequer. Basically, however, because he, too, was entangled. In effect he had been involved, he calculated, taking in the tussles of his father, for close on half a century.

Elephants, the terrain demanded.

He had, earmarked for his personal use, one trusty working animal, a peaceful cow elephant tolerant of all manner of human tarantara, conches and bugles among them, into whose howdah, a four-seater with jade trappings, he climbed with distinctly sacrificial feelings when obliged to. There were nine such occasions, all to do with the State: the Dassara procession, the King-Emperor's Birthday Parade, the Maharajah's Birthday Celebrations, and a half dozen ceremonial visits to the temple tied in with religious festivals.

Should he subject himself a tenth time in the space of a year? The Dewan debated, and could not bring himself. That rolling elephantine gait, seeking out, and wrenching, every shrinking muscle. Over unceremonious distances. No. Only alternative, wise men insisted, a bullock-cart. Settled for it, dewans cannot be choosers. Folded himself into this jarring vehicle, immaculate as usual though he feared it could not last, his gloom alleviated only slightly by a sight of his secretary, folded opposite (no room for the finer distinctions) in a state of shock.

And there was Rabi, waiting to greet him. In some kind of faded khaki, such as lesser *chaprassis* might wear, sleeves rolled up over arms that were (somewhat carelessly, one couldn't help thinking) burned to a dark cork. As cool as if he were in his father's drawing-room, receiving guests. Ah, youth! The Dewan had some moments for poetry while he waited for suitable boots for his town feet. Lissom youth, what it was to be in one's springtime!

Springy, this young man, but collected. Coming forward to greet his crumpled mentor, hand stretched out (hand like a ganger's: must have a word; only gangers forgiven such callouses) to aid his descent.

'Good of you to make the journey, Dewan Sahib.'

That touch of formality that irked the Maharajah. Not unpleasing, from a younger to an older man. Deference, the Dewan felt, that was only one's due as preceptor and principal.

'A pleasure, my dear Rabi.'

But standing, duly booted, under the tossing trees, he was jolted to find that the balance of dues and receipts, the working formula within which people function, this delicate equation was altered. In this wild place—in which he could see himself, creaking a little, his thin clothes blowing—the khaki figure commanded. Quite loomed over him, he felt, though it was not simply a matter of height, but control as well.

It was Rabi who controlled, or dominated; to whom he, the Dewan, must (so to speak) touch his snowy turban.

As Rabi, too, was aware, human commerce being more than a matter of speech and appearances. Something was equalising, he felt, slashing idly with the switch he carried, a peeled margosa wand that one of the labourers had presented him with, to ward off eye-flies, the man said. This was after he had been around awhile, and the Maharajkumar halo had worn thin and they remembered one was human, suffering from these minute persistent creatures that tirelessly and insanely assaulted the eyeballs. One day up came Baldev, pick over his shoulder, wand in his hand, bent on his mission. Humanitarian, speaking up boldly in a humane cause.

'For you, Sahib.'

'Are you sure it'll work?'

'O, very good, Sahib. Working very good. You please try.'

Try anything. Slapping at the suicidal things, feeling suicidal oneself, crushing the merest bleep from one's city scepticism to experiment in the interests of sanity.

Faith rewarded. Or the swarming season was over. Like the rains, two lots, blown in from different directions. And the worst of the blistering season. Weathered, all of them, and primed with the new authority that came from finding out, teasing out the vexed strands of innumerable problems, here in the heart of it.

Unlike, clearly, the Dewan, fluctuating gently beside him and attempting to mould himself to the climate. Unusual for him, one could see that quite plainly, but managing, and managing with some aplomb. He warmed to the billowing, indomitable figure.

'Well, Dewan Sahib, what do you think?'

'I congratulate you, Rabi. I had no idea, that is to say, no real notion,' the Dewan answered, grappling with language to convey what he felt, namely, that somewhere in all the paperwork he had regrettably mislaid the reality. The reality of running water, that simple adjunct to living which not all the fine white tracery of blueprint, nor all the progress reports that had thudded regularly onto his desk, had quite succeeded in delivering up.

'You mean you expected no progress at all?'

Rabi was, yes, grinning. A holy light spread over his countenance. A small matter, the Dewan saw, of pupil twitting his master, having smartly taken his place. He cleared his throat.

'Not at all, Rabi,' he said primly. 'A case, since you ask, of word made flesh, by which I mean I see our plans are coming to fruition.'

And there in the scrub, beside the rangy figure, among the assembled men, of a sudden the Dewan felt that glut, like a warm infusion of sunlight, that will sometimes envelop men who are joined in a valid and pure endeavour.

'Worth it, I think, don't you?' he said, somewhat gruffly.

(Every hour, every bit of juggling with the revenues, every inch of the hideous journey: so why ask? unless simply for something to say.)

'Coming along, yes.'

Rabi laughed. Exquisite sensations, not for exhibition. Wrapped up in word made flesh, this vast undertaking that had risen up out of blueprint and some visionary promptings. Sometimes it roped them all in, from labourer up—a common astonishment, one could only suppose. Even the Dewan. Doing his best, but those pinkish flecks betraying him. Seized, it was clear, in this odd upsurge that was making his own face burn.

'Coming along well,' he repeated, and clapped an affectionate arm about the Dewan's shoulders.

Then they were walking easily together, in the orderly chaos, shouting at times to make themselves heard above the sound of blasting and the cataract of water, among the lines of sweaty men and baskets of earth that jogged past on the heads of women with, it did strike the Dewan, the bearing of divinities. Coolie ants, whose activity, according to situation, could gladden the heart or arouse the blackest introspection.

The Dewan was gladdened. He did not tote, after all, the burden of the Resident.

'Good workers.'

He grunted, chary with compliments, compliments consequently falling like manna. Received, however, soberly. The air, as both men were discovering, precluded the fulsome.

'Fired, I think,' said Rabi.

And moved on quickly to physical detail—inflow, outflow, rockfill, turbines, diversion channels—all the minutiae, which the Dewan allowed to wash over him, as generals must. Impressed however. Since this kind of intelligence—not at all within the compass of maharajkumars—could only be gleaned by sustained effort, working with experts here on site, during the grinding months, while the gilded body went to cork.

It quite moved the Dewan.

* * *

Fired.

Jolting along on his way back to civilisation the Dewan pondered. Head drooping, chin, by now heavy with the celadon hues, touching his chest—how anyone could slumber, the shattered secretary marvelled, between envy and indignation, himself as wide awake as a bat from the punishment this tumbril was meting out.

The Dewan however was not asleep but engaged in those interior gyrations out of which worlds are spun, although the nebulous cloud cannot be guaranteed to shape into words.

For, it seemed to him, man must be quickened.

Fired by mystery, and the impossible, the far-off star that lures him, awesome heights and enchanted distances not on the map but in the mind. This is what leads him, rocking wildly between the heinous and the most tender and devout.

Man's nature, cloven straight down the middle.

No equal for rapacity, lusting after the universe itself; but striving also for illumination, those cracks through which he hankers to glimpse the infinite. A human craving that redeems him, soothing those desperate convictions that he is a howl in the wilderness. A part of man that, coming upon some bleak tundra of earth or soul, boldly calls it Paradise Valley.

Or Dilkusha.

Or The Residency, for a temporary habitation.

Rocking gently, his mind browsing in regions where workers like princes were fired and quickened, a look of singular beatitude crept over the Dewan.

Some pleasing dream, the numbed secretary inferred—incorrectly, for it was more in the nature of a vision, with earth attachments.

13

The two enterprises, the Maharajah's Expeditionary Force and the Maharajkumar's dam and irrigation project, were thriving, absorbing men and money and the energies of the highest in the land, when the new (acting) Resident arrived.

A downright man, the Honourable Mr. Buckridge, hand-picked, Princely States too important a runner in the imperial stakes not to command the cream, or at least such as was available in wartime; but selected for qualities and purposes different to those embodied in Sir Arthur.

Sir Arthur came out in the tranquil heyday. Harmonious prospects as far as one could see, stretching at least as far as the North-West Frontier. Those unruly tribesmen, of course, one never forgot Kabul;* and fanatics here and there (the poor Viceroy, blown from his howdah on his State entry); and latent memories of the Mutiny. But generally speaking peace, spreading regions over which the Flag serenely flew and on which the sun never set, lit now and again by Jubilees and Durbars, Accessions and Coronations.

A responsible post, his. No one could have supposed otherwise. Nor did Sir Arthur, not even at the beginning, as Secretary to another Resident. Only the assumption of authority was so ingrained he seldom paused to consider it.

Somewhere, true, a knowledge lurked of his power. He had,

*The British set up a puppet in Kabul, backed by a British force. The Afghans rose, toppled the puppet, and drove the British out of their city. One man was allowed to survive to bring back news of the disaster.

he would allow, full discretion; enjoyed, he supposed, carte blanche (of an order, the sarcastic Dewan was fond of suggesting, when they had their differences of opinion, that precisely imitated the scale of an Oriental despot). But to have applied more than a touch of the rein would have branded him in his own eyes as a failure.

Sir Arthur reflected on these aspects of his, well, rule, more than once on his way Home, in his cabin on the boat deck aboard the *Oceanic Empress*, before the delights of Shropshire, and Sophie, overtook him. Persuasion. That was his watchword, and, he believed, not a bad one for the country either. He had preferred to persuade. Good old Waji, always open. Perhaps, at most, lean on him a little. The small matter, for instance, of the Maharajah (greedy young Waji) attempting to augment his privy purse by curtailing the expenses of the Residency . . . and later on (young Waji still, the Maharajah had taken his time about growing up) the proposed Grand Tour with the attendant and frightful expenditure, though even then he had done no more than express a mild disapprobation. But compel? Sir Arthur was perfectly well aware he was not incapable, but the very thought made him shudder.

Mr. Buckridge's appointment was of a different order. He was despatched from England after the outbreak of hostilities, charged with certain duties, and bristling with explicit instructions. Sir Arthur's instructions, in their way, had been no less explicit; but there is a certain leeway in peacetime, scope, in a leisurely heyday, to ease, or mask, the more vehement exactions while preserving the framework of an independent State. No such opportunities were available to the acting Resident. He was, in any case, differently cast, with little patience for niceties and garnishes.

A stern man, this Buckridge, they saw, peering apprehensively from chinks in the barracks and (rather more aloof) from behind the Palace marmore. Few felicities, it seemed to some, the tentative tendrils they had put out withdrawn, or withering; no charm, and hardly a grace to redeem the saturnine figure that stalked about the place. Straight-lipped. Booming at poor Bawajiraj, who was too loyal to reveal the true architect of the lamentable state of his Lancers.

The Maharajah accompanied his Adviser palely. A mistake, he saw, that very first day, to have called out the ceremonial. Should have stuck to the fighting force. His officers had advised him but he—stickler for a correct reception and all that—had overruled them. His fault. He bowed his culpable head to take the searing syllables and, feeling somewhat sneaky, compared the Hon'ble Mr. Buckridge to his friend Sir Arthur.

While the Resident's heart sank, inspecting the martial talent drawn up on the parade ground. Pike-men. Archers. Men on *stilts*, for god's sake. Did they really expect Germany to field elephants? the amazed Mr. Buckridge asked himself, mesmerised by the striped poles, like seaside rock, that these elongated warriors were twirling. And his long face grew longer, even vindictive, debating how he could carry out his brief, which was to ensure the fullest possible contribution to the war effort, given this medieval collection. As he was determined to do, Maharajah or no. Already, parade barely over, he had begun to address crisp letters to the appropriate quarters (Quetta, and even Aldershot) for certain secondments.

Bawajiraj, though culpable, was not entirely vanquished. He had the pride of his race, and resilience, and the honour of the State, of which he was Head, to consider. He ordered a full-scale review of the Expeditionary Force, at short notice, once again overriding his army commanders who were already at full stretch, men with battle in their sights, and disinclined for pointless manoeuvres in the name of kudos.

The Force by now was shaping up—military energies had borne fruit—though not yet as ship-shape as it would have been, given the fullness of time the Maharajah had unwisely banked on. But it was of respectable proportions, overflowing, the citizens afterwards recalled, the whole of the People's Maidan to the North of the city, and taking up half the morning to march past the saluting base.

It moved the Resident, who had earlier been badly shaken, perhaps from relief to utter a compliment or two, and even to murmur (the Maharajah distinctly heard) that so fine a body deserved better arms and equipment. The Maharajah absolutely agreed, and was encouraged to drop a reproachful aside, which did not escape the Resident. Something to do with imperial forces, like imperial cities, not being built in a day, a statement of such devastating truth that Mr. Buckridge barely deigned to endorse it. Only what, one wondered, had His blinkered Highness been at all these years?

Manners, and the memory of his tutor, forbade Bawajiraj remarking on this *volte-face*. He smothered the meaner emotions and instead dwelt lovingly—his warrior blood stirring, woken from some ancient slumber—on the satisfactions of seeing an old object attained. At last, at last the Devapur State Forces could aim at that summit seen and admired at the Durbar of '03, and yearned for ever since.

No such restraints impeded his caddish Minister, who, to Bawajiraj's disgust, presumed to discern a certain agility in British high places.

'Their battle, our men. When it suits their strategy,' dared to murmur this ignoble Brahmin whose own community, if the Maharajah was any judge of these matters, would not yield so much as a brace of combatants. It quite incensed Bawajiraj, who could barely bring himself to enquire whether the illustrious Dewan had heard of the atrocious Hun? and he smacked down reports he had received from unimpeachable sources. To which the Minister's response was to cross his arms on his virtuous breast and give his odious opinion that atrocity, if not inherent in the situation, was inevitable on all sides.

Bawajiraj took himself off. Nothing could poison the air for long. These days the worst aggravation slid quite soon from his happy shoulders. For word had come. His tender had been noted and accepted in the highest quarters (there was a gracious little note of thanks, signed by an exalted hand, appended to the formal communication) and he would shortly be going abroad, exactly as he had envisaged it, as leader of the Expeditionary Force. It brought him back to his old form, somewhat mangled since the events of Bombay.

Cock-a-hoop, Mohini saw, and melting kind, hovering over her after delivering the dreadful news. She dropped what she was doing and sat, somewhat loosely, as if supporting cords had begun to give, looking out over sunlit lawns with the hibiscus borders, which had already begun to darken.

'Do you mean field service?' she asked, calmly. Gone to marble, she and the terrace were one for coldness.

'That is my hope and belief.'

Sizzling. How could he not feel the ice floes forming in her veins? It incited her to cruelty.

'Aren't you too old?'

It came out dully, when she had intended flaming arrows. She could not blame him if he barely felt it.

'Not at all. In my prime.'

She would have disputed it, but his glassy determination, she could see, would easily foil similar thrusts. Linking her hands in her lap she moved from another, desperate, angle.

'What about me. Have you thought?'

328

'My dearest, what do you think? Every provision. The Dewan has been fully instructed—'

'I don't mean in that way.'

'What way do you mean?'

'I'm in my prime too. Aren't I? Look at me. What do you expect me to do?'

If she had stormed at him he could have coped. He was used to his passionate partner. Challenging him where no one else would have dared. Fighting him over Rabi, Sir Arthur, that motheaten Pandit of hers, hectic colours in her cheeks that made her desirable in the very middle of vexation.

But this marble. If only she would rage.

Instead, she invited him to look.

He did, rather shiftily; and he saw. His companion in love, and other things. Lips that curved sweetly, giving, and taking, so much pleasure. Rounded arms, and breasts that could never be contained but pushed up out of the cups of her bodice—or perhaps the bodice was cut to this end? Quiet now. As if carved from stone. Hands in her lap, lap always clad in some frothy nonsense of voile or lace. Rose-scented. Collapsing in dry bubbles under his head, delectable frou-frou going on somewhere down there as she settled him in. Sometimes for dreaming, her thighs a pillow. Sometimes converted for loving. Turning on him as he lay peacefully, her hands steering his head, his head twisting, face now buried in foam. Smell of milk of almonds rising strongly, subduing the roses.

Against his will it struggled up. That desire was embedded there too. In her. In women. In sexual flesh, whether man or woman. That woman had her physical needs no less exigent than his own. Ripe, as he was; and, he managed to remember, a good bit younger.

It was in a way a dismal awakening, because having conceded desire he had to crown it with the freedom for fulfilment. He found it detestable. What he would really have liked (he tracked it down, in this mood of crackling honesty) would have been to lock up her genitals while he went crusading, chaining the key to his breastplate.

He killed this, after another tussle. Somehow he was fair, as she had invited him to be, justice glimmering palely on his forehead as he said, thickly,

'I don't expect you to—to—not to. While I'm away. If you must have lovers. But don't tell me. I don't want to know. Anything. Ever. Never, do you hear? Never.'

329

His vehemence rose in an inflamed if monosyllabic crescendo—needlessly, as it happened.

For Mohini there was, and there would be, no other man.

* * *

She sat on, on the terrace, after he had gone, waving away the waiting woman who would have kept her company. Racking her powers. Trying to visualise what it would be like and her owlish imagination unable to stretch to anything but an 0. That hollow and resounding pit that Dowager and Maharajah before her had faced. Each in turn incredulous. So much going on, how was it possible to feel as one was feeling? Bereft. Absolutely alone. Merely to look at the horizon was enough to ensure that it rapidly emptied. Birds, trees, sun, sky—all sucked into some black hole.

It was so stark that she shook herself into a semblance of life. Moving her cramped limbs. Taking up what she had dropped. Mechanical means, not to be despised, for spiritual ends, man too weak to dispense with such crutches. The Pandit's favourite axiom, she recalled, smiling at a recollection not without pathos. One came upon him in the old days, eyes closed, reciting couplets, in that poky room of his, after some crushing encounter with His Highness, the subject (always) *his* pupil, though also the Maharajah's son. Magic, perhaps. But it worked. The Pandit emerged uncrumpled, fleeting hints of rose-leaf about his smoothed-out person.

Some such process she now felt in her, the barely audible hum of minute dynamos precariously starting up. Squeezing paint onto the palette, working gamboge into vermilion for the desired tint, in the middle of such preoccupations the empty sky slowly became populated. Kites, she saw, with streaming tails, bucking in unseen currents, connected by invisible strings to small, intent children. Parakeets, wheeling above the fretted pavilions, come to share in the feast of corn spread for Palace doves. From the Residency, distantly, the clashing of bamboo canes, their masts grown tall and lordly since the departure of the Resident's lady.

Things going on. As she would go on, she supposed. Mohini bent to her task, applying paint in rough daubs with the palette knife to the hideous papier-mâché mask she had earlier put aside. This mask was the first of a half dozen that she had promised to have painted and ready—anguished and ringing pleas from Usha, the Dewan's youngest—by opening night of some play the children were putting on.

* * *

Usha was, as ever, the driving spirit. She loved theatricals. She couldn't wait, she told her music master, to get away from him and his boring fiddle. This patient man had long given up rebuking his pupil. He was paid, and he continued to impart some rudiments, but it grieved him sorely to listen to what she could do with an instrument he loved. Other tutors received similar messages. Earnest, pained men, who wished to do their best by this eminent family, but were thwarted. Except the history tutor and the dancing master, who wondered aloud if their colleagues were going about it in the right way? They themselves found no cause for complaint in so assiduous a pupil, flatteringly attentive, no lesson too long. . . . Whereas the rest, smarting, received the clearest contrary signals. Their pupil had no patience for them or what they sought to impart.

Usha was impatient for a good many things. She could hardly wait, she told her mother, to grow up and become an actress. It appalled Vatsala. She kept her thoughts to herself, for fear of activating stubborn streaks that might be lurking; but she shivered to think of an actress in the family, a scandal of scandals, sufficient to wreck all hopes of a good marriage. What had she done, she sometimes asked herself, in some previous existence, to deserve this dramatic daughter? As she could not imagine, she had to suppose it was her husband. Some crime, committed in his past life, for which they would all have to pay.

Luckily there was time. Give it time, it will work itself out, she said to herself; but she did not seek these assurances in the depths of her daughter's eyes.

The Dewan did not unduly agitate himself about these tendencies that his wife brought to his attention. Partly the cares of State; its finances, these days, a cause for some anxiety. Partly because it was, really, up to his wife. His duty was by his sons. Stroking a dispassionate jaw, probing as clinically as a father is capable, he felt he had done it to the best of his ability and even, he dared to plume himself, not too badly. His eldest, the budding future Dewan, somewhat insipid perhaps, but coming along nicely under his personal direction; the second in finance, no complaints there either; the third boy doing well in law. Boys had to learn from the earliest age that life was earnest, that it had a purpose. One needed to be strict, even stern, where they were concerned. But girls? What, Tirumal Rao asked himself, was the point of parenthood if a man could not indulge his daughters a little? Already Vijaya was gone from under his roof. Vimala was shortly due to go. That left only Usha.

The Dewan's steel became butter when he thought of this last-born child of his (an unintended conception that he ceased to regret the moment he held the infant). He indulged her, he knew. Fond father to all his children, but this child had a special place. He found time for her. Put aside the State, took her on his knee. Little girl unimpressed by august personage, enchanted by her father. Demanding. Sunny about it though. Huge smiles and airs of ravishing expectancy. Huge appetite for stories.

'What kind of story would you like?'

'About battles we fought.'

'I don't think I know—'

'Please!'

Hint of desperation, plus some suggestion of thumbscrew, but countenance nothing if not charming. But battles. Most unsuitable for a girl. One obliged, however. To the best of one's ability, can't do more. Despite a certain dearth, in one's line, of martial deeds and doers. Except for the lone General. Hauling out this handy ancestor, daughter cannot hear enough, eyes are sparkling, rosebud mouth is open, oneself puts forth petals in this sunshine and outdoes oneself—some kind of Scheherazade at the very least. Quite limp at the end. Story-telling exhausting, who would have guessed? Sprouts of respect for one's wife, who has coped all these years with all the other children.

But Usha prefers her father.

Father's pet, her siblings might have said, only they were all a good deal older, an amiable crew who took time off from their own engrossing concerns to pamper the baby of the family. Usha undoubtedly takes advantage of them all.

'Tell me another.'

'I've just—'

'Please!'

The Dewan often sighed.

But when she began to read for herself he missed these sessions where she perched on his knee and made him feel, rapt face upturned to his, that he was the centre of her universe.

* * *

First reading, then plays. Filled with animals, these early
enactments, flushed children emerging out of, or disappearing
into, curious sack-like garments with ears and tails. Then,
romances, sad tales of languishing princes and princesses, the
Maharani's wistful daughters barred from the leading roles on
the ground of their real-life situation. This phase coming round
to battles. Epic themes, with large casts, co-opted from the Palace
and Court as well as Dilkusha.

But Dilkusha was short on wardrobe and properties, a place of
orderly elegance that did not yield the kind of treasure of which
the unbridled Palace was chockful. Could afford to be, carpers
said, well over a hundred rooms, not including ante-chambers
and enclosed balconies, no one was quite sure exactly how many,
those who counted never arrived at the same number.

Simply everything, breathed Usha, eyeing her stolid parents,
stuck in a house which boasted not even one brass breastplate.
Parents eyeing back, composing lectures on conspicuous waste,
to be delivered later on, at a time of maximum impact, when the
child's critical faculties were developed, themselves shuddering
at the truly magnificent lumber sometimes glimpsed in the indiscriminate mansions of profligate rulers, sometimes revealed by
the innocence of children.

Spears, said Usha, and a silver cannon, and there's a palanquin
made of gold, it's so heavy hardly *anyone* can lift it, and a kind of
canopy-thing, a thousand people—well, (catching an outraged
eye) at least a hundred people could get under it, and a huge
chest full of iron balls—for muskets would you suppose?

Ferreting, thought Vatsala, in other people's houses.

'I hope,' she said, severely, a woman intent on bringing up her
children properly, 'I hope you always remember to ask Her
Highness's permission first.'

'Of course. Her Highness says don't bother to ask, go anywhere you like, except the Pearl Suite. The Pearl Suite,' Usha
explained meticulously, as meticulously as it had been explained
to her, 'doesn't belong to Her Highness.'

Vatsala drew her lips together tightly. Everyone knew to
whom the Pearl Suite belonged. So flagrantly made over. She
did not wish to go into it with her daughter.

Usha, being the age she was, did not need to go into it. The
Pearl Suite belonged to Rabi's mother, that was the simple fact.
From her, then, she had long ago secured the necessary permis-

333

sion to rove on the upper floor, which had once been cleared by superhuman effort to serve as a sickroom. The lumber had long since crept back, an unwieldy sea of wooden and metallic components, glinting here and there where brass burst through the dull coating of time, or copper from casings of verdigris. Among this debris spiders scuttled, mice, for unknown purposes, and white ants. Cones of peppery dust revealed their industry, in a heap by the piano legs, spilling out of the gut and handles of the Maharajah's tutor's abandoned squash and tennis racquets.

It was here, wading somewhat dreamily, and stubbing her bare toes painfully against queer but alluring objects, that Usha came upon the javelins and the rusty armour that, she saw at once—she was good at spotting possibilities in the most forbidding material—would fill the bill for her forthcoming production. She had been searching for equipment for her characters to go with the masks Rabi's mother was painting for her. What she had found looked ideal. Tucking her skirts up—her mother would disapprove, she knew, but then she wasn't there to see—and not bothering to call up a servant, she began to haul at the blackened and somewhat buckled suit of armour in which it was not easy to imagine inserting a human form.

But she would try. You could do anything if you tried hard enough, her father took pains to inculcate. Usha took up this sword and had begun to beat and temper it in flames of her own, slow-burning fires that she guarded, drew screens around when anyone approached for fear of having them extinguished by careless feet, or even breath. For she had had some intimations—the faintest tapping on a windowpane—that they would blaze up in her one day, become most brilliant and illuminating, like a chandelier in which all the candles were alight.

* * *

Mohini, co-opted into helping, was putting the finishing touches, now and then with the flitting impression that the paper-mush models had taken charge of painter and medium. Surely she alone could not be responsible for these vicious strokes, these gobbets of pigment that had resolved into gloating moustachios and popping, bloodshot eyeballs? But the effects were suitably bellicose for what the play portended.

When she could improve no more she carried them out carefully, one by one, and set them out to dry in the sun on the terrace. Like a row of severed heads, she felt, those scowling countenances, and was touched with something of the pleasure and excitement of a child.

Humming, by then. The waiting woman noted, and stole back, announcing her presence with a string of awed exclamations for her mistress's handiwork, a theme that was presently taken up by Usha.

'They're frightful, Auntie. You *are* clever.'

Inspired, rather, Mohini felt; her hand guided during temporary absences of herself. Maybe to poetry. Perhaps to massacre?

Need, there, to watch it. As you would a falcon. Watch what takes possession, at whatever cost, from whatever distance. The jess, after all, is to your hand, finally. She said:

'It just happened. I can't really take all the credit.'

'I know. It's scary when it happens, don't you think?'

It halted the older woman. What do you mean? she almost gasped, but took control in time, time to tone it down for the sake of the child. Although the flat planes of the face this child presented were ageless, her eyes were opening and opening, down to sea-bed if you cared to dive, between the stark, spiky fringes of her lashes. Mohini shifted a little, rearranging herself as if to get it right, and said,

'Don't you think we like to frighten ourselves, sometimes, by imagining things?'

But now Usha was retreating. She would not reveal herself. She hugged her knees closely together and rested her chin on this bony plateau and said,

'I don't know. I suppose some people might.'

Her eyes were quite shallow, Mohini noticed.

Sari drawn over her head, for it was now past noon, and sultry, the waiting woman was turning the masks round, so that they could dry evenly, and flapping at a dragonfly that hovered, drawn by what she could not think. Must be the linseed, she said to herself, in which the pigments had been thinned, but not sufficiently, that was clear, or perhaps it was the livid colour? and she went away to rummage for some kind of wire coop in case the silly insect settled, just possibly mistaking those horrors for blooms. She could not bear it, she knew, if wings got gummed up, together with wriggling and gasping owner.

The place seemed very empty when she had gone. Just the woman and the girl, on a bleached plain where bones might have been strewn, Mohini felt. Usha's knuckles jutted, although she was lounging. Craggy apices, thrusting up under the skin, though the arms were thin and childish. It compelled Mohini to try to leaven it a little, whatever had stranded them in this grim place. She said, light and brisk, nodding towards the lopped heads,

'Are they fierce enough?'

'For what?'

Usha would admit nothing, she put up defences and crouched behind them.

'For battle. That's what your play's about, isn't it?'

Usha withdrew still further. She was positively bundled up, arms wrapped around knees, knees nudging chin, head tucked down. In a different species she would have shown up as a carapace.

'I don't know,' she mumbled. 'I don't know what men look like in battle. Do you know?'

Bawajiraj interrupted this scene. He was breezing along, showered and tingling, on his way to luncheon, and hoping to inveigle Mohini to accompany him, himself famished after the morning's manoeuvres on the maidan, when the masks took his eye.

The Dewan's daughter, he guessed. A lively child, given to dressing up and leaping out at people. But now, he saw, quite remarkably still, for her, only rising when he approached (nice manners there, well-behaved children, got to hand it to old sobersides). He waved her down, onto the pink silk bolster from which Rabi, when younger, had reigned over him.

'For your play?' he enquired amiably.

Of which everyone had heard, and quite a few were assisting. A good deal of dragooning had gone on.

'Yes.'

'I must say, they look fierce enough for anything.'

'Well, soldiers can be called upon, can't they,' said Usha, 'to do anything at all.'

Found her tongue, thought Mohini, and would have been relieved but for certain inflections, which also struck Bawajiraj, but more of a glancing blow. What an odd thing, he felt. But he was glad to confirm.

'Naturally,' he said, comfortably. 'That, my dear child, is the whole object of discipline.'

'It's very important, isn't it?'

'Yes, certainly.'

Usha was unwinding herself. The bones that had jutted were subsiding. She nudged the buckled mail she had lugged down with her.

'More important than armour, or anything?'

'Well, proper equipment is helpful.'

'But discipline's what counts.'

'I would say so, yes. Most decidedly.'

'So would I!'

Quite animated, Bawajiraj saw, and really rather pretty.

'A born soldier I can see,' he said, genially, and with a side swipe at the absent and unwarlike Rabi. 'Make you one of my commanders when you grow up, eh? What d'you say?'

'No, your Highness,' said Usha, rather flatly, if correctly. 'Not that kind of soldier.'

'No? Then what kind of soldier would you like to be?'

Bawajiraj could be endlessly patient and tender with children.

Usha's lips trembled. Her longings were subtler, and were not to be commanded, or even coaxed, into uniforms. Except, she did perceive, in their own time. So she sat, quivering before these shapes she could hardly grasp herself that hung in the future, at immense distances, and glimmered under some shiny gauze of promise.

Full of secrets, prerogative of childhood, never delve roughly, Bawajiraj said to himself. With children his instincts ran true, a pure flow that he trusted.

'Well, just let me know when you've made up your mind and we'll see what we can do,' he said kindly, and wagged a finger.

'Helping people, you know, one of the few privileges we Maharajahs enjoy.'

He really meant it, Mohini saw.

As did Usha, if in a different light, and was moved to requite the kindness.

'I'll send you a special invitation,' she offered, 'for my play, when it's ready. Would you like to come?'

'I shall be delighted,' said Bawajiraj. 'And I'll tell you what—' he was inspired to continue, warmly, generosity breeding generosity, 'why don't you hold your performance in the Durbar Hall? My dais is as big as a stage. What d'you say?'

'The whole Durbar Hall?'

'Why not?'

'That would be lovely!' Usha breathed, velvety eyes adoring the benefactor.

Bawajiraj marched away, beaming. How pleasing children were! Conversely, how tiresome were Councils of State! Having sat out some exceedingly tedious sessions of late, he quite looked forward to the pleasing diversion that the children offered.

14

It was morning, shortly after this, and the Minister sat at his embellished desk absently fingering an inscribed china egg that had been Sir Arthur's parting gift, and jigging his foot in a manner that, although not calculated to do so, would have driven every thought from that envoy's mind except, perhaps, the need to step gingerly.

Opposite him sat the new Envoy, who was built more ruggedly, and incapable, or at any rate loth, to receive any signals except of the most ringing kind. Open, it liked to think, this Occidental mind; none of your Eastern nudges and winks. Consequently he overlooked, rather than bore with, the Minister's distressing habit.

The Dewan, for his part, was driven to invoking the word *feringhi*, which had not figured intrusively in his mind's vocabulary for a considerable time.

This jarring foreigner, he felt, fished from the sea—a torpedo, via the heinous Wilhelm, had been responsible for Mr. Buckridge's delayed arrival—to sit here dripping with authority and imagining that he, the Dewan, would disrupt intricate and smooth-functioning revenue systems to oblige. Or to order of proconsuls upon whom the lustre of the distant Crown filtered palely, these days. This Mr. Buckridge, in his shiny shoes with the bulldog toes planted squarely—not on his Herats, true, since this was his office—but on an equally beloved Qum.

His very presence a shade improper. Seldom, the Minister mused, china gliding smooth and oval under his hand, had Sir Arthur. Immense power, and the sense of it, but scrupulous, his Excellency. Or, it did come to him, courteous. However bent on

338

confrontation, and seething (that is to say, icy), he would not have presumed upon these precincts except by invitation. Precincts in which the Ministers of Devapur State conducted the affairs of Devapur State which, whatever the reality, was deemed to be an independent realm outside British authority.

At his most urgent, or riled, Sir Arthur's P.A. arrived to invite the Dewan Sahib to invite the Resident, or, more often, to present the Resident's compliments and desire his attendance at the Residency offices. Best of all they strolled, unattended, where distances became immaterial, if they could not be altogether obliterated, in some neutral pleasure garden or park.

Tirumal Rao could have sighed for those days, benign stretches interspersed with tart acrimony, stirring times studded with passages of arms that left them both blanched, their voices hushed with rage. But done well. Between men of caste. Even if, at the time, he had (extravagantly, he now feared) privately classified the imperial envoy as a resident infliction.

What, then, was his successor? Rumours had reached his ears. Certain tidings, arriving circuitously: that army of clerks, indispensable to British administration, of ambivalent affiliation, only the British supposed (perforce) unswerving loyalty to, of all things, the paymaster. Disturbing reports of the slant of the Resident's thought.

The Dewan, composed on his own ground, leant back in his chair and waited to discover.

The new Resident, in his own estimation, was a blunt man. No liking, ever, to beat about the bush, and even less inclined in the middle of a war. He had come to raise the smouldering question of the Garrison Force, or more specifically its finances, or even more plainly to talk about money. Resting his arms on the unvarnished deal of his chair (the carved rosewood waved away, to the astonishment of the *chaprassi*, dealwood being reserved for petitioners, those of the less inferior quality who were permitted to sit in the Presence), he began to expound in a manner and at a pitch that, perhaps, the occasion warranted, but which, in the Minister's sensitive estimation, verged on the excessive. Hectoring on, he said to himself in amazement; but the matter being money he gave it his full attention.

* * *

Money at this time was at a premium. It always was, of course, but especially at this juncture. Vast sums were needed, what with

Education, and Water Supply, and the Expeditionary Force for His Majesty, apart from general funding of the State, not to mention expenses of His Highness, and those of his Household, and of the Resident, and of *his* Household, Palace and Residency running, as usual, neck and neck.

And there was the Garrison Force, thorn in the flesh of innumerable Officers of State, including especially the Dewan, but combined *vade mecum*, solace, balm, and defender of British susceptibilities. Its absence was unthinkable, its presence guaranteed by treaty wrung from Bawajiraj's predecessors and ratified by him.

Tirumal Rao had long ago retreated from direct assaults on this stronghold. Even his sniping was tepid and desultory. The annual subsidy was duly paid as negotiated.

Difficulties, however, had now arisen. Sums found ample at the beginning of the reign would not stretch to ensure that excellence envisaged by the Resident. The British Garrison, in his stern eyes, evinced signs of slipping into that picturesque desuetude from which the Maharajah's Forces, for pressing reasons, had been but lately plucked. An increase in the subsidy was essential to avoid this disaster.

More urgently, Mr. Buckridge had detected signs of disaffection in the country. He therefore considered it his duty to double the strength of the Garrison, for only thus could guarantees given to the State be met. He saw it as a reasonable request: not as an abrogation of treaty or a variation of its clauses, but as a sensible up-dating of an ancient contract to keep faith with its original intention.

Mr. Buckridge had, correctly, first broached the question with the Maharajah. At least he had cornered him, for Bawajiraj could be, as Mr. Buckridge discovered, quite nimble at dodging any discussion of finances, which he loathed.

Cornered, however, he had been tempted simply to assent to whatever the Resident proposed. Anything for the sake of peace. One was tired of being hounded. Of late the tedious T. Rao had been at him, long discourses on the need for economy: why not close down the Summer Palace? dispose of Magnolia Lodge? sell a couple of Guest Houses? retrench on his racing establishment? decimate his fleet of motor-cars? This cut and that chop, he could see himself reduced to clutching a begging bowl . . .

Some scraps of caution, however, restrained the Maharajah. Best, he had learnt, leave all this kind of thing to the Dewan, his department, what he was there for, leave him to battle it out. Thankfully he fell back on this stratagem.

'My Chief Minister, you know,' he said vaguely, to the annoyed Mr. Buckridge. 'I'm sure he—you—er—we, can come to some arrangement.'

'If we do, I trust I can rely on you to ratify the arrangement,' said the Resident, and barely managed to add, 'your Highness.'

'If you do,' said the harassed Maharajah. 'If the Minister . . . that is to say yes, by all means you may, if the Minister . . .' And fled.

Buck-passing, the Resident pronounced it, and bearded the Dewan in his den.

* * *

'If we could come to some arrangement,' Mr. Buckridge now said. Squared up for contest, his jaw like a pugilist's, the Minister noted.

'It is not impossible,' he said.

Tension there, some overstrung instrument, was the Resident's fleeting impression, and was misled into linking tension with, if luck held, breakdown and capitulation. But luck not holding, the Minister proceeded intact.

'As I say, Mr. Buckridge, it is not impossible, but there is the question of funding. As I feel sure you will readily appreciate, further borrowing at this juncture is inappropriate. If, therefore, you would indicate those areas in which retrenchment is feasible, or in which further revenues can be raised, no doubt we can progress in the direction you wish.'

Here he relinquished the tranquil egg, which had served its purpose, and banged a gong. That was Mr. Buckridge's impression. In reality there were no bangs. The gong was a miniature, three inches in diameter, a charming silver object crafted by the Palace silversmith to order of the Dewan, who disliked vehemence in any form. Partly, his threshold was low. Partly, results did not, he was persuaded, necessarily rise in proportion to sound effects. Consequently he did no more than set the silver disc shimmering with a diminutive striker.

After which there was, in Mr. Buckridge's opinion, an invasion, a jade green and flowing white procession of writers, clerks, *chaprassis*, and what appeared to be ballboys in green tunics carrying bundles slung in nets.

341

And presently, spread like some picnic, were the ledgers of State, bound in buckram (morocco anathema to the Minister and his staff) and transparently open for the inspection of the Resident, should he care.

Mr. Buckridge might have been compared to his disadvantage, but he, too, was chosen: was one of the Lord's Anointed*: and could sift and glean at speed. He cast a swift eye, seeing, he suspected, what he was intended to see, although even this, the vast detail of running a State, could have been overwhelming. All of it meticulously entered, in the neat and even loving hands of clerks under neat headings. Palace expenditure, he saw, skimming: thrones, horses, cheetahs, doves, saddles, banners, motorcars, musicians, women's apartments, perfumes, parks, gardens, pavilions. All untouchable, this Aladdin's cave, he reminded himself, and passed on to military accounts: bodyguard and garrison, infantry, cavalry, bands, Expeditionary Force, and Lancers. Finally he came to the revenue statistics: tariffs that ran to page after page of tolls, taxes, imposts, and levies under which the citizens of the State, groaning but alive, somehow contrived to pursue their activities.

The intention was clear to Mr. Buckridge. Blind one with detail, he said to himself, and considered his opponent, who seemed to embody a quality, characteristic of India, which he had unearthed and carried away from a previous stint in the country; the quality of low but ferocious cunning. Like a cat, he described it, with claws sheathed.

The Minister observed the drift. In his time he had been compared, he had gleaned, to many creatures. Fox, jackal, jackass, gazelle (in his leaner years), stoat, and weasel, all had figured. But this one eluded him. Searching himself he could not discover, in his cultivatedly mild interior, evidence for those tigerish accusations that seemed to spring at him from the Resident's bulging countenance.

Which Mr. Buckridge subdued, by sheer force of will.

'The gist being?' he enquired bluntly, but calmly, waving a hand over the clutter of folios.

'That revenues will not stretch,' said the Minister, equally bluntly, against his grain, which always had run to scrollwork.

There was a pause, in which the Resident began edging towards what his darting mind had already picked out, in that gilded and bewildered jigsaw, as the missing piece.

*Popular term for the old Indian Civil Service from which 'politicals' like Residents were selected.

Salt.

He had seen no figures. This essential, collared in many a quarter in the name of the Crown for its tax potential, known indeed as the King's commodity, had not appeared anywhere in the elaborate cards ostensibly laid on the Minister's table. A rich yielder. But an emotive subject: upheavals in British India, more or less endemic, over the substance. Mr. Buckridge cogitated, and presently said, rather thinly, from sensations in the pit of his stomach that warned he was playing with fire,

'Salt, of course, would be, may I suggest, a source of revenue . . . although it is, naturally, a matter entirely within your jurisdiction.'

Then the Minister did indeed discover those traces of tiger that he had earlier hunted in himself in vain.

'That avenue is closed. Salt is already taxed to the extent it will bear,' he said, brusquely.

'I do not see the figures,' said Mr. Buckridge.

'You will have to take my word. I cannot recommend an increase,' said the Minister, and rose to terminate the interview.

* * *

The Resident left. He had right of direct access to the Maharajah, which he immediately exercised.

The Maharajah, concluding from a certain harshness in Mr. Buckridge's demeanour that there was to be no escape this time, paid attention to his English Adviser. He never revealed what passed between them. He had his pride, and was at least as susceptible as the Resident to those pit of the stomach warnings.

Court opinion was unable to decide what pressures had been applied. The least of these was the withholding of honours (the Maharajah known to be angling) and a curb on the Grand Tour (at last within the Maharajah's sights, and planned to follow the successful termination of the war). No one, however, doubted that even more powerful sanctions touching the throne itself were invested in the Resident, and had, in this crisis, been invoked.

Mohini conceded that pressures had been brought to bear. More disturbingly, she also allied his action to the process she glimpsed, at night, with something like anguish, a hardening, as it were, of clear resins.

* * *

The Minister, to begin with, did not know what to make of it. He stood in the Throne Room, to which he had been summoned for interview, discounting what he had heard until the Maharajah, glaring by now, repeated his instructions. Only this time round they had assumed the crystal, needle-sharp qualities of a command. Then the Minister, oddly for him, since his own flame burned steadily, began to be chilled, somewhere in his marrow, for the wanton manner of it, this dabbling in lives with consequences that could not be calculated, either by him, or the Resident, or this closed man the Maharajah.

Still, he tried. It was what he was there for.

'An enhancement in the salt tax—' he began.

And faltered to a stop, his own emotions threatening to rise and swamp him. For, he saw, and quite openly now, that he was as entangled as the least of the Maharajah's subjects. Felt like them. That the King's commodity rested on ethereal plinths like air or water, unlike tobacco or tea. Himself as passionate as any peasant; of the same soil, composed of similar elements.

What, then, was the Maharajah?

A *feringhi*, for the second time that day, rose to the Dewan's lips. A stranger in his own land, he felt, with an overflowing disdain, and was able to finish.

'—is unthinkable, salt being an essential commodity,' he said.

'Like many another,' said the Maharajah.

'Not entirely,' said the Dewan, almost absently, to the deracinated man who stood and glittered in the jewelled chamber. 'Not entirely, your Highness. If it were, it would be different. As it is, I do not think the people will stand for it, for long.'

'The people,' the Maharajah repeated, and his hand went up to the welt on his forehead, which still, now and again, throbbed fiercely. 'There are lessons, Minister, and disciplines, that the people must learn, or be taught, in their own interests.'

Then it was indeed confirmed to the Dewan that the sparks he had seen were not idle or stray, but had been struck from iron that had entered and set hard and would be re-encountered; although, of course, it was open to question who would suffer the most damage: the Maharajah, or those who presumed to tangle with him.

It was at this point that the alliance between Dewan and heir to State was finally ratified.

* * *

The Minister retired. He shut himself up for a week.

No one, except the Resident, who disapproved of people laying off when they felt like it, considered it strange. It was natural for a man to fast, and go into retreat, when the need came upon him to sort out his resources, or re-examine the goals he had set before him, or simply to refresh his soul.

Into this cell—actually a large, if bare, room, kept ready for the purpose, dusted and aired and regularly inspected by Vatsala—Tirumal Rao surrendered himself for a spell.

Simply sitting, with the blank wall for company, in a silence less absolute than warbling (bee-eaters and koels upon the windowsills), to clarify his thought. What he should do, and why, and the nature of the promptings, which could as easily be wily as veracious. Sipping his milk, which Vatsala prepared and carried to him once a day, while he tested his conclusions. About Devapur State, and his links with it. About war, and its brutal transformations of landscapes and the men in them, and the restraints that it butchered. About his country, and his son, and the Maharajah's son.

Oddly enough it was Rabi who swam up most strongly.

In a khaki shirt, sleeves rolled up over biceps, skin gone to cork. Ribbing him, the Chief Minister, in the casual confidence of his own power. Laughing. Impassioned. Passion in that long rangy body that lounged, as it could afford to do in its own territory. Leafy lights playing about the Maharajkumar's head, Maharajkumar unconcerned save for leafy lights, turning his back on the intense radiance beamed at him from the Throne. Casual as a labourer in employment.

One never, the Dewan was moved to feel, smiled again as freely, never walked as light and springy as young men did. For now Rabi was joined by his son Narayan, shoulder to wheel as bidden, but entitled to hope his own father would not crush him with burdens laid on him too early.

No. Now was not the time. When it was ripe for departure he would, he believed in all humility, know, and like his forefathers go without a backward glance. But now was not the time to abandon Devapur State but, rather, to combine his skills with their strengths to nurse its inherent power. Himself able, and, unless he deluded himself, in his prime.

Eased and lightened by decision the Dewan's mind skipped nimbly over a generation and presented amiable pictures of his son, the new Dewan, and the new Maharajah, of a calibre different from that of his father . . . this sinewy pair advancing

345

Devapur State to heights that no Englishman could ever look down upon, nor dare to mulct, or thwart, or hector, stalking about as if in some seedy ownership of the land and the souls it supported.

At which Tirumal Rao rose, somewhat stern about the mouth from certain presumptions, certain plebeian indisciplines and flippancies he detected in his thought, and set off for the temple in a trap he drove himself—or rather was whisked along to his destination by a plump and enthusiastic little pony.

Here, in the adytum untenanted save for himself and his god, he prayed, or atoned for, the flaws of his nature; and presently made his peace.

Vatsala saw it was over and ordered a feast.

'Will you resign?' she asked, fanning him as he ate; he looked quite thin, as fined down as a lath.

'I think not,' said her husband.

* * *

'Been vegetating?' asked the Resident.

'You may call it that, if you wish,' the Dewan replied to, as far as he was concerned, plain Mr. Buckridge.

For *honour* and *honourable* had long been eschewed. Now he withdrew even *excellency*, an appellation found for men who, from qualities intrinsic to themselves, had risen above the estate of resident overseer.

Tranquil about it, however. Even contemplative, simply eyeing this plain, offending alien.

'I believe, Resident Sahib, you have the Maharajah's ear, and also possibly the upper hand,' he said at last.

So calm that every fibre in Mr. Buckridge's body leapt. Something odd there, he felt. Caving in like that, it smacked of—well, something not altogether aboveboard, or even healthy.

'I prefer not to consider the matter in those terms,' he replied in a careful, clipped way, and reserved his defences.

* * *

Mr. Buckridge returned to the Residency.

This magnificent pile, in the opinion of many whose duties took them thither, was that it was not what it had been in the days of the previous incumbent.

346

Lifeless, the servants said as they approached its imposing portals, a hushed note entering their voices, which were already down to piccolo as prescribed in Household Regulations; and they drew their draperies about them as if the corridors were cold, although they could also swear, really, that nothing was changed, not so much as a brick or stick of furniture had been moved or altered. All in place, and all of them at full strength, all the peons and gardeners and glass and silver, and sentries slapping and stamping as hard as ever they had and reveille and last post as regular as anything. . . .

But somehow it was different.

They couldn't tell why. They shot sidelong glances at Buckridge Sahib, from a distance usually, and the bolder, or more kindly, dared to wonder if it was to do with the Sahib's being single. Mostly they didn't pause; they felt it best to vanish when they heard him coming. Except, of course, those who had to wait at table, who did find that the china shot out of their experienced hands in a truly extraordinary manner, and who told, with a kind of expiring warmth, how the Sahib had refrained from barking, even when it was the best china.

But they could not take to him. They, too, reserved themselves and passed the dishes silently, apart of course from those resounding crashes, now and again, which sounded the louder for the silence.

Mr. Buckridge did not notice. He was not in the practice of noticing the servants. He sat in the room with the dimensions of a tennis court, which overlooked the lawn where fountains played, and ate his dinner in state, if also in solitary, which did not bother him. When he had finished, and not till then, for he was a methodical man, he went up the stairs to his study to pick at it.

For, he felt, this stern, shrewd man with experience of innumerable outposts behind him, that the Minister's equanimity had foundations. Some kind of platform, or base, that enabled him to sit there presiding calmly over his own defeat. Composed as a cat, and conceding upper hands while, he was convinced, not giving a trick away. One needed to get to the bottom of it; neglect these elementary precautions and you could let yourself in for some exceedingly nasty surprises. But, he had to admit, it was no easy assignment. What gave the man his composure? his airs of insufferable assurance?

Chin in palm, elbow on table, table lamp angled away from his gingery head, he worried at it, alternately giving the devil his due and despising the, he suspected, underhand Minister whose springs of behaviour he could not for the life of him uncover. Until, presently, a distinct impression grew of being storm-tossed. He, the Resident, pitching like some frail caique in fearful seas, while the Minister watched, unmoving, from the still eye of this hurricane.

It was so disagreeable, and powerful, that he gave up. On the table, next to the lamp, reposed what he called his Journal, a leatherbound tome with a brass lock and his name on it in gold, but sober, calligraphy.

ALFRED BUCKRIDGE, ESQUIRE

He drew this towards him and, after some care, as his thought for the day, wrote in a forthright hand:
> There is something about the Indian Mind
> that is Absolutely Unintelligible.

He read it over, reflected a little, crossed out 'Indian' and substituted 'Hindoo,' and read this over. It rang so true that he was cheered, feeling that one thing at least in a baffling encounter had been captured and nailed down. Closing the Journal with a modest *crump*, he rang for a brandy and, glass in hand, strolled out onto the terrace.

* * *

The Residency terraces were favoured by many people: in Sir Arthur's day, and especially for birthday parties, by the children, who raced flushed and rapturous along the broad marbled avenues trailing balloons and ayahs.

Those whose racing days were over were nonetheless enchanted by the pleasing impression of air and space ensnared by the lightest of hands, barely enclosed within a tracery of pearly baluster and parapet. Evenings the best, the sun mellow and clement in the west, zephyrs rising in the east and wafted in over rose-gardens and cupolas to smooth surfaces that the Indian day so often roughed up. They lingered then, cherished in a filigree of cane, cushions with flower designs, slots in the wicker for the tumblers . . . and even a view of Eastern excess (domes, gold-leaf by the maund, not to mention the surrounding warren) was not too unsettling for English sensibility.

There were those (callow, or imprudent, in the opinion of older hands) who would have preferred not to have this native city, albeit built round a resplendent Palace with a well-disposed Ruler, within their sights at all; but they were people with a poor grasp of the past, who forgot that the Residency had been purpose-built to keep an eye on Palace. Palace knew. Residency knew that Palace knew. They glared at each other, these two utterly different and utterly magnificent structures, over the stretches of Native and British terrain, over the decades, until passion could not be sustained at this devouring pitch and the glare became neutral, if slashed with suspicion. Suspicion could never be laid to rest, not while folk memories persisted and English bones had yet to crumble to dust in Indian graveyards (centuries still to go); but people and eras change, and in these urbane later years the glances exchanged were mostly tolerant, and not without touches of civilised emotion.

* * *

Mr. Buckridge was encouraged, like many before him, to linger in this charming anchorage. He leant on the parapet, glass in hand, and watched the smoke rise from the cooking fires in the servants' quarters. Banished to sufferable distances, these, but the smoke still drifted, carrying watered-down smells of spice and goat-curry that mingled, not disagreeably, with the bouquet of flower scents that rose from the gardens. Until, as evening wore on, all these flavours and scents were subdued or quenched in the essences that streamed from Queen-of-the-Night. Of paradise, the watcher felt, this nightingale-shrub that poured such unbearable notes into the darkness, drenching the night in perfume. And presently, across from the *hatikhana*, in the scented stillness, came an air, a tender solo, someone young singing, the pure clear voice of a young boy encompassing a love and a longing that were beyond his years.

> *There's a boy across the river*
> *Whose cheeks are like a peach . . .*
> *Alas, I cannot swim, I cannot swim*

So pure, it seemed to the man who listened, so clear, these blue mosque notes that rose from forbidden minarets to summon him to forsaken delights.

Then Mr. Buckridge began to shiver, and ache, and to wrestle, as he accepted he would wrestle to the end of his days, with the urges of his nature, which had fallen wretchedly outside the norms approved by society.

The watchman, on his rounds, saw the figure on the terrace, which by now was washed in moonlight. Ordinarily he would have raised his staff in salute, but now he passed on, muffling himself up, chilled in turn by the chilled figure.

* * *

While the Residency continued along controlled paths, the Palace in the opinion of inmates and observers alike lurched into even more anarchy than usual.

Children, under the Maharajah's fiat, had invaded the public Durbar Hall.

They poured in, after lessons, for rehearsals, eager actors and actresses and their supporters and camp-followers, enthusiasm kindled by the theatrical properties so magnificently afforded by the great audience hall. The sounds of battle (not a few real sabres and such) rang through ante-rooms and corridors, and penetrated the most hallowed sanctums, causing a good many to question the wisdom of the Maharajah, while granting his motives were entirely kind. Officers of the Court, in particular, sighed, especially those whose own children did not figure prominently on the cast list. So much business to be transacted, so many durbars and audiences before His Highness departed, the hall essential for putting citizens through their paces, the Maharajah the first to notice any flaws in performance—indeed, no courtier better versed than he in the punctilio of the Court— but one could barely think for the commotion.

They would not have believed, if told, that all these alarums and aggravations were the mildest of harbingers.

Nor would the Minister, currently basking in the prowess of a nephew, prominent member of the cast who was proving, under tuition, a fencer *par excellence*.

He did not know, although he could have, if he had paid attention, that round the corner his own child was waiting, armed with a bludgeon, ready to deal him a body blow. Nor, more understandably, did the Maharajah.

Almost anywhere else, possibly, it would have been less of a disaster.

In the Pearl Suite—in Dilkusha—in any one of the nobles' mansions—masques and charades were enacted and went unnoticed except by participants and parents.

The Durbar Hall spurred everyone to greater endeavour and expectation.

The Maharajah persuaded the Minister's daughter to invite the Resident. The Resident shanghaied his Personal Assistant, a Military attaché, an anti-Bolshevik officer who happened to be passing through the kingdom, and numerous cronies from the regimental mess. The Maharajah was there of course, and so were the Maharani and, suitably distanced, Mohini, the mask mistress. The Dewan and his wife naturally, their child the moving spirit; and the Maharajkumar came up from the wilds to combine theatricals with discussions with the Minister and imminent farewells to his father. A distinguished company that inevitably exerted its own powers of attraction, so that the Durbar Hall was filled.

All of them did splendidly by the children, the women in Benares tissue, the Maharajah in satin, his nobles in silk with gold-lace turbans, the Resident in a dinner jacket, the attaché sporting his decorations, the officers in uniform, and even the heir-apparent parted from his khaki and buttoned into a passable coat. All of them, in a mood to be indulgent towards the youngsters, and perhaps reflecting the ambience of the occasion, sat smiling and easy, the cares of war and State laid aside, embossed and beribboned programmes in their laps, waiting to be gently amused and entertained.

The curtains parted . . .

This play that the children are enacting, on the stage which is the Maharajah's dais, his own golden Throne a prop by gracious permission, is morally unexceptionable in that it is divided uncompromisingly between Good and Evil. The Rulers, evidently, are Bad, while the ruled are very Good. No one is left in any doubt as to who is what. The King and his Guards lurk behind masks of such evil genius that even hardened adults wince. His downtrodden subjects, who do not wear masks, in contrast offer, above their peasants' tatters, such young and flower-like visages that it positively wrings the heart.

The action is brisk. In Scene 1 the Good, but poor, are ground into the dust by unjust demands. In Scene 2 the Good, dusting themselves off, armed only with righteousness, are challenging the Bad king. In Scene 3, the finale, the Bad Rulers are won over, and mumbling behind their masks promise to do better in future.

By now backs that had rested easily were angular.

Only utter discipline and training, its grounding from cradle up, enabled this polished audience to applaud the revolutionary performance as it did, with commendable vigour, and creditable smiles. So well was it done, indeed, that the company, convinced of success, retired flushed and triumphant to the wings. Nor were its members made aware of the ripples that spread, or the wrangling that followed. No one, after all, however incensed, wanted to massacre children. Some, it is true—notably the Military attaché—flitting back to robust earlier days, found themselves endorsing old customs, like holding noble children hostage for their parents' good behaviour. But on the whole they exercised restraint and took it out on each other.

* * *

Mohini was sullen, which was unusual for her.

'I'm no judge of these things. The child asked and I obliged, that's all.'

'They were monstrous.'

'They were meant to look fierce. That's all I know. That's all I can tell you.'

'Tell me this then. Are we monsters? Those of us who are born to rule, and do our duty as we see it? Is that how you see *me*?'

Mohini did not; but she would not budge, some flint in her soul which set her against this man who was, almost, beseeching her.

'The play was about monsters,' she maintained, sourly.

* * *

Next the Maharajah interviewed the Dewan.

'In the worst possible taste, Minister. Granted the play was Usha's . . . but some responsibility, as parents . . . Quite appalling, considering the public nature of the performance.'

'If I may be permitted,' the Minister took refuge, 'the suggestion for public performance in the Durbar Hall was entirely your Highness's.'

* * *

The furious Resident came straight out with it.

'Is it necessary, Minister, to use children to fight your battles?'

The Minister was so outraged he could not utter. He had to recite a quatrain to himself before the art of speech would revive.

'I am unable, Mr. Buckridge,' he said finally, 'to take your meaning.'

'Then I will make it plain. You have objected to certain taxes, and you have elected to make known your resentments within the framework of a play depicting a peasants' revolt.'

It was so awful that outrage in the Minister was converted to the coldest, most icy fury.

'Another interpretation, Mr. Buckridge,' he said, a polar chill to the words that struck at the Resident's innermost fears, 'an equally feasible explanation is that that framework has an historical pedigree, since peasants' revolts are, are they not, a common feature of history.'

The Resident went away and brooded. After some time it came to him and he sent for a clerk and dictated a Memorandum:

> Under the authority promulgated by the Dramatic Performance Act, 1876 (check that, will you Krishnan) all further performances of the Play (get the name, Krishnan) are forthwith forbidden as being likely to incite feelings of disaffection within Devapur State.

This memo was duly circulated. As a consequence effects which had been returned to various almirahs and armouries were disinterred, and the Play was enacted at least a dozen more times, in private premises to which the Resident and his Staff had no access, until the cast had to return to school.

* * *

After some thought the Dewan interrogated his daughter. Perturbed.

Because sometimes one garnered from the air, children good at it, all sensors whirring, superb receptors of what was brewing. Ahead, sometimes, of what the most subtle network of intelligence could bring in. One did not, definitely, want premature upheavals. Or, more particularly, punitive exercises.

Usha reassured him.

'No one suggested anything. I just thought it up, I don't know why. Why, didn't you find it interesting?'

Transparent eyes. A clear, golden brown like her mother's.

Paddling in these harmless shallows and suddenly up to one's neck. Vatsala was sparing of, but good at, this trick. Were tricks, like eyes, inherited? Here the image of the egregious Resident floated into the Dewan's sights and made him pull up sharply. Possibly, also, it was the thin, anxious look on his child's face that banished these shameful suspicions of deceit.

'I enjoyed it very much,' he said warmly.

'Did you find it interesting?'

Interesting, when you caught the inflection. The Dewan, who had been about to embark on further eulogy, desisted.

'Most. Most interesting,' he said, after some thought.

* * *

'Did you like it?' Usha asked Rabi.

'Loved it. Didn't you see me clapping?'

'Doesn't mean a lot. You have to do these things, Maharaj-kumar.'

'Who says?'

'I do.'

He caught her by the shoulder and spun her round, none too gently, although he was fond of her. For sometimes it rankled.

'If you mean because I'm a king's son, that's over.'

'Is it?'

The bones under his hand were sharp and quite stubborn. It surprised him into letting her go. His empty hand hung clumsily while he took fresh stock, as he needed to, those bones were convincing him.

'I can try,' he said, simply.

Usha's face began to glow, in an affinity of sentiment, or perhaps fired by those trials of strength that seized her imagination and had already caused such havoc in more vulnerable constitutions.

'So can I. If I don't try, I shall never find out.'

'Find out what?'

She hugged it close, not sure herself, only now and again she had to take off the lid and look inside to see how it was coming along.

'Well, there are things, aren't there,' she said, vaguely.

By now her bones were visibly softening.

* * *

Soon it was time for the second round of farewells, this time for the Maharajah and his Expeditionary Force, from which units, on the fields of France, were destined to be incorporated into the 2nd Indian Cavalry Division.

The date of departure was more or less decided by Mr. Buckridge, who voiced his view that the war might be over, and all hope of imperial service overseas dashed, unless the Maharajah got a move on.

It seriously perturbed Bawajiraj, who had caught the mood of his princely comrades, and could hardly wait to get at the Boche. Accordingly he set a date for departure, although it meant lowering his sights somewhat, for to his finicky eye, indeed superb judge of these matters, the cavalry could have done with a spot more training, that dash and zest without which one's cavalryman's heart could never rest entirely content.

It also meant he would miss the coming of age of his heir.

'Set my heart on it,' he told Mohini, theatrically, hand on breast, but with a genuine emotion beneath the theatre. 'But when Duty calls—'

Mohini perceived the capital, and was briefly antagonised. Your Duty is here, with your people, she wanted to say, sharply, but she could not bring herself. In the short time that was left to them, and loving him as she did, welt and all. And, Maharajah or not, he was, she felt, as entitled to his delusions as any man.

While Bawajiraj was consumed by duty. The substance of *devoir* began to flower and fill his mind, as honourable as ancient treaty given under one's royal mark, entrusted to cloth-of-gold, closed with crimson strings, sealed with royal seals of rosin and lac, as unthinkable to renege on it as on this unwritten compact. His gaze grew misty thinking of it.

'A privilege,' he said. 'It's a man's privilege, to do his duty, the highest to which he can aspire . . . for what is he without it? Although,' he said, gently, and all his features were touched and softened, 'I would have wished . . . I had nourished the hope, all these years, ever since His Excellency, you know, was gracious enough . . . to present my son, when the time came, to my people.'

Then Mohini was wrung, as much for him as for herself. She clung to him, without a word, while fiery trails seemed to run through her demanding to know why this man should forsake his hearth, his home, his son, his lifelong partner, to serve a foreign country. For what, she cried, *for what*? But, sensibly or through weariness, it was a silent cry.

The last durbar, the last dinner in the Palace, the last stroll around the nenuphar, which was now at its best, the heavy blooms thrown wide and bright right across the water. That night there were fireworks, reflections in the pool like falling stars, followed by cannon and mortar to bid goodbye to His Highness and the departing hosts.

* * *

The Maharani Shanta Devi lay in her bed and listened to the clamour with the passive bitterness that all the years had been unable to expunge. She was the Maharani, the lawful wife of the Maharajah. She would not have minded a second Maharani, or a third, or a concubine who pleased a passing fancy. It was not unknown for Maharajahs, or unfamiliar to their Courts. Palaces were built with sets of apartments for wives. But this constant woman who had usurped her place, borne her husband a son, appeared at his right hand on innumerable occasions, yielding it only for the most public appearance, that was a different matter. But in these later years she made him ask her before she would consent to appear with him on public display. As he did. The State forced him, sometimes. Sometimes the State forced both of them.

On this occasion Bawajiraj had formally requested her, and she had as formally acceded to his request, to stand by his side in the formal arrangement known to appeal to the British, family-worshippers to a man. She would have kept her word. She was a Rajah's daughter, pride and discipline would have upheld her; but her body, rebelling, struck her down.

Travel inadvisable, the Court physician pronounced, and took it out of her hands. The mischance was taken by those concerned as a small and unexpected mercy.

* * *

In the morning they left for Bombay: the Maharajah, the Maharajkumar, the Minister (reluctant and unconvinced) in case of last minute words of wisdom and guidance His Highness might wish to impart.

Also the Regent, incorporated into the person of the Dewan and added to his numerous portfolios. Not because he wanted it, particularly. Maharajah, Resident, and Minister himself were dubious. But, simply, there was no one else. Mr. Buckridge conceded it, after considering the Dewan in his customary manner. The devious Hindoo. So sharp you had to have your wits about you unremittingly, a process that wore you out. So many facets—no, faces—to the man. Man like his innumerable gods, which you saw lush and immoderate on his temples. At every turn a different face. It made Mr. Buckridge queasy.

But there was no one else.

The Resident recommended, the Viceroy confirmed, the Maharajah, sighing, surrendered his Seal, voicing his earnest wish that the Regency should pass to his son on his twenty-first birthday.

Now, with mixed feelings, and minus the Resident, who saw no reason, windswept farewells not his forte, they took their places in the special carriages.

* * *

Bombay.

It might have been yesterday, Rabi felt, though the years had fled. Same hotel, same beaches, same (better behaved) people. Somewhere among them the blithe little dancer, and the girl who had taken his virginity.

Same quayside, if wearing a different aspect. Even the steamer was familiar: the *Oceanic Empress*, the same brave vessel that had conveyed Sir Arthur and was now steamed back for the Maharajah (among others). The three of them in the shadow of this noble boat, awkwardly isolated despite the trammels and trappings that surround such embarkations and adventures; and of course a certain melancholy.

'Well, Rabi, my boy.'

Bawajiraj cleared his throat, hoarse from innumerable adieux, he pretended to himself. 'Look after things, won't you.'

'Yes, sir. Try to, yes.'

'And yourself, of course. And the people. *Your* people, my boy. Don't let anyone tell you otherwise. The old dictator, you know (here he all but dug the staid Minister in the ribs)—he's apt to think they're his.'

'Not at all, Highness . . . wouldn't dream . . .'

The Minister lowed, small discreet disclaimers that couldn't be held against him, later.

'Well, if you do, there are worse crimes, my dear fellow.' (For, no doubt about it, such occasions did induce a mellowing.)

'Most kind, your Highness.'

'Well, goodbye, Dewan Sahib.'

'Goodbye, your Highness. A safe voyage by God's grace, and a safe return home.'

The Dewan stepped back, because after all it was now between father and son. He engrossed himself in the anchoring of his turban, which the sea breezes were threatening, and listened to the band which, though the military air (actually it was 'Tipperary') was incomprehensible to him, mercifully drowned the private exchange.

While the salty wind whipped at the two who were left, stinging their eyes, leaving a taste of brine on their dried-out lips.

'Your mother,' said Bawajiraj, rather thickly, but winning over wind and band. 'Bound to miss the old man, Rabi. Women are lonely creatures, you know, don't really have our resources. . . . Cheer her up, there's a good chap.'

'Try to. Of course.'

'Know you will. And spare a thought for your father, now and again, eh Rabi? Proud of you and all that you know, my boy, even if it's not turned out *exactly*, you know what I mean. But proud, no question. Always was, from the time you were so high. Had you up with me on Tantivvy—no, before his day, it was Punch— and you insisted on grabbing the reins! Bless me, you couldn't have been two at the time.'

'I remember Punch.'

'Good times, Rabi.'

'Marvellous. Couldn't have been better.'

'More of the same, my boy, when I'm back. What d'you say?'

'It'll be something to look forward to. Goodbye, father. Good luck.'

And Rabi too was rubbed up, raw inside, for all the distance that now separated them, as he fell back and allowed it all—flags, band, entourage, standards, colours and crisp commanders—to surround his father and bear him away.

Dewan and heir walked back together to the sleek ministerial motor-car that waited, pennants flapping, State plates burnished.

('Remember you are the Chief Minister, Minister. I don't intend to be seen off by a fakir!'

'I fully appreciate, Highness. I have often, in the past, been reminded of my status by Sir Arthur.'

'I do believe, Dewan Sahib, at times you went out of your way to provoke his Excellency.'

'When it was unavoidable, Highness. Otherwise our relations were most cordial.')

Now the two settled back, not ungratefully, in the limousine decreed by the Maharajah, in a silence that contrasted pleasantly, both felt, with what had but lately buffeted them; and presently the Dewan said, pensively, and with certain airs of studied neutrality,

'Well, Rabi. I understand from your father that the people belong to you.'

'Belong?' said Rabi.

And laughed. Sometimes, though rarely, the Dewan could be quite transparent.

'I understood you were the Regent, Dewan Sahib,' he said. Softly.

So soft that it alerted the Dewan, who was unprepared, or perhaps unused, to being taken on by young men.

But not worsted. By no means.

He did, however, cast aside his pensive airs.

'People seldom yield their allegiance to Regents, although they may belong body and soul to Maharajahs and their sons,' he countered, keeping watch.

While Rabi who did, now and then, rejoice in sword-play, felt no inclination to prolong the trial.

'A slight exaggeration, Dewan Sahib,' he said, easily, and stretched his stiff, richly encumbered legs. 'They belong to themselves in the first place, and after that it's up to them, really, don't you think?'

Then the Dewan, relieved in one sphere, began to be dogged by the sense of history repeating itself that had earlier trapped Rabi. For years, it seemed to him, they had battled over Rabi; now the struggle was to begin for the loyalties of the people. Although, of course, it could not be joined until the Maharajah's return.

So unsettling were these feelings that the normally upright Dewan sagged a little, and even rested his dizzy head against the plush, determinedly making the most of the peace and ease so staunchly provided by the motor-car's suave interior.

15

The Maharajah missed Gallipoli—luckily, as it was a disaster, although it did provide unrivalled opportunity for gallantry in the face of strategic withdrawal—but he did make the Western Front.

Letters came weekly in batches, though often at much longer intervals, owing to the exigencies of war. For Rabi. For Dewan and Resident and Dowager and Mohini. Mostly for Mohini.

> Whizz-bangs all night [he wrote to her from the Somme]. It was like Deepavali Fireworks! We are in the most chivalrous company (P--na Horse, Pooky's L----rs, Dr----n Gds!) . . . You will be glad to hear our squadrons have acquitted themselves Worthily.

And from the château in Querrieux to which the field ambulance had ferried him,

> I have as they say here Copped it, my Beloved, but Nowhere that Matters, and am consoled by the Distinguished Company in which I find myself.

And later, recovered (but for how long, Mohini wore herself out wondering), writing from the trenches,

> We were, this Day, honoured by the presence of His Royal Highness . . . H.R.H. was good enough to enquire after our

Wives (as you are, my Treasured One, although you have refused me the pleasure of bearing that title) and to hand round his packet of Abdullas, of which I took one, although I do not smoke, and shall cherish it, having received it from his Own Hand.

'He is well, I trust?' The Dowager enquired of the pinched woman who had come bearing this latest missive.

'Well enough,' her ward replied. 'He is alive, Highness, and that is the utmost, in the circumstances.'

And traced with a listless finger those indomitable flourishes, wrought in a far country on buff paper, in the shadow of destruction, the habits of a lifetime gaily prevailing over a mindless havoc, although it could not thereby afford any warranty of survival.

Gutted, the Dowager saw, and quite ugly. Or perhaps it was the morning light that fell upon the several attributes of her beauty but could not bind and kindle them into a blaze.

Nor were the illuminations of evening any better. They could not hoist the plain and lifeless woman to her proper state, even if they did provide opportunities. The Dowager seized them, from a memory of what it had been like, and an affection for her ward, whom she saw, besides, as mother to her true heir.

'There is Rabi,' she said. 'Dewan Sahib is persuaded, of late, that he takes after his mother.'

'One or two features,' said Mohini, and thought of the father, lodged in some ditch, the fine head that could have lain in her lap presenting like a hideous target.

'In temperament. Looks did not enter into it,' the Dowager persisted. 'Current affairs have brought to the Dewan Sahib's mind certain early tussles with his mother.'

'He said so?'

'Came specially.'

'Old battles. Old days.'

'The Dewan was transported back. Brick walls, he confessed, was what he was forcibly reminded of. Butting his head against them.'

'I do not recollect the Brahmin,' said Mohini acidly, abruptly abandoning her ditch, 'ever submitting his precious crown to such injury. My remembrance is of a presence on the sidelines, bleating.'

'But sidelines are no longer accessible to the Regent,' said the Dowager. 'He is directly concerned with the coming of age celebrations.'

'It's Rabi's concern and Rabi has decided to postpone them.'
'That is precisely what agitates Tirumal Rao.'
'He admitted it?'
'In as many words, wine gone to his head.'
'The Regency?'
'Not at all. Merely the time of morning. The Dewan sparkles at sunrise.'
'And is aware of it.'
'But was not helped, particularly,' said the Dowager. 'Even assuming a grandmother's influence, which the Dewan was at some pains to stress, I would not undertake to badger Rabi. And if I did—'

The two women were joyous by now, from a closer acquaintance of Rabi, and in a sly if mild triumph over the Dewan who could not after all approach, for all his gimlet qualities, their flesh-and-blood knowledge and intimations.

'Even as a child,' Mohini began.

Prised up at last, the Dowager perceived, and was moved to wheel out the record of it, in a lavish album, on its lacquered stand, the pages opening on charming chronicles of children.

'Here he is, taking the fence the *syce* swore he couldn't.'

'And in his Durbar dress. He only wore that outfit once. I never could get him to put it on again, not for anything. Some story about how it had turned into a viper.'

'Full of stories, and avid for more,' said the Dowager, peering, barely able to concede herself in the faded sepia, while the child on her lap seemed to bound out of the frame, impatient and clamouring: *What happened next? And after that? And then?*

'I told him every tale I knew,' she said, 'as they had been told to me, before they could reach him garbled. Although it displeased his father.'

And glimmered, those strange rays that could put Bawajiraj off his chosen course, sending him stumbling from his mother's presence to polo, or cricket, or iced cup, or durbar, or finally even to war, to get back on to that wide, bright, shadowless, and infinitely preferred path that unwound like a crimson carpet before his correctly pointed feet.

While Mohini was revived, and dwelt with an equal affection on past turbulence as on the images of pleasure that the album preserved. Since, being only human, her heart was infinitely accommodating, cherishing both lover and son who marched in different directions.

362

The following day, at dawn, for she shared this penchant with the Dewan, the Dowager rose, rather stiffly, from her bed, and waving aside the sleepy woman who came forward to assist her left the chamber and made her way to the upper storeys above the Pearl Suite. Here she paused for breath, and to muster her strength, before attempting to scale the narrow stairway that spiralled up to the circular gallery below the gilded dome. Presently, her breath coming easier, she began to ascend, gripping the slender rail, the lacy silvered rungs icy under her soles, until she was standing in the gallery.

An unearthly place, this crystal gallery, full of extraordinary lights from its enclosure in glass—jewelled flashes, curls of shaved ice, diamond-edged, sweeping up to the golden dome— less a gallery than a walk, more a gazebo than either. Its views drew her, rivalling any available to the Residency watch-tower, or even the hill that Rabi favoured, the Hill of Devi, crowned by a ruined fort, that dominated the city.

The Dowager Maharani could not gaze enough.

She strolled, transcending her age, her eyes returned by miraculous gift to a younger, clear amber that mirrored the parks and courtyards and fountains and forts, the indestructible lands that stretched beyond the city, the forests and rivers and the distant lake, and even more distant a glimmer of limpid reservoirs; and was soothed, in her crystal belvedere, by images of an inheritance that going beyond actual rights and titles awaited, it seemed to her, its proper heirs.

Her reflections consoled her even when, quite shortly, she was struck from these dizzy heights; a fall appropriately diagnosed as a stroke. A mild one, the doctor said, exclaiming over follies that precipitated such disasters, and in half a mind to take it out on the frightened underling except that the woman was already distraught.

The Dowager continued serene, reconciled to blood-warnings that at her age could hardly be called unexpected. She received, quite soon, the Dewan and Rabi, forbade the sending of alarming telegrams to the Maharajah, and after that she rested, husbanding her powers which, confounding the doctors, were even now not wholly consumed.

* * *

The Dewan's agitations meanwhile waxed and waned—a moon that took its phases according to the length of time that separated him from last sojourn in his calming cell—but would not wholly vanish.

It was Rabi, with Usha in the wings.

This otherwise sensible young man was bent, he did believe, on thwarting the Chief Minister.

It upset one's orderly mind. Offended one's sense of the fitting, he put it to himself, that the Maharajakumar's majority should not be celebrated (give or take a few days or weeks to placate priests and planets) on the due and proper date.

'Why not, Rabi?'

'No particular reason.'

'There must be.'

'Nothing to speak of.'

At times like these the Dewan's sympathies, possibly for the very first time, went winging to the absent Maharajah. One had an inkling at last. One was, after all these years, being made to realise what one was up against.

'Maharajkumar, it is illogical to refuse, without a particular reason, a reasonable request leading to a reasonable course of conduct.'

'Not in the mood, Dewan Sahib.'

'Rabi, only artists have moods. I, too, believe me, cannot pen a verse to will, I have to wait for illuminations. But when it is a case of ordering grain or appointing judges, can I afford to fold my hands and wait for inspiration?'

'You can't,' Rabi commiserated. 'I can.'

And departed.

So casual, this generation. Winning arguments—if you could call it winning—in this casual fashion. Sly, brittle, blunt, velvet glove that the British were so fond of extending—one had weapons for these approaches. But this cool armour that deflected the best steel?

When he next tried, Rabi, in different mood, was slightly more intelligible.

'Later, Dewan Sahib. When the work is finished. Can't concentrate on junketings before that, somehow. But I'll let you know in good time.'

'Which means more than a couple of hours, you know,' the Dewan grumbled. 'All the preparations—you princes haven't any notion, Rabi—and besides we have to ensure adequate response—'

'Do you mean drum up enthusiasm?'

It was so abrupt that the Dewan, ill-prepared, felt almost assaulted. It might have been disabling, except that somewhere over the years the relationship between them had been tested and—

The Dewan dragged at his lip, rather surprised by his conclusion. Tested and ratified, he acknowledged.

'I do not think,' he said then, straightly, 'that in your case drumming up will be necessary.'

As there might be for the Maharajah. For there was no point in pretending that all was well between Ruler and people, whatever might be developing between the people and their servants. Like this one in, he was sorry to see, his ragged coolie-type turnout, which, had he been a low-class woman, he would have ached to mend.

* * *

Next it was Usha.

Madam had taken herself off to her sister's. She had a legitimate excuse—one suspected she had furnished herself with it—in the shape of an invitation from Vimala and her husband.

It was not the *fact* of her going—to a select Brahmin household of nobility and learning, no dearth of chaperons on whom you could absolutely rely—but the manner of it. A plain announcement, as if she were a train, departing.

While Vatsala looked to him, silent signals passing over the imperilled head of their last-born. But what could he, the second most powerful man in the State, *do*? He felt it was unreasonable of his wife. Her domain. A case, as it were, of pitting will against will, so why couldn't she? He tried, however; and discovered that the adolescent Usha's will was very strong indeed. In the circumstances he did what he could. He removed the priceless ring, set with a diamond of the purest water, from his little finger and placed it on her third.

'To remind you,' he said, severely.

'If I tried I couldn't forget my dearest father,' said the sunny Usha, and bent to touch his feet.

The sweetest of children, always had been, the Dewan

reflected, placing the tips of his fingers on her bowed head in the blessing she sought from him.

But he was also aware that she had turned his meaning.

Not brazenly, it was obvious, but standing wracked and speechless on the edge of some confessional, twisting the ring, which was too big for her and had slipped to the first knuckle of her finger.

Wasting virtually before his eyes, and wearing, the Dewan saw, the cheapest, most deplorable of saris. Another of the same ilk, he said to himself, preparing for the climate; and of a sudden was wrenched by the pity of it, as one must be when whole generations are called up for testing.

Usha would have pulled back then, if she could. One owed so much, and loved so dearly. But she was irresistibly drawn, excited by possibilities of unique rebellion against an oppressive and alien government at which her sister had hinted, and which she, Usha, could not divulge. Did not fully know herself but was eager to discover, voyages of exploration whose exhilarating promise had already begun to round out her crestfallen face; and quite soon it polished off her parent.

* * *

The Dewan often pondered, these days. He sat at his desk, often late into the evening—the *chaprassi* was on the brink of rebellion—and dwelt on the forms and manifestations of warfare. Not the Great War, to which the Princes had rallied as one man, and which was cropping its own generation, but the upheavals that had begun in less infatuated territories that fringed the State, of which news came regularly, and with increasing frequency.

One such evening there was a manifestation. That is to say it took on the attributes of a manifestation, for the man was real enough. He came in without announcement, blinking a little in the bright electric light and obviously unused to it, but advancing confidently down the long room until he was standing before the desk. A cultivator, the Dewan surmised, dark-skinned, gnarled hands, a posture that made you look for hoe, or spade, some heavy earth implement that he would normally carry, resting in the shoulder-groove it had hewn for itself.

The Dewan was a little surprised, at this late hour, but not alarmed. Anyone could approach him: it was the point of the durbars he held daily, scrupulously, in the tradition that held that officers of State should be accessible to the public. He put away the ledger he had been studying—it was a statement of the State's cash reserves—and made himself available.

'You wish to see me?'

'That's why I'm here. Didn't expect to get in so easily, but your guard was asleep.'

'My *chaprassi*. I'm afraid I overwork him sometimes.'

'You ought to be ashamed.'

The Dewan's breath snagged, slightly; but recovering, he drew the fuse of whatever was working up to explosion in this intrepid peasant.

'I am ashamed. When I have the grace, and leisure, to think about it,' he said.

'You're a busy man, then.'

'Look around you.'

'Sahib, I—'

'Did not think. No matter. It's a common failing.'

'Sahib, I mean no disrespect.'

'I seldom take unintended meanings.'

'But I, too, am a hardworking man, like all my clan.'

'The land is a hard taskmaster.'

'You know what I am?'

'It's not difficult to guess.'

'A cultivator, Dewan Sahib. That is my walk in life, to which God has called me. I am content with it. I work my land and I pay my dues, the collector never has to call twice. But now—'

He stood, a basalt figure with the pictogram engraved in the stone, a raw monument raised to inhumanity. The Dewan saw the lines of strain, thrown into relief by the sharp light, and the gristle jerking in the scraggy neck; and was moved to help this strangled petitioner.

'I am here to listen,' he prompted, as calmly as he could, since by now he had an inkling.

'I came here to speak,' the man responded. Impediments had melted, he enunciated clearly. 'There is a new levy on us. The Salt Tax is doubled. In God's name I stand here and I tell you it is not a just measure.'

And waited.

While the Dewan listened to a barrage of sound that seemed to fill the room without in any way impinging on the quiet night.

'Do you think,' he said at last, quite low, when the roaring that filled his ears had subsided. 'Do you really think you are telling me something I don't know?'

And rose, in no great haste, but since there was no more to be said, to accompany his opponent, or ally, to the door. Here he did pause, for a link was forging, like that between survivors who, confronting each other when the echoes are dying, become aware of the strange grey volcanic ash in which they are identically coated.

'What is your name?' he asked his companion.

'My name is Ramdas. Remember it,' said the man, quietly, and went out as quietly as he had spoken, so as not to wake the overworked and slumbering *chaprassi*.

The *chaprassi* did not rouse, but stirred and mumbled in his sleep, and in the morning related how, though wide awake, he had seen a ghost; a recital to which, to his vast surprise, he found his sardonic employer unusually sympathetic.

* * *

At this time Bawajiraj, like several hundred thousand others, was still bogged down in the mud and mire of the Western Front. The Maharajah continued indomitable.

Our Cavalry were brought up for the Charge!

he wrote, from Cambrai, where the division was entrenched; and in the same bundle of mail, in a note of earlier date, was a paean about a Rolls-Royce, a breed especially favoured since its baptism in the Bombay docks.

A Real Beauty,

he wrote, feet braced against the duckboards of his dugout, crested pad in the crook of an elbow.

Armour Plate, which is better than Platinum, as you will agree when I tell you it has withstood Shellbursts.

So that Mohini was left with confusing images of her beloved, mounted sometimes on a charger, sometimes riding smoothly in a plated Rolls similar to the half dozen more or less laid up, together with the English mechanic to nanny them, in the Palace mews. Both images were truthful. The fearless Maharajah did charge at the head of his Lancers, to the astonishment of German tank commanders; and he did foray behind enemy lines in a plated Rolls, acts of valour which earned him a mention in dispatches and subsequently the G.C.B. Bawajiraj, modest to a fault, could not bring himself to speak of it, so that his dear one had to hear the news via the Dewan, via the Resident, via the War Ministry in London who, mindful there was a war on, did by-pass the Viceroy's office.

Not all the excitements of war, however, could make up to Bawajiraj for the absence of his family. Often, in that dreadful winter, soaked to the skin, or his tunic dried stiff as parchment upon his back, he drew out of webbing pouches the precious photographs, poring over the cherished features of Mohini, his son, his daughters, with as much love and longing as any conscripted private.

Nor could the mud and misery of the trenches obliterate the Maharajah's sense of occasion. As soon as he could—it was spring by then—he journeyed to London, his mind bursting with designs, and used up the whole of a precious three days' leave haggling at Asprey's.

Not money, of course: only bounders; nor any difficulty in the matching of execution to design in this treasure house of elegant craftsmen. It was the creation itself that gave rise to prolonged engagements, and even to muted conflagration, for the gentlemen of this courtly establishment were as determined as the Maharajah to produce a work of art and significance.

Only, they did not see eye to eye. Blue and amber flashed. Blue had in mind a Key, which in the circumstances might be thought appropriate. Frosty amber thought it singularly inapposite, considering the ten entrances to the grounds, each guarded by a sentry with a dagger at his belt. Then there was the question of bejewelling . . .

But in the end, by attrition, it was done. The bulky present, packed by the makers, too cumbersome (and precious) for anything else was despatched in a special reinforced diplomatic bag to Rabi.

Back in his hole, a cramped billet in a shell-damaged French farmhouse, the Maharajah penned a letter:

> My Dearest Son and Heir,
>   I send this gift as a Token of my Joy at the attainment of your Majority, tempered by the loss I feel that I shall not be present in Person. It will not, my dear boy, reach you in time, but the Exigencies of War . . .
>   Your Loving and Devoted Father and Maharajah.

It was, indeed, a token. For long before he sailed Bawajiraj had journeyed to the Jewel Chamber and allocated for his son and heir a generous portion of his private treasure. Compared with the trayfuls of precious stones, the solid gold ingots, the cummerbund of matching pearls—beside these the latest gift was certainly the merest trifle.

The thought however was tremendous.

* * *

The Maharajkumar received his Golden Spurs months after his twenty-first birthday, which had yet to be officially celebrated. He admired the exquisite object and put it in a cupboard.

Mr. Buckridge was less cavalier, and accustomed to consider almost any circumstance in terms of possible advantage. The handsome gift, delivered through diplomatic channels and of which he had caught a glimpse, conjured up scenes of a matching magnificence in his mind. He saw himself presiding at the specially convened meeting of the Minority Council, in the great Durbar Hall, himself enthroned to the right of the Maharajkumar, a position to which he was entitled as Resident, while the outgoing Regent took his place in a chair on the left, and perhaps half a pace behind. Thereafter came, in the vaguest outline, a hazy picture of kingdoms being handed into the care of the new young Regent, or at least underwritten, British seals on the document, for which no doubt procedure and precedent existed and could be unearthed in due course by his Staff.

Rabi dashed this golden cup from the Englishman's lips. He wrote from his jungle fastness declining to participate in the ceremony.

It was a short letter, which Mr. Buckridge considered plain to the point of brusqueness, though a plain man himself, but one did expect flourishes from Orientals . . .

More irksome still was what it gave rise to: a nasty feeling that this physically pleasing (one regretted to admit it) and potentially puissant young man was educating him in what he could and could not do. While close behind—hauntings impartially handed out, left, right, between English and Indians—walked another ghost, a lurking fear that the Maharajkumar was outgrowing desire, and would not be easily tempted or won or kept by pleasures and privileges the Raj might dangle, or even soberly provide.

Nor could intransigents be brought to heel, as once one had been able. Mr. Buckridge's thoughts hovered like a plaintive bee over a flower, while accepting there was no question, these days. But take him down a peg or two, this bumptious princeling, he felt, and set his mind to the task. Presently it came to him. Sitting down at once he drafted a letter conveying his decision to defer the formal transfer of the powers of Regency from Dewan to Maharajkumar, notwithstanding his attainment of majority.

It took some courage. Mr. Buckridge had to resurrect Regulation XXV, somewhat mouldering by now but still on the Statute book, before he could reassure himself that he did indeed possess the necessary power for the care and control of refractory Indian princes. After which he despatched the letter.

Dewan and Rabi studied the document together, since it concerned them both.

'The Khan,' said the allusive Dewan, 'sent Shah Ismail of respected memory a begging bowl, and received in return a spinning wheel.'

'War followed,' said Rabi, who was not uneducated, even if he could not compete with his mentor. 'But that was not the purpose behind my refusal, since I have not, Dewan Sahib, your subtlety.'

Though, now, he did wonder. For his opinion of Mr. Buckridge closely resembled the Resident's opinion of him.

More than ever now, since the decision over the Regency flouted his father's fond and declared wish.

* * *

Summer came. The skies were blinding, the shadows grew tall and black and fell sharply on the scorched plains.

In the cities lugubrious citizens began to prepare for the annual siege. They brought out mouldy black umbrellas for airing, and mended the thatch of their huts, and despatched their women, hung about with a motley collection of pots and pans and leather bottles, to a variety of water-points to lay in what they could before the water supply, immemorially unreliable, ran out on them.

Hope, unsoundly founded on prayer in the candid opinion of the Chief Minister, was what usually buoyed up these parched citizens. This year was added an ingredient of tremulous expectation—although they didn't really believe, but no harm in wondering, was there?—in that water was said to be coming from the hills, where mighty labours had been expanded.

But when the sluice gates were opened, and the water did actually flow, in thin streams since the scheme was not yet fully functioning, and instead of stony beds there was a finger's depth of water and as much again in the canals that criss-crossed their fields, it still came as an astounding, if pleasant, surprise.

True, they had never given up hoping, and perhaps it was beyond human power; but they had all but ceased to believe.

The following year the miracle was repeated, more efficiently, the water flowing down in controlled cascades and boiling up creditably in the water-courses. The citizens marvelled. They treated it as a divine answer to their prayers, while prepared to acknowledge, and in due course bent on fêting, the human factor.

A deputation waited upon the Dewan.

* * *

At this point Rabi had returned to the capital.

To visit his grandmother, whose sands were running out, the grains visibly numbered in her tranquil glass; and for other reasons.

And stayed a while, the short visit lengthening itself, seized as he always had been by the manifestations of the season.

The hot season, the hottest of the year, the land blasted by torrid westerlies, splitting under a pewter sun. A lancing light. It laid open the countryside, you saw through to its skeletal forms, quartz made plain under the crust.

On these searing plains men had mustered and fought, choked by dust and heat, skins blistered by their own armour, while over the tossing plumes and helmets the indifferent blossom drifted. Frail indestructible showers, falling softly season after season.

The paths were thick with the creamy surf. He scooped up a handful from where they had fallen, behind the stables where he had gone for a mount, and thought, gently enough, of the little girl (but her breasts were beginning, and she had been proud of them: how clearly one saw what had been blurred to her smaller companion, himself that innocent, peremptory playmate) whose job it had been to clear these walks.

'Shall I ride with you, *huzoor?*'

The *syce* had saddled up as bidden, his not to question, and come round leading a roan.

'Not today,' said Rabi, and caught the glint of relief before it could be masked by the obedient salaam; and was tempted to needle.

'It's too hot for you,' he said.

'*Huzoor*, if you wished'—began the indignant, but perspiring, *syce*; but they were away, mare departed with perverse master.

Rabi rode alone, along the gravelled paths, past the most obscure of the ten exits manned by a wilted sentry, across the parched plain and up the hill crowned by the ruined fort. He dismounted here, looping the reins over a thorn bush and leaving the docile mare to crop in the shade of the crumbling walls while he ascended to the obelisk that marked the point of highest elevation. From this pinnacle the country was open to him: great sweeping arcs that stretched to the curve of horizon, views that surpassed, he liked to tell her, any available from the Dowager's crystal tower.

Rabi stood in this lonely eminence, gazing, and soon entranced, and presently felt that exchange between man and landscape that persuades one of unity, a process which, if carried far enough—and lifetimes can be insufficient—will end in resolutions of the nagging enigma.

Only a sip, however. The sun had shifted, and the toasted roan whinnied for attention. The sound, borne up clearly, restored the patchwork and he saw once more the city spread before him, the palaces and temples, the remains of the wall that enclosed this ancient capital, the fields and the brimming channels that watered them and the river that flowed lazily, sun silvering its winding surfaces. It pleased him, this natural yet composed panorama; a deep pleasure that seeped in gradually and engulfed him. He could, perhaps, face them now, he felt: tormentors like Das, with his armoured, insolent eyes, and the thin women with pots balanced on the bones of their haunches, trekking; and even the tender child for whom he had cared, and who had cared for him even in those heated moments when he tore her torn bodice into irredeemable tatters.

* * *

The Dewan saw the silhouette on the hill; and when it was accessible, and in his judgment sufficiently rested and refreshed, the flaring russet reduced to less alarming hues, he cornered his quarry.

'I know you're not an enthusiast,' he said, 'but if the people want a fête then you must think of the people.'

'Too hot to think,' said Rabi, and moaned a little, assuming a defenceless foetal position in his canvas chair.

'Why, are you English?' enquired the Dewan.

Rabi sat up, to extract this barb.

'Neither are the cattle,' he said, 'but, you may have noticed, even the Brahma bulls are dozing in the shade.'

'I also noticed you,' pursued the remorseless Dewan, 'at high noon, on the crest of the Hill of Devi.'

But then barriers fell; he saw he was entering some forbidden territory and changed his tack.

'I am your Adviser,' he said, simply.

'English?'

'Indian.'

'Odd, the difference.'

'Not odd.'

'Natural then. Very well, Dewan Sahib.'

'We go ahead?'

'As you wish.'

'As you wish too.'

'Yes. As I do too.'

'Will you name a date?'

Because one didn't take it this far, virtually rolling a boulder uphill, without clinching the matter.

'Am I an astrologer?' said Rabi, exhausted. 'You get your people to juggle with the charts. It's their job. You can't expect me to do everything.'

'My officers,' said the Dewan, pleased, if also slightly winded, 'will take care of all the detail.'

So the celebrations were held; for the dam, not the Maharaj-kumar's majority, although the two seemed to blend, or were made to by the people in defiance, or more probably innocent, of Mr. Buckridge's wishes.

The Dewan cast an eye, which grew sober, rather in the manner of Sir Arthur, reflecting that the numbers of people assembled augured less well for the father than the son, and not at all well for Residents. He also detected in the acclamation more than the formal airs of durbar, or even those notes of extravagant joy sounded by people grateful for any break in their simple lives. Certainly the Maharajah could not have asked for, nor received, more fervent *Jai's*, which far surpassed those which, from time to time, he had happily imagined greeting his only son.

The Dowager had not been able to attend the ceremony; her body had failed her.

It failed her increasingly. Some days she could not leave her bed but lay, propped up on pillows, watching the rose-red stains creeping up the marble, and peopling the courtyards with children now grown, with concerns too pressing to dwell on these slow tides. At times, however, she was conscious of revival, a grant too brief, and rare, not to pursue. Then she would rise, and make her way to her favourite anchorage on the verandah shaded by morning glory, and take up a neglected piece of embroidery, or string together jasmine or marigold in a garland for the shrine in the little prayer-room adjoining her bed-chamber. Or even, greatly daring, walk the length of the verandah and down the steps, and along the avenue between the flower borders, aided by her stick and the waiting woman.

That morning—a fine day in June, hot weather ending, the first rains fallen, the pick of mango orchards on Palace tables— Rabi had joined her, after an early ride, so fresh and glowing that she felt herself infused.

'Shall we walk, Rabi?'

'If you would like to.'

He was smiling.

It made her feel she could walk for miles, like any young woman, willing for anything.

But when she rose, blithe as the day, and took the arm he offered, suddenly it struck at her. Some treachery of arteries, or heart, she thought resentfully, and would have fallen but for his arm, which supported her and eased her back onto the cushions.

He would have gone for help then, but she stopped him. Since it had come, she recognised, her resentments fading; and she wanted no doctors, purveyors of ruthless aids that prolonged the act of dying and robbed it of its inherent decencies.

So she rested, to recover her breath, which was snagging badly in the wake of the pain, closing her eyes against the light which had become oppressive.

When she came to again it was dark, or seemed to be. She could not see what she wanted and had to grope for it, and he, too, was lost in the shadows that converged, although she felt his presence.

'Rabi?'

'I'm here. Beside you.'

Her vision returned briefly then. She saw him with a great

375

clarity, bathed in an intense light that also irradiated her, and with a vast effort, for she was infinitely tired by now, raised herself up from the pillows and reached for the withered petal circlet and laid it on his shoulders. In some way the act satisfied her, although the nomination would have to be ratified by others, and the nominee had yet to signify acceptance. After this she simply lay, drifting, without the strength to speak; until presently she felt him touch her feet, and then his tears, falling and scalding the backs of her hands, which he had taken in his.

But she could not comfort him.

Soon there was no need to. She was thirteen years old, and he, or someone very like him, was holding her hand and they were laughing as they raced up the valley to their house, and entering grew merrier still, listening to the solemn Envoy who had come from the distant capital.

There was one reminder, however, which rose disturbingly from the torchlit procession that wound, a mile long, out of the Palace gates. She had to remind him while she could.

'No fuss,' she said, distinctly, putting aside, momentarily, the delightful pursuits that engaged her.

'None,' he promised, and continued to kneel, and chafe her hands, and could not believe she was dead until their utter stillness convinced him. Then at last he rose, and closed her eyes and drew up the covers himself, and did not know what state he was in until someone, one of the women who had gathered around them, reached up and dried his face.

It was coming up for noon by then, the shadows were at their sharpest.

* * *

So, without fuss, he lit the pyre, performing a duty which had skipped a generation to devolve on him.

16

Poppies blew on Flanders fields.

Scarlet against azure skies, an astonishing sight from a shell-hole but serene and absolutely normal now that Armageddon was over.

The Maharajah lingered, filled with proud and melancholy memories of fallen comrades with which, somehow intertwined, was the death of his mother.

Although they had never been close. But they might have been, he felt a little wistfully, only something had seemed to twist, quite early on, between them. Nothing to be done about it now, however. So he laid the wreaths he was bearing and turned on his heel, putting it all, as others were doing, briskly behind him.

Sirens were calling: Paris and Rome, and Deauville and Biarritz and Baden-Baden. The eager oppidan answered them all, as busy as ever he had been in his kingdom answering the calls of State, often in a quandary as to which of these delicious cities should be awarded the palm.

But London, without doubt, wore the crown. An incomparable city, cool but glittering, grey façades of monumental stone opening upon glowing interiors of immense and solid wealth risen upon the efforts of, among others, the Honourable East India Company. A city that offered diversions from the most chaste to the dizziest. Filled delightfully, Bawajiraj found, with soul-mates: people who spoke as he did, same language, same accents, enchanting harmony of aims and interests, many of them old cronies (dear old Pooky among them, and not a few Governors and Residents he had put up at his shooting lodges), or friends of cronies.

He made it his base, secured by an account opened at Coutts, sallying out to Henley and Ascot to sample the joys of the season, or to polo at Hurlingham; week-ending in the country, or proceeding, in good shape and civil company, to the Cavalry Club, or to the Travellers', or somewhat more gaily to the Cabaret Club; and also on one spectacular occasion (some misunderstanding on his part, he felt sure) to the Bag o' Nails where, rather pink about the gills, he found himself among a bevy of gilded young Hussars scarcely less astonished than he at his penetration of the portals of this élite educational establishment. And pleasing beyond anything—a treasured privilege—was to be received at the Entrée Entrance of Buckingham Palace.

It was all very agreeable. How charming people were! How welcoming everyone was! There were times when, somewhat basely, he could not help comparing the hospitality that flowed in kindly abundance from the most exalted quarters with the invitations that issued somewhat sparingly from excellencies in India. But then, he told himself charitably, in India there were Five Hundred like him, one simply could not expect; and besides, there was rather a lot of jostling and jealousy, especially among the lesser Houses, one had seen it with one's very own saddened eyes.

Finally, to fill the Maharajah's cup, there was Sir Arthur, back from the wars. None other than dear Sir Arthur, inviting his old friend Waji to his place in the country, which turned out to be a mansion of palladian splendour set in numerous and rolling acres in Shropshire. Nothing to one's own princely State, of course, but of a pleasing sufficiency, and affording a green and wooded seclusion, and many enchanting views. They lingered over the brandy, exchanging notes about the day's bag, and the week's polo (both of them still able to show the younger ones a thing or two), and capping each other's memories of the old country—meaning India, whose heat and dirt and other aggravations Sir Arthur handsomely forgave. And presently the Maharajah, warmed as never before, was moved to lay bare his innermost thoughts.

'I do wish, you know,' he said, rather huskily, and not without persuasions of verging on treason, 'that someone else. Not that we don't get on. Not at all. We do. Mostly. But Rabi. I did want him to—quite looked forward—subject to approval. But it— um—wasn't. Don't quite know why. Excellent reasons I'm sure, but—'

From which Sir Arthur had to deduce, and did, since after all he understood English, that his successor (now who was it, one couldn't quite place these wartime appointments: ah yes, one Mr. Buckridge) was making poor old Waji's life a misery. But one couldn't criticise one's own, well, kind. On the other hand there was Waji. Decent old stick. One of the best. In the end he felt it best to dwell on the satisfactions his own term of office had afforded him. He did so, most warmly, only a quiver or two of the golden spirit in the globe he held betraying the actual passion he felt.

It was now, on this visit, on his friend's native heath, in the aftermath of what had been kindled, that the Maharajah was encouraged, or perhaps it came naturally in the English climate, to call Sir Arthur Arthur.

Bawajiraj returned to London. Being London it was not difficult to execute his plan, whereas in Delhi there were all those corridors and channels. He had a word with His Majesty's Private Secretary and in no time at all an invitation from His Majesty, receiving from him the most gracious and cordial assurances. After which, well pleased, the Maharajah set sail for India.

In a satisfactorily short space of time thereafter Sir Arthur called to present the Letters of Recall of his predecessor and his own Letters of Credence as Resident at the Court of His Highness the Maharajah of Devapur.

No one in the State said much, they had all become a bit numbed, but there was something like a corporate sigh of relief, for Mr. Buckridge without a single calculated act of aggression and simply by being himself had created an area of psychic disaster. All from sweeper to Dewan had suffered in some degree; and people like sweepers, unlike the Dewan, had no weapons with which to retaliate. Things were not at their happiest in Devapur State, was the consensus, but that Mr. Buckridge would have rendered them intolerable everyone was unshakeably convinced.

Sir Arthur perceived the burden of goodwill and was almost ashamed. Indians asked for so little, he felt, and if you gave that little the response was out of all proportion.

The difficulty was that the greedy Indians were no longer satisfied with little. They wanted the lot. They wanted to rule themselves.

These were the thoughts of British India.

Sir Arthur cosily imagined, though now and then he prayed, that they would be confined there. He continued to see his role as that of a shepherd, doing his best by his flock, and he confused the manifest goodwill towards him with the previous unquestioning acceptance of his slot in the State. Certainly a good many people—servants, pensioners, petitioners, even some in the countryside—did see him as a shepherd. Only sometimes their thought slid sideways, under the influence of Gandhi-wallahs, wandering to other sides of the business, in fact precisely to the business-like qualities of shepherds. For Gandhi had roundly proclaimed that a state of affairs that allowed the Viceroy to earn five thousand times as much as the average Indian was both immoral and intolerable.

No one knew what the Resident earned. But the Residency provided evidence.

Not that there were many Gandhi-*wallahs* in the State, the Maharajah discouraged them. It was their thinking, winds that blew in over the border, which was not all that distant as the mind flies, and little more than an imaginary line drawn over the land manned here and there by a post and a sentry.

The truth was that a war had intervened.

Except in higher conclave no one had cared to dwell overmuch on maintaining the supremacy of Britain as a naval power, or the need to curb the expansionist ambitions of Germany, or the desirability of preserving the huge and profitable captive market of the Empire for the British, which were among the causes for which Britain fought the Great War. It was considered wiser to concentrate on the nobler objectives, the liberty and freedoms of nations and peoples, which appealed more readily to the simpler emotions. Certainly it appealed to Indians, who believed that the freedom of nations applied equally to their own. They said so loudly and persistently.

Britain, as many annoyed Englishmen perceived, had been hoist with her own petard.

But Britain—a view reinforced by profound and wishful misconceptions—could not conceive of India as a nation. The British could not believe the unruly Indians, non-cooperating wildly on all sides, could possibly rule themselves. They could not see where trained and experienced cadres—after years of turning out *munshis* and *babus*, and two centuries of rebuffing the nobility—would come from to man the administration. They felt the time was not ripe. They said it would be an abdication of responsibility. And what about our chivalrous feudatories, the Native Princes?

Excuses, excuses! rang round the land.

Agitation and repression followed. In this cycle one act stood out, whose effects were to be at least as haunting as the events of the Mutiny. It was the action of a British officer, one General Dyer, who opened fire on unarmed Indian civilians. He and his troops killed 379 people and wounded 1200. The wounded were left where they fell. Compatriots presented the General with a purse of £20,000. A band of Englishwomen, quite carried away, contributed a Sword of Honour. After this the notes of official disapproval sounded very thin indeed. Further cooperation with this kind of Government was clearly impossible.

These feelings crystallised around Gandhi. He began to forge a unique instrument (its news appeal was worldwide) to challenge the detested rulers. It involved disciplined, non-violent resistance to an imposed and untenable order. It included strikes, the withdrawal of services, and the withholding of taxes: a total non-cooperation with Government. It was this campaign that sent shivers down the spines of virtually everyone in authority from Viceroy to sub-inspector of police. It encouraged further repression, which led to further rebellion.

The struggle for independence had begun in earnest.

* * *

The Dewan was aware, not merely through what was released through official channels, but more reliably through his own network.

He was made even more sharply aware, that morning, by the bombshell that had landed on his desk. It was a telegram informing him that his daughter Vimala was in prison. His high-born and beloved daughter and her high-born and carefully chosen husband had both been incarcerated in the women's and men's wing, respectively, of the same prison across the border in British India.

He could not believe it. But here was his beloved youngest to confirm the unbelievable, summarily returned from the latest of her frequent and lengthy visits to this very household.

Since it was some time after the delivery of the first blow, the Dewan had recovered himself a little. He sent his peon to pay off

the bullock-cart (bullock-cart!) in which his penniless child had
arrived and then he said, calmly, arranging the roly-poly to
support the small of his back, which he suspected might sag,
  'What for?'
  'Well.'
Usha stood, and twisted. Her fingers had worked themselves
into a tight, bloodless trellis. Her sari was torn and skimpy, a
four-yard peasant garment, his shrinking eye saw, barely yielding a meagre pair of pleats, and tied ungracefully high like a
peasant's to exhibit ankles that were swollen and discoloured. It
was so out of place, so painful against the flowing and delicate
abundances of Dilkusha, that the Dewan could not continue.
Not, at least, on the disciplined lines he had set himself, which
were all swept away in the flood of concern for this washed-up
wraith, flesh of his flesh, twisting itself into knots on his hearth.
  'My dear child,' he said, 'sit down. You look dreadful. Are you
all right? That's all that matters. That's all I want to know.'
  'Really?'
  'For the moment.'
  'I'm all right.'
She sat down, grimy against the Herat, but exquisitely folded
in her old manner. That, at least, was intact, the Dewan noticed,
grateful for crumbs; and was further persuaded that despite
appearances so, basically, was his daughter. Reviving already, he
saw, cheeks rounding out, those appalling hands still. Composed, now, like the rest of her person. In the interplay of caring
flesh she had been racked, he clearly perceived, for him, not at
all for her state. Which continued, however, to distress him, as
well as others. Vibrations were reaching out from the servants,
hovering, too disciplined to enter until summoned, but holding
themselves at the ready, their breath all but shivering the bugle-
bead curtain. He had scarcely to touch the bell before they were
streaming in, ewer-bearer, maidservants, even the lordly cook,
honeyed offerings on wide platters under immaculate covers,
murmur of kindly voices for the bruised fledgling, child of this
house.
  Usha sighed. She was lolled, almost, against silky cushions.
  'How lovely it is to be back. In all this. It's heavenly.'
  'All this heaven is yours. Why did you leave it?'
  'Well, there are some things, don't you find, that one has to
do?'
  The room, which had throbbed and murmured—beads
trembling, birds in the garden, the passage of attentive feet—

grew very still. The Dewan looked up. Outside, he was surprised to see, the sun still shone.

'I do find,' he said, steadily, and very tenderly. 'But then, you see, I am that much older.'

Time went by after that, without jarring, marked only by the hour-glass that stood on a little silver pedestal, filled with coloured sand brought back by the children from the sea-shore at Cape Comorin, one holiday. Dried out long since and running freely in the globe blown by Feroze, the glass-blower from Damascus. Employed by the Palace, this magical man, and sent round by the Maharajah, that day, to charm the Minister's children as his own had been charmed.

The Dewan was content to watch the sand, and wait. He was a man of cultivated patience. And presently Usha was describing events.

'A meeting. To protest. Quite peaceful, but of course meetings are forbidden. That was what we were protesting about. One of the things. The police came very quickly, truckloads. And a magistrate. They ordered us to leave. Naturally we refused. Because basically, you see,' said Usha, massaging her ankles, 'it was an experiment. To see if discipline would hold, whatever.'

The Dewan saw, very well. The exercise of power, and its disciplines, were ancient and dynastic and these days national concerns. Only, one had somehow hoped young girls would not be saddled, his own at that, so early.

'And did it?' he asked, not without curiosity, apart from the desirability of knowing.

'It did,' said Usha, and rose above her state, so calm, so pure, that she seemed to him to be wrapped in some kind of rich and inviolable mantle instead of the deplorable cloth that his eye continued to see.

'It did. It was like a revelation. We didn't believe, you know, never really believed how much force there could be, if you trust yourself. But there is. I've never felt like that before. So powerful. All of us. All the fright gone. They couldn't have touched us whatever they did. I think they knew,' she said, 'but they arrested us.'

'All of you? How many?'

'Scores. Everyone except a handful. The magistrate didn't want it. I suppose he thought we weren't old enough. He came up to me,' she said starkly, and felt again the mundane ache in her ankles, 'and told me to go home.'

The Dewan, who was torn, whom indeed the recital had considerably mangled, managed to dredge up something of his own canons of order.

'I hope,' he said, with restraint, 'that it was not too painful a decision.'

Usha could have fallen at his feet. She felt she had never cared so much before. All smiles now, she unclasped her hands and flashed the ring he had placed on her finger.

'I wore it all the time to remind me,' she said. 'Although I was terribly afraid it would get broken.'

'Broken? No,' said the Dewan, remote, but gentle. 'You need a diamond to break a diamond.'

Then he made a great effort and wrenched up from abstractions.

'And who,' he asked tartly, 'in that company would have worn an equivalent stone?'

But he was comforted, in a spare way, that reminders he had thought to provide continued to uphold the disciplines he treasured, even if demonstrably powerless to act as the checks which he had also intended.

Vatsala cut short her annual pilgrimage to Kasi and returned to take charge of her daughter. But Usha, she found, had advanced, and was not to be in anyone's charge but her own. Not unruly about it, or defiant, but totally controlled in a manner that dismantled her mother, she went her own way.

Since you cannot fight for freedom, which is indivisible, without support citadels coming under siege; or on one front only, without challenging further frontiers. Or so Usha believed, not a shrill belief but a quiet and truthful inflow that built up her strength, gave her airs that Vatsala considered unsuited to her age. Though, being in part of the spirit, it was in fact an ageless matter.

Who would have thought? Vatsala often said to herself, and joined her thoughts to her husband's. They sat, one each end of the rosewood swing and rocked, gently. All their memories. All that care. Horoscopes and emissaries, and even the lands neglected while the squirrels (no doubt hearts thumping) feasted on the verandah. And in the outcome one child in a common jail while the other—

Yes, well, the other.

'Have you noticed,' said Vatsala, and traced with a finger the demure lotusbud carved in the rosewood. 'How Usha. And Rabi. So close these days.'

'It's natural,' said her husband. 'Their attitudes are not dis-similar. It's bound to bring them together.'

'But is it desirable,' said this matron, and closed up her lips.

Because she had no solution to offer to the intractable problems the times were creating, blowing them up like balloons that soared away out of one's control.

So she went about the house, carrying out domestic duties that had accumulated in her absence, which soaked up some of the fractious conjectures about Usha: coming up for seventeen, and not one arrangement concluded. Now and then she attacked her husband, in a subdued way, longing for bright and clever solutions to stream from him—attacks he bore with fortitude, the mind that could flash and dazzle, a saw with diamond edges, deliberately placed, it seemed to her, under a black velvet cover—and not really surprised when they didn't.

More frequently, and satisfactorily, she flew at her companions, the half dozen indigent relatives who had returned with her from Kasi. These ladies ran about in turn, distracted, asking what the world was coming to, the abode of bliss was full of their flustered notes (until the returning Dewan shut them up) but could not achieve what was intended.

There was even a point at which Vatsala considered approaching Mohini. Middle age had soused, if not finally extinguished, those indignant and jealous flares of earlier years. But, more realistically, she suspected that the irregular concubine would not intervene. Besides, she was these days, as anyone could see, absorbed in the Maharajah as much as he seemed to be in his (Vatsala jibbed at the word, but finally conceded it) constant concubine.

* * *

While the pair of them strolled, not merely in the supervised acres of Dilkusha, but in the unmanageable and spreading estates of the Palace where Vatsala could not follow. Not so much asserting, or even claiming, but simply assuming a liberty of thought and association.

They had, it is true, grown up, somewhat tentatively, side by side. It amused Rabi to remind Usha.

'Taught you to walk. No one else had the patience.'

Usha was plopping pebbles (small and selected, so as not to massacre the inhabitants) into the ornamental lake and feeling sorry for the carp who swam up, gaping, expecting bread and receiving stone.

'I suppose,' she said, 'I would have learnt eventually, as people do.'

'But it helped, don't you think?' said Rabi, mildly, and passed her half the loaf he carried, to stop her maltreating the fish.

'Too young to remember,' said Usha, pushing fish bread into her mouth, and glazing her eyes to smother a glimmering, of thumb enclosed in fleshy fist, that did remain.

'Well, I do,' said Rabi. 'You were always asking, straight from the shoulder. Like an empress. A child's gestures are superbly simple to understand.'

'Why,' said Usha. 'Is it so difficult now?'

'Sometimes,' he admitted. 'There's been a whole experience, hasn't there? For both of us? Sometimes it is difficult.'

'Not really,' said Usha. 'Well, a little. One's adult repertoire is bound to have grown, but it isn't basically less comprehensible than a child's, is it?'

She rose, brushing crumbs off her lap. Her gaze had altered, and now possessed a total clarity that drew his mind with its promise of a truthful response. If he asked, he felt, she would always answer; if you made the right appeal, at the right time, she would not hold back but would make herself available. More than ever it seemed to him that they were flowing along some common stream, in which fluid exchanges were not so much possible as inevitable.

It was after this, one of those long lucid days that come after the rains, they were out walking, the river a distant objective, when he stopped to show her, a spot near the verges of woodland where the grass grew tall.

'I was conceived here,' he said, watching her, that pared profile that sometimes presented nothing but bones, but at times resembled some exquisite sculpture. 'My father told me. When I was about fifteen, and he thought he ought. Or my mother made him.'

'Here, exactly?' She turned her face to him. She could have been filled, he saw, with the mystery, or the beauty, of how things happened.

'Hereabouts,' he said. 'You know my father. One of his lordly waves.'

'He's a lucky man,' said Usha. Grasses reflected in her eyes touched them with limpid greens. 'Or brave. They both are. It's been a free union.'

'Yes,' said Rabi, and drew a long breath. 'It's the only way he's been free. Through my mother. She was—is—the one who lifted the veil. Made him see what it could be like. In one area.'

'One area's been rich enough,' said Usha. 'You can see it a mile off, when they're together.'

'Yes. But think what it would be like,' he dreamed, 'if it could be extended into every corner . . . just one isn't really enough, is it?'

'No,' said Usha, who saw the tender conversions that were overtaking him, and herself began to be filled with longings, soft if heady desires woven into distances that his vision was spinning.

'Perhaps not for us,' she said. 'We've been spoilt. But your mother—did what she could, at the time. As one does.'

'Would you?' he asked. Very dry, in case she declined to answer.

'Yes,' she said, and pulled him up from the grassy knoll on which, perhaps hopefully, he had thrown himself. 'Yes, I would, if I felt I had to.'

They continued to walk, towards the object of the expedition, although this object was tacked on rather than integral to their purpose of enjoying the day, which had turned out to be one of clarity, and full of the finest scents and lights.

'All yours,' said Usha, once, as they were passing through an orchard.

'In due course, possibly,' he agreed. 'But I shouldn't bank on it.'

Though he did reach up and snap off a branch on which the sapodilla clustered, it being a day that invited these liberal flourishes, and the fruit being ready for eating.

Woodland and orchards behind, now the plain began to tilt, straining towards the river which was soon in sight. Here women were gathered, with their water-pots and washing, and children with smaller children straddling their hips, and away from all this human flap waders and fishers on pale, circumspect stilts. All of a piece, it seemed to him then, these tender figures in a familiar landscape, and not least the girl, or woman, who walked alongside him in sandals, and a sari that barely covered the bones of her ankle joints. She fitted into the countryside.

He would have said so, except that by now they had begun to communicate less in words than through breath, and skin, and silence, and other eloquent but improbable instruments. She, too, preferred to give no sign but spread her skirts and settled herself on the riverbank where children stood, but soon came up, some bold, some shyly, to present their smiles and compliments.

Since both were perfectly well known, having, roughly speaking, grown up in these parts.

* * *

The Dewan was aware. He could scarcely remain unaware, what with his wife, and the suppressed but nonetheless eloquent women, and sightings in the distance. As, however, there was little he could do, he set this daughter aside while he dwelt on her gaolbird sister.

This matter festered until finally one day he apprised the Resident. For what reason he could not entirely fathom, but connected, he discovered, with acrimony. It became plain with the first word he uttered.

'Your Government,' he said, and paused as it struck him, but went on, 'your Government, Resident Sahib, has imprisoned my daughter.'

The Resident frowned. He was a preoccupied man, engaged, at that moment, in personally reviving a cineraria. There was mud on his trousers and also somewhere, grittily, inside his shoes. But for shoes, and skin, he could have passed for a gardener.

'Prison, yes, only place,' he said. 'It's these hot-heads, kicking up a fuss. There's a lot of it about, Dewan Sahib.'

Then it came to him, and he ceased to be a gardener, or even rejuvenator of his wife's loves.

'Your daughter! My dear fellow, why didn't you say so! I'll get her out at once. No difficulty at all. At once, drop everything.'

At which point he did indeed let fall the trowel.

It so shamed the Dewan that he felt totally unable to pursue the vendetta. Especially since the cineraria was now clearly doomed.

'I am grateful, Excellency,' he said, 'but it would do no good . . . since the objective has not been realised she would merely court arrest again. Our young people are determined, and ardent.'

'It's a time of life, Dewan Sahib.'

Sir Arthur was quite melancholy, remembering the pretty infant, now apparently grown and tedious; and also guiltily aware, his mind embowered around his own returning child, of a touch or two of *schadenfreude*.

'The times themselves, Excellency,' the Dewan corrected, not to injure, but to keep the picture straight.

The Resident informed the Maharajah, who had already heard directly from his Minister, who conveyed the facts in one brief neutral sentence and retired.

Sometimes I think the man has no human feelings whatever, the Maharajah said to himself. These thoughts, and others, were robust by day and resounded convincingly.

It was the nights.

* * *

Nights were clear at this season. The rains had laid the dust. Moons of a polished perfection rose and slid over the city, slung low in the sky. People came out to look at the gleaming scimitars of new moons, or when full, to bask in silver floods before turning in. Once in, however, there were those who could not sleep. They lay, restless between sheets that grew stale with their pitching bodies; or rigidly, staring up at the blackened rafters of their bare dwellings.

Ramdas was one of these. He had dragged his charpoy to the front of his hut where the moonlight straggled in, and he lay, somewhat cruciform on the strings, and wondered how far his spirit could be counted on to carry him. Sometimes it sprouted a very fine pair of wings indeed, such as those that had swept him into the presence first of the Dewan, then of the Maharajkumar himself. But sometimes it cringed, earthbound, a thing of clay; nothing would make it soar. At which point Ramdas began to toss and feel the ropes under his back, for it seemed to him the height of foolish presumption to have pledged himself to the Maharajkumar on the basis of this fluctuating quantity. He had to think of the man to whom he had made these pledges—half his age, stroking the ruffled plumage of the falcon he carried on his glove—before he could replace the terrible clay images with bird avatars; and so, finally, compose himself for sleep.

Rabi was another. Some nomadic strain, his father suggested, that made him want to sleep in the open long after the hot season was over. Not sleeping however, but merely lying on his bed, within stone's throw of the tent his bearer had pitched and crawled into with distaste. Far from a nomad, this man; his city soul longed for palatial corridors on which to stretch his carcase; but he was incurably distrustful of the guards who were posted. So he did his best, under canvas, which he hoped would deflect the worst of that lunar light, to personally safeguard the prince. Poised for protective sorties, he nevertheless contrived to sleep, envied by the object of his concern who guessed, from an impression of subsiding flounces, that this faithful guardian had at last succumbed.

While he continued sleepless, his mind roving. Thinking of his father, the pivot, on whom the phalanx of troops wheeled in this ceremonial, or military, movement. Of Usha, and the disciplines she advocated and practised to aid the campaign they were developing in Devapur: disciplines that, reflecting his own, appealed to his nature. Thinking of Devapur State. That word *state*, nothing could be more fitting for that interlocking of abstract and physical, land and the people on it, a mesh that approached in intricacy the bonding of body and mind. The pair of them spliced together, not too well, one or the other forever sighing over the deficiencies of its sluggish partner. Usha often sighed, complaining of her pampered flesh, which felt the blows too easily.

So did Ramdas. Foolhardy man, rising up out of the ground like some genii, where any other would have soberly carried his petition to one of the durbars at which the Maharajah conscientiously presided for this very purpose. Himself shouting at this apparition. Apparition announcing it was armour-clad by virtue of spirit.

It wasn't this nebulous mail that saved him, however. It was the horse, scenting mania, unwilling to injure a creature not in its right mind; and in superb control of its muscles and nerves.

Ramdas admitted it, later.

Then it was Rabi's turn to wonder.

At this stage he became conscious of the dew that was falling, a light fall, but sufficient to make him pull up first a sheet and then the *paschmina* shawl that had belonged to his grandmother. Under which, presently, he slept.

Bawajiraj could not escape either; possibly there was communication.

He lay motionless out of consideration for Mohini and watched the moonlight streaming in and tangling with the mother-o'-pearl on the scalloped alcoves in a bluish and ghostly contest. Baulked of sleep, his mind picked over the days, sometimes as rough as a scavenger, sometimes holding its breath for fear of what might escape too ruthless a lunge.

Looking. Listening.

To silences. Or rather a thinning of sound; what had been full-throated once whittled away, so cunningly done you would not realise, but for comparisons. His son. Swelling crescendoes, people putting their heart into it when this candidate appeared, straw in his hair so to speak, shirt open to the navel; and for himself, in his robes of state, huge kettledrums beating from hill to hill, crowds who shouted politely with their lungs.

All he had ever wished for for his son, coming true. Prayers answered. Only, this devilish twist to divine requitals.

Then Bawajiraj began to feel afraid. A thin sweat pushed up evenly, head to toe. If he stood up now, naked, there would be a steamy nimbus about his body, he became convinced. But when he did stand up he discovered, somewhat surprised, that he was wearing pyjamas, a stout striped pair acquired in England, which mercifully concealed any peculiar effusions there might have been. It consoled him, somewhat. He got back into bed, between the sheets, and fitted himself around the sleeping Mohini for those flesh-to-flesh reassurances she continued to provide, and he to need, in what they comfortably called their spoons position.

It was funny how different everything looked in the morning. When he woke, sharp at seven, the sun was throwing enchanting clover patterns through the pierced marble. The room was cheery and bright, the smoky alcoves were gleaming but sane, the only notes of deathly hush were what the servitors were commanded to provide until the Palace was up and had gathered its wits.

It was all so pleasant and reassuring that Bawajiraj dismissed certain quakings of the night. Imagination, he felt, or indigestion; greedy Waji should have known better than to feast on quail for dinner. He got up briskly, pausing only to kiss Mohini (fast asleep, incorrigible slugabed, no State duties to claim *her*) before departing to make ready for his duties.

It was a Tuesday, durbar day. Mondays, Tuesdays, and Thursdays were durbar days, when from eight till eleven he placed himself at the disposal of his subjects. He enjoyed these days. It was a privilege, he felt, coasting along the polished corridors, to receive petitions, to listen to grievances, to do all in his power to mitigate the blows of fate, to fulfil legitimate desires, and to dispense justice. It was privilege and pleasure and duty rolled into one: what Sir Arthur fondly called, on daring incursions into the language, one's *mai/bap* functions. Father and mother to his people. By now Bawajiraj's heart was so full, so eager to give, that it was disappointing to see how few had arrived to receive.

The Durbar Hall was barely populated. A matter of mere hundreds. Whereas the day before (a Wednesday: Rabi presided on Wednesdays) he distinctly remembered the crush gates of the farther courtyard having to be closed.

The Maharajah was pleased for his son, naturally. But the misgivings of the night were rather horridly revived when the pattern began to repeat, run-of-the-mill occasions equalling special events in reacting to his presence with something less than fervour.

* * *

Bawajiraj mentioned it in passing to the Dewan.

'Have you noticed, Minister,' he said, casually, 'how the Maharajkumar. Huge audiences, of late.'

The Minister, fresh and starched, and crisp these days from satisfactory alliance with Rabi, said, briskly,

'It is to be expected, Highness. The common mind identifies the Maharajkumar with Water, whereas your Highness is identified with Salt.'

And made deprecatory gestures dissociating from responsibility, while heaping coals.

Bawajiraj, struck speechless, thought it typical of this Brahminy biscuit. Implying these revenues went to keep him, the Maharajah, in comfort, and ignoring the fact that they were necessary to meet the obligations of the State to the Crown. *The honour of my State*, he felt like reminding the odious man; only one knew from experience it would be a waste of breath.

It fell to the representative of the Crown, the Resident, to sustain the besieged Maharajah. Wise, Sir Arthur agreed, to keep the Permanent Garrison at full strength. Only sensible, with all this unrest. Act of a statesman. A reduction of these forces, he frankly revealed, would be as unacceptable to him as it was to Waji. Indeed, he had to concede his predecessor had had a point. Indeed, privately he felt he owed the man a debt, relieving him of the necessity for the deed and saddling himself with the obloquy. However, he did feel he could have thought of something better than the Salt tax, people were inordinately touchy about it.

After this they turned to more agreeable matters, namely the instituting of a croquet court. It was the Maharajah's idea. He had been much taken with the gentle sport during his stay in England, and the happy thought had come to translate this game of summery English lawns to Devapur. It would, he ventured to hope, please Lady Copeland, who had been civil to him in London, and who was due out soon, together with the enchanting Sophie. The picture was already forming, in pastels more or less, of a table set for tea, in the garden on a fine afternoon, with floury scones under silver domes, petal-thin bread-and-butter on rose-pink doyleys, cherries in golden bowls from the railhead at Chaman; and from somewhere less distant the blissful click of mallet on ball.

Sir Arthur had agreed to assist, after some hesitation; but continued to feel the grass was different.

However, he accompanied the Maharajah. They strolled, side by side, towards the crew who were mustered on the lawn, drooping but ready, armed with a wide selection of implements that would, they hoped, take care of orders of the most freakish, mind-bending variety, such as were known to flow when Palace and Residency combined.

17

Sophie.

Sophie Sahiba was back. The servants ran about, faces split foolishly, telling each other. The Lord Sahib's daughter had returned to her home. Ayah could not speak of it enough. Even Copeland Sahib's dreadful cruelty in sending his own child away was forgiven, redeemed by this act of blessed if tardy restoration. One cannot, she told the *syce*, live without one's kith and kin forever, as had been revealed to the Sahib in his later years, since God in his mercy set no age limits to the acquiring of wisdom.

The *syce* agreed, with half his mind. He had come out of some dungeon of retirement, and stood blinking in the sunlight, wrestling with the problem of what he had done with Star's bones. He would be asked, he knew; he knew Europeans' obsession with bones; he would have liked to devote his mind to it only there was this woman, gabbling. After a little he succeeded in detaching from her, and fixed his gaze on the ground, searching it desperately for clues in these last few minutes before the Sahiba's lightning felled him.

But Sophie had yet to place him. She stood in the portico, surrounded. The severed ends of her life, sealed since her abrupt departure, were, she was discovering, not incapable of regeneration. The dark faces that had hovered, blurred by distance and different skies, and been finally treated as figments, swam up boldly in this bright light and declared themselves to be real.

That face, for instance—how could she have forgotten?—belonged to loving Ayah, whom she had loved fiercely, once.

There was even a sense of *them*—who, exactly, was gone—unplaiting her fingers, which were desperately locked about a desperate neck. Next to her the *syce*, his face refused recall but his hands came back, laced into a supporting cradle for her foot. And after him a memory of the bearer, herself astride his shoulders, reaching up to retrieve a shuttlecock. If she walked between these ranks now, round the verandah and past the canna beds, she would, she knew, come upon the tree, a golden laburnum, in whose trailing racemes the shuttlecock was snared. And if she kept on there would be roses, climbing up a trellis, and a tangle of greenery in which a new life was beginning to crack its shell. All of it was hers, all of it was rushing back, the whole bright immense tapestry with herself worked into the design.

She looked so dizzy that it disturbed the young cavalryman who had escorted Miss Copeland (in a motor-car) and her mother to the Residency. He wondered if he should tender some advice about the impact of the Indian sun, until luckily he remembered this was an Indian family. Three generations, if he recalled aright, had served the country, and Sophie—as he thought of her—had spent seven years of her life here, to his one. Blushing slightly at this close shave, the attentive officer cleared his throat and said,

'You must be tired, Miss Copeland, after your journey. May I suggest that we postpone the formalities until later?'

'Formalities, Captain Lomax?'

Sophie was still wrapped in her tapestry. Reaching her through its tight weave the young man's words sounded woolly.

'Well, this er . . . reception committee.'

He waved a hand at the giddy company, some of whose members had flower garlands concealed like weapons behind their backs, and leaning a little closer to his dazzling companion said, confidentially,

'These people do tend to overdo the jubilee . . . I'd dodge 'em, Miss Copeland, if I were you.'

And cupped an elbow, firmly, while not presuming.

Sophie, still dreaming, obeyed; it was an authoritative touch, inculcated in Captain Lomax quite possibly from infancy, coming to full bloom on these juvenile shores. As she was turning away, however, something made her stop, and release herself, and reach for the desperate bouquet, trussed up like a fowl in silver thread, with a lime in the centre, that some diminutive and invisible well-wisher was urgently waving above the crush of heads. After which they proceeded.

Lady Copeland had already been conducted by even more highly seasoned entourage (Colonel Wilmot: dear devoted Charles, a tower of strength, what would one do without one's old friends?) into the formal drawing-room. He had handed her into a chair where billows from the ceiling fans soothed, rather than buffeted, the occupant, and now stood on the hearth, on the polished porphyry, and wondered at the courage of women who came out time and again to join their husbands in serving a hot and thankless country. He was, indeed, more than a little concerned by the pale tones Mary Copeland displayed, which nearing Port Said had begun to make inroads, and east of Suez were devastatingly in evidence. Some delicacy, however, prevented him from remarking on a pallor which, strictly, more closely approached those appalling mongolian yellows most dreaded by his countrywomen. Instead he said, bluff but kindly,

'Done my poor best, Mary. I hope you'll find everything as you want it.'

'Thank you, Charles. I'm sure I shall.'

Mary Copeland replied gently, raising eyes which, whatever eastern encroachments disfigured her skin, would continue flawless and steadfastly to assert her own heritage. Looking into those blue lakes Charles Wilmot became convinced of a beauty that did not in fact exist, but which would never fail to cast its spell over him and those in similar exile.

'Arthur would never forgive me, you know,' he murmured, 'if anything . . .'

'Everything is perfect, Charles, I do assure you.'

Lady Copeland spoke softly, very soft in a mist of hyacinth, easing off her silk gloves by the tips while contemplating the arrangement of urns upon the verandah.

'Because you're to summon me at once, if anything. You do understand, Mary, don't you.'

The Colonel searched the features on which the light fell so harshly, and was moved by the frailty they often conveyed to add with a genuine anxiety, although he was not one to flap,

'I hope, my dear, it will not prove too arduous a time for you.'

'Arduous, Charles?'

Because when was it not arduous? The heat, the dust, the disease, the people with their terrible suffering eyes. Lady Copeland all but glimmered.

Colonel Wilmot found it magnificent, and entirely in keeping. Arthur, he felt, was fortunate in a wife who exemplified the qualities that were needed out here. Arthur's absence, however (he was conferring urgently with the Viceroy in Delhi), placed on him responsibilities that prompted him to pursue it further.

'More so than usual,' he said, and laid a protective hand on the back of her chair. 'I'm afraid, my dear, it's going to be a difficult time for all of us.'

'Difficult?' Lady Copeland laughed, and patted the hand that rested above her shoulder. 'When, my dear Charles, are things on this continent ever easy?'

Colonel Wilmot said no more. A little local unpleasantness, he could see, would not be allowed to ruffle a single hair. He would have liked to pour his unbounded admiration into some small bearable tribute, but he did not find it easy at the best of times, and now the young people had come in: his delightful god-daughter, and Sebastian, whom he had specially selected to escort her on, so to speak, her debut.

'Well, Sophie. Everything to your liking?'

He twinkled at her; she really was quite a beauty.

'Oh yes, thank you. Everything's absolutely lovely! Why didn't anyone tell me?'

Sophie flung herself onto the formal crimson, herself anything but formal. Her cheeks were flushed, and her hair clung damply to her forehead, but she was not conscious of heat in the wealth of other emotions. Strong citrous and tuberose scents rose in an intemperate mixture from the nosegay she carried, and into which she had plunged her face.

Unbridled, was the adjective that came to Lady Copeland's mind. She did not approve of unbridled reactions, which one met at every turn in this country. She would not, however, deal with it now. Sophie should be enlightened, later. Told of the truth of India, treacherous Mata Hari. Warned to keep clear. For to love would only result in a trail of ruin and disaster.

But it could come later. At this stage she only said,

'Sophie, dear, what is there to tell?'

Dryly, and clasping a square of cambric to deflect the extravagant scents which the fan-blades were slapping in her face.

'Especially, Miss Copeland, since you have been over here for seven years,' said the Captain, to whom seven years did seem a long time, and with whom it was beginning to rankle. He would so much have enjoyed showing Sophie round virgin territory.

'I'm sure there's a good deal nevertheless, Sebastian,' the Colonel soothed the young man, 'to which you can introduce Sophie.'

'Indeed, sir. I shall be delighted.'

'There you are, Sophie.'

The Colonel was himself delighted. He was not, heaven forbid, *matchmaking*, but one did enjoy bringing together the children of one's lifelong friends.

'You may depend on Sebastian, my dear,' he said, 'to place himself, military duties permitting, entirely at your disposal. That right, Sebastian?'

'Certainly, Miss Copeland.'

The unfortunate Captain blushed even more fiercely, waves of colour poured rather touchingly down his neck and vanished into his military collar. But Sophie did not see. She was still caught up in her past, its waves swept over her as ungovernably as Sebastian's scarlet.

'Seven years,' she dreamed. 'I can hardly believe it. It seems like yesterday, some of it. So clear. But some of it's completely gone.'

'What do you remember, Sophie?'

'So *many* things. Ayah. My pony. You, Uncle Charles, carrying that huge doll you bought to console me, when all I wanted was to go to—was it the Delhi Durbar?'

'Bless my soul, yes! I scoured the entire bazaar, my dear girl, for that doll. Anything to stop you crying your eyes out, since your mother had left me *in loco parentis*. But,' said the Colonel, rather flatly, 'it didn't. Never saw such floods.'

'Well, I didn't want to be left behind. Everybody was going. On elephants—*imagine!*'

'In perfectly ordinary trains.'

Lady Copeland glimmered again, as she corrected her daughter.

'Yes, I remember now,' said Sophie. 'The servants told me—no, it was the prince, Ayah called him the prince.'

'The prince,' said Colonel Wilmot, emerging rather suddenly from his bazaar rambles, 'is becoming something of a nuisance.'

'Nuisance, Charles?' Lady Copeland raised an eyebrow. 'We met him at home. I must say Arthur found him unexceptionable.'

'I mean the son,' said the Colonel.

'Rabi,' said Sophie, with the pleasure of suddenly placing a memory.

If there was some effect of a stone being lobbed into a placid, if polished, millpond, no one except the young officer gave any impression of having heard the splash. Bit much, Sebastian felt, Sophie on terms of such intimacy when he and she had yet to progress to Christian names. He trembled a little, and had to put down his tea-cup. Colonel Wilmot continued to sip at Darjeeling with a steady hand. Mary, he felt sure, could take care of anything.

Lady Copeland, certainly, was capable. Later, she promised herself, later. Aloud she said,

'You mean the Maharajkumar, Sophie dear. The heir-apparent, as he is now. At the time he was, of course, a nobody. More tea, anyone?'

While Sophie continued to grope, disturbed by ripples that were spreading, lapping at shores on which she stood.

'A nobody,' she said, 'a Maharajah's son?'

'Sophie has a good deal to learn,' an amused Lady Copeland informed the room. To Sophie she said:

'He wasn't designate then, you see. One or two irregularities. We didn't confirm his position until—well, years later, really.'

And inflected, slightly, so that Sophie became aware of dark presences, mounted on ballbearings, engaged in conjuring away the ceremonial of tea. *Not in front of the servants* rose up strongly, and effectively muted her.

Lady Copeland might have been relieved, except that one did not even remotely expect anything else. She had drifted to the window, where the view continued to distract her. That extraordinary clumping of urns, not to mention the jumble inside them!—which made one fear for the rest of the garden, if not the Residency itself. But she, superb choreographer, would put it right, gardens and residence and that special retreat within it in which they could pursue their lives unmolested by India.

Already in her mind she was supervising the unpacking of the crates and trunks that she could see jogging past on the heads of coolies through the West gates. Soon she would settle to arranging the contents, in cool rooms that would close round them softly, offering no quarter to intruders.

The picture was coming along nicely, rounded out with mementoes of trophies and photographs in silver frames, when, unaccountably, it lurched out of control, giving way to strange impressions of siege. Certainly the admirable arrangement was in disarray, and all these objects, the components of her vision, were taking on more than a passing resemblance to sandbags, piled up under windows against rising and disagreeable tides.

Only Lady Copeland's considerable skills enabled her to restore, presently, the original consoling design.

* * *

Salt, elsewhere, continued to rub into wounds.

Mohini was so incensed when she finally discovered the details that she refused the Maharajah her bed. Bawajiraj had to stretch out beside her on a camp-cot, which in the jungle on hunting trips he took to like a duck to water, but found insupportable within the Palace. It creaked dreadfully when they quarrelled. They were quarrelling now. Since his return, in the sweetness of reunion, the Maharajah had forgotten how tigerish his consort could be, and now, he felt, was to be reminded. Mohini was up on an elbow, on her queenly couch, which gave her height and advantage.

'Do you know how long a peasant has to work to pay your tax?'

'Not *my* tax.'

'It *is* your tax. You could abolish it tomorrow if you wanted.'

'I can't. I'm not as free as you think.'

'Exactly. You're bound hand and foot.'

'Nonsense. I'm a perfectly free agent but there are limits.'

'What limits?'

'Limits placed upon one by one's obligations.'

'What obligations?'

'Is this the time to go into it?'

'I don't care about the time! But if you want to know, yes, it is the time. High time.'

'Mohini, you know I haven't been sleeping well—'

'It's your own fault. If you had a clear conscience—'

'My conscience is perfectly clear.'

'Then why can't you sleep?'

So he did try. He closed his eyes. When the strain proved too great he rolled up the shutters and she was still angularly poised, and waiting to re-engage.

'It takes a peasant three weeks' labour in the fields to earn enough to pay your tax, do you know that?'

'Do you expect me to carry all this kind of detail in my head?'

'Why shouldn't you? You call yourself the Head of State, don't you?'

'I *am* the Head of State!'

'Then you should know.'

'I suppose he told you.'

'*He?* Do you mean Rabi?'

'Of course I mean Rabi.'

'Then why can't you say his name? Can't you get your tongue round your own son's name?'

'Don't be so *absurd.*'

'I'm not being at all absurd. Your English friends have that difficulty and you get more like them every day.'

'Is that so awful?'

'It's *frightful!*'

'Civilised people.'

'Civilised wolves. No, not wolves. I *like* wolves.'

'Mohini, you're so prejudiced—'

'So would you be, if you were in your right mind. And if you want to know, Rabi didn't tell me. It's common knowledge, the smallest bazaar urchin. You'd know too if you weren't so rarefied.'

No, no one in the kingdom. Bar one. Say two. Nowadays the Dewan had lapses, forgot he was a salaried employee.

'I sometimes wonder,' Bawajiraj was inspired to say, 'if you are in your right mind.'

'I am. *We* are. It's you. Your mother would have been ashamed if—'

'Please leave my mother out of it.'

'Why should I? Your mother was my guardian. She warned me not to take up with you.'

'Then why did you?'

'I loved you.'

'What did she say?'

Bawajiraj could not restrain his curiosity. His mother had always been a mystery to him.

'She said we were incompatible.'

'But we're not! Couldn't have been closer. Couldn't *be* closer, mostly.'

'That's flesh.'

'Are you telling me it's not important to you?'

'She meant spirit.'

'I have reason to think that my spirit—'

'It's monstrous. I thought not, but I've changed my mind. You're a monster to your people.'

'I think I can safely say that my people—'

'*Your* people! They *were*. *Now* you can count your people on the fingers of one hand and all of them are toadies. They're Rabi's people.'

'Of course they are. I rejoice at it. In due course, when I'm gone. It's the natural order.'

'Now,' cried Mohini. '*I mean now.*'

And trembled. As one must when the natural order is upset. As did Bawajiraj, though not for himself.

'Have you,' he said, very quiet and anguished, 'no respect at all?'

'For what should I have respect?'

'For me. For me as occupant of the *gaddi*.'

Her tears were flowing. Huge drops of a total misery, welling up out of an anguish hardly less than his.

'You cannot command,' she said. 'Highness, you cannot command respect.'

'I'm not commanding. I'm asking.'

But she could not bear to answer. She stuffed her face in the pillow, and soaked it; seeing which he rose, creaking frantically, and brought her another and plumped it up tenderly, cradling her head while he shovelled it into place. She could no longer hold out then. She dried her eyes and made room for him, and rather thankfully, constitutionally incapable of harbouring a grudge, he got in readily beside her.

She had not answered, however; and he was careful not to ask her again.

* * *

Rabi saw the blotches that his mother could not always hide from him. There were barriers, however, that she, not he, would have to surmount. She tried, that day.

'Your father,' she said, warily, walking the tightrope of her split loyalties, 'can be a stubborn man.'

'Oh? When,' said Rabi, 'did you make the startling discovery?'

It surprised them all, from time to time, how much that was fair, with invitations to tenderness and laughter, was left even between these riven families.

Mohini pressed her advantage.

'I wish,' she said, and watched him whittling at wood—it looked to her like a boomerang—'I wish, Rabi, you would be kind to him. Gentle. He does take it to heart.'

'It was not I,' said Rabi, 'who ordered camp-cots to be sent in.'

And continued to whittle.

While they continued to nag, certain strictures of his which were valid, and perhaps even inevitable in the circumstances, but which abraded incessantly. One in particular, a curt refusal to call on the Resident, a small ambition of the Maharajah's, framed with some ardour not on politic but entirely personal grounds. So that presently he put aside other concerns and went round to his father's apartments to make amends.

Bawajiraj was in his bath, an imported tub that squatted square and somewhat barbarically on original and exquisite tilework. He modestly floated a square of towelling on the soapy water before greeting his son.

'Ah, Rabi. Take a pew. Be with you in a second.'

'No hurry,' said Rabi. He hoisted himself onto a ledge on which essences lurked in bottles and began unstoppering and snuffing each in turn. Steam, which had risen purely, began to turn variegated.

'Just came round to say I've reconsidered,' he said, to get it over quickly. 'Perhaps I ought to call on the Resident.'

'My dear Rabi, how very sensible of you!'

Bawajiraj, battling against a rainbow of vapours, coughed and beamed through the clouds. 'Never mix your flavours, my dear boy, if you will permit your father a word of advice. Yes, as I was saying—hand me my towel, there's a good fellow—courtesy costs so little and it gives such enormous returns.'

'I don't expect any kind of return,' said Rabi, gloomily, but passing the towel. Already he was beginning to suffer misgivings.

'No, of course not. Only bounders. I meant in terms that are ineffable and quite, quite incomputable. No, don't run away, Rabi. So many preoccupations, we hardly have an opportunity—'

And marched, commanding in his toga, with his captive in tow, to the glistening palaestra where they sluiced him again (after all that nasty swilling in a bath-tub) before his masseur would accept his flesh. Body on slab, face twisted sideways on the padded block, he continued to discourse between kneadings and pummelings. About his belief in law and order, and the marvellous kindness disbursed him from all quarters in England; about the proposal for the appointment of an ADC to the Viceroy (guess who, Rabi) with which Sir Arthur had returned from Delhi; about the superb stallion that Pooky, soul of generosity, had despatched as a gift, and about the training of falcons.

At which at last they began to move together. Certainly Rabi revived, surfacing from depths into which preceding observations had plunged him to punt along in these easy reaches.

'Prithviraj?'* he said. 'He's coming along well. A reckless lover, but what can you expect with that name?'

And smiled, at an evocation of the little tiercel that rode with

*Prithviraj, dashing twelfth-century ruler of Delhi who carried off the daughter of the king of Kanauj. A popular hero.

him, the extraordinary beauty of its markings, and the relationship that had worked up between them, juddering and suspicious at first, on both sides, resolving into a trust that brought the magnificent predator back from a free flight to glide, jesses trailing, and fold its wings and compose itself on his fist.

Clean young prince, Bawajiraj beheld, even from his sideways position. From which he was tempted to consider, a little wistfully, what it would be like if that profile were always as clear, so that his words could flow without sticking and catching as he was often conscious they did; and, more robustly, to be convinced by the uncluttered countenance that there were no impediments that could not be chiselled away, with cunning and patience, and smoothed off afterwards, enabling them to proclaim a common affiliation and purpose.

While the bird that had balanced like a dancer suddenly dug in its talons, talons sharp through the leather, feathers ruffed up, mewling shrilly as it glared reddish and furious at Ramdas.

Then Rabi would have retracted, had he been able. As he could not, he began to resent the deal which had just been concluded, as one must every concession of critical territory.

* * *

Rabi believed that but for this he would not have met the Resident's daughter as he did, informally, in a garden, where the air played natural tunes rather than the correct symphonies elsewhere exacted.

Possibly he was right. Possibly the ropes of enclaves, which children skipped over, recovering their designed function might have restrained their adult persons. Certainly he had no desire otherwise; the schism was deepening, visibly sown with glassy splinters. But here he was, in the Residency compound, his father's hosannahs disagreeably close to the tolling of cracked bells, to wait on the Resident and his lady; and coming upon the Missie Sahib instead.

Poised in herself, and at the head of the noble flight down which she would swoop, blue ribbons flying.

There were no blue ribbons, however. Sophie was older. She came down the stairs soberly, but welcoming, one arm girding the inevitable animal, the other extended to greet him.

'Rabi.'

The deep pleasure of framing a memory: raising it, fleshing it, robing it, writing down the name with a gold pen and ink.

'Sophie,' he responded.

To the small girl who had been his pupil, or partner, in this very arena. She flooded back. The enamels that had been dulled were suddenly blazing. The sunbonnet turned into this delicious hat, while no more able to contain those flares which alone had remained bright in his mind. A host of memories were breeding in their clasp.

Then Rabi recollected himself, this girl, her father, the place, the attendants in Residency livery.

'Welcome to Devapur, Miss Copeland,' he said formally, and released her hand.

'This *hat*,' said Sophie. 'Here, hold him will you? He won't bite, I hope.'

And bundled some curly auburn object into his arms while she attacked the straw with skewers.

At least she didn't fling it down and trample on it, saw thankful Ayah, who had been half expecting it of her baba, and was prepared to rush, old bones permitting.

'He does bite,' said Rabi, and shortened the leash so that the puppy should not turn and snap again. 'I came, actually,' he said, 'to call on your father, Miss Copeland. I gather he's out.'

'Beastly cur,' said Sophie, taking him back to her bosom. 'Yes, he's out. Should I,' she asked, 'address you as Maharajkumar Sahib?'

At which he had to confess he had no wish to go back on their past. The past was valid, whatever the present, for all that its fabric had evolved in the formidable innocence of another age.

'Not unless you insist,' he said, and dredged up some grace and added, 'I hope you won't insist.'

'Bargain,' said Sophie, and jiggled the lead. Her shoulders hinted at impatience. 'One feels compelled, don't you find? A hateful sense of compulsion.'

'About what?'

He could not imagine. He had not tried to, as yet.

'All sorts of things. Big, small, middling. Just now,' she said, 'I had to resist an overwhelming compulsion to offer you a sherry.'

'Should one,' he suggested mildly, 'go that far?'

'If you're dying for a sherry—'

'Not dying. I'm perfectly happy.'

For by now they were walking easily, rid of assiduous attendants, dog gone to dog-boy, along shady, bordered, sweet-smelling paths.

'So am I,' said Sophie, and drew long breaths, as if to cure some crimping of which she had become conscious. 'I'm so happy to be back. I wish I'd never been sent away. But it's all coming back. Well, nearly all. What's this?'

'Frangipani.'

'And this?'

'Mimosa. Cousin to mimosa. Closes up if you touch.'

'I knew I knew it. Isn't it enchanting?'

'It used to entrance me as a child. I closed up a whole plant once.'

'I'll try, shall I?'

'Why not? The day's young.'

'Don't watch then, or I shall feel foolish.'

He could not believe that. He watched her crouch beside the plant, touching crazily, leaves were folding. The closed leaves were a dusty silver. Silver transmitted surrealist tinges to the bush, which was peevishly shaking itself back to an orderly green almost as fast as she touched.

'Come and help!' she cried.

But they could not win. They stood, rather hot, and even ridiculous, over the composed foliage. Laughing, however. The simplest things revealed edges of laughter.

'Tell me,' invited Sophie, as they resumed their stroll, 'more.'

'More about what?'

'Anything you like. Interesting, amusing things.'

'For instance.'

'What you do, for instance.'

'I wouldn't dare to.'

'Why not?'

'Doings of an heir to State are a State secret.'

'Is there,' she enquired, 'a word to express utter disbelief?'

'You could say *"shabash,"* ' he replied, 'or even try *"wah, wah."* '

'It's totally irresponsible,' said Sophie, 'to tell people wrong things.'

'I feel irresponsible,' he confessed.

'So do I,' said Sophie.

She had, indeed, regressed a little. She had removed her straw, and was engaged in crowning various pieces of formal topiary they passed. Now and then she invited his opinion.

'There. What do you think of that?'

'Um. Pretty, but unsuitable.'

'Even for a hedge horse?'

'For any unfortunate horse. Your pony, I remember,' he accused, 'used to wear one summer and winter. I thought it reprehensible, even at the time.'

'Star,' said Sophie. Softly. And paused, caught up in the diffuse rainbow of her past. 'I loved her,' she said. 'What happened to her, in the end?'

'She died of old age. Bharathi was inconsolable.'

'Bharathi?'

'My sister. My half-sister. She inherited the pony from you. She loved it too.'

'But Star,' said Sophie, the filaments of her dream still wound round her, 'wasn't very old.'

'She was when she died,' said Rabi, gently. 'It was a long time ago. Bharathi's married now, she has two children almost the age you were. I might too,' he found himself saying, 'except that there've been other things.'

'So could I, I suppose,' said Sophie. 'It seems strange to think of it, I never have. . . . It's a different tempo here, isn't it? Things get burned up so quickly, and yet you feel, somehow, there's all the time in the world.'

And seated herself on a bench that tempted with promises of vistas, set on a plinth of polished stone, in a setting dappled and splotched with the gold of crotons.

'Isn't it perfect? Such lovely views,' she said lazily, inviting him to share, her hair falling intensely gold in the clash between leaves and evening light. It moved him to offer her his own.

'There's a fine view I'd like to show you some time,' he said 'from the hill west of the Palace; it's called the Hill of Devi. You can't see it from here.'

'You can from the terrace,' she said. 'I've often seen you riding there.'

'It's a favourite spot of mine. The whole country opens out at your feet. It's magnificent.'

'It's a magnificent country,' she said. 'These huge skies, they go on forever, you feel you could begin to grasp what space really means, if you looked long enough. Sometimes it's all I do. I sit and look and it's almost too much . . . so much beauty, the people, the colours, the light; it's lovelier than anything one imagined. I'd forgotten,' she said, her eyes reflecting horizons and perplexities, 'what it was like. I'm glad I've come back to find out.'

Then he saw, and it wrung him to see, that she was in love with India, sharing his passion for the country without the taproot of birth that was his, that sturdily provided support and sustenance during the worst seasons of doubt, dislike, confrontation and even at times hatred.

She would love, until they taught her to keep it at bay. Close the shutters. Snap at the flies, and the servants. Ride in a car, looking down at faces on a lower level, remarking on the impenetrability of countenances. Ferret out the ugly to provide excuses, and the ridiculous and the pathetic to make a light comedy.

Sometimes, pondering the need for it all, he came to such bleak and writhing secrets that he retreated in distaste.

Now he felt a concern, not experienced before, to ensure a fair hearing.

Now, however, they had come full circle and were almost back at the Residency; sentries were snapping, and discouraged anything but formality.

'I'd like to show you round, a little, if I may,' was all he could say, somewhat baldly.

* * *

The Cantonment saw, and so did the Civil Lines.

Calling in droves to inscribe their names in the Visitors' Book, in anticipation of an era of entertainments that might reasonably be expected to follow the arrival of the ladies, to which they hoped, some more confidently than others, to be invited, they happened to see.

The Maharajkumar, more or less invisible in his place, not a patch on his colourful father, leapt into view when accompanied by the Resident's daughter.

The Resident's daughter. Quite a catch, vulgar elements said, slitting their eyes at what they saw. Not a part of the fishing fleet, not by a long chalk, not Miss Copeland. The entire regimental mess anxious to escort her, while she accepted the attentions of this commoner-princeling. In his homespun clothes, which were a studied insult. In whom they could see nothing; though one or two, more honest, did. Whose inclinations ran (tell a man by the company he keeps) to the country's disaffected riff-raff. In whose presence (rare, but it occurred) they felt they were squashed on a slide, squirming under some amused, but powerful, scrutiny.

It was all very upsetting.

The memsahibs in particular were indignant, on their own account, and on dear Lady Copeland's; but mostly Lady Copeland's. They did not, however, dare to tell her distant ladyship, even those who had the opportunity, since they were, actually, a little in awe of this slender woman whose dry ice could silence the boldest brass. She would never, they stoutly allowed, deny her own kith and kin, but somehow she did give an impression of gliding past them, her hem barely brushing their camp.

There were, nonetheless, a great many lively discussions. There had not been such a succulent bone since the Maharajah had publicly taken up with his concubine.

Lady Copeland needed no telling. She saw for herself. In a curious way she agreed with Rabi in believing it was the country.

Sophie, it became clear, was bewitched by India, India personified in the heir to State. Only, under the intense illumination bequeathed by her past it was a personification of its haunted and destroying elements that Lady Copeland perceived in the Maharajah's son.

Sometimes the view wavered. Sometimes she remembered the distressed child who had come to her, begging for what she did not know, an appeal she had not been able to answer. But mostly it held steady, and at times even grew menacing. Then she would put aside what she was doing, the flowers, or the menu, and go up to the Blue Room, the sanctum that enclosed her in soft resonances, and sit at her little escritoire to compose herself, and practise the rite of exorcism. Thinking of the land . . . this land in which she would contrive to live, and exhale hot breath, and forbid encroachments. . . . And presently take up her pen, when at last her shaking hands were stilled, to inscribe subtle denigrations, allowing the soft poisons to flow onto the pages of her diary.

But the poisons could not be entirely drained, nor what was substantial be exorcised.

She continued to see.

In bordered walks.

Or side by side on burnished horses, a pair who complemented each other with the particular hues and distillations of their two countries, in that disturbing polarity that had once bludgeoned Sir Arthur.

Under, one day, the Teardrop Chandelier.

It was, actually, one glittering evening, the great doors of the ballroom flung wide, scarlet manning the portals, huge swags of greenery and music and magnums to launch the season.

Sir Arthur and his wife had taken the floor, and were amiably revolving, when Mary Copeland said, quite quietly,

'Shall we stop, Arthur?'

He did, of course. Mary, he accepted, seldom lasted out an evening, although he did think it a little early for her. However, there was a slight pearling at her temples which he noticed.

'No, Arthur, it's nothing at all . . .'

She calmed his anxiety. 'Yes, perfectly well. I just feel I'd like to watch for a while. Do go along, Arthur, and enjoy yourself. I shall be perfectly happy with Charles.'

Towards whom he had, rather cunningly, steered her, and with whom he could leave her with good conscience while he found himself another partner, since he did rather enjoy dancing.

While Lady Copeland continued, as she had said with perfect truth she wished to, to watch.

The room, which was full, as far as she was concerned might have been empty except for the pair in the centre, lit by the hundred candles of the centrepiece.

Mary Copeland was no superstitious woman, nor young girl numinous with half-beliefs in the sway of charms, or birthstones, or the rays that stream from crystal drops. Yet she could not evade the fear that struck from the sharp glass. Heart fluttering, frantic captive, in its cage, she stood frozen, in her gown of watered silk, whose folds would not betray the smallest tremor, beside the frozen reefs of ice and fern which cooled the whirl of dancers.

Charles Wilmot followed these tracers easily, but did not quite pinpoint the target.

'Some kind of bolshie,' he said. 'Wouldn't think it, would you, from looking at him? Looks, I must say, eminently civilised.'

Lady Copeland shivered a little, coming out of trance. Her shoulders were bluish and cold.

'That is the point,' she said. 'Is he? Who knows? Can anyone tell with Indians?'

Rabi felt her glance. It struck between the shoulder-blades, as glances will. He ignored it, being engaged by his companion.

'Of course you can,' Sophie was saying, smouldering in blue, her bare shoulders beautiful under the Waterford masterpiece.

'I haven't for ages,' he parried, truthfully. 'I can't remember a step.'

'It's perfectly simple. It's like swimming or riding. Once you learn you never forget,' claimed implausible Sophie, neglecting at least six young subalterns to devote herself to Rabi. 'All you have to do is follow me.'

She had the confidence of her class, and was besides an accomplished dancer.

* * *

That night Mary Copeland lay like an effigy in their bed, very slender, very straight, perfectly still except for a hand that played with the lace at her throat, the narrow ribbons slipping endlessly between her fingers until her husband could not resist their plea. Covering her hand with his, quieting the restless picking if not the pulse that beat unevenly below, he said gently,

'Worried, Mary?'

'Just thinking.'

'Sophie?'

'Yes.'

'She's a pretty girl. Bound to have votaries.'

'The Maharajkumar, though. She's often with him, have you noticed?'

'No more often than with other young men. I'm sure Sophie can be trusted to look after herself.'

'Trust,' said Lady Copeland, and stiffened into the effigy from which he had patiently coaxed her. 'How far can one trust, in our terms, in terms which have any meaning, when his outlook is so different?'

'I don't think he would—' said her husband, and stopped there firmly. Because one did not quite know how to put it, even to one's wife.

'Besides,' he said, 'there are enough self-appointed chaperons, I would have said, to avoid anything like that.'

As well as those his wife of course appointed, not to mention Lady Copeland herself.

So that he felt entitled to turn on his side to sleep, pleasantly tired after dancing practically half the evening, including two waltzes he had managed to snaffle with his adorable daughter, snatching her away like a cad from two furious, but junior, young officers.

PART III.

Bodies you can move from one place to another, but souls you cannot compel . . . Calanus, Hindu gymnosophist, to his friend Alexander the Great

18

Far, far away from these realms Devapur was recklessly testing its wings, preparatory to soaring away to glory in one view, or to sinking into perdition in another.

There were pickets these days. The Maharajah had to pick his way between people who seemed to have nothing better to do all day than to loaf around his State carrying placards.

They prevented his loyal subjects going about their lawful, peaceful duties.

They prevented him. They surrounded his motor-car, one ghastly morning, and stopped him from proceeding on his tour of inspection of the Maharajah's School. It brought back to Bawajiraj the most vivid memories of the riotous and disgraceful scenes in Bombay, which not for a moment had he envisaged witnessing in his own firmly guided State. This was worse, if possible, because this time he was not inside his Rolls but outside, trying to get in. Also, this time Rabi was not with him (brief shots of his son defending the Ruling Chief whirred through the Maharajah's mind) but could be seen on the fringes of this mob, observing if not superintending proceedings, in fact so engrossed in this frivolous activity as to ignore his father's predicament. It was, Bawajiraj felt, both incomprehensible and profoundly irresponsible.

The guard was summoned and turned out at the double; weary men who looked back with nostalgia on the era of peace, when the most lively action of the day had been to round up some stray petitioner who had lost himself in the courtyards of the Palace. Some, indeed, were thinking of giving up and going back to their villages, to sit cross-legged on charpoys, under shady trees, and listen to their wives churning up the buttermilk that would presently be borne out to refresh them; instead of all this chasing about in the sun.

Now, however, they were brisk and efficient. The Maharajah proceeded on his stately way, rehearsing not only what he would say to the schoolchildren but also to his son, directly he got back. Tawker, the unhappy private secretary, had already been thrown into the thick of the scrum to issue the Maharajah's summons.

'What is all this nonsense, Rabi?'

He came straight to the point, in full panoply, in robes of some state, his turban emphatically formal, addressing not his son but an erring heir. It was to be, the offender perceived, an interview that adhered strictly to the Timurid maxim: a king has no relatives. Vassal and sovereign in their strict and appointed station.

'Your Highness,' he said then, 'We feel—'

' "We," ' cried the outraged Maharajah, 'Who is "we"?'

'We, the people,' said Rabi, without display, but very plainly. 'We feel that insupportable levies and treaties must be rescinded, whatever the consequences. We shall continue the struggle to that end.'

'In the process you will tear the State apart,' said the furious Maharajah.

'Not I. We,' said Rabi, who was equally furious but more contained. 'We rajahs and nawabs have rent the country apart for a century and more and in the process traders and soldiers of fortune have been elevated into emperors. The people are attempting to repair the damage.'

And folded his arms, which by now were solid with assurance.

It convinced the Maharajah that he had on his hands not an errant heir but a disruptive subject on a scale and of an order worse even than anything he had suspected. Jails, even, flitted through his mind, but no, there was the rebel's mother, not to mention the Devapuris. His people, who were now, apparently, being coolly and formidably subverted.

At which point he grew, or appeared to grow, in stature. Certainly the robe was totally justified.

'My people,' he said, and flashed, those sparks struck from the powerful metal that invests the incumbents of thrones. 'My people have not forgotten, although they may have to be reminded, where their allegiance lies.'

416

It was indeed the truth, the source of this great strength that infused him, transforming the common elements of blood by quasi-mystical process into an infinitely richer substance. For the people worshipped their Maharajahs, upheld their divine birthright, gloried in their benevolence as they submitted to their excesses, and would not be budged from their stand except—

Except, possibly, when their loyalties could flow to a prince of the blood.

It was not for nothing that the British insisted upon their right of confirming the succession.

Maharajah and heir exchanged this knowledge silently. It might have ruined both except that this family had devoted its considerable energies to preserving itself, subduing the deliberate and sustained centrifugal forces pitted against it.

The old cement held, and worked.

Rabi recovered first.

'Who can tell what the people are capable of doing?' he said easily, and put an arm about his father's shoulders. 'Would you allow me to demonstrate Prithviraj's skills?'

Tawker, trembling in an ante-room, was presently delighted to see his two masters strolling amicably in the direction of the falcons' mews.

* * *

Nor was Sir Arthur spared.

Moving like a muted sun in deference to the prevailing temper, he nevertheless found himself assailed, his satellites dislodged here and there (a peon, a brace of outriders): and one tiresome day the flag was missing from its pole. There was a spare, of course, run up in a matter of minutes , the Raj nothing if not efficient; but it was upsetting.

Especially considering who was involved, as rumour had long maintained, and the facts had now to be faced.

Waji's son. (How one sighed for the tutors who had never been appointed. How infallible one's instincts that had warned from the beginning of the dangers of Waji's liaison—bad enough with a commoner, worse still never regularised, it left one without a single thumbscrew.)

The Chief Minister's daughter. (Not one but, unforgivably, two quasi-criminals in that stable.)

Ringleaders, these two. People from whom you might reasonably have hoped for better things but, these hopes dashed, you could not quite treat like other people.

Not in Devapur State, with the Devapuris watching.

This was something he had endeavoured without success to convey to the robust Viceroy. Not even after he had delved into history and come up with that lamentable episode in the reign of Nabob Hastings.* Although H.E. had been of the utmost help. Categorical assurances of the most fortifying kind. His old and trusted friend Charles winkled out of Delhi at his, Arthur's, special request, and sent at once to take command of the Garrison Forces.

It was, however, a thoughtful man who sat in his study, late into the evening, drafting his notes for the Residency Records. For Sir Arthur could not share in the confidence maintained in high and remote places.

* * *

Worse followed. The ice-factory ceased to function. Palace and Residency were united in misery.

The Maharajah sent for his Minister.

'I thought,' he said, at his most exquisite, the rings on his fingers throwing the most slender lances, 'correct me if I am wrong, Minister, but I distinctly remember instructing you to introduce legislation to outlaw strikes.'

'It is not a strike, Highness,' replied the Minister, peddling technicalities in the Maharajah's view. 'It is a lockout.'

And made those motions of washing his hands that were intended to remind the Maharajah of where ultimate responsibility lay for this latest disaster.

Despite these victories the Dewan also was a thoughtful man. True, Maharajahs must stoop to touch a Brahmin's feet, but nowadays Maharajahs had organised themselves into a trade union. One did not want one's sons blacklisted throughout the union of princely states, to which men of birth and capability must look, since every top post in British India was reserved for Britons. Yes, circumspection needed, especially with the Maharajah tipped as the next Chancellor of the Chamber of Princes. . . .

*In 1780 Warren Hastings, Governor-General of India, placed the Rajah of Benares under arrest in his own palace. The Rajah's troops then rose and massacred the British force.

418

So that he thought it prudent to approach the composed party who now and then honoured his house with her presence.

'Ice-factory?' said Usha. 'Just testing. It'll be called off soon. Ramdas doesn't think we're ready for anything full-scale yet.'

'What do you think?'

'I agree with him. One cannot rush things.'

The Dewan agreed, but not aloud. A man of infinite patience himself, he detected his own quality in his daughter. Only, in the circumstances, admiration had to be tempered.

* * *

'I suppose,' said Rabi, 'your father's been asking a few questions.'

'Yes. Your father's been at him about the ice,' said Usha absently, and continued to flick sand, rather finically, from her toes. She had been paddling in the river. Its banks were often a site for councils of war, its waters frequently resorted to for subsequent cooling off.

'Let me,' said Rabi. He could not bear those ineffectual flicks. 'You're so fussy,' he groused, holding her feet firmly and efficiently deploying the towel.

'I'm a Brahmin, I can't help being fussy,' said Usha. 'Besides, I don't like sand between my toes.'

'Can't do this, can't do that, can't clean your own feet, it's ridiculous,' said Rabi, dusting brutally. 'You'll have to give up a good deal of that nonsense, you know.'

'I know. I shall. And so will you,' said Usha.

'What will I have to give up?'

Baffled, because of persuasions of perfection.

'Being so haughty,' said Usha. 'You can't just seize things, you know.'

'What have I ever seized?'

'My feet, to name one. Just now. I might have fallen over.'

He was so astonished that he returned them at once to their prim sandals, and locked his arms about his knees. But his mind worried at it, cur with a slipper would not let go.

'I did ask,' he said at last, and caressed with a penitent finger the tender blue-veined arch in its lattice of leather. 'Next time I'll wait for an answer.'

'It's not you, it's me,' she responded at once, and generously. 'My fault, I shall have to learn to be quicker. It's all a question of adjusting.'

There was a silence after this, which lapped about them pleasantly, for it was a nice day, and they were pleased with each other.

'I daresay,' Rabi said presently, 'we shall soon all be doing a good deal of adjusting.'

'Exactly what his Highness said.'

'His Highness? Are you on speaking terms?'

'Why not? You are.'

'I'm his son!'

'Well, we are. My forbearing nature allows it.'

'Or his.'

'Or his. Anyhow he asked me to his croquet party.'

'Bribery.'

'Reward. He's so grateful the ice strike's been called off.'

'Will you go?'

'No.'

'Why not? They can be fun.'

'Too many English,' she said honestly.

It made him sit up, and oddly enough it was a speech of the Dewan's that rose to the surface, words which, from injections of truth, prevailed at times over his own convictions of schism.

'They're here, interwoven,' he said. 'You can't write off the past just like that. We think English, many of us. We'll get them out in the end, they won't be the first ones we've ushered out, but there's no point in hating them while they're here. It's so corrosive, such a waste of energy.'

'*Hate*,' said Usha. She was so shocked that her face was quite bloodless. 'We don't *hate*. We leave that to princes and emperors. It's just better not to have friends in the enemy camp, that's all. It avoids unnecessary suffering.'

'Is that a warning?' he asked, and drew patterns in the sand.

'If you like,' she answered.

A light breeze had sprung up, fanning their hot faces. Their emotions were further calmed by dhobi sounds from the river, a braying of patient donkeys, and the *sho-shup* dhobi shanty counterpointing the *thwack-thwack* of cloth hitting stone. One upstream, pounding the Maharajah's household linen; one downstream, attacking the Resident's household's.

Just once, briefly, during Mr. Buckridge's reign, the pattern had been overturned. On the Sahib's instructions the upper station had been appropriated for the Resident's dhobi, dislodging the Palace dhobi from his immemorial upstream seat. Subsequent and widely reported exchanges between washermen's factions had rejoiced all Devapur hearts, except possibly those of Mr. Buckridge, and the residents of the dhobi-khana.

This ridiculous but treasured memory began to retrieve the situation between the cool couple.

'A strange man,' said Rabi.

'Yes. I remember my father used to call him a *feringhi*,' said Usha, effortlessly picking up a common thread. 'It was the most offensive thing he could think of.'

'Mr. Buckridge offended,' said Rabi.

Usha would not dispute it. Their agreement was total now. The atmosphere, which had clouded, was assuming its usual concord and clarity.

* * *

Days went into weeks, weeks became months, aggravations not only did not cease but escalated.

'When I am dead,' Waji confessed to Arthur, 'you will find Salt engraved on my heart.'

Sir Arthur's sentiments closely coincided; but, rather unjustly, he added 'Mr. Buckridge' to his engraving.

The Maharajah was so fed up that from time to time he made sacrificial offerings: a College, a Hospital, one Elected Member to his Council of Twelve. Only Salt, which was tied to Defence (and his survival, he shrewdly suspected), was, he instructed his Chief Minister, to be regarded as sacrosanct.

'Too little, too late,' the tiresome Dewan had taken to murmuring.

He had picked up the refrain, which came clearly over the border, endorsing it wholly and with utter identification. He felt he could have coined the words himself. He went further.

'No taxation without representation,' he dared to utter in the Maharajah's hearing.

It made him shudder, after a lifetime of autocracy, almost as much as the Maharajah.

However, he would learn. Learning was the hallmark of a Brahmin.

If you could learn to put up with the British you could learn to put up with anyone, even his countrymen, he felt.

Concessions also flowed from the Residency.

There were sedate tea-parties on the lawns, at which Lady

Copeland presided, to which ladies from the Indian Community were invited, and sometimes came, to sit precariously on folding wooden chairs provided by the Indian contractors, and partake of tea and iced lemonade in striped and airy marquees. At numerous Residency luncheons—in the festive run-up to Christmas—Indian gentlemen, and occasionally a conscripted wife or two, were to be seen. Not just the few, shaped by the hands of devoted tutors, who could be trusted not to smear their knives with honey for the garden peas, but a few who could be persuaded, whose manners had not been vetted, and would have to be either overlooked or endured in the overriding interests of preserving the Raj.

But, sadly, the steel also showed. Shadowy presences whom the city had scarcely seen—no more than smart silhouettes at Residency balls—resolved into the alert and ominous forms of adjutant, major, commanding officer, coming and going under prudent escort to conferences at the Residency, and other military places.

All of them observed, being meant to: a lamentable necessity, but there it was. So they saw: Rabi, Usha, Mohini, the Devapuris, among them Ramdas, who trembled less and less as, like athletes, they limbered up their inner strength. Discipline, some called it. Others, less inhibited, had taken to calling it soul-force.

Christmas, like Dassara and Ramzan before it, passed in peace. No one had expected otherwise.

Devapur State was fortunate in that its rulers, the Resident, the Maharajah, and the Dewan, were tolerant men who shared a lively distaste for fanaticism. The Resident could not, except in brief but telling flashes, interfere in religious matters; it was not policy, and anyhow one loathed dabbling in that kind of thing. It was left to the Maharajah and his Minister to make it perfectly plain—which they did in their inimitable manner—that they expected their Hindu, Muslim, and Christian subjects to co-exist without coming to blows. The Devapuris, with varying degrees of enthusiasm, complied. They observed each other's festivals from a distance, and with marked disdain, while continuing to respect these unholy events. It had become a tradition much appreciated by all, especially the children (by now all of them firmly netted in the Dewan's compulsory-school mania), from the plethora of holidays in the Devapur calendar.

After Christmas it was the Maharajkumar's Birthday, closely followed by the Maharajah's Accession Celebrations, which not the most rabid soul fighter would have dreamed of disrupting.

422

For Rabi, like others, it was a welcome break from organising campaigns, attending meetings, participating in demonstrations—activities more arduous than they might have been from the pained reproaches, visible though nobly suppressed, of his father.

With his mother's exhortations ringing in his ears—*Be gentle!*—and not altogether clashing against his own human inclination. Be gentle. The Maharajah in purple and the British in scarlet. Wealth accumulating while men decayed. Be gentle.

Sometimes, at vulnerable moments, waking shivering in cold dawns, the horizon stretching emptily, he pondered on how much easier it would be to follow the impulses of his kingly caste—wage war, kill, destroy, die if necessary—than to adhere to patient Gandhian principles. Mostly, and more lucidly, however, he had a growing sense of the immense power they carried within themselves, more effective than the violence to which he was drawn, and more powerful than anything Palace and Residency combined could field.

* * *

Often he envied Sophie. No conflict there, as far as he could tell. A divine chain that linked Sophie Sahiba to Resident Sahib to Viceroy Sahib to Kaiser-i-Hind in a perfect unity. An undivided family. Its confident sheen rubbed off on to Sophie, who larked through the gardens trailing dogs and the incense of devoted admirers, herself ready to fall instantly in love with anything.

Rabi loved this rapturous companion whose presence convinced of the existence of secular heavens. Life, she demonstrated, was intended to ravish the senses. Life was created for—who else?—young men and women. Like this enchanting creature in a striped blue dress, slim green bottles leaning enticingly in a wicker basket, mouth-watering shapes lurking under snowy napkins.

'What have you got there?'

Sniffing. Cold repast, expertly bundled up, refuses to release a single clue.

'The entire larder. Cook surpassed himself.'

'Let me see.'

Attempting to lift a corner, damask and wicker are whisked away smartly.

'No. Not until we get there.'
'Where?'
'Where's a good spot to picnic?'
'Here.'
'One's own garden?'
'If it's as big as a province—'
'Rabi.'
'Uh?'
'Can't you do better?'
'No.'
'You're not trying. *Think*.'
'I am—uh—thinking. Distant places . . . don't want to bring down dear Mama's wrath.'
'Dear Mama won't be wrathful.'
'No?'
'No. Well. Somewhere closer then.'
'You say.'
'The river.'
'The river is—uh—sort of a meeting place.'
'You and your girl?'
'What girl?'
'You must know girls.'
'A few. Like you know men.'

Lids are coming down, brown-gold fringes on flushed cheeks. One's having admirers is quite, quite different, Mama hints, and could be right, from a Maharajkumar having women.

'Actually—' (he can't bear what is spinning)—'it's political meetings.'

'Oh, *political*.' Sophie's radiant again. Her radiance is inspiring.

'I know where we'll go,' he says, homing straight in on this sunny beam. 'Boating on the lake.'

The lake is a distant glimmer from the Palace. In no time they are at the boathouse, Palace boatmen are, under orders, keeping their distance. They intend to do this thing by themselves. Sophie, not dressed for boating, is angling, skirts hitched up, for a safe descent. At this point he has to tell her.

'Milk-and-sugar,' he says.
'What?'
'Your dress.'
'Seersucker.'
'Same thing.'
'Really?'

'Yes. Seersucker. Milk-and-sugar.'

'Rabi, how *enchanting!*'

She, yes, *pirouettes* in her silly shoes. She's falling, napkins flare open, precious green bottles are sliding.

'The *basket*,' he screeches.

Sophie rights herself miraculously and belts him one with the wicker.

'All right, *you* manage.'

He does.

This royal barge is basically a quinquereme, needs five banks of slaves, but he manages. What is propelling a ton weight to erstwhile dam-builders? Swans follow, gliding like queens, not a quill out of place, eyes incredulously beaded on the straining oarsman. You wait, my beauties. Teach you not to swan it. Not one solitary crumb between those flaming bills.

But ire refuses to fuel him, once he is fed. He leans back bloated, feeding duck morsels to swans. Swans are eating, beaks clapping, they can't have enough. Cannibals, he says, disgusted, and closes his eyes.

Sophie wakes him. To look at the view. There is only the Palace to see.

'Isn't it beautiful?'

'What?'

'The Palace.'

'Yes.'

'How can you be so casual about something so beautiful?'

'I'm not being casual. I've seen it before, that's all.'

'Rabi?'

'Mm?'

'Is your mother very beautiful?'

'I don't know,' he says.

Must be some kind of moron not to know, but he scents what's coming.

'I'd like to meet her sometime.'

'I can't think why,' he says, amazed at the depths to which he can sink.

'Just would. I'm not likely am I,' she says realistically, and dabbles a hand in lake water, 'to just bump into her.'

'No,' he agrees.

'Besides, you've met my mother,' she says accusingly.

'Yes, I have had that pleasure,' he agrees.

They're both wide awake now. The sun is going in, and their vision of each other is dimming.

* * *

'Be nice,' he bullies his mother.

'I wouldn't know how to be anything else,' claims Mohini, not batting an eyelash.

'You know all right. Just remember she can't help her father,' he says.

'I know. Neither can you, my sweet,' says sweetly poisonous Mohini.

* * *

'A delightful girl,' says his mother after the meeting. 'You must look after her until she really gets used to the climate.'

'What do you mean?' he barks.

'So fair,' she answers. 'Bound to burn easily. Then they get jaundiced.'

'Sophie couldn't possibly—'

'You have only to look at her mother,' says Mohini definitively.

'I know about the mother. I'm not concerned about the mother,' he says, controlled.

'The daughter,' says Mohini, 'is extremely pretty.'

'Is that all?' he says. He is barking again.

'Isn't it enough?' says wide-eyed Mohini.

She makes him feel he wants sun, moon, and stars combined, when all he wants is—

Well, what *does* he want?

* * *

He took his problem, covertly, to Sophie; who had problems of her own, she was discovering. The smooth binding chain, that made her the object of his envy, existed, but was kinking here and there. The short, impatient tugs she gave did not help either, merely adding a discordant jangle without straightening a single twist.

'If only things were *simple*,' she said, sighing, and looking back.

She had been out long enough, in a matter of months, to look back with nostalgia on the marvellous simplicity of lakes, and gardens, and innocent excursions into safe and captivating corners of the landscape.

426

'Do you really,' he said, 'find it difficult?'

A touch, there—the faintest dash—of astringency. Things are made easy for some. Ease is an unknown dimension for others.

She had to consider her answer. She was, besides, preoccupied. They were riding up the hill that morning, and it was not an easy passage.

'Not *difficult*,' she said at last, when she thought she was clear. 'Tedious. No. I don't mean that. It's just that everything's so unnecessarily complicated.'

Complicated. Complications are bred by haughty seizures of territory, no less than persons, he felt, somewhat shortly.

'Let him have his head,' he advised, of the pony she was riding, which happened to be his. 'He's used to the terrain, you'll find he'll make his own way.'

When the pony had stopped slithering and they were out of the gully he said:

'I wouldn't say unnecessarily. Inevitably, perhaps. It's an inherited situation, bound to throw up endless problems.'

'Yes, I suppose,' said Sophie, doubtfully.

She was riding rather slackly, the reins bunched loosely in one hand. Problems, she thought, and it brought to mind the *sadhu* she had seen when out for a drive one afternoon. Absolutely motionless, this holy man, under a banyan tree, smeared with ash, colour matching the banyan bark, she wouldn't have noticed him except for the flies crawling around his eyes. To which he remained completely oblivious.

But why? Why not flap the disgusting things away? Even a beast—this hill pony she had been lent—would not stand for it. It shivered its coat whenever midges settled, or whisked its tail, the sensible animal. Luckily there were no flies.

She was frowning now, and shading her eyes from the sun. She had straggled so far behind that he wheeled his mare round sharply and clopped back to her.

'Tired, Sophie?'

'Not really. Perhaps a little. Sun's a bit strong.'

'Would you like to rest for a little? I've a spare saddle-cloth.'

'Is it safe? I mean snakes and things,' she said, and laughed a little, nervously. She hadn't meant that at all. She bent her gaze on various boulders strewn about the hillside, to add verisimilitude, which took in neither of them.

'You're quite safe,' he said, and having begun ploughed on. 'You're as safe with me as you would be with your father.'

He began to feel a little helpless then, as the words twisted in the air. Whatever they uttered seemed to turn, like clasping a serpent by its tail, it came up smartly in a loop and bit the hand you had thought was safe.

'I mean,' he persevered, 'safe in the sense that, if there were to be a—uh—disturbance, no one would touch you. If you were with me no one would lay a finger.'

There was no one to lay a finger; the place might have been a desert; but Sophie pretended. There was, after all, a dark side to this hill that they were ascending. She even felt lightened of some load, for it so happened she had taken a stand on precisely this subject. In fact she was at odds with Sebastian Lomax, who confessed to being far from *au fait* with these matters, while stoutly behind any action Colonel Wilmot might take. Sophie could not accept that force was ever the answer, except for criminals and one or two other categories; but certainly not for Devapuris, like sweet devoted Ayah.

'I hate violence,' she said at one point, when a vulture had swooped and was bearing away a hapless lizard, which had carelessly come out to bask on a rock.

'We don't intend to use violence.'

He took her up at once.

'I meant us,' said Sophie, weaving around in the saddle. She did not feel at ease, leaving the pony in charge. She looked, she was convinced, like a sack of potatoes, which was also what she felt like.

'Sebastian Lomax,' she said, rather leadenly, 'thinks that force would be justified, under certain circumstances. He would consider it his duty.'

This dutiful Lomax. How one loathed the bull-necked, unsubtle Captain.

'Well,' he said, 'there are always people who won't look beyond blunt instruments, aren't there.'

They toiled on.

The track had narrowed, and Sophie's pony had taken the lead. Following behind he observed and approved her seat (which she had improved, herself detesting the sense of a lumpy sack), and also noticed the rash of freckles sprinkled on her arms, visible below the short sleeves of the silk shirt she was wearing; and could not avoid comparison with Usha, whose skin ran as smooth as his mother's cream, not needing to push up these blotchy defences.

He loathed himself by now; and was glad when at last they arrived at the crumbled fort. From this point on, he resolved, he would be nice in word, deed, and thought; and he sprang down to help her, and tethered their mounts, and unfurled with a flourish the rather rich saddle-cloth (it came from the Maharajah's stables) on which they could sit. It would, he hoped, bring them closer—a cloth of average size stitched for one horse, spread on the shale for two humans—while they rested and recovered before tackling the further climb, up this rocky hill, to the obelisk.

'I love this spot,' he said, when they were seated, reviving flasks of iced water between them. 'I often come up here when I need to unwind. When I have the time, of course.'

'Unwind, Rabi?' said Sophie, with some, but not utter, incredulity. 'I wouldn't have thought you had a care in the world.'

Thinking of him like some cut gem cosily bedded in its plush if indigenous setting, while she was sentenced to coming up, unpleasantly, in the course of an ordinary drive, against all manner of confusing and flinty aspects in otherwise heavenly surroundings.

'Perhaps one or two things,' she allowed, from peeks into another's wilderness. 'There are always those. But there's hardly anything you want, is there, that you can't have? That's as ideal a state as anything I can think of.'

It disconcerted him to have his state described in terms which closely resembled those he had chosen for her.

'It's not that easy,' he fell back. 'What does anyone want? I'm not sure I know.'

If Sophie didn't know, she had vague yearnings, which were nowhere connected to the stony plateau he was offering her. She yearned for swans and lakes, clear turquoise water in which slender fingers could trail, leaving a feathery spoor on the placid surface.

So did Rabi; only his longings went further, grew subtler, more encompassing, and possibly less transparent.

He was, he recognised, a product of two schools. But he had no right to lumber her, he convinced himself.

'I suppose the truth is,' he said, 'I want the moon. A full round moon, nothing less will do.'

Sophie began to flower again. She understood about moons and moonlight. Or perhaps it was the water, stone-cold next to fragile mirror linings. She had splashed a good part of her flask on her complaining wrists.

'The other night, did you see,' she said. 'Huge. Raining down silver. You could have read a book.'

And leaned, temple resting on palm, hair falling away like a curtain from her nape, which was beaded, he saw, with a golden moisture. He was tempted, then, to caress the tender isthmus uncovered by that fall of gold; but some infallible instinct warned she would leap at his touch. While his fingertips created instant deserts. So he got busy elsewhere, dusting his knees, and corking up the flasks.

'Come on,' he said, 'time to move on.'

'Where?'

'To the obelisk.'

'Can't we just stay here?'

'No. I insist on sharing my pleasures.'

Sophie might have resented these orders, except that resentments seldom curdled her nature. She had, besides, felt feathers stroking, and the fine hairs rising in soft insidious response along her nape, when the last thing one wanted, she felt, and had been told, was to yield to one's impetuous impulses. So she got up as bidden, and hoisted up into the saddle, and only glanced back once at the little patch of shale on which the colours of Herez had briefly glowed.

They rode on. Sun was hitting at glittering rock. Sophie began to regret the topi her advisers had recommended, as well as the scarf, like the checked cotton kerchief Rabi had knotted about his neck. At one point, since he was leading, she even had to call to him:

'Is it far?'

At this very point, it appeared, they had to dismount and continue the exhausting ascent on foot.

'Not very far,' he answered, and this time he did take her hand.

Quite soon thereafter they achieved their goal, this high pinnacle on which the obelisk was planted, and beside it a slab of stone to take care of aches and pains and other physical interjections while catering for spiritual feasts.

'There,' he said, when they were seated. 'Isn't it magnificent?'

Spreading before her what was virtually the fabric of his life.

'Yes,' said Sophie; and made an effort and subdued sundry arid features that were lunging up for inspection. 'It is rather splendid.'

'You can see for miles,' he said, possessed, as he often was, by the dusty gold of the panorama. 'It's easily the finest view of Devapur. My grandmother, though—'

And lingered, as she still had the power to make him, over reflections of those obstinate resins which would not be converted, while melting into the most liquid amber under his gaze.

'I never could convince her,' he said, and Sophie saw the great tenderness his mouth and eyes could assume. 'I tried, but she had a view of her own, from the crystal gallery, from which I could never shake her.'

Then Sophie, too, was caught up in these clement, if misty, evocations.

'Your grandmother,' she said warmly, 'must have been a remarkable woman.'

'She was,' said Rabi. 'Some people even found her a little formidable.'

The formidable Dowager. Fragments of conversation, splintery with disapproval, to which she had not paid attention, returned and began to slash at Sophie.

'She was, wasn't she,' she said, feeling her way, and frowning a little, 'the power behind the throne?'

Incredulity at this surreal grasp of the actualities of power made him eye her, quite sharply. But she was still enclosed. Innocence gave her a candour and grace which made it difficult to impeach her.

'There wasn't much scope for that,' he said diplomatically. 'But she influenced me a lot. When I was a child she used to tell me the most tremendously inspiring stories.'

'So did mine,' said Sophie. 'I loved her. More than my parents really, darlings though they are. But I saw them so seldom. Whereas she—'

So they retreated into childhood, whose weave and substance is charming but cannot really carry the weight and vigour of maturity.

* * *

The Dewan also regressed, if not quite to childhood.

'When I was your age,' he told Rabi, 'everything stretched. As far as eye could see one knew (God willing, of course) what lay in store, and how one would act. One could plan (naturally bearing the Almighty in mind) some way ahead. But now. You young people.'

'Some old ones too,' said Rabi affectionately. 'Greybeards and whatnot. Not all hotheads, Dewan Sahib.'

'I'm aware of that, Rabi,' said the Dewan, and could not resist a plume or two. 'I'm glad to note that your years as my pupil have not been profitless. But young blood, you know.'

'If there wasn't, we might be scared out of our wits,' said Rabi.

The Dewan agreed, silently. He could not see those venerable uncles of Ramdas (impressed, one shouldn't wonder) standing up to police, Lancers, or (he shivered) Garrison troops. Or Rabi's middle-aged and mildewed old tutor, the Pandit, for that matter. He wondered they had the nerve to enter the fray, considering their proportions. Whereas Rabi, of course. Flesh-eater's physique. Plus one or two other dimensions.

At times the Dewan could not quite decide whether it was Rabi who loomed over him, or whether it was he who had untimely shrunk.

It was, this morning, the first of the westerlies singeing the plains, something of a family conclave. Leaving his sons to hold the fort the Dewan had retired for one of those periodic retreats, and blandishments of the soul, which he found essential to his sanity. He had just emerged from one such session. Vatsala prepared and brought him his glass of spiced milk, and then she sat with her two daughters, and one grandchild, on the rosewood swing, leaving the main arena to the men. Not entirely, however. During lulls, she spoke.

'In my day,' she said now, 'you could not take these liberties. Sitting on river-banks all day long. I don't know what you talk about.'

'Oh, tactics,' said Usha.

'Politics,' said Vimala.

'Yes,' said their mother, 'and see what it did for you. Six months, in that dreadful place. Each time after visiting you I had to have two head-baths before I felt clean again. Now your sister has to court the same fate.'

'Not in Devapur,' Rabi dared to say.

'Rabi, you are not the Maharajah,' Vatsala shut him up.

But then, brooding over him, she was once more overcome.

'Men and women,' she said, 'mingling like that. On river-banks, and where all else I don't know. In my day it would have been a right scandal.'

'In your day it was different,' said Usha. 'This is a revolution. Who ever heard of a revolution for men only? No, it's everyone. Men and women. They do belong to the same species.'

Bolder if possible and even less womanly than her sister, her mother felt; and she smoothed her lap, and pulled down the skirts of her active grandchild who was clambering on and off the swing. But she kept sensibly silent, deprived as she was of allies, and unable to detect any censure from other quarters for behaviour that offended the proprieties. Younger quarters, certainly, were united, and were exchanging glances of the most supportive, and annoying, kind. As for her husband, she had almost given up hope.

At this point the Dewan rose, to usher his guest on to the verandah, for the air. It was his custom to do so when the atmosphere grew charged.

They stood, the two of them, on this wide avenue of delicate tiling, under a colonnade designed to attract the most elusive of breezes; and presently the Dewan took up a favoured theme and said:

'In all this, Rabi—as in all affairs—the watchword is discipline.'

'Yes. I've gathered,' said Rabi.

Wryly.

He felt he had, or had had thrust upon him, reserves of that commodity, on all sorts of fronts.

* * *

Sir Arthur also sped back, to pre-war days. When, if you gave an order, you didn't wonder if. Some things jammed of course; India wasn't England, basic mistake to imagine. But not for want of *will*. Whereas now. So many things that jarred. Were even hurtful, for one had tried.

'When I first took up my appointment,' he said to Waji, and sighed.

And stopped. One did not wish to be maudlin, even in one's cups. In any case Waji understood, there was hardly anyone, outside one's circle, who understood as well as he did; a compliment that Waji fully returned.

One piece of intelligence they did not share. Sir Arthur preferred to keep his worries to himself. It was that levers were vanishing. The heir, however disruptive, could not be removed to Calcutta,* or Burma,** or other safe and distant corner. Days were gone when a Maharajah could be compelled through his heir, or heir invited to contemplate the loss of heritage. His blood, and solid backing, saw to that.

It even occurred to him, briefly and unpleasantly, that only Waji's loyalty, and of course force, retained the Resident at Court.

Sir Arthur discounted the one, and was not and had never

*Tipu Sultan's sons, incarcerated in Calcutta.
**Emperor Bahadur Shah, exiled to Rangoon.

433

been enamoured of the other. A man of some ideals, and great and convinced moderation, he detested violence as vehemently as the Dewan.

* * *

Ramdas was another who contemplated the past. He thought about the time, only a few seasons ago, although it seemed altogether another age, when his life had run calm. Then, in that era, all he had to do, regular as the sun, was to rise of a morning and harness up the bullocks, and amble down to his patch of land for a bit of ploughing; or perhaps sally out of an evening, to the sugar-cane field, and cut a few canes for the children to crunch, the sweetest imaginable juices running from the fibre.

These images, rinsed free of grit, were familiar and reassuring.

Whereas current preoccupations were of an immeasurably different and even frightening composition. So much so that at times he sat back on his heels, hands dangling loosely between his bony knees, and gave himself up to unreality. Was it really he, Ramdas, engaged in such doings? Was he, Ramdas, a peasant farmer, and his fellow peasants, really attempting to challenge the established order of Maharajahs and Lord Sahibs? It passed belief. He had to restore the grit to green and peaceful scenes— failed harvests, creeping rot, ruinous taxes, famished, crying children—before he could renew himself, before he could resume training for the arduous campaign they were developing.

For which discipline was the key.

Fashioning it was the problem.

'No discipline,' Ramdas often groaned. He gave displays of patience exhausted, and of a strong man reduced, and resorted to prayer, especially after outbreaks of disorderly behaviour from his troops.

But he exaggerated, it was generally felt. Discipline was beginning to tell.

434

19

The days went by. Events were building, everyone accepted. The main event, that is to say, for there were still these exasperating side-shows.

The Maharajah rose above the vulgar clamour. He had his own standards, and would not be pushed. He felt the gusts of reproof that rose from his subjects, and more keenly the silences, but was not, he declared, to be swayed from his course. Even Mohini could not bring herself to suggest that this course had been charted for him by others. She saw him without his robes, and the bruising was plain, even bloody. So she simply took him to her bosom, without questioning, and the minimum of quarrel.

Only, now and then, her fiery nature refused to be muffled. Then she would break out, words and objects bursting like shells. Even *that* they have taken, she raged at these times; his own people, his *birthright*, they have robbed from him, *robbers*! But somehow she contained herself in the Maharajah's presence; while her women silently cleared away the shattered pottery and porcelain.

* * *

The Maharajah, awaiting developments like everyone else, maintained a befitting calm. Sometimes a melancholy overtook him. He felt a need for his son, and since, humanly speaking, he had no false pride, he often summoned the Maharajkumar from what he referred to, with distaste, as the 'other side,' to consult him about State programmes.

'You're sure, Rabi, my commanders will not be subjected?'

'Perfectly, sir. I've checked with my—uh—people. Not a thing planned for that day.'

Sometimes, unfortunately, there were hitches. Through all these trials Bawajiraj continued imperturbable, Lady Copeland herself could not have faulted him. He did not flap even when, on the eve of his croquet party, the very last one of the season, an ashen Tawker arrived (he was of a race that, in an earlier age, would have fully expected his head to be struck from his shoulders for bearing such tidings) to convey that vandals had wrecked the court.

'I wish, Rabi, you would keep your chaps under some kind of control,' the Maharajah controlled himself, got over to his son, before getting on the blower to alert his guests.

'Some splinter movement, the zealous bastards!' Rabi groaned.

His woe was not feigned, for the Copelands were coming.

* * *

The Copelands, the Wilmots, a married Wilmot niece, whose husband was serving on the North-West Frontier, and her twin children; Sebastian Lomax, and his friend and fellow-officer Peter (Pip) Aspinall; and dear old Pooky, who was hardly a guest, one of the family really, who was shortly due at the Lodge; and his smart son Ranjit.

This round dozen, chosen to do agreeable battle, must now be content with tea and conversation.

'Maharajah Sahib.'

Lady Copeland surrendered a cool hand, smiling palely, in a pale Lanvin dress. Thank goodness the Suez was navigable, and dependable, once more. It spared one so many trials, including that wretched bazaar *durzi*.

'Dear Lady C! Arthur! So glad you've come, despite everything. Too ghastly, I don't know *what* to say.'

'My dear chap, you mustn't blame yourself. Might have happened to any of us.'

Sir Arthur was cheerful; he did not shine at croquet, he believed it was the grass. Whereas Sebastian, a dab hand at the game, was disconsolate.

'Rotten luck, sir.' The golden young man shook hands. He was in flannels, which set off his gilding to perfection. 'Perpetrators deserve to be horsewhipped.'

'Just what I intend, when I catch them.' The Maharajah beamed at the sensible Captain. 'Now let me see, do we all know each other?'

They did. They moved in much the same circles. Except, it turned out, Rabi, who had to be introduced to Mrs. Ramsden, the Wilmot niece, and to Lieutenant Aspinall, both newish arrivals in the station.

But not even Rabi could wreck the air of tranquillity. He was not really trying, yet. Nor even the Maharajah, the martial Sikh, advancing on the mild company with his equally splendid and military scion, and booming as he came.

'Waji, you old rascal! What ho, Rabi! Still on the right side of Savile Row, I see.'

'Yes, sir. As you see.'

Rabi felt lazy, and cheerful, and, besides, he still nurtured hopes of Sophie who, this afternoon, had chosen to look adorable in a dress of jonquil linen.

Sebastian Lomax nursed similar, cunning hopes. He was planning, with Pip's aid, to execute a pincer movement that would deliver her up to him for a few brief, but exclusive, minutes.

'I'm not entirely convinced,' he said, 'that a game's out of the question. Shall we recce? What d'you say? With his Highness's permission. I wonder, sir, if—'

'Of course, of course. Treat the place as you would your own, my dear young man. But I'm afraid you will find,' said the melancholy Maharajah, 'it is quite beyond redemption.'

'Cut to ribbons,' said Rabi. 'Had a look this morning.'

But the Captain had already risen, and the Lieutenant was taking up position on the left flank, so that he sat back prepared to admit defeat. Sophie, however, had other ideas. She had many devoted English attendants, but, in Devapur at least, only one Oriental.

'Come along, Rabi,' she said. 'Come and show us. We shall be quite lost without a guide.'

No one believed in this artifice, not even Sophie. But the group proceeded civilly, Sophie twirling the hat on which her mother had insisted, her thoughts idling on the charming prospect of being lost somewhere with the prince, some remote place, but not as remote and rocky as the Hill of Devi.

Until, quite soon, for the court was neither hidden nor distant, they came upon the scene. Certainly it was harrowing. The grass, which had been mown, and mown badly, and grown and mown again and watered and rolled to a baize perfection, had been raked up over the entire surface. By means of a plough, at very least. In places there were unsightly mounds of mud and turf, on which the green was already shrivelled.

'Blackguards!' said Sebastian Lomax, rather huskily, and tightened his belt.

'How horrible,' said Sophie, shuddering. It seemed to her the most pointless, wanton deed. 'Do you think anyone can have really *meant* to do it?'

'It was meant, all right,' said the tight-lipped Captain.

'Feelings are running high,' said Rabi, himself low, and somewhat cool.

'But how *could* they!' cried Sophie, and felt obscure assaults, unaccountably, here in the open. 'I mean,' she said, 'how could anyone get past the guards? They're posted at all the gates.'

'Must've shinned over the wall,' said Pip Aspinall.

'Through the breaches,' said Rabi. 'Innumerable holes.'

'But who—?' said the Lieutenant, who was newly out from England, and as bewildered as Sophie.

'Your people, I'm afraid, Mr. Aspinall,' said Rabi, lifting his shoulders. Innocence of this order, in a man, invariably tempted him to goad.

'I suppose we did,' said Captain Lomax. He was rather stiff, he considered it in bad taste, this kind of thing, especially inflicting it on a woman. 'Historically speaking. No reason, of course, why they should be left in that state.'

'Well, one or two treaty—um—obligations,' said Rabi, mumbling, siding entirely with the chivalrous young Sebastian in a wish to cocoon Sophie, a desire many young men who met her shared, but not quite prepared to let it go. 'Shall we,' he proposed, 'return?'

The Maharajah meanwhile was gently entertaining the gentlemen, and the ladies, of whom there was the usual dearth. Usha, Shanta Devi, Mohini (more understandably, Lady C still chilly about her), these three presentable people had been cordially invited, and all three had declined. If only, he felt, wistfully. Nothing like a woman to grace a table as, say, Lady C did for Arthur.

And was driven to apologise.

'My wife,' he said, and coughed, and added for the new Mrs. Ramsden's benefit, 'my wife, the Maharani, sends her salaams. She is—er—not in town.'

Most of them knew she was; but no one was so churlish as to challenge him.

'She often goes,' said Bawajiraj, who often felt this urge to embroider, 'to her temple, somewhere in the wilds. I must say I'm seldom tempted to accompany her.'

'Nor would I be,' said Mrs. Ramsden, utterly believing in these mythical excursions. 'Not in these times. The Maharani must be a very brave lady.'

'The Maharani,' said his Sikh Highness, who loved games, 'would naturally have been provided with a suitable escort, eh Waji? A squadron or two, crack cavalry?'

'Naturally,' said Bawajiraj, whom Mrs. Ramsden had somewhat bemused, but reflated by dear old Pooky. 'Though not a squadron, my dear fellow. One or two Lancers, would be more like it. Devapuris, you know, not Sikhs. Don't need an army.'

'Bearded warriors,' roared Pooky, positively revelling by now. 'Unbeaten in the field.'

'Poona Horse,' said Sir Arthur, who was also enjoying himself, 'beat your team, Pooky, in—my memory's going to pieces—when was it, Charles?'

'Pindi, '09,' said the Colonel. 'Best game I ever saw.'

'The year your Lancers took the Cup, wasn't it, Waji?' said Sir Arthur.

'Indeed,' said Bawajiraj, suffused, yet sober. 'And kept it for the next three years against all comers.'

Giving the facts, while not allowing himself to boast.

They were all enjoying themselves hugely.

So were the ladies, while contemplating the agreeable scene. Enchanting, or should one say magnificent, Cicely Ramsden debated. She had an artist's eye for colour, and found it ravished by the fire of red sandstone and pure marble, against an emerald cloth of lawns and cypresses. She would bring her easel one day, she resolved, and set it up here, and record the magical scene.

'I really must,' she said, and changed it. 'I would very much like, if the Maharajah Sahib, and of course the Maharani, have no objection, to put it all down one day. In oils, I think. Oh, I don't know. Water colours might be better, the lights are so subtle. What d'you think, Margaret?'

Mrs. Wilmot didn't know. She had no artistic pretensions, unlike Cicely.

'You know I'm not the slightest good at these things, Cicely dear,' she said, leaning back in her basket-chair, the honeyed afternoon was making her feel deliciously languid. 'I'm sure to give you the wrong advice.'

439

Then some goblin got into her.

'Except, Cicely, to suggest the sooner the better. Before the whole thing goes up in smoke.'

It sounded extreme, even to her ears.

'I know it doesn't sound *likely*,' she defended herself. 'But, you know, worse things happen. It wasn't all *that* long ago the Officers' Mess in Lyallpur was burnt to the ground. Poor lambs had *nowhere* to go for months. It was Pindharis, I believe.'

'Pindharis, m'dear,' said the Colonel briskly, briefly abandoning Quetta, 'were crushed by the Marquess, in 1818.'

'Do I mean *dacoits*?' enquired his wife.

'Cracked down on 'em,' said the Colonel, 'in '05. Not a one's dared show up since.'

He lingered over these and other civilising missions, perhaps to reassure the ladies, one of whom at least was more concerned about her boys, who were treating, and loving, leopards as if they were lambs.

The Maharajah suffered no such anxieties. The cheetahs were on silver chains, which were stronger than they looked, and, for good measure, were muzzled and gloved. However, he soothed Mrs. Ramsden while thinking about his tea, and wondering how much longer the croquet quartet would be; air, and conversation, had sharpened his appetite. Now and then, in his post of host and hostess combined, he scanned the horizon keenly, and as soon as he glimpsed the returning party (a flash through the flower beds of Sophie's jonquil linen) he said, somewhat coyly,

'Shall we pour?'

Experimenting, as it were. He had heard one or two hostesses, in England, pronounce this formula, and even suit deeds to words. Not that he would dream. Not with those platoons lined up discreetly, one behind the tables, the reserve behind the cypresses. However, he began to direct, skilfully, by means of a system of silent signals that would have earned the admiration of a Sabutai squadron.

Rabi, eye on these manoeuvres, said, vulgarly,

'Better hurry, before they scoff the lot.'

'Really, Rabi,' cried delighted Sophie, who fell less easily, now she was more established; but the Lieutenant turned crimson, suffering terribly for the Maharajkumar, who proceeded to make it unbearable.

'I'm afraid, Sophie, you simply don't know my father,' he was saying. 'He can be a pig without trying, a real old porker.'

However, everyone was waiting, including the famished and blameless Maharajah, who had not allowed greedy Waji to so much as think of downing a single morsel. They watched the four young people advancing up the lawn, Cicely Ramsden feeling that she really must, one day, sketch the Maharajkumar. So striking, in that simple white, not a touch of colour except the gold haft of some weapon he carried in his belt, on which the sun was glinting.

'Is that,' she said, as he came up, 'a bazooka you carry, Kumar Sahib?'

Ranjit tittered, before he could smother it. He was a version of the Saxon Sebastian: bronze, say, rather than flaxen. Nevertheless his heritage was different, and sometimes it peeped through.

Rabi, meanwhile, found himself at sea.

'Bazooka, Mrs. Ramsden?' he said, doubtfully. He really had no idea.

'Perhaps I mean tomahawk,' said Cicely, desperately.

'It looks like a dagger to me,' said Mrs. Wilmot, eye cocked on the shiny hilt.

'Oh this,' said Rabi. 'It's a—'

And made to draw it.

And stopped. Hand arrested as it dropped and gripped. That old sense of a command ringing out, while a wrist was rapped; and an aura of chill constriction reaching out from childhood which as far as he was concerned could emanate only from Lady Copeland.

His resources, however, were greater than those of that child. Nor could Lady Copeland indefinitely continue her grip. As both emerged slow, and even shaken, from the thickets of their past it became clear it was she, rather than he, who now stood in need of help. She was, he saw, really afraid, strands of hair, that must once have resembled the stunning golds of her daughter, clung to her forehead. It moved him to a certain pity.

'It's a boomerang,' he said then, quite gently, and drew out the object and passed it to her for inspection. 'One of the tribesmen, when we were working up in the jungle, taught me the rudiments . . . but I'm afraid I've a long way to go yet.'

'It's beautifully fashioned,' responded Lady Copeland. Her fingers moved steadily over the goldsmith's handiwork, she could have been wholly absorbed by it. For all his impulse of pity he could not but salute such powers of recovery.

'Yes,' he agreed. 'The Palace does still employ some extraordinarily fine craftsmen. But the arabesques are entirely the goldsmith's idea, all I asked of him was a capping to increase the weight and range.'

'Does it?'

'Around twenty yards, I'd say, at a rough guess.'

Water closed over the incident. It had barely been allowed to infringe and now was buried by the company, most of whose members were glossy and experienced.

Colonel Wilmot, after a frisson of anxiety for Mary, for whom he steadfastly nurtured a soft spot, was adducing weighty reasons for his preference for Darjeeling over the Orange Pekoe favoured by his wife, while the Maharajah was embarked, somewhat hazardously, on a description of the forthcoming Holi for the benefit of Sophie and Cicely.

'It's a very jolly festival,' he was saying. 'Though it's religious too. A bit of both, d'you know what I mean? A little worship, and a lot of hurling things about.'

'What sort of things?' asked Cicely Ramsden, bulging with visions.

'Well, water, mostly,' said the affable Maharajah, who, in youth, had loved it. 'Coloured water, and various powders—don't ask me what—and flowers, and rice, all sorts of missiles. They pelt you like demons.'

'*You*, Maharajah Sahib?'

'Oh yes certainly, my dear lady. Everyone's equal on that day, you see. We're all Maharajahs together. Or all ordinary folk, if you like that better. And it is absolutely forbidden to take umbrage.'

'It sounds delightful,' said Sophie.

'Fun,' said Cicely, whose postings up North had so far yielded only some fierce sword-dancing by alarming Baluchis.

'Actually,' said the Maharajah, cosily, but innocently, 'it provides an excuse for everyone to let their hair down a bit.'

'More than a bit. It's a saturnalia,' said Mrs. Wilmot, severe about the mouth. She had once observed proceedings from a window.

'I'd love to go,' said Sophie, disregarding these stuffy opinions, and addressing herself to the country's interpreters. 'Can anyone, your Highness? Someone like me, for instance?'

'Oh yes, absolutely, my dear child. Absolutely anyone can go, it's a free country,' said the liberal if incautious Maharajah. Then he suffered a twinge, either self-manufactured or, more likely, from picking up obscure signals emitted by the British party.

'However, if you do decide to attend, my dear young lady,' he said, interpreting hurriedly, and a shade off-centre, 'I trust you will not think of doing so without a suitable escort. In these unsettled times. A guide, shall we say . . . someone who knows the ropes . . . in case of any eruptions.'

So that Sophie, naturally enough, turned to Rabi.

Rabi, it appeared, would be honoured; but goblins were at work in him too.

'There's really no need,' he said. 'It's a perfectly harmless festival, and there won't be any eruptions.'

'If there were to be,' argued the Maharajah.

'There won't be,' said Rabi.

'Just in *case*,' said his harassed father, 'of political disturbances.'

'No political disturbances,' said his son, firmly. 'There's a truce until Holi is over. But, if you wish, I'll keep an eye on Sophie.'

Since it was settled they went on with their tea. Powers of recovery were not confined to Lady Copeland, although in her they did reach superb heights.

'From Kabul, via Chaman,' the Maharajah was saying, and even himself handing round gold bowls whose gilt interiors bloomed with the luscious cerise of cherries picked at their best. 'Lady C, I insist on your sampling the first of the crop . . .'

* * *

The Dewan was invited to coffee by Sir Arthur. He declined the invitation. Then he was simply summoned. Sir Arthur's patience was wearing thin. His intelligence—which in private in milder times he dubbed his *Cavalerie de St. Georges*—were sending in distinctly disturbing reports.

'I understand,' he said bluntly, 'the Palace is to be the next objective.'

'Who knows what next?' the Dewan wondered, billowing on the verandah. It was quite a hot wind, for March.

'If you don't I'm sure your daughter has an excellent idea,' suggested Sir Arthur.

'I am not privy to her plans. Our children, Excellency,' said the sententious Dewan, 'are a law unto themselves. They do not confide—'

'Ours do,' said the Resident.

'In the Establishment,' said the Dewan.

'Parents,' said Sir Arthur, coldly, 'hardly fall into that category.'

443

The Dewan held his peace. The Resident perambulated. A fair-minded man, however, he could not indefinitely forbid glimpses, from which sympathies sprang. One's dilemmas, he felt: the highest in the land; and he was not even thinking of himself or the Maharajah. Quite soon he stopped pacing.

'Very well, Dewan Sahib. Have it your way,' he said, and sighed a little. 'But tell me this, if you will. Is your Holi or whatever safe for my child?'

The Dewan unbent. Human tinges under the statuary, Sir Arthur was relieved to see; these days he could not bank on them, he had a niggly feeling, as he had once been able.

'Entirely, Excellency,' he said. 'A somewhat rowdy festival which gives a lot of pleasure to feebler minds; but your daughter will not come to the slightest harm.'

'But a religious festival,' said Sir Arthur, whose custom it was to keep well clear. 'Can it not—er—give rise to frenzy?'

'Of what *sort*, Resident Sahib?'

'Well, religious,' said Sir Arthur, who was not too clear what he meant either. 'I mean, if it were to get mixed up with these soul-force *wallahs*.'

'Ah, but that is a different kind of religious experience, Excellency,' said the Dewan kindly.

Sir Arthur left it.

'Well, if you say so,' he said, dubiously, and mused a little and added, a thought off-key he sounded to himself, 'I suppose the fact is, Dewan Sahib, we all have to fulfil our own destiny.'

There were times, like this one, when he felt he was oddly close to turning into an Indian; a process with which he was not wholly out of sympathy.

20

The Holi party resolved itself into four: Rabi and Sophie, Cicely and the Lieutenant. Lady Copeland had prevailed upon Cicely Ramsden, who was not unwilling, and besides was an obliging young woman; and she in turn had coaxed Pip Aspinall. The Maharajah would be going, separately, as a Maharajah, though naturally he would fall in with all the other one-day Maharajahs when he got there. Of the two others hoped for the luckless Captain was on duty, and so in a manner of speaking was Usha, who was preparing to go into retreat prior to the campaign.

The quartet, it was clear, must soon part along natural lines; transparent bonds attached Pip to Cicely, and even Rabi to Sophie; but for the moment presented an impression of party. For it was gathered on the Residency lawn, an exposed position at any time, even now under a moon.

'This festival, it seems to me,' Cicely was attempting to clear her mind, 'is a celebration of Spring, and Lord Krishna, and the idea of Fellowship, all rolled into one.'

'Anything you please,' said Rabi.

He was in one of his moods, not lazy but contained. These explanations, he felt, when one should absorb meanings through senses and the pores of one's skin. His own was taut and luminous. Full moons are handmaidens to festivals.

Under the same moon Sophie had been nudged into silver. Her skin, the strands of her hair, were netted in shining scales. The soft stuff of what she was wearing might have been woven to soak up these silvery falls.

'Will I do?'

It was not Sophie who asked, but Cicely. Sophie, perhaps, had no need. It was, however, her whom he addressed.

'You look ravishing.'

Cicely wondered, some deflection scratched for attention; but decided it was intended for her, fulsome though she considered the compliment. The light, however, excused excesses.

'That is kind, Kumar Sahib. I hadn't a notion what to wear. I've never been to a festival like this. I'm so excited, I feel all trembly.'

She looked all trembly, in a shot-silk dress with bead fringes, and several ropes of beads about her neck; but he warmed to her, coming up out of his own lucid cave to respond to some honesty in this pale-eyed, artless woman. Eagerness made her shine.

The Lieutenant, next to Cicely, could not shine, he was over-conscious. It was his rig. He had put on khaki, whose thick dull twill resisted, it took in and gave back nothing. He felt, in this shimmering company—for Rabi's mull also ran silver—a bit of a blot.

He was impelled to defend himself.

'It can be messy, his Highness was kind enough to warn me,' he said. 'I dug out my oldest togs. Luckily it fits.'

It was patently not old, but it did patently fit, without a crinkle, his slender, civilised back. In other lights, on lawns, Pip Aspinall was only a shade less handsome than Sebastian.

'Never mind. It won't matter what we've got on by the time they've finished with us,' said Cicely, and giggled. 'Isn't that so, Kumar Sahib.'

'Oh entirely,' said Rabi, fending off the clashing of her beads. 'We shall all end up all colours of the rainbow.'

Lieutenant Aspinall was relieved to hear it. He was a nice young man, he sincerely wished to fit in, he did not want to put a damper on proceedings which Cicely, at least, seemed to think would be a riot. The thought of playing skeleton at anyone's feast filled him with absolute horror.

'Do you think,' he said, 'we ought to get moving? Don't want to be late, or anything.'

'Yes. Why not?' said Rabi, lolling, somewhat, in a deck chair.

'But has it *started*?' asked Cicely, her nails clattering on the little glass table. 'No point in going till it's warmed up.'

'It's going on now,' he answered. 'Just goes on, join when you feel like it.'

'I feel like it,' said Sophie, rupturing some fastness of her own.

'Let's go then,' he responded, and rose from his chair, which he had converted into a hammock at sea, forcing from it sounds of straining canvas and cordage. In the stillness what he had wantonly stifled came back: a distortion of air currents, rather than plausible sound, distant rhythms that got into the turf. The lawn was close to a sprung floor, although it struggled gamely, thick green pile, against such conversions

By now he was impatient to be gone, limbs were itching; but there were bags and wraps, and other amazing paraphernalia. Finally, however, they were fully equipped and on the move.

'Is it far?' Cicely thought to ask. She didn't really care, her beads were swinging recklessly.

'Not by car.'

Motor-cars had, reasonably, been provided: Rolls by the Palace, Daimler from the Residency; were selecting gear, low, purring, these discreet pewter ghosts, preparing to shadow the cavalier foursome.

None of the four, from another brand of reason, favoured ghostly or sobering shades. For the rhythms affecting them now were clearer and clearly concerned with the exuberance of living.

'Let's walk,' said Sophie. Her slender jaw was finely, invincibly structured.

'It's a fair way.'

'*Walk,*' said Sophie.

She would blaze the way. Her cloistered silver had begun to fizz and spark.

The Lieutenant, falling in behind with Cicely, in spite of distractions did think to wonder. He hoped Sophie knew what she was doing. However, she was in sieved, select hands: firm, and even powerful hands, he had happened to notice on other occasions; while the strength of his own seemed strangely compromised. On the whole he felt he would have his work cut out—distant drums impressed it on him—keeping hold of himself and Cicely.

* * *

All the way the country came up against them in soft and swelling flurries. Leaves, dust, blown petals thrown up like moths against flaming torches. People. Bright rings of people who moved with them, brushed with shy dark fingers, slid away into bashful ellipses, regrouped at distances. Poured back like surf, pressing on them the warmth of their bodies, their smiles, their gifts.

'What shall I do?'

Sophie is clutching a pyramid of fruits of the earth.

'Hand them back.'

'No.'

The pyramid is lurching. Limes tumble out. One huge green coconut rolls like a head. Sophie gets down and scrabbles in the dust for this outsize skull, bare toes cringe and retreat at her touch.

'Sophie, do you *want* to get trampled to death?'

He is sweating.

'No.'

She comes up, triumphant, fine act of balancing there. The coconut is on top of the pyramid.

'Give it back.'

'No.'

'They expect you to. Touch it and hand it back.'

'No. They *want* me to have them.'

'*Anyone* can *see* you can't take it all.'

Suddenly she gives in. Her face is radiant, distributing this bounty.

But, really, she wants to hang on. She is yearning to hold all of it, the warmth, the loot, the laughter. Her eyes, sealed under crescents of heavy gold lashes, have become a mystery to him. Are they dreaming or daring? He is not at all sure. She is not going to help.

A wind gets up. It brings the odours of evening, of herds, of jasmine, of watered earth from this little walled garden they are skirting. It stirs the women. Women's skirts swirl into bell-tents and are slapped down. Boys and girls are helping. Tents flap and collapse, subside gracefully into parachutes of crumpled yellow and scarlet. Girls are laughing. Sophie's hair streams, she is running with the wind.

'*Sophie!*'

'Yes?'

'Stay close.'

'Why?'

Why. He races to catch up. He has his problems, a cwt of garlands dangling from his neck. He catches up, and cups an elbow fiercely. Bones are sliding flimsily in their chiffon sheaths in his palm, he is made to feel a thug.

The wind begins to gust. It carries the pungent odours of camphor, oleander, burning oil, oiled bodies, incense. Hectic smells. It brings music. A great sheet of music has collected just past the lip of this bowl over which they are skimming. It arcs over a huge pool of water, the tank in the town which is the epicentre of this movement of giggling assassins and victims.

In mid swallow flight they actually catch her voice. Miraculous, considering the shindy.

Cicely's voice, calling faintly, not too hopeful, not too anxious. Doing her Duty.

'Not so fast! Wait for us!'

Mother of two, her senses are leaping like fish. Sex in this land is tied up with religion, she's heard. Doesn't really care, she's in safe hands, she offloads the burden and shimmies along in shot-silk beside Pip, who instinct informs carries a level head on a pair of splendid shoulders.

The two in front cannot wait. Not on this rip-tide. Do they *want* to? Humanity engulfs them.

* * *

Over the bowl the scene explodes on them.

Kettledrums, flutes, fifes, fireworks. This vast pool of water and light. Upside-down palaces in it, bits of enamelled sky, polished bodies, jewelled faces. A floating temple, pyramid of flowers and precious metals, rides at anchor, a ship of light.

More lights on shore. Fizzing, crackling, showering on people. People are everywhere. The place is thick. Sophie has never seen anything like it.

'I can't breathe!'

'Yes you can.'

He hauls her out of the fray onto this square in front. Sort of a watered-earth desert, comparatively speaking, set up for weaker disciples. Sophie can breathe, she discovers. Breathing rather fast she watches this amazing foreign scene. It seems to be play. Horseplay. People pinch and run, are chased and caught and pinched in turn. They tweak each other and are tweaked back. They have pails and scoops, they scoop up water and slosh each other. Girls fly shrieking and are pursued and bombarded. Powder-bombs burst, spill brilliant colours on soaked shoulders, on dripping hair. The air is full of whirling motes.

Looking round for ammunition it comes up on trays, piles of

the stuff: red, pink, yellow, opal, oriflamme, moon-grain, fish-scale, gold. This thing's really organised. Someone, grinning, puts in a thumb, pulls it up smothered. She can feel the straw-berry flaming in the middle of her forehead. Her cheeks, wrists, temples, the parting of her hair, all are daubed.

'What is it?'

'A custom.'

'Can I?'

She doesn't wait, she's into the velvety stuff which flakes like ash between finger and thumb. Daubing, hurling with the best of them, her cheek-bones grow hectic.

But what does it signify? These jokes, the exploding laughter, slapped thighs, diaphanous hymns in an unknown tongue, these loops and cusps of coded legends unfolding on sinuous banners?

Occupied as he is he receives the transmission.

'What does it mean?'

What meaning does she *want*?

Absorb, absorb, suck it in. It's not laid down you can shake yourself eternally into meanings. Being is its own kind of sense. Earth assimilates all, water, oil, the sweat of devout foreheads and feet, the oblations they pour on it, the bones of the dead.

'Blood!' shrieks Sophie.

'Where?' he snarls.

Not that he can't stand the sight. But can't Diana? But it isn't the *place* for it.

Lunar blade ascends, gleams, descends, cleaves a coconut in half.

Sophie uncovers her eyes, shrieks, covers them up again. Eyes, ears, head, all are cowering in an igloo of desperate chiffon. He's half frightened himself.

'Sophie, for heaven's sake! We're not *savages*, it's only *birds*!'

Birds indeed, assorted. Fantails, parakeets, sulphur-crest cockatoos, are all being impressed into the scheme of celebra-tion. Wicker cages open, bells ring, inmates are poked out of bondage. Flapping sleepy wings the emancipists straggle off to roost, some quiet tree away from homo sapiens. *Sapiens!*

The music stokes up. Atonal to Sophie, it has begun to peak into shrill falsetto. Drums are another matter. Any pair of feet can answer drums. She is longing to answer, but afraid. She is both afraid and longing to mingle with what she doesn't under-stand. It is taken out of her hands. Girls are laughing, nudging, inviting, pulling her into their circle. They clap and stamp and break her into their dancing.

Rabi is roistering in his own ring. Rings edge closer, now and again. At one point they are dancing together, room is made, clapping eggs them on.

This girl's an accomplished dancer, but she can't get his beat. He can't fall into hers, for that matter. They are zigzagging wildly, when they are not stalking each other. He doesn't know what's gone wrong, he cannot follow her moods. If he could get at her, he feels, but she has retreated, enclosed her face. Moving badly she is tripping the rhythm.

'Let yourself go,' he says.

'How?'

How!

'Try this.'

Suddenly she's into it. Laughing at him, loving his antics, eyes deepened to fantastic blues she swirls past him and is swept up into the circle of applauding dancers.

Rabi rejoins his ring. It's his scene, he's free to soak it up, his skin has begun to quicken.

'Ram-Ram, Rabi *bhai!*'

This man who claims him as brother has been a dancer from so high. It gives him advantages. He's wearing bells, and a codpiece under the finest, most intricately pleated gauze. The bells are about his ankles. He's shaking his bells and clashing a pair of cymbals, plus all kinds of snaky movements, you can see he's inspired, he's well known for his inspirations. Youths come from near and far to emulate, but he's a master of the art, tantalises one pace ahead, the quicker they catch on the subtler he gets.

Musicians pick up the score, they're adroit practitioners themselves. They're scaling up, playing with, daring each other, together they're converging on some shining core, these performing wizards and the wily virtuoso.

Horseplay begins to slide. It glissades sly and glossy up the slope of this powerful roller.

Elsewhere it's subtler too.

Except for Sophie, who's fighting a hose.

Some maniac's found one and turned it on, the water gushes like a bore from the bucking nozzle, Sophie is leaping in and out of the powerful jets gleaming and wet as a fish. The special woven dream-stuff of her dress glistens like a second skin, it clings to and points up the whole of her body.

There's a good deal of nakedness around, but it's brown. Sophie's revelations are different. People are too polite to take a good look, but their indecent eyes are squinting at this lewd moonflower.

Sophie looked as women do with their men; in private.

It made him furious. With them. With her. He pushed through to her side.

'Sophie, let's go.'

'No.'

'Come on.'

He found her wrap and threw it about her, swung her round, away from the music and the dancing, guiding her back towards the calm evening.

While his own fever mounted. He could hardly bear to touch her now, he had to drop his arm. It had become a matter of trust.

They walked slowly, Sophie limping, space between them; crossed the dip in the land, breasted the rim, were cutting across the small walled garden when she stopped.

'I must sit down.'

'Not far to go now.'

'Please.'

He could not control her any more.

She was bending, pulling off her oozing shoes, heavy gold curtain swinging and parting, moonwashed nape, slender columns of legs hoisted onto the low stone, burning feet on the cool slab ascending to silvered crests, dizzy sweep from crest to petalled hollow.

He looked away. He saw her shadow on the rough adobe wall, insubstantial and very slender, or possibly it was the future that was forming, to which the preliminary had been the roll of drums.

'Rabi,' she said, 'it's been—it is—so lovely.'

Turning to him. He revolving to meet her. Her face upturned, sleeves sliding, riding up the lovely slopes of her arms, arms opening, purest alabaster in moonlight.

Caught in the same light, balanced on this dazzling trampoline of stretched skin and tension, he could not control himself.

He did not want to. Her arms were open, he knew where he wanted it to end.

She realised too, and began to be afraid, striving in the time that was left to crush what she had had a hand in constructing.

'What is it?' she asked, and shivered in her thin dress.

'What do you think?' he answered.

Softly.

Coming for her, she saw. One of these same wild people who had rubbed up against her for so long. Meanings that had gnawed all evening suddenly stark. What had been stalking her was finally out in the open.

She began to struggle.

He could not open her lips.

Because of the strength of his passion or possibly what had gone before, it took him some time to realise that he was, in her view, attempting rape.

Certainly it was her view.

Wrong side of the sheets, sprang from her mother's lips. *Plurality of women. A pagan race, not one of us.*

Because she was civilised she could not actually say these things. Not that there was any need, not with this powerful osmosis working. While Sophie shivered and flinched, although it was finished. Her lips were blue.

So were his, for that matter. It took him some time to recover, but he did. He was not, as it happened, interested in rape: finer things, when one had come out on the other side.

'Sophie,' he said, 'listen.'

Like an uncle. Why not. He had held children in his arms before, actual children, and children whose only maturity was in their bodies. Girls who tantalised and ran but made up for it when caught, or tried to. All kinds of experience.

What was new was the re-coding of a mind, until it responded with perversions.

'Sophie,' he said again. He had to try, her gold too fine, he felt, to heft such dross. 'People aren't different, in the things that matter.'

She could almost believe it. Some inklings had already begun to batter at her, painfully.

'I'm sorry,' she said. 'I don't know why I did what I did. It was unforgiveable. Do you think you can forgive me, start again from the beginning?'

Turning to him, lit by her honesty, the sweetness of her nature was not to be obscured.

Now, however, it was he who retreated, seeing, unfairly but clearly, in the sweetness she offered the nucleus of seductions and abductions that had finally claimed his father. Besides it was, quite plainly, over.

He took her face in his hands and kissed her trembling but tender and beautiful mouth.

'Nothing to forgive,' he said. 'It has been very lovely.'

And lifted her up and carried her back. She could not walk, the soused shoes had finally come to pieces; and it pierced him to see her limp.

* * *

Leave them alone
And they will come home
Bring-hing their tails behind them,

Cicely was singing, rather tipsily, but otherwise intact. Pip Aspinall had seen to it. The pair was ensconced in the Residency Daimler, which had trailed after and waited like a faithful collie.

Pip could see, even by moonlight, when the missing two arrived. Decently he refused to look, one did not goggle at the disarray of one's fellow-man. Been socked one, or something, he said to himself, and glazed his eyes before asking:

'Aren't you coming back with us?'

'No,' Rabi answered. 'I'd like to walk a little before calling it a day.'

So Pip helped Sophie in, and was made to sit in his polychrome tunic like a thorn, as Cicely said, between two roses.

* * *

Rabi walked.

Walking it off, the Pandit had called it, never specifying what *it* was, while recommending this course, in an agony of embarrassment, to the adolescent in his care.

Walking it off and, like falling asleep, entering a new state without placing at what point exactly. The land taking over now, this plain he was traversing which, dark or light, he knew like the back of his hand. It waited, or was there, like a comfortable glove that he could slip into when the spirit had been savaged.

Savaged? Not by Sophie. Her race. A golden race seduced by an arrogant philosophy and tainted by pride, but the sin was contributory. Victim and aggressor collaborating in the shabby process. Both diminished. Until one withdrew. Ducked out of the damaging compact and clutching its bedraggled soul for strength gave notice of intent to quit. An end and a beginning, as one came of age. All manner of things and people come of age.

Soaring high, the cry cut him down.

'*Arré baba! Haré Krishna!*'

A lone reveller, as pained as he, each imagining the earth his own, the squawk wrung from indignation and fright.

It was the dancer, respectable in a shawl, but betrayed by his bells, taking a last fling. Discovered, the pair, each in a state of

454

deshabille, but allowing themselves a rag or two and passing gravely, with dignified salutes, each to his sphere of lunatic rhapsody.

Rabi was walking easily now. Panditji and the leaping dancer had proved their worth. The easy pace, extinguishing fatigue and distance, brought him round in a wide circle from the Holi grounds to the hill. His world. A world of desert and dreams into which he fitted.

As Usha fitted.

Her form began to take shape in the luminous and drifting mists of pre-dawn light. Exquisitely put together, by infinitely subtle but sane processes. Not a doll to dress and undress. Not a child, nor some quivering turban ornament. A woman of a pared and lucid grace with whom he could talk, or be still, who could move him, and move with him, effortlessly picking up where he left off their common strand. A woman who was at one with him, their lives interlocking at more than one level, with whom, it pleased him to feel, he could wait, or not, to come together. In their own country, in their own time.

The sun was rising. First rites, all manner of hints of hues to come.

He found a boulder and sat down to watch. There was an engaging spell when sun, moon, and stars were all three visible. It was a good combination, to which his mother had implied he aspired.

He did. He would go after it, after breakfast.

21

St. George's Cavalry had got it right; but not entirely. The Palace was one objective. The Residency was another. Both were surrounded. The whole of Devapur appeared to have come out on strike.

The Resident turned back rapidly into an Englishman when he saw the multitude in position.

People. God, where did such hosts spring from. This utterly deplorable fecundity. Made a nonsense of one's sober planning. Not even the bodyguard, hacking (butts only) at elbows and shins could uniformly guarantee a stately passage for him through the congestion.

Never, however, say die. He sought, or rather fought through to, the Maharajah.

The Maharajah was similarly confounded. He had not realised he had quite so many subjects, subversive at that. The hinterland where all this breeding had taken place had chosen to shed some of its mystery. Those durbars and Dassaras, he began to perceive, had revealed nothing at all of the capacity and purpose of his kingdom.

It was at this nadir of gloom that the Resident arrived with some trenchant suggestions for His Highness, the Commander-in-Chief of the State Forces.

The Maharajah trembled. He could not order the Devapur Lancers.

Not with the child of one's loins squatted out there like a stone buddha.

As much to the point, they might not obey.

Sir Arthur was furious. No discipline, he wanted to, well, yell, and did, inwardly. However, he saw it was no use. His own force, luckily, or wisely, was recruited from the North-West Frontier (Waziris) under Colonel Wilmot. He went off to confer with that tower of strength, who had long since drawn up contingency plans to stem the march of a nation.

* * *

'What did Bania Sahib want?' Mohini wanted to know.

'The same as I do. To be allowed to live in peace,' said her wilted consort.

'But what is to *prevent* you, my sweet,' wheedled Mohini, soaping her knuckles to aid the passage of some small but extra-pretty bangles. 'All you have to do is go down, to that square there—it's your square remember, named after you, not Bania Sahib—and tell them you'll give them the peanuts they're asking for. They look on you as their father. Why can't you behave like one?'

It was very tempting. It was no fun at all, being cooped up like this. All right for a woman, bangles and things, but a man got restless. However, it could not be done. However badly one longed to be a father to one's people.

'I'm afraid you simply don't understand these matters,' he said firmly, while squirming a little, viscerally, in case she did have more than a glimmering.

Conversations

'Dewan Sahib. I—er—Usha. We—.'

'Never known you to lose your tongue, Rabi.'

(Enough to clam one up forever. Start again.)

'Dewan Sahib, I know what you'll say—'

'Rabi, I'll let you into a family secret. My great-great-aunt was permitted to honour a Mughal harem.'

(Other times, other diplomacies and compulsions. A *mleccha* blot on the escutcheon. But even one's Brahmin wife, one hoped, would not run to the extreme of declaring this union a *mleccha* alliance. One so wished one had not—ah, encouraged these extremist tendencies.)

'You mean—?'

'My dear Rabi, of course I mean. I will—ah—approach my wife to arrange for emissaries.'

'Now? In the middle of all this?'

'Why not? Life goes on, does it not? It will, besides, occupy his Highness, take his mind off current unpleasant developments of which you, my dear Rabi, will be even more fully aware than a mere Minister.'

(Back to his curlicues. Forgiveable, just, if one kept in mind the circumstances.)

* * *

'We can't just live together.'

'We are practically living together.'

'Doesn't signify, *does* it, surrounded by thousands!'

'Well, your parents do.'

'Does one have to copy one's parents in everything?'

'If you're going to shout, Rabi, we can't discuss anything.'

'I'm not shouting. No more than is necessary to make you hear.'

'Your parents have managed all right.'

'The effort! Have you any idea? I don't want you to struggle like my mother.'

'Did she struggle?'

'Fiercely. I realise that now.'

'Frankly, I'm not keen.'

'If you want me to pay court to win your hand, just say so.'

'I don't want anything so ridiculous. I don't want the British to have any levers on me either, or on my children.'

'What British, what levers! What do you *think* we're all doing, playing games?'

* * *

'Thing is, Rabi, I don't think I could stand all that savagery you go in for.'

'*What* savagery?' (He can hear his teeth grinding. This is the second time a woman has accused him.)

'Hunting and so forth.'

(This is almost amusing.)

'Have you any notion what it costs?'

'Nothing. You don't even think. Snuffing out life means nothing to you.'

'In money terms. What it costs to mount a tiger shoot.'

'I daresay there're ways to wring money out of stones.'

'Not if you—uh—want other things.'

'What things?'

'Well. Everyone has desires, haven't they? Not ready for airing?'

* * *

'My dear, I do think you and Sophie ought to get away for a bit, until this little exhibition's over.'

'Do you think, Arthur, I would even consider it?'

'I suppose not. You know, Mary, I am grateful. . . .'

* * *

'Since you ask—'
'When?'
'Since you haven't asked, I have to say there is the question of
the plurality of women.'
(Oh God, not again.)
'*What* plurality?'
'D'you think the doings of princes can be kept secret?'
'Not a race of eunuchs, you know!'
(Got to make a stand somewhere.)
'No. Such a thing as a happy medium.'
'*Whose* happiness?'
'Rabi, a square like this is for *public* assembly and *public* discus-
sion.'
'I know. I'm only saying I'm as much in control as you.'
'I know. You've learned from me. Self-control is a keynote to
this movement. Here.'
'What?'
'Lime squash.'
'Nectar.'
'Any liquid would turn, at high noon. Secret of transubstantia-
tion.'
'I wonder how long it'll last.'
'The siege?'
'Self-control.'
'Long enough.'
'Not easy, when some oaf's thumping you.'
'No.'
'I wish this was over. Must be better things than sit here and
fry.'
'Yes. By the river would be lovely.'
'Yes.'

* * *

'Never seen such a grim lot.'
'Troops aren't prepared for this kind of action.'
'You know what they look like? The bad characters in that play
you put on. Same kind of expressive faces.'
'Weren't faces. Masks your mother painted.'
'They horrified everyone.'
'Yes, I realise now. I was innocent in those days.'

'Everyone in the audience. Never seen such a crowd of paralysed martyrs.'

Almost paralytic themselves.

* * *

Glad someone was able, the beleaguered Residency felt. They
could see nothing in the situation that warranted laughter. In
this horrible month of May. Macabre. Wasn't it the *Chinese*,
actually, who laughed at funerals? Muddling. No doubt the heat,
one couldn't think straight. One's nerves, moreover, were like
chewed cord as hopes of Simla retreated.

Lady Copeland did not have the heart even to order the Simla
trunks to be brought down.

* * *

'Are you afraid?' Usha asked.

'I was thinking,' he replied. 'Of that strike I got mixed up in. In
Bombay. There was a girl who helped me, a millhand. She was
on strike too. It didn't last long, they were broken in the end.
They didn't really expect anything else, she told me, because that
was how it had always been for the empty-belly race. That's what
she belonged to, she said. Not this or that caste or craft, or sex, or
anything. She belonged to the empty-belly race. A race that
would always be defeated. I feel afraid when I think of that, yes.'

'But that was before,' said Usha, composed on the ground, and
folded together as elegantly as if resting on one of her father's
beloved Persians. 'That crowd didn't know its own strength. This
one does. There have been one or two discoveries since.'

Very sleek, he saw, from the confidence that such discovery
brings: hair like a polished stone, and herself involved in some
process of truth, or revelation, that clothed her in shiny skins.

A sheen did seem to invest those who waited. Perhaps it was
sweat, it was a broiling sun.

* * *

The crowd that had assembled to challenge the Palace and the
Residency and beyond these two an untenable order was, certainly, different from those that had gone before.

462

These people have not come here for justice. Justice, according to what its high priests have told them, is meant for the people. They know better. They have learnt it is window dressing, for display purposes. Ordinary sensible mortals, they fly from it at speed—its stunning cost, which will cripple them to the third generation, its delays, its mystery, its airs of sanctimony, its palpable and mountainous injustice.

No. They have done with justice, and have come instead to claim their natural rights. What is more, they have a supreme confidence in their ability to succeed in their claim.

This crowd is not going to make the mistake of the mill crowd, or any other crowd, or strike. It has discovered muscle. Further, it has found out that muscle is a mesh of physical and mental fibre. It intends to use this strength, which is founded, even more basically, on its human spirit.

It intends to stay. It, or, if not, its heirs and successors. Time is on its side.

This is the force against which, somewhat half-heartedly, and with a dismal conviction of bullying, they are attempting to pit the tinny might of soldiers.

Sir Arthur grew irritable, thinking of it. That Garrison Force, nannied all these years with God knew what effort, completely spiked by these inadmissible tactics.

* * *

Then it became dreadful to endure.

These numb, dumb people, sitting it out, all round the clock. In protest, or condemnation. Owl-eyed, exuding silent reproaches.

Indefensible, Sir Arthur felt. Nothing but moral blackmail. Infinitely preferable would have been a straight, clean fight. Colonel Wilmot was all for it. One machine-gun, it had been his experience, would take care of a thousand spear-toting natives. Sir Arthur had to curb him, although he too longed for a straightforward battle with upright opponents. Instead of all these squatted opponents who offered themselves up like sacrificial cows.

The Resident would have liked to continue furious but he was, he felt, too weary. It was wearying merely to see.

Day in, day out, people. Parked out there like so many bales of cotton.

Insensate? One knew better.

At noon all these white humps put up umbrellas with which they had come thoughtfully provided and turned into flocks of crows.

It was the nights though. Then it was rows of tombstones.

After an initial alarm Sir Arthur was not afraid, day or night. Military training enabled him to recognise, and fairness to pay tribute to, the exemplary discipline that informed the thin and unlikely forms of the rebels. He soothed his wife, turned over and slept soundly. But, simply, he saw no end. Volunteer squads came in endlessly to take the place of those who were clouted and carried away. Unlike the Viceroy, he did not find it amusing. It was hateful to watch, these ordinary, decent people. An altogether wretched business, which was made even more intolerable by elements of admiration he could not wholly avoid, sneaking in through cracks that attachment to the country had opened up in him.

* * *

'I suppose, Maharajah Sahib,' said the Resident, 'we must try different tactics.'

'Military, d'you mean,' said the Maharajah, recoiling.

'I mean you will have to yield,' said the blunt Sir Arthur.

For the first time in their long association it took away Bawajiraj's breath.

Sir Arthur was also struggling, as his infernal fairness jostled up officiously.

'I suppose you could say we,' he said, 'will have to yield a point or two.'

* * *

'I suppose,' said the gloomy Maharajah to his Minister, 'we shall have to give in, in the end.'

'Yes, Highness, you will. As a beginning,' said the Dewan, gently. 'Yes, I think a beginning.'

* * *

'Are you pleased?' Rabi asked Usha.

'Yes. Aren't you?'

'It's a beginning,' he said.

'Yes. A splendid beginning,' said Usha. 'Now, what next, d'you think?'

She was radiant. He thought he had never seen a more beautiful woman. He drew her closer, so that they could plan.

* * *

'But what is there to grump about?' Mohini wanted to know. 'For once in your life you're behaving like a father to your people. You're actually letting them keep a fraction of what's theirs, instead of grabbing the whole lot for yourself and your *bania* friends. You ought to be pleased for their sake.'

'I am pleased.'

'So am I. So is your son. Everyone's pleased. Why you couldn't have stood up to Bania Sahib years ago I simply cannot fathom.'

'Affairs of State—'

'I know all about affairs of State.'

'You *think*—'

'I know.'

'You're entitled to your opinion.'

'My opinion is shared by the entire nation.'

'If you want to know—'

'If *you* want to know—'

It made the Maharajah sigh. That fault of hers, always insisting on the last word. But really he was quite glad to be squabbling with her again. They were back, he happily imagined, to old times.

Epilogue

India became independent on 15 August 1947.

By Independence Day the Princes of India, with two exceptions, had signed the Instrument of Accession, their States acceding either to India or to Pakistan.

Note

It would be difficult for the general reader to follow the confused workings of the British official mind in the nomenclature of its agents and agencies in India. It resulted, for example, in the British Head of the Government of India wearing different hats at different periods and for different occasions: that of Governor-General, Viceroy, or Crown Representative. On at least one occasion the Government succeeded in confusing itself.

To simplify, the Viceroy was head of the Indian Political Service, which more or less dominated the Indian States through Residents and Political Agents under them. These 'politicals', reflecting the important and military nature of their posts, were recruited in a proportion of two-thirds from the Indian Army and one-third from the Indian Civil Service, the principal political officers being personally appointed by the Viceroy. The senior ranks of the I.C.S. and the Indian Army were, of course, almost exclusively British, certainly for the period in which the novel is set.

In the interests of the novel, and to provide demarcation, I have kept to 'Agent' for earlier and 'Resident' for later sections of the book.

Acknowledgements

I would like to thank the Librarian and staff of the India Office Library, Mrs. Katherine Bell, of the Department of Prints and Drawings, I.O.L., and the Librarian and staff of the Royal Commonwealth Society Library for their kindness and courtesy in answering my many queries, and for making available much material of absorbing interest.

I have drawn extensively on I.O.L. archives for the chapters on the Delhi Durbar of 1902/03, and for the material involving Lord Curzon during his viceroyalty of India, although the interpretation of events and reactions is, of course, my own.

The quotations in the Prologue are taken respectively from *The Oxford History of India*, Third Edition, by the late Vincent A. Smith, C.I.E., edited by Dr Percival Spear; and *Lord Randolph Churchill* by W. S. Churchill (Macmillan, 1906).